They met on the run.
Then they became partners.
But which side of the law are they on?

THE PRINCESS AND THE PEA
Kathleen Korbel

IN SAFEKEEPING
Naomi Horton

FUGITIVE
Emilie Richards

Guilty of love…

KATHLEEN KORBEL

lives in St. Louis with her husband and two children. She devotes her time to enjoying her family, writing and avoiding anyone who tries to explain the intricacies of the computer. She's garnered a *Romantic Times* award for Best New Category Author of 1987, the 1990 Romance Writers of America RITA Award for Best Romantic Suspense and the 1990, 1992 and 1995 RITA Awards for Best Long Category Romance.

NAOMI HORTON

has written 23 books for Silhouette in the Desire, Intimate Moments and Romance lines. In July 1996, she launches her first Intimate Moments miniseries, WILD HEARTS, with *Wild Blood.* Among her notable achievements, Ms. Horton won the *Romantic Times* Special Achievement Award for Series Book of the Year in 1986. In 1990, she won the *Romantic Times* Lifetime Achievement Award in the Romantic Suspense category. For Silhouette's 1991 Christmas collection, Ms. Horton contributed "Dreaming of Angels," and that collection earned the B. Dalton Booksellers' Award for the Bestselling Contemporary Collection of 1991. And she's been nominated twice for the Romance Writers of America RITA Award in the Short Contemporary category.

EMILIE RICHARDS

has gone on to write more than two dozen novels since her first novels were published in 1985. She won the 1986 *Romantic Times* award for Best New Series Romance Writer, a 1988 *Romantic Times* Reviewer's Choice Award and, in 1994, a RITA Award for Best Long Contemporary novel, *Dragonslayer.* In 1995 she won the prestigious Janet Dailey Award. In 1996 her first mainstream novel will appear. Emilie enjoys writing about complex characters who make significant, positive changes in their lives...and she heartily approves of happy endings.

OUTLAWS and Lovers

Kathleen Korbel
Naomi Horton
Emilie Richards

Published by Silhouette Books
America's Publisher of Contemporary Romance

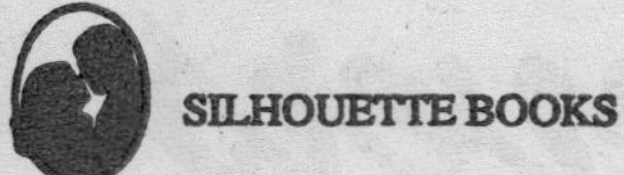

by Request

OUTLAWS AND LOVERS

ISBN 0-373-20126-5

This edition published by arrangement with Harlequin Books S.A.

Printed in U.S.A.

CONTENTS

A Note from Kathleen Korbel

Dear Reader,

Funny how a character is born. Paul Phillips was born as two lines in my previous Desire novel, *A Prince of a Guy*. Princess Cassandra von Lieberhaven had a bigger part, but not a much more sypathetic role. Cassandra, in fact, was a terminally spoiled young woman who spurned her birthright and walked away from her throne on her very coronation day. The challenge to redeem her was just too great.

I ended up writing *The Princess and the Pea* to rescue Cassandra's reputation and to find out just where Paul went all those years ago when he walked out on his family. As hard as this may be to believe, I was more surprised than anyone by the answers. I did, however, have a great time working them out along the way. I hope you never look at Oreos and milk the same way ever again.

To be perfectly frank, I also wanted another visit to the tiny Alpine country called Moritania I invented over which Cassandra and her handsome cousin Eric ruled. It is a good thing to have your own country, even if it's only on paper. I hope you enjoy your visit. I hope you will also keep in mind that as its founder, from now on I am entitled to be curtsied to at all royal functions. Just in case you run into me. At a royal function. In Moritania.

Kathleen Korbel

THE PRINCESS AND THE PEA

Kathleen Korbel

To Edna.
A daughter-in-law couldn't
ask for a bigger fan or a
better friend.

One

He didn't see her until it was almost too late.

Dusk had fallen, and rain spattered listlessly against the car windshield. Somewhere toward the south, the Alps blotted out an already dark sky. The Porsche's windshield wipers slapped out a hypnotic dance, and the headlights cut a dreary swathe through usually breathtaking countryside.

Paul Phillips tapped a syncopated rhythm against the steering wheel as he drove. There was a Gershwin tape playing and a long night's driving ahead of him. A few long days before going home.

For the first time in fifteen years, he went without haste. There was no one to chase, no one chasing him. Paul took a last drag from his cigarette and added the butt to the pack or so already accumulated in the ashtray. Then he reached to downshift for a corner.

If he had waited a split second longer to slow down, Paul would have hit her. She came out of the dark so fast that he didn't even have time to swerve. A white face and wild black hair. A whiter, flowing garment streaking out into his headlights. Not hearing his own hoarse cry, he slammed on the brakes.

Paul wasn't sure if he'd hit her. He just knew that suddenly she wasn't there anymore. He skidded the car to a stop. The engine died. With reflexes honed by long practice, Paul swung out of the car and went into a protective crouch. Reached for his gun.

His gun wasn't there.

His first day without it, and he'd forgotten. His heart hammered against his ribs. He struggled to bring his breathing back to a controlled, even pattern. The rain had already plastered his hair against his forehead. Running a quick hand through to force it back, Paul edged around the front of the car.

It could be a trick. A setup. Even though he wasn't in the business anymore, old grudges sometimes proved the deadliest ones.

The moment he caught sight of her, Paul knew it was no setup. Gut instinct. Nobody could act that terrified. Not even a pro could get her eyes that wide or sob so brokenly. He saw the pasty white sheen of panic on that beautiful young face and reached out his hand.

Crouching at the side of the road, the woman backed away. She was shaking her head, her hands in front of her as if to ward him off. Paul began to murmur to her, as he would to one of his horses.

"Here now, it's all right . . . I won't hurt you."

There was something about those huge, dark eyes and fine-boned face that tugged at emotions too long dormant. A wild desperation that crept in beneath his defenses. Paul now saw that she was dressed in no more than a slip. As soaked and disheveled as the rest of her, it clung to her, offering no protection against the bite of the winter wind. She didn't even have shoes on. Paul was surprised by the irrational ache she set up in him.

"I didn't hit you, did I?" he asked, finally reaching her. His voice seemed to soothe her. She flinched at his touch, but didn't draw away.

Her skin was like ice under his hand. Straightening a little, he quickly shed his own coat. "Here, let's get you warm. How did you get out here?"

Out here was the middle of the German countryside, miles from a village, from the possibilities of threat or rescue. No lights blinked anywhere in the deepening night. No cars passed on the lonely stretch of road. Paul couldn't imagine where she'd come from. She was still sobbing, her breathing ragged and hoarse as she looked questioningly up at him. Gently reaching out, Paul brushed a lank strand of dark hair from her forehead.

"Where are you from?"

Still nothing. Maybe she didn't speak English, he thought. He tried again in German, Italian and French. No answer. He wasn't having any luck at all. He was also getting wetter by the minute. The time had come to either coax her into his car or forget her altogether. The problem was, the minute Paul had first seen her flash across the beam of his headlights, the second alternative had ceased being an option.

Still murmuring to her in all four languages with a little Croatian and Russian thrown in for good measure, Paul got her to her feet and over to the passenger door. The woman went along without protest, her eyes never leaving his face, her sobbing slowly beginning to ease.

It wasn't until he had her safely belted into the passenger seat and had gotten behind the wheel that Paul finally thought to wonder what he was going to do with his surprise passenger. Should he find a village with a local constabulary? Should he head east toward Munich and try there? Maybe somebody somewhere was missing her. Maybe she wanted them to.

Paul flipped on the overhead light and frowned at his new charge. "I don't suppose you want to tell me where you belong."

"Not particularly."

He started. She was facing forward, tears still streaming down her cheeks and her chest heaving erratically with gulping little sobs. Amid her distress, the sound of her voice was surprising. In control. In charge. She sounded as if she were addressing an employee. As if she were *used* to addressing employees.

"Well, so you can talk," he mused with a smile.

"Of course I can talk," she snapped without changing position. "And please put those filthy things away."

He hadn't even realized that he'd pulled out another cigarette. Taking a rather stupid look at it, he dropped it right into the tray.

"Anything else?"

"Yes. Do you have anything more comfortable than this jacket?"

Now Paul was shaking his head. "No. But I'd be happy to take it back if you're more comfortable in just your slip."

That got a reaction out of her. She turned to him, a ghost of fear darkening what he now saw were lustrous hazel eyes.

"Mind telling me what you were doing wandering out in the rain in just a slip?"

She turned away again, her head down, her hands clenched in her lap. "Trying to escape." The anguish that colored her whispered words was real.

"From what?"

"I don't see where that's any of your business."

Again Paul heard a sudden hint of imperiousness, as if he had been the first one to ever question her. Paul wondered at the incongruity, at the stark white of her face, the trembling frailty of her body and the Queen Victoria tone of her voice. "Other than the fact that I'm the one who pulled you in, you're probably right. If you'd rather not tell me anything, that's okay. I'll be happy to let you out—"

"No!" Her reaction was swift and sincere. The thought obviously terrified her. "Please."

Paul waited, watching the secrets she kept shift and settle in her as she decided what to tell him.

"What's your name?" he asked gently, knowing all about terrified people. It made him wonder how close to the truth her answer would be.

Again, a pause. She looked even more forlorn swimming in the oversize leather jacket, more childlike with her thick hair half falling in her eyes. She was no child, though. One look at the long, lithe legs that stretched from beneath the sodden slip proved that. Not to mention the taut, firm breasts that were covered by no more than a layer of fine silk. She lifted a trembling hand up to her hair as if checking a chignon for loose strands. The action was obviously from habit, which meant that her disheveled state was an unaccustomed situation.

Paul felt the sudden gnaw of desire and wondered at it. Lost waifs were usually not his type at all. His eyes straying back to the sweet body so deliciously outlined by wet material, he realized that he wanted to know all about someone—*this* someone—for the first time in some fifteen years. She intrigued him. He liked a little fire in a woman, a solid backbone. He also found a sudden taste for hazel eyes and delicate, expressive hands.

"You must have a name," he prodded gently, reining in an impulse to reach out to her again. "Almost everyone does."

"Emily," she finally said, turning to fix him with a "dare me to deny it" look. "What's your name?"

"Paul."

"You're an American, aren't you?" She waited for his nod before motioning to their surroundings. "What are you doing out here?"

Paul offered a shrug. "Waiting for half-naked women to run in front of my car. You're my fourth, so far. I must be having a lucky streak."

What she gave him would have been, he was sure, a withering look at any other time. Right now, though, it looked endearing. The growling of a tiger cub.

"I suppose you think you're funny," she retorted archly.

He grinned, flipping the light off and reaching for the ignition key. "Amusing, maybe. Definitely not funny."

"What are you doing?" The anxiety was back in her voice.

"Well," he allowed, turning over the engine to a steady, throaty purr. "I personally think goose bumps suit you. But I'm sure you don't want to keep the look just to please me. I thought maybe you'd like a little warm air."

"Oh—" she deflated a little, not sure just how to react "—thank you."

"And then I thought you'd like to talk to the police."

"The police—" She was turning again, even as he threw the car into gear and edged back out onto the deserted road. "No...no, not the police."

Paul turned to catch a new unease in her posture. "Afraid of being caught?"

"What?"

"Caught. Are you a second-story man or a Peeping Tom?"

That brought her shoulders right back and her head up. "A thief?" she demanded with hot eyes and voice. "You think I'm a common thief? I'll have you know I'm—"

But the revelation never came. Just as quickly as she'd straightened, she slumped, turning away in silence.

"You're what?"

"None of your business."

"Then where do you want to go?"

A small hesitation, then an even smaller voice. "Where are *you* going?"

Paul looked over, not only thinking about what kind of reception his surprise companion would get in her state but about what kind of reception *he'd* get. It wouldn't look very good no matter where he went.

"A wedding." My sister's wedding, he thought unhappily, the sister I haven't seen in fifteen years. Who must be grown and pretty and sassy as hell by now without me. God, he wished he felt better about coming face-to-face with her again after all these years. However, Emily might just be the distraction that uncomfortable little reunion needed. He imagined the conversation. "Casey, this is Emily, whom I just happened to run into on the highway coming here. Emily, this is my sister Casey, who is about to marry some kind of king. At least, I think it's Casey. I haven't seen her in fifteen years. Isn't life amazing?"

"Where are we now?" his passenger asked, scanning the darkness for some sign of life.

Paul turned back to her, eyebrows lifted in surprise. "You don't know?"

"They didn't tell me." She answered before thinking, before retreating behind her frosty shell.

Paul's attention was immediately back with her. "Emily?"

No reaction. Not her name, then. No real surprise to him. He tried again. "Emily."

Finally she turned.

"Did they hurt you?" Paul couldn't even consider the accusation he was contemplating. She looked so small that it was the first thing he thought of. God, he hoped not. Not to this fragile lioness of a woman. The distress in those dark eyes was enough to tear at him.

It took her a moment to understand the full implication of his question. When she did, her eyes widened even more. Not so much at the query, but at the gentle concern in his voice. "No," she answered with a definite, reassuring shake of her head, a fleeting smile crossing her lips. "I wasn't raped. They treated me well—as far as that's concerned anyway. They just took my money and held me... held me in a dark, stinking little room where—"

Paul saw new tears and relented, touching her badly trembling arm to reassure her. Her skin was a bit warmer with the heater on full blast. She hadn't lost her pallor. She evidently hadn't grown passive yet, either. The minute she felt his hand on hers, she yanked it away with very real outrage.

"How dare you?" she seethed. "To touch me without my permission!"

Paul again raised an eyebrow. "Excuse me?"

"You take liberties, sir, that not even *they* thought to take!"

Paul's lips curled in wry amusement. "Must have been a hell of a kidnapping." Giving her one last challenging look, he reached deliberately over to retrieve his cigarette and punch the lighter. "Might as well get some rest. You're gonna have a lot of explaining to do when we find those police."

"I told you—"

Paul turned, the cigarette dangling from his mouth, to let his eyes take slow pleasure in the sight of her. "This may not have occurred to you yet, but I'll be damned if I'm going to explain how I got a woman in my car wearing only her slip and a smile. That one's up to you, honey. And it's for the police. The German police."

Her Highness the Crown Princess Cassandra Catherine Anna Marie von Lieberhaven turned away and closed her eyes. Oh, God, she thought, waves of relief and terror still washing through her with equal effect. What am I going to do? He's going to take me to the police and then they'll know. Eric will find out just what a mess I made of my big play for independence.

No more than three months earlier, she had been standing in St. Cyril's Cathedral in Braz waiting to be married. Waiting to be crowned Queen of Moritania. The entire country had been there, cheering and waving and singing. The cathedral had shimmered in the afternoon sunlight and glittered with the trappings of ritual and wealth. It would have all been hers—if she'd only married Rudolph and assumed her duties by once again doing what everyone expected of her. Well, no one else had to face living with that pimply-faced mannequin or spending the rest of their days counting curtsies.

By now, Eric would be king. A more popular monarch than she, Cassandra knew in her heart. A more fitting one. Eric had always held the strings of power in the country. It had been Eric, her god as a child and her nemesis as an adult, who had truly captured Moritania's loyalty and love. Cassandra, born to a title she didn't know how to assume, had never been able to match her uncle's more impressive talents. In the end, she really hadn't wanted to.

Now she would have to go back to face him . . . to face her grandmother. Fresh tears welled in her hazel eyes at the thought, but Cassandra squeezed them back. A princess did not show weakness. She did not allow herself the frailties which most humans assumed as their right. Cassandra tried her best to overcome the momentary lapse by concentrating on her rescuer instead.

For a moment, she toyed with the idea of taking a sidelong glance at him. More than just curiosity drew Cassandra. There was something about him that made her feel at once safe and unsure. He'd catch her watching, though. He seemed to anticipate her with deadly aim.

Her first sight of him had terrified her. She'd thought he'd been one of the terrorists. He'd moved like a jungle cat, a black panther against the harsh illumination of the headlights. He was lean and quick, with thick sable-brown hair. Long, she realized now as it began to dry, almost to his shoulders, and wild. It looked almost like a mane, giving him a slightly dangerous look. He hadn't shaved in a day or two, and his eyes were tired.

His eyes. They were so soft, so sweetly blue like a lake in early spring. Cassandra had seen terrible wariness in them at first, then laughter and compassion. Those eyes seethed with life, with energy.

Paul wasn't a handsome man. His angles and slightly off-plumb features made him look as if he'd taken his share of knocks—as if the wariness in those eyes had been well earned. All the same, Cassandra reacted to him more intensely than to any of the dandified, educated men she'd known all her life. Just sitting next to Paul in the confines of the small car set her skin humming.

A panther, Cassandra thought once again, finally succumbing to the urge to take just one look. What an appropriate image. What a dangerous one. He wore a black turtleneck and jeans, slung low over lean hips. Cassandra didn't know whether to feel comfortable with him or at peril. She had only an instinct that this man wouldn't put her in an even greater danger than the one she'd escaped. And truth be told, Cassandra and her instincts had not really been reliable.

One thing was sure. She was away from that bastard Erhardt. To that there was no looking back. Even though there was no looking forward either, for now she was warm and dry and away from the nightmare she'd stumbled into. And more than anything, right now, she wanted to know about the man who'd rescued her.

"What do you do?"

Paul turned, the dashboard lights barely illuminating his eyes. "I thought I told you to get some rest."

"Many people wouldn't have stopped. I want to understand why you did."

His answer was delivered to the road, his face crinkling in wry tolerance. "I was a consultant."

Cassandra tilted her head a little. "A consultant. At what?"

Paul sent another quick look her way that left fresh goose bumps in its wake. "Safety. Now get some sleep."

The car swept on into the night, the wipers clicking steadily, the water thrumming beneath the high-speed wheels. Occasionally a car passed on the lonely road.

"You said 'was.' What did you mean?"

This time he sighed. "I didn't pick you up because I was in need of conversation."

"I want to know."

Again, the assumption of compliance.

"I'm sure you do," he retorted. "I'll tell you what. You tell me who you were running from and I'll tell you why I said was."

"Did they fire you or did you quit?"

She got a look of exasperation this time. Cassandra smiled and curled up a little tighter in his jacket. She wasn't about to tell him from whom she was running—or who she was. He probably wouldn't believe it, anyway. There were days when she didn't believe it herself.

There I was minding my own business, she could see herself saying, just doing the things a crown princess does the week before her wedding and coronation. A little shopping, a bit of innocent escape. Who'd know I was going to be kidnapped? Who'd know I'd fall in love with one of my captors? Hans, gentle, idealistic Hans. If only he hadn't been so very weak, I might love him still. I was freed, you see, by my Uncle Eric and some distant cousin he plans to marry, but instead of being crowned, I ran off with Hans. Well, I thought that's what I was going to do. I was going to find the freedom my title never afforded me with a man I thought loved me. Instead, I ended up at the mercy of his new boss, Erhardt, a terrorist with no ideals and fewer manners. And for the past two months, after stealing the fifty thousand pounds I was bringing to Hans, Erhardt locked me up in a room because he knew a royal hostage could come in handy, although he hadn't yet figured out for what.

Cassandra looked at the hard edge of experience in Paul's features and knew that he'd feel no pity for a self-centered, lost little princess who didn't know where she was going now that she wouldn't be a princess anymore. She'd have to put off the pleasure of formal introductions as long as possible.

With a small sigh, she eased back against the seat. A frown immediately took over her features. "You're quite sure you don't have anything other than this jacket? I think it's lined with rocks."

"I put them in on purpose," he retorted with a straight face. "Keeps me from getting too comfortable. I have marbles beneath my shirt."

Cassandra straightened. "You don't believe me."

"I believe that you're tired and overwrought. Besides, that's the only thing I have right now to keep you warm."

"Overwrought?" The look in her eyes was dryly affronted. "Tell me, have you by any chance taken to reading Victorian romances? It's the only reason I can think of to account for that archaic attitude of yours."

Paul grimaced. "I said 'was' because I'm retired."

Cassandra couldn't help laughing, delighted with the image. "Well, then, that explains it. You're actually sixty and dye your hair. Going to spend the golden years fishing, are you?"

She coaxed a fresh grin from him. "Something like that."

She nodded, anticipating him. "Now, go to sleep."

"Why didn't I think of saying that?"

Surprisingly enough, she did sleep. Nestled in the warm cocoon of the car, fortified by the security of Paul's presence and lulled by the steady rhythm of the windshield wipers, Cassandra found herself nodding off. She'd been awake so long—trying to find a way out, bloodying her hands trying to break down that damned door, screaming until she was hoarse. It had been over two months since she'd been able to sleep without fear, since she'd been able to eat and move and relieve herself without an audience. It still hadn't sunk in that she was free...

"Emily?"

Cassandra felt the hand on her shoulder and instinctively snuggled closer. Her head hurt and her back was stiff, but she'd been dreaming in fits and starts of her jumper, Merlin. Merlin was a liver chestnut, sixteen hands high, Cassandra's favorite. There had been times when only Merlin had expected no more than she could give. He had forgiven her her weaknesses and patiently waited for her to try again.

"Emily?"

This time the shake was none too gentle. Cassandra jerked upright, the gentle memories of her horse shattering before the memories of Erhardt and his guttural German commands. She cried out, and her hands automatically came up to protect herself.

Something was holding her back. Holding her down, its bite sharp across her chest.

"No!"

"Emily, it's all right." Not Erhardt's voice. A gentle sound, this. A murmur of reassurance. Cassandra reined in her terror and tried to open her eyes.

It took her a moment to focus. Everything was indistinct and hazy. She thought she was still in her room, the light only the thin beam of a flashlight. Cassandra saw the man bent to her and lashed out.

He caught her hand in his own gentle ones and smiled at her. "You're safe, little one. It's just me. Remember?"

Her heart still thundered. She couldn't quite control her breathing. The seat belt, that harness that had so constrained her, held her snugly against the leather seat. Cassandra fought against it with what was left of her irrational panic. Paul reached across her and let her loose.

The quick brush of his forearm across her breasts brought her upright. Her mouth snapped open along with her eyes, the sudden shaft of lightning from his touch searing her to the toes. In the back of her mind she knew she should reprimand him—should at least protest his unintentional intimacy. All her tumbling, overloaded brain could do, though, was beg for more.

Cassandra drew her arms across her chest, pulling the jacket closed around her. She felt the tips of her nipples, button-hard from the memory of Paul's touch, and scowled. She definitely did not need an absolutely irrational reaction to a man she had to depend on—a man she had no reason to see again once she returned to the palace.

The palace. She really had no place left at the palace. No place anywhere. A new sense of loss stabbed her.

"Where are we?" she finally managed, realizing that Paul was now crouched next to her on the ground, a pair of socks in his hands. It was still dark out, the only light the pale glow of the overhead light. A brisk breeze cut through the warmth of the car and she started shivering again. Then Paul took hold of one of her feet and started off a new set of shivers that wasn't at all as unpleasant.

"At an inn," he allowed, sliding an oversize black sock onto her foot. Cassandra thought of the valets at the palace and stifled a giggle. She couldn't imagine Uncle Eric hiring as disreputable a man as this to see to his bodily needs. Uncle Eric would do no more than show Paul the border of Moritania in a fast-moving car.

Cassandra looked around, trying to discern some landmarks in the gloom. There were a few squares of light off to their right, and the hulking shadows of other cars alongside theirs. "An inn," she echoed uncertainly. "What about the police?"

Paul looked up from his task to grimace. "Couldn't find any." Not exactly true. But after watching her sleep for the past two hours, whimpering and frightened even then, Paul had decided to at least let his mysterious guest get some uninterrupted rest before she had to go through the rigors of interrogation. As he well knew it wasn't the logical thing to do, certainly not the prescribed. Somebody was going to be mad at him by the time he got this young lady to the authorities. But then, if Paul had been logical and dispassionate, he'd still be plying his trade over the continent instead of running as hard from it as his fast car and inheritance allowed him.

He noticed that she was warily scanning the darkness. Understandable. For all she knew, she'd walked from one nightmare into another. Paul finished slipping the sock over the bruised, lacerated foot and straightened to offer his hand.

"You're safe now, Emily," he assured her, restraining himself from showing any of the protective urges just the feel of her sleepy body beside him had aroused. "I'll get you to the authorities in the morning. Right now, there's a nice, soft bed waiting for you upstairs. The owner's an old friend of mine."

Cassandra couldn't help the sudden stab of fear his words ignited. "No, I don't..."

He wouldn't allow her hesitation. With a gentle smile, he took hold of her hand and pulled her from the car. "Well, I do. The owner is an old army officer. Sure to keep the bogeyman away. And his wife is just about your size, so we can get you some clothes. Trust me, Emily—" the soft blue of his eyes held even more support than his words "—you're safe now."

It was like an omen. An evil sign. Paul had no more than gotten the words out than a set of headlights stabbed across them and swung around. The sudden roar of a powerful car shattered the peace of the countryside. Cassandra cried out, jerking away. Paul turned to the lights, already in a crouch. There was a staccato of coughs, the sharp ping of metal against metal, and suddenly Paul was shoving Cassandra back into the car.

"Paul...!"

She got no more than a quick look at the car as it screeched in alongside them. A pale globe of a face and a short glinting barrel were all she saw before Paul had tumbled over the hood of the car and back into his seat.

"Get down!" he yelled, pushing her. Glass shattered. Cassandra curled up on the floor, trying her best to get her head under the floor mat. Beneath her, the engine roared to life and Paul slammed the car into gear.

As they skidded onto the road, Cassandra lifted her head, all the disdain she could muster in her shaking voice. "If this is safe," she said, "would you care to define danger to me?"

Two

"I think I've lost them."

Cassandra brought her head up to see Paul check the rearview mirror. "Does that mean I can resume a somewhat civilized position?"

"Assume whatever position you'd like," Paul offered with an absent wave of his hand. "And then tell me exactly who that was chasing you."

Cassandra did her best to resettle onto the seat with a modicum of grace. Unfortunately, in a small sports car traveling along winding mountain roads at a brisk pace, that was more easily said than done. She knew that by the time she was once again upright, Paul had been allowed more than his share of provocative views.

She couldn't imagine why the heat of his eyes on her set up such a thrill of response. He didn't say a word or reach out to take advantage. Yet it was as if his hands had claimed her as boldly as his gaze.

Cassandra caught his eyes straying again and pulled the jacket more closely around her. She was by now upright and less exposed, even though her nipples had once again decided to betray her. It infuriated her that Paul could drive with so little apparent concentration. He handled the car as if it were another part of himself, adjusting steering and speed while his eyes remained most comfortably on her.

"You're going to hit a tree," she advised dryly.

"You want to tell me who it was we ran into back there?" he countered with a crooked grin.

Cassandra fought returning his smile. She could watch his face for hours, the lean hollows and strong features, the sky blue of his eyes. Daybreak was closer, and she could see a scar along his right cheek, a wicked, jagged streak that couldn't have been that old. It only served to make him more appealing. More dangerous.

"You shoved my head into the floor before I got a chance to recognize any of them," she retorted, automatically smoothing the remnants of her slip as if it were a tailored suit. "How did you let them catch us?"

He never took his eyes from the road. "I probably forgot to insist that you identify them for me. You didn't want to tell me, and I didn't want to risk messing up the car by beating it out of you."

Cassandra stiffened again, her head up. It was an instinctive position of rebellion. "You don't need to know." An instinctive answer. She regretted her words before she ever got them out. She really didn't want to alienate Paul as she had everyone else in her life.

Cassandra was set to apologize when Paul swung the car around and flipped off the lights. She automatically looked about. The sky was lightening to dawn pearliness. The mountains surrounded them, dark and sudden and silent. And empty. They sat on a small track in the trees, the black Porsche virtually invisible from the road. Her eyes widening in involuntary panic, Cassandra turned back to her savior.

Paul was occupied with another cigarette, his hands cupped around a match. It lit his face with almost demonic effect, sparking in his eyes and slashing yellow along his cheeks. Cassandra reacted without thinking.

Paul didn't realize she was going to bolt on him. The first thing he knew, he was looking up from his cigarette to find an open door and a blur of white stumbling into the woods.

"Damn!" With movements born of years of long practice, he was after her.

In the end, it was no contest. Cassandra had no idea where she was heading, and she was trying to get there on bruised, stocking feet. She was cold and frightened and exhausted. Paul caught up with her after no more than half a dozen paces.

She felt his strong hands clamp around her waist and fought harder, succeeding in bringing both of them to the ground.

"I'm beginning to wonder if this is worth it," Paul grated, landing atop her. His body pressed hers into the damp, cold earth. His hot breath whispered sweetly against her neck. Chills raced through her. Cassandra could feel the thud of his heart and the steely length of his legs. She wasn't sure if she wanted to fight her way free or nestle even closer, and that frightened her even more.

"Would it have occurred to you," she asked in the most controlled manner she could assume, "that I don't particularly enjoy being thrown to the ground?"

That only succeeded in getting her flipped over to face him. He was so close, his hands so sure against her, his eyes on fire. Cassandra couldn't breathe, couldn't think past an overwhelming certainty that he was going to kiss her.

"Would it have occurred to you," Paul countered, nose to nose, "that I don't particularly enjoy chasing you around the countryside?"

Paul Phillips had never been a man to take advantage of women. He'd been raised on old-fashioned courtesy and practiced a code that had seemed quaintly outdated to most of his peers. Yet, here, struggling with a terrified, fractious woman he'd stumbled across only hours before, all he could do was stare at the sweet bow of her lips. He found himself thinking how very much he wanted to taste them, how much he wanted to feel her lithe young body come to trembling life in his arms. The desire he'd been surprised to find in himself earlier suddenly kicked him like a horse. Here. In a field at dawn in the Alps on the run from this woman's unknown assailants. He was nuts. He was an idiot. He kissed her.

Cassandra had never known such command. The men she had known had treated her with all the deferential respect due a crown princess, touching her only with her permission and kissing her as if waiting to be scored for future reference. Paul dragged her to him as if she had no say in the matter. He took her mouth with lips so soft and sure that she forgot her objections. Cassandra felt his hands close tighter around her and brought her own to him, suddenly sure that if she didn't hold on she'd fall far and deep and never pull herself up again.

He stopped as abruptly as he'd started. Cassandra felt him pull away and whimpered, adrift and alone without understanding why. She looked into his eyes and knew that if he hadn't stopped, she wouldn't have objected. Her body sang with shivery delight. Her breasts longed for him with aching fullness, begging for his touch. She had never whimpered for a man in her life. The fact that she could for this man should have angered her. But it only fed her anguish, her confusion.

"You're . . . touching me again," she accused uncertainly, the attack the only way she knew to protect herself from the maelstrom this man was unleashing.

She expected anger. She received humor. Paul's eyebrows lifted and his mouth quirked. Bringing one hand around, he traced the corner of her mouth with a quick, callused thumb.

"So I am," he retorted easily. "But you don't have to thank me. I'm trained in the treatment of hypothermia."

Cassandra stiffened, trying to push his hands away. Her lips tingled from his touch. "I'm sure this is grossly unfair of me," she snapped back, "but if you don't mind, I'd prefer borrowing a pair of pants and a sweater. That would be much more comfortable on me than two hundred pounds of arrogance."

Still he didn't move, pressing her back against the loamy earth with his weight. So close, so warm and intimate against her. Cassandra was having trouble thinking when he watched her intently like that—when her body still so obviously betrayed her.

"Are you going to tell me who was chasing us?" he asked, resting an elbow on either side of her head and bringing his own face close to hers once again.

"Are you going to get up?" she answered, the smell of him surrounding her. Soap, a tang of sweat and leather. A masculine, enticing fragrance that was so much more compelling than any she'd known. Damn him.

"When you tell me."

Cassandra's expression was as dry as dust. "Then I guess we'll be here awhile."

Paul shrugged. "You're the one with the blue legs, lady."

He didn't mention that he could coerce the truth from her. Paul didn't want to think about it. Just that brief taste of her had set him on fire. Her mouth had been so delicious, so responsive. He'd felt her wrap herself around him and recognized how close to the precipice he was. Another minute and he wouldn't have stopped at a kiss. That troubled him.

He should have let her up right away. There were jeans and a sweater in his duffel he could lend her right now. But the feel of her beneath him was like a narcotic. The fire in her eyes was a stimulant. This woman pulled at him like a magnet, and he didn't want to get away just yet.

Cassandra finally let her gaze drift, struggling to keep her breathing even and her pulse steady. "You've heard of the European Liberation Movement?"

She didn't see the lift of Paul's eyebrows. "The latest in organized terrorism," he answered evenly. "I've heard of them."

She nodded a little, still facing away, toward the fog-shrouded mountains. "It was some of them. They kidnapped me, took the money I had on me and . . . and threatened my family."

"Who's your family, Emily?"

She took a small breath, trying to pull her thoughts together enough to lie. How could she tell him who she really was? If she did, he'd only take her back, maybe demand a ransom. And maybe he'd turn out to be just like all those other earnest young men who had courted her. For the first time in her life, even held at bay on the cold, damp earth, even unsure about her immediate future, she'd managed to leave the palace and its burden behind. Even though that left her isolated and alone, she wasn't quite sure she wanted her former life back.

"My father is a manufacturer," she finally said. "Emil Fredricks, from Switzerland. They wanted him to pay a ransom."

"How did you get away?"

Now she smiled with a certain pride. At least this part was true. "I hit one of them over the head with my supper dish when he came to fetch it. Then I ran."

"Why are you so afraid of going to the police?"

Cassandra turned, a stark expression in her eyes. "If I can just get to Switzerland," she begged, "I'll be all right. Please."

"Why, Emily?"

"I can't tell you."

To a certain extent, Paul knew the scope of her lies. There was no Emil Fredricks in Switzerland with a daughter in danger. He would have known. But he knew, too, that she really had been in the hands of the ELM. Paul had learned to trust his instincts, and they pegged that as the truth. Her escape, her fear, were all real. The rest would still have to be sorted out.

"Why would you dye your hair?" he asked, fingering the surprising silk that tumbled to her shoulders.

That was the question that stiffened her spine. He'd taken a step over an invisible line that somehow brought him too close. "It went better with my wardrobe," she snapped, pulling away from him.

"Now let me up before I scream loud enough for every goatherd in these mountains to come running."

"Y'know something?" he responded. "I never thought I'd see the day when I'd feel sorry for a bunch of terrorists."

Cassandra stood up with a regal grace that belied her situation. Before walking back to the car, she turned a glinting eye on Paul. "Then imagine how difficult I can be for just one person."

Paul laughed. "I don't have to imagine anything. Let's get you those jeans."

Cassandra had never worn a pair of jeans in her life. Her intense indoctrination in the proper wardrobe for a crown princess had developed into a sincere dislike of denim. Cassandra saw no reason to emulate Annie Oakley. As her mother and her grandmother had often explained, a crown princess had a proper image to maintain, and ranch wear was not part of it.

That was why she was so amazed to find the jeans Paul handed her so very comfortable. Soft and supple and well-worn, they rode low on her hips and hugged her bottom like gentle hands. She cuffed up the excess length and took a few experimental steps to find that maybe the Americans did, in fact, have something here.

The sweater, a large cable knit, hung well over her hips. Its sleeves had to be rolled up farther than the jeans. Even so, Cassandra had to admit that she was almost more comfortable than she'd ever been before.

The scent of Paul clung to his clothes and surrounded her in an embrace of wood-smoke and musk. The slightly scandalous aroma, dark and unique, was like Paul. Just the hint of it, constantly close, set up quick chills in her. Just the feel of those snug jeans against her legs insinuated the image of Paul in them, lean and long and masculine. It unnerved Cassandra in ways she couldn't name and set up a hunger she'd never experienced before.

"Paul..."

He turned at the sound of her voice, the signal that she was finished dressing and decent again. Cassandra saw a new light in his eyes, a warm possessive approval that made her feel absurdly defenseless. She felt a rare pink reach her cheeks and wondered at it.

"You wouldn't by any chance have a brush," she asked. She had never felt so at a loss in her life.

"I think it could be arranged. After all, you want to look your best for the gendarmes."

Cassandra took an involuntary step closer. The sun struggled closer to daylight, the trees a black curtain around them. The road was invisible and silent beyond. Far off the first bells of morning were beginning to sound.

"Don't you think we could..."

Anticipating her, he shook his head. "You're being chased. Until we go to the authorities, it won't stop." He tossed her a hair-brush. "Now, brush your hair."

Cassandra caught the brush and turned away. There had to be some way to get past the police to keep from revealing her identity to Paul. As she brushed she thought, and as she thought, she fumed, because at this juncture Paul held all the cards. He had the car, he knew his way around. Cassandra was caught in a situation that would be impossible to get out of. She could always walk away to the nearest farmhouse, but then she'd have to leave Paul behind. And, she realized with one final, frustrated tug of her hair, she didn't want to do that at all.

"What about going to the Swiss police?" she asked, turning back to see him watching her. Leaning back against the side of his car, he had his arms crossed across his chest, his lips crooked in an appreciative grin. His whole body exuded a cocky, self-assured masculinity that made Cassandra's pulse jump.

"You make that an art, y'know?"

She stopped. "What?"

"Brushing your hair." Paul walked up to take back his brush. "If it weren't for a couple of very cranky men with guns, I'd be very tempted to waste the rest of my day watching you do that." The expression in his eyes boasted the fact that that wasn't the only thing he'd do.

For a moment, Cassandra didn't know how to react. She stood before him, her eyes wide and her mouth pressed shut. Why was he doing this? Why would he one minute be so gentle and the next so forward? And why, in the name of God, was she so attracted to him?

"What a relief," she finally said, making it a point to hand his brush back with deliberate ease.

"What?" He was close enough to set off new alarm bells.

Cassandra didn't budge. She did smile, though, a frosty gesture that carried as much triumph as satisfaction. "To know that I didn't have to be so worried about treating you like a gentleman, after all. I hate nothing more than wasted effort."

Paul reached out to run a slow hand along Cassandra's hair. "I didn't know it was ungentlemanly to appreciate beauty."

Cassandra had to force herself to keep still when she felt the delicious chills his touch unleashed. "Boldness may be a desirable trait in America. It is not where I come from."

Still he didn't move. He touched her hair again, testing it, savoring it within his fingers. "What color *is* your hair, Emily?"

A dangerous languor seeped through Cassandra at his touch. She came very close to closing her eyes. "My name isn't Emily." She couldn't believe that her voice was no more than a whisper, her statement unintentional truth.

"I know."

She blinked. "You do?"

"Sure." More shivers, more struggle against the desire to fit her body neatly next to his. "You never did strike me as an Emily. That isn't the name for a lioness. I figured that it was like your hair. Changed for a reason."

Cassandra couldn't think. Now the rough edges of his fingers had dropped to the tender flesh of her throat. Her body was betraying her, aching, anxious for the thrill of that gentle rasp against every inch of her.

"What reason is it?" he asked, his voice throaty and intimate, his eyes almost as dark as hers.

Cassandra involuntarily shook her head, still sure she shouldn't tell him. "Escape."

"From whom? The ELM?"

"From myself. From . . ." Her eyes found his and battled him, struggling for control. "One never knows from whom she'll need to escape, does she?"

Now Paul's smile was delighted, his fingers coming to rest along her shoulder. "From me?"

The hard planes of Paul's body were close enough to emanate heat. Cassandra felt the ache of her breasts as they strained for his touch and realized that this was a man she was glad she hadn't met as princess. She would have handed her country over to him without so much as a whimper.

"You most of all," she admitted. "You're more dangerous than any of them."

Paul thought that he should take his hand back. She was right. He could be more dangerous to her than any of the men she'd faced. None of them had touched her. None, it seemed, had been so mesmerized that they couldn't keep their hands off her. But he was, and he couldn't understand it.

He'd certainly dealt with his share of beautiful women. Beautiful and shrewd and strong, all practiced in the ways of their craft. More than one had attempted to play on his weaknesses, sure that the easiest way for him to betray his position was in the bedroom.

Ever mindful of his hazardous situation and guided by a rare common sense that had made him the best in the business, Paul had resisted, confusing more than one adversary. Now, within forty hours of his retirement, he stood in a lonely field in a foreign country with an enigmatic woman he'd rescued and he couldn't drag himself past thoughts of how intoxicating she was.

Nothing made sense. She wasn't a stunner, especially in the half-dressed, half-wild state in which he'd found her. Even now, her face was too pale against the wild black of her hair. Her features were sharp with deprivation, her eyes overlarge.

She wasn't the sweetest rose he'd ever encountered, either, that was for damn sure. But something—be it the sudden freedom he anticipated enjoying, or the uncertainty of his future that still unsettled him—had him acting with unnatural abandon.

"Blond," Cassandra finally said, her smile precarious. She couldn't remember ever having less composure.

Paul's head jerked up, as if her words had dragged him back from a distance.

"Blond," he echoed blankly, his hand cupping her face, his eyes on the honey-brown glint in the green sea of her eyes. "Your name or hair color?"

Cassandra laughed, nestling a little against his hand. "The hidden me," she answered with delight. "The only woman in the world to decide that blondes have less fun."

"And your name?"

"Is not Blond."

"And you're not going to tell me what it is?"

Cassandra's expression was sly. "Don't you like a little mystery in your life?"

Paul smiled, the banter in her eyes heady. "I've had more than enough mystery in my life, thanks. I think we'll let the police settle this." Giving her cheek one last caress, he moved to take hold of her arm. "They might have better luck at you than I have."

Cassandra balked. "Did you ever stop to think that maybe I don't want them to?"

Paul tugged her right after him. "Of course. Which is why we go straight there without passing go."

"Without what?"

He shook his head, dragging her unceremoniously along behind him. "A woman without a cultural upbringing. Too bad. Well, what do I call you now that you're not Emily anymore?"

"Emily. I really don't want to go."

Paul opened the door and slid her in. "Why?"

"Don't I want to go? I told you, I'd just rather not deal with the police right now."

"Why, Emily?"

Cassandra answered when she thought Paul wouldn't hear. "Because I like it."

Paul heard her though, as he opened the car door. He fought the urge to look at her, knowing what would be in his eyes and how she would react. He had never heard such a forlorn sound as those last words. As if they had been uttered by a lost little girl who dared the darkness. Who was she? he wondered. Why was she on the run, and who missed her? Why was she more comfortable with a stranger than the family from whom she'd been taken?

Cassandra was still trying to talk some sense into Paul when they pulled into the constabulary. She saw a police car with its blue lights parked alongside the door. There was revelation in that building, an admission she didn't want to make. Suddenly it seemed more important than ever not to make that move. I can't go forward, she thought in desperation, and I can't go back. What's wrong with staying a little longer in the comfort of this limbo where I can feed myself on the attraction in Paul's eyes and salve myself with a fairy tale?

"What if I told you that I lied?" she asked as he opened her door to let her out.

"I'd say it was a good try. We're still going to the police."

"But I wasn't really kidnapped," she protested, straining against the hand that pulled her steadily from the car. "I decided to take a long walk and got lost."

"In your slip."

She was on her feet. Paul's hand felt like a vise around hers as he led her inexorably toward that door. "I often walk in my slip. It's . . . cooler."

"Especially when there's a cold rain and frost warnings out."

Cassandra saw Paul's patient grin and balked again. There had to be some way. She resorted to another proven method.

"I'll pay you to take me to Switzerland."

Paul nodded. "Fine. Right after we talk to the police."

Three steps and a doorway to go. Cassandra panicked. "Please. I'm allergic to police. I faint at the sight of a uniform. Don't make me go in there."

Paul gave her a broad grin. "I'll catch you when you drop."

He had his hand on the door handle. Cassandra closed her eyes, trying her best to maintain her composure, wanting to scream and rant and demand just as she'd always done. But she knew it wouldn't do any good. Not with this man. He'd more than likely laugh if she lifted her chin at him.

Suddenly she realized that something was amiss. One minute Paul had been walking forward, a hand on the door to open it. The next he was whipping around and heading back down the steps.

"What are you doing?" Cassandra demanded, tripping after him, her arm still in the steel of his grip.

"Be quiet. You got your wish."

Cassandra tried turning around, but that only succeeded in tripping her up again. Paul was moving too fast. "Why? I thought you were so all-fired determined to get me to spill my guts to the police."

Paul took one last quick look over his shoulder before opening the passenger door and ushering Cassandra in. "You've been watching too many gangster movies," he advised dryly. "Ruins your vocabulary."

"At least I still have manners!" she accused hotly. As he walked around to get in, she took a last look at the police office. It was a quiet, unassuming cinder-block building with vague signs of life. Certainly no commotion. The way Paul had turned tail and run, Cassandra fully expected to see a swarm of angry police following them out like a disturbed hive.

Paul was barely in the car before getting it into gear and out of the driveway.

"Don't talk to *me* about being uncommunicative," she accused, turning on him. "I've been a veritable encyclopedia of information compared to you."

"We can't go to the police."

"That's what I was trying to tell you. What changed your mind? The money?"

Paul grinned and shook his head, as he aimed the Porsche down the mountain road with practiced precision. The little town disappeared in their wake within minutes, the road winding back into the mountains.

"The bad guy."

Cassandra turned again. "Bad guy? You mean the one who shot at us?"

He nodded. "Exactly."

"Where? In the station?"

"In a uniform."

Cassandra stared at him, unable to quite comprehend. "What uniform?"

"The kind that make you faint. Our not-so-friendly visitor was standing just inside the station in full uniform when we walked up. And from what I heard, the driver who'd been with him belongs to the same union."

Cassandra gaped. "Police." She shook her head, a hand up to push her hair back. "How could that be? Could the ELM have infiltrated them?"

"Possibly. It could also be someone else. I know you said you didn't get a good look at the men in the car, but I did. Were any of your assailants middle-aged?"

Cassandra thought a moment as Paul pulled out a cigarette and lit it. "No. There was the general, but he was captured."

Paul looked over.

Cassandra waved aside her earlier remark. That explanation came under the "too complicated to merit" category. "They were all young men. In their twenties . . . and quite unshaven." The last was offered with an air of distaste.

Looking over with a wry glint in his eyes, Paul made it a point to rub at the stubble on his own face. "A disgusting state to be in, to be sure."

"It is." Just in time, Cassandra relented. Casting a sidelong glance to see Paul's amusement, she acquiesced with a graceful smile of her own. "These were also unwashed. It makes a difference."

"I can imagine."

"What are we going to do?"

"I'll be happy to shave if you can find us someplace safe to stay."

"Stay?" she retorted, sitting more fully upright. "We can't stay here. We have to get to Switzerland."

"Why?"

"Because . . ." She faltered. She didn't really have a good reason, except that Switzerland was where her only friends lived. Cassandra had survived the past two months by anticipating her reunion with them when she got out. They were all she had left, now that her family was lost to her. Her school chums, fellow boarders from her teen years were the only people who might enjoy seeing her. She'd depended on that all the while she'd been locked up.

"It's just away from here. Away from the German police." She shook her head, sending her mane of hair to trembling. "I don't know. Maybe we can get help there."

Paul nodded noncommittally. "And here I thought you were going to say you wanted to go home."

Cassandra started, caught again. "Well . . . that, too."

"Your family must be worried sick."

She nodded, not seeing the loss in her own eyes. "Terrified." They weren't, of course.

"Exhausted from the strain," he prodded, his eyes still on the road. "All those sleepless nights—"

"Hours of waiting—"

"All the false hopes. Y'know, I'd venture to say they'll greet you with the proverbial fatted calf, Emily old girl."

When he didn't get an answer, Paul looked over. Cassandra looked straight ahead, her eyes blind to the passing scenery. There was such pain in those dark, tear-swollen eyes. He'd only meant to goad an answer out of her. Somehow he'd opened a wound that saw no sign of healing.

Paul had seen that expression before, in the eyes of the lost, the survivors left behind alone. He realized now that his castaway felt a desolation that lay in something more than just the kidnapping.

Paul knew that kind of loneliness. He opened his mouth to offer comfort and knew it wouldn't help. They really shouldn't stay around here. There was no way of knowing just who among the police was legitimate. They might very well stand a better chance of getting help in another country. Austria was just a border away, and Switzerland another fifty miles or so southwest. And even if Cassandra didn't have any family there, Paul did—after a fashion.

The pain in Cassandra's eyes now tearing at him, Paul turned back to the brightening sun and made a promise he could never have anticipated.

"We'll go to Switzerland."

Three

"We can't go to Switzerland."

"What do you mean?" Cassandra demanded, turning in her seat. "You promised."

Paul took a drag from his cigarette and ground it out in the ashtray. "I overlooked one small problem."

"Which is?"

"Your passport. I don't suppose you have it with you."

The look on Cassandra's face was all it took to resurrect her former state of attire. "I keep it strapped to my thigh," she retorted dryly. "Just in case I want to swim across the border on a whim."

"Then what do you plan to say to the border guard?" he asked with a small smile. "We have to make it past a set at Austria and Switzerland, y'know."

"Don't be ridiculous. They won't bother me. I'm the crown—" Horrified, Cassandra stopped. She'd reacted instinctively to his gentle goading, tossing her title before her like a buffer and weapon. She'd almost given herself away. Her heart thudded in her chest at the nearness of her betrayal.

It was getting easier to talk to him. Too easy. The truth tended to inadvertently slip out when you didn't pay attention to what you were saying. She was going to have to guard herself against the comfort Paul induced.

"The crown what?" Paul asked quietly, his voice a shade too careful.

"The crown princess of Bavaria, of course." Cassandra smiled deliberately, facing him once again. "I've been known to bluff my way through sticky situations before."

Paul took a last look at her and went back to his driving. "I believe that." He nodded with conviction. He didn't tell her that he was ahead of her again. The slip had been unintentional, and therefore revealing. The crown. The crown what? Who was she that she assumed so much and expected even more? What kind of an upbringing could produce someone so commanding yet so painfully unsure at the same time?

"How did you get out of Switzerland in the first place?" he asked.

Cassandra gave him a baleful look. "I was kidnapped."

Paul returned the glance with a painful grin. "I know that. I'm talking about the mechanics. How did they get you past the borders?"

"In a box. I hated it."

"A box," he echoed, absently tapping the steering wheel. "Not a bad idea."

"Guess again," Cassandra retorted. "I have no intention of getting back in a box."

"You don't have to," he said.

When Cassandra saw what she did have to get in, she rebelled. "Oh, no you don't," she protested, at the sight of the tiny trunk space. "A spare tire couldn't survive a short trip in there."

"Better ideas will be entertained for the next five minutes," Paul countered easily from where he leaned against the side of the car. "After that, I'm leaving. With or without you."

When she clambered into the negligible trunk space, Cassandra made it a point to deliver a scathing look in Paul's direction. "Why do I have the feeling that this isn't so much the more practical consideration for you as the more enjoyable?"

Paul gave a final delighted smile, his hands poised on the trunk lid. "I like a woman with perception."

Then he shut her in.

From past dealings with borders all over Europe, Paul knew that it would take no more than a flashing of his U.S. passport at the gate to gain entrance to Austria. The guards there didn't even bother to so much as stop an American to stamp his passport. A search of the trunk would be unheard of. He set off in optimistic spirits.

Those lasted until he spotted the helicopter. A sleek, insectlike aircraft, it hovered low beyond the pass Paul was negotiating. He could see it beating its way back and forth, following a classic quartering search pattern. It bore no specific markings—no military insignia, no company logo. Something about its anonymity set Paul's teeth on edge.

Instinctively, he knew it was after him. He had, after all, survived for fifteen years in the espionage business by relying on his instincts. An early retirement didn't erase a knack like that.

He had that gut feeling that anticipated ambush. The hairs on the back of his neck bristled, and a seeping cold settled into his belly. Paul could read the signs well enough to know just what to expect. He also read them well enough to know exactly who was laying this particular trap. Running a hand through his hair, he thought of the innocent woman in his trunk and cursed himself for what he had to do.

"This part of Austria looks an awful lot like Germany," Cassandra observed as she eased the kinks out of her cramped limbs. She and Paul were parked along yet another back road in front of a quaint chalet. The area was deserted, with only the march of high tension electrical towers just alongside, betraying the encroachment of civilization into the mountains.

"That's because it *is* Germany," Paul admitted, his eyes scanning the ridges to the east where he'd last seen the helicopter. He couldn't hear it anymore. It must have continued north.

Cassandra turned to him, astonished. "I know I've been locked in the trunk of a car for a long time, and I've been jostled about a bit, so my hearing might not be quite up to par. I could have sworn you said we were in Germany."

He didn't look at her before heading over to the chalet. "I did."

Cassandra followed behind, limping a little on a foot that was still waking up. "This isn't going to be another one of your attempts at humor, is it?"

"As a matter of fact," he admitted, taking something out of his pocket and bending to the door. "It's going to end up being an apology. As soon as I get us inside."

Cassandra looked around, trying to get her bearings. "Inside? No, I don't think I want to go inside, thank you. I just managed to get *outside* for the first time in two months. I don't think I quite trust myself to go back in yet.... What's that?"

Paul continued his task, the slim metal instruments tinging against the stiff metal. "Lock pick."

"You know how to use a lock pick?"

"Tools of the trade." With a final flourish, he nudged the door open.

"Security." Cassandra nodded suspiciously, her eyes on his handiwork. "I know. I don't suppose now is the time to ask just what side of security you worked?"

Paul gave her a nudge in the right direction. "No. After you."

Without exactly knowing why, Cassandra walked on in. The house was simple, with a kitchen and living area, bedroom, bath. The furniture was rough-hewn, the walls whitewashed. There had been a recent fire in the fireplace, and heavy boots stood by the door.

"Who lives here?" she asked, feeling absurdly like Goldilocks.

"Shepherds," Paul said, closing the door behind him. "It's used when the sheep are in the high meadows during the summer. With the snows coming soon, the sheep have been moved lower down, so we have the place to ourselves."

For the first time Cassandra allowed a shadow of fear to touch her eyes. She didn't, after all, know this man. He had happened upon her by accident and been kind to her. Cassandra couldn't really be sure that his kindness wasn't about to abruptly end. She'd certainly seen that happen before.

Not Paul, she thought instinctively. A person with eyes that gentle couldn't possibly deceive with the same aplomb as Erhardt and his bunch.

Cassandra found that she wanted to believe in Paul. She wanted to let him lead her along until she could see her way to leading herself. Increasingly, she wanted to see the heat of desire in his eyes when he looked at her. But then, she'd once felt the same way about Hans.

"I'll tell you what," Paul offered, blithely ignoring the question in her eyes as he paced the small rooms. "We can stay here during daylight and head back out tonight. I'll turn the water back on while you get some food together."

"Food?"

"Yeah." He smiled brightly. Too brightly, but Cassandra didn't notice. "Aren't you hungry? I sure am." He was back out the front door before she had the chance to do so much as protest.

For a moment, Cassandra stood in the middle of the room looking after Paul. Automatic instincts came to call, but she pushed them away. He wouldn't leave her, she told herself. And he wouldn't lock her in. That was all over. But so much had happened so quickly that she had difficulty assimilating.

It had been late when she'd squeezed out past the hulking, unconscious form of the guard Otto. They had kept her in her slip just so she wouldn't think to escape, but after almost two months in a locked box, Cassandra would have run out stark naked. The cold rain had felt good against skin that hadn't felt sunlight in so long.

At first Paul had seemed like a dream—a vision sent to torment her with hope. That he could really be so caring seemed impossible. The fact that he had taken charge and physically pushed her where she needed to go only served to make him more appealing. Right now, cast adrift without purpose or goal, Cassandra knew she didn't have the courage or willpower to push herself.

Now she was alone in a house with a man she knew nothing about, who ignited frightening responses just with a touch, who sheltered her with the gentleness of a father and taunted her with the sly humor of a friend. To Cassandra, ever isolated by position and responsibility, such a luxury was like the first taste of ice cream to a starving child. There was a world out there, and Paul was her first real taste of it.

"What about that food?" he asked, stepping back in with a pair of old shoes in his hands.

Cassandra looked up from her perusal of the cabinets. "What food?" she asked with some bewilderment. "There's nothing here but cans."

"Cans of food," Paul amended. "Just enough left for a couple of hungry travelers, looks like. Why don't you throw something together while I get the stove going? I even think I found a pair of shoes that'll fit you."

All Cassandra could do was deliver a look of helpless confusion at the stacks of neatly arranged cans. "Throw what together?"

Paul looked around. "Whip up some breakfast. Right now, I'd even settle for beans."

She took a can in her hands and studied it. "But how do you get them out?"

"What?"

"The beans."

His answer was delivered with a certain amount of confusion. "You open them."

Cassandra turned the can over, searching for some clue as to how to breach the metal, desperate to ask for help but stubbornly refusing to make the move. She had to do this on her own. She had to figure out how to *live*. There were no more servants always waiting at the periphery to provide the most basic needs.

Cassandra didn't want to admit that she had never so much as taken the time to learn to cook. She hadn't even drawn her own bathwater in her life. Standing forlornly in the center of the room with a simple can of beans in her hand, Cassandra felt more at a loss than she ever had in her twenty-three years. She felt as if she were an egg, cushioned her whole life in a plush nest only to be sent tumbling to the ground by an errant wind.

"A can opener," Paul prodded gently, stepping closer.

Cassandra's head snapped up. "I know that." The fact that she looked aimlessly about her simply proved she didn't.

Cocking his eyebrow quizzically, Paul set the shoes on the table and walked over to relieve her of her burden. "Just how long did you say those kidnappers had you?"

He immediately regretted his words when he surprised bright tears in her eyes.

"I've never been . . . good in the kitchen," Cassandra bluffed, struggling mightily to keep her composure.

"You've never been *in* the kitchen," Paul amended and took the can gently from her hands. "Your father must have had a lot of money."

She gave a miserable nod, feeling perfectly useless. "He did."

"Why don't you look for some plates then?" he asked. "I'll set the beans free."

Surprisingly enough, Cassandra stood her ground. "No," she disagreed. "I have to know how to do this."

Paul grimaced. "I could starve by then."

That only brought the tears closer. "You don't understand. . . ."

Setting the can down, he gently lifted her chin until she had to face him. The tears gave her eyes a luminescence that beguiled. "Then tell me," he prodded, his voice like a caress.

"I . . ." Still the trust wouldn't come, the courage to offer herself up. Cassandra hadn't known a completely supportive person since she was thirteen. It was almost impossible for her to recognize one now. Even so, a slice of the truth wiggled its way out.

"The . . . the ELM didn't kidnap me from home. I kind of walked right into them. I was trying to get away on my own. To go someplace I wasn't smothered. I didn't know it would mean . . ."

Paul wanted to tell her she had no business being on her own. He didn't. There was the most intoxicating determination struggling to be heard in that uncertain voice. A fledgling courage that had too long been stifled. If she wanted to learn to cook, who was he to object?

"Anything else you haven't learned how to do?" he asked.

Cassandra had enough presence of mind to grin. "Alphabetically or chronologically?"

Paul smiled back, dropping a kiss on her upturned forehead. "Well, then, we'd better get started."

"You never did say," Cassandra said sometime later over a plate of beans and tomatoes. "Why *did* I waste all that time in the trunk?"

"You mean why aren't we in Austria on our way to Switzerland?"

Cassandra gave a cat's smile. "Is this where I hear the apology?"

Paul sipped coffee that tasted suspiciously like dust. "I know you're going to take all this with grace."

"Don't count on it."

"I was afraid of that." He waited to swallow another mouthful of breakfast before continuing. The two of them sat at the table, the morning light streaming in through the dirty window behind them. It glinted on the rich brown of Paul's hair and lit the sky of his eyes. "When I explain, just remember who hauled you out of the rain."

"Hard to forget. You're the only person I've seen since. Well . . . almost."

"Exactly the point I'm coming to," he conceded with a stab of his fork. "The gentlemen in the police station might not have been looking for *you* after all."

"But they shot at us," she protested, trying her best to keep her eyes away from the delicious texture of his hair. She wanted to run her fingers through it.

"They did that," he agreed. "But I have the feeling that you might have been the innocent bystander instead of me."

For a moment all Cassandra could do was stare. She hadn't had much sleep in the past few days. She hadn't had much stimulation in the past few months. It took a minute for the tumblers to click into place.

"They were after *you*?" she asked, her sense of security doing a fast nosedive. "Why?"

Paul shrugged and gazed toward the window. "There are a few people in Europe who aren't too fond of me."

"Does this have to do with your security work?"

He nodded.

Cassandra stared. "Spies? Spies are after you? Does that mean you're a spy? I escaped terrorists to wander around with a spy?"

"A retired spy," he corrected.

"But if you're retired, why would they still be after you?"

"Well, they—"

"Who are they? I mean, are they on our side? On your side, I mean? Are *you* on your side?"

Cassandra's rapid-fire questions elicited a chuckle from her breakfast companion. "I assume you mean did I work for the U.S." When he got her agitated nod, he nodded back. "And others. Kind of a lend-lease deal. The gentlemen in the car seem to be with someone I never worked for."

"The other side."

"In a manner of speaking."

"But what do they want?"

Paul shrugged, sincerely mystified. A grudge would have possibly brought on the scene with the other car. It wouldn't have brought out high-tech helicopters. There was something going on about which he hadn't a clue, and because she'd been seen with him, his lovely companion was just as much a target as he was.

Cassandra leaned forward, her expression just shy of terrified. "What are you going to do?"

"Cross the border tonight. Then I'm leaving you with some friends of mine while I take care of this."

Without thinking, Cassandra reached a hand across to him. "Paul, don't. Call your embassy. Call the army. You shouldn't have to bother with that anymore."

Paul saw the sincere concern in her eyes and smiled. "Emily, don't worry. I know how to take care of myself. If I don't get this cleared up, I won't be able to enjoy my retirement."

Cassandra grimaced, then shrugged. "Cassandra."

That brought Paul up short. "What?"

"My name. It isn't Emily, it's Cassandra."

Paul sat very still, his gaze sharp and careful. "Why tell me now?"

Cassandra shied from his consideration. "I don't know. I suppose because I suddenly feel like a twelve-year-old playing games and insisting on using a false name."

Alarm bells jangled in the back of Paul's memory. Something about the name. It wasn't a very common name, certainly not one he'd forget. Besides, it was his kid sister's name. The same sister who was about to get married.

Suddenly Paul stiffened. His heart beat a little faster. He sat very still, the expression on his face passive. Cassandra. The Crown Princess Cassandra of Moritania. Good great gods. The woman sitting across from him was the woman who had been rescued from her kidnappers at the Moritanian Socialist Movement earlier this summer—the band led by none other than her chief of security, General Mueller. This was the woman who had been freed, only to abdicate on the day before she was to be crowned. The day she was to have been married. Boy, he'd heard of leaving a guy at the altar. She'd evidently done it with style.

Paul had been apprised of the whole situation when several members of the Moritanian Socialist Movement had escaped into neighboring countries to join up with the ELM. He'd also heard about her in the letter his mother had sent begging him to come to his sister's wedding. It turned out that the Crown Princess Cassandra was the niece of the man his sister Casey was going to marry.

He couldn't believe that he hadn't seen the resemblance before. His mother had written that the crown princess was a dead ringer for Casey. He recognized it now, in her eyes—those wide, deep, hazel eyes that could pack such a wallop. He hadn't seen Casey since she was ten, and even then her eyes had promised to be something special. So this is what Casey had grown up to look like. Paul wondered if she was a third as compelling as her near-twin.

"Paul?"

Cassandra looked up as Paul hauled himself to his feet and walked to the window. He was already pulling out his cigarettes.

"Paul, what's wrong? Did I say something?"

Did he tell her? Could she really think he wouldn't know once she told him her name? Of course, she'd been out of circulation for a couple of months. She'd probably figured that no one had missed her, that she didn't make the news. She also didn't know that he was Casey's brother.

It turned out that Paul didn't have to say a word. Cassandra saw the new set to his shoulders and sagged in her chair.

"You know," she whispered bleakly. "Oh, God, you know."

Taking a long pull of smoke into his lungs, Paul nodded out toward the mountains. "I know."

Four

"What are you going to do?"

Cassandra sat rigidly on her hard chair, her hands flat against the table, her heart in her throat. Disaster threatened. She could see it in the set of Paul's shoulders, in the fact that he refused to face her with his admission but continued to watch the scene outside. She could hear the wind suddenly, a low, keening sound as it swept the tops of the trees, and the far-off jangling of bells. There was so much silence here. So much solitude. It would have been perfect without her stupid blunder to ruin it all.

Now he knew, and everything was different.

"I guess I'll just have to call you Cassandra." He shrugged, his face still turned away. "And here I was just getting used to Emily."

"No," Cassandra disagreed, getting to her feet. "What are you going to do about me?"

Now Paul turned to her, the light in his eyes calculating. Cassandra was too upset to notice the glint there, too.

"What is the reward these days for rescuing a princess?"

Cassandra bristled, bringing herself to her full height. "A princess who's *abdicated*," she retorted icily.

Paul shrugged and dropped his cigarette beneath his heel. "I guess that means half of all your land is out of the question."

"I have no land."

"A bauble or two from the crown jewels?"

She scowled. "Do you see any on me?"

"Can't say that I do."

"Then that's all I'm entitled to. And twice what you're entitled to."

Now he scowled. "You take all the fun out of a rescue, princess."

"You'll be well compensated, I'm sure," she snapped, finally turning away. He wasn't disappointing her. He was becoming everything she'd feared. "Just turn me in at the nearest Moritanian border."

"Kind of like recycling, huh?"

Cassandra spun on her heel to see Paul grinning at her, a winsome, teasing light in his eyes. "They just don't make princesses like they used to. I bet Cinderella would have laughed ten minutes ago."

Cassandra didn't have enough practice to back down. "Cinderella wasn't locked up in a windowless room for two months."

"And you've never had to wash the floors and take care of stepsisters. I'd say you're pretty even. What if I asked for your hand?"

Cassandra stopped, not at all sure she'd heard correctly. "My what?"

"Your hand. The part of your anatomy you use for waving to adoring crowds and bestowing knighthoods." His grin broadened. "And slapping forward suitors. What if I asked for it? Isn't that what all fairy-tale heroes ask for?"

"The lands and the jewels usually come with it."

Paul shrugged, leaning back against the window. "I have enough land, thanks. And I look silly in emeralds."

Still Cassandra couldn't quite tell just how much he was joking. "What would you do with my hand?"

He managed to answer with a straight face. "It'd probably come in handy when I have a lot of packages to carry, or if I have to open a door and my arms are full—"

"Paul!"

An eyebrow arched. "Yes, Cassandra?"

"Why are you doing this to me?"

He laughed now, easing away from the window to approach her. "Because you're so all-fired intense. What do you think I'm going to do with you now that I know you're a princess? Drop to my knees and ask for an audience? Hand you back to the terrorists? I can't drop you off at the police station on my way out of the country. I don't know how many of the police are involved in my little escapade, and they already know you're with me. I can't leave you in the cabin. You'd die of starvation in a week."

He was standing right before her now, his hands reaching up to her arms as if to support her, to comfort her.

"Then what are you going to do?"

"I'm going to have to take you with me," he answered, his eyes honest and regretful. "I'm sorry. You're not really safe either with or without me, but we haven't had a choice since I saw that 'copter. The big guys are after us." He smiled now, and bent a little closer, his voice softening more. "There's just one thing."

She couldn't take her eyes away from his. A heat was building that mesmerized her. "What's that?"

Paul leaned closer, his breath on her cheek now, his gaze intense. "Don't expect me to back out of a room just because you're royalty. I'd kill myself."

"You . . . !" Unable to think past instinct, Cassandra went into a windup for the slap of the century. Nobody had ever treated her the way this man did.

"See what I mean?" he retorted, easily catching her hand before it met his cheek. "One of the hand's more useful purposes, especially for people with no sense of humor. Next time you do that, could I at least earn it?"

"I think you just did," she snarled, still smarting from his gibe.

"No," he disagreed, inexorably drawing her closer. "For that I deserved to be laughed at or called a jerk. Slaps should be reserved for something more important."

Cassandra couldn't take her eyes from his, and her breath caught somewhere in her chest. "More important . . ."

Paul nodded, his smile enveloping her. "Like this."

Before Cassandra could voice a protest, Paul pulled her into his arms. He caught her with her head back, her mouth open to object. His arms snaking deliberately around her already softening body, he bent to taste her lips. To savor them. He breached her defenses with quick, skimming kisses, his lips no more than a caress that pulled her closer, his hands gathering her to him, to fold her against the hard planes of his chest and meet his heart.

Again Cassandra yielded, almost before she knew what was happening, her body betraying her, her mind reeling into senselessness. All she could feel, all she could taste or smell or imagine, was Paul—his touch, his fragrance, the thrumming of his heartbeat and the sweep of his breath against her cheek.

Her defenses thoroughly crushed, Cassandra felt him return to more fully explore her mouth. His lips were so soft, so sure and compelling. He nibbled at her lower lip and outlined the edges with his tongue. Fire, wind, a rush of water—all these swirled through Cassandra's mind at the maelstrom he unleashed. A great devastation had been loosed in her body, a conflagration that melted her insides and churned her blood to boiling. Damn him, but she couldn't keep her senses about her. She'd always been able to before. But she'd never been reduced to molten liquid with just a kiss before.

"Now *that*," Paul whispered, lifting his face to offer a wry, almost apologetic smile, "merits a slap."

"That," Cassandra countered acidly, her eyes still soft and dark, her heart still stumbling, "deserves a trip to the guillotine."

Paul made no move to distance himself. "Is that how they take care of poachers in Moritania these days?"

"No," she admitted. "But for you, I'd be happy to reinstate it."

"Queen Elizabeth I knighted the men who excited her."

Now Cassandra could smile. "And *then* she beheaded them."

Paul lifted a finger to once again trace the lips he'd just tasted. "I hope you'll wait until I can at least get you back to civilization before you do that."

"I'll wait until we reach the first guillotine."

He smiled then, the wry light in his eyes self-effacing. "In that case, maybe I should make the most of the time I have."

Before he could even think about acting on that thought, Cassandra pushed him away, her posture rigid and erect, her head held regally. "I may not have my title anymore," she warned, determined to keep from falling into another, even more deadly trap, "but I do have my knees. And my fingernails. Make one move in my direction, and I promise I'll use both to full effect."

Paul wanted to laugh, glad to see the real backbone finally surface in her. So this is what the Princess Cassandra had looked like. A rare opal, she'd been all fire and light, delicious and intoxicating no matter how the light struck.

He'd heard she could be a real bitch if she wanted. For the first time, he saw how. She had the kind of bearing that by itself could send the unfortunate objects of her wrath scurrying for cover. Lady Macbeth in full raiment.

So the tiger cub had real claws. He was glad. She was going to need them in the next few hours. Rather than flinch beneath her icy regard, Paul swept a courtly bow before her. "In that case, Your Highness, we should get on with the business at hand . . . the *other* business. You clean up and I'll do a final security check outside before we get some sleep."

Cassandra's eyebrows arched with a measure of disdain. "I'm getting a bath before I nap, thank you."

"Fine," Paul agreed, turning for the door. "The dirty dishes should leave a very neat trail for the bad guys to follow."

He was ready to go out. Cassandra stood her ground, her jaw clenched in fury. She'd never had to back down in her life. Learning how to do it gracefully was going to take some practice, especially when she still couldn't think past the sudden fire Paul had ignited in her.

"You didn't let me finish," she grated, closer to tears than at any other time except when she'd been imprisoned in that damn little room. "I'm going to bathe *after* I've cleaned up the dishes."

She braced herself, waiting for Paul's comeback, sure he'd make fun of her. God, how she hated being at a loss.

Instead, the smile he offered when he turned was simple, honest. "Thanks. We'll make better time if we work this deal together."

His generosity forced an unwelcome admission from her, the humblest she'd ever offered. "I'm trying."

Paul nodded, his support sincere. "I know." Then he opened the door and walked out.

Paul took a moment after he closed the door to just savor the bite of the air. To regroup. He'd come too close, let his emotions get the better of him. There was something about Cassandra that set his blood at a quick boil, throwing his brain straight into shutdown. What began as play suddenly ended up in deadly earnest.

He wanted her. He wanted her more than any other woman he'd ever known. Paul wasn't sure if it was that beguiling waif who had first attracted him, or the glimpse of the tiger beneath. All he knew was that the minute he got too close to that sleek, supple body, his hormones took over. He felt like a moth drawn to its death by the flame in her cat's eyes.

Walking from the cottage, Paul lit a cigarette. The snow wasn't far away in these mountains. The clouds that built along the saw-tooth horizon absorbed the morning light into gunmetal gray, harsh and dark against the cerulean of an autumn sky.

They were only a few miles from the border, only hours away from friends. If only there were another way around that damn border crossing. Even if Cassandra had been an operative, a courier like the ones he'd dealt with through the years, he wouldn't want to put her in such an untenable position. But Cassandra . . .

It wasn't just her eyes that had captured him so quickly, or the life in her body. It was the challenge of her. She battled him, honing herself against him like a sharpening stone, and he liked it. He'd never had that kind of relationship with a woman before—a proud, willful, determined woman who would only retreat kicking and screaming. The duel between them stirred Paul to life. More than the glint in her eyes drew him back like that moth. It was the bite of her tongue. Paul drew another lungful of pungent smoke into his lungs and walked on, scanning the quiet mountains and wondering just when he'd get around to telling her the rest of what he knew. . . .

The bathtub in the cabin was ancient, its taps stiff from disuse. No matter what she did, Cassandra couldn't get them to budge. She stood naked, trying over and over to determine which way the little knobs turned to get the water to go on. She'd been so sure of herself when she'd stormed away from the palace two months ago. All set to prove herself to the world. And here she stood, her first real day out on her own, and she couldn't even figure out how to bathe.

Tears threatened again, the release of exhaustion. Unused to them as she was, Cassandra stiffened and assumed her most regal, most unforgiving posture.

The last thing she could do was ask Paul for help. He thought her enough of an idiot as it was. How could she explain to a man who lived by his wits that she had spent all her time learning how to run a country instead of how to take care of herself? He made her feel so inadequate, so helpless with his offhand assumptions.

The old Cassandra would have never stood for it. She would have heaped abuse upon Paul's head, battering him with her titles and privilege until he'd backed away. The old Cassandra wouldn't have prayed that Paul wouldn't walk back into the cabin until she could find whatever was used to wash dishes.

I know the exchange rates of fifty different currencies and their importance in world economy, she thought miserably, seating herself on a cold loo. I have no idea how to get a damn bathtub to give water.

"Princess?"

Cassandra jerked upright, just as full of dread as exhilaration at the sound of Paul's voice on the other side of the bathroom door. "Don't call me that," she answered stiffly, keenly aware of her state of undress. There was no lock.

"You want to go back to Emily?"

She could hear the smile in his voice. It stiffened her spine. "No," she allowed, staring straight ahead at the rough wall, tears again close. "Just Cassandra. What do you want?"

"Whatever you say, Cassandra. Are you about finished in there? You should manage to get some sleep before we head back out."

Miserably Cassandra took in the state of the tub. It was badly scarred and scratched, with chunks of porcelain missing. There were patches of rust on the outside, and one of the claw feet had been replaced by a block of wood. The tub was nothing like she'd ever used in her life. Still, it seemed the most enticing comfort she'd ever anticipated. If only she could get it to work.

"I, uh, haven't . . . well, I'm not finished. I can't get the taps to turn."

"Probably hasn't been used in a while. Want me to help?"

"No!" Turning quickly around, she made a grab for her clothes. "I'm . . . not dressed."

"Then get something on. We don't have time for formalities. Just put your slip back on."

She did, and just in time. Paul edged through the door as she backed into the far corner of the tiny room. It only left enough room for him to get in.

Paul realized his mistake the minute he walked in. He should have told her to put the jeans back on. And the sweater. And his down jacket and boots. The sight of her in broad daylight wearing just that length of silk sent his pulse rocketing.

Her hair tumbled around her pale shoulders, and her arms were crossed. The pose just served to accentuate her breasts, high and full against the sleek material. Paul jerked his gaze away from her and tried his best to pull his desire back under control.

"And don't ever wear just that again," he warned, bending to the taps.

"But you . . ."

"Don't want to get kneed and clawed in a small bathroom." It only took him a quick turn of the wrist to unstick the taps. Water spilled into the tub, echoing like a rapids in a canyon. Like the blood in his veins. All the precious objectivity that had kept him healthy these fifteen years had just been swept down the drain with that brackish water.

For someone who carefully guarded his distance while on assignment, Paul suddenly had none. He found himself on a mission with no landmarks and no instructions, and he couldn't keep his mind clear for strategy.

He couldn't think of a better way of ending up in a box.

"Thank you."

Paul turned to see the subdued light in Cassandra's eyes and watched the rest of his distance disappear. Damn her for being so alluring.

"The taps turn counterclockwise, by the way," he informed her, straightening. "The one on the left is usually hot, although there isn't any hot water here."

Cassandra's eyes widened.

Paul grinned. "Just in case you ever want to bathe again."

"No hot water?"

"These are shepherds, princess," he informed her, unable to stand away from her. "You're lucky they have a tub at all."

"I told you—"

He nodded. "You prefer Cassandra."

"You don't make that sound as much of an insult."

Paul shrugged. "Princess helps me remember that your frame of reference is different from that of most of us."

Cassandra shook her head, hair trembling, chin set regally. "You make it sound as if I have no frame of reference at all. As if I've been a leech all my life. Do you want to know the gross national product of Moritania? The banking codes for Switzerland and the Grand Cayman? The mean salary for a waitress anywhere in Europe?"

"Not really."

"Well, neither did I," she snapped, ignoring the water that still cascaded into the tub. Her eyes were hot and defensive and focused only on Paul. "But I do know. I also know European history dating back to the first caveman who clubbed a meal, and the name and religious preference of every world leader who has enough money to use a bank."

"You also might want to know that if you don't turn the taps in a clockwise direction, you're going to be cleaning water up off the floor."

Before Cassandra even had time to turn to look at the water swirling so close to the edge of the rim, Paul scooted out the door and closed it behind him. She was left in the room with just her anger and a tub full of cold water.

"I thought you were going to get some sleep."

Paul looked up from where he contemplated the scene out the front window to see Cassandra walk into the room. She was back in sweater and jeans and was trying to towel her hair dry with one of his undershirts.

"I couldn't find a towel," she admitted sheepishly.

He got to his feet, the sight of her blue lips and mottled skin propelling him. She was shivering like an old man with the ague.

"You washed your hair?"

"Of course I washed my hair," she retorted dryly through chattering teeth. "Do you know how long it's been since I've been able to bathe?"

He nodded, reaching across to pick his jacket up from a chair. "Of course. Cold water probably doesn't mean as much to a woman who takes regular walks through the rain in just her slip."

She nodded back, a grin teasing the corners of her lips. "Exactly."

He wrapped his jacket around her and eased her down into a chair near the stove. "I thought you were going to get off the topsoil. I didn't know you were going in for the whole make-over."

"I did go for the topsoil," she retorted, grateful for the warmth of not only his jacket but also his hands. The bath had been an exercise in torture, designed, she was sure, to make her appreciate the small things in life. Like hot water...and thick towels. Her science tutor had once informed her that forty percent of body heat was lost through the head. Sitting in an unheated cabin in the first days of autumn with a head of wet hair, Cassandra was suddenly inclined to believe him.

Reaching up to set the oven, Paul opened the door and walked to the bedroom to swipe a quilt.

"This is quaint. Kind of electric campfire. What do we do next, tell computer stories?"

"You really know the banking codes for Switzerland and the Grand Cayman?"

"And the finance ministers of over a hundred countries on a first-name basis. What I don't know is why it's preferable to sit in front of an electric oven. Wouldn't a fire in the fireplace give off more heat?''

Returning with the blanket, Paul draped it over Cassandra's shoulders. Then he took another of his undershirts and continued to towel Cassandra's hair dry.

"It would. It would also give off smoke. Which can be seen from the air and alert someone that the cabin is being used.''

Against her will, Cassandra felt a sweet lassitude stealing through her at the feel of Paul's hands against her hair. His movements were brisk and businesslike, but his hands were the gentlest she'd ever known. Just the pressure of his fingers against her scalp sent showers of sparks racing through her.

"Paul, I can do that myself,'' she objected with not as much affronted dignity as she would have liked.

"I know. But you're shaking so badly you wouldn't do any good. The last thing I need on my hands is a woman with pneumonia.''

She grimaced, her body warming more quickly than the heat from the oven provided. "Your concern is overwhelming.''

She was weakening, her body almost melting against the agitation of his hands. Cassandra didn't know whether she wanted to ease off into sleep or into his arms. She knew she should have been more worried, at least more outraged. The magic his fingers worked was wearing down her defenses along with her strength.

As she relaxed against the pressure of his hands, Cassandra eased back into the chair, her body relaxing. Whatever he was doing was working. She didn't even mind so much the sharp little edges that kept digging at her back from whatever that was he'd squirreled away in his jacket.

Paul knew that he didn't have to keep rubbing her hair. It was dry enough now not to cause any trouble. But the feel of it in his hands, like heavy silk, enticed him. Its color enchanted him, a dark mink that winked richly in the morning light. He liked its texture, its smell, and the way it tumbled about Cassandra's face. Paul knew he was only asking for more trouble, but suddenly, alone with her in this little cabin, he didn't care. He just wanted to bridge the distance between Cassandra and himself.

"If you knew all that stuff,'' he asked, his movements slowing a little. "Why did you leave?''

Drained by the new warmth Paul and the stove provided, Cassandra answered with her eyes still closed, her head resting in his hands. "Freedom.''

His hands stopped. Cassandra could feel his uncertainty. "You're a princess," he retorted. "Not a Russian ballerina."

"When you were five," she said, opening her eyes again and seeing more than the battered old stove before her. "What did you want to be when you grew up?"

Paul didn't have to think long. "A fireman."

Cassandra nodded. "And what did your parents do when you told them?"

"They took me to the fire station and let me sit on the pumper." It had been June, and the streets outside had been sweating with the heat. Paul remembered his anticipation when his mother had told him, the breathless exhilaration when the fireman, in Paul's memory so very tall and strong, had bent way over to set the helmet on Paul's head. He'd been sitting atop the truck when the bell went off. To the day that he'd finally left home, his mother had never tired of telling the story of trying to get him back off that fire truck before it went careering out of the station on a call.

"When I was five," Cassandra said, her voice suddenly far away and a little small, "I very much wanted to be a ballerina. I'd seen the Bolshoi at a state function the night before, and I couldn't think of anything more magical than *Swan Lake*."

When she stopped, lost in her own memories of footlights and lithe, soaring dancers, Paul pulled a chair alongside and sat.

"What did your parents do?" he asked.

Cassandra turned to him. "My mother hired a dancing tutor. My father told me to always remember that no matter how many lessons I took, or how brilliant I became, there was only one career for me. I was to be queen, and nothing was to overshadow that. When I was fifteen, I wanted to be on the equestrian team for the Olympics. I really was that good. My father was furious. He reminded me—again—what my position in life was. I was wasting my time with my silly fantasies, he said. I had obligations to fulfill that should take up all my time. From that day on, they have."

"And now? What do you want to be now?"

She smiled, her eyes sad. "I'll tell you what I don't want to be. Queen. I spent all those years learning and learning, and sitting in on one conference and conclave after another, and it didn't do any good. No matter what I was born to be, I don't have the talent for it."

"But talent doesn't necessarily fit into it, does it?" he asked. "It hasn't throughout history."

When Cassandra faced him this time, the weight of the past few months lay heavily in her mind. "I'll tell you something, Paul. I left on impulse. I thought that I could live a better life with a man who loved me than by ruling a nation that could get by without me. But after sitting alone in a room for two months, I came to an unpleasant realization. I didn't go because of Hans. He was an excuse. I went because I realized after I'd been freed from the kidnappers that my uncle and his fiancée were the ones who made a difference in my country. He ran it from his office at the bank. He projected the proper image of Moritania, not only for our people, but also for the rest of the world. He was the one who inspired confidence and loyalty. All I'd managed to inspire in twenty-three years was disdain. If I'd stayed, it would have only gotten worse."

Paul settled an arm around her, and the tightness of her shoulders telegraphed the grief her words brought. A lonely child had grown into a lonely woman. And that woman had lost her ability to bridge the distances in her life.

"I hear you were pretty much of a hellion," he remarked. "Surely that didn't help."

"Yes," she conceded with no little pride. "I was. I did it just to drive Uncle Eric and my father nuts. They couldn't tolerate it."

"What about your mother?"

The grief returned, an injury that had never been allowed to heal, a loss that still festered. "She died when I was only thirteen. After that, there wasn't anybody."

"So you set out to prove all of them right."

She shook her head, her hair trembling about her. "I don't know. I think I just wanted them to pay attention to me. To Cassandra instead of the crown princess. They never saw me that way, though. Only Mama did. And then she died. . . ."

Paul understood what it was like to forfeit your mother early. No matter what your age, the only person with whom you could always be a child was your mother. Only she would cushion your fears and understand your uncertainties without expecting anything of you. To have been in such an unforgiving position without even that support must have been devastating to an unhappy thirteen-year-old.

"Cassandra," Paul said, settling her more closely in his embrace. She accepted the closeness willingly, the solid plane of his chest comforting her. "What do you want to be when you grow up?"

She thought a moment, quiet against him, her head nestled beneath his. "Happy," she finally admitted.

The single word weighed more than any other admission Paul had ever been privilege to. Maybe because he understood it so well. Even after all these years, he foolishly held out for the same thing.

"Then you will be," he promised. "You will be."

A stupid thing to guarantee, he chided himself, still unable to draw himself away from her. You don't believe it's possible yourself. How are you going to manage it for her?

Five

"You can't steal just *any* car," Paul said as they drove by yet another candidate.

It was dusk, the clouds deepening the gloom and a cold northerly wind whistling at the car windows. Quitting the little cabin at sundown, they'd been cruising the streets and restaurant parking lots in and around Garmisch-Partenkirchen for the better part of an hour trying to find a likely car to steal. The chances were Paul's car had already been identified, leaving them vulnerable at a crossing. In a new car, though, he still might get by with just flashing his passport.

"What difference does it make?" Cassandra asked, scanning the other side of the street. The car Paul had just turned down had been a Citroën, ugly but serviceable. "The speed?"

"The style. There are certain cars I wouldn't be caught dead in."

She turned to him then, disbelief in her eyes. "Well, now that certainly makes sense. Just what car would you like to be caught dead in? It might come to that if we don't stop fooling around, you know."

Cassandra was feeling better for the five hours' sleep she'd managed that afternoon. For the first time in over two months, she'd felt safe in a bed. She'd been secure enough not even to dream. Paul had kept his vigil by the front window, claiming not to be tired. Cassandra realized that he was just watching out for problems. Shamelessly, she'd let him, and slept like a newborn beneath the delicious down comforter.

"Porsche, Ferrari, Lamborghini. Mercedes Sport if I'm really pressed."

She shook her head, delighted. "And I'm the one with the difficult reputation. Right now, I'd settle for a horse-drawn cart."

"You wouldn't if you'd ever had to outdrive the competition on a mountain road," he assured her with an unrepentant grin.

"A Volvo can do the job."

"But not with as much class. A man has a reputation to uphold."

"Who did you work for before your government?" Cassandra asked. "A chop shop?"

Paul turned on her, surprised by her terminology.

"Contrary to popular belief," Cassandra informed him archly, "the modern-day princess is quite well informed."

"She also seems to watch *Miami Vice*."

She relented with a smile. "Only after the banking conferences are over."

"There it is."

They'd pulled into the back of a small parking lot, away from the lights of a restaurant where dinner was most likely being served. In the corner, crouched like a nocturnal beast, sat a black Ferrari. It was wedged between a Volvo and an old model Peugeot.

"Aren't you asking for trouble?" Cassandra demanded, instinctively liking the line of the expensive sports car. "The owner of that Ferrari is going to scream a lot louder about his car being missing than the Peugeot's owner is."

"We'll only need it for a few hours."

"And then we'll give it right back?"

"Of course not. By then we'll be in Switzerland. But we'll leave it there safe and secure. I'll even let the police know where to find it."

"What about your car?" she asked. "How are you going to get it back?"

"I'll leave it in the lot at the train station. Then in a couple of days, I'll have a friend pick it up."

"You have those?"

"Friends? Yeah. And they all like fast cars. By the way, do you drive?"

Cassandra concealed a dry smile of triumph. "Oh, I get by."

"A stick shift?"

"Uncle Eric taught me on the Daimler."

Paul rolled his eyes. A Daimler was a great car. It was not, however, a Porsche or Ferrari. "Do you think you could drive my car down to the train station and park it without running into anything?"

Cassandra nodded, now thoroughly enjoying herself. "I think so."

He nodded, pulling to a stop before the Ferrari. "Okay. I'll meet you there in ten minutes. Try not to get kidnapped again before I get there."

Paul stepped out and handed over the driver's seat to Cassandra. He was just about to lean back in the window to give a few final warnings, when she slid the car into reverse and backed to the end of the parking lot at about thirty miles an hour. Yanking on the emergency brake and spinning the wheel, she executed a perfect 180-degree turn and sped out onto the street, her taillights disappearing quickly down the mountainous road.

Back in the parking lot, Paul could only stare. He'd never managed such a precision move in such a small area himself. "Well, I'll be damned," he breathed, a grudging smile playing on his lips as he turned back to the task at hand. It seemed the princess had a few talents of her own.

Cassandra reached the train station lot in five minutes. It was only about a third full, with the station itself nearly empty.

Shutting off the engine and killing the lights, she sat in the car and grinned. Her last sight of Paul had been satisfying. Very satisfying. It didn't hurt at all to surprise someone, especially when it was so generally assumed by the world that she was a worthless commodity. She could, in fact, do some things very well. Driving fast cars was one of them.

She'd been sitting there for a few minutes, watching a few passengers wander past the brightly lit station windows, when a new car pulled into the lot. And not the Ferrari. It was a Mercedes station wagon, with muddy license plates and a long scrape along the right front door.

Cassandra froze. Hans. How could he be here, driving the car he'd brought to the ELM with him? Was it chance, or had he somehow found out where she was?

Slumping down in her seat, she did her best to assume invisibility. Her heart raced, and her palms grew damp. The terror that she'd thought she'd put away only that afternoon ignited a hot fire in her chest and the pit of her stomach. She couldn't go back. She couldn't live through another session with Erhardt and his cold hatred.

The wagon was now parked a row away, but no one got out. It sat just as inconspicuously in its spot as the Porsche in which she waited. It seemed as if the car was watching her, as if it knew just where she was and was waiting to pounce.

She wanted to run—to sneak away from that car and dash out into the woods where no one would find her. Cassandra was working the door open when a new set of lights stabbed the darkness.

The Ferrari pulled up right next to her. She stopped, her hand still on the door handle, not knowing what to do. Paul saw her hesitation and motioned impatiently over to her. He was looking around for possible problems. He didn't realize that a problem waited for him along the next row, silently watching, waiting for someone to make a move. Cassandra still sat, frozen.

Rolling down his window, Paul leaned toward her. "Get a move on, princess. We have a couple of borders to cross before sunrise."

His voice propelled her. Swinging open the door, she crouched down out of sight. "I'm not going to tell you again . . ."

He watched her with bemused eyes. "Yeah, I know."

She yanked the door open and climbed in. "We're being watched."

"What?" His head swiveled again, his eyes as sharp as a hawk's. "Watched by whom?"

"The Mercedes station wagon over there. Hans is sitting in it."

"Hans? Hans who?"

"The man I ran away with. He's a member of the ELM now. That's the car they took me over the border in."

Even as he watched, Paul was slipping the Ferrari into gear. "Hans, huh? So, what did this Hans have that made you want to start a new life with him?"

Without even taking his eyes off the other car, he imitated Cassandra's move in the other parking lot, coming out onto the street with a definite screech at some forty miles an hour.

"Is he good-looking? Intelligent? Does he know the gross national product of Moritania?"

Cassandra kept her eyes on the parking lot behind her. They had no more than reached the street before the wagon followed, his lights coming on as he hit the street.

"He was sweet," she retorted, now very afraid. "How fast can this thing go?"

Paul laughed. "Oh, *now* you want a fast car. What happened to the Peugeot?"

"I hadn't seen my nightmare come back when I saw it. By the way, you drive very well."

"So do you. Where did *you* work before your government?"

Even with the threat of recapture hanging over her, Cassandra couldn't help but admit a certain satisfaction. "I went with the chauffeur to his terrorist evasion classes. And then I drove. He was just a little too old to want to try daredevil tactics."

Paul took a quick look in the mirror and turned onto another side road. The back spun out a little on the gravel. "How did they get you the first time?"

Cassandra grimaced. "The old bicyclist-down-on-the-road gambit. I fell for it like an amateur."

His eyes kept swiveling from mirror to road. "It's happened to the best of us," he assured her, his forehead creased. "Of course, if you'd marry me, you could put it all behind you."

Cassandra's answering laugh was dry. "I'd just be trading terrorists for spies. Thanks anyway. I was looking for something more along the line of peace and quiet when I left."

"May I remind you," he answered, swerving along a narrow mountain road with the ease of the pro he was, "that those are your terrorists rather than my spies following us."

Cassandra turned to take another look. The Mercedes still followed. "And may I ask just how they know where to find us?"

"Hold on." Slamming on the brakes, Paul turned abruptly into a tiny gravel path. Instead of following it, though, he killed the engine and lights. Then he turned to Cassandra. "I don't suppose you've been dropping breadcrumbs."

Before Cassandra had a chance to answer, the Mercedes sped right by them, continuing on along the road without seeing the Ferrari hidden in the dark trees. Paul only waited until the Mercedes had cleared the next bend before backing out and heading back the way he came, the car whining and roaring as he negotiated the difficult turns.

"They'll know we've turned around," Cassandra fretted, glancing over her shoulder. No lights appeared yet. It didn't lessen her dread.

Paul nodded, his own eyes on the course ahead. "By the time they turn around we'll be out of reach."

"How do you know?" she demanded. "They've already found us once."

"Twice, actually. I think there's a bug on the Porsche."

"A what?"

"Homing device. I think that's how they found us at the border."

"But they had plenty of time to catch up to us at the cottage," she protested.

"Did you notice the high-power wires over the cabin?" he asked. Waiting for her nod, he nodded back. "We followed them pretty much up that mountain. The very thing to scramble a homing device of any kind. The minute we came out of that field, they picked us right back up."

"Who, Hans?"

"No. The agents after me. They have the technology and had the opportunity. The station parking lot was the first time I saw that bunch from ELM."

Cassandra shook her head, truly confused. "But Hans—"

"Might have been in touch with the people after me about something completely different. It's well-known that the ELM is partially funded by them. They might have just decided to join forces on this one."

Now Cassandra's eyes widened, the news like a giant stone in the pit of her stomach. "Then we really are in trouble."

"In a manner of speaking."

"What do we do?"

"Well—" spinning the wheel with deft movement, Paul turned them back onto the main road and south "—first we get across the border. I have some friends there I can trust, and we can get this all sorted out."

"And I," Cassandra groused, "go back in the trunk."

"Nope." Reaching up onto the dash, Paul lifted another American passport. "Ferraris don't have trunks. But thanks to our unknown benefactor, we have two passports to flash, not just one. You stay where you are."

"Thank heavens," she breathed, reaching out to claim hers. It was when she opened it that the situation took on its look of doom.

"William Feldman?" she demanded, looking down at a picture of a fifty-year-old man with mustache and glasses. He looked like a banker. She'd have loved to see him in his Ferrari, as out of place as an accountant on a racehorse. "If these are examined we'll be strung up."

"I'll tell them that we just got married," he responded. "You changed your name and shaved the mustache for the ceremony."

"And what did I do about the five o'clock shadow?"

"The miracles of modern makeup."

She snorted, closing the passport. "I'm certainly glad you're enjoying yourself."

"Of course I'm enjoying myself," he countered easily. "Driving my lovely new bride to the border in a stolen Ferrari, anticipating my first kiss without her mustache—"

"You're disgusting."

"Thank you."

"What last name?"

Paul turned to her. "What?"

"You said you'd changed my name when we got married. To what? You've never told me your full name."

He turned back to the road, the darkness masking the calculation in his eyes. "Well, I figured that your uncle would at least award me a title when I took you off his hands. You know, the Duke of Earl or something?"

"We do not make peerages of old songs," she informed him. "Besides, he wouldn't do it until after we married. I'd get your name first. What is it?"

"Is that them?"

Cassandra turned to take in the flash of lights that had appeared behind them and forgot her line of inquiry. It wasn't their pursuers. She didn't see the appraising look Paul shot her or hear the soft escape of breath as he turned his attention back to escape.

"Oh, damn." Paul sighed.

Paul downshifted the Ferrari to join the line of cars at the border. A dozen vehicles waited before him, the first in line with trunk open and a swarm of officials searching every inch. Farther along in line, people leaned out windows or stood in the road to better assess the commotion. In the dead of night, the road was lit up like noon.

"What do you think?" Cassandra asked in a very quiet voice. She desperately wished that her stomach could just once have the chance to climb down from its position in her throat. The unease she felt at the roadblock changed into fresh fear as she saw the look on Paul's face.

"I have a feeling that this party is being thrown for me," he admitted, slowing the car to a stop. "I just don't know why."

She took another look at the activity. "Are you *sure* you're the innocent party in all this?"

Surprisingly enough, he took no offense. "I was when I got up this morning."

"Well, what do we do?"

After another few moments spent watching the scene, his fingers absently rubbing against the bristle on his chin, Paul turned to Cassandra. "Do you think you could go talk to them?"

Cassandra's eyes widened. He was serious. "About what?"

"Just ask what's going on. Say you're going to miss your reservation, and if it's going to be a while at the gate, you'd like to call ahead. They might not recognize you."

"And if they do?"

His expression bore nothing but encouragement. "Run back here. I'll get us out."

"Paul—"

He took her hand, anticipating her objection. "You escaped kidnappers, Cassandra. You made it on your own. So don't tell me you can't do this."

Cassandra couldn't quite pull away. "And to think I keep expecting protection from you."

"You're also the Crown Princess Cassandra of Moritania. If worse comes to worst, call your Uncle Eric and get his help."

"What about you?"

He smiled. "I've survived on my own before."

Cassandra walked along the road with her head high and her hands clenched at her sides. Paul was right. She could just call Uncle Eric and be done with it. Maybe she should admit the truth to these guards, ask for their help and leave Paul to his own devices. He certainly seemed to have enough.

She knew she couldn't. It wasn't just that Paul had been the one to rescue her, treating her with more care and concern than she'd ever received in her life. It wasn't just that he set her on fire with his touch or that she couldn't seem to get enough of the sly humor in his eyes. Within a period of hours, Paul had reacted to her with more honesty and support than any single person in her entire life. He'd believed in her. He'd bullied her like a sheepdog to show her the right direction. And he'd done it all before he'd known who she was or what she could be worth to him.

Even more important, since he'd found out, he hadn't treated her any differently. Cassandra couldn't abandon someone who had so stubbornly refused to abandon her. First she'd find out exactly what was going on, and then, if the situation warranted, she'd find them some help.

"Excuse me." She smiled with all the sleek charm she could muster. The guard she approached turned. When he caught sight of the tall, slim, beautiful woman assessing him with frank attraction, he smiled.

"How can I help you, *Fräulein*?"

Cassandra stepped close, struggling to keep the fresh anxiety out of her voice or stance. "I was just wondering what the holdup is," she said, her voice deliberately soft. She knew precisely what effect that ploy usually had and wasn't disappointed now. The guard leaned even closer, only too glad to help. "We're running late, you see, my friend and I," she went on. "We should be reaching our hotel within the hour. If we're going to be late, I'd like to notify them."

Nodding importantly, the guard motioned to the line. "We're sorry for the delay, of course. But we have reason to believe that a pair of terrorists is making for our border. They were spotted near here."

"Terrorists," she breathed, eyes wide. "Heavens, how exciting. Do you know what they look like, then?"

"No. Just that the woman has no passport. We have reason to believe that she's the former princess from Moritania, Cassandra."

"But—" Cassandra couldn't help her astonishment, her initial denial. Dear God, who could possibly think that?

"I know," the young man replied, his attitude one of weary acceptance. I've seen it all, he was saying to impress her. Cassandra knew he hadn't. "Who could imagine giving up a life like that to blow up buildings? The girl must be crazy."

"Blow up buildings? Don't be absurd."

"This morning," he said emphatically. "In Garmisch. The police station was attacked."

This morning. They'd been setting up camp in the mountains above the little town, secure that they couldn't be found, that once they reached the border everything would be all right. While they'd been out of touch, someone had committed an act of terrorism and signed their names to it.

"Was anyone hurt?"

"No, thankfully. But we've had the roadblock up since."

Cassandra was stunned into silence. There was nothing to do then. Claiming her rightful title wouldn't garner help, as she'd hoped. It would drop them right into the net that was being laid. Smiling her thanks to the guard, she walked slowly back to the car.

"Hey, there! You, wait!"

With her hand on the door, she turned to see her informant approaching, another, older guard in tow.

"We want to talk to you!"

Before Cassandra had a chance to answer or act, the door she held swung open.

"Get in!" Paul snapped. "We've been made."

Still she couldn't quite move. Too much had happened too suddenly. Cassandra was still trying to assimilate the charges against her.

"Cassandra!"

She turned at the sound of her name. He reached way over and gave her arm a good yank. Cassandra cracked her head on the roof, but she ended up in the passenger's seat before Paul turned the Ferrari in a tight circle and back up the road.

Behind them, the border staff had already swung into action. Sirens set up a wailing and uniforms bustled into a variety of vehicles. The Ferrari left them all in the dust.

"What happened?" Paul demanded, his attention once again on his driving.

Cassandra paused from rubbing the lump that was growing over her left ear. "Yes, my head hurts," she snapped. "But I think I'll be okay."

"And I'd like you to stay that way," Paul retorted without patience. "What happened back there?"

She looked ahead as lazy mountain meadows swept by the car in a blur. The sky was a midnight blue, sprinkled with autumn stars, and a half moon rode the tops of the mountains. A beautiful night for a ride in the country.

"They think I'm a terrorist." She hadn't meant her voice to sound that small. It was just that suddenly she realized how vulnerable she was. She was at the mercy of the man next to her, at the mercy of the men after her, at the mercy of her ignorance. For the first time in her life, Cassandra had no one behind whom she could hide her inadequacies.

Paul took a considering look over at her. "What else?"

"They think we blew up a police station in Garmisch this morning."

"No kidding. Did we?"

She wasn't in the mood for his humor. "Someone did."

"The guard said it was a man and a woman?"

Cassandra turned to him then. "The guard said that it was a man and the Princess Cassandra of Moritania. I got a lecture on the morals of proper royal conduct."

"Well, after blowing up a police station," he said with an easy grin, "you probably deserved it."

"After *what*?" she demanded hotly. "How dare you make fun of this. You've put me in a perilous situation, damn it." Tears threatened again, and Cassandra blamed Paul for them. "Just what do you plan to do to clear my name?"

His eyes were back on the road. "I don't think you want to know."

"I demand to know. And I demand to know now. I'm in this up to my abdicated crown, and I have a right to find out just how we're going to get out of it."

"All right." Paul shrugged. "We're going back into Garmisch-Partenkirchen, break into an office building and tap into the CIA's computer."

Cassandra's mouth went dry. "Oh, my God."

"And then," Paul continued, unfazed. "We're going to do something illegal."

Cassandra turned back to the road and sank dejectedly into her seat. "Why do I have the feeling that my life would have been a lot better right now if I'd just stayed in that little room?"

Six

"But I don't want to be your wife."

Paul shrugged. "You could be my husband, but I think that would be stretching our cover a little too much."

Coming to a stop on the sidewalk, Cassandra glared at him. "Why do you do this to me?"

Paul continued walking. "Because you're so much fun to tease. Do you know that your eyes get all squinty when you're mad? And you add about two inches to your height."

Cassandra couldn't believe her ears. It was difficult enough to deal with the fact that she was running for her life not only from terrorists but also spies. But now she found herself standing on a sidewalk—dead center in the town of Garmisch-Partenkirchen, whose police station they were supposed to have blown up—finding out how funny she looked when she got angry. For just a moment she considered cornering a passing pedestrian to ask his help sorting the whole situation out.

"I simply don't see the sense of going right back into the town we're supposed to have sabotaged and spending the night there in a hotel, where anybody can catch us," she argued.

Paul took her arm to guide her into the *gasthaus*. "I'd appreciate it if you'd list specifics in a quieter voice."

Cassandra wasn't finished. "And my eyes do not get all squinty."

"Good," Paul countered with a nod and a grin. "For a moment there, I was afraid with all that's been going on that you'd lose your perspective. I'm glad to see that your priorities are still in order."

"Since safety still tops that list right now," she retorted instinctively, "perhaps you'd care to explain all this to me." She supposed she would have sounded a lot more forceful if she weren't being propelled up a short flight of steps to the hotel's front door.

Paul held the door open for her. "The minute we reach our room. Darling."

Cassandra was feeling disoriented and not a little frantic, but she wasn't stupid. The minute she walked into the lobby, she followed Paul's lead and played the proper newlywed, cooing and smiling every time Paul looked at her. They registered without any problem.

"Perhaps you'd care for some supper after you've made yourself comfortable," the owner suggested with a smile as he pocketed Paul's prepayment. "I can reserve you a place in the restaurant."

"I don't know," Paul instinctively demurred. "It's been a long day, and we're—"

"Starved," Cassandra cut in. The only substance that had met her stomach in the past twenty-four hours had, after all, been warm beans. And not very good ones. The mention of food set up an ache in that very empty place. "I would adore something to eat. You have caviar, of course."

Paul turned on her, his astonishment showing. "Caviar?"

"Caviar?" the proprietor echoed uncertainly.

"I haven't had any in two months," Cassandra all but whined. "Two months! Do you have any idea what it's like to go completely cold turkey like that?"

"Perhaps some pâté," the gentleman was suggesting diffidently.

"Caviar," Paul informed Cassandra with laughing eyes, "is out of the question. Your father isn't feeding you anymore. I am."

Cassandra was surprised by an urge to smile back. "If you loved me, you'd feed me caviar."

"Then I guess I don't love you. Wonder if I can still get this thing annulled."

Paul was walking Cassandra forcefully up the stairs, leaving the proprietor watching from the desk in some confusion. "Salmon mousse?"

Their room was a quaint little one right up under the eaves. Cassandra walked in without noticing the heavy, dark antiques that filled the room. Her eyes were only on the bed.

"Mr. and Mrs. Peter Piper?" she asked, sinking into the mountain of goose down. It nestled her like a mother's arms, soothing the aches of weariness and inviting sleep. Cassandra closed her eyes. "Who's to blame for a name like that? You or your parents?"

"No," Paul answered from somewhere over by the windows. "My name isn't Piper. I was never good at making up names on the spur of the moment."

Cassandra grinned. "Obviously. Next hotel, let me pick the name."

"We'll be divorced by then."

"We will if you don't find me some caviar."

"This is definitely a peanut-butter-and-jelly operation, lady."

Cassandra snorted disdainfully. "I'd rather eat rocks."

She heard Paul chuckle. "Did it ever occur to you that you worked hard for that reputation of yours?"

She opened her eyes then, not sure whether she heard humor or censure in his voice. Her Uncle Eric would have offered that opinion with so much exasperation. Grandmother would have been able to slice glass with the tone of her voice. Paul only smiled, actually amused by the idea. Cassandra couldn't understand it.

Sitting up, she faced him. "My preferences are that entertaining?"

Paul turned from his view of the town to see the uncertainty in Cassandra's eyes masquerading as offense. How could anyone have let her build such a prickly fence around herself, he wondered. She was like a high-walled garden, hiding the most delectable flowers behind a near-impregnable boundary. The roses planted there were beautiful, but no one had been allowed to see them for too long. And no one, he knew, realized how fragile the glass was that made up Cassandra's boundary. An offhand comment was all it took to shatter it.

"Endearing," he disagreed with a gentle voice. "Everyone has his own bids for attention. I'm amazed no one recognized yours."

For just a moment, Cassandra lost her footing. The ground beneath her seemed to slip away and the world spun. How could he assume so much? How could he see through her so easily as no one else had?

"What did *you* do for attention?" she asked a little stiffly, still not sure she wanted to admit her own weakness.

"Me?" He smiled, turning back to the windows. "Oh, I did some beauts. Mostly I took things."

Cassandra sat up straighter. "You were a thief?"

"Apprentice thief," he amended, objecting finger in the air. "I'd passed hubcaps and was well on my way to purses when Uncle Sam made me a better offer."

"I don't understand," Cassandra said.

"The service," Paul clarified. "I joined the army."

"Not that," she countered with a brush of her hand. "Your attitude. You seem so...I don't know...objective about yourself."

"Don't count on it," he told her, once again gazing out at the street. His eyes were as dark as the night sky. "Remember how you said you had two months to think about what you'd done?"

"Yes."

"Well, I've had fifteen years. A lot begins to make sense after enough time has passed. I've dealt with the things that I chose to."

"The things you chose to?" she responded, leaning forward, pulled by the quiet revelation in his voice. "You have your life so cleanly divided that you can differentiate?"

"Everyone does," he said. "They just don't always realize it."

And tonight isn't the night to address that, he thought. There were too many people still at the periphery of his life who called for an accounting, too much truth that couldn't yet bear to be told. Yet he would have to do it soon. When he met his sister, he'd have to give an explanation for his absence that would satisfy her. Either that or he'd have to forfeit her again. Even after considering his options for the past fifteen years, Paul wasn't sure he could afford to do either.

Sitting in silence behind him, Cassandra suddenly saw the weight that pulled at Paul. He was rubbing at his eyes with the heel of his hand and slumping a little as he leaned against the wall. There were new strain lines on his handsome face, and she saw shadows of weariness that hadn't been there when she'd first met him. She remembered then how little sleep he must have managed in the past twenty-four hours. He couldn't very well do as he'd planned without at least some rest.

"Why don't you lie down?" she asked, trying to interpret the sweet pain the sight of him set up in her. She'd never experienced that kind of bittersweet ache that made her want to hold him against her. She wanted to ease those lines away, erase those shadows and see that impish grin light his eyes again.

"In a minute, I guess," Paul agreed without turning. "I'm just getting oriented from the ride in."

"But you look so tired."

With the sound of Cassandra's hesitant words, Paul finally turned to her. Tell her who you are, his conscience demanded when he saw the concern in her eyes. Explain the whole setup and let her make her own decision.

After what she's been through she at least deserves the truth, Paul thought. Isn't life just full of coincidences? Only two days ago I was on my way to my sister's wedding, and here I stumble across her double—the woman she stood in for when she was kidnapped, the woman she'll replace. What's my sister like? Is she bright and beautiful, like you, Cassandra? Is she sweeter, or thornier, happy only if she could keep a spark lit in her relationships? Will I like her as much as I like you?

"I thought you wanted to know why we came back," he said instead, his hesitation eating at him. What was wrong with telling her? It wouldn't necessarily mean she'd think less of him. It did mean that she would demand the explanation he would soon enough have to give to Casey. And after fifteen long years of running from the truth, he still didn't have the courage to face it.

"It can wait until you at least get some rest," Cassandra said. "You can't possibly go much longer without sleep." What was that hiding in his eyes, she wondered. That darkness, the furtive sadness that refused to be allowed. She realized then that for all she trusted this man, she knew nothing about him. Not even his last name. He was a spy, recently retired, and he knew how to drive a car like Andy Granatelli. He could also incite fires and soothe aching hearts like no man she'd ever known. Not much to bring back to her Uncle Eric. But his eyes were more full of empathy than any others and whatever lay at their depths compelled her.

"I'll tell you what," he compromised, leaning back against the window corner and pulling out his cigarettes. "I'll let you in on the plan, and then I'll catch a few hours shut-eye until the town goes to sleep."

"How can you do that?" Cassandra asked, distracted.

Paul lifted a cigarette. "Easy. Breathe in, blow out."

She shook her head. ''Not those, although they are a disgusting habit—''

''So you told me.''

''I mean lean up against the corner like that with your jacket on. Isn't it uncomfortable?''

Paul turned his head around, as if expecting to see shards of glass plastered into the windowsill. ''Hurting is sleeping on a glacier in February. Leaning against the wall doesn't even come close.''

''But your jacket. Don't you feel it?''

''Cassandra.'' Paul sighed. ''Don't tell me we're going to start on that again. There is nothing wrong with my jacket.''

''But there is,'' she insisted, getting to her feet. ''I feel it every time I have it on.''

Walking up to him, she turned Paul around.

''You don't have to protect your reputation with me, y'know,'' he advised, grinning at her over his shoulder. ''I *already* think you're difficult.''

''I'm telling you I felt it,'' she insisted, running her hands over his back. ''I probably have the most pampered skin in Europe. It can certainly feel lumps the size of dice in the lining of a coat.''

What confused her was that she couldn't feel anything except the lean strength of Paul's back. She pressed harder, intent on proving her point.

''Would this work better if I lay down?'' he asked, his eyes gleaming mischievously.

''It might . . .'' Then Cassandra saw what he meant. Jerking her hand away, she glared at him. ''Fine. Don't believe me. It doesn't make any difference one way or the other to me.''

''But it does, or you wouldn't keep bringing it up.''

''I just don't enjoy being called a liar.''

''Not a liar,'' Paul assured her with a tempting smile as he turned back to her. ''Simply delusionary. Besides,'' he continued, to prevent the fresh outburst he saw coming, ''after tonight you won't have to worry about wearing it anymore.''

Cassandra's reaction was predictably dry. ''We're flying to Brazil?''

''Better. I'm getting you some new clothes. Which—''

Cassandra nodded. ''Is part of the plan. Could we at least talk about this over some food?''

Paul scowled, taking a drag from the cigarette. "Back to that again, huh? This is hardly the kind of conversation one has in a public restaurant."

"Room service?"

"This is a *gasthaus*, Cassandra. Not the George Cinq. The only things we're paying for are clean sheets and a short walk to the bar."

She raised imploring eyes to him. "But I'm starving."

He just grinned. "What about that sleep you talked about?"

"All right," she conceded. "Tell me the plan, and I'll find some food while you get some sleep."

Paul thought about that for a minute. "Should I let you out by yourself, do you think? Ask the wrong person for caviar, and we'll both find ourselves on the inside of a German prison looking out."

"I'll be good," she promised, sitting on the edge of the bed and patting the space next to her. "Now sit down and tell me just why we walked right back into the town we were supposed to have just escaped."

Instead Paul paced, the cigarette smoke curling into a soft blue haze after him. "Ever read *The Purloined Letter*?"

Cassandra watched him as he walked. "By Poe? Of course."

Paul nodded to no one in particular. "The letter was best hidden by being in plain sight. It's a method I've found quite useful over the years. Hide right under your opponents' noses."

"And since we're supposed to have run from here, they'll figure we're still trying for the border."

"Especially since I led them off east toward Mittenwald before turning back. We'll stay here until tomorrow night and then make for the border west of here, at Linderhof."

"And until then?"

"Until then, we selectively visit a couple of clothing shops and food markets to stock up without being seen and then visit the insurance office I saw down the street to borrow their computer."

"But what if somebody finds out?"

"Hopefully, we'll be long gone by the time they figure out what we've done."

"What do we do when we cross the border?"

"Head south to stay with some friends who'll watch you while I take care of the rest of this."

Again, Paul's words ignited fear in Cassandra. The playful light in his eyes had completely died with his last words, leaving only a chill purpose. The professional was speaking now, the man who had spent every day of the past fifteen years dancing a knife's edge from death. Cassandra thought he must have been unnerving to face, a man devoid of emotion, of compassion, when necessary.

All that she could see in the brief glimpse she had. Calculation, control, ruthlessness. The eyes of a killer. The same eyes that had looked on her with such gentle humor. It awed her, unsettled her, reminded her yet again that she didn't really know this man at all.

"Will you sleep now?" she asked, her voice unaccountably hushed.

Surprised, Paul turned to her. He had the butt end of his cigarette between finger and thumb, just an inch from his mouth. The hesitation in Cassandra's eyes stopped him. The uncertainty in her voice. I'm something to know, aren't I? he thought disparagingly. A man who was so good at his trade that no one was sure they could quite trust him. A man no one thought could retire. God, how he hoped they were wrong. How he hoped that the legacy he carried with him from his earliest days would melt away like ice with the coming of spring.

Throwing Cassandra a careless smile he hoped would cover his silence, Paul took that last drag from his cigarette and crushed it out in a brass ashtray on the old trestle table by the window.

"Now," he acquiesced with a nod, "I'll get some sleep. Are you sure you don't want to join me?"

That fast the humor was back, the sly gibing that kept Cassandra on such an exhilarating edge. She returned his teasing with a knowing smile of her own and a shake of her head. "Not until I've had some food, thanks. And not until I get these beds apart."

"Apart?" Paul gave a very good impression of a disappointed man. "Whatever for?"

"For whatever you think," she allowed, standing and bending over to move the heavy oak frames. The beds, two heavy singles, had been moved together to simulate a double. One huge comforter had been thrown over both.

"We could pretend we're Clark Gable and Claudette Colbert and raise the Walls of Jericho," he suggested, nestling closer.

"We could not," she retorted and sidled away.

"Don't you trust yourself?"

That brought her fully upright. The last thing she could afford right then was to tell him the truth. "I don't trust *you*," she said instead, her smile widening deliberately. "Now shove."

A lot of good it did her. After heaving and shoving the two beds a respectable distance apart, Cassandra returned from her meal to find them right back where they had been before. A pair of jeans and a turtleneck were thrown over the chair. Paul was nestled dead center on the bed in a fetal position.

"Dammit, Paul," Cassandra groused, walking over to push his shoulder.

She got no response. He slept away, his breathing even and deep. In the soft womb of darkness, he looked younger, tousled, like a little boy resting after play. Cassandra was surprised by that sharp ache again, that feeling that brought her unforgivably close to reaching out and pushing his hair back from where it tumbled over his forehead.

She didn't think she'd ever seen a man asleep before. She'd certainly never had the chance at the palace. Protocol forbade barging in on anyone's private room, no matter what their station. Even her captors had slept apart from her. Cassandra had no idea whether all men or just Paul looked this innocent when they slept. It didn't seem to matter. Within moments, she'd lost her objections to climbing in under that marshmallow comforter next to him.

Cassandra pulled her slip back on to sleep. She slid in beneath the sheets and kept what distance she could from the heat of Paul's body. She didn't see the slow smile that crept over his face.

Lying next to Paul was such a companionable feeling, a warmth like that of an open fire that made you want to ease yourself up next to it. Cassandra lay for what seemed like a long while, her body stiff and uncomfortable, the temptation and the reservations battling in her.

Paul finally made the first move. Murmuring in his sleep, he turned over, ending up completely on her side of the bed. Cassandra tried to protest, but that seemed to just draw him closer. Turning completely toward her, he drew her against him with an arm. Cassandra groaned, the contact of his body unnerving her.

He had undershorts on. That was all. She could feel the smooth skin of his arms and the bristle of hair on his chest. His legs, hair-covered and solid, insinuated themselves along hers.

"Please don't," she begged, struggling to break away. "Please, Paul."

His bristled chin nestled against her neck. She could feel his breath fan across her throat, like the wash of a summer breeze. His arm wrapped around her waist, bringing her closer. Cassandra pushed it away, but the brand remained. Her skin sang with it, her muscles shuddered. With just that brief contact, she felt as if he'd deposited a hot ember in her belly, and all it took was the ebb and flow of his breath to fan it.

Terrified, exhilarated, Cassandra found herself frozen. No matter the reputation she'd managed to build over the years, she'd never found herself in a position in any way similar to this. Common sense told her not to be found in it much longer. Exhilaration told her that she'd never known anything like it before.

It was intoxicating, ennervating. She couldn't get away from it, couldn't fight it. Almost without thinking, she nestled closer to Paul's hold, instinctively seeking the reassurance of his heartbeat, the turmoil of his touch.

Immediately his arm sneaked around her again. Cassandra turned toward him. Her own hand sought the sleek line of his chest. Her legs settled against his. Her heart hammered suddenly, and her lungs couldn't keep up. The ember leaped into flame, its tongues dancing up her chest and along her limbs. The last vestige of defense raised itself, warning against her rashness. Paul nuzzled against her neck and the warning died.

"I told you not to wear that slip," he whispered.

Cassandra started. "You're awake."

"Either that or I'm having the best dream I've had in fifteen years." Gathering her closer, he tested the silk with lazy hands, tracing it along the line of her hips and up to her waist. "You're being unfair."

Cassandra felt his hand edge toward her breast and held her breath. "I'm not the one who pushed the beds together."

Paul dropped kisses along the back of her neck, unleashing hot sparks in his wake. "Fire code," he murmured.

Cassandra couldn't help but giggle, her blood racing through her veins. She ached, feeling swollen and uncertain, her body trembling for wanting to know what would happen. What would his hands, his lips, his tongue, feel like against her? He reached up to tempt her breasts with racing fingers, and with a gasp, she knew.

"Why am *I* unfair?" she demanded, her voice throaty with surprise.

"Because by now," he countered, brushing a palm across her nipple and returning to tease it, "you know what silk on you does to me."

Cassandra couldn't think. Fire leaped from his fingertips. Just the suggestion of his touch through the silk sent shafts of lightning to her toes. How could a body she'd lived with all these years have this in it, when she'd never known it? She'd stored quicksilver in her, which only Paul could unleash. Fires and tempests swirled through her with a fury that was astonishing.

Paul raised himself above her, edging his knee between hers and dipping to taste her lips. With a hand as gentle as sunlight, he brushed her hair back from her forehead. Cassandra arched against the play of his hand as it slid back down lower across her belly, seeking contact with its fire, instinctively beckoning. He kissed her again, his mouth urgent against hers, his tongue clever. Cassandra felt the terror rise with the excitement and couldn't breathe.

He was sapping her resistance, melting her with the art of his hands and mouth. His tongue tasted like tobacco and mint, and greeted hers with insistence. His hands anticipated her, outrunning the molten heat that coursed through her. As he pulled her closer, Cassandra felt the hard, unyielding length of him against her and suddenly panicked.

Not now, her mind told her, her hands coming up to his shoulders. Not yet. You don't know him. You don't know how much you can trust him, and a princess never . . . a princess never . . .

"Paul, no," she gasped, finally pushing him away. "Please, I can't."

Paul reined himself in. Looking down at the sudden fear in Cassandra's eyes he reached out to her. Once again, he brushed her hair back, his action as caring as that of the dearest of friends.

"What's wrong, Cassandra?"

She couldn't face him. Turning away, she looked out toward the moonlit gray of the window. "This shouldn't be a surprise. It shouldn't . . . outdistance me."

"What shouldn't?" His heart still pounded, but he was getting his breathing back under control. He wished he could say the same about the rest of him. If Cassandra hadn't set him off so fast, he might have been making better sense of what she was trying to tell him.

"Maybe you're used to this kind of thing," she accused defensively. "Maybe twenty-four hours is enough to know . . . or maybe you don't care. But I've been taught differently. I've been raised to expect . . ."

With a shuddering start, Paul finally caught on. "Cassandra, look at me."

After a moment, she did.

"You've never . . . made love to a man before, have you?"

Paul needed no more than the painful uncertainty in her eyes for his answer. "What difference does that make?" she demanded.

But instead of the censure Cassandra seemed to expect, Paul offered only a smile. "All the difference in the world. You're right. It shouldn't outdistance you. It almost outran me, and I'm a pretty fast runner."

Cassandra arched an eyebrow at him. "Now is hardly the time to be boasting."

Paul sat up next to her, his body still trembling with the cost of control. "I'm trying to apologize," he said. "You've been setting my short fuse from the minute we met. I guess tonight I just kind of let my guard slip. I wanted you, and I decided I was going to—"

"*Have* me?" she demanded acidly, sitting up herself. "Don't you think I should have had a vote in this?"

Paul's grin was sheepish. "I kinda figured your reaction *was* your vote."

"My reaction had nothing to do with my vote," she snapped, pulling a fallen strap back up to proper position, as if that was all it took to regain her propriety. "My body seemed to short-circuit tonight." Without looking at him, she completed her admission. "Just the way it has since I met you."

"Then you'd like to *have* me, too?" Paul teased, leaning back against the headboard and watching her with laughing eyes.

Cassandra wasn't quite ready to be mollified. "In a warped manner of speaking, I suppose."

"Then let's give it a chance," he suggested gently. "With time and patience is how this lesson should be taught. I'm willing to put in my share after we get a few of these distractions taken care of."

"Oh, so it's a lesson, now, is it?" Cassandra countered, facing him down. "Another little slice of life to feed poor, deprived Cassandra?"

"Stop being so defensive," he retorted, reaching out to her. "It gives you wrinkles. I'm sorry about tonight. I'll do my best to make amends in the most pleasant way I can when this is over. Deal?"

"I'll let you know when all this *is* over."

Paul nodded, satisfied with the compromise, certain he couldn't promise more. To promise he would leave his hands completely off Cassandra would be more than even a saint could hope for.

"Since that's settled, how about getting a little more sleep before I have to go out again?"

"Will you stay on your side?"

He crossed his heart. "On my honor."

Cassandra nodded, her body betraying the fallacy of her determination. "In that case, I'll try. But one hand on me . . . anywhere on me . . ."

Paul nodded. "I know. Teeth and knees. Good night, my lovely bride. The honeymoon so far has been more than a man could dare dream of."

"Drop dead." Cassandra smiled brightly and sank back beneath the covers.

Seven

Outside, the world slept. Night was creeping on toward morning, the stars in the sky outshining what few lights still dotted the streets below. Even the birds were still, pausing between the night and early morning. Watching from the dormer window, Paul knew that now was the time to go.

He hadn't needed an alarm to wake him. These were the hours of the day he'd always found most useful for his work. Now he instinctively awoke in the deepest hours of night.

Taking a final drag from his first cigarette of the day, he looked over to where Cassandra still lay nestled amid a mound of snowy white linen. God, he was going to have to be more careful. Move more slowly. He hadn't even stopped to consider when he'd pulled his little game on her that she might not have been as experienced as she was touted to be. Who could have possibly guessed that the jet-set princess, seen everywhere with the best and brightest of companions, was as innocent of lovemaking as she was of anything else in life?

Paul shuddered to think of how close he'd come, how relentlessly he'd pushed her toward that foregone conclusion. I want you, you want me, so what difference can it make? Except, in the insular world of Moritania, it made a great difference.

Not that he'd been much more than a monk himself these past few years. His occupation had made sure of that. If he tried hard enough, he could blame his unaccustomed impatience on that. But Paul knew that wasn't the reason for his actions. He'd been attracted before. He'd been more than sorely tempted. Not once had he put himself in the kind of vulnerable situation he had tonight. The reason for tonight's performance was none other than the lady who still slept in the disheveled bed behind him.

Was she such a kindred spirit, this woman who'd had no real childhood? Did he look at her and see a reflection of himself? He wasn't sure. All he knew was that he understood her better than she understood herself. He shared in her loneliness in a way he didn't want to acknowledge. He and Cassandra were a pair of vagabonds who had built strength from confusion, who had finally worked up the courage to flee what they couldn't abide. It had just taken Cassandra a little longer to do it.

She still sang in him, even these hours after he'd held her in his arms. What was it she'd said about the most pampered skin in Europe? All he knew was that her skin was the softest, the sweetest, he'd ever touched. It had felt like rose petals and velvet, alive to his hands, sparking a kind of heat he'd never met before.

He ached, sitting alone in the dark. The memory of Cassandra curling into his arms, lifting her lips to greet his, the heat of her body, still imprinted on his like a burn, ruined his sleep and gave him no peace. He felt himself drawn to her as inexorably as a ship to the Lorelei, and knew that, for better or worse, it would be he who would finally teach Cassandra that final lesson of love. And it would be he who would suffer for it.

Giving the thought its due with a shake of the head and a sigh, Paul finally got to his feet and began to dress.

"I hope you're not trying to sneak out on me."

Balanced on one foot as he worked his other leg into his jeans, Paul noticed Cassandra sitting up in bed. The ache in his gut sharpened and took form with the sight of her sleep-tousled hair, her pale face in the darkness. Her slip had bunched a little, leaving a strap dangling and the top drooping low over one breast. Paul couldn't drag his eyes from the sight. With a silent curse, he bent to his task.

"I won't be long."

As quick as a cat, Cassandra was out of bed. "You're not leaving me back here waiting for you to get arrested or something. I'm coming along."

Paul glared at her. "Would you just for once do something without arguing about it?"

Cassandra's answer was a knowing smile. "I have a reputation to uphold, too, you know. I'm coming."

He shook his head impatiently, zipping his jeans and fumbling with the snap. "Well, whatever the hell you do, I wish you wouldn't do it in that slip anymore. Aren't you getting just a little tired of wearing it?"

She looked down at it. "I washed it back at the shepherd's hut," she protested, as if that were the problem. It had taken her fifteen minutes to find the soap. Finally noticing the slipped strap, she repositioned it. "Besides, even for a girl who likes a brisk walk, I figured that the proper attire for robbery would probably be something closer to pants and a shirt."

So saying, Cassandra began looking around for the self-same objects. Cassandra wasn't as comfortable working in the dark as Paul. Rather than risk one more crack of her shins she opted for the lights. She had her hand only an inch from the switch when Paul moved.

"Don't." Before she knew what was happening, he had her hand in his own, pulling it away.

"But I can't see," Cassandra objected, turning to challenge him. She shouldn't have. Paul was still in only his jeans, the frail window light liquid along the sleek lines of his chest. He smelled like sleep, warm and musty and enticing, and she suddenly found herself battling against the same instinct that had had her nestling up against him in bed no more than a few hours earlier.

It had infuriated her that Paul had drifted off to sleep so easily after that. She'd lain stiff and silent on her side of the bed, losing the battle against reliving the sweet familiarity she had found in his embrace. How could he have been so unmoved when she had been in such turmoil?

But then, she decided even as her chest had tightened and her heart lost its rhythm, he's probably much more used to that sort of thing than I. At least, she thought, easing closer to the heat of his body even as her better sense shrilled against the movement, he probably doesn't have quite the control I do.

"The less attention we draw to ourselves the better," Paul murmured, his eyes like pale gems in the darkness, their intensity belying the calm pragmatism of his words.

Cassandra could have sworn that she heard his heart, felt it through her fingers. Abruptly, she jerked her hand away. She had no throne to protect anymore, the voice of insanity told her. No duty, no honor worth upholding. What reason did she have to ignore the frightening chemistry between them? Why not just dive in headfirst and see how long it took to come up?

Because Paul had fallen asleep when she hadn't been able to. The inequity troubled her too much to ignore.

"Then if you'll be kind enough to show me the way to my pants," she finally acquiesced with regal control, "I think I'll be able to take it from there."

"Your pants," he told her, his body impossibly close, his words frustratingly cool, "are right behind you. Don't trip over the table."

Cassandra gave him a chill little nod, her body at terrible odds with her brain. "I won't take long at all." And just for perversity's sake, before she turned away, Cassandra lifted a hand and oh, so gently raked a nail along the length of Paul's chest. His sudden, sharp intake of breath satisfied her enough to smile.

Without another word, she turned to the task at hand.

"Where do we go first?" she asked a moment later as she buttoned an oversize flannel shirt.

"I'd still rather you didn't go at all," Paul retorted from behind her. From the location of the sound of his voice, she assumed he was donning shoes. Or praying.

She smiled again, at least more firmly possessed of her own powers. "I told you. It isn't a choice. And you know how contrary I can be when I don't get my way."

From behind her came a most ungentlemanly oath. "I'm beginning to find out."

"What kind of stores are we going to hit?"

That provoked a groan. "I'd really appreciate it if you didn't sound quite so enthusiastic. When I hand you back to your uncle, I'd rather it not be with a whole new set of problems."

"My uncle?" she countered, spinning on him. "You aren't really going to deliver me back to the lions, are you?"

Paul smiled with some satisfaction. Cassandra could just catch the gleam of his teeth in the dimness. "Smack-dab in the middle of the pit."

"But I don't want to go back. I told you."

He got to his feet, picking up his jacket and slipping an arm into it. "And how else am I going to be reimbursed for all the money I'm spending on you?"

"Spending?" she retorted archly. "You've just been talking about robbing stores."

"Not... robbing," he disagreed. "Merely creatively procuring. I plan to leave extra money behind in the bottom of the till. And what about dinner tonight? Who paid for that little repast?"

"But you don't have to go to Uncle Eric. I'm worth..."

When Cassandra's voice trailed off, Paul grinned. "The price of one well-worn slip and some pretty good hair coloring. By the way, do you want to pick up some more when we go out? You're growing roots."

Cassandra couldn't think of anything more to do than glare. He'd managed to regain the upper hand. "I can't wait to see you come face-to-face with my Uncle Eric. He'll have you back out the door so fast that your wheels will be spinning. Besides," she added with perverse satisfaction, "the last person on the face of the earth he'd pay to get back is yours very truly. You'll walk out of that interview as empty-handed as when you walked in."

Again Paul surprised her. Instead of escalating the argument, heaping challenge upon challenge, he simply walked up and cupped her chin with gentle fingers. "In that case, I pity Moritania. They have a ruler with very little sense."

"But we're so close. Why not just make a little side trip?"

"I told you. No caviar."

Her thoughts still on the display in the window one door down the street, Cassandra snorted with disdain. "You'd sing a different tune if we were talking cigarettes."

"Thanks for reminding me." With swift movements, Paul plucked a couple of cartons from the shelf and deposited them in his backpack with the other staples they'd been collecting.

"Why don't you quit smoking?" Cassandra demanded, following behind. In the darkness, she could barely make out the labels on the various boxes and cans, but the variety stunned her. She couldn't imagine how anyone ever made a choice in a place like this.

"Why don't you quit caviar?" Paul countered, scooping up a couple of loaves of bread.

"It seems I just did," Cassandra pouted.

Walking closer to the shelves, she peered at the multicolored-wrapped packages, praying she'd see even a tin of low-grade Romanian. Anything. Cassandra positively craved the salty decadence. She knew darn well that she'd lost weight this past two months because she'd been denied her favorite treat. Or her attention-getting device, as Paul would say. Well, what was wrong with an attention-getting device that tasted good?

The way things were going, though, she was going to have to find a substitute.

"Ooh, this looks intriguing," she mused, coming to a halt before a box with a dark wrapper. "Are these any good?"

Paul turned to look. "Are you kidding? They beat caviar all to hell."

"But what are they?"

He seemed genuinely surprised. "You mean you really don't know?"

Cassandra instinctively stiffened. "I didn't do the shopping. And I don't remember ever having been served these."

Paul nodded, picking up the package and adding it to his booty. "Yeah, come to think of it, I guess you're right. There's only one problem."

"What's that?"

"You can't eat Oreos without milk."

Cassandra picked up another package, scanning the label for some hints. "Why?"

"Why?" Paul echoed in disbelief. "Why? Would you eat duck without l'orange? Would you eat strawberries without cream? Would you—"

"I get the picture. Find some milk."

Cassandra enjoyed their trip to the little store enormously and found herself looking forward to visiting stores in the daylight. There was so much there that she hadn't ever even seen before, so much world she'd never been allowed to taste. She followed Paul around and questioned all his "purchases," and then helped him stow the food in what trunk space there was in the car. From there, they went on to the kind of shopping Cassandra was more familiar with.

Paul was absolutely brutal with his limitations, allowing Cassandra to pick up only enough to get her comfortably through the next couple of days—underwear, jeans, shirts, shoes and jacket.

"You wanted the simple life?" he asked with a wry grin when she protested the exclusion of a beautiful patterned sweater from the collection. "This is the simple life. No more than one outfit for any occasion."

They compromised with a couple of extra blouses and left it at that. From there, it was a short walk up a steep hill to the insurance office Paul wanted to visit.

Having looked at the clock in the little store, Cassandra knew it was closing in on three-thirty. She'd never been alone outside at this hour before. Until now there had been security and companions and servants, all hovering, all too close. As she walked through the silent streets of Garmisch-Partenkirchen with Paul, she discovered yet another world she'd never been privileged to.

The earth took on a mystical quality this early in the morning, quiet and waiting, as if watching for the dawn. The moon had almost been swallowed by the mountains, but the stars still blazed in a blanket of light that swept across the sky like a vast glittering cyclone. The wind, ever present, brushed sweet music through the tops of the trees. A few leaves danced along the street and into the gutters. The buildings, whitewashed to a pristine white, glowed softly in the starlight. Cassandra could smell late flowers and pine and hear the mutterings of the first birds.

Just that simple sight, like a revelation always there for her to discover, threatened to overwhelm her. For the first time, she realized she had the luxury to stop and savor it. For the first time in her life, she had someone with whom she felt she could share it.

Without a word, she slipped an arm through Paul's. He didn't answer as he continued to scout the streets for trouble, his tread light and anticipatory. Even so it seemed to Cassandra that he knew just what she meant. Pulling her just a little closer against him, he squeezed her arm and smiled.

This time it took Paul all of twenty seconds to get inside the building. Clucking over the lax security in the little village, he swung the door open and ushered Cassandra in before him.

Cassandra took a moment to look around her, but found nothing of real interest. They entered what was merely a sectional office with unremarkable furniture, a computer terminal on each desk and assorted well-tended plants in the windows. A few framed prints were hung on the walls, but she couldn't make out the artist in the dark. The whole place looked well tended and well moneyed without standing out in any way.

Paul led her directly to the nerve center, a room toward the back that had no windows. Cassandra lost all sense of direction in the enveloping blackness and walked right into Paul's back.

"Oh, sorry."

"Here," he offered, guiding her through. "Let me get the door."

Cassandra saw that he meant to close them in and turned in Paul's general vicinity. "We broke in to stand in a closet together?"

He chuckled. "Seemed like a good idea at the time."

But when he flipped the light switch, Cassandra understood. The room was small, with only a few desks and chairs. The prints, she saw now, were Impressionist and Postimpressionist, good quality. A Pissarro and a Cézanne hung in this little room, bringing vivid slashes of color to an otherwise Spartan decor. There weren't even any plants to share space with the overwhelming technology.

The secret here was in the concentration of computer equipment. There weren't any huge banks, all whirring and blinking like in the movies. All it took these days was several desktop models, bracketed by printers, phones and files. The insurance company's link to the world.

"How did you know where to look?" she asked, impressed by Paul's ability. She'd seen no more than the planters and the sign above the door when they'd driven by earlier. How had he unerringly known what the building would hold and where to find it? And in the dark? She'd no more than said it when she caught the amused glint in Paul's eye and shook her head. "Secrets of the trade," she conceded with a grin.

"Standard stuff," he admitted, already seated at the closest terminal. "Princesses have 'em, too."

"Of course," Cassandra retorted dryly. "We're renowned for our professional ability."

Paul smiled without taking his eyes from the flash of green on the computer screen. "I don't know the first name of any of the finance ministers of the world," he reminded her. "And if you put me in the same room with any of them, I'd probably end up provoking an international incident within a matter of minutes."

"Well," she acquiesced, mollified. "If you put it that way, maybe I wasn't all that much of a worthless leech, after all."

"I didn't say anything about that." He grinned easily, eyes still on business.

Her attention already on the incomprehensible material Paul was calling up on the computer screen, Cassandra pulled up a chair and joined him. "Thanks for the vote of confidence. What are you doing?"

He tapped a few more keys and the computer responded. "Just getting acquainted. I have to get this little beauty to call a friend for me."

"To call a friend? How?"

He took a second to deliver a look of consideration. "Didn't they teach you anything in that princess school you attended?"

Cassandra shrugged. "Computers intimidate me. We don't seem to think alike."

Paul actually laughed. "I can believe that," he admitted. "All right, this is how it goes. I hook up the modem and have the computer contact the computer at Langley."

Cassandra watched the interplay take place on the screen, listened to the whirring and clicking of the computer in action and found herself no more enlightened. "What are you looking for?"

Paul punched up a final message and leaned back a minute. "Some kind of clue as to why somebody's after me. I'm checking my file and the records of the last two... transactions I made. Maybe there's something there that I missed."

"Why not just call the CIA and ask your boss?"

"This is much more fun. Besides, if there's a problem he doesn't want me to know about, he'll be the last to admit it."

"You mean he could tell you everything's all right and let you walk around as bait so they can catch the Russians that are following you?"

"Or call me back to Langley to discuss the problem someplace secure, and bring the agents with me... who are East German, by the way."

"But why don't you do that?"

"Langley's in Virginia. A lot can happen between here and there."

She nodded, easily able to appreciate that. "So, what's going on now?"

Paul peered at the screen, his concentration almost excluding Cassandra as he scanned the pages of text that flipped across the screen. "My last couple of assignments. If you don't mind, this might be a good time to appreciate the Cézanne over there."

"You mean you don't trust me?" Her outrage was quite real.

"I mean I'd rather you not know anything anyone might consider valuable enough to hurt you for."

Cassandra didn't need to be told twice. Launching herself from her chair, she walked over to study Cézanne's still life.

Cézanne had always been one of her favorite painters. If Cassandra had ruled, she would have replaced the saccharine Fragonards in the palace with Cézannes, Monets, Pissarros, Van Goghs, maybe a Picasso or two. She'd bring some fresh life into that stuffy old place. But she wouldn't rule. Her Uncle Eric would, and he'd see no reason to break with tradition any more than any other person in that incredibly claustrophobic place.

It was probably better that she would never get the chance to reign, she decided with a wry smile, her hand up as if to absorb the bold energy in the print. It would have only been a matter of years before she would have demanded Jackson Pollocks and then the tradition-bound Moritanians would really have thrown her out on her ear.

"Any surprises?" she asked over her shoulder.

Paul sounded disappointed. "Not a one. Everything went just the way I remembered. No loose ends that should pop up to haunt me."

"And you didn't do any free-lancing on your way to southern Germany that might have ruffled any feathers?"

"None. All I did was stop for a drink at a friend's house in Berlin on my way out of the city. We didn't even talk shop."

"Another . . . spy?"

She heard him chuckle. "If you want to be terminally cute about it. We started about the same time. He's on the diplomatic side of things now, with a wife and daughter to make him respectable."

"And you?"

"I quit, remember?"

"But what do you have? What are you leaving for?"

When Paul didn't answer right away, Cassandra turned. He still faced the computer, still scanning the words, but his eyes were miles away, tallying up the burden of his experience. Cassandra saw the ghost of his past in his expression, memories that would never be hers to share.

"Another old friend," he finally admitted, his eyes briefly meeting hers over the terminal. "He made me a bet that I couldn't pass up."

"You're going to work for him?"

"No. He died a few months back. Left me something in his will if I promised to get out of the game then and there."

Cassandra's eyebrows lifted. "Really? What did he leave you that would make such an impact?"

Paul shrugged, already back to his task. "Some land in Ireland. It's peaceful there. Simple. Hard work and honest people and no more looking over my shoulder."

"Ireland," she breathed, tuning in to her own pictures. Cassandra had been to Ireland once, on a goodwill tour. She remembered the legendary green, so vivid in the sunlight that it hurt her eyes. She remembered the people, so kind and simple that they seemed transplanted from a different era, caught in a kind of time warp. While shaking hands and accepting flowers from rosy-cheeked children, she imagined herself walking such streets, free of all the stress of the real world. Had she been born to another life, she might have tried it. "Do they have computers in Ireland?" she asked.

Paul looked up, a bit confused. "Of course. I have a feeling they have more pubs, though. Why? Do you want to go with me?"

"Just think—" she smiled brightly "—if I gave you my hand, you'd be the one who'd have to divide up your land. Speaking as a princess, I find that idea rather attractive."

Paul scowled. "You would. Of course, on these lands, you'd have to help milk the cows and groom the horses."

She nodded, considering. "It would certainly be a new experience. I don't suppose we could have a trial run."

Paul chuckled. "You'll get that when I drop you off at Brian and Gerta's in a couple of days. They have plenty of farm animals to care for."

"Brian and Gerta?"

"Another old friend. He's the caretaker on my farm, but he and his wife are watching Gerta's parents' farm while they're on vacation."

Cassandra nodded. "A lot of imagination. I like that in a man."

She'd wandered over to the Pissarro, a little street scene from Paris. It was a print of a painting she'd seen in the museum she'd almost come to call her second home. When Cassandra traveled and no one knew where to find her, she'd go to the museum or the countryside. Oh, to be able to absorb the light and form of the world around her and create something this brilliant from it. To be able to create at all, bringing life from nothing. A word on a page, a splash of color on a canvas, a muscled torso from marble so lifelike that you waited for it to take its next breath.

Cassandra was not an artist. She did not create and that lack haunted her. If only she'd been able to offer some form of art, she would have suffered more gladly the imprisonment and stifling boredom of her position.

She'd been so wrapped up in the regrets the paintings conjured up for her that she didn't realize how quiet Paul had become. It was only when she heard a soft oath behind her that she turned.

"Bad news?"

He nodded. "Bad news. They've closed my file."

Cassandra came closer, the expression on Paul's face unsettling her. "But you've retired. Wouldn't that make sense?"

"No. The information's always available. This says that my file's being revised . . . which doesn't make sense."

He hit a couple of other keys, but the results didn't satisfy him.

"Your *personal* file?" she asked, still unsure of the ramifications. "The one about birth and marriage and hair color?"

He nodded again.

"You haven't changed the color of your hair lately, too, have you? Maybe they're just catching up."

"This is not catching up," he retorted. "This is some kind of housecleaning. I think it's time to make some calls."

"But I thought you said that you wouldn't find anything out."

"I'm not calling the boss." That was all she got out of him as he reached for a phone and began dialing.

"This insurance company is going to be a little upset when they get their phone bill next month," she observed dryly.

"Justin?" he barked into the phone. "Phillips. I know I woke you up, but something's wrong. Are you secure? Okay, here it is. Where the hell's my file?"

"Your file?" he heard the sleepy voice answer from five thousand miles away. "What are you talking about?"

Suddenly feeling unbalanced, Paul gripped the receiver more tightly. "You know, Justin, my personal file. In the computer. Somebody's screwing around with it, and I want to know why."

"Why are you looking up your file, Paul?"

It was the tone of voice. Careful. Calculating. Paul found himself running a hand through his hair. "Stop jerking me around, friend. Just tell me why I'm suddenly a nonperson."

"Are you having problems over there, Paul? I thought your retirement went through this week."

"Just tell me. I don't have time for games."

A pause, then real worry in a voice he knew too well. "You haven't been taking two paychecks lately, have you?"

"What!"

"We've had a mole problem here. Deep level. The search showed up a bank account for you we didn't know you had."

"Then I don't know about it, either. The only money I've gotten in the past fifteen years is the inheritance from Williams. And everybody in the company knew about that."

"Might be a good idea to come in and check it out, Paul."

But Paul knew better. Somebody had set him up, and the answers weren't in Virginia. They were right here.

"When was this found?" he demanded.

"Just this morning."

"They move fast."

"Who?"

"I'll be calling, Justin. There are some things to settle over here first."

"But, Paul . . ."

"Just try to keep the hounds off me until I get it figured out. I'm clean, Justin. You know it."

Before Justin could do more to convince him against his course of action, Paul hung up.

For the moment, he completely forgot about Cassandra. He was tapping into his own mental computer, calling up years of experience and training. Remembering incidents as far back as a year that might have had some bearing on the present situation. For the life of him, he still couldn't think of anything.

The word in the business had been that Paul Phillips couldn't be blackmailed. The very best had tried at one time or another, and all had failed. Who had blindsided him, and how were the East Germans involved? True, his last two assignments had involved the Potsdam mission in East Germany, but he'd already turned in his reports, and neither had contained anything all that startling. If they were trying to discredit him, it was for almost worthless information. Even the East Germans wouldn't waste that much time for that.

The question was what to do now. He had to get over the border as soon as possible and make contact with Brian and Gerta. He couldn't warn them beforehand, just in case their line was tapped. He'd just have to drop in and beg their indulgence.

In his time, Brian had been the best. He'd been retired three years now, sidelined by injury and happily relegated to Paul's farm in Wicklow. But Brian was an old fire horse. A hint of smoke and he'd be more than willing to help. Paul wished he felt better about asking him.

"I guess it's safe to say that the plot has thickened?" Cassandra asked gently.

Startled, Paul looked up. God, how he wanted a cigarette. He'd left them in the car. Besides, he didn't want to leave the hint of smoke in a smokeless office to trace his steps.

"It's congealed," he answered with a slow shake of his head. "Somebody has gone to a lot of trouble to set me up, and I don't know who or why."

"How are you going to find out?"

He pulled his hand through his hair once again, still calculating, and then moved to shut down the computer. "I'm going to do just what I'd planned. Drop you off with Gerta and ask Brian to help me locate the source of my problems."

"And after that?"

Looking up from his task, Paul was surprised to see the concern in Cassandra's eyes—a concern that centered solely on him. "After that," he retorted, flashing her an impudent grin, "maybe I'll ask you to marry me again."

Eight

"I wish you'd stop saying that," Cassandra said as she and Paul walked down the street. Daylight had begun to edge out night, and the birds had awakened. Soon the farm animals would begin to drift out to pasture, accompanied by a symphony of bells. The moon had finally disappeared. The stars, so bright only minutes before, had begun to fade, and the border between earth and sky had grown indistinct.

Cassandra walked with her head down, her eyes on the sturdy walking shoes Paul had picked for her. If all the soothsayers in the world had pointed to this moment in her life, she would have laughed at them. Nothing in her well-protected existence could have prepared her for the time she'd find herself on the run with an espionage agent, clad in down jacket and slacks, and happy to be in shoes she would have once relegated to Miss Marple. The woman who had once graced the covers of more than one fashion magazine for her trendsetting had regressed to functional, and she was surprised at how much she liked it.

Maybe it was the company. She looked over at Paul, but his attention was on his problem. With his cigarette clamped between tight lips, hair dancing in the early morning breeze and his eyes as dark as the predawn sky, he looked even more disreputable than dangerous. Cassandra could have spent the better part of the day feasting herself on the sight of him.

"What?" he asked, finally focusing on her.

"I said," she repeated with a smile, "that I wish you'd stop proposing just to fill in the dead space in a conversation."

For just a moment, it seemed as if he hadn't followed her train of thought. His brow remained furrowed, the line of his jaw as taut as she'd ever seen it. The strain of that last phone call vibrated in the very timbre of his voice.

Cassandra was surprised by a renewed urge to reach out to him. To run her fingers over those brutal creases, to edge away the taut set of his mouth with gentleness. She hurt to see him like this.

Finally, just when Cassandra despaired that she could get any kind of reaction from him, Paul plucked the cigarette from his mouth and tossed her a grin. "What makes you think I'm not being sincere?"

Cassandra flushed with her small triumph. Paul's eyes had lightened just a little. "Proposals are made on one knee, with a ring in hand. And from where I come from, a very sizable ring."

"Sorry," he answered with a shake of his head. "I'm all out. I do know where I can get a can of caviar, though."

Cassandra groaned, sincerely tempted. "That's not fair."

They reached the car and Paul helped her in. It was no more than a three-minute ride back to the *gasthaus*. Cassandra settled into the leather seat and smiled, her satisfaction growing. It amazed her how powerful the pleasure could be from simply making a difference in someone else's frame of mind. Laughter, support, companionship. How had she survived without that all these years? How could she possibly look forward to a future without it? She'd felt more of a sense of accomplishment the minute she'd seen the mischief reappear in Paul's eyes than she had all the times she'd created news or made policy.

"Where's the canary?" Paul asked, sliding in and reaching for the ignition. The car turned over to a throaty purr, and Paul pulled out.

"Canary?" Cassandra asked, just a little confused. He had quite a superior smile on his face.

"You have feathers all over your face. Why do I have the feeling they're mine?"

Cassandra let an eyebrow slide up, her smile now self-contained. "I was just thinking about what kind of dowry the two of us would be able to put together."

Paul nodded, chuckling. "Foodstuffs and underwear."

Cassandra laughed back. "It would certainly be a first for the Royal House of von Lieberhaven. Well, no, on the other hand, it wouldn't. Eric's fiancée is only bringing him season tickets to some baseball team in New York and something called Space Invaders."

When Paul laughed this time, it was with pure delight. He had to admit that sounded like Casey.

"It's an interesting story, really," she went on, her eyes on Paul rather than the passing scenery. "Uncle Eric met her strictly by chance, and it turns out she's a distant cousin. Her name is also Cassandra. She is also, we found out, much to my grandmother's discomfort, the real heiress to the throne."

Paul turned on her, almost running the Ferrari into a wall. "She's *what*?"

Later it would amaze Cassandra that she hadn't picked up on Paul's astonishment. Sitting in the car, though, she nodded, her interest only in entertaining him. "Our family was a branch that came down from a . . . well, a royal liaison, if you will, back in the 1800s. Casey—that's her nickname—is from the true branch. Her ancestor was the heir apparent when he ran away to America during a war—a man after my own heart, it would seem. Anyway, Casey never knew. You see, her family took the prince's middle name, Phillip, as their surname. Phillips . . ." She'd been about to turn away, when something clicked. Phillips . . . Phillips . . . she'd just heard that somewhere.

Cassandra made the connection at the same moment that Paul brought the Ferrari to a jarring stop.

"Phillips!" she accused, the coincidence more than she wanted to believe.

"Damn!" Paul snapped, his attention out into the predawn gray as he ground out his latest cigarette.

"Would you care to explain?" Cassandra demanded, still not aware of what had made Paul stop so suddenly.

"We've been made." Slumping back in his seat, he slammed a fist against the steering wheel. "Dammit!"

That got her to turn around. A little more than a block uphill, the little *gasthaus* was basically quiet, just as they'd left it, with a light on over the porch and another inside by the front desk. The building glowed that soft white, and window boxes overflowed with late flowers. Cassandra could discern no difference other than the addition of a few extra cars scattered around it. The only sounds she heard were the birds and the first distant bells of morning.

"How do you know?" she asked, looking about for something a bit more obvious.

Slipping the car into reverse, Paul edged up against the curb and killed the engine. "Stay here," he commanded. "I'll be right back."

"Where are you going?"

"To find out what's going on."

"But the car," she protested. "That's probably what they're looking for. What if they find me in it?"

Easing the door open without a sound, Paul slid out. "Call your Uncle Eric."

"I told you not to take it!" she whispered.

"You told me you didn't care what we were in as long as we got away from your friend Hans!"

Paul didn't even have to get out of the car. Just as he was getting ready to scoot away, two men walked around from the corner of the *gasthaus*. Because of the topography of the street, sound carried unusually well. Paul and Cassandra could hear the conversation up that block as if it were just a few feet away.

"It was good of you to call us." The taller of the two men spoke.

"I tried to convince the local police, but you know how they are. They didn't seem to make the connection between the caviar and the princess. I imagine they don't read magazines."

Paul and Cassandra turned to each other, Paul's expression fatalistic and Cassandra's sheepish.

"Well, I don't think you have to worry about them returning, Herr Becker. They're probably on their way to the border, and we have every crossing between here and France under surveillance."

Paul waited only long enough for the two men to part company before slipping the Ferrari into neutral and letting it slide back down the hill. Once they were out of view he started the engine and headed the other way.

"I guess the only route left open is Czechoslovakia," Cassandra mused.

"We'll get across."

"I can't fly, Paul," she said. "And I lied about swimming."

"We won't have to swim," he answered, the strain back on his features. "We'll walk."

"I beg your pardon?" she retorted, turning on him. "I thought for sure you said we'd walk over the border."

"I did."

"Over the border that lies across the Alps."

Paul never took his eyes from the road. "The very same."

She nodded, turning to the front again. "Send me a postcard."

"Cassandra," he patiently reminded her, "without me, you have no plausible explanation for why you're wearing stolen clothes and running from a village where the police station was blown up."

"And with you I'll end up doing ten to twenty for car theft, espionage and arson. I don't really see the choice."

"The choice is," he retorted, "that if you come with me, I can promise a lovely day walking in the mountain air, followed by a safe retreat where you can soak your feet while I solve all our problems."

Her scowl was heartfelt. "Seems to me you promised a safe retreat once before. Right before we were shot at."

"I'm always open to suggestion."

"And then you do what you damn well please."

A dry, hard smile quirked his lips. "When we're in a financing conference, I'll let you make the decisions."

Cassandra surrendered by changing the subject. "Are you going to explain about Phillips?"

"When I have some uninterrupted time."

"All we're doing now is driving."

He scowled, punching the lighter and reaching for the inevitable pack of cigarettes. "I'm also trying to plan an escape involving myself and a woman who hasn't had to perform any exercise more strenuous than turning for fittings."

"The way you smoke those cigarettes, you're going to be the one keeping up with me."

"If you must know," he snapped, lighting the cigarette in his mouth. "I'm quitting the day I walk onto the farm in Ireland. Until then, I'd appreciate it if I didn't hear any more on the subject."

"All right," she agreed. "The same goes for the caviar."

She got a grin out of him. "You'll quit when you reach the farm?"

"I can assume that caviar is not one of Ireland's largest imports?"

"Not in County Wicklow."

"It's a filthy habit I've been trying to break for years, anyway. This will give me the perfect excuse."

"An entire generation of baby fish will thank you."

Cassandra chuckled. "The Russians will be inconsolable. I think I was responsible for a sizable part of their yearly gross national product."

Turning off the main road, Paul again headed south toward the mountains. "We'll just have to find you another bad habit."

"I can't eat Waterford crystal, Paul." She scowled, thinking of the dearth of culinary delights for which the Irish were famous.

"You don't necessarily have to *eat* a bad habit," he said with a sly grin.

Her skin tingled with just his words. Cassandra hazarded a look over to see a frank anticipation in his eyes. He could see something that made her suddenly breathless. Cassandra found herself thinking of his hands as they'd sought her out the night before, so strong and callused and delicious against her skin. She remembered the sweet fire in his eyes as he'd turned to her in that cloud-soft bed . . .

There had been mastery there, in both his hands and his eyes, knowledge that Cassandra didn't possess. But there had also been a hunger she'd recognized in her own heart. She knew how he felt. It was as if he stood on one side of a long bridge and something he longed for dearly stood just out of reach on the other. His hands had sparked a fire in her, but the brief vulnerability in his eyes had claimed her.

Cassandra found herself wanting to see that look in his eyes again. She wanted to be what he longed for. And in those brief, breathless moments in a speeding car on the edge of daylight, she could almost believe she might be.

"You're Casey's brother, aren't you?" she asked, deliberately sabotaging the moment for fear of its import. "The one she doesn't ever talk about."

Now Cassandra didn't have to imagine the pain in Paul's eyes. When he looked at her, it was as if she had deliberately pulled his crutch away from him to let him fall.

"That's me," he agreed without noticeable inflection. "Black sheep of the family."

Did Cassandra imagine it, or did she see a kind of accusation in his eyes? Had he shared the memory of last night with the same apprehensive regard, knowing all along how tenuous his grasp was on their special magic? Had he wanted to hold on to it for just a moment longer?

Cassandra couldn't bear to think of the possibility that her own growing dependency on Paul could be returned. No one had ever needed her. She had been a superfluous person in an anachronistic position, and she hadn't even garnered respect for that. She wasn't even sure that anyone since her mother had loved her. How could someone like Paul feel that way?

"Why didn't you say something before?" she asked. "You've sidestepped the issue as if you were the second son of Hitler."

"Occupational hazard," he retorted with deliberate ease. "People in my profession like to think of themselves as mysterious. You get my last name, and you know all about me."

"I don't know *anything* about you."

He took a long drag from an already short cigarette. "Then I guess I didn't have to worry about it, after all."

"Paul—"

"The question now," he went on, adding the butt to the pile in the once pristine ashtray, "is whether to lie low today or try for the border."

"I don't suppose I could talk you out of that idea altogether."

"Not a chance," he answered easily.

"In that case," Cassandra suggested, "let's wait until next week. How did you find out about the wedding? Uncle Eric said that Casey hadn't heard from you in years."

He scowled now, the impatience in his eyes more clearly visible in the growing light. "I'm a spy, remember? I can find out what Gorbachev had for breakfast fifteen minutes after he's eaten."

Uncertain why she should feel suddenly protective, Cassandra acquiesced to Paul's discomfort with the conversation by reverting to form. "Caviar, probably. I don't suppose we could find a pair of bicycles to get across that border."

Paul didn't acknowledge her concession. He didn't need to. Cassandra saw the tension ease from his shoulders, heard the patience return to his voice. As they drove farther into the mountains, they settled into a silence that lay comfortably between them.

The mention of his sister, her connection with him and his absence from her, was what had set Paul off. She represented some pain that weighed heavily on him. Cassandra wondered what had kept him away from her and home for all those years.

She was surprised to recognize his isolation, the same kind of loneliness that had fed her youth and eroded her self-esteem. She was more surprised to realize that Paul's pain hurt worse than her own. Cassandra hadn't had a lot of practice empathizing over the years, so dwarfed had her growth been by the burdens and limitations placed on her. To feel it flower now unsettled her. To feel it link her with the passionate, compassionate man next to her unnerved her. It was as if each moment she spent with Paul, each new facet she discovered about him wove another thread of commitment between them that Cassandra couldn't imagine either breaking or strengthening. She was a child walking new ground, and the new experience had begun to terrify her almost as much as it exhilarated her.

Cassandra decided that she wouldn't probe further right now. She'd wait for when they had some time, some peace and a stronger bond between them before she would ask him to bare that wound again.

She would have been surprised to realize how closely Paul's thoughts resembled her own. He'd been safe for so many years. Anonymous, just like everyone else in the business. The particulars were down on paper, but no one out in the field cared because they had particulars they were running from, too. Paul had been able to build a life away from his past, and he'd almost reached the point where he thought he could stay there.

Then this.

It wasn't just Casey. He'd been bracing himself to face her for weeks now. If it didn't go well, he'd just slip back into his other life and leave her with her own. He'd go on to the farm where all that mattered was an honest day's work and the companionship of friends over a pint in the evening.

For years he'd kept a deliberate separation between his two worlds, a line he'd crossed selectively and carefully. But suddenly, in a matter of hours, his barriers had been breached, and he was going to have to straddle his own fence.

It wasn't just that he owed Cassandra an explanation. She'd taken his real identity quite well, all things considered. It wasn't just that he was afraid she'd be curious. He was afraid that he'd want to include her. He turned briefly, masking his attempt to assess her in an adjustment of the rearview mirror.

She was so young. So open to the world. It was as if he'd found a fairy child and been given the gift of introducing her to the world. His lioness had an appetite for life that was breathtaking. His lioness would also lack the experience to comprehend what he would want to share with her.

He'd seen the concern grow in those luminous hazel eyes, like a flower, wanting to help, to protect, to nurture. He'd seen a surprising pain ignite there when he'd neatly sidestepped her questions about Casey. What had so overwhelmed him was that it wasn't a hurt look, as if he'd excluded her. Instead, he'd seen clear, sweet empathy. She'd known somehow that the place she'd tapped had been a poison well for him. She'd known and ached for him.

He could still feel the corresponding ache in his own chest. God, how long had it been? He couldn't remember the last time he'd wanted to take a woman home. Not just to his bed, but to his soul.

But he was afraid. Would he end up relying on her support too much, only to find that she didn't understand, after all? Cassandra leaned back in her seat, her eyes closed, her lashes like pale shadows across her cheekbones. She looked deceptively frail and small in the morning light. Paul knew the fire behind those eyes. But did he know the depth of her comprehension? Could he bear to gamble so much when the stakes were growing so large?

Maybe he should stop right now. Back off. Get the relationship back to a professional level, where not only he but she could be protected. Wouldn't it be easier never to tell her than to see the censure in her eyes? Paul turned his attention back to the road, jerking his cigarettes out of his jacket and setting the lighter, no nearer to a solution than he'd been ten minutes earlier.

Nature had given them a reprieve. The day that dawned was a mild one, more reminiscent of early spring with its pastels than the crisp hues of fall. Lacy white clouds raced before a west wind, and the earth smelled full and sweet. If it were any other occasion, the walk in the mountains would have been delightful.

"Are you *sure* there isn't any other way to do this?" Cassandra asked, her eyes cast up the long incline they would have to follow. They were walking a dirt path that wound its way in leisurely fashion through pasture and forest and then over a relatively low ridge between two peaks. The walk would still be miles and hours long, and Cassandra had no desire to be there at its end.

Hitching his backpack up a little higher, Paul took Cassandra's arm and started her on her way. "I don't believe in miracles, and that's what we'd need about now. Barring that, we walk."

At least they were starting out in the shade of a pine grove. The needles crunched pleasantly underfoot, and the air carried a pungent sweetness on it.

"Is this how Girl Scouts feel?" Cassandra asked, her head back to take in the size of the trees and the mountains that surrounded them.

"How's that?" Paul asked, grinning at her uncustomary position.

Cassandra shrugged. "Small. I've never felt so . . . insignificant before."

"You'll get over it," he promised. "First designer salon you hit."

Cassandra scowled, an easy sense of camaraderie stealing over her. "You have such faith in me," she protested without much conviction.

"I have all the faith in the world in you, Cassandra," he retorted, an arm over her shoulder. "That's why I'm so sure you can make this hike with no trouble."

"And no more complaining?" she asked sweetly.

He smiled. "See? I knew you'd understand."

"How far do we have to go?"

"I'll tell you when we get there. It'll give you a feeling of accomplishment."

Cassandra's shoulders slumped noticeably. "Feel free to inscribe that on my tombstone."

Noon brought them to the highest stand of trees. From that point, all Cassandra could see was grass, rocks and sky. Her feet ached, and her calves shrieked in protest. She'd already allowed Paul to tie a bandana around her forehead to keep the perspiration from her eyes. Oddly enough, when she looked back at the deep valley she'd left, she felt a real pleasure.

"Ready for some lunch?" Paul asked, coming up to slip his arm around her once again.

Cassandra settled easily against it, her eyes still on the valley and the sharp mountain beyond. Civilization lay down there. It didn't seem to mean so much from here.

"A person could almost get used to this," she admitted quietly. "Mind you, if you tell anyone I said that, I'll help them put you away."

"If they saw how you look now, they'd be jealous they weren't here."

Cassandra looked up with a scowl, certain he was joking. He wasn't. His smile was easy, open and charmed. She didn't realize that the exercise had brought a soft color to her cheeks, or that the glow of perspiration enhanced the porcelain of her skin. And Cassandra would have been the last to admit that her eyes shone with discovery and accomplishment. The Cassandra who had first tumbled into Paul's life wouldn't appreciate just how seductive that combination could be.

Paul dragged himself back from the precipice just in time. All he could think of was how delicious her lips looked, full and ripe.

How he wanted to taste the salt on her skin and share the excitement that fueled her.

This was the last place in the world he could take advantage of her. She was completely dependent on him. No matter what happened, they couldn't escape each other until they'd reached the other side of this mountain, and Paul had learned long ago just how devastating unfair advantage could be. He'd never abused that privilege in his life, and he wasn't about to start now. Still, his hands ached to gentle the pulse he could feel just below his arm. He wanted to nestle her against him as her breathing eased and stir up the molten emotion that bubbled in her.

"There is something patently unfair about this," she was saying, her gaze still over the vista.

"What's that?" he asked, even though he had very definite ideas of his own. His heart rate had picked up noticeably in the past few moments, and he found himself having trouble concentrating on anything but Cassandra.

"Tell me if I'm wrong," she said with a scowl, her words still coming in short stretches as she waited for her body to get over its recent forced exercise. "But you're the one who's been filling up the Ferrari's ashtray at a rate of a cigarette a minute or so, correct?"

"Broadly speaking, I guess."

"And I have never had so much as a puff of smoke in my life, since it is both unladylike and unqueenly."

"If you say so."

"Then why am I the one huffing and puffing like the Little Engine That Could?"

"Could it be," he countered with gentle amusement, "that you're out of condition?"

Cassandra scowled, slipping beyond the reach of his arm. "Have you taken patronization lessons from my Uncle Eric?" she asked dryly. "If so, you're an apt pupil."

"I didn't mean it that way," he apologized, his attention more on the slowing of his heart rate and his body's sudden longing to increase it again. "I meant that you don't have a physical occupation. I do."

"I may not have spent the past fifteen years dodging bullets and fast cars," she objected, "but I've been an athlete in my own right."

An athlete who shouldn't have been out of breath. After all, Paul hadn't set a grueling pace. But then, her heart *had* slowed dramatically since she'd slipped out of his hold. And her lungs now seemed much more at ease with the oxygen content of the atmosphere. Could it have been that her physical reaction had nothing to do with the exertion?

Without quite knowing why, she turned to look at Paul and found herself locking gazes with him. Silence fell between them, in a sudden, charged moment when even the birdsong seemed to die. Cassandra felt the blue of his eyes trap her like the seductive waters of the sea, shipping over her, luring her deeper until she wouldn't find her way back to the surface again.

His gaze swirled about her just that way, inviting her into its depths where emotions seethed and secrets lay buried. And as she found herself succumbing to their sweet invitation, Cassandra felt her body respond.

Her pulse jumped again. Her breath caught somewhere in her throat. Deep within her, a spark of desire lit, ignited by no more than the silent wonder in Paul's eyes. Tiny frissons of excitement rippled along her limbs and sought to close the gap to Paul. She felt the chills in her fingers, tingling as if with magnetic attraction, seeking his skin, the rasp of his days-old beard, the impossibly soft line of his lips. Cassandra wanted to see that wonder in Paul's eyes ripen to satisfaction, and she wanted it to be at her hands.

"Oh, dear," she breathed, sincerely stunned. She was still out of reach, held rigidly apart by the warring emotions in her body. Held immobile by the desire she'd finally named.

"Oh, dear, what?" Paul asked, his voice husky and unintentionally abrupt.

Cassandra smiled, a small declaration of surprise that brought new depth to her expression. "I just realized something."

Paul couldn't move, snared by the light in Cassandra's eyes, glowing suddenly like a new star in the heavens. A decision, a milestone that marked her passage from princess to woman. He knew what it was before she spoke, and the magnitude of it took his breath away.

"I just realized," she said, "that I've wanted you to make love to me all along. And that it's about time I did something about it."

Nine

"Here?" Paul asked, still holding his distance.

She nodded, her eyes even wider. "Here."

"Now?"

"Now."

She saw him tense, almost trembling. Cassandra saw his effort and was awed. She saw his pupils dilate, saw the quickened rise and fall of his chest, felt the sudden thunder of his heart. She knew enough to realize how unfair it would be to tease him. She was still innocent enough to be honest about what surprised her. Delighted her. Tormented her.

Even as she seemed to be held rooted, she felt drawn inexorably to Paul. Cassandra knew for certain that merely the feel of him would bring her that unique sensation that could only be felt in one man's arms.

Instinctively, she reached out.

"Paul..."

"Don't do this," he grated out, tensing against her touch. "You don't know what you're asking."

Her lips quirked in a wry smile. "I'm asking you to make love to me. You were ready enough to last night."

"Last night was different," he said.

"And because today you know I'm a virgin you would treat me differently?" she asked, knowing that she was being unfair, but wanting the truth in the open where they could deal with it, wanting him and knowing no other way to cross the distance. Deliberately drawing her hand away, Cassandra stood before him with the manner of a queen born. "Wouldn't that make you a man with a double standard?"

"No. It would make me a man who refuses to take advantage of someone who isn't used to the rules of the game."

Cassandra's expression grew dry. "Just because I haven't spent time on the court doesn't mean I'm not acquainted with the instruction manual," she retorted. "I'm twenty-three, not twelve."

"I'm the last person you need to tell that," he reminded her with a tight smile of his own.

Almost of its own volition, his hand came up to cup her cheek, to test the petal softness of her skin and soak in its warmth. "When I make love to you, Cassandra, it will be right. I'll have the time to make your waiting worthwhile. When I make love to you, it will be with all the care and tenderness and passion you deserve. It won't be here on a hillside in between lunch and an afternoon hike."

"Then, when?" she asked, her voice husky with surprised tears.

Paul stood very still before her, caressing her with his care, with the depths of desire that colored his eyes. Cassandra felt the wind tug at her hair and swirl about the fingers at her cheek. She heard the birds again, high in the trees, and the chattering of squirrels. The rich aroma of autumn filled her nostrils, enhancing the salty spice of Paul's scent. The elements of the moment seemed to fuse into Paul's words, the smile he offered with his promise.

Cassandra couldn't believe he'd done it again. Turned her around and turned her down, and somehow done it so that he made her feel all the more special. When was she ever going to understand him? When was he going to stop surprising her so completely?

Never, she hoped, the sting of tears unaccountably sweet.

"It will be," he promised, "when I can give you everything I promised. And not before."

She held her position, even as her own emotions buffeted her like a windstorm. "Would you at least kiss me?"

Paul knew he shouldn't even dare that. The sun glinted in Cassandra's eyes and warmed her skin. The wind danced through her hair, lifting it about her shoulders in silken banners. Paul took her face between his hands and thought how very dear she had become to him. Scowling in anger, haughty in disdain, open in amazement, Cassandra had moods that never seemed to tire him. Those same colors made up her very unique spectrum. He would be a very old man, he thought, before she finally stopped surprising him.

"Yes," he acquiesced with a smile. "I can kiss you."

Gathering her into his arms, he dipped to taste her lips like the rarest of nectars. At first skimming, nipping, he stopped to savor the sweetness of her mouth. Raising one hand, he brought a thumb up to stroke her cheek, indulging in the velvet of her with the rasp of his work-chafed hands. He drew slow circles against her skin, tracing the line of her jaw, venturing along to her ear and wandering along her throat.

He'd only meant to kiss her. He'd only meant to seal a promise. The moment he'd touched her, he'd created a new promise, different, greater than the one he'd thought. Because the moment he had met her lips, Paul had discovered a pliant intensity in her he'd only imagined before.

Cassandra brought her own hands up, spreading them across his chest as if she could capture him between her fingertips. She melted into his embrace and met his lips with the softest, most delicious little moan of surprise. Paul caught the erratic trip of her pulse just beyond her jaw and let his fingers follow it down.

His body was betraying him. His hands moved of their own accord. Deep in his gut an ache sharpened, flared. He felt the soft swelling of her breast beneath his hand and almost lost the strength in his legs.

God, he wanted her. She bubbled in him like champagne, like a fountain of light, like a great wind that tore through him without cease. The feel of her intoxicated him. The smell of her hypnotized him. When Paul held Cassandra in his arms, he couldn't think past the very essence of her.

By the time he managed to pull away, Paul was gasping.

"You did that on purpose," he accused, holding Cassandra at arm's length. He wasn't sure what reaction he expected. She smiled. Her eyes were still soft, languorous, a honeyed brown. Her lips lured him with their swollen promise.

"I guess I just wanted to make sure it wasn't a fluke," she admitted huskily.

"What wasn't a fluke?"

Cassandra made a little waving motion with her hand, as if she were too drained for big gestures. "What I felt for you last night. What I feel when I get too close. It isn't a fluke, is it, Paul?"

Smiling down at the surprise in her eyes, Paul gave in to temptation and drew a finger along those lips. "No, Cassandra. It was no fluke."

She nodded, as if settling something for herself. "Good. I'm glad. I mean, after years of not trusting my instincts, it's good to know I can start again."

"You really never trusted your instincts?" Paul asked a while later over cheese and baguettes.

They had spread their bounty out over their jackets and scooped water from a nearby stream for lunch. Sitting now in the shade of the pines, the two found themselves able to recapture the easygoing camaraderie that had waited beyond the unexpected passion.

Thinking back over her life, Cassandra offered a wry laugh. "How much do you know about my past, Paul?"

Slicing a piece of cheese and handing it over on the blade of his knife, he shrugged. "About as much as anyone who reads *People*, I guess."

"Hmm." She nodded over her first bite. "Emmenthal. Quite good." Then she shrugged. "The magazines generally only hit the high points—the brief forays in the direction of fashion design and cultural engineering, the string of well-known and equally notorious gentlemen friends, the public scenes in a scrupulously private royal household. They didn't cover the generally stupid blunders I made in financing, unfortunate taste I had in friends, the times my maid rescued me from public humiliation during one or the other idiotic relationship or rebellious snit. Poor Maria," she lamented with a sad shake of the head. "What that dear woman had to put up with. I begged her forgiveness a thousand times when I sat alone in that little cubicle reviewing all my sins."

"Sins are transgressions against people," Paul said. "The only thing you did was try and find your place."

"My place was on the throne," she retorted easily. "Just as my father told me. Only I didn't have the courage to assume it."

Breaking off a hunk of bread, Paul shook his head. "I'd say you had more courage than most. You knew you wouldn't make a good monarch, and you got out."

"History hasn't been terribly kind to the abdicators among us," Cassandra reminded him. "Even the ones, like me, who knew they couldn't handle the job." For a moment she concentrated on her lunch. Her expression had become wistful, melancholy, as if she were speaking of a great chance she'd missed in life, instead of one she'd turned away. Carefully spreading a slice of pâté on her bread, she turned back to Paul. "I met the Duke of Windsor, you know, when I was a very little girl. He and the duchess were fond of our gaming tables. He seemed such a sad man—like a little boy who couldn't find his way home again. I never forgot him."

Paul's gaze was empathetic. "And now you feel like that little boy?"

Cassandra's smile was small. "Every time I've come close to quitting in the past, I saw him there. Never at peace, never at home. I couldn't bear that."

"And now?"

Her head came up a little, as if protecting herself against his question. "What about now? Where will you find your home?" Paul asked.

It seemed for a moment as if Cassandra had ignored him. She munched on her bread, her attention on her actions. What could she tell him? That she'd finally reached the crisis point and run without thinking, and now she had nowhere to go? That, once again, her instincts had failed her? Dear God, how this future ached in her like a sentence.

Finally, still not able to look at him, she shrugged. "I don't know. I was thinking to go to some friends in Switzerland."

"And after that?"

Cassandra faced Paul, her eyes sparking just a little. "I told you. I don't know."

"What do you plan to do with your life?" he persisted, his eyes on her as he sliced more cheese. "Now that you're not going to be queen, you must be planning to go into some other line of work."

"I was trained to be a monarch," Cassandra retorted. "Which means that I'm not qualified for any other line of work. I'm useless, Paul."

"Hardly useless," he contested with maddening calm. "You drive a car like a stuntman."

"Fine," she snapped. "I'll just head off to the Grand Prix circuit and get a job. I'm sure they wouldn't mind letting me loose around Monaco in one of their Formula Ones."

"You could be a chauffeur."

"Where?" she demanded. "How many people I know would give me a job? I'm not really sure I could even get references."

"Your chauffeur from the palace would write you something nice," he said, smiling. "After all, you got him out of a lot of work. Besides, you've already taken the training."

Cassandra lifted a finger, ready with an idea of her own. "I could move to America and drive a truck," she suggested with a tentative grin, Paul's goading provoking some effect. "How do you think I'd look with a cowboy hat and a tattoo?"

"That's the girl," he said approvingly. "Keep your options open."

"Or I could open the I Was Almost the Queen and These Are Almost New Clothes shop with my castoffs. I don't think I'll be needing all that formal wear anymore."

"Call an agent in Hollywood and let them do a miniseries about you. I hear this glamour-and-adventure stuff is all the thing."

"What adventure?" she said, scowling. "I sat by myself in a five-by-ten room in my slip for two months."

"Not after Hollywood gets through with you."

Rolling her eyes at the idea, Cassandra found herself laughing. "And I thought Uncle Eric was angry before. After this he wouldn't let me in Europe, much less Moritania. No, I have a better idea. Since Casey was from the real royal family, that means that *you* are the real heir apparent. Let's sue for the throne."

"I look terrible in ermine," he said, busy with his cup of water.

"Oh, come on," she protested, feeling better than she had in a long while. She still had no future, but for the first time she could joke about it. "Where's your spirit of adventure? There's nothing like a little battle for succession to stir things up. Europe has been doing it since we first figured out how nice crowns looked. You could gather an army of all your old spy friends—"

"I beg your pardon?"

But she was really getting into it. "I could go to the U.S. and plead for aid. I'll tell them Uncle Eric is really a closet Communist and that American interests are at stake."

"Not to mention the president's private bank account."

Cassandra's eyebrows lifted. "How did you know about that?"

"I'm a spy," he retorted dryly. "Remember?"

"Oh, yes." She nodded enthusiastically. "What do you say, Paul? We'd only have to mount a small army. Moritania doesn't have any... especially since General Mueller was prosecuted for helping kidnap me."

Paul couldn't help chuckling. "I say you're just looking for something more exciting for your miniseries. Why don't you just pretend you're a White Russian and open a tea room in New York?"

"You're the White Russian," she countered. "Casey told us. A real Romanov. If anyone was going to open the shop, it should be you."

"I told you. I look terrible in ermine. The Russians wouldn't have me. I stuck to the Irish side of the family."

Making a show of studying him, Cassandra tilted her head, still munching on a piece of bread. "You really don't have that royal attitude, you know. The air of noblesse oblige, that distant look in the eye that people mistake for regal disdain and really means you're as dumb as a brick...the inbreeding, you know. Maybe old Berthold was right in getting out when he did."

"Berthold. Who's that?"

"Your great-great-grandfather, you dolt. The man who could make you king for a day. The one who ran off to start the Phillips line."

"Oh, Berthold," he mused. "And here I always thought Nana Anna was more than enough royalty for one family."

"Nana...Anna?"

If the name hadn't been given in childhood, it would have sounded ludicrous to him, too. Paul smiled. "The Romanov. Enough royal attitude for the entire lot of us. She used to hound us mercilessly about how an heir to the throne of Mother Russia should deport himself."

Cassandra's eyes widened. "You had a grandmother like that, too? I thought Grandmother Marta was the only royal left schooled in the Gestapo School of Decorum."

"A rap on the knuckles for using slang?" he asked with a smile.

"A schoolbook on the head for deportment." Cassandra got his nod and laughed, truly delighted. It was difficult to impress on anyone who hadn't lived through it what a disadvantage a grandmother like that was to a teenager. All her friends had been able to see was that her grandmother was a queen. Come to think of it, she thought with a wry smile, that had been all her grandmother had seen. "I used to have to sit for hours reciting the von Lieberhaven lineage to her. She put me in my room for a week once for being too familiar with the butler. I called him by his nickname."

Paul laughed. "A good employer is not supposed to know her employees' nicknames. It promotes familiarity, which breeds anarchy."

"Yes! Oh, Lord, almost to a word! They must have known each other." She shook her head at the delicious irony of two royal grandchildren finding each other over an escape attempt. "The only person who stood up for me was Mother. She used to let me sit with her in her sewing room when Grandmother went on one of her rampages, and we'd giggle together about how absurd some of the protocol could be."

Paul agreed, his own memories vivid. "My mother balanced out Nana's lectures with little anecdotes about the Romanov court that showed me that no teenage boy could be more barbaric than a tzar. Nana had trouble forgiving her. After all, my mother was just shanty Irish."

"What about your father?"

Cassandra saw him closing off as if a door had shut. Reaching away from her, he began to gather together the lunch supplies. "He was her son. He listened."

Cassandra felt the chill of his voice, the sudden distance, as if even he weren't allowed too close to those memories. She wondered at it, hurt for the look that appeared on Paul's face, but she kept her silence. It wasn't the time. It wasn't the place, just as Paul had known, for intimacies of any kind. She would wait—and she would hope she recognized what that place would be. It still hurt, though, to see their easy camaraderie die so suddenly.

"What about those biscuits?" she asked, doing her own gathering.

"Biscuits?" Paul repeated, looking up from his chore.

"You know, the ones from the store that you said were so good."

The tension eased a little. "Oh, those. I have them, but we had to leave the milk behind."

"Water wouldn't work?"

Paul grinned finally, the amusement almost reaching his eyes. "Not at all. We'll be making Brian and Gerta's soon. They'll have milk, and I'll teach you how to eat Oreos properly."

"Your friends wouldn't have—"

"No," he answered, anticipating her. "They don't believe in slaughtering innocent fish to supply expensive habits."

Cassandra made a face and got to her feet. "Beast."

"And while you're up," he continued, holding a few pieces of the battered camping gear they'd used to lunch from. "You can wash these in the stream over there."

Cassandra arched regal brows. "It occurs to me," she accused, "that besides being a spy, a car thief and taskmaster, you are also a chauvinist. Why is it that I seem to always be doing dishes?"

"Because you can't break into computers," he answered evenly, piling more equipment into her hands. "Fair division of labor. Of course, if you'd rather I wash the dishes, I'd be happy to let you guide us over the mountains."

"The next car we steal," she retorted before turning away, "I drive."

Behind her, Paul laughed. "It's a deal."

Cassandra wasn't at all sure just how one washed dishes in a stream. After all, it had only been a day since she'd learned to do it with a tap and soap. She supposed she could dip them. Maybe beat them against a rock. Wasn't that how primitive women used to wash things? No, come to think of it, that was how they washed clothes. Cassandra was sure Paul wouldn't want his eating utensils beaten against a rock.

Finally giving up, she crouched alongside the chattering brook and immersed the tin plates and cups one by one in the rushing water, satisfying herself that just that action got rid of the majority of residue. This is a far cry from the palace, she thought, reaching around to set the things in the grass behind her to dry. She wanted to be in the room when someone told Maria that she, Princess Cassandra, felt a real sense of accomplishment just seeing food drift off plates. It sounded like a bad American commercial. Maria, she was sure, would smile her private, enigmatic smile and say nothing.

Cassandra was turning back to dip the last utensil when she lost her balance. Perched on her heels, she wasn't very stable to begin with. When she turned, she found herself faced with the choice of getting her shirt sleeve or her face wet. She chose her sleeve.

A good decision, too. The stream was bitterly cold. Cassandra drew her hand back from where it had landed on a rock and gathered her things together. She was getting to her feet when she first saw the blood.

It was on one of the plates, a streak of bright red across the battered, scratched tin. For a moment, Cassandra could do no more than stare at it, as if waiting for some kind of explanation. Then she saw more on her pant leg. Still, no reason. She turned the plates over, intent on finding some kind of source. It was then she saw her hand. There was a steady flow of blood dripping from her palm, crimson against the pale white of her cold flesh.

Cassandra stared, then dropped the plates in a clatter. The blood couldn't belong to her. Her hand didn't hurt; she didn't feel cut. Yet still the blood dripped steadily down her wrist and onto the sleeve of her yellow oxford blouse.

"Paul..." Cassandra suddenly felt clammy, nauseated. Frozen. She was going to faint, and she couldn't think what to do about it.

"P-a-u-l!" Now her voice rose, its shrill edge betraying her panic. She ended up on her seat, shaking and gray and still staring at her hand as if it were alien to her.

"Cassandra?"

Cassandra heard the rustle of leaves. She felt Paul take hold of her hand, bend close to her head. She could smell him, that rich muskiness that was so like the fall leaves.

"What did you do?" he asked, lifting her hand for inspection.

"I'm...going to...faint..."

Without ceremony, he shoved her head between her knees. "No, you're not."

"Don't tell me what I am or am not going to do," she retorted instinctively, her nose inches from the grass. She already felt marginally better, but she wasn't about to tell him.

"You're a wimp, Cassandra," he admonished with a smile in his voice, rubbing her hand with something.

The nerve endings in her hand woke with his ministrations. "Ouch," she protested, trying to pull away, with no luck. "I am no such thing."

"Can't even stand the sight of a little blood."

"May I remind you once again," she snapped, "that we don't have similar backgrounds. Princesses, unlike nurses and espionage agents, aren't trained in bloodletting."

"Physical bloodletting, anyway."

That brought her head back up with a snap. "Oh, is that how it's going to be?" she asked acidly. "Am I that much fun to insult?"

"To antagonize," he corrected. "I already told you. Besides—" now he flashed her a rather triumphant smile "—it brought the roses back into your cheeks."

Cassandra glared, not ready to forgive Paul for the bright humor in his eyes. "What are you doing?"

"Applying a little pressure to stop the bleeding," he answered, bending to his job again. "Then we'll wrap it up in something I have."

"You always carry a first-aid kit with you?"

He grinned. "Bloodletting precautions."

Cassandra ended up watching with concealed interest as Paul worked. He was good, his actions economical and gentle. This was something Cassandra had the feeling he'd done before.

The cut wasn't deep, just long. Paul applied some kind of ointment and then wrapped her hand in a bandage he pulled out of his backpack. And then, he announced, as he situated the same backpack to his satisfaction, he was going to take a nap.

Cassandra watched him in fascination. Paul stretched out on the ground next to her, used his pack as his pillow, and within seconds, was relaxed and asleep. He hadn't had much of a chance to rest since she'd met him. Cassandra couldn't imagine how he'd gone as far as he had. At least she better understood now how he functioned. This must have been a trick he'd perfected over the years. She wished she could do the same. Unfortunately, if she drifted off right now, he wouldn't get a coherent movement out of her for the next six hours.

She wasn't sure whether it was the sunlight or the sleep, but he looked so much softer lying there. So open and beguiling, like a little boy resting from a hard day at play. Cassandra wanted to reach out and brush his hair back from his forehead, or cover him with her jacket.

Sitting with her back against a tree, she smiled at her musings. What a switch. For the first time in her life, she found herself wanting to put someone else's comfort first. And she wanted to tend to it herself, like a wife or a mother. The funny thing was, it was the most pleasurable feeling she'd ever known, like a sweet ache in her chest—an ache she didn't want to lose.

As she sat alone in that high forest on the slopes of a mountain, watching the man she'd only met days before sleep next to her, Cassandra came to a stunning realization. She loved him. Not the way she loved Uncle Eric, looking up to him as an example, or Maria, for her kind wisdom and forbearance. Not even like gentle, unfortunate Hans who hadn't had the backbone to protect her. Cassandra found that this struck her deeper, more intensely than any emotion had. And it demanded less.

She didn't find perfection in Paul but complexity. He didn't match any ideal she'd been raised to respect. His was rather a seething, contrary, seductive life, the likes of which she'd never known.

She loved Paul for his bright humor and dark secrets. She loved his passion and his patience. Cassandra wanted, more than anything she'd ever wanted in her life, just to stay alongside him and watch him when he slept. And then when he woke, she wanted to bicker and laugh and make love with him. Only him.

"Oh, dear," she mused, eyes wide. She stood, wanting to get away before she woke him with the sudden turbulence that hammered through her chest. It wasn't just the lovemaking, the sweet touch of his hands and honeyed taste of his mouth that she wanted. It was him. All of him.

Was this what falling in love meant? Was it what had been happening to Uncle Eric when he'd looked at his fiancée with such affection in his eyes? When he'd fought like a tiger to save her life, that man who had been raised to be a banker? Cassandra wasn't sure. She had no experience in this. Even her own erstwhile fiancé, Rudolph, had been picked not by her, but her father, an appropriate choice she'd acquiesced to out of duty. No man had ever excited her, had unnerved her as much as Paul Phillips. No man had made her want to cry just with gentle words. She'd always been the one in control, knowing exactly what she wanted from a relationship. She'd always called the dance and then sent the partner home alone. Suddenly Cassandra found that it was she who stood alone in unfamiliar territory without a guide to get her through.

There was one thing she was certain of, though. Paul wouldn't love her in return. It had happened before. He might be amused by her, be excited by her. But Cassandra knew what would happen when he really got to know her. He'd turn away, just as everyone else in her life had.

She was unlovable, just as her father had always said. Just as Uncle Eric and Grandmother implied with their arched eyebrows and acerbic words. Cassandra wasn't sure she wanted to wait around for Paul to reach that same conclusion. She didn't know whether she could bear his rejection.

Taking one last look down at Paul, feeling the tears that once again stung the backs of her eyes and lodged in her throat, Cassandra gave in once again to impulse. Grabbing her jacket, she turned and walked away.

Ten

Paul's internal clock woke him almost on the stroke of three. The sun had edged closer to the horizon, its light yellow against the mountains. The breeze had picked up, edged with a sharper chill that forewarned of the return of autumn. Paul could hear bells off in the distance and the chatter of the brook beside him. Other than that, the mountains were silent.

He lay still for a moment, looking up toward the distant treetops and the sky they seemed to pierce. He felt better, rested. Alert. These short naps had seen him through more than once. When he was traipsing across the other side of that mountain tonight, he'd be grateful for this one.

It was time to get on. Sunset wasn't going to wait for him, and he preferred not to be too close to the top of the mountain when it came. Paul was in the process of stretching out the kinks from a hard ground when he first heard the munching. He stopped. Listened. There was something going on, and Cassandra wasn't the only one involved. Unless, of course, she had suddenly grown some very big teeth.

Paul sat straight up and looked around. He stopped when he got to a spot just downhill from him, his eyes widening in surprise.

Cassandra sat, her back against a tree, smiling at him. Alongside her stood two horses. She was feeding an apple to the smaller one, a bay with stockings. The other, a dapple, was nuzzling her shoulder for similar attention. Both were unsaddled, but had some kind of rope bridles on, the reins hanging to the ground.

"Have a nice nap?" Cassandra asked offhandedly.

"Where did they come from?" Paul asked, raking a hand through his hair. Suddenly he didn't feel as alert as he'd thought.

Cassandra grinned up at him. "They followed me home. Can I keep them?"

The gray nudged her again with more insistence, and she laughed. "You are a pig, young man," she informed him, reaching for a piece of castoff baguette to feed him. He whiffled happily and munched away as she stroked his muzzle.

Paul got to his feet, intent on inspecting this new acquisition. The minute he moved, both horses shied. He stopped. Cassandra stood, put a hand on each horse and spoke in a low murmur that settled them. Ears back, they kept an eye on Paul, but they allowed his approach as long as Cassandra was there.

"You've found some friends," he observed.

"Aren't they sweet?" she asked with a real smile. "I asked, and they said they'd be happy to take us across the mountain tonight."

Stopping before her, Paul took a considering look at the horses, then Cassandra. "Who do they belong to?"

"I don't know." She shrugged. "I didn't ask."

His eyes widened again. "You *stole* them?"

Cassandra grinned. "Well, you got the cars. I figured the least I could do was get the horses."

"But don't you know what can happen to you?"

The gray butted her for attention and she laughed, more at ease than Paul had ever seen her. "I understand that in your Texas, I could still be hanged. Isn't it amazing? When I ran away, I thought I'd have to learn new skills. You know, things like shopping and cooking and working for a living. Who'd have guessed I'd also learn the fine arts of breaking and entering and rustling? I find it all quite stimulating."

Paul scowled, edging closer to her and her new friends. "You would. Where did you find them?"

"In a field a little way down the mountain. I went for a walk, and there they were. Once my tired and aching feet reminded me that I still had a mountain to climb, the decision about what to do about such a serendipitous discovery became a moot point." Cassandra lifted an eyebrow at Paul. "That is, of course, unless you can't ride. I hadn't thought to ask."

"I can ride."

"Bareback?"

"I was a circus rider in a former life."

Cassandra smiled, her attention still on her new companions. Paul saw a new hesitancy in her, a kind of shyness toward him he hadn't noticed before. She acted as if she had drawn away somewhat, retreated somewhere. She was contented with the horses, and comfortable enough with him, but something had changed without his knowing it.

He reached to her and drew a gentle hand along her cheek. "Cassandra?"

Cassandra didn't face him. Turning to the little bay, she drew the reins back over his neck. "I'll ride this one. I've named him Harry. You go ahead and take Porky, but be careful. He likes to bite until he gets to know you."

Paul stood where he was, wondering why Cassandra should suddenly back away from him. Grabbing Harry by the reins and the mane, Cassandra easily swung herself up on his back. Harry turned his head back to her, as if he was checking to make sure she was all right. Paul was amazed at the communication Cassandra seemed to have with the animal.

"You're not going to tell me what's bothering you?" he asked her.

She sat easily on her horse in a fusion of animal and rider that few manage, as if one spirit complemented the other. The bay picked up his head and pranced a little, and Cassandra laughed, her hands easy on the reins, her head erect and her hair trembling in the afternoon light.

Paul saw a new side to her. She possessed a commanding self-sufficiency that brought a new, even more alluring light to her eyes. Never had he seen her so satisfied, so attuned to herself. Whatever in life she had been made to do or allowed to do, this was something she'd loved—something she understood far better than royal protocol and financing.

"What could be wrong?" she asked as she turned her horse up the hill. "We have a lovely trip ahead and some wonderful transportation. Ready to go?"

Quickly scooping his backpack up off the ground, Paul swung up onto the dapple—making sure he was out of the way of those big teeth—and trotted along after her.

Cassandra let Paul take the lead. She was glad to be off her feet, although she was sure she'd be sore in other places by the time this was over. It had been too long since she'd been on a horse, much less ridden bareback. But Lord, how good it felt!

Cassandra had come upon the horses by surprise. She'd been heading down the hill at a fast clip, unsure where she was going or how she'd get there, certain only that she didn't know what to do with her new knowledge. The minute she'd broken out into the meadow, though, and seen the horses, her indecision had died.

They had been a gift. A sign. It had taken Cassandra no more than five minutes to win them over, and another ten to fashion their bridles from the crude halters they wore. If there had only been one horse, she would probably have continued back on down the mountain, propelled by all the insecurities that had accumulated over the years. Maybe she'd have actually run away from Paul. But seeing the horses made her realize that the only real way out of her jam was over that mountain. With Paul. She still depended on him to clear her name, if nothing else. There was nothing she could do but bear with her growing dependence on him, and try to not unduly embarrass herself in the process before he was able to find the answers to their problems.

Cassandra had returned to find him still asleep. Her chest tightened again at the sight of him. She felt that pull, drawing her to him, to his warmth, his smile, his touch. Stopping across the small clearing she'd deliberately sat with her horses and paid attention to them instead. It hadn't made her situation any easier.

The feel of a horse beneath her settled her, though. She felt as if for the first time during these long months, she was finally on familiar turf. Cassandra knew nothing so well as she knew horses, had grieved for nothing so much as her jumper Merlin when she had left her life behind. Whatever other privileges her life had afforded her, riding had been the one that had more often than not saved her. When she really did enter the real world, she was going to miss it desperately.

That long trip over the mountains, instead of being the grueling trek Cassandra had anticipated, evolved into one of the most pleasant rides she'd taken. The horses were surefooted, their gaits as fluid as ships on soft swells. The weather held, the sky deepening with the dying sun and stars beginning to peek out by the time they reached the road on the Austrian side.

Cassandra felt the ache in her arms and her legs where she gripped Harry. But the fresh air and exercise went a long way to dispel the stale residue of the past few months.

"How far to your friends'?" she asked, pulling up beside Paul as they trotted through a shadowed meadow. The cows had already returned to the milking sheds, and the farmers were at dinner. She and Paul now had the hills to themselves for a while.

"About another thirty miles," Paul told her. "We're going to have to trade these in for faster models."

Cassandra pulled Harry to a halt. "No," she said with a definite shake of her head. "We can't."

Pulling Porky alongside her, Paul jerked a bit on the reins to keep the horse still. Porky wasn't nearly as cooperative with him as he had been with Cassandra. "Cassandra, it would be incredibly difficult to sneak over the Swiss border on horseback. Besides, not only would it be unfair to ride them even half that distance, but we'd end up spending another night out on the road."

"But we can't just let them loose," she protested. "Besides, we already have one car, two horses and a good deal of groceries on the arrest warrant. Aren't we pushing our luck?"

"We'll hitch a ride," he suggested. "Everybody does in Europe."

He caught her attention. "Hitchhike?" she asked, eyes brightening suspiciously. "I've never done that."

He scowled. "It's another habit you shouldn't get into. There's a little town down the road a way. We'll leave the horses in the field just beyond the first house. Somebody will be bound to find them."

"But what about their owners?"

"When this is all over, we'll come back personally and reunite them all. Okay?"

Cassandra still looked as if she were being torn from her best friend. "I wouldn't really mind sleeping out another night."

"Well, I would. Now say your goodbyes. You can make new friends when we get to the farm. Gerta's family has a couple of horses there."

When they reached the place where they were to leave the horses, Paul watched Cassandra. The two horses migrated to her, as if they really knew she was leaving, each in turn dipping his head to her hand like a gentleman bidding farewell. And Cassandra, her eyes bright with new tears, spent her few minutes silently stroking them. She stood between the two great animals, who acted like small children with her. Her own grace was amplified in her communication with them. Paul could almost imagine a kind of dialogue between the threesome, as if she could truly read their minds, or they could really project their own thoughts to her.

She really was making him fanciful, he thought with a shake of the head. Pretty soon, he'd imagine the two of them flying out over the moon. If he told Brian any of what he'd thought in the past few hours, the Irishman would roar with laughter and tell him he'd been visiting with the shee—the wee folk who wove spells and snatched away unwary humans.

"You're really good with horses," Paul admitted a while later as he hiked with Cassandra along the darkening road.

Lost in her own thoughts, Cassandra nodded. She walked, hands in pockets, head down, her shoulders just a little more slumped than before. "That was the dream that hurt the most," she said quietly. "When my father took away my real chance to ride. I always felt as if I was invincible when I was riding. As if no one could touch me."

"Why don't you use that for your career?"

"What?" she demanded. "Mucking out someone else's stalls for a living?"

"Breaking and training horses."

Cassandra laughed, her head thrown back to the evening sky. "The same people who need chauffeurs are the ones with enough money to have good horses. I'd run into the same kind of credibility problem. 'Oh, Princess Cassandra train horses?'" she mimicked brutally. "'Why, I remember when she tried to be a fashion designer. And an author. And a revolutionary. No, my dear, we need a *real* trainer.'"

"In Ireland nobody cares."

"They care more for their horses in Ireland than anyone else."

"But they respect anyone who handles a horse well, no matter what royal house they're descended from. I'd let you work for me."

"I thought you had cows."

"Two cows. Fifty horses."

Cassandra looked over, stunned. "What?"

His smile ghostly in the dying light, Paul chuckled. "It's not really a farm. More a stud."

"Flat racers?"

"And chasers."

Cassandra came to a dead stop in the middle of the road. The giant hole in her chest filled with possibility, dread and the disaster of hope. "Why didn't you tell me?"

Paul shrugged, enjoying himself. "You didn't ask."

Cassandra tilted her head. "Do I have to marry you?"

"Only if you want to change your name."

She mused on it a moment, her heart tripping in her chest with Paul's new offer. This one she wanted. A stud farm with steeplechasers. Please, God, she thought, don't let him be teasing. Let this be for real.

"Cassandra Phillips," she mused, trying her best to keep the desperation out of her voice. Then she shook her head. "It's been done."

"But it won't be in use for long. That Cassandra is going to be a von Lieberhaven...like you. Don't you think two Cassandra von Lieberhavens is one too many?"

Cassandra scowled, back on familiar ground, more comfortable with Paul as the darkness pulled its protection over them. She was suddenly wanting too much to let him see it.

"You're much too romantic for me, Paul," she admonished. "I can't take advantage of you."

"You really want me to get on my knee?" he asked dryly.

She actually smiled, aching for the ease with which the two of them played. Yearning to always have that. "I'd hate for you to strain something. Let's flag down that car."

But people weren't in the habit of driving frivolously in the evenings around these parts. Two cars and a truck passed before Paul finally gave up using his thumb and used Cassandra's leg.

"What are you doing?" she demanded when he tugged up her pant leg.

"I saw this in a movie once," he informed her. "Worked great."

"I bet she wasn't wearing jeans," Cassandra retorted. The pants made it as far as her knee. The next car stopped anyway.

Cassandra's first reaction was to despair. Brian and Gerta weren't home.

After riding in a number of successive cars across the Austrian Alps, she and Paul had managed to squeeze across the border in an American's rental car by flashing the passports from the back seat. Cassandra had never sweated before in her life. She had when that border guard had hesitated before waving them through.

Deep night had once again settled over the mountains by the time that same car, filled with college kids with too much money and not enough to do, had dropped them off in the village below Brian's place. They'd walked the rest of the way, Cassandra's muscles by now protesting vigorously.

But the house was silent and dark. And locked. No one home. No help. The minute Paul rattled that unyielding door, Cassandra found herself fighting frustrated tears.

"No problem," he assured her, producing the lock pick again. "We'll just go in the back door."

The house was a little chalet that overlooked a steep valley and the mountains beyond. Cassandra could smell the farm animals and hear rustling in the connected barn. The place was neat, tidy... and empty.

They found the note on the kitchen table.

"See?" Paul grinned, waving the paper with relish. "What did I tell you?"

Cassandra snatched it from him and read.

> Knew you'd come, old son. Went off to get started on the problem. Make yourself at home, and give the young lady our best.
>
> Brian

"Are you sure it's for you?" she asked suspiciously. "It's a fairly generic message."

"It's for me," Paul answered, walking farther into the room to flip on lights.

The simplicity on the outside was reflected inside. A basic living room area with huge stone fireplace took shape with the illumination, and a kitchen was tucked away beneath the balcony that overlooked the fireplace. Two doors led off the balcony, evidently to bedrooms. Cassandra thought it was charming, all whitewashed walls and warm woods and thick area rugs, the colors basic earth tones with a few woven wall hangings in bright basics to offset it.

It made her think of hardworking people with the taste for simple things. It also reminded her how very far she was from her frothy pink room she'd inhabited in the palace.

Had she really liked that decor, with enough excess to nauseate Marie Antoinette? Had it reflected her the way this place must reflect its owners? The thought did not make her think highly of herself.

"What's wrong with you?" Paul asked suddenly.

Cassandra answered instinctively from where she stood looking out a darkened front window. "Nothing."

"You're walking like you have rocks in your shoes."

"Oh," she said, turning a little toward him. "That. I'm just sore. You would be, too, if you'd gone from zero to sixty in the activity department the way I have in the past few days."

"Easily taken care of, my princess," he teased.

"Don't call me that," she snapped before thinking. She didn't see the lift of his eyebrows in return.

Paul walked up and put his hands on Cassandra's shoulders. They were as tight as stretched leather. Something besides physical discomfort was weighing on her, and he wanted to know what. Without thinking, he began to gently massage. Cassandra pulled away.

"I don't think Brian will be home till it's time to do chores in the morning," Paul suggested diffidently, keeping carefully away. The feel of her taunted him, now that he had the chance to luxuriate in it. "That means you could probably afford a long, hot bath before anyone caught you."

Cassandra turned, the temptation lighting her eyes a moss green in the soft light. "A bath?"

Paul couldn't help a smile. "A hedonist to the end, aren't you?"

Cassandra managed to smile in return. "I haven't asked for caviar in at least six hours. What do you want?"

"I want to make love with you."

He surprised even himself. Paul wasn't one to make bald statements. He wasn't one to let his desires rule his mouth—or any other part of him. But suddenly, here where he instinctively felt safe, where they were alone and isolated and comfortable and he knew he could give Cassandra what she deserved, all his bottled-up longing came crashing through. His palms began to sweat. He physically ached for her. He needed her as if she were oxygen to his system, as if she were the very essence of life, without which he would wither and die. Paul wanted that wild, silken hair in his hands. He wanted that fine, strong body in his arms, tasting it, touching it, bringing it to life and watching its glow reflect in her smoky cat's eyes.

But all he saw in those eyes now was fear.

"A bath sounds fine," Cassandra finally said, her eyes wide.

"That's not what you said this afternoon." He didn't realize that a soft note of hurt had crept into his voice.

Cassandra's answering smile was no more certain. "This afternoon I hadn't spent hours on horseback. I smell like a ranch hand, thank you, and I'd like to rectify that."

He nodded. "All right. The tub's upstairs. I'm sure Gerta's left a robe in the room to the left."

Paul was surprised to see a glint that looked suspiciously like tears in Cassandra's eyes as she turned away.

Cassandra had been lying in the hot, steamy water for twenty minutes when she heard the knock on the door.

"Wait your turn," she called, eyes closed, body automatically tensing with Paul's proximity. "I'm making up for two months of deprivation."

"Then you'll probably want what I have," came his voice. It sounded suspiciously sly.

"Don't deceive yourself," she automatically retorted, grinning against her will. How could she react so strongly to just his voice? Fire lit in her belly and flowed through her limbs. Those odd chills settled in her breasts and tautened her nipples. Suddenly she wanted to move; the soft timbre of Paul's voice excited her.

Cassandra realized it wasn't going to get better. Her attraction to Paul was going to grow, her dependence on him deepen, until it would kill her to have him turn away.

Cassandra heard the doorknob turn and straightened in the water. He was coming in. She hadn't thought to lock the door. She'd never had to do that before. But now she was just letting him walk in on her at her most vulnerable.

"Turn your eyes," he commanded. "I'm coming in."

"I'm not the one who's supposed to turn her eyes," she snapped, looking around for some kind of cover and coming up short. Both towel and bathrobe were across the room.

She needn't have worried. The first thing she saw peeking around the door was a champagne flute, filled. Paul edged through behind it, backward, his eyes carefully averted.

"I knew there was some trick to this I'd forgotten," he said, handing the glass back to her. "Thought you'd like a little something to celebrate."

"Champagne," she breathed, reaching out without thinking. "Where did you find it?"

"Languishing in Brian's refrigerator. I figured it would be wasted on those two. They drink beer."

Cassandra took the glass in a slippery hand and sniffed the golden liquid, eyes closed with pleasure. "Oh," she breathed, truly in ecstasy. "Dom Perignon. You're a miracle worker."

"I'm a spy," he answered with a chuckle, producing the bottle for a refill once she'd had a sip. Then, reaching out past the door, he produced another glass for himself.

"You could just leave the bottle," she suggested, not trusting him.

"And have you hog the whole thing? I don't get as much of a chance to drink half a bottle of Dom Perignon as you do, lady. I'm getting my share." With that, he kicked the door shut and settled himself quite comfortably on the floor in front of her, his back resolutely to her.

Cassandra giggled, relishing the tickle of the bubbles, the dry, crisp taste of the champagne as it slid down her throat. She'd sat in that lonely, cold little room for too long dreaming of a moment just like this.

"Thank you, Paul," she finally said. "This is awfully sweet."

"Yes," he answered with a nod. "It is, isn't it?" Then he drained his glass and refilled both, hers over his shoulder until her squeal told him he'd overdosed her a little.

Cassandra licked the cool liquid from her wrist and considered him. The back of his neck where his hair curled in wild disarray enticed her. She wanted to taste it, running her tongue over that sensitive skin right above his collar until he groaned. She longed to tangle her fingers in its thickness. Startled not so much by the thought but the resulting reaction in her own body, Cassandra drained the rest of her glass in a gulp.

It didn't help. The restlessness didn't die. The ache didn't ease in her breasts. And suddenly she wanted to see his eyes.

"What happened this afternoon that changed your mind?" Paul asked softly, stretching his legs out before him and leaning back against the tub, the champagne bottle balanced on his leg.

Cassandra nudged him for a refill. He complied without question, spilling just a little more of the wine.

"Why do you want to make love to me?" she asked.

Cassandra saw him lift the glass to his lips and remembered how very soft they were. How delicious.

"Probably for the obvious reasons," he answered.

"Thank you." She scowled. "I needed a little brutal pragmatism right about now."

"You mean you want me to tell you how much I want to hold you, to feel your skin beneath mine and teach you just how beautiful your body is?" When Cassandra couldn't find the voice to answer, Paul took a sip of his wine and continued. "Maybe you want to know that I have had the damnedest time keeping my hands off you since I met you—and that that hasn't happened to me in the past fifteen years. Or that when we slept in the same bed last night, I lay there the whole time aching for you."

She found her voice then, barely. "You did?"

"Of course I did," he grated, wrapping his hand around the neck of the bottle. "What did you think, I fell asleep? I couldn't have fallen asleep if you'd been in another country."

She didn't take her eyes from him. He didn't move, but Cassandra could have sworn his hands were already on her. Hundreds of tiny shivers raced across her skin. "So... you want me?"

Paul's answering laugh was harsh. "I think you could pretty well classify that as an understatement."

Cassandra's next question could barely be heard, so important was it to her. "Is that all?"

For a moment, Paul didn't answer. He merely sat where he was, sipping the wine in his glass. Cassandra held her breath. She was sure her heart stopped as she waited for his answer. The champagne had given her false courage. It had also fueled her desperation, her desire. If Paul didn't answer soon, she'd go to him no matter what he said.

"If it were all," he said, his voice almost as quiet as hers, "do you think I would have waited?"

When Cassandra held out her glass again, her hand trembled. "I think I need a little more champagne."

This time when Paul poured, a little splashed across her breasts. The chill startled her, ice against burning skin.

Paul put the bottle down on the floor next to him. "Don't wipe that off," he said, still not looking at her. "I'd like to do it."

Cassandra finally looked up to see that he'd been watching her all along in the mirror along the wall. She locked gazes with Paul's reflection, a small circle of glass that held him suspended, his eyes like hot gems in the steamy light, his body as tense as a guide wire. He wasn't smiling. Cassandra felt the touch of his eyes like the champagne, the sudden surprise skittering across her skin and sinking into her belly where that fire grew.

Now she knew what anticipation meant. "I'd like you to."

Eleven

Paul kept his promise. From the moment he turned to Cassandra, he carefully and tenderly taught her what it was like to make love.

Cassandra could have lived a long time on nothing but the delicious surprise in his eyes when he'd seen her rise, sleek and wet, from the sudsy water. He smiled, his eyes dark with desire, his hands gentle around hers. It was Paul who dried her, stroking her with the big, fluffy towel until her skin glowed with his ministrations and she was breathless from waiting to have his hands against her skin. He rubbed slowly, deliberately, drying her arms, her back, her legs and belly, letting the thick cotton entice her, and finally—finally when she almost begged him for it, he sought the softness of her breasts.

Paul didn't take his eyes from hers, as he slowly fitted his hands against her.

Cassandra couldn't imagine a more intense yearning, a sweeter hunger than the one he unleashed. She allowed herself to succumb to the invitation in his smile and the temptation of his hands. She let him lead her to the huge old bed with its down comforter and crisp, cotton sheets, and place her gently before him. Her heart thundered at the sight of him. Her lungs couldn't get enough air.

Everywhere he had touched her a separate fire raged, tormenting her for release, for a higher, hotter fire.

Cassandra had seen naked men before. She was no child, after all. None had ever stunned her the way Paul did. There was a power in him, an energy that radiated from his lean lines. His body was taut, hard, well used. Even in the dim light of one lamp, Cassandra could see the scars of old fights, and those enticed her even more. She looked up to see the soft light running along his muscles, the sharp ridges of his hips and flat of his belly like a soft rain on a statue so that it defined its beauty and sharpened its strength. Cassandra wanted to know that body, to taste its secrets and fan its flames.

"Do you know how beautiful you are?" Paul asked in a hushed whisper, standing just over her. He let a hand trail along her arm so that it raised goose bumps, his fingers a delicious rasp against her skin.

"May I say the same?" she asked with a smile, the hunger liquid in her eyes. "Don't stay away, please."

Paul smiled, softening the chiseled angles of his face and melting the ice of his eyes. "I've wanted you since I first set eyes on you, Cassandra."

Cassandra held her arms out to him. "Make love to me, Paul."

For a man who made his living dodging the darker corners of life, Paul was the gentlest of lovers. Cassandra felt a field of energy surround her, like heat lightning on a dry summer night when he came close. Trembling with the effort of control, his hands praised her, courting with an unhurried attention that took Cassandra's strength away. She felt the fire melt throughout her, seeping into her bones and liquefying them beneath Paul's touch. She gasped at the sharp thread of pleasure he wove through her with his fingers and tongue, dancing along her throat, the soft contours of her shoulder and arm, the gentle concave of her belly, the rim along her pelvis.

Her hands came up to hold on to him, clutching his corded arms for balance against the maelstrom he unleashed. She felt the cool air brush the sheen on her forehead and wanted relief. She felt the graze of his tongue across her nipple and cried out for more.

Cassandra had never known the pleasure of simply feeling such a body against hers: so coarse and fierce, deliciously rough against her fingers, muscle and tendon in her hands, beard chafing her cheek. She drew a finger along the slash at Paul's cheek, soaking in its feel, its import. She accepted his murmurs of endearment and offered her own, blind, breathless words incited by his care. Then his fingers tested her, slipping over the velvet core like quick wings. Cassandra gasped, moaned. It felt as if glass were splintering in her. She rocked against him, clutched him, searching his eyes for a sign.

He smiled, and she shuddered, the waters his swift fingers stirred hot and roiling. Her body arched against him, arched again, movement inciting movement. Her mind seethed. Paul lifted a hand to her hair, brushing its wet tangle back against the pillow, and bent to taste her mouth. Cassandra felt him move over her and instinctively welcomed him home. She urged him closer, wrapping around him, arm and leg to ensnare him. And when he entered her, she cried out with the sharp pleasure, the surprising sweetness of the pain, and then begged him to return.

Paul found himself drowning in the hurricane of Cassandra's passion, entangled in her eyes and captured by the soft honey of her hands. He had never lost himself in a woman before, but he felt himself falling, spiraling deeper and deeper into blind oblivion with just the whisper of her surprised sighs. He had meant to offer her fulfillment, carefully bringing her to the satisfaction she deserved. His body was already slick with sweat from the effort of waiting. But the minute he slipped into her, his control exploded into need.

Paul crushed Cassandra to him, his hands filling themselves with her softness, his mouth feasting on the dark flavor of hers. He called out to her, his words mingling with hers as he vaguely felt the scratch of nails at his back. The storm that had been building in him ever since he'd first seen her mounted, seethed in him, the lightning so close. He eased into her and drove deeper. Her cries gathered, intoxicated. Paul lost his intentions within the sound of those cries, and let the storm overtake him.

That same storm swept over Cassandra. A shock jolted through her body, and then another. Her eyes opened to Paul's, as wide and wondering as hers. Her head came back, and her mouth opened. The room was lost to her, the cloud-soft bed that smelled like lavender, the cool mountain air, the silver moonlight that spilled in through the window. All she could see was Paul. All she could feel was the wave after wave of lightning that racked her. All she could want was for Paul to be impossibly closer, even as he met her and followed her rhythm to the top. She brought his head to her breast and felt him shudder and knew that the storm had passed. And in its wake, she thought how very glad she was that it was Paul for whom she'd waited.

"So," she murmured a little while later as she lay against him, her head on his chest. "That is what it's all about."

"No, it's not," he answered, one hand touching her hair and the other around her waist. He'd fitted his angular frame around hers with delightful effect. "That was only the beginning. Making love is like fine wine. It only gets better with time."

Cassandra ran a slow nail across his nipple to see it immediately harden. "And practice?" she asked.

Paul smiled and dropped a kiss to the top of her head. "And a lot of practice."

She nodded, assessing the sweet, satiated glow that eddied through her. "I like your attitude."

Stretching, Cassandra was surprised to feel the heat flare in her again, as if stretching out could stoke it. She'd remember that, just as she'd remember the fact that Paul shuddered when she ran her hands across his belly.

There was so much about him that she still wanted to know, so much to explore. The way he talked, it would take a long time to discover it all. Cassandra wasn't sure whether that should make her feel much better or much worse. Paul hadn't promised that they would have a chance for that time.

"How did you get that scar?" she asked, her eyes on the whorls of hair on his chest, so surprisingly soft against her thumb.

"Which one?" he asked.

She grinned. Good point. He did have enough to catalog. "The new one, along your cheek."

"Oh, that." He shrugged it off as not important. "Temporary lapse of attention. I was watching one way, and the man with the gun came from the other."

"How long ago?"

"A few weeks."

"How many times have you been . . . hurt?"

Paul was running a contemplative hand along Cassandra's arm now. She snuggled closer, delighting in the rasp of his chest against her still-tender breasts.

"Enough to decide that a farm would be a good idea about now."

"Have you ever been afraid?"

He took a moment to answer. When he did, Cassandra heard the ghosts return to his voice. "Yeah," he said flatly. "I've been afraid."

She lifted her head, wanting to see his eyes. They were opaque, hard, like sheet metal. It made her want to shiver. She'd never seen such a barrier before.

Instinctively, Cassandra reached out to him, lifting her finger to his lips. "Want to talk about it?"

For just a minute, Paul seemed not to hear her. His attention was miles or years away. Then, just as quickly, he smiled and the curtain lifted. Taking her hand in his own, he kissed the tip of her finger and laid it back against his chest.

"I just thought of something I bet you'd like," he offered, pulling her to him for a savoring kiss. "Stay right here. I'll be back in a flash."

"Paul..."

But he was already out of bed. Cassandra remained where she was, curled into the mountain of white, wondering how she could break past that barricade of his. Whatever his secret was, it directed his actions. It had to do with his sister, Cassandra decided, and his father and fear; but Cassandra had no idea of how to bring it to light.

"Voilà!"

Startled, Cassandra looked up. Paul stood in the doorway, his naked body gilded in the gold of lamplight and the silver of moonlight. He held a tray in his hand. Cassandra wanted to tell him not to move, to stay there where she could enjoy just the sight of him. Instead she sat up and scooted over to make room for him.

"The ultimate in decadence," he announced, sliding in under the sheets and settling the tray on his lap. "Oreos and milk. Once you taste this, you'll never crave caviar again."

"That," she retorted dryly, "I'll have to see."

Cassandra reached over to pick up a cookie, but Paul smacked her hand. "This has to be done correctly. There's a certain ritual."

Cassandra lifted an eyebrow. "Like a Japanese tea ceremony?"

Paul grinned. "Better. Now, observe."

He made great show of pouring two glasses of milk from the pitcher and handing Cassandra hers. Then, setting the pitcher aside, he set the plate of cookies between them.

"Address your cookie," he instructed.

"Hello, cookie," she said, giggling.

Paul scowled. "You know what I mean."

He picked up his glass of milk and a cookie and held them out as examples. Cassandra followed suit.

"Now there are two ways to eat Oreos," he informed her. "The final choice must be yours. The first is the dip. Follow my lead."

So saying, he dipped the cookie in the milk and took a small bite. Cassandra did the same. Then she smiled. The taste was as delightful as the texture. Soft chocolate and vanilla cream.

"Now take a sip of milk to cleanse the palate."

She followed the ritual until the cookie was gone. All that did was make her want more. No wonder Paul said that these were so wonderful. They were. It amazed her that she'd never tried one before.

"Ready for the next method?"

"But I like that one," she protested, ready to dip another.

"This next one," he continued, barring her way to the cookies, "is considered the connoisseur's choice. A much more subtle approach. Take cookie in hand."

She did. The milk was set on the table for the moment. It was all Cassandra could do to keep from giggling afresh. Never in her life would she have thought that she would be celebrating the loss of her virginity with cookies and milk. Suddenly it seemed the only way.

"Pay attention," Paul commanded, holding his cookie out with a flourish. Cassandra did likewise. "Don't try anything until I tell you. This must be followed precisely."

Then Paul unscrewed the two halves so that some of the cream was left on each half. He held each up before proceeding to lick the filling from first one half, then the other. Only then did he deign to eat the outer chocolate layers.

"Some," he informed her with disdain as he licked leftover crumbs from his fingers, "prefer to try to eat the chocolate first. They are barbarians. Of course, you do have the option of assisting the chocolate with sips of milk."

Cassandra tried that way and found that it took some practice to get the cookie to come apart to Paul's satisfaction, with the cream equally divided. The exercise involved a lot of laughter and a few unacceptable attempts pitched over shoulders.

"Well?" he asked when she'd finally had her taste, the bright glint of amusement in his eyes belying the severity of his voice. "What is your judgment?"

Cassandra assumed full regal dignity, although without the robes her bearing lost some of its formality. "An unqualified success. I shall have this delicacy at my next state function." The thought gave rise to pictures of men in tails and medals decorously dipping cookies in goblets of milk. Cassandra promptly dissolved again into giggles.

"I want to be there when the famed Uncle Eric tries it," Paul agreed with a chuckle.

Cassandra nodded, immensely tickled by the whole thing. "And my grandmother. She'd drop dead of mortification."

"We'll have them for the wedding reception."

Cassandra shook her head. "For the honeymoon."

"The honeymoon?"

She nodded, widening her eyes with mock sincerity. "They have great aphrodisiac powers, don't you know?"

Paul's answering smile was less playful.

"If I may," Cassandra suggested, picking up one of the last cookies, "I'd like to introduce a variation on the rite. The two-person method." Never taking her eyes from the rising heat in Paul's, Cassandra put both their glasses aside and set the tray on the table. "I call it 'the toast.'"

Without taking her eyes from Paul's long enough to watch what she was doing, Cassandra slowly twisted the cookie to perfect separation and held each piece up. Paul couldn't so much as look at what she was doing. There was such invitation in her eyes, in the slow smile on her lips. She sat before him, the snowy comforter nestled at her hips, the rest of her naked and inviting. Her skin seemed to glow in the soft lamplight. Her breasts were high and firm, lifting as her breath quickened. Even her arms, smooth and slim, held up in demonstration, tempted him. As she made her offer, the desire that suddenly bloomed in her eyes, the fun they'd shared crystallized into new passion.

"It's done just like the best toasts," she instructed in a voice that was suddenly husky. Reaching out, she held the cookie before him. "Each partner feeds the other."

Leaning forward, Paul slowly licked the filling from the cookie, all the while holding Cassandra's gaze. He never touched her, never moved to take her in his arms. All the same, his reaction was as swift and potent as hers. Her nipples tightened. Her pupils dilated. Paul felt the rough edge of the cookie along his tongue, thought of what else he wanted to taste, and he knew she understood.

The thought only served to stoke the madness in him. His gut was on fire and his legs were putty. His arms ached with the effort of keeping to themselves. When he had finished the center, Paul ate the cookie. He ended up by slowly licking the crumbs that still clung to Cassandra's fingers.

Still he kept his hands to himself. Still Cassandra gasped, as if stunned by electric shock. She did not take her hand away, though, until Paul had licked the last crumb from between her fingers.

"Now," he said, holding his hand out, "it's your turn."

Paul took the other half of the cookie in his hand and held it out to her, leaning close so that she couldn't avoid him. Cassandra almost found herself unable to move. The charge of his tongue against her palm still coursed through her, like the champagne on her skin, ice against fire. She was shaken, stunned, breathless. What had begun as a game had changed. And Cassandra knew that even Paul had never experienced anything like this before.

At first she wanted to stop, terrified by the swift fire that raged through her. But Cassandra had never been one to fall before a challenge. Deliberately offering a smile that smoldered back to her from Paul's eyes, she leaned forward. Her breasts deliberately brushed against his arm. Slowly she slid her tongue over her lips, anticipating.

Cassandra could smell him, dark and musky and dangerous. She could feel the fan of his breath across her cheek, and it was ragged. Edging just a little closer, Cassandra tipped her tongue toward the cookie and began to lick. Paul trembled. She could feel it. She wondered if he could hear the triphammer of her own heart. She nibbled the cookie, her eyes still locked to his, and ate it until she nipped his fingers with quick teeth.

Still he didn't breach the distance with his hands. He reached out behind him for a glass and offered her some. Cassandra took it, sipping the milk as if it were the Dom Perignon they'd had earlier. And just like the champagne before, she managed to spill some of the milk.

"Don't bother to wipe that away," Paul offered, finally reaching out to run a slow finger along the trail the lone drop of milk had left between her breasts. "I'll take care of it."

Almost gasping with impatience, Cassandra deliberately eased back onto the crisp sheets and smiled. "Please do."

Cassandra thought before that she couldn't have asked more from Paul. He had been generous and caring and gentle. Caught now in the whirlwind of his passion, she knew that she could have asked for this.

He consumed her, exhausted her, his desire a white-hot flame that couldn't be quenched. Cassandra felt at once battered by his intensity and invigorated by his power. Her body unfolded to him, welcoming his hot touch and hungry mouth. Her hands roamed with a ferocity of their own. Cassandra accepted his groans and offered her murmurings. She drove him with a frenzy of her own, and then, when she couldn't bear it any longer, took him with trembling hands and guided him home.

The moon had disappeared by the time they lay quiet again, wrapped tightly in each other's arms and waiting for racing hearts to ease. Cassandra wound herself around Paul as if afraid of falling.

The bed was a disaster, the bedclothes tumbled and half off. If she weren't still trying to cool off, Cassandra would have cared more. As it was, her hair was damp all along her neck, and she felt the air stir across the sheen of perspiration on her forehead. She felt absolutely spent and found herself smiling.

"So tell me," she finally mused. "Do you think the 'Princess Cassandra toast' has a chance?"

Paul chuckled, the rumble comfortable against Cassandra's cheek. "The cookie world salutes you, Cassandra. I think that variation will definitely go down in the official rule book."

"Thank you. I was thinking of giving the formula to Uncle Eric and Casey for a wedding gift. I'm just not sure how to go about it—or how Uncle Eric would take it."

"We still have a little time to work on that," he consoled her. "The wedding's not for a couple of weeks yet."

Cassandra lay still for a while, her ear to Paul's heart, her thoughts on his sister's wedding.

"Moritania's only about five miles from here," she said quietly. "Did you know that?"

Paul went on stroking her hair. "Uh-huh. We could make it across and stock up on cookies at Braz before the wedding. The problem would be keeping the milk good until the wedding night."

"*You* could stock up on cookies," she corrected him. "I haven't been invited to the wedding."

"They just didn't know where to send the invitation," he assured her. "You can come as my date."

Cassandra's laugh was sharp. "I'm not all that sure my family would let me pass the gates."

Paul held her just a little more closely. "In that case, I'd be more than happy to punch them out for you. Especially since they don't have any sense to begin with anyway."

"It's not sense they lack," she said softly. "It's charity."

"Now you're indulging in self-pity. There's no reason in the world you can't go back and work things out right now."

"Except for the small matter of international arrest warrants."

"Well, yeah . . ."

Instinct propelling her, Cassandra raised up on her elbow. "Why didn't *you*?"

Paul's eyes softening at the sight of her, tousled and sleepy from his lovemaking, he reached up to tuck her hair behind her ear. "Why didn't I what?"

Cassandra eased around for a more comfortable position against him. "Go back and work things out? What kept you away for fifteen years?"

She was watching this time and saw that wall go up. Paul didn't move, didn't tense or ease or shift position. But Cassandra saw something in his eyes close off as if iron gates had shut. Still she persisted.

"Are you that mad at your sister that you haven't been able to talk to her for all these years?"

Paul started, looked down at the sincere question in Cassandra's eyes. "Casey? Why the hell should I be mad at Casey?" he demanded.

"I don't know," Cassandra answered truthfully. "But I do know that you haven't seen her in fifteen years, and you haven't once asked about her. You don't talk about her. And she didn't talk about you. What did you two do to each other?"

"Casey didn't do anything," he insisted. "I told you. She was only ten when I left. What can a ten-year-old possibly do that's that bad?"

"There were times when I was ten that I wondered that," Cassandra answered with a wry smile. Then she kept her silence.

A war was raging in Paul. Cassandra saw it in the sudden set of his jaw, in the hard, almost bitter glint in his eyes. She wanted so much to reach out to him, even knowing that he wouldn't accept it. He stood alone before this, and Cassandra wasn't invited along yet.

Finally, unable to hold it in any longer, Paul slipped out of Cassandra's arms and got out of bed.

"I'd better take the milk back," he said, gathering the things.

Cassandra watched, once again bewildered, once again silent. How could she get closer to him? How would she breach that wall he'd built? She sat rigid and alone in the big bed and watched him turn from her. It was only when he closed the door behind him that she gave in to frustration and tears.

Cassandra was sitting in the same position when the door opened again. She wiped furiously at her eyes, but the tears still glinted on her cheeks. She hoped Paul wouldn't notice.

Paul saw them and his resolve shattered. He had no choice. He'd received more trust from her than he had from any other person. It was time he gave a little trust of his own. Still, this would be the hardest admission he'd ever have to make. It was the admission he really hadn't even made to himself until he'd answered his mother's letter inviting him to the wedding.

"The reason Casey doesn't talk about me," he said without preamble, walking right over to the window and the anonymity of a night sky, "is probably because I ran out on her. Her and my mom. I ran out and left her behind to face what I couldn't."

"Paul," Cassandra commanded in the gentlest of voices. "Come here."

He turned to her to see only question in her eyes. No judgment. Support. Understanding. Anxiety. She wanted to help, and it ate at him.

Even so, he walked over and sat next to her. Without a word, she drew him into her arms and bid him tell the rest.

Paul rested his cheek against her silken hair and closed his eyes. He'd never known such comfort, like having one place that was home and coming back to it after too long a time. It tempted him so sorely.

"I . . . had problems with my dad. It wasn't that uncommon in my neighborhood. We didn't have two dimes to rub together when I was a kid. My dad had trouble finding work. Sometimes when the frustration got to be too much, he . . . took it out on me."

Cassandra stiffened. "He beat you?"

Paul's laugh was harsh. "Like an old rug. I'm a lot like him, and we used to fight. I guess sometimes I egged him on. By the time I was sixteen, he knew I was going to be bigger than he. He...I think it scared him. He really started going after me. When I couldn't take it anymore, I left."

"What about your mother? Didn't she try to stop it?"

He shrugged. "She didn't know how. She was afraid if she challenged him, she'd be on the street with nowhere to go."

"Did he . . ."

"Hit Casey? Never while I was there. He adored her. It happens, I hear. One kid gets singled out for all the trouble. I seemed to be the one."

Cassandra felt the ambivalence and guilt that fifteen years had nurtured boil up in him. It angered her for him, hurt her with him. That a man could do that to his son.

"Why did you stay away?" she asked.

"Ah, that's the question." He took a breath, facing the ghosts that had followed him. "I want to think it's because I didn't want to disillusion Casey. She worshiped him. I mean, how could I tell her that the man she loved more than anyone in the world spent his Fridays beating up his other kid?"

"She didn't know?"

"Never. It was kind of like a secret pact in that house. Nobody let Casey know. She was such a special little kid. All sunlight and mischief."

The loneliness, the longing to rediscover that place in his life, escaped into his voice. Memories that could still be special, even from a hell like that.

"What about your other reason?"

"For staying away?" Paul shook his head. "Less noble. I just didn't want to face any of it. I didn't want to live with the fact that I'd run out and left my sister—or my mother—to maybe take up where I'd left off. I'd always thought it was me in particular Dad couldn't tolerate, but who knew?"

Cassandra thought of the ferocity in Paul, the dark edges that peeked through sometimes. But then she thought of the patience and gentleness he had showered on her. Two children isolated in different ways, she by tradition, he by violence, and the child of violence had grown to be the better person. It only served to make her love him more.

Paul sat very still for a moment, silently stroking Cassandra's hair and waiting for her judgment. He'd finally opened the door. Breached the dam. Emotions and memories boiled in him like a hot caldron of acid, the years of ignoring them only serving to make them more potent. Casey as a baby, toddling after him, calling in that insistent little voice of hers when he strayed too far away. Pauly, her big brother, her idol. The person she'd depended on and confided in and unabashedly adored. The brother who had walked out of the house one summer night and never returned.

How did he reckon with that? How could he possibly deal with her? The pain of his betrayal ate at him anew, a deep and festering wound that he'd shoved away for too long. He held on to Cassandra more tightly and wondered when she would turn away.

"You've been in touch with your mother all these years," she said quietly, the tears that had begun to streak her face not yet in her voice.

Paul's laugh was bitter. "Nothing salves the guilty conscience so well as the regular contribution."

Those were the words that brought Cassandra's head up. Angry, glaring, fiery. Paul saw the tears in her eyes and the sudden indignation in her spine, and despaired. Here it came, then.

"How dare you?" she demanded, gulping a little on a sob. "You escape a hell no one should have to live through, and then you blame yourself? Do you also administer the lash when you convict yourself?"

Still waiting to hear much different words, Paul hesitated. Gaped a little. "What?"

Now it was Cassandra's turn to gape. She read his expression as if it were typed in bold print, and it angered her all the more. "You really think it was all your fault, don't you? You can't forgive yourself for getting out when you did and then protecting your sister from the truth all these years?"

"I ran out on her!" he retorted, the pain now there to see on his face. He was contorted with it, his own tears too close to bear, Cassandra's defense too unexpected to understand.

"You did nothing of the kind! You were sixteen, for God's sake, not thirty! You got out before it got worse. Before you were hurt—and before Casey found out. Give yourself a break, Paul."

Paul stared, the turmoil in him almost unbearable. He could see it now, there in her eyes. She was angry for him, not at him. Cassandra glared like a lioness facing down a threat to her cubs.

She didn't see his point at all. But she understood instinctively what he'd been through. She knew the isolation, the humiliation, the pain. It was almost as if she had sat with him in his bare bedroom all those years ago, as he'd sobbed his heart out and nursed his wounds, wondering how he could be so bad that his father couldn't love him.

He still couldn't believe that she'd be looking at him in such a protective, loving way now that she'd learned the truth. A new door had edged open, and there was a light behind it, a new light he'd never seen in all the years of his life.

"You really mean it, don't you?"

Cassandra huffed, giving his arms a shake. "Of course I mean it. Paul, I know what it's like not to have anyone on my side. But that didn't happen to me until I was thirteen. I can't imagine what I would have done if I'd spent my whole life without help...without hope. How did you get through it?"

Paul smiled now, and the light from that new place in him brightened. The tentative hope in him eased many of the harsher angles of his face. He still couldn't understand why she hadn't turned away from him. He wasn't yet sure whether he could hope for more.

"A guy could easily fall in love with you," he said, running a quick finger down her nose.

Cassandra crinkled it in response, the import of Paul's words stirring its own fire of hope in her. "Not according to my grandmother."

Paul smiled. "She's never eaten Oreos with you."

Now Cassandra laughed. "Nor is she ever likely to."

"We'll bring her some when we go to the wedding."

"I told you," she objected, turning her face away. "I don't think I'm invited."

Reaching around, Paul cupped her chin in his fingers and turned her back to him. "No excuses. I'm not going to face that crowd without a little support, and you're the only one I can think of to fill that bill."

Cassandra caught herself just shy of smiling. "Really?"

Paul didn't. He beamed for her. "Really. Come with me?"

Lost in the sweet plea in Paul's eyes, Cassandra found herself nodding even before she'd made her decision. "Of course I will. After all, who's going to fight for your throne?"

"*My* throne, huh?" he countered softly, his eyes melting, his hand straying along the line of her throat. "Does this mean that I'm your liege lord and master?"

Cassandra eased toward him. "In a manner of speaking."

"And you must follow my commands?"

She scowled, at once exhilarated and wary. "That depends."

Paul only smiled as he took her hand in his and brought it to his lips. "Pretend you have a cookie."

"Oh," she murmured, her heart tripping, "that..."

Twelve

He was a bear. A giant, red-haired, laughing bear. Cassandra came upon Brian O'Shaughnessy the next morning over breakfast and promptly found herself in a crushing hug.

"Well, then," he almost shouted in her ear. "So you're the fairy princess Paul's brought home to the old folks, are ya?"

"Well . . ."

"And a good choice it is, too. You're a fair beauty of a lass, you are."

Cassandra was still getting her breath when she found herself back on her feet and spun around. She caught herself against the table before she landed on her nose. "Thank you."

"Can ya cook or clean or dig the praeties, then?"

"Pardon?"

Brian laughed again, a great booming thunder that fairly shook the rafters. Cassandra couldn't help but smile at him, infected by his good humor and vitality. She didn't realize until she'd been back in one place for a few seconds that a woman stood in his shadow.

"Don't play with Paul's friends, Brian, dear," the woman admonished easily as she laid a heaping plate of eggs on the table. "You might break them." The tiny, dark-haired woman walked with a limp and spoke with a Germanic accent. A greater antithesis of the giant Irishman, Cassandra couldn't imagine.

"Now, mother," Brian protested, "I was only saying my hellos to the girl. Surely she can endure that."

"Sit down, my dear," the woman advised Cassandra with a sweep of her spatula, "and eat an egg or two before himself here finishes off the rest."

"What about Paul?" Cassandra asked diffidently. She'd left him in the shower.

"He ate his breakfast when we got in this morning. You were still asleep. So," she added with a glower toward her husband, "did this human waste system. He claims to need more."

"A fighting machine, mother," Brian said without rancor, "needs its fuel."

Ignoring the protests, the little woman spooned two eggs onto Cassandra's plate and physically sat her in one of the oak chairs. "He takes a little getting used to," she remarked with a dry grin. "But he'll grow on you . . . rather like warts."

"I heard that!"

"I fully intended you to. My name," she said, returning to Cassandra with hard rolls, "is Gerta. You've met my husband, Brian."

Cassandra nodded, still a bit stunned by the whirlwind across the table from her. "Thank you for your hospitality. I'm sorry we had to break in."

That provoked another laugh from her host. "Himself your partner would have been insulted if I'd left the door open for him. That much of an artist he considers himself."

"I *am* that much of an artist, you old turf digger."

Cassandra looked up to see Paul descending the steps. He was in jeans and gray pullover, his hair still wet from his shower, his eyes laughing.

The minute he saw that Brian was intent on getting up, Paul held up a warning hand. "And don't you dare try to inflict one of those Gaelic tortures on me. The last time you said hello, you broke two ribs."

Brian waved it off. "A grand exaggeration. Nothing more than a bruise or two, it was."

Pulling out the chair alongside Cassandra's, Paul reached over to drop a kiss on her forehead before sitting. "Did you survive him?"

Cassandra wanted to tell him that she was sore, all right, but certainly not from Brian's hug. Instead, she smiled. "About as well as I survived meeting you."

Both of the men laughed at that. Cassandra assumed then that explanations had previously been served up all around. Except for her. She was still in the dark.

"Excuse me," she spoke up between eggs. "But how did you find out about us? We didn't call."

Brian shook his head, intent on his own breakfast. "Didn't have to. It's kind of a tight clan we have here. Word spreads fast."

"But I thought—"

"That I was retired? So I am. I still have a good ear, though."

"What did you find out?"

Not only Brian and Paul, but Gerta exchanged glances before answering that one. A nod of Paul's head decided it. While Gerta poured coffee and eased herself into the remaining empty chair, Brian took up the explanation.

"Well, it seems the two of you landed yourselves in the middle of a fair spider's nest. The East Germans profess an interest in you, the ELM want to resume your acquaintance, and the fair mother of our former employment herself would like a word with you."

"Not to mention the German police for torching one of their stations," Cassandra added dolefully. Then she leaned over to place a hand on the Irishman's arm. "Are you sure Paul is a good guy?"

"A good guy?" he retorted with another rolling laugh. "Oh, lass, the boy here couldn't do a bad deed if it were the only way through the gates of heaven. He's been the despair of more than one enemy agent looking for an easy blackmail target."

Silently occupied with drinking his coffee, Paul allowed a heartfelt scowl. "The ten dollars will be in the mail, Brian."

"But what do they want us for?"

Brian shrugged, sincerely mystified. "That I don't know. It seems to all generate from the East Germans, who are swarming over the continent like an army of red ants—if you'll pardon the pun."

"Not likely," Paul mumbled.

Cassandra turned to him. "You said your last two assignments were in East Germany."

Paul shrugged. "We've been through it again this morning. None of us can come up with anything they might have objected to from those assignments."

"Then why shoot you over it?"

Paul's fingers went to the scar as he offered up a wry smile. "Principle."

She looked around with a scowl to see three faces that seemed a lot less concerned about this whole thing than she was. Maybe being used to all this had its advantages. Maybe their stomachs didn't churn with the thought of jail or worse.

"Well, what are we going to do?" she asked.

Immediately, Paul set his coffee cup down and turned to her. "I told you. *We* aren't going to do anything. You are staying here with Gerta while Brian and I go see some friends who might help us."

"But, Paul . . ."

He held up a finger. "I bet you're about to say that you're as much involved in this as I am. True. But you've just received your diploma in basic life-support tasks. This takes the advanced class. You'll be safe here. Brian and Gerta are supposed to be up on the farm in Ireland, and only a few people on our side know about Gerta's parents. My guess is they'll think we went right on through to Moritania and look for us there."

Cassandra's mouth went dry with the thought. Her heart hammered. She'd never had to be afraid for anyone else, and the feeling truly threatened to overwhelm her. "And you?"

Paul took her hand in his and squeezed it, his smile easy and soothing. "I'm going to be doing what I've done for the past fifteen years. And if I know that you're safe here, I can put my full attention into it. Okay?"

She saw his logic, understood its merit. It didn't make her feel any better. "Once you hit that stud farm, you don't leave it for anything," she insisted. "Promise?"

Paul grinned. "Promise."

The first time Paul and Brian left they were gone for two days. Cassandra spent the time helping Gerta with the farm and getting to know her better.

It amazed her that the little woman could go about her chores with such a placid attitude, knowing all the while that her husband was out risking his life. Cassandra didn't think she herself had the stuff to be that way. Her heart leaped every time she heard a car pull close or the telephone ring. She paced when she wasn't busy and drank cup after cup of coffee when she was. Gerta, on the other hand, seemed perfectly contented to sit for hours on end working the delicate needlework pattern she carried with her. She hummed quietly to herself when she cooked and spoke gently to the animals. If nothing else, the force of her calm pervaded the household and settled Cassandra somewhat by the second day.

And then Brian breezed back into the house.

"Where's the nourishment due a hardworking man, then?" he bellowed from the back door, sending Gerta's head up from her needlework and Cassandra up from her chair.

Paul wasn't with him.

Cassandra had made it to the door before Brian caught her with surprisingly gentle hands. "No, lass, don't worry. He'll be home before nightfall. We went separate ways today, and his was the longer. I heard from him on the way in, though. Everything's going well."

"What have you learned?"

"Oh, much. We'll have it over dinner when he gets home. Until then, let's pass a drop and talk about the life of a deposed princess. Has Mother been treatin' you well, then?"

Passing the drop turned out to be the best Irish whiskey, something else Cassandra had never tried. By the time Paul finally walked in the kitchen door to shed his jacket and throw it over a chair, Cassandra and Brian were laughing together and trading barbs. She accused the Irish of having no sense of order, and Brian accused the Moritanians of having no music, for the Irish a much more serious accusation.

Cassandra giggled, downing a bit more of the fiery liquid, and nodded. True. The Moritanians had no traditional music. They'd stolen theirs from the Austrians, just as they'd stolen their currency from the English. Both served just fine, thank you.

"Too bad you two don't get along," Paul observed, coming upon them before the roaring fire. Gerta lifted her head from her own beer and more needlework and smiled at him in greeting. Brian bellowed something in Gaelic that Cassandra couldn't understand.

"No, you can't have her," Paul told him with a shake of the head. "You have one of your own, remember?"

"We'll have dinner, now," Gerta decided, setting her linen aside and getting up. "Before we find ourselves in a reenactment of the Cattle Raid of Cooley."

Cassandra turned then, the whiskey in her causing the room to turn with her. "You know Irish mythology, then, Brian?"

The Irishman's eyes lit with true wonder. Paul sat with a groan.

"As well as yourself, lass?" the big man demanded, taking her hand. "You have a knowledge of it?"

She nodded. "The Irish were much more fanciful than the Moritanians. I think the only national literature we can aspire to is in essays on fiscal responsibility. I studied other countries' folk histories instead."

"Oh, it's a rare beauty you are, then," he praised, helping her to her feet for dinner. "And a loss on the heathen, here, who can't even name the high kings."

"And an Irishman at that," Cassandra admonished with a silly grin. Paul responded with a set of arched eyebrows.

The table had been set for a while. In her desire to help somehow, Cassandra cleared Paul's jacket from where it had landed on Gerta's chair.

She had a hand on it when Gerta turned around next to her with a platter full of sausage. The men were refilling their nourishment over at the sink. Running her hand over the battered leather, Cassandra smiled up at her new friend.

"When is Paul's birthday, do you know?"

Gerta shrugged. "He never would tell us."

Cassandra just nodded. "Then I'll make one up. I'll get him a new jacket for it."

"A new jacket?" Gerta asked with raised eyebrows. "Whatever for? Paul wouldn't part with that one, anyway."

Cassandra picked it up in her hands. "Lining's getting bad. Or maybe the leather, I couldn't tell. Anyway, he needs a new one."

Gerta just shook her head. "He's like a baby with a favorite blanket, that one. Give his jacket away, and he won't sleep until he finds it again. He's had it since I've known him."

Cassandra was about to answer when it finally sank in that the jacket she held was suddenly much heavier than before. A quizzical expression crossed her features as she weighed it again, her eyes on it. She didn't see Paul come up behind her.

"I'll take it, Cassandra."

Cassandra looked up to see caution in his eyes. "What's in here?"

"Besides the rocks?" he asked playfully.

But the grin was a little too tight. Cassandra put down her drink and patted the pockets. The minute she felt it, she knew she shouldn't have searched. She felt worse—if possible, more terrified for him. Maybe when he hadn't had one she could have pretended the whole situation wasn't quite so serious, or that no one would really hurt him. Now she believed it. The giddy feeling the whiskey had created now died a cold death, and she was afraid she was going to cry.

"What did you find out today?" she asked, handing Paul his jacket without taking out the gun.

He faced her without balking, knowing what she'd found and what it meant to her. "We're on the right track. I don't think anybody has picked up our trail yet, but I don't want to take chances."

Cassandra turned to help Gerta put out the rest of the food.

"What could you have brought out of East Germany with you?" Gerta asked sometime later. Brian had done the filling in so far. Cassandra, still feeling the weight of that gun in her hands, was only half paying attention.

"It's the plans for some kind of electronic guidance system the East Germans and Russians have put together," Paul answered, his eyes still on Cassandra. "The word is that they think I somehow walked out with them."

"Did you?"

He shrugged, taking a drink of beer. "I don't see how. We have Justin at Langley looking through the papers and film I brought in to see if there are any surprises I don't know about. I already looked through everything else I have to see if something ended up with me. It didn't."

"And the problem with the company?" Gerta asked, her eyes alert and calculating.

Again, a shrug. "Our pet theory is that the East Germans are trying to discredit me so that if I show up with anything it won't be counted seriously."

"Justin is working on that, too?"

Paul nodded. Gerta nodded in return, a contemplative little move.

"And tomorrow?"

"I retrace my steps." Cassandra's head came up and Paul corrected himself. "Figuratively."

"You haven't been doing any free-lance work since Potsdam?" Gerta asked carefully. "Anything they might have misconstrued?"

Paul shook his head. "None. I didn't even retire in person. Just handed in my stuff with my last report."

"And after that?"

"I started to drive through Germany to see my sister before I hit the farm. The first person I ran into except for gas station attendants and *gasthaus* waitresses was Cassandra."

"You haven't been dallying around any East Germans lately, have you, lass?" Brian demanded, sensing her anxiety and trying to work her free.

Cassandra couldn't work up to her previous enthusiasm. "Not unless they're married to an economics minister."

"There you have it, then," Brian finished, waving his hands in brief summary. "The boy hasn't been around anything or seen anything, and was good enough to pick up top secret information doin' it."

"You forgot your friend," Cassandra said.

Paul turned to her. "My friend?"

"The one you stopped in to see in Berlin."

Paul shook his head. "That wouldn't be it. I just stopped in for dinner. We didn't even talk shop."

"Who?" Brian asked.

"Elliott Weiss."

Those two words electrified the couple across the table. Stiffening as if they'd been shot, Gerta and Brian exchanged alarmed looks. Brian let out a low whistle.

"I think we have something here, lad."

Paul shook his head. "I told you, Brian. I only stopped in for dinner. Took his kids some dolls and ate pork roast. We talked about football and the cost of moving his family back home to live."

Gerta was the one who put her hand on Paul's arm. Cassandra, suddenly attuned to the new tension, saw the compassion in the other woman's brown eyes. "Elliott's dead, Paul."

Paul turned on her. "Gerta, I only left him six days ago."

"He was shot Wednesday night. A professional job."

Paul stared at her, stared at Brian, waiting for a denial. He'd laughed with Elliott less than a week ago, drank his brandy and danced with his wife around the kitchen while she cooked. He couldn't be dead.

"What did you bring away from his house?"

Paul was on his feet, though, heading for the other room. He had to give motion to the surprise. The anger. The outrage. Elliott was a decent man, a low-level man, careful for the sake of his family. Who could have considered him that dangerous?

He reached the fireplace and found he had no place to go. Leaning his hand against the mantel, Paul stared into the flames. He didn't hear Gerta and Brian clear the table or Cassandra walk up behind him.

"I'm sorry," she said, her hand on his back, her voice soft.

"He wasn't even in the field anymore," Paul protested blindly, his mind racing. "I've got to call Justin and find the connection."

"You just got back," she protested, easing closer. "Can't you sit for a minute?"

Paul turned on her then, and she drew back. His eyes were like steel. Cassandra knew better than to argue.

"I'll be here with the cookies and milk when you're finished," she offered with a hand to his cheek and a smile.

Reaching out to her in kind, Paul relented. "You're too good for me."

Cassandra looked pleased. "That's what my grandmother will say."

It turned out not to be cookies and milk, but marshmallows. While Paul used the phone in the upstairs bedroom to call Justin, Gerta and Brian treated Cassandra to her first-ever marshmallow roast over the open fire. It would be years before Cassandra realized that the regulation marshmallow roast did not entail liberal helpings of Irish whiskey. By the time Paul got back downstairs, she was once again helplessly giggling.

"Brian, the king of Moritania is not going to understand when his niece comes home a lush," Paul warned.

Sitting on the thick ecru rug in front of the fire, Cassandra bent her head way back to take in Paul above her. "I beg your pardon," she said, slurring her words ever so slightly. "I am not a lush. Have you ever had burned marshmallows, Paul? They're wonderful!"

Paul just rolled his eyes. "I thought if I got her away from caviar she'd be more manageable. I think I've created a monster."

Gerta just smiled. "Cassandra has asked how to cook marshmallows."

"And how they grow," Cassandra said sagely. "I want to have some on the farm."

"We can't," Paul told her with a tolerant smile. "The horses would just eat them and get fat."

Cassandra blinked. "Oh."

Pulling the latest batch from the fire, Brian waved a flaming stick in Paul's direction. "Have one, lad. You have some catchin' up to do."

"Thanks, I'll just have one," Paul demurred, blowing at the stick as it passed under his nose and then picking the sticky goo off with his fingers. "I'm driving."

Cassandra giggled again.

"No more for her," Paul admonished, easing down on the floor next to her.

Cassandra knew she was just a little tipsy. She hadn't meant to get that way, but Brian had been hard to refuse. It was he who had calmed her fears about Paul's being able to handle himself, and just what they were up against right now. And it was Brian who had helped her dispel the hurt she'd felt for Paul and his friend.

"Doesn't do you any good, then, does it?" he'd demanded. "The dead are dead and there's nothing we can do about that. If you can't get past the sadness, you find yourself without the attention to deal with the matters of the living."

"The Gospel according to St. Brian," Gerta had intoned from above her sewing hoop. Cassandra heard the wry timbre of her voice, but she also saw the fond smile in her eyes. Life must have been one long road show with the big Irishman.

"Now then, lad," Brian said, passing a glass over to Paul. "What did Justin have to say for himself?"

Paul finished licking the marshmallow from his fingers and took a sip of whiskey. "That Elliott had been in contact with Langley before he died. Said he had something for them. Then he didn't show up for a scheduled drop."

"The day after you were there," Brian remarked.

Cassandra nestled against Paul and was rewarded with an arm around her shoulders. This business was beyond her, and that's where she wanted it to stay. She was beginning to realize enough by now to know that she could only hurt their efforts by interfering in their discussion. She let them talk around her, contented to luxuriate in Paul's touch, his scent, the sound of his voice. Contented to sit on a hardwood floor munching on blackened, gooey marshmallows and sipping old whiskey. More than caviar had changed in her life since she'd met Paul.

"Justin was saying that whoever did it made it to look like a terrorist attack," Paul was saying. "Slogans on the wall. That kind of thing."

"So when are you going back out again?" Cassandra asked.

Paul turned to her. "First thing in the morning. While you're sleeping off your marshmallow jag."

"In that case," Gerta was saying above her, "I think it's time for the O'Shaughnessys to be getting to bed."

"To what?" her husband protested.

Cassandra didn't see the two exchange pointed glances over her head and the Irishman smile. She didn't see the look in Paul's eyes as he held her. Her eyes were on the fire, her thoughts on leaving and returning.

By the time Cassandra finally lifted her head, Brian and Gerta were upstairs.

"Did I scare them off?" she asked with a blink or two.

Chuckling, Paul pulled her more tightly against him. "Nah. I told 'em to get lost so I could propose."

"Not again," she groaned. "Are you going for a record or something?"

"You don't believe me?"

Her smile was dust dry. "See me when you have something more substantial in your hand than a marshmallow."

Paul laughed, the light in his eyes delighted. "Is there anything else you can think of to do—all alone—in front of a roaring fireplace?"

Cassandra thought a moment. Her body had already given its answer. She just hoped Paul wouldn't recognize it for a moment.

"Yes," she replied. "Eat."

She was spearing another marshmallow when Paul caught her hand. "You're going to get fat, young lady."

Cassandra just shook her head. "I have months of deprivation to make up for."

"That excuse is only going to last for so long."

Then she smiled up at him, and all the longing he'd unleashed was reflected in her eyes. "Then I guess you won't want to hear the one about the years of deprivation I also have to make up for."

Paul smiled back, a hand still on hers, the stick caught between them forgotten. "Now that," he informed her, dropping a kiss on the tip of her nose, "is an entirely different matter."

Cassandra straightened, eased herself against Paul until she could feel the hammering of his heart against her breasts. The soft ache that always lived in her around him blossomed, brightened within her. Her breasts tautened against him, and she reached out to touch him.

"Want to satisfy a craving together?" she asked in a whisper, the hard rasp of Paul's cheek caught in her palm.

Paul's smile was so intimate that it sent fresh shivers racing along her spine. "I don't like marshmallows," he answered.

Somehow the stick had fallen to the floor. Paul had a hand in her hair, twisting his fingers into it so he could pull her closer. Cassandra shivered at his touch. His kiss.

"Then I guess you won't like me," she answered with a relentlessly seductive smile. "I'm just as soft... and sweet..."

Paul lowered his mouth to hers, effectively cutting off the description, tasting it instead. He had her securely in his grasp, one hand snaking around her back to pull her even closer, his lips enticing her even more than his hands.

Cassandra felt the sigh collect in her, a delicious sensation that filled her like sunlight. Lifting her own hand, she took in Paul's face, the edge of his scar and the feathering of lashes at his eyes. She tasted the whiskey on his tongue and inhaled the musk on his skin. So contrasting, so compelling. Letting the sigh escape, Cassandra melted into Paul's embrace and forgot how she was going to seduce him.

"As soft and sweet as a cat," he whispered in her ear as he eased her back onto the rug.

Cassandra's eyes opened to see humor mingle delectably with desire in Paul's gaze. Shadows deepened the creases at his cheeks, luring her to explore them. The lines of worry on his forehead eased. The crow's feet at the corners of his eyes spread with his smile. Cassandra loved those best of all, because they were the measure of his strength.

"I think I'll take that as a compliment," she decided, running a nail up to where his top button waited to be free. She could feel the brush of hair beneath, and it both delighted and awakened her. The glowing grew in her, pulsating like the core of a fire, curling out from her belly and along her legs, skittering along her spine. Cassandra anticipated the pleasure of his hands and the heat of his mouth.

"Take that however you want," he agreed, spreading a cool hand along her throat and easing it down. "I find cats a lot more interesting than marshmallows."

Cassandra chuckled, reaching now with both hands to bare his skin. The soft firelight shuddered along his features and tinted his eyes the color of dawn. The thick rug cushioned them from the chilly touch of wood. The heat from the fire danced with cooler air to create a delicious breeze over sudden gooseflesh.

Paul looked down to see gold in Cassandra's hair where it fanned out over the tan rug. Her skin glowed in the soft light, so pale it seemed a fragile veneer. Her eyes, so dark and luminous, enticed him with their awakening desire. She had grown so much since the night before, her hands more sure, her satisfaction more complete. It maddened him to see the confidence, the fulfillment born of assurance, build in her.

Her body danced beneath him, welcoming and enticing, giving and taking. He'd never known such satisfaction before. He'd never been so hungry for the taste of a woman, for the crescendo of anticipation beneath his fingers, the fervor that built like a sweet fire in hazel eyes. Paul had never known such excitement in the soft rasp of cloth against his fingers, the slick heat of satin over hidden pleasures.

His fingers trembling with the delicious agony of waiting, Paul slipped Cassandra's buttons free. He felt the shudder of excitement in her, saw the soft swell of breast, washed in firelight and straining against the lace that constrained it. His eyes devoured her long before his hands reached for her. Paul returned to feast on Cassandra's eyes and let his fingers find her breast.

Her nipples were taut, her skin soft and warm. He felt her skin through the lace of her bra, taunting himself and her with that last barrier. Cupping her breast and tracing sensitive skin with a callused thumb, he bent to taste her through the material.

She groaned. Arched. Paul laid a hand against her belly and felt the fever take hold of her. Saw her eyes go wide. Recognized the sudden power in her new smile.

That was the moment Cassandra took over. She turned Paul on his back, and tormented him the way he had tormented her, with hand and tongue and quick, clever mouth. His soft groans of pleasure drove her on. The harsh strength of his hands, reckless with the passion she stoked, compelled her. Cassandra discovered the joy of participation and relished the sharing. She drank in his escalating passion and offered herself.

Guiding the way with age-old instincts, Cassandra led Paul up to the heights and followed him over the edge, where passion exploded into brilliant shards of sharp light. And when she lay in his arms, spent and glowing, her cheek nestled against his chest and her arm across his belly, she told him something she had never really known how to tell anyone. Cassandra told Paul that she loved him.

Thirteen

Cassandra felt Paul go very still. She waited, eyes closed, wondering how he'd react. Terrified he'd turn away.

She shouldn't have said it. She shouldn't have opened herself up so much. She'd only invited rejection, and Cassandra was much too familiar with that to expect anything else.

But she *did* love him. Suddenly it seemed important he know that.

"How was that again?" Paul asked, his voice very quiet.

Instinctively retreating, Cassandra shook her head. "Nothing."

Instead of letting her off the hook, Paul pulled her up to face him. "I wouldn't call it nothing," he challenged, the expression in his eyes undecipherable, hands firmly around her arms.

Cassandra avoided his gaze. "I'm sorry. I shouldn't have..."

Letting go of her arm, Paul lifted her chin with a finger. He saw the tears in her eyes and smiled. "That's what I thought you said."

The firelight trembled in Cassandra's hair, tipped her breasts in gold. Paul saw the painful uncertainty in her and thought that he'd never seen a more beautiful woman in his life.

"I'm really embarrassed," he admitted with a crooked smile.

"Embarrassed?" she asked carefully. "Whatever for?"

He edged her mouth with a gentle thumb. "Because," Paul told her, his eyes melting with the emotions she'd unleashed, "the ex-princess has a lot more guts than the ex-agent. I've been falling in love with you from the moment you appeared in my headlights, and I haven't had the nerve to tell you."

"You have?" she asked numbly. "You haven't?"

"Kind of hard for somebody like us to stick our necks out like that. You had the courage to do it without a net."

"You love me?" Cassandra echoed, missing his point.

Paul leaned forward to prove his words with a kiss. "I love you."

Funny, now that he'd admitted it, he felt a weight lift—a weight he hadn't even known he carried. Knowing for so many years that that kind of vulnerability brought pain. It had been so long since he'd taken that kind of chance. He'd forgotten, though, that it had also brought delight and peace. Paul found a haven in Cassandra's eyes he'd never known anywhere else.

"You're not just after my title?" she asked a bit breathlessly, a new self-assurance already in her eyes.

"I could say the same," he retorted with a wide grin.

Cassandra giggled, the headiness of not only Paul's admission but her own lifting her, filling her. "Or my money?"

"What money?" he demanded. "The last I heard you had a set of underwear and some stolen shoes."

"Do you?" she asked.

"Have money?" He shrugged. "Not a cent. It's all tied up in hay and tack. I do have a classy car, though."

Cassandra smiled. "And a great set of buns."

With a soft chuckle of satisfaction, Paul pulled her close again. "Let's compare assets tomorrow. Right now, I think I'd like very much to fall asleep with you."

Cassandra couldn't help it. "You won't sneak off in the night?"

"Not on your life," he promised, nuzzling against her hair. "I think you're stuck with me, princess."

"And you me, prince."

But when Cassandra awoke the next morning, Paul was gone.

Her first reaction was to panic. Had he inadvertently promised too much and lost his enthusiasm in the waning hours of the night? Had he just turned away, like everyone else, sure he wouldn't want to know more about her? Had she driven him away somehow?

But when she made it down to breakfast, it was to find out that the men had merely already left for their next leg of investigation.

Gerta bustled quietly in the kitchen, sunshine pouring in the windows and the smell of coffee filling the little rooms. Cassandra joined her and began to fix some breakfast.

"What have you done to our Paul?" Gerta asked from where she chopped vegetables for soup.

Cassandra lifted her head. "What do you mean?"

Gerta's smile was possessive. "I mean that in ten years I have never seen him so happy. You must work miracles."

For a moment Cassandra concentrated on the egg she was frying, nudging its edges with a spatula and savoring Gerta's words. They stirred the most delicious anticipation in her. A sudden promise, as if a new door had opened in front of her where before the future had been nothing but a nondescript gray wall. Her life had a new scope to it, a vast horizon that was tantalizing.

Then, her eyes still on her work, Cassandra shook her head. "No," she disagreed. "He's the miracle worker."

At her side of the sink, Gerta responded. "Good. Then we don't have to worry about you hurting him, do we?"

Cassandra offered a startled look. "Paul?"

"He is a very special man. More...sensitive than most. He would have to be to survive this business with his kindness intact. He is also a rigidly private man. I think he opened up to you, and he wouldn't do that to anyone. He never even did to me."

"To you?" Cassandra asked quietly, forgetting the egg that popped and sizzled to a crisp before her. "If you'll pardon my saying so, why would he open up to you?"

To that, Gerta just smiled. "Because," she explained, "until this leg relegated me to farms, I was his partner."

Five hours later Cassandra was still mulling over this latest revelation about Paul's life. She wasn't really all that surprised, the more she thought about it. It was just that she hated always being the last to know. When Paul got back, she was going to have to take it up with him.

She'd been out visiting with the two Belgians Gerta's family kept in the barn, great, golden horses with the temperaments of easygoing children. Gerta had taken a walk up to a sick neighbor's to drop off some soup. The day had stayed quiet, the sky bright and high, no clouds to speak of, the air crisp and dry. Not a bad day, all in all, except for the waiting.

As Cassandra walked back in the house, she was thinking more about the horses in Ireland than the ones in Switzerland. It might have been why she didn't notice that the door was just slightly ajar or that a couple of the cabinets were open in Gerta's usually immaculate kitchen. Her mind still preoccupied with the idea of a future, Cassandra walked right into the trap before she knew what happened.

"Well, *liebchen*, you're looking good."

Cassandra came to a shuddering halt. There was no mistaking the voice. Or the lanky frame draped over the chair by the front window.

Erhardt.

Smiling with that obscene Cheshire cat smile of his, he lounged easily in the chair, absently tapping an Uzi against his crossed leg. Cassandra turned to bolt, only to find another of her old friends already stationed at the door. Smiling. And not with welcome.

She turned back to her old foe, the sight of him threatening to turn her knees to rubber.

"What are you doing here?" Bile rose hot in Cassandra's throat.

"Me?" he asked, easing himself up from the chair. "Why, I came to see you. And your friend."

"He's not . . ." She stopped, afraid. Unsure what to do. Gerta would be back soon. She'd have to see that something was wrong.

Erhardt was approaching with that familiar sick, satisfied air, his perfect white teeth sparkling. He was pale, with clean good looks that had fooled more than one person. Erhardt Zimmerman was a ruthless killer with the face of an accountant.

"He's not here," he said, coming closer. It was all Cassandra could do to keep from backing away. She knew better now. "He will be, though. Soon. He'll come save you, won't he, *liebchen*?"

"I thought your interest was just in me, Erhardt," Cassandra managed, amazed that her voice could remain so quiet. The last time she'd communicated with this man, it had been with tears, with threats and curses and pleas. "Why don't we just get going?"

"Ah, would that I could." He'd reached her now, circling her slowly. When he walked around behind, he reached out to touch Cassandra's hair, running it slowly through his fingers. "But I have a bigger fish to fry this time. Greater goals for the good of mankind."

Cassandra snorted unkindly. "More money."

If anything, Erhardt was amused. "Exactly. Of course, I am disposed to make certain . . . provisions with you if you would be so kind as to help."

Cassandra froze, the feel of his hands on her more of a message than his words. He had never touched her before, never bothered to come this close. She was suddenly very afraid. Very certain that the stakes on Erhardt's little game had been raised.

"What . . . provisions?" she said in a tight voice.

He'd walked around to face her now, his finger trailing a last tress of hair slowly across her throat. Cassandra did all she could to keep from flinching, from crying out. Erhardt's touch terrified her.

"I'm sure you'd rather not come back with us, now, would you?" he asked quietly. "Especially since Hans is no longer there to protect what virtue you had."

Cassandra's head snapped up to see there was no emotion in Erhardt's eyes. "Hans? What happened to him?"

Erhardt merely shrugged, hitching the Uzi to a more comfortable position. "An unfortunate lesson. He lost you, so we lost him."

Cassandra's mouth went dry. Her hands began to tremble. "You killed him?"

"As I said—" he stopped, standing very close to her "—unfortunate. Which brings me to my offer. If you could see your way to giving a bit of assistance to a worthy cause, we might be able to see our way to letting you go free."

Cassandra could hardly think. He was offering to let her go to keep her from returning to that dank, cold little room where only Erhardt's disdain had kept her from being harmed. There was no question now that he proposed to call that little truce off if she refused to help.

He knew what could frighten her enough to comply, and he was doing it. The Cassandra who had left his company only a few days ago would have gladly complied.

Taking a slow, shaky breath, Cassandra looked around her. Otto was still on the door. Another man, one she didn't know, was slowly and systematically searching the house. They moved as if they knew they had all the time in the world.

"How did you know where to find us?" she asked, stalling for inspiration. Praying for help.

Erhardt laughed. "Your friend is just a bit too trusting of his friends. Now, all we want are the microchips. Tell us where he's hiding them, and we'll be on our way. Alone."

Cassandra ran a tongue across dry lips, tried to think of something. She didn't have the training, the experience. All she could think to do was stall until Gerta got back.

"Microchips?" she asked, finally screwing up the courage to look Erhardt in the eye. It didn't help. There was ice in those eyes, death. They were the eyes of a man with no soul.

"Don't play games, *liebchen*." He stepped closer again, bringing the Uzi around until it nudged her just between her breasts. "The guidance system. A lot of people are anxious to get it back, and I, for one, plan to have them in my debt. Now tell Erhardt before he makes you. Because if he is forced to do that, all deals are off."

Cassandra didn't see it coming. Neither did Erhardt. He was so intent on terrorizing Cassandra that he found his back to the window. The first shot shattered the glass. The second spun him around.

Cassandra cried out. Felt the sting of glass across her face and turned to run. There was an explosion behind her as the plate glass disintegrated. The back door slammed open. Otto went into a crouch, training his weapon on the door. The man on the balcony turned to the window. With a sudden sputtering, almost no louder than the egg frying earlier on the skillet, five guns opened up.

Cassandra hit the kitchen floor and curled up. Otto didn't notice her. His attention was on the sudden company.

Brian. Cassandra saw him roll behind the couch, swinging his weapon up to the man in the balcony. Plaster spattered from the ceiling in an arc and the man crumpled with a cry. Cassandra crawled behind the table and looked around for Paul. He had to be here somewhere.

He was. He must have come in the window. Cassandra saw him now, locked in a hand-to-hand struggle with a bleeding Erhardt. Brian and Otto both turned to them, also wanting to help. The fight was too close, though. Whatever happened between Paul and Erhardt would, for now, have to be settled between them. Brian and Otto turned back to each other. Fired. Peppered the furniture with holes and the walls with bullets. It was like a deadly hailstorm, and Cassandra was caught square in it. She flattened, trying to get her head into the tile, trying to cover up with anything that was handy. She saw the open cabinet door, then and spotted the skillet. Not perfect, but something. Cassandra pulled it out and covered her head.

It was so surrealistic. So silent, except for the gunfire. Cassandra didn't hear any shouting or grunting, just the scuffle of shoes and the patter of bullets from those deadly automatics. Once Cassandra felt a pinging against her impromptu helmet and yelled an instinctive "Watch out!" It was the wrong thing to do. Otto promptly remembered her, huddled over in the corner, and decided that she would make a wonderful hostage.

Cassandra's attention was only on Paul. His eyes were flat, opaque, as if his soul, too, had died. His face was slick with sweat. His hands, straining against Erhardt's, were white and taut, the tendons like slashes along his wrists. The two of them held each other's gun at bay, high over their heads. Erhardt's left sleeve was soaked with blood, his arm beginning to bend with Paul's pressure. Cassandra wanted to cry out, to offer support, to scoot over somehow and tip that balance for good.

She didn't even notice Otto until Brian yelled. Cassandra turned in the direction he'd pointed, but Otto was ahead of her. Before she could move, he had a hand clamped over her free arm and was pulling her against him. The skillet fell from its protective position, thunking to the floor beside her. Across the room, Paul witnessed the action, and lost his concentration. Cassandra saw his eyes turn to her, saw the fear take hold and realized that the advantage had gone to Erhardt.

"Watch out, Paul!" she shrieked.

Otto yanked her again, turning her toward Brian, and shoved a gun into her ribs. Cassandra saw Brian go very still, saw Erhardt begin to smile. Losing her fear in a surge of blind anger, she made a grab for her skillet. She imagined that Otto would have guessed her the last person to make a stupid move like that. It also kept him from anticipating it.

"You will throw down the weapon," he was instructing Brian. "And tell your friend to do the same."

The skillet hit him in the side of the head with a resounding clank. Turning a stunned look to Cassandra, he slumped to the floor.

"Oh, and it's a rare fine girl ya are!" Brian shouted in glee, leaping from his hiding place.

Cassandra did the same, picking up Otto's gun as she did. She was about to turn back to Paul when she heard the quick chatter of gunfire. Then a flat silence.

She whipped around, the gun up and ready, thinking somehow to protect Paul. Alongside her, Brian did the same. Paul and Erhardt stood where they had, each still with a hold on the other. Each unyielding and silent. But there was only one gun now, and it was caught between them.

Cassandra's heart stopped. The two of them stayed rigid, eyes locked in combat, fierce determination holding them together. Then, as slowly as if in a dream, Erhardt began to topple.

Paul let go. Looked down, first at Erhardt, inert on the floor, and then at the automatic pistol in his hands. He seemed surprised. There was a spatter of Erhardt's blood on his shirt and a rip in his good jacket where he'd come in through the window. Otherwise, he seemed intact. Cassandra didn't wait for an in-depth appraisal before launching herself into his arms.

"Oh, God, you scared me!" she accused, tears suddenly loosed and spilling down her cheeks. "I thought he'd killed you."

"Hardly," Paul reassured her, pulling an arm around her. "Are you okay? He didn't hurt you?"

"He thought I'd trade you in for a chance to pass up a return visit to his summer camp." The words came out in a rush, half sob and half laugh.

"You almost sound surprised that you didn't take him up on it."

Cassandra shook her head, still safely nestled in Paul's embrace. "I think I am. I'm not altogether used to the altruistic me yet."

"Or the action-adventure you." Paul smiled, reaching for the Uzi she still held behind his back. "Just what were you planning to do with this?"

Letting go of the gun, Cassandra raised her head. "I'm not sure. Help, I guess."

Something was wrong. Something about the way Paul was smiling. Had she done something wrong?

"And where is that fine wife of mine?" Brian demanded, coming over to relieve Paul of the weaponry and check on a very still Erhardt.

"Right here," came Gerta's voice from the door. "I saw all the excitement and decided to call in a little help. Especially since you two were obviously having too much fun to let me interfere." Gingerly stepping over the prone body by the door, Gerta approached.

"We didn't have time to warn you, Mother," Brian apologized.

But Gerta wasn't intent on abusing her husband. Her attention was on Paul. As was Cassandra's.

"Paul?"

He looked up at his former partner with a small smile. "Did you see Cassandra with the skillet? She should receive an honorary agent's pin, don't you think?"

Really confused now, Cassandra stepped away a little. There was something just a little off. The tenor of Paul's voice was forced. The smile on his face was stiff. And he was still sweating.

When she stepped away, she saw her own shirt. "Oh, Paul," she instinctively admonished. "You got Erhardt's blood all over the front of my..."

But that was when she realized that it wasn't Erhardt's blood at all. It was Paul's. Her head came up in a snap just at the moment Gerta and Brian reached them.

"What have you bloody well gone and done now, old son?" Brian demanded.

Paul's smile sickened a little. "I think I got myself shot, Brian."

Cassandra's knees almost turned to water. "Oh, dear God—" The blood had gathered on the front of his shirt, a dark pool of it. "Oh, dear God, Paul."

"About time to sit down, isn't it?" Gerta asked pragmatically, taking hold of one of Paul's arms.

"Time to lie down, if you ask me, woman," Brian retorted, grabbing the other.

Paul shook them both off as he eased his way onto a chair. "I'm all right. Get the guy by the door taken care of."

"But Paul..." Cassandra objected instinctively.

There were flashing blue lights coming up the hill now, and the keening of sirens. A brisk afternoon breeze filtered in the shattered window, but no one seemed to notice.

"My jacket," Paul instructed, leaning forward. "Get it off."

"Of course," Cassandra acquiesced, thinking to make him comfortable. He leaned carefully forward and let her slip his arms free. Cassandra did so with shaking hands as Brian walked away to tie up the awakening Otto and greet the police.

"Now rip open the back," Paul instructed. His voice was even more quiet than before as if by conserving it, he could conserve his strength.

"Paul," Cassandra objected, the garment in her hands. "You shouldn't be bothering, really. You have to get some help. Brian's right. You should lie down."

Paul smiled fondly. "Trust me, Cassandra. I'll live. This has to be taken care of before I go anywhere. Now rip it open."

There were tears in her eyes now, a hard knot in her throat and a storm in her stomach. How could he be so flippant with his life? Didn't he know how awful he looked? His skin had taken on an ashen quality that frightened Cassandra far more than any threat

Erhardt could have made. Even so, starting at the tear the window had made, Cassandra ripped. When she got to the back, a thin card slid to the floor.

Picking it up, she looked up to Paul.

"The microchips," he informed her with a grin. "It seems that just like in the fairy tale, you proved to all of us that you really are special. You felt them when nobody else did."

"Those lumps in your jacket were microchips?" she demanded breathlessly.

He nodded. "Elliott's wife sewed them in while we were talking in the other room. He knew he was being followed...knew that..."

Cassandra shook her head. "Paul, that's enough. Brian can take care of all of this. I'm getting you to a doctor."

But again he shook his head. "Not yet." Holding out his hand, he nodded to her. "The jacket."

Cassandra balked, blinked. But in the end she handed the jacket back to him. When she did, he reached into one of the pockets.

"Now, scoot back a little.... I need room...."

She did so without thinking. Caught up in her conversation with Paul, she didn't see the police arrive and swarm over the other end of the room, didn't notice that Gerta watched Paul like a hawk, or that Brian took care to keep the other business away until Paul was finished. Cassandra's eyes were only on the terrible toll being taken on Paul. Her heart and her attention were only on him, because nothing else mattered.

His hand still in the pocket, Paul edged off the chair. He ended up on his knees.

"Gerta, help..." Cassandra pleaded.

Paul took hold of her hand to quiet her. "Would you relax? I'm here for a purpose."

Cassandra faced him and saw that even as his face began to tighten with the pain, his eyes held a sweet amusement. He was leaving her way behind again.

"Cassandra," he began, on one knee and one of her hands in his. "I have something to ask."

"What, Paul?" Still preoccupied with his condition, she really didn't see it coming.

With what flourish he could, Paul pulled a can of Beluga caviar from his pocket and held it out to her. "Will you marry me?"

For a minute Cassandra could do no more than stare. She felt the clammy touch of his hand, so she knew she was really there. She could even feel the cool mountain air swirling in from the window, and hear the sudden hush from the police. But she couldn't possibly be hearing what she'd thought. It was just too much.

"Make up... your mind," Paul said, the hand with the can wavering a little. "I'm not going to... be able to keep this up much longer."

"Yes," she whispered, tears overflowing and her knees giving out. Suddenly she was on her knees, too, holding on to him as if her life depended on it, laughing and sobbing at the same time. "Yes, you great big idiot. I'll marry you."

He nodded against her. "Good. In that case...I think...it's time to... lie down...."

And with that he slumped against her, unconscious.

Fourteen

For the first time in her life, Cassandra found herself cold and rational in a crisis.

"I am damn well not waiting fifteen minutes for a helicopter to arrive," she announced, brandishing a can of caviar at the chief inspector. "I'm taking him to get medical help now."

The gentleman in question lifted hands in the air, obviously not thinking much of the beautiful young woman's powers of logic. "But where?" he asked. "The nearest hospital is too far away."

"The nearest *Swiss* hospital," she amended with the can to his blue-clad chest. "Braz is no more than ten minutes away." And then she turned to take in Gerta and Brian, who were stationed by Paul on the living-room floor. "I'm taking him home."

"We'll come with you," Gerta said, getting to her feet.

Cassandra shook her head. "You stay and clear this up. I don't want all that nonsense hanging over Paul's head. If Brian's Porsche is anything as good as Paul's, I'll get him there faster than you. And I don't have to worry about the border guards. Now, help me get him in the car."

With a grin, Brian took hold of Cassandra by the arms. "I'm beginning to get the measure of the queen you would have been, lass. It's a shame you left."

"It's not, really," she said, smiling gratefully in return. "I don't care half as much for fiscal policy as I do for Paul. Moritania would have gone bankrupt."

It wasn't until she was turning onto the road to Braz that Cassandra allowed herself the luxury of fresh tears. There had been just enough room in the back seat to lay Paul down. He was scrunched up, it was true, but he was horizontal, and from what Gerta had told her, that was what was important. They'd strapped him in to protect him from bouncing along the mountain roads and applied a pressure bandage to the bullet wound that bracketed his left side and still bled much too steadily. Now all Cassandra had to do was reach the palace in the ten minutes she'd promised. Briskly wiping the tears away with a shaking arm, she downshifted with businesslike attention and turned into the curve, the can of caviar sliding a little across the passenger seat.

She didn't have any problems until she reached the border. It was the first time she realized just how much she'd changed. The border guard, a middle-aged little man with stiff propriety and an oversize nose, had held this station since she'd been a child. He didn't recognize her.

"Please, Franz," Cassandra insisted, suddenly thinking how this all resembled an odd musical comedy. Franz was attired in the time-honored traditional uniform of gold-and-black-striped garb with plumed hat. He looked more like a troubadour than a guard. And Paul was losing his precious blood to the back seat. "I have to get him to the palace for help. Let me through."

"Excuse me, *Fräulein*," he demurred, the sight of the inert form squeezed in the back seat noticeably unsettling him. "I need your papers."

Cassandra's eyes lifted. "For heaven's sake, Franz, I'm Cassandra. Now stop stalling and let me through."

Franz barely took a better look. "I'm sorry, *Fräulein*, but you're not..."

His hesitation cost Cassandra what was left of her patience. Without further ado, she pulled herself to her full height and packed every ounce of cold disdain she could muster into her expression.

"How *dare* you not recognize me, you little pimple?" she sneered, this time praying for his forgiveness at a later date. "Open the gate at this very moment and call ahead to the dowager queen to tell her of my arrival and my needs or I will personally see your head served up for tonight's dinner!" Nailing him with a particularly scathing glare, she put the finishing touches on the performance. "Is that perfectly clear?"

Franz was no fool. He very nearly slammed his forehead on the car door in an attempt to bow low enough. "Yes, Your Highness. Of course, Your Highness. Right away."

"Then stop stammering and open the gate!"

The gate was opened and Cassandra sped through.

"You're beautiful when you're a bitch," she heard from the back seat. Paul's voice almost sent her into a guardrail, she was so relieved to hear it.

"Saved precious time." She smiled back to him in the mirror, feasting on the sight of his open eyes. "I'll apologize after I get you some help."

"After seeing that, I might just take my proposal back." His voice was still so quiet, so careful. Cassandra hit the gas a little harder. The first buildings of Braz began to whiz by the window.

"I had to convince him who I was," she said to defend herself.

"And you did. In spades. He's probably back there...changing his shorts."

"Are you all right?"

"Until Brian realizes that I've bled over his best leather upholstery. Where is he?"

"Back with the police. I decided that you didn't need to wait around for the questions to all be answered before they took care of you."

"And I appreciate it." He stretched a bit against the constraints of the seat belt and winced. "Are you sure you're going to be able to get me back out of this?"

"The other choice was a fifteen-minute wait for a helicopter."

Paul nodded again, singularly unruffled for a man with a bullet in his stomach. "Good. I hate heights."

"Did you really mean your proposal?"

Cassandra could see a ghost of a grin on his face. "I wouldn't have gone to all that trouble if I hadn't."

"You had a roomful of witnesses, you know."

"To keep you from backing out later."

The tears threatened again, but Cassandra wouldn't let them take over. She still had to get Paul to the palace. The car took the twisting roads with grace, easing around each with barely a shudder. The steel and glass of Braz's downtown area slid past and the road climbed into the forests around the palace.

"I hope Uncle Eric is busy at the bank," Cassandra thought out loud.

"Why?"

Her laugh was a dry one. "Grandmother is going to be difficult enough on her own without Uncle Eric goading her on."

"Are you sure they won't mind my bleeding all over their palace?"

"I'll convince them."

Paul actually managed a chuckle. "Like that poor old guard back there?"

Cassandra smiled back, new determination in her eyes. "If necessary. My notorious past comes in quite handy sometimes."

"Remind me of that later when I'm paying for your caviar habit."

Cassandra turned the car into the entrance lane and shifted up, the tires spinning a bit over the carefully graveled lane. A vast expanse of trees flanked them for almost a quarter of a mile before they reached the palace, a great, grand old building of gray stone, glass and timber. Cassandra hadn't realized how much she'd missed it until she caught sight of it again.

One of the grooms was waiting for them when she pulled the car around the circle drive. Cassandra pulled the car to a stop before the front steps and yanked open her door.

"Get help, Heller," she called, pulling the seat forward for Paul. "I have an injured man."

Heller nodded, stepping up alongside her. "Franz notified us. The Queen Mother said to take the gentleman to the green bedroom. She awaits you in the Rose Room."

Hands appeared from nowhere, unbuckling the belts and gently prying Paul loose from his prison. Cassandra supervised, her hand always in Paul's, her eyes on his face.

She saw the movement take its toll. He gasped once, and his hand clutched hers. She wanted to cry out for him. She didn't. When Paul looked over at her, he winked the import of his discomfort away. She knew better than to challenge him.

Werner met them at the door. A formal, precise kind of man, Werner was her Uncle Eric's secretary and the household's unofficial organizer. Cassandra had never really taken the time to know him before.

"Princess Cassandra," he said, greeting her with a stiff bow as if she showed up with gunshot victims every day of the week.

The strength of dear old Moritania, Cassandra thought dryly. The idea of allowing surprise was considered an insult. Life Goes On should have been inscribed in Latin under that very fancy family crest over the great front doors.

Cassandra was so intent on getting Paul to a bed that she didn't notice the extra cast in the foyer. A couple was just walking in from the library. The commotion effectively stopped them in their tracks. The sight of the injured man brought a gasp from the woman. She stepped forward, suddenly almost as ashen as Paul.

"Pauly...?"

Paul managed to get his eyes up to find his sister before him. He straightened, unwilling to frighten her on top of everything else. "Hi, sweetie. I thought I'd come for the wedding." Even the smile he offered was costing him now.

"Paul..." Cassandra admonished, hot on his trail.

But Paul was still watching his sister. Waiting for the anger to take the place of surprise. Waiting for her condemnation. When he caught sight of the man who stood beside her, Paul knew Casey wouldn't have any choice but to hate him now. Especially after what he was going to do.

"So is this the infamous Prince Eric?" he asked, pulling free of the supporting hands. It took all his strength to stay upright, but he had a certain score to settle. There was a young lady who had spent her life trying to live up to this man's expectations and torturing herself for not being able to. Suddenly Paul wanted to tell him how he felt about it.

"I am Eric," the man said without much comprehension, his gaze flicking in growing irritation from his niece to her surprise guest.

Paul nodded back. "Just wanted to know."

And then he hit him. Full square in the jaw, almost sending Paul to the floor right behind him. He felt the action tear along his side, felt the fresh flow of blood. And recognized a sense of satisfaction at seeing the prince on the floor, rubbing his jaw.

"Since Cassandra couldn't see her way to doing it," he told him, "I thought I would."

"Sir," Werner gasped behind them where the servants still clustered openmouthed and aghast. "You have just struck the king."

Paul didn't really care. He was going to pass out, anyway.

Cassandra turned on Werner with as much impatience as distress. "We'll hang him later, Werner," she snapped. "*After* we've cared for his wound."

That was all it took. The men who had supported Paul in helped him straight through to the back where the green room—a downstairs bedroom for the monarchs who got too old for the stairs—was located. Cassandra was all set to follow him when Werner discreetly blocked her path.

"The dowager queen is waiting on you in the Rose Room," he reminded her.

"The queen can—" Cassandra bit off her retort and turned to him. "I'm sorry, Werner. Of course I'll go see her. But make sure Paul is well taken care of."

He agreed with a little bow, his eyes down and his brow up.

Cassandra was set to continue down to the Rose Room when her uncle addressed her from where his fiancée was helping him back to his feet.

"Cassandra, I hate to ask just who that was," he said, rubbing his jaw. "But I suppose I must."

"That," Cassandra informed him with a silly grin, the sight of Paul outraged on her behalf one she would cherish for a long time, "was my fiancé."

And even knowing how unfair it was to leave Casey without an explanation, Cassandra walked away.

The dowager queen sat in regal silence on one of the Queen Anne chairs before the fire. The Rose Room was where she held her audiences, did her correspondence and kept her small family treasures.

Cassandra looked around as she entered and realized how much warmer it was than she'd always thought. Aunt Anna Marie's harp sat in the corner, lush Oriental rugs covered the glossy hardwood floors, and ranks of framed pictures crowded on the couchback table. There were even flowers in a vase by the queen's elbow. Cassandra saw her grandmother and thought suddenly that she was old. And that, unbelievably enough, she'd missed her.

"I don't suppose I should be surprised by anything you do, Cassandra," the old woman began, her eyes on the fire rather than her granddaughter. The bejeweled hands rested quietly on the arms of her chair. The regal gray head was held as formally as Werner's. The queen embodied that great Moritanian tradition of propriety. Her voice bit with annoyance. "But this time I have to admit that you have quite outdone yourself."

"I know I have no right to come here, Grandmother," Cassandra began, finally moving into the queen's range of view.

She got no farther. The queen saw the blood all over Cassandra's blouse and came abruptly to her feet.

"Oh, my child," she gasped, her hand instinctively out, the steely blue eyes that had offered so many reproaches suddenly liquid with fear. "Are you . . . ?"

"No, I'm fine," she insisted, taking the thin old hand in hers and easing her grandmother back into her chair. "It's Paul's. Please help him, Grandmother. He saved my life."

But the queen couldn't quite get over Cassandra's appearance. "Your . . . your hair . . ."

Cassandra saw then how much Paul had changed her. For the first time she saw the uncertainty beneath her grandmother's steel, the emotions locked up within that rigidly proper exterior.

Her heart went out to the old woman, left with only a son and granddaughter in her old age, and thinking that the granddaughter had been a botch of it. Cassandra very suddenly wanted to put her arms around her grandmother's shoulders, but she understood that just holding her hand would be enough.

"It's all part of a very long story, dear." She smiled, kneeling before the chair.

"Well," the queen said with a set of arched eyebrows and a recovery of her brisk manner, "considering that the doctor arrived just before you did, I'd say we have quite enough time to hear it. Ring Rolph for tea."

Paul woke to find he wasn't alone. He'd half expected to see Cassandra there. She had been every other time he'd awakened, always with a hand on his, her eyes tired and strained. He tried to tell her that this was just the way he mended, that the gunshot was no worse than most of the rest. She hadn't believed him. He imagined the fact that the doctor had ended up transferring him to the Braz National Clinic for surgery and back again under Cassandra's close scrutiny didn't help his case any.

The healing process was now well under way. He didn't feel so much like pulverized silly putty, and his appetite was coming back. It was, anyway, until he opened his eyes to find his sister, Casey, seated in Cassandra's chair.

He expected anger. What he got was uncertainty, brittle eyes and a crooked grin. "I don't suppose you could have just shown up on your knees begging forgiveness, could you? I've had more than enough drama for one life already, thanks."

She would have been beautiful even without the royal make-over, her honey-colored hair in a soft upsweep, her frame encased in very fine silk. There was something that transcended the new wealth, though, a spark that refused to be extinguished. A real rebellion that he was sure Moritania wasn't quite ready for yet.

Paul knew her because she so closely resembled Cassandra. Yet at the same time they looked nothing alike.

"I guess I should apologize for slugging your fiancé," he greeted her back.

Casey waved his apology aside. "If Eric can't take a joke, the heck with him."

"That's my Casey," Paul replied, smiling. "Are you sure this guy knows what he's getting into?"

Casey laughed, taking Paul's hand in her own. "If he didn't figure it out right after the first time I pushed him in the fountain, he'll never learn. And that's his problem."

He smiled. "You love him?"

She nodded, glowing with a satisfaction that only a woman can. "You love her?"

Paul nodded back with a wry grin. "Hard as it may be to comprehend."

"Oh, Cassandra's okay," she assured him. "Just a girl with some unique tastes. Do you know that she was down in the kitchen asking if they could get in some Oreos? And I thought the caviar was odd."

Paul laughed, clutching at his still-tender side. "That was my fault. I decided that if I was going to be supporting her habits, at least Oreos were cheaper."

Casey gave him an impish grin. "We sat up all night in her room eating cookies and dishing dirt."

Paul rolled his eyes. "I think I've created a monster."

"Nah. Just a real person. My question is, how are we going to explain this all to Mom?"

Paul squeezed Casey's hand with meaning. "To tell you the truth, kid, I don't think anything I do would surprise Mom."

Suddenly Casey's face clouded over, and Paul knew the time had come. He didn't feel up to it, but then he never would.

"We have to talk, huh?" Casey asked, tilting her head just as she used to as a girl.

Paul nodded, holding on to her more tightly. "We have to talk."

And pray, he thought, that you'll forgive me for what I'm going to tell you.

* * *

The Grand Ballroom glittered beneath the huge chandeliers. The exalted company of guests eddied about, chatting to the accompaniment of the string quartet on the bandstand, refreshed by the endless procession of waiters bearing champagne-laden trays.

The best and brightest of European society was here tonight. Generals and deposed kings and oil barons. In one corner the Prince of Wales discussed architecture with the American ambassador. By the window, James McCormac, internationally acclaimed actor, traded stories with Sandy Perone, a secretary who had worked with Casey. King Eric II, resplendent in his full white uniform of the Moritanian Guard, was to be found by one of the few chairs in the room speaking with his niece and brother-in-law. To Eric's left stood his new wife and queen.

"So you mean to tell me you discovered that this Justin was actually the double agent when you found out he knew more about that man's murder than he should have?"

Seated in the chair in full evening attire, Paul took a sip of champagne and nodded. "The usual idea in a murder is to hold back certain evidence from the public. The Berlin police knew that there had been a message scrawled on Elliott's wall by the ELM, but no one else was supposed to. When I contacted the police, they demanded to know how I'd found out."

Eric nodded. "Justin."

Paul shrugged. "It began to make sense. Especially since there had to be a real mole in the company to lay the trail to me. So I got in touch with my old boss and let him in on it. I also decided to return to get Cassandra out before Justin had time to get in touch with his friends and let them know where we were."

"Well, Cassandra," Eric toasted his niece, "you have certainly kept busy since I've last seen you."

"I'm not the only one," she countered. "Did I actually see a Renoir in the entrance foyer today?"

Eric laughed. "Casey's idea."

"In that case," Cassandra announced formally, lifting her own glass to her new aunt, "I will say again how much I underestimated you. You're just what this country needs."

"I think a few people have underestimated you, too," Casey responded with a grin and a meaningful nudge to her husband.

"Yes, dear," he immediately replied.

Paul looked up with his own grin. "What, you, too? I thought kings had a better chance of holding out against female whims than the rest of us."

Cassandra would have none of it. Leaning over, she slid a kid-gloved hand around Paul's throat. "It wouldn't take all that much to put you back in the hospital, my love," she cooed.

Paul laughed up at her and thought how he had to get her off the farm once in a while just to see her dressed like this. She wore a strapless gown of electric blue that was belted at the waist and flared out into a lovely, swirling skirt. Around her throat were diamonds, and her hair was swept up much as her new aunt's. She'd kept it dark, at least for the time being, and Paul had to admit that it flattered her. She glowed tonight. Outshone everyone in the room with the possible exception of his kid sister in her ivory-and-lace wedding dress and sixteenth-century lace veil.

A long way from Brooklyn, he thought with a wry smile. A very long way. Casey caught his expression and smiled down at him. There were still ghosts in her eyes from the burden he'd had to finally share with her. But there was also joy, fulfillment and happiness—enough, he hoped, to balance out.

"Pauly, you're not going to believe this."

Paul turned to see his tiny mother approaching with a scowling Brian in tow.

"According to this barbarian," his mother announced, "we're related. On the O'Hanley side."

Paul groaned. "Don't believe a word he says, Mom. He's a pathological liar."

But his mother, turning back to her new friend, reached up to tweak his cheek. "I think he's cute."

Brian groaned. Gerta, alongside, chuckled. Paul laughed.

"You'll dance with me, then, my love?" Brian asked Cassandra with gentlemanly hand outstretched.

"A little later, Brian," she said, perfectly happy to stay in the corner with Paul.

He conceded with a gentlemanly bow, although with his girth and looks, even a tux couldn't tame him. "A sorry loss it is to the party, lass. I'll just have to take this young lady here, then."

Even kings turned to smile at the great bear of an Irishman twirling the tiny Margaret Callan Phillips around on the dance floor.

"Are you sure you won't change your mind?" Eric asked his niece a few minutes later as his wife danced with the eminent Mr. McCormac.

Looking out on the crowd of swirling, gliding dancers, Cassandra shook her head with quiet contentment. "I'll visit, of course, Eric," she decided. "But I think I'm much more suited to the life my husband has planned for us."

Eric straightened, gaped a little. "Excuse me?"

Exchanging fond looks with Paul, Cassandra turned to her uncle and king with a broad grin. "Well, you were so busy getting ready for all this that we had to settle for Brian and Gerta as witnesses. I'm surprised Werner didn't tell you. He arranged the whole thing." But then, she'd threatened Werner with his well-organized life if he'd mentioned one word to the king. The dowager queen had promptly backed up the threat.

"Witnesses?" Eric turned on a placid Paul to find him sipping champagne and holding hands with his wife. "Are you telling me you've been married?"

Paul made it a point to check his watch. "For five hours and seven minutes."

"Without my permission? Without the archbishop?"

"Eric, my dear—" Cassandra grinned with real delight "—you're getting stuffy in your old age. We had Grandmother's permission. And of course the archbishop was there. Who do you think married us, Werner?"

"But Cassandra," Eric objected, still not understanding. "Why sneak away like that when you could have had a true wedding?"

At that, Cassandra laughed. "If you remember, dear, I wasted the last one I had. Believe it or not, I was much happier with just the few of us in the Rose Room."

And she was; truly happy, and more contented than she'd ever been in her life. She'd finally come home to her family and found a new one in Paul's. And she'd come to find her own place in life. Looking out on the vast wealth and privilege collected in this one room, Cassandra could honestly say that she wouldn't miss any of it. She had Paul, and she had a future she could look forward to. And that, she realized, was all she needed.

"Caviar, Your Highness?" a passing waiter asked, bowing with a laden tray.

"Oh, maybe one last time," she demurred, reaching for the hors d'oeuvres. "And then it's definitely marshmallows for me."

"So," Casey spoke up as she approached, dance partner in tow. "Have you ever had moon pies?"

Cassandra's head came up, her eyes avid. "Moon pies?"

"No," Paul groaned.

"They're wonderful. Chocolate and marshmallow..."

Cassandra didn't even notice her new husband get to his feet beside her. "Dance, Your Highness?"

Cassandra looked up, still savoring the salty taste in her mouth. "You dance, too?" she demanded in delight. From one delicious taste to another. From one life to another.

Paul's grin was almost piratical as he held out his hand to her, the tux giving him a dash of elegance that made women's heads turn all around the room. "You think I can only drive a fast car?"

"No," she assured him with a smile that said it all. "I think you can do anything you want."

Paul drew her out onto the floor and slipped her into his embrace. "And you," he countered, kissing his wife with as much tenderness as passion, "can do the same."

"I know," she agreed, closing her eyes and laying her head against his chest, savoring the strong, whole feel of him against her. With Paul beside her, she'd never doubt again. She'd never wonder again just what Cassandra Catherine Anna Marie von Lieberhaven was worth. Because when she looked at Paul, she saw her worth in his eyes. And it was enough. It was more than enough.

* * * * *

A Note from Naomi Horton

Dear Reader,

Even as a child, I hated fairy tales. No wimpy, wan princesses whining about peas under their mattresses for me! You can blame my father and James Fenimore Cooper for that, not to mention Zane Gray, Robert Louis Stevenson, Edgar Rice Burroughs, Jack London and a dozen others. No fairy tales for my dad—he loved gung-ho heroics, and when he read me stories, he read whatever he was reading at the time. Same with movies. No cute cartoons for us. If it didn't have cowboys or fighter planes, we didn't go! (My mother, needless to say, knew nothing of this or we'd both have been grounded.)

Tarzan, Hawkeye and the Lone Ranger, John Wayne and Jimmy Stewart—they all had one thing in common. They were heroes. Cool-eyed and taciturn, they knew right from wrong, ignored temptation, fought evil without question, were good to their horses, kind to children and, if they were very lucky, earned the love of a good woman. And no frail princesses for them, either! Can you see Barbara Stanwyck or Lauren Bacall complaining about a lumpy mattress?

I still hate fairy tales, and I still love heroes. Heroes like Trey Hollister in this story, a lone wolf used to making his own way in the world but who can't turn his back on trouble, even if it means risking his heart. But heroics aren't just for guys! Linn Stevens is the kind of woman I like in real life: brave, resourceful, smart and funny, able to take care of herself but still woman enough to recognize love when she finds it. And willing, when the time comes, to put it all on the line for the man she loves.

If you're reading this book, you obviously share my love for outlaws and heroes, and I hope you enjoy Trey and Linn's story....

Naomi Horton

IN SAFEKEEPING

Naomi Horton

Chapter 1

"There's a man following us."

Linn's heart did a distinct somersault. On her knees beside the tide pool that she and Nathan had been examining, she looked up and saw him staring at something behind her, his small face pinched with sudden fear. She dropped the shell she was holding and got to her feet swiftly, trying—for the boy's sake—not to appear too concerned.

"It's probably just someone out for an evening stroll, like us," she said offhandedly. "We can't always expect to have the whole beach to ourselves." But she scanned the wide sweep of sand behind them nervously. It ran on for miles, the hard-packed sand glistening where the retreating tide had washed it clean. The setting sun had turned it to scarlet and gold, but the colors were fading now and in a few more minutes the grayed dusk would be upon them.

There was no one there. Linn eased her breath out. "Well, whoever it was, he's gone now. He's probably staying in the campground or one of the motels."

But Nathan shook his head, still staring down the beach. "He went behind that big pile of logs."

Linn looked around again, trying to ignore a jab of raw terror. Odds were the man was simply a tourist, enjoying the sunset and a few minutes of solitude before retiring for the night. Odds were...

She wet her lips and stared hard at the weathered logs lying in jumbled piles along the foot of the steeply rising shoreline. Some of them were whole trees, torn off the rugged coast by winter storms, their tangled roots rising like frozen coils of rope. But most were strays that had slipped free of the big offshore log booms. They'd been tossed ashore by the relentless waves and wind and lay in huge drifts, jammed so tightly that they built an almost impenetrable wall running the entire length of the coast. They looked for all the world like a set of pickup sticks cast down by a giant's hand, and they created a rabbit warren that could hide anyone who wanted to stay hidden.

Sternly she hauled in her runaway imagination. The odds that he had followed them this far were all but impossible. She and Nathan had left Florida three weeks ago, and she'd laid a dizzying crisscross of false trails across eight states that was guaranteed to lose the most determined pursuer.

Something gave a sharp cry from the tall, silent pines hemming the beach. Some night bird probably, out for the hunt, but it made her start badly and she swore under her breath as she realized that her own nervousness had transmitted itself to Nathan.

Suddenly he looked very small and defenseless, his eyes shadowed with a weary kind of fear far at odds with his age. He stepped nearer to her, the delight and laughter that had lighted his face only minutes ago gone now. As always, it made Linn's heart ache. This nightmare was taking a horrifying toll on everyone it touched, but perhaps the worst was the effect it was having on Nathan. Boys of five were supposed to be filled with laughter and the reckless joy of just being alive, but Nathan had become withdrawn and silent over the past few weeks, his small face growing paler and more pinched as the days went by.

Linn caught the sudden bite of anger and swallowed it, knowing from experience that giving in to either the anger or the relentless dread behind it would accomplish nothing. She smiled at Nathan and touched him on the shoulder. "I'm about ready for a cup of cocoa," she said lightly. "Do you want to head back now?"

He nodded vigorously, reaching for her hand. Two months ago, like any rambunctious five-year-old, he wouldn't have been caught dead reaching for the security of an adult's hand. But all that had changed.

His sea-damp fingers fastened anxiously around hers. "Let's walk by the edge of the water." He tugged her toward the lower beach where long combers were spilling across the sand. Away from the jumbled piles of logs and whatever he'd seen there to frighten him.

But there was no one waiting for them. The shadows where Nathan had thought he'd seen the man were empty, and they walked on undisturbed. Nathan seemed to relax after a few minutes, and after a while Linn managed to shake off her own unease. They were safe. Santos couldn't have tracked them this far. As long as she didn't get careless, there was nothing to worry about. Nothing at all.

> She was raven-haired and blue-eyed, and from the first time he saw her, Steele knew she was the kind of trouble that no man needed. It came like that sometimes, gift-wrapped in satin and sin and long, smoldering glances that kept you coming back for more. The kind of trouble that left good men dead.

Raven-haired and blue-eyed . . .

Trey gave a snort. It wasn't difficult to tell where *that* had come from. He raised his eyes from the computer screen and looked out at the beach. It filled his entire view from the expanse of glass that made up the west wall of his study, blood-red now in the setting sun. The restless Pacific swept onto the shelving sand a few hundred yards out, but he gave the long, foamstreaked combers only a cursory glance, more interested in the empty beach stretching southward, curved and clean. And empty.

Damn it, where was she?

He glanced at the clock on the bookcase. It was nearly nine, well past the time she and the boy were usually back. Suddenly restless for no reason he could pin down, he got up and wandered across to the big windows, frowning slightly as he stared along the tide-damp beach. Where was she, anyway, his raven-haired, blue-eyed mystery lady?

If she *was* blue-eyed, Trey reminded himself. He'd never gotten close enough to her to find out. As elusive as sea mist, she ventured out only in the evening or early morning to stroll the deserted beach with the boy he presumed was her son. She'd rented the beach house beside his about a week ago, but he'd never caught more than the occasional tantalizing glimpse of her since. And although he'd asked around the village, no one knew anything about her.

The big German shepherd lying on the rug in front of the fireplace lifted his head and whined softly, ears pricked. He got to his feet and walked over to stand beside Trey, staring out at the beach as though he, too, sensed that something was amiss.

"It isn't any of our damned business," Trey reminded the big dog irritably. He reached down to rub the puckered scar running diagonally across his left thigh, kneading the aching museles almost absently. He'd gotten *that* by not minding his own business, by being in the wrong place at the wrong time and taking a bullet meant for someone else.

He swore under his breath and walked back to the desk. The woman wasn't his problem. Getting this damned book written *was*. He sat down again and forced himself to reread the last paragraph, frowning again.

Steele was in trouble. Not the usual kind, the kind that a bit of heavy armament and natural guile could get him out of. No, the trouble was closer to home than that. The truth was, after eight books, Steele was bored.

Correction, Trey reminded himself with a faint smile. Author T. C. Hollister was bored.

There *was* a difference, in spite of the efforts of various critics and media types to convince the reading public that Steele, cold-eyed hero of the Man of Action espionage novels, and T. C. Hollister, ex-marine, were one and the same.

Eyes narrowed, he reached for the cigarette sitting in the ashtray and drew deeply on it, realizing with annoyance that he'd smoked it half down without even tasting it. It was the second—and last—of the day, the one he looked forward to most because it *was* the last, and the fact he'd wasted a good part of it irritated the hell out of him. He drew on it again, slowly this time, forcing himself to concentrate on the acrid bite of the smoke as he contemplated the words staring back at him.

Not bad. Although where she was taking him, this raven-haired beauty, he had no idea. She'd appeared out of nowhere a few hours ago, taking Steele as much by surprise as she'd taken her creator. And as he'd typed the words, something had happened. Suddenly he'd found himself wanting to get the next sentence down and then the next, wanting to know what was going to happen. Wanting to know who she was, this blue-eyed woman who had captured Steele's imagination as she'd captured his....

He glanced at the clock again. Where was she? She'd never been this late coming back before.

After looking down at the computer once more, he swore softly and stabbed a finger at the keyboard, clearing the screen. He turned the machine off and ground what was left of the cigarette into the ashtray. To hell with it. He'd finish it tomorrow.

Trey walked downstairs and into the kitchen and poured himself a cup of coffee, trying not to look at the pack of cigarettes lying on the counter. It had been a mistake, taking his precious last of the day early like that. He'd thought the familiar ritual might help jar loose some sudden bolt of creativity, but all it had done was underscore how little he'd accomplished today.

She was raven-haired and blue-eyed....

In spite of himself he smiled. Maybe the alchemy of caffeine and nicotine *had* worked. He was on to something there. Something good. Maybe *Steele on Ice* was going to get written, after all.

He strolled onto the wide sun deck and took a sip of the coffee, squinting as he scanned the beach through rising steam. The shore was completely deserted, nothing moving but the long, white-frilled breakers rolling up the beach. A lone gull sailed overhead, its cry desolate, and Trey's frown deepened as he stared southward, eyes narrowed. It would be dark in another few minutes. She should have been back by now.

Finally he caught himself and turned away from the railing with a soft oath. Hell, it wasn't any of his business if she stayed out there all night! He didn't even know her. Not where she was from, not how long she was staying, not even her name. Just that she and the boy were alone. And that she was scared to death.

He'd recognized it the moment he'd seen it in her eyes that day he'd come up behind her on the beach, unseen and unheard. She'd turned around and had found him standing only a few feet away. He'd said something to reassure her—what, he couldn't even remember now—but she'd hurried off and now would only come out when no one else was on the beach.

But there had been no mistaking the terror on her face. He'd seen fear like that before and had hoped never to see it again: the wild, frightened look of something hunted.

And that was when it had started, this habit he'd gotten into of sitting out here on the deck each night with a coffee and his last cigarette of the day. Not that he was watching over her, exactly. But the truth was that he rested easier when he knew where she was.

Just habit, he told himself. Watching over people was his business, and he was damned good at it. As he was at anticipating trouble....

Murphy whined softly, and Trey glanced at him. The big dog was staring intently down the beach, every muscle of his body taut. "You feel it too, don't you, old fella?" he murmured, staring at the long, dusk-grayed stretch of sand. "Something's wrong. She should have been back by now...."

Murphy responded with a whimper, then turned and trotted toward the steps leading down to the beach. He looked over his shoulder at Trey and gave a quiet bark, as though wondering what was taking so long, and Trey whispered an oath under his breath. This was crazy, damn it! She'd made it pretty plain that she wanted to be left alone. If he went wandering out there and met her in the dark, he'd scare the daylights out of her. And for all he knew, she was carrying a gun....

He rubbed his aching thigh, unable to stop a grim smile from lifting one corner of his mouth. That would be the ultimate irony, all right: T. C. Hollister, original man of action, getting shot by a mysterious raven-haired, blue-eyed beauty on a deserted beach in the middle of the night. Hell, it would probably double his book sales. If he lived to enjoy it.

The man stepped in front of them with no warning at all.

Nathan had been telling her about starfish, and Linn, concentrating on the boy's story and lulled by the rhythmic surge and ebb of the waves washing around their feet, had relaxed her watchfulness. Head down, hands tucked into the pockets of her windbreaker, she'd been strolling along with her mind on the mysteries of tide and sand and shell instead of possible danger, which was why she hadn't spotted him until he stepped from behind a huge, tide-tangled pile of weathered logs right into their path.

Linn stopped so abruptly that Nathan, who had dropped behind a step or two to look at some piece of tidal debris, very nearly ran into her. He saw the man and stopped as abruptly as Linn had, his eyes wide and frightened.

The man grinned at her. "Hi, gorgeous."

Linn swallowed. Common sense said she had nothing to fear. Common sense said he was just a local resident, looking for clams or doing a little illegal fishing. It couldn't be one of Santos's men. There was no way he could have tracked her this far....

"I been waitin' for you." The man's grin widened with anticipation. It was as though he could sense her fear, fed off it. "You're late tonight."

Linn could taste the panic now, felt light-headed with it, but fought it desperately, knowing that she couldn't afford the luxury of falling apart. "I think you've made a mistake," she said coldly.

"No, I don't think so." His words sounded faintly slurred. "You're stayin' in one a' them ritzy beach houses up a ways." It was less a question than a statement, somehow all the more threatening for its certainty.

"What do you want?" She snapped the words out, her mind racing. He was big, damn it. And beefy, with wall-to-wall shoulders and arms like tree boles, biceps straining at his shirt sleeves. If he got his hands on her, she wouldn't have a chance. But she had to keep him away from Nathan. A weapon ... if only there was a rock, even a piece of driftwood ... anything ...

"Jus' wanna talk." His grin widened sloppily. "I been watchin' ya. You don't come out much, do ya? 'Cept at night."

There was something about his voice that made Linn look at him sharply. He grinned back at her congenially, weaving ever so slightly in the soft sand, and suddenly she gave a gasp of strangled laughter. He was drunk!

He wasn't one of Santos's thugs at all, just a local barfly with a couple too many under his belt. Reckless with relief, she put her hand on Nathan's shoulder and started to walk around the man. "Perhaps some other time. It's gotten cold and it's past my son's bedtime, so—"

"Pas' my bedtime, too." Still grinning, he stepped in front of her. He glanced at Nathan. "You go on home, kid. Your mom an' me are goin' to have a party."

"You're drunk," Linn said icily. "Get out of my way."

"Not too drunk to show you a good time, honey," he assured her with an ugly laugh.

"You leave her alone!" Nathan's voice rose with indignation; he pulled away from Linn's hand and planted himself squarely between her and the man. "My daddy's a policeman, and he'll put you in jail if you—"

"But your old man ain't here, is he?" The man's grin widened and he aimed a lazy swat at Nathan. "Now you get before I—"

"Get away from him!" Linn grabbed the man's arm and wrenched it down. "Nathan, run!"

The man gave a grunt of surprise and Linn caught a glimpse of Nathan stumbling back out of reach just before the arm she was holding pulled her sharply off balance. She tripped in the soft sand and would have gone down if her assailant hadn't caught her. He grabbed both wrists and wrenched her upright, giving an unpleasant laugh. "Well, well, looks like I got me a real little spitfire." He laughed again, enveloping her in a bearlike embrace. "You jus' go ahead and fight all you want, honey. I like it rough."

He tried to kiss her, but Linn gave a yelp of disgust and wrenched her face away. He stank of diesel fuel and stale beer and the combination made Linn's stomach heave as she struggled futilely against his powerful grip. The fear was back now, a more basic, primitive kind; she realized with a sudden, sickening clarity that by walking the beach at night to avoid one danger she'd left herself wide open to another.

"You leave her alone!"

It was Nathan's voice, the anger in it overriding the fear, and Linn heard her assailant's breath sucked in on a gasp of pain. He swore and swung his left arm around and Linn caught a glimpse of Nathan stumbling backward to avoid the blow, a heavy piece of weathered pine clutched in both hands. His footing betrayed him and he fell sprawling, but as Linn's assailant made a lunge for the boy, she flung herself sideways with every ounce of strength she had.

Caught by surprise, the man made a wild grab for Linn. He caught the back of her jacket and wrenched her back so violently that she tripped in the deep sand and fell heavily.

"Run, Nathan!" she shouted. "Get out of here! Run!" The man snarled something and reached down for her, his face twisted with anger, and with more instinct than rational thought she grabbed a fistful of sand and flung it squarely into his eyes.

He threw up his hands with a roar and in that instant Linn was on her feet, screaming to Nathan to run, run, even as she herself was running. But not fast enough. Her assailant was on her with a bellow and as his hand clamped down on her shoulder, Linn tried to twist free. She stumbled heavily, her feet sinking into the deep, loose sand, and then she went sprawling facedown, landing against two posts, embedded firmly in the sand.

It was only when they moved that she realized they weren't posts at all, but legs. Sun-browned and well-muscled male legs, wide-spread for balance. They were bare, as were the feet in front of her, and it took Linn a befuddled moment or two to realize that they didn't belong to her attacker.

"Just what in the hell," a husky baritone above her asked very calmly, "is going on here?"

"Nothin' that's any of *your* business," Linn's assailant warned with drunken bravado. "Butt out before I—"

"By the look of it, buddy," the baritone went on conversationally, "I'd say the lady wasn't interested."

"She's interested, all right. She comes out here every night, looking for company. Figured I'd give her some of what she's bin lookin' for, that's all. But I ain't in no sharing mood, so get lost."

Linn heard a throaty growl above her, so animal-like it made the hair on her neck stir. She went motionless, terrified to move, not even daring to look up as another growl rumbled around her, the sound filled with deadly threat.

The legs beside her stirred. "I don't think so," the husky voice said, deceptively soft.

"This ain't got nothin' to do with you," she heard the other man say belligerently. "You an' the mutt don't scare me none." He took a step forward and Linn recoiled. "Come on, doll-face. The party's just started. We're goin' to—"

Linn wasn't too sure what happened next. There was a spitting snarl behind her, then something large and black shot out of the shadows just as the tanned legs moved. The stranger stepped across her in one smooth stride, bracing his right foot in the sand and pivoting on it. Linn blinked as his other foot rose in a clean, sweeping arc, lashing up and around so fast that the movement was just a blur.

The kick caught her attacker solidly in the solar plexus; he gave a grunt of surprised agony and staggered backward. The stranger, both feet on solid ground again, stepped forward lightly. His fist shot out and landed on the man's jaw with a satisfyingly meaty thud, and Linn watched in astonishment as her assailant went sprawling across the sand.

"Murphy, watch him!"

The black shadow that Linn was only starting to realize was a huge German shepherd pounced on the prone man with a snarl.

"Get him off me! Get him off me!" The man's voice lifted in a shriek of terror.

"Lie still or he'll tear your throat out," the newcomer snapped. "Guard, Murphy!"

The big dog stood fully astride the downed man, lips curled back, the wet, gleaming fangs hovering mere inches from the man's face. The fur across the dog's shoulders stood up like a brush and Linn could see him quivering with anticipation, poised like a cat over a mouse, every muscle as tight as coiled steel.

Her attacker was babbling something, his voice just a wordless squeal of fear that was all but lost under the dog's snarls. Linn swallowed and sat up very slowly, dazed, brushing a tangle of hair out of her eyes. "Nathan?" she whispered hoarsely.

Another dark shape detached itself from the deepening shadows and hurled itself at her with a low wail. Nathan's arms went around her neck in a stranglehold and he clung to her, shaking so badly that Linn could hear his teeth chattering.

She hugged him fiercely, holding back her own tears of fright through sheer force of will. "Are you all right, Nathan? He didn't hurt you, did he?"

Nathan shook his head, snuffling and sobbing against her neck. "I hit him, b-but he wouldn't l-let go!"

"I know, honey, I know." Linn buried her face in his damp, tangled hair and squeezed her eyes shut, too shaken to do more than simply rock him against her. "I know you were trying to help me, Nathan, but you should have run. We talked about what to do if something like this happened, remember?"

"B-but he wasn't trying to hurt *me*," the boy sobbed, his arms clasped so tightly around Linn's throat that she was having trouble breathing. "H-he was trying to hurt *you*, Aunt Linn. He was—"

"Nathan!" She spoke his name with quiet urgency, praying the stranger was too occupied with her attacker to have caught the boy's slip. She felt Nathan flinch slightly and hugged him even tighter. *He's just a child,* something in her cried out. He was too young to understand the implications of even one tiny mistake, and yet—for his own safety—he *had* to understand. The charade had to continue, no matter what the circumstances, no matter how afraid he was.

"It's all right, Nathan," she murmured reassuringly. "And I'm all right, too. He didn't hurt me."

He drew back slightly to look at her, his eyes blurred with tears. "W-was he one of the bad men after my daddy?" he whispered. "D-did they follow us here?"

The fear on his face made Linn's heart ache. "No, honey," she said softly, knowing the stranger was listening but suddenly not caring. "He was just some man who wanted to scare us. He had too much to drink and was being obnoxious, that's all. We'll never see him again, I promise."

Nathan drew in a deep, unsteady breath and wiped his eyes with the back of his hand. His lower lip was still trembling but he held the tears back manfully. "Are we going to put him in jail?"

"Damned right," a gruff baritone muttered behind her. "The cops are going to *love* finally getting something solid on this guy."

Linn swallowed, a sudden smothering panic washing over her again. She fought it again, only half-successfully, and glanced up as the stranger walked around and into view.

He looked, she found herself thinking inanely, like someone who'd be more at home on a battlefield in ancient Gaul than a modern-day beach. She had a sudden, crystalline image of him on the back of a war chariot, a plumed helmet on his head and good Roman iron in his hand. She could almost smell the horse sweat for an instant, could hear the clash of weaponry. Then it all vanished and she was back on the cool, tide-damp sand, Nathan tight in her arms and the stranger standing there silently, looking down at her.

Except he wasn't a stranger.

She'd seen him before. On the sun deck of the big beach house beside hers, as a matter of fact. And once on this very beach. She'd turned around one evening and had found him standing not five feet from her, startling her so badly that she'd still been shaking an hour later. He'd said something to her—she couldn't remember what—but she'd grabbed Nathan's hand and had headed for the safety of her beach house at a near run. She'd seen him two or three times since then, but always at a safe distance, and to her relief he'd never attempted to approach her again.

But it was definitely the same man. He had the kind of face a woman wouldn't easily forget. His features were strong and straight and ruggedly male, with just enough sensuality in the mouth and around the eyes to send a little tingle through any female old enough—and woman enough—to recognize the promise it held.

His hair was long and thick and tousled, and it lay in wind-tossed waves around his ears and neck, almost but not quite hiding the glint of gold in his left ear. It gave him a rough, slightly dangerous look she wasn't sure she liked and she swallowed, holding Nathan a little tighter. He was taller than she would have liked, too, and lean and well-muscled enough to be real trouble if he wanted to be.

And he was fast, she already knew that. He moved like a street fighter, quick and sure on his feet, not making a single move that was wasted, and there was something about the way he was just standing there now, loose and relaxed yet quietly alert, that put her nerves on edge. It was as though he were waiting for her to make the first move, as though whatever happened next was going to depend on what she did—or didn't—do.

It was only then that she realized, even more uneasily, that he was all but naked. He was wearing nothing but a deep golden tan and a pair of very brief denim shorts that had in an earlier life been real jeans. Threadbare and tattered, they rode so low on his hips and hugged his contours so audaciously that it was impossible not to notice he was wearing nothing under them.

And for the first time since he'd appeared, Linn found herself suddenly wondering *why* he was there. What had brought him out to this far end of the beach? It was almost as though he'd known she was going to be there. As though . . .

Without warning, he dropped onto one knee just in front of her and she flinched, her arms tightening around Nathan.

"Easy. . ." His voice was just a murmur of reassurance and he made no move to touch her. "Are you all right?"

Wetting her lips, Linn nodded. She drew in a deep breath, trying for Nathan's sake to sound calm and in control. "I—I'm fine," she managed to whisper, her voice so rough it didn't even sound like her. "Thank you. For c-coming when you did, I mean. For helping."

"That's me. Trey Hollister, man of action."

She looked up at him uncertainly, hearing the edge of bitterness to his voice, and Trey gritted his teeth against the pain. It was like a physical presence, pressing on him, blurring his vision. It felt as though he'd just torn part of his leg away, and through the haze of agony it occurred to him that he might have done just that. The wound in his thigh had gone bone deep, the layers of muscle and tendon and ligament and flesh were only just starting to draw together, and that damned kick he'd used on Rolfson had sure as hell ripped *something* loose.

"I don't suppose you'd mind telling me what the hell you're doing out here this time of night?" He bit the words out, teeth still gritted.

She flinched, saying nothing, and Trey swallowed the rest of his tirade, not even sure why he was so angry. Maybe it was the way she'd risked her own life; maybe it was the way she'd risked the boy. And part of it was just the realization, like a stone in his gut, that if he hadn't decided to come out here after her, he'd have had to live with that on his conscience, too. And he had enough there already without some damned woman deliberately putting herself in danger.

He kneaded his throbbing thigh with his hand, half expecting to bring his palm away bloody. But although it felt as though he'd ripped his leg open, he hadn't, of course. The ridged scar merely stood out red and ugly against the tanned skin around it.

She was still kneeling in the sand, her head so low that her face was hidden by a silken curtain of hair, and it was only when he saw the tear splash onto the back of her hand and glitter in the moonlight that he realized she was crying. He stared down at her, feeling his fierce anger dissipate. It all but disappeared after a moment or two, leaving nothing behind but a bone-deep weariness and an emptiness that seemed to go on forever.

For a split second he found himself tempted to slip his arms around her and cradle her against him, to just let her cry and get it all out—all the terror and anger and pain—but he managed to catch himself. First off, odds were that she'd figured he was planning to finish what Rolfson had started and would claw his eyes out, and second, nowhere was it written that Trey Hollister had an obligation to take on the mantle of savior. Whatever was scaring this woman half to death went beyond this moment and this beach, but that wasn't any of his business. He'd done what any man would have done under the circumstances, but his responsibilities ended right here.

Slowly he eased himself to his feet, teeth clenched against the pain in his leg. The boy in her arms gave him a quick, uncertain look and then, to Trey's surprise, broke into a tentative but very real smile. Trey smiled back, a private smile passed man to man over the woman's head that made the boy practically beam with pleasure. The fear in his eyes vanished and was replaced by such utter uncomplicated trust that Trey groaned inwardly.

Now what in the hell had he done! The kid's mother had taught him that fear for some damned good reason, and she wasn't going to appreciate having it tampered with.

He wheeled around with a muttered oath and limped through the loose sand to where Murphy was still standing guard over the woman's attacker. The dog hadn't moved so much as a hair in the intervening few minutes and was still rumbling threatening growls. Trey had to smile at his enthusiasm. Murphy always had taken his heroics seriously, but tonight he'd pulled out all the stops. Obviously as big a pushover for ladies in distress as his owner.

Trey didn't find the thought particularly cheering. "Okay, Murph, back off," he ordered gruffly. The big dog whined and looked up. The man made the mistake of moving slightly and Murphy gave a coughing snarl and snapped the air inches from the man's face, spraying him with saliva and hot, canine breath.

The man gave a squeal of fear and covered his face with his hands, and Trey chuckled and nudged Murphy aside. "Let him up," he said quietly. "You've done your part. It's my turn now."

Murphy whined again a couple of times but did move back a few steps. He circled slowly, bristling and growling, obviously hoping the man would make a break for it and try to run. And for a split second or two, Trey was almost hoping the same thing, wanting nothing more than some excuse to work off some of his remaining anger and adrenaline. He reached down and grabbed the man's shirtfront and pulled him to his feet, feeling disgust rise like bile in his throat. It took all his willpower to keep from planting his bruised, aching fist solidly in the man's face.

Breathing a little quickly he released him instead and flexed his fist. "You should have stayed home tonight, Rolfson. Because you just bought yourself some jail time."

The man gave a derisive snort, trying to keep one eye on the circling dog and glower at Trey at the same time. "And *you* just bought yourself some serious trouble, chump. You can't go around punching people for no reason. The lady 'n' me were just having ourselves a friendly visit, that's all." His scare had sobered him up considerably, but he still sounded badly shaken.

Trey smiled grimly. "Save it for the cops, *chump*. But I wouldn't count on it getting you anywhere. They've been trying to get something solid on you for months—I figure they'll give me a good citizen's award for getting you off the street."

"She was asking for it." Rolfson gave the woman an angry look. "No woman goes walkin' on the beach at night unless she's looking for some action."

Trey's right fist itched, but he drew in a deep, calming breath and kept his hand by his side, satisfying his urge for violence by giving the man a ferocious shove toward the piles of driftwood. "I told you to save it. Now get over there and stand real still or I'll let my dog have a go at you. Murphy! Guard!"

The big shepherd sprang forward with a snarl and stood in front of the man, legs widespread and braced, hackles raised. The man paled slightly and swallowed, licking his lips, seemingly transfixed by the dog's burning stare.

Trey turned to the woman. She hadn't moved, but the color had come back into her cheeks and the wild panic he'd first seen in her eyes was gone. In its place was an odd mixture of emotions: fear, suspicion, relief and, just perhaps, a hint of gratitude. Or maybe he'd just imagined the gratitude, he decided as he got closer. There didn't seem to be anything in the troubled gaze now but wariness and mistrust.

Which was fine by him, he reminded himself impatiently. He didn't want her thinking she owed him anything. Debts just made things complicated. "If you're ready, let's head back. Your place is closer. We can call the police from there and—"

"No." She said it quietly, but the one word, crystal clear, seemed very loud. "I won't . . . be pressing charges."

Trey stared down at her. "What the hell are you talking about? He tried to rape you, for—!"

Her chin lifted fractionally and she held his glare without faltering. "I appreciate your help, but it ends here. You can call your dog off and let him go."

"Like hell I'm letting him go," Trey said heatedly. "Damn it, lady, I don't know what your problem is, but you're not turning this guy loose to prey on some other unsuspecting woman! If you're afraid he'll get off and come after you and your son, don't be. The local cops have had their eye on him for over a year—they'll be only too glad to get him behind bars."

"No." She said it much too quickly, the fear back in her eyes again. She swallowed and looked away, hunching her shoulders slightly as though suddenly chilled. "No police."

Trey's eyes narrowed. There was a sudden awareness between them, a silence filled with a thousand unworded things that both were aware of, yet neither acknowledged. It seemed to grow, filling the night, and Trey shifted restlessly. The woman clearly felt it, too. Suddenly she seemed smaller and very vulnerable, and when she finally looked back up at him, her eyes were filled with misery and desperation.

It held and caught him, that look. It was the look of something trapped and afraid, something that's been pushed almost to the end. "Please," she whispered, hugging the boy more tightly against her. "I... I know you're angry. But I can't get involved. I just can't...."

Chapter 2

Her voice trailed off, lost under the rhythmic wash of surf on sand, and she looked away again, her eyes sliding from his as though she knew exactly what he was thinking.

Hell. Trey drew in a deep, angry breath and exhaled it noisily, staring out across the darkening sea. Common sense said he should get out now, before whatever trouble she was in sucked him in, too. But he'd chucked common sense out the window the minute he'd decided to follow her tonight. In fact, it had probably gone out the window when she'd first turned up a week ago and he'd let himself get slowly entangled in the web of mystery around her.

His oath was short and pungent, and it made her blink. She flinched slightly as he strode by her, flushing at the unspoken anger and censure in his face.

Her attacker smirked as Trey approached. "Told you it wasn't none of your business. You're goin' to pay for this, buddy. Nobody's goin' to take a swing at me and not—" He gave a squeal of surprised fear as Trey's hand shot out and grabbed him by the shirtfront.

Trey lifted him off his feet and threw him back against the pile of weathered logs, hard, then moved in close and fast before his opponent could do more than struggle to catch his breath.

He put his splayed fingers lightly on the man's chest and leaned in close. "One more word, and you're dog meat. I'm going to let you go because that's the way the lady wants it, but that's not the way I want it. I'll be watching you, Rolfson. And I'll be waiting. One wrong move and I'm taking you out. Fast and clean, with no witnesses."

"Y-you can't do nothing," the man babbled with false bravado. "It's harassment. I'll go to the cops. I'll—"

"You do that. I'm sure they'll be real worried about what happens to you." Trey gave the man another violent shove. "I'm dead serious, Rolfson. Right now I'm the biggest problem you've got, understand? If I see you hanging around this beach or find out you've been bothering this woman or her kid, I'll kill you."

Once again he wrapped his fists around the man's shirtfront and hauled him to the end of the pile of logs, then gave him a ferocious push that sent him sprawling into the sand. Murphy pounced on him with a snarl, stopping only at a sharp command from Trey. The man clawed himself to all fours and started scrambling away. Finally he managed to get his feet under him and headed down the beach at a dead run without so much as a glance over his shoulder. Murphy was dancing with excitement, yelping in frustration as he watched the man speed away without being given the command to go after him.

"Lie down," Trey told him sharply, knowing exactly how the big dog felt.

Something moved behind him and Trey looked around, finding the boy—Nathan?—standing there wide-eyed with awe. He looked up at Trey. "Wow! Is your dog a police dog, mister?"

The small, dirty face gazing up at him was filled with such undisguised worship that Trey felt something inside him catch. He thought of another little boy looking up at him in that same way. That had been nearly eighteen years ago. The boy was a man now, close to twenty. Maybe even married with a son of his own....

Trey forced the thought away brutally, trying to ignore Nathan's gaze. That was exactly what he needed, some hero-worshiping kid underfoot every time he turned around. Not bothering to answer, he strode by the boy without looking at him.

But even as he tried to ignore it, Trey couldn't miss the way the boy's face crumpled with hurt, the way the small shoulders slumped under his denim windbreaker. He blinked hard, as though fighting sudden tears, and Trey swore again, silently this time, and dropped stiffly onto one knee with an inward sigh. "Come on over here," he said gently. The boy looked at him mistrustfully, and Trey impatiently motioned him to come nearer.

"Nathan..." The woman's voice was vibrant with warning.

"Look, lady, would you lighten up?" Trey gave her a mildly hostile look, not knowing if it was her suspicions he was annoyed with, or himself for giving a damn. "Murph here is worth his weight in marines when it counts, and when he's around I can guarantee that nothing's going to happen to the kid. Or to you. So do me a favor and just ease up a bit."

She flushed and looked away, her mouth tightening with what he figured was instinctive anger. But to Trey's relief, common sense won out over raw pride. "It's all right, Nathan," she said in a hoarse whisper, not looking at Trey. "Do as he says."

Nathan walked over slowly, clearly still uncertain after his initial rebuff. Trey smiled at the boy, knowing the woman was watching him, her eyes dark and private in the deepening dusk. "Murph, come here." Trey snapped his fingers and the big dog came bounding over, tail windmilling, tongue lolling. "Sit." Murphy did so instantly, giving Trey a goofy, good-natured look, as though wondering what kind of game they were playing now. "Murph, this is—" Trey looked at the boy. "What's your name, kid?"

"My name's Nathan Val—" He stopped abruptly. "Nathan Stee—" Again he stopped, giving the woman a stricken look.

"Stevens...son," she said, stumbling awkwardly over what was obviously a spur-of-the-moment alias. "Nathan Stevenson."

Her eyes dared him to argue. "Stevenson," he repeated, holding her gaze just long enough to tell her he knew damned well that she was lying. She held his gaze steadily, refusing to rise to the bait, and he nearly had to smile. "Okay. Stevenson it is. Nathan, this is Murphy." Hearing his name, Murphy beamed. "Well, Nat...does anyone call you Nat?"

The boy smiled. "My daddy sometimes calls me—" He bit it off, sliding his mother a quick, nervous glance. "Sometimes," he whispered, looking down. His fingers twisted in the hem of his windbreaker and he dug at the sand with one small, sneaker-clad foot. "Most people call me Nathan."

"How about me?" Trey asked gently. It was a judgment call, and he didn't even know why he was bothering, but the look of desolation on the boy's face tore at him. "Would you like me to call you Nathan or Nat?"

"Nat... would be okay," he whispered, looking up shyly. His words were casual enough, but he was still too young to be able to disguise his pleasure at the nickname.

Careful, Hollister, Trey warned himself, knowing the woman was watching him with a cool, speculative expression. He found himself thinking of lion cubs and their mothers, and the fate awaiting any man foolish enough to come between them. "Okay, Nat. Hold your hand out so he can get used to your scent. That's right." Trey nodded as the boy hesitantly extended his hand. Murphy, as though sensing the boy's nervousness, reached out very gently and nudged the waiting fingers with his nose, then, even more gently, ran a large, wet tongue across them.

The age-old gesture of acceptance made Nathan giggle with delight. "Can I pet him?"

"Sure. You're friends now. If you're ever in trouble and need help, just sing out and Murph will be right there."

"Wow." Nathan's eyes shone as he ran his hand down Murphy's broad head and between his ears. The dog wriggled with pleasure and eased himself a little closer, giving the boy's face an enthusiastic swipe with his tongue.

Nathan gave a sputter of laughter and wiped his face with his arm. Grinning, he looked up at Trey. "Thanks, Mr. Hollister."

"Trey, to friends." Trey held out his hand. Nathan took it and they shook solemnly. "Okay, kid, I think it's time I took you and your mother home."

"Is that man going to come back?"

"He won't be back," Trey assured him. "That was a pretty brave thing you did, trying to drive him off with that piece of driftwood. But your mother was right—it *was* dangerous. If anything like that happens again, you clear out, fast, and get help. Understand?"

"Yes, sir," Nathan said firmly, looking very much older than his four or five years. He scrubbed a handful of tousled hair off his forehead and for a moment Trey almost thought he was going to salute. Shoulders back, he looked Trey straight in the eye. "I think we should go home now."

Trey looked down at the boy curiously. "Your daddy wouldn't happen to be a soldier, would he?"

"No, sir," came the prompt and proud reply. "My daddy's a pol—"

"Nathan." The woman's quiet voice silenced the boy abruptly. Nathan gave Trey a nervous glance, as though aware he'd said too much, and turned to walk back to his mother.

My daddy's a policeman, Trey finished for him thoughtfully. Now that was interesting....

His gaze met the woman's almost by accident, and he could see the fear in her eyes, the mistrust. She was still kneeling on the sand and looked scared and cold and miserable, arms wrapped around herself as though trying to hold out the chill. The sea wind had whipped her hair into tangles and the small oval of her face seemed even paler than usual, the dark pools of her eyes haunted as she stared up at him, as though uncertain of what he was going to do next.

What in God's name was she mixed up in? he found himself wondering. She didn't strike him as the kind of woman who would frighten easily. She'd been shaken up over tonight's ordeal, for instance, but was far from hysterical, so whatever had put that kind of fear in her eyes must be pretty serious. The kind of seriousness that a man didn't want to get mixed up in if he didn't have to.

"I don't know about you," he said quietly, reaching down for her, "but Murphy and I have had enough excitement for one night. Let's go home."

He felt her flinch slightly as he took her by the upper arm and lifted her to her feet, but she didn't argue or even pull away. Probably too damned cold to make the effort, he decided as a spasm of shivers ran through her, making her stumble slightly. It was shock, mainly. If he didn't get her home soon, he was going to wind up carrying her.

"Let's get this jacket buttoned up." He reached for the front of her windbreaker, but she recoiled from his touch like a horse shying from the whip.

She clutched her gaping jacket and started walking away, so stiff with cold that she stumbled again. "I'm all right," she mumbled, hunching her shoulders. "Nathan and I c-can get back by ourselves."

"You're not all right," Trey told her bluntly, catching her by the shoulders and swinging her around to face him. She gave a squeak of shock but he ignored it and zipped up the jacket, then turned the collar up around her ears. "Quit being such a hard case, Stevenson. You don't get points for stubbornness."

She stared up at him, half frightened and half outraged, and Trey watched her struggle to make up her mind which to give in to first. But in the end, much to his satisfaction, she resisted both of them. Her shoulders sagged, she simply nodded and started walking, shivering so badly he could actually see the tremors as they ran through her.

I'd like to know your story, lady, he told her silently as he fell into step beside her. What's out there that's scaring you so badly?

The walk back to her beach house took hours.

In reality, Linn knew, it couldn't have been more than twenty minutes. It had taken Nathan and her nearly an hour to walk the same distance, exploring salt pools and drifts of tidal debris along the way, and it was only when she started to realize how far they'd gone that she also became aware how much danger she'd put herself and Nathan in.

Rolfson would have known how deserted the beach was at night. Hers was the nearest house, nearly a mile from where he'd attacked her. There was nothing out here but eagles and gulls and the endless keening of the wind. The forest rising into the mountains from the beach was so thick and wild that there were no campgrounds, no hiking trails. Nothing. No one would have heard her screams. No one would have come.

She shivered violently. The tears flooded her eyes so unexpectedly she couldn't even blink them back and she stumbled heavily against Hollister, blinded. He steadied her, then wrapped one large, warm hand gently around hers. "Almost there. How are you doing?"

"Okay," she lied bravely, dabbing at her nose with her sleeve. The shivers just wouldn't let up and all she wanted to do was sit down in the cold sand and burst into tears. But aside from the fact that it would frighten poor Nathan even more, she was also damned if she was going to fall apart in front of Hollister. Half of it was the stubborn Irish pride that had gotten her through worse situations than this, and half of it was—perhaps—a matter of survival.

The timing of Hollister's rescue still bothered her. He must have been right behind them to have gotten there that quickly, yet neither she nor Nathan had seen him.

Unless he'd been waiting for her, too.

She glanced at Hollister uneasily. His fingers were still meshed warmly with hers, but was he holding her hand simply to reassure her—or to keep her from escaping?

Her heart did a quick little flip-flop and she wet her lips, wondering how far she'd get if she wrenched her hand free, scooped up Nathan and started running.

Not far at all, she advised herself grimly. Not even on her best day, and without the burden of Nathan. She'd seen Hollister move.

She shivered again, more violently. God, the expression on his face when he'd had Rolfson pinned against those logs! He'd spoken about death as though it were something casual, his words less a threat than a promise, delivered in a flat, calm voice that had chilled her to the bone. And there had been something in his eyes, something cold and still and lethal, that made her shiver again just thinking about it.

She dared another sidelong glance at him. If he *was* working for Santos, she'd escaped one nightmare tonight just to fall into another one—this one far more deadly than attempted rape. They wanted Nathan, not her. To Santos she was just someone who was in the way, someone who had something he wanted.

And yet, if Hollister's plan was to kill her and kidnap Nathan, why go through this silly charade?

Unless he hadn't wanted a witness. Rolfson had been drunk, but not that drunk. If her body washed up on the beach in a few days, he'd have no trouble remembering Hollister's face. But that didn't make sense, either, because if Hollister was on Santos's payroll, he'd have no qualms about killing Rolfson, too. In fact, that probably would have been ideal, setting the whole thing up as a murder-suicide or something. It wouldn't have been difficult. Rolfson hadn't been much of an opponent; she'd have been even less so. A quick judo chop to the throat, and—

"You and the boy are staying with me tonight."

Hollister's voice made Linn blink, and she slowly realized that they were in front of her rented beach house.

It was set back in a stand of pines on the embankment overlooking the beach, low and weathered, looking so much a natural part of the rugged landscape that most people didn't even notice it. A sun deck jutted off the front, wide enough to hang over the bank, supported by huge pilings.

From the deck ran the wooden steps that were the only access from the beach, complete with the large No Trespassing sign nailed to a post at the bottom to discourage sightseers and tourists. There was another sign under it, smaller and obviously added as a whimsical touch. Until now Linn had always found the graphically drawn skull and crossbones amusing; tonight it just made her shiver.

The house was dark and silent. And oddly ominous. She swallowed and put her foot on the bottom step.

"I said—"

"I heard you," Linn replied. "I appreciate the offer, but we'll be staying here tonight."

"Not so fast." Hollister's hand caught her wrist and Linn's heart gave a leap of raw fear. "You're in no shape to be here by yourself tonight."

Linn twisted her arm free and stared up at him defiantly. "I'm perfectly all right."

Hollister's eyes narrowed. For an instant Linn thought he was going to try to force her to go with him and she braced herself. "Damn it, lady, you really are a pain in the—" He swallowed the rest, his eyes glinting dangerously in the near darkness. "Wait here, then. And don't come up until I tell you it's clear."

Linn had her mouth half open to argue, but it suddenly seemed like too much trouble. Numbed with cold and the residue of what she supposed was shock, she simply nodded and watched as he padded lightly up the dew-damp steps, silent as a cat.

He gave a sharp whistle after a moment or two and motioned her to join him, and Linn started climbing the stairs slowly. He was waiting by a big sliding door leading into the living room when she finally reached the top. He held his hand out and wiggled his fingers impatiently. "Give me the key."

Wearily Linn fumbled in the pocket of her windbreaker. Her fear had vanished under the leaden weight of exhaustion, and suddenly all she wanted was to get inside and into bed. "You don't have to do this," she mumbled through chattering teeth. "I'm okay now. Nobody could have—" She frowned and went through her pockets again, more slowly this time, aware that Trey was looking down at her impatiently.

She looked up at him, stricken. "I can't find it." He whispered a soft oath and Linn checked the pockets of her jeans. A feeling of hopeless despair washed over her and she had to bite her lower lip to hold it steady. This was too much! Sudden tears welled, threatening to overflow. "I—I had it. I know I had it!"

"It probably fell out of your pocket when you were struggling with Rolfson. Hang on a minute—I'll be right back." He vaulted the deck railing and vanished around the side of the house.

"Trey'll get it open," Nathan said confidently.

"But the front door's locked. There's no way he can get inside to—" The faint tinkle of breaking glass stopped her.

Nathan smiled up at her knowingly. "Told ya."

"But he can't just break in like a . . . a thief!" He was too good at this sort of thing: from martial arts to breaking and entering, there didn't seem to be anything he couldn't—or wouldn't—do.

The curtains on the inside of the glass were pulled aside and Trey looked out at her. He unlocked the catch and slid the heavy door open and Nathan scurried through, glad to be out of the cold, and Linn unhappily followed a moment later. "You broke a window," she said accusingly as she stepped by him.

"Give me a break," he said wearily as he pulled the door closed behind her and locked it. "What did you want me to do? Leave you and Nathan out there in the cold while I went back to look for your key? Hell, I could have just gone home and let you find your own way in. You could have walked back up to the end of the beach yourself and looked for the key. There's only about twenty square miles of loose sand out there to sift through."

It cut through the cold and misery, as it was probably supposed to. Linn felt her cheeks color. "I'm sorry. You're right," she whispered, so cold and tired that she was having trouble holding back the treacherous flood of tears again.

Damn it, what was the matter with her! She wasn't a cryer. Bursting into tears when all else failed was Kathy's way of coping, not hers. But right now it was taking every bit of willpower she had not to do just that. "But I'm all right now, so you d-don't have to s-stay." She could sense more than see him moving through the darkness, and flinched when he turned on one of the table lamps.

"Like hell you're all right," he growled, striding across the room toward her. "You're scared and you're cold and you're this far from losing it." He held his hand up, thumb and forefinger a scant inch apart. "Now I'm going to take a quick look through the rest of the house, and I don't want you or the kid moving out of this room until I get back. I'll leave Murphy with you in case I scare something loose. Then, once that's done, you're going to put the kid to bed, and you and I are going to have a long talk. Got all that?"

If she'd had the strength, Linn thought wearily, she'd have gotten a lot of satisfaction out of telling Trey Hollister to go to hell. As it was, it took almost more strength than she possessed just to nod. He had to be one of the most overbearing men she'd ever met. If she got out of this mess alive, she was going to take the time to tell him off properly.

If she got out of this mess alive...

She looked around the room miserably, only to discover that he'd vanished. As promised, the big shepherd was still there, sitting by the door with his ears pricked up and his chocolate eyes alert and watchful. Keeping watch or standing guard? If she walked across to that door, would he hold her at bay until his master got back? And had Trey gone to check for intruders, or just to ensure that the house was empty before—?

Stop it, Linn told herself angrily. Enough was enough. She couldn't go on like this, second-guessing herself and everyone around her, or she was going to drive herself crazy. Staying alive and keeping Nathan safe depended on keeping her wits about her, and she couldn't do that if she worked herself into such a knot of panic that she couldn't even think straight.

"Okay, the place is clean." Trey was suddenly there again, startling her slightly. "Everything's secure—both doors and all the windows, except the one in the kitchen I broke to get in. But I jammed the lock on it. Do you have a gun?"

"A *gun*?" She stared at him blankly.

"I just figured that under the circumstances—" He shrugged, leaving the rest unsaid. "Probably better that way. Guns have the bad habit of killing the wrong person, anyway." He turned and looked down at Nathan. "Okay, kid, time to hit the hay."

"I usually get a cup of hot chocolate," Nathan said doubtfully. "With mushmallows."

"I'll bring it in to you, honey," Linn said through chattering teeth. "But it is past your bedtime."

"Can Murphy stay with me?"

"Honey, I don't think—"

"Sure," Trey interrupted smoothly. "Just don't feed him any of those marsh—mushmallows. Even if he begs."

"Promise! Come on, Murphy!" Nathan was out of his windbreaker in a flash, and he and Murphy raced down the hallway to the bedrooms.

"One down, one to go." Trey turned toward her. He reached out and unzipped her jacket, then deftly pulled her arms out of it and tossed it onto the sofa. "I'm going to make Nathan's hot chocolate, and while I'm doing that, you're going to get under a boiling-hot shower and stay there until you thaw out."

Linn wrenched away from him. "Damn it, you c-can't just come in here and—"

"Either you get those clothes off and get into a hot shower on your own," he said in a dangerously calm voice, "or I'll take them off and *put* you in."

"Just because you rescued me from Rolfson tonight doesn't give you any right to—" Linn stopped dead, stumbling back as Trey started toward her. "Come near me and I swear I . . . I'll . . ."

"Call the police?" he asked dryly. "Lady, I'm just about done arguing with you. You've got to the count of three. *One.*"

"I'll . . ." Linn sputtered to a halt. Damn him! He'd called her bluff, and she was fresh out of options. And there was something about the set of his mouth and the way he was moving, slowly yet deliberately, toward her that made her think that he just might carry through his threat if she gave him enough provocation.

"Two."

"Hollister, I'm warning you!" Linn looked around for a weapon. She spotted the set of brass fireplace tools and snatched up the poker, brandishing it like a saber. "Come another step closer and I'll spit you like a cocktail olive!"

"That's it, by God," Trey rumbled, his patience evaporating. "Lady, I don't need this! I'm tired, I'm sore and I just want to go home and lose myself in a very large glass of bourbon—but I can't do that. And you know why? Because I'm stuck here, watching over some scared, stubborn woman who's too damn obstinate to admit she just might not be able to hold it together much longer."

He took two long strides toward her, grabbing her wrist in one hand and the poker in the other, and had wrenched the weapon from her before she'd even had to time to to react.

"Enough is enough!" He tossed the poker away and it ricocheted off the stone hearth with a clatter. Her eyes had gone wide with terror and Trey inwardly sighed, the agony in his throbbing leg forgotten for a moment or two as he realized he'd frightened her half to death.

"You're close to frozen and you're in shock," he told her quietly. "By tomorrow morning all of this will just be a bad dream, but you've got to get through tonight." He released her wrist and she stumbled back, pale and wide-eyed, staring up at him through a haze of fear. "You're not in any condition to take care of yourself, let alone that boy in there. And I'm not leaving here until I know you've gotten things under control and that he's safe. Got that?"

He watched her struggle with it. She was smart enough to know he was right, but could she overcome her fear and suspicion of strangers long enough to trust him? "If I were going to hurt you or the boy," he told her softly, "I'd have done it by now."

She stared at him in silence, mouth tight with anger, eyes still mistrustful. Then she drew in a deep breath, releasing it through clenched teeth. "The cocoa," she said with chilled precision, "is in the cupboard above the stove. Make it with hot milk, not water, and he likes exactly five miniature marshmallows in it." Her chin went up a notch and eyes filled with defiance held his. "And I do *not* appreciate being bullied, Mr. Hollister, regardless of how well-intentioned. I am quite able to take care of myself and my son, and I don't need—"

"Like you were taking care of him down on the beach with Rolfson?" Trey held her stare just as defiantly, feeling the anger flare through him. At her, or at himself? Or was it just rage at an imperfect world where women lived in fear and little boys never saw their fathers again?

He thought she was going to say something, but at the last moment she bit back the words and drew herself up to her full five feet three inches. The effect was spoiled by the fact that she was shivering so badly she could scarcely stand, but she made the best of it as she turned on one heel and strode across the room.

"This backwoods he-man routine may endear you to the women around here," she said icily, "but it doesn't do a damned thing for me." She paused in the corridor to turn and glare at him. "I want you *out* of here before I get back, Mr. Hollister. Out of my house and out of my life. Do you understand me?"

Trey nearly laughed. She reminded him of a stray kitten he'd taken in once, so small it fitted in the palm of his hand but full of enough spit and hiss to hold Murphy at bay. "Two and a half . . ."

She wheeled away and marched down the corridor, back ramrod straight, and he had to wince as the bathroom door was slammed with enough force to rattle the windows.

He had a roaring fire going in the big fieldstone fireplace by the time Linn got out of the shower. His back was to her as he added another pine log to the flames, and as she stepped into the room and saw him, Linn's breath caught.

Her shock lasted only a split second. Just long enough for her heart to give an odd, quick little twist of recognition before her mind, always logical, always practical, reminded her that what she was seeing was quite impossible.

Jack was dead. He'd been dead for nearly four years now. And that tall, dark-haired man across the room from her right now, moving catlike and quickly and wearing that achingly familiar old plaid shirt, was a stranger.

Damn.

The old memories hadn't caught her unawares like that for a long, long while; she was surprised how sharp the pain of loss could still be. It wasn't Trey's fault. He'd obviously found that old shirt of Jack's on the back of the chair where she'd left it that morning and had slipped it on without even thinking. And why should he? He didn't know anything about her or the man she'd once loved, or the memories that faded old shirt held. . . .

Chapter 3

Trey didn't know if Linn had said something, or if he had just sensed her standing behind him. But whatever the reason, he suddenly knew she was there; he straightened and turned around, mouth half-open to ask her if she wanted a drink.

The question turned to dust in his mouth as his eyes met hers. She was looking at him with an expression of such radiance and love that his heart literally missed a beat and he completely forgot what he'd been about to say.

Then, abruptly, the look was gone. A flicker of what might have been pain crossed her face and then she was looking at *him*, Trey Hollister, and not the man whom, for one magical heartbeat of time, she thought she'd seen.

She held his gaze for a moment longer, her expression curiously vulnerable, then lifted the towel she was carrying and started rubbing her hair dry. "I thought I told you to get out."

"And I told you to stop being such a hard case." Trey eased his breath out tightly, feeling a sudden, violent surge of jealousy for the man that look had been for. Where the hell was he? Trey found himself thinking. Why wasn't he here, taking care of his woman? And what was he? Husband? Lover?

He swore under his breath and turned back to the fire, shoving another log into the crackling flames. It was crazy, being jealous of a man he'd never met over a woman he hardly knew. But if a woman ever looked at *him* that way, he'd damned well be there when she needed him. If it had been *him* . . .

But it wasn't him. Trey swore again and roughly closed the fire screen. He straightened and turned away from the fire, trying to ignore a treacherous little feeling of wistfulness. No woman had ever looked at him like that. No woman but Diane, anyway, and even then it had only lasted three months.

It had taken her that long to realize the man she'd married was a marine first and a husband second, and by the time his orders had come through for Vietnam, the rift between them was already irreparable. She'd stayed another year, then she'd left, taking with her the only family he'd ever known. And the son he scarcely knew. . . .

He shrugged the memories away impatiently. Linn was sitting on the wide stone hearth, vigorously rubbing her hair, and he poured her a generous shot of the scotch he'd found in one of the kitchen cabinets.

"Here." He touched her on the shoulder and she drew the towel from her hair and looked up warily. "Drink as much of this as you can get down. It'll help stop the shakes."

To his surprise, she smiled faintly as she reached up to take the glass. "You're very good at this, Mr. Hollister."

"Trey," he reminded her quietly. She'd changed into slim-fitting jeans and a hooded sweatshirt pulled over a turtleneck sweater, and with her hair all tousled and her cheeks flushed and damp from the shower, she looked about sixteen.

She cupped the glass between her hands and stared down into the amber liquid. "I . . . uh . . . I've acted pretty badly tonight. If you hadn't come along, that man would have . . ." She drew in an unsteady breath and shuddered, looking up at him. "I'm sorry."

Her eyes were almost violet in this light, deep enough to drown in, and for the second or third time that evening Trey found himself consciously fighting their spell. "Anytime," he said easily. Then he gave a snort of laughter. "On second thought, forget I said that. Either my fists aren't what they used to be, or I've forgotten how damned much it hurts to smash your bare knuckles against some drunk's teeth."

He rubbed the bruised knuckles on his right hand, smiling reminiscently. He was going to regret that impulsive swing at Rolfson's concrete jaw, but by God, it had felt good at the time! There had been a lot of frustration pent up in that one punch, and even if it meant typing with one hand for the rest of the week, it had been worth it.

He suddenly realized that Linn had been watching him, her expression thoughtful. "You're very good at *that*, too," she said quietly.

"I have my moments." He rubbed his knuckles again and glanced up a moment later to find her still watching him, "If you're planning on continuing these after-dark walks, you might consider learning a few moves yourself."

She smiled faintly. "I've learned my lesson. No more nighttime walks." She stared into the glass, brows pulling together. "It was just dumb, blind luck that you came along when you did. If you'd come out twenty minutes earlier or later, or if you'd gone the other way instead of..." She shivered again, not bothering to complete the thought.

"It wasn't luck. I followed you."

She shifted her gaze slowly. He could see the sudden doubt in her eyes, the beginnings of what might be fear. "I'd seen Rolfson hanging around the beach earlier," he said quietly. "When you and the boy didn't come back from your walk at your usual time, I decided to check things out."

There must have been something in his expression that reassured her slightly, because after a moment or two she nodded. Her eyes were still shadowed with worry, but of a different sort now. "I didn't realize I'd fallen into such a predictable routine," she said, perhaps more to herself than to him.

"Predictable enough." He held her gaze evenly. "The best routine to follow when you're on the run, Mrs. Stevenson, is no routine at all."

She caught the faint stress he put on her name and frowned, obviously annoyed by the jibe. "It's Linn," she said sharply. "And what do you mean, on the run?"

She was damned good, Trey found himself thinking. A bit *too* blasé, maybe, and she'd have to learn to do something about that worried little frown that settled between her brows, but those were things that only an expert would catch. She'd learned to control the fear; that was good. And she had a mind like a whipsaw, always assessing and analyzing and checking the exits.

"Why don't you tell me?" he asked bluntly.

For a moment he thought she was going to bluff her way through it. But at the last instant her gaze faltered and slipped away. "It's nothing," she whispered. "Just a . . . domestic problem."

He gave a snort of disbelief. The only kind of domestic problem that would put that kind of fear in a woman's eyes was a crazed husband with a gun and a court-bruised ego.

Which wasn't impossible, he reminded himself thoughtfully. She wouldn't be the first woman to take her kid and hightail it. Diane had done it. His eyes narrowed slightly. Except Diane hadn't been running scared, like this woman was. She hadn't flinched at every sudden noise or touch, hadn't looked at strangers with terror in her eyes.

He found himself thinking of Rolfson. He'd had the advantage of height and weight and drunken bravado, yet Linn had fought him like a wildcat, protecting the boy as well as herself.

And she'd held up better afterward than he'd expected. Although he knew that was just another kind of fear. Fear of him, this time; of what he might do to her or the boy should she show the slightest weakness or vulnerability.

I don't know who you are, Linn Whatever-Your-Real-Name-Is, he mused, but you are one tough lady, "I don't like the idea of leaving you here alone tonight. Is there someone I can call who can come and stay with you?"

She shook her head. "No," she said in a soft, hoarse voice.

Her tousled hair was starting to dry in the heat of the fire and he watched the flames play across it, bringing the highlights out. Abruptly he shook himself free. He finished the last of his drink in one swallow, then set the glass on the wide mantle. "I'm going to leave Murphy here tonight."

Linn blinked, Trey's voice working its way through a thousand whirling, muddled thoughts and bringing her back to the present. "You don't have to do that. I'll be all right."

"I'm sure you will be," he told her calmly, "but I'm not leaving you alone."

"But you already said you don't think Rolfson will—"

"It's either Murphy," he said flatly, "or me."

His eyes met hers directly, and Linn bit back the rest of her protest. He had the same expression on his face that Jack used to get when he was convinced he was right about something. Arguing with him when he'd been in that mood had been like trying to shift a mountain with a teaspoon, and what she did or did not want didn't seem to have much effect on *this* man, either.

She nodded, swallowing her annoyance. Having Murphy underfoot all night was one thing; having his tall, gray-eyed owner here was quite another. She'd already let him get closer than she could afford.

Trey walked to the glass door and slid it open, and she followed him thoughtfully. Friend, Mr. Hollister, she asked him silently, or foe?

The question was redundant. Until this business with Santos was over, she had no friends. And everyone, even Trey Hollister, was suspect.

She stepped into the salt-scented night and took a deep breath of the cold air. Moonlight glinted off the restless surge and ebb of water beyond the beach, and the air was filled with the distant boom of breaking waves.

Trey suddenly remembered the borrowed shirt and slipped it off, handing it to her. "Lock the door behind me."

She nodded, hugging the shirt against her. In the months after Jack's death, that shirt had been her magic talisman, protecting her, keeping her from going crazy with grief. It had been the first thing she'd reached for when they'd called from the hospital that night, and in the weeks afterward she'd worn it to bed, able to sleep only when swaddled in its comforting folds. It had still held the scent of him, and even now, four years later, she felt so close to him when she was wearing it that she'd often find herself laughing at some remembered thing he'd said, half expecting to feel the touch of his hand on her arm or the warmth of his breath on her lips.

But its magic didn't seem to be working tonight. For one thing, the shirt carried Trey's scent, not Jack's, and although she couldn't say it was unpleasant, it *was* disconcerting. It still held his body warmth, too, but even that didn't keep the night chill at bay. The wind had picked up and was sighing through the big cedars that sheltered the house, making them moan and creak. The boughs moved restlessly against the moonlit sky, casting ragged shadows across the deck and the steps down to the beach, and she hugged the shirt a little tighter.

"Are you sure you're going to be all right here by yourself?" Trey's voice was quiet. "You had a hell of a scare tonight, and I still think you should call someone to—"

"I'll be all right." She spoke much too quickly and could see both impatience and disbelief play across his face.

"I wrote my phone number on the pad by your phone. If anything strange starts going on, I want you to use it."

"Okay." She nodded again, her voice a subdued whisper.

"And you know where I live." He inclined his head; a corner of his beach house was just visible through the trees, silhouetted against the sky. He looked down at her seriously. "I mean it, Linn. Don't take any chances. Independence is great, but there's such a thing as carrying it too far."

For some reason it nearly made her smile. He thought he knew what was going on, but he didn't. He thought it was about a drunk and a woman on a lonely stretch of beach, but things were a lot more complicated than that, a lot more dangerous. If he had any idea of the secret she was hiding, of the real reason she and Nathan were out here, trying to disappear into the crowds of summer people, he'd wish he had never ventured off his sun deck to play hero tonight.

An owl hooted in the darkness and she started slightly. Trey lifted his head like a stag scenting the wind and gave the moon-silvered beach and trees a sweeping look. He didn't seem in any hurry to leave and Linn found herself half wishing he wouldn't.

She shook off the thought, realizing he was once again gazing at her thoughtfully. His face was hard-edged in the darkness and moonlight cascaded across his bare shoulders, making his long, wind-tangled hair gleam blue-black and catching the glint of gold in his left ear.

For half an instant it wasn't Trey Hollister standing there at all, but someone out of a different age, a Barbary pirate, who had just come ashore seeking a resting place for himself and his weary crew after months at sea. In that moment it wouldn't have surprised her in the least to look beyond him and see his ship at anchor in the bay, to imagine her decks stained with blood and her hold fat with plunder. He'd have brought some of it ashore to barter for food and drink and weapons: gold coins from kingdoms to the south and west, jewels, spices, fine silk and perhaps even a woman or two, virgin doe-eyed daughters of kings to be ransomed for whatever live flesh would bring.

And he was gazing down at her, Linn realized uneasily, as though he wouldn't mind adding her to his booty.

He shifted slightly, eclipsing the moon, seeming to draw closer without moving at all, and Linn stiffened, certain for one bizarre moment that he was going to try to kiss her. His eyes were very dark, full of tangled emotions she couldn't decipher, and once more she became very aware of the warm, male scent of him through the essence of sea and pine. There was an odd tension between them that hadn't been there moments before, another level of awareness so unexpected that it took Linn a moment or two to recognize its subtle but unmistakable sexual undertones.

It took her so by surprise that she simply stared up at him, more amused by the absurdity than alarmed. It had to be simple shock, she decided. Maybe there was some genetic synapse in every woman, automatically triggered by acts of masculine bravery, which produced a flood of hormones that would send her swooning into her hero's arms.

But she didn't have the time for swooning these days. Even if she *could* risk the chance that Hollister was indeed the hero he appeared to be and not a devious and all too charming dragon in disguise.

Just for a moment, for the tiniest heartbeat of time, she almost wished . . .

A black, furry presence suddenly squeezed by her and Linn gave a violent start. But it was just Murphy, coming out to see what they were doing.

Trey took a deep breath and shrugged his shoulders as though relaxing tight muscles. Murphy looked up at him questioningly and Trey dropped onto his right knee, wincing. "You're staying here tonight, old fella," he said firmly. "Stay, Murphy. And guard. Understand?" The dog whined and aimed a wet lick at Trey's face that he deftly avoided. He looked up at Linn. "Give me your hand."

Linn held her hand out and Trey meshed his fingers with hers. "Guard Linn, Murph. Stay with Linn and guard her." He drew Linn's hand down and Murphy sniffed at it damply, then licked her fingers and looked up at her with a sharp bark. "Guard, Murph. Guard Linn and Nathan. Got it?"

The big dog threw his head up and gave a series of deep-chested barks, then rubbed his face against Linn's blue-jeaned leg with a soft whine. Trey nodded and got to his feet. "Nobody's going to get near you two tonight," he said with quiet assurance. "Or at any other time, if he's within shouting distance. He stays on my sun deck or within the perimeter of the yard, but I don't keep him chained. So if you ever need him, just sing out and he'll be on an intruder like a terrier on a rat."

Murphy gave her free hand a nudge with his nose and Linn scratched between his ears. He leaned against her leg with a sigh, tail thumping on the wooden decking. Trey was still holding her other hand and to Linn's surprise, Murphy reached out and took his master's wrist between his huge jaws and gently but firmly pulled.

Trey gave a snort. "Murph, you bonehead, you're supposed to be protecting her from *bad* guys, not from me."

"Maybe he knows you better than you think," Linn said dryly, her fingers still tingling from his warmth.

Trey turned his head to look at her, his eyes catching the moonlight, and for an instant he reminded Linn of that Barbary pirate again, dark-eyed and dangerous. "Maybe he does, at that," he said very softly, his eyes holding hers long enough to let her know that he, too, had felt the subtle electricity that had passed between them.

Then he turned away and walked across the wide deck. "Just turn him out in the morning and tell him to go home. He may want to hang around and play with Nathan, but if you're firm enough with him, he'll get the message."

"Does that work with his master?" Her words seemed to hang in the night air, and Linn regretted them the instant they were out. She should have ignored what had happened, or pretended she hadn't recognized it for what it was. Acknowledging it only heightened the unwanted intimacy between them.

Trey paused on the top step and glanced around, his gaze holding hers for a long, still moment. Then one corner of his mouth tipped up. "Good night, Linn Stevenson, or whatever your name is. Sleep well." He turned and padded down the steps and into the darkness.

"Good... night," Linn replied slowly, frowning as she ran one of Murphy's silky ears between her fingers.

What *had* just happened, anyway? She was so out of touch with the intricacies of sexual politics these days that she could have simply misread the entire incident and imagined something that wasn't even there. Were all the subtleties and rituals the same as when she'd been dating? Had everything changed during the three years that she and Jack had been married, or the four since his death?

Odd, she'd never given it much thought before tonight. She'd simply never been *interested* in knowing.

She still wasn't interested, she reminded herself firmly. She smiled at Murphy and gave him a pat. "Do you need to go for a stroll before bedtime, big guy? Because this door is going to be locked tight all night."

He seemed to understand exactly what she was saying and bounded back into the house with a wag of his tail, pausing to look around as though making sure she locked the door securely behind them. Then he put his nose to the floor and trotted into the kitchen, looking very businesslike. Linn followed him and put a bowl of water down, but it took her only a moment to realize he was just checking his perimeter, as every good guard should do at intervals.

He gave the door leading from the kitchen to the carport a thorough sniff, then continued his patrol, making a quick circuit of the living and dining rooms before heading for the bedrooms.

A sudden wave of exhaustion washed over Linn and she yawned, quite content to let Murphy do the rest of his patrol on his own. To her surprise, the horror of Rolfson's attack was starting to fade. It was amazing how resilient the human mind was, she mused as she checked the fire, closing the damper and making sure the screen was tight. Either there was a limit to how much terror one person could absorb, or she was getting better at handling the fear.

She yawned again as she walked down to her bedroom, pausing to glance in at Nathan. He was sound asleep, one arm thrown around the furry neck of the big dog stretched out beside him. Murphy lifted his head as she peeked in and she smiled at him, winning a wag of his tail. Then he put his head back onto his paws and closed his eyes, seemingly relaxed, although Linn had no doubt those big ears were listening to every sound within a quarter-mile radius.

Feeling safe for the first time in weeks, she smiled and went to bed.

It was the hammering that wakened Linn. And the sound of someone softly whistling.

She was out of bed and into her jeans and sweatshirt in one motion, and in the next had slipped silently into the corridor and across to Nathan's room.

He wasn't there.

Linn fought rising panic as she stared at his rumpled, empty bed. She was going to stay calm, she told herself forcefully. It was late—nearly nine—and he'd just gotten up to play. And Murphy was with him. Nothing would happen to him as long as Murphy was there.

The hammering started again. Linn looked swiftly around Nathan's room, then snatched up the tall lamp sitting on his desk, giving the cord a wrench to pull out the plug and discarding the shade. It was one of a pair of living-room lamps, solid brass and heavy as sin, and it settled into her palm with satisfying solidity as she moved silently down the corridor toward the kitchen.

There was a man there. He was standing with his back to her, dressed in filthy jeans and a ragged blue pullover, his stringy gray hair curling around his shoulders. He was bent over the kitchen table, seemingly engrossed in whatever he was doing, and Linn padded a little nearer, brass lamp at the ready.

"What the *hell* are you doing in my kitchen?"

A tape measure went flying across the room as the man shot into the air with a startled oath. He whirled around to skewer her with a hostile glare. "Damn it, lady, you don't go creeping up on a man like that!"

Linn stared at the clutter in her kitchen with a growing sense of unreality. The pane of glass in the window above the sink that Trey had broken had been taken out, and there were tools scattered across the table and floor. "Who *are* you?"

"Toomey," he replied with some annoyance, eyeing the lamp in her hand suspiciously. "Don't need that. Got enough light. Just fixin' the window."

Linn stared at the mess on the table, then at him. "How did you get in?"

"Key, a' course." He gave her a look that said more clearly than words that only an idiot would have to ask the obvious.

"Key? What key?"

"The key *he* gave me," he said acerbically, turning his back on her and picking up the tape measure.

"He?" Linn echoed thinly.

"Hollister, a' course." He pinned her with one impatient eye. "You gonna stand there yammerin' all day, or can I get back to work?"

Linn took a breath and set the lamp down carefully, resisting the growing temptation to pitch it at him. "Have you seen my son?"

"Boy's outside."

Linn gritted her teeth, wondering if Hollister had inflicted this man on her out of revenge or just as some macabre joke. The door leading to the carport was open and she walked outside, looking around for Nathan and Murphy. They were nowhere to be seen, and she felt the familiar panic starting to build, but refused to give in to it.

She walked around to the deck and stood on the top step, staring intently through the trees to the beach. The tide was out and the pale sand seemed to run on for miles, glinting damply in the hot morning sun. And then she saw them—a small boy and a big dog, playing in the sand near the high-tide line.

Her heart gave a thump of relief and she ran down the steps lightly, pausing for a moment under the big trees at the bottom. It was cool in the shadows, and it took her eyes a moment to adjust to the sudden dimness as she made her way along the short, root-strewn path to the sand.

The wide beach was hot and bare and completely empty, except for Nathan and Hollister's big dog. They were racing around in ever-widening circles, involved in some game that seemed to involve a piece of driftwood and a good deal of wrestling and shouting and running. Nathan's cheeks were flushed and he was laughing, the sound of his young voice rising above the muted roar of the surf.

How long had it been since she'd heard him laugh with such happy abandon? Damn Guillermo Santos!

And damn Rodrigo Valencia, too, she found herself thinking with unaccustomed heat. What had ever possessed him to play the hero, anyway? And why couldn't Kathy have married a banker or an accountant or some other peaceful, sane man instead of the dashingly handsome Latino who looked more like a border bandit than the Miami vice cop he was?

It was Rod's single-minded dedication to law and order that had put them all in this danger: his wife and himself in hiding, literally running for their lives, their son smuggled out of Miami to Linn's Fort Lauderdale home. And from there to a wild, windswept beach on Vancouver Island, still in danger from the Colombian drug lord who was trying to kill both his father and Kathy.

Linn caught the anger and swallowed it. Rod couldn't help being a good cop—she knew all about that, being a cop's daughter herself. And she *had* volunteered to take Nathan; it wasn't as though she'd been coerced into it. All she had to do was keep him safe until Santos's court date, when Rod's testimony would put him away for good. Then the danger would be over.

Murphy's excited barking distracted her from her brooding, and she shook the mood off. She smiled as Murphy snatched up the driftwood and took off with Nathan in hot, noisy pursuit, and for half a moment she was tempted to let them continue playing. It had been too long since she'd seen Nathan so carefree and happy, the constant fear momentarily forgotten.

But she couldn't afford to get careless. One slip, that was all it would take. Santos's men could be anywhere....

She was just going to step into the sand when the tall form moved out of the shadows in front of her; a strong hand gently encircled her wrist.

"Leave him," a quiet voice said. "He's all right."

Linn recoiled so violently that she stumbled over a loop of exposed root and would have fallen if the hand holding her wrist hadn't held her upright. She snatched instinctively for support and grabbed a handful of soft chambray shirting, and in the next instant found herself in the circle of Trey Hollister's very competent embrace.

Chapter 4

"D-damn you!" she managed to gasp, her heart cartwheeling with shock. "You scared me half to death!"

"Sorry," he murmured. "I thought you saw me standing here."

"Well, I didn't!" She closed her eyes for an instant, trying to catch her breath, then realized she was still clutching his shirt-front. She released the fabric and stepped away from his supporting arm. "What are you doing here, anyway? And why is there a perfectly horrible little man in my kitchen who says you let him in with a key?"

"That's Toomey—sort of a local jack-of-all-trades." Trey let his fingers slide from her wrist and stood looking down at her, his dark, handsome face thoughtful in the shadows. "He's replacing the glass in that window I broke last night."

"Why didn't you warn me you were sending him around? And what are you doing with a key to my place, anyway?"

"I have a key," he said calmly, "because the owner gave me one—I keep an eye on the place when it's empty. And I didn't wake you this morning to tell you Toomey was coming in because I figured you needed the sleep."

"So you sent him in to scare me to death instead," she said with annoyance.

He smiled faintly. "I told him to wait for a couple of hours, but I guess he just got impatient. I'm sorry."

Linn found herself even more irritated by his sudden and unexpected civility. In daylight, she realized that his dark hair was shot with silver, the effect emphasizing his rugged good looks. And his eyes were the oddest color she'd ever seen, more pewter than gray, with darker flecks of what might have been blue in a different light. They were still private, watchful eyes, but they lacked the underlying savagery she'd seen last night, indeed were almost amused as they held hers; he obviously knew damned well he'd taken the rug out from under her.

"Excuse me," she said with precision, stepping by him. "I've got to get Nathan."

The sand was hot and dry and she curled her toes into it as she walked down to where the boy and dog were playing. "Nathan!" Her tone was sharper than she'd intended, and Nathan's head shot around in alarm. "Nathan, you know you're not supposed to be out here by yourself."

"But I'm not by myself," he protested. "Murphy's here."

"You know what I mean. Come on back to the house. You've got plenty of toys there to play with."

"But, Aunt Linn, we're just—"

"Nathan!" Her voice snapped across the sand, warning and rebuke both, and she saw him pale slightly at his slip. The fear was back on his face again, extinguishing the laughter and joy, and Linn ached with sudden guilt.

He was just a little boy, she reminded herself wearily, and little boys and big dogs were *made* to play with each other. It had been weeks since he'd had anyone's company but hers—and twenty-seven-year-old aunts, no matter how loving or well-intentioned, just weren't the same as a large, rowdy dog.

"Being a little hard on him, aren't you?" Trey suddenly appeared at her elbow. His voice was mild enough, but his eyes were narrowed slightly as he watched Nathan walk slowly toward them, feet dragging, face forlorn.

"Mother's nerves," she replied calmly, only half lying. "I guess I'm still a little shaken up by what happened last night, that's all." Which wasn't quite a lie, either. Although it was getting harder and harder these days to tell truth from fiction, so adept was she becoming at swathing every word in distortion.

"That stands to reason." He watched Nathan for a moment, then looked down at her. "Let him play out here for a while longer," he said quietly. "A kid that age can stay cooped up only so long. And nothing's going to happen to him. I've been watching over him."

"What do you mean?" she asked sharply.

"I mean," he said gently, "that I've been babysitting while you've been catching up on your sleep. I looked out about seven and saw him sneaking down to the beach with Murph, and I figured it wouldn't hurt to keep an eye on him."

He spoke as though it were the most natural thing in the world, but it left her momentarily speechless. It was like something Jack would have done, the kind of thoughtful gesture that was all the more precious for its honesty and spontaneity.

The rest of her anger was defused, and she looked up at him with a faint smile. "You must be getting awfully tired of coming to my rescue every time you turn around."

"I don't think keeping an eye on Nathan for an hour or two this morning constitutes a rescue."

"Maybe not, but last night did." Linn gazed across the sand, rubbing her arms. Nathan had stopped to play with Murphy and Linn opened her mouth to call him again. Then she sighed instead, and looked up at Trey. "I never did thank you for that. Properly, anyway. In fact, I behaved pretty badly, all around. You had every right to be angry with me."

"No." He eased himself onto the stand, wincing slightly. The scar across his thigh was reddened by the chill morning air and he kneaded it slowly, as though it was aching. "I was rougher on you than I needed to be."

She watched his fingers massage his thigh, remembering that swift, clean martial arts kick that had sent Rolfson flying. Remembering the way Trey had been limping afterward. It had been pain as much as anger that had made him lash out at her, she realized suddenly. The pain of scar tissue torn too far too soon, of damaged muscles and tendons pushed past their limits.

Sighing, she sat down beside him. "I'm sorry about that, too," she said quietly. She reached out without even thinking and placed her hand on Trey's. "Did you hurt it seriously last night?"

He seemed to go very still. She could feel the tension and latent power in his hand, as though he was forcing himself not to pull it away, and Linn very carefully withdrew her own.

"No," Trey said roughly, not looking at her. The unexpected touch had unsettled him more than he wanted to admit, and he massaged the deep ache in his thigh angrily. It wasn't her fault he'd ripped into Rolfson like some high school football hero last night. Hell, he knew better! The doctors had told him it would be months before the leg was sound, and not a night hadn't gone by since he got out of the hospital when he wasn't reminded of how close he'd come to losing it.

Maybe that had been part of his anger last night. He'd taken on Rolfson with a recklessness he'd hardly recognized as his own, luxuriating in the tear of healing muscle, in the crunch and pain of bone against bone. His right hand was swollen and stiff this morning, his knuckles cut and bruised from where he'd landed that punch on Rolfson's jaw, but even that had been worth it. He'd relished the sheer physicality, the violence, as though he'd been lashing out not only at Rolfson but at all those months of pain and anger and bad memories.

And in some strange way it had worked. He'd awakened this morning feeling better than he had in weeks, the gloom that had been hanging over him all but gone. It was like this after every tough assignment; the physical and mental exhaustion, the letdown that always followed weeks of intense physical activity and danger. It had been worse this time simply because the *job* had been worse. A few more weeks of R and R on this beach and he'd be back up to fighting trim again.

If he didn't wrack himself up first, keeping his mysterious new neighbour out of trouble, that was.

What the hell was it about her that had resulted in this sudden—and uncharacteristic—urge to play hero? Those eyes, probably. She had the bluest eyes he'd ever seen, so wide and clear a man could get lost in them. Or maybe it was just that stubborn way she had of looking at you head-on, just daring you to confront her on the obvious lies. Even last night, so damned angry that he could have strangled her, he'd had to admire her, too. A woman who'd fight that hard to protect her child deserved a man's respect.

He gave her a sidelong look and found her staring across the sand, a frown creasing her forehead, shoulders slightly hunched.

She looked small and vulnerable, almost lost, and again he found himself thinking of something wild that had been chased and harried and hunted. She'd been holed up here with her son like a fox in a den, licking her wounds and catching her breath but never relaxing, ever vigilant for the hunter with the gun she knew was out there somewhere.

Suddenly she gave her head a shake, as though breaking free of whatever she'd been thinking about. "I've got to go in."

She stood up and started brushing sand from her jeans. Well-fitting jeans, Trey couldn't help noticing, the soft, worn denim hugging her in all the right places, in all the right ways. As she bent over, he also couldn't help noticing that she wasn't wearing a bra. The heavy wool sweater she was wearing almost but not quite disguised the contours of an unrestrained breast as she brought her arms forward.

Of course, Trey mused: she'd just gotten out of bed. The first thing she'd have done was check on Nathan, and when she couldn't find him she'd pulled her clothes on and raced outside to look for him. That was why her hair was still uncombed, her milky complexion still devoid of makeup.

There was something subtly erotic about it, as though she'd just come tumbling out of *his* bed, all naked and warm and tousled. It took no effort at all to imagine her still in that bed, thick hair spilling like water across the pillow, those incredible eyes almost sapphire in the shadowed dimness of the room. And God, she smelled good! Even from here he could catch the scent of warm female skin and hair, knew instinctively what she'd feel like against him, every inch of her like satin. Satin and sin....

He caught the rest of the thought with rough impatience. Cool down, Hollister, he told himself irritably. The last thing you need is woman trouble. And son, you'd better believe that's what she is! One look at her, that's all it takes. Just one look and a man knows... trouble, gift-wrapped in satin and sin....

He shook himself free of it again and stood up, wincing at a jolt of pain in his thigh. He'd ripped something loose in there last night, sure as hell. It would mend, of course. They always did. But it was going to be reminding him regularly and painfully for the next few days that he was getting too damned old for this kind of abuse.

He knew Linn was watching him with faint concern and forced himself not to limp as he walked back along the beach beside her, smiling grimly at himself. They made a good pair, one of them refusing to give in to age, the other refusing to give in to fear.

Linn paused at the bottom of the steps leading up to her rented house, waiting for Nathan to catch up.

Trey had followed her, was standing looking at her now. "You know where I live. If you need a hand with anything, don't be too shy to sing out."

Linn nodded, slightly bemused. He was still gruff and abrupt today, but she had the distinct impression that he was making an effort to be civil to her. It touched her for some reason, and she found herself suddenly contemplating asking him in for breakfast. Or even just coffee. Nathan would love it, and she...

No. She caught the impulse in time, unnerved by how easily it had sneaked up on her. Loneliness was perhaps the worst part of this nightmare with Nathan, the one thing she'd never anticipated. It made her vulnerable and it could make her careless. She couldn't take that risk. She'd kept Nathan safe this long through luck, guile and not taking a damned thing for granted; it was silly to start taking chances now, just because she was hungry for the sound of another person's voice.

He was still looking down at her, a curiously thoughtful expression on his face. Even standing on the bottom step, she barely came to his shoulder, and he seemed much broader through the shoulders and chest than he had last night, much more solid. A real flesh-and-blood man this time, not a swashbuckling hero conjured up out of moonlight and desperation.

He was so close she could smell the heathery scent of his aftershave. His cheeks and square, hard jaw were cleanly shaven, the tanned skin silky and smooth, and she could see a faint scar running diagonally across his chin. It ended just under his lower lip and she found her gaze riveted there. His mouth was full and sensuous—remarkably so, she found herself thinking idly, for so rugged a man.

Trey damned near kissed her then and there. The urge came right out of left field, hitting him so solidly that it took every ounce of willpower he had not to cup her upturned face in both palms, turn her mouth toward his and kiss her so deeply and thoroughly that it would have left them both reeling. She was so close he could *taste* her, knew exactly what her mouth would feel like under his, could anticipate the first startled hesitancy, the slow yielding. And it wouldn't be any formal, chaste little kiss, either, but deep and slow and deliciously erotic, an enjoyable prelude to the loving they both knew would have to follow.

But he managed somehow to resist that tempting little mouth and everything it promised. "I wouldn't stay out here in the sun too long, if I were you," he said quietly, daring to brush a tangle of dark hair off her cheek. Her skin was as warm and soft to his touch as he'd known it would be. "You can pick up a wicked burn before you realize how hot it is."

She put her hand up as though to touch the spot where his fingers had lingered, but checked the movement halfway. "No," she whispered, her eyes wide and dark. "I...won't."

"That was a damn fool thing to do." Toomey nodded toward the kitchen window, fastening one faded blue eye on Linn. "What 'cha go do a silly thing like that for?"

"*I* didn't break the darned window," Linn said heatedly. She was still shaken by what had happened on the beach a few minutes ago, could still feel Trey Hollister's gentle touch on her cheek.

"Not talkin' about the window," he grumbled, opening a vast tool chest that looked as though it weighed more than he did. "Talkin' about losing your key. Woman should know better than to be careless with her house key. Just invitin' trouble. Never know *who* might pick it up."

"Mr. Toomey, will you please just fix the—?"

"Just Toomey," he snapped. "I'm not no mister!"

Linn, to her surprise, managed to restrain herself. Nathan was sitting at the kitchen table, supposedly eating his lunch, wide-eyed in wonderment at the stranger's colorful vocabulary.

"Well, it makes no never mind," Toomey muttered as he rummaged through the toolbox. "About the key, I mean. I'll be changing all the locks, anyway."

"Changing the locks?" Linn looked at him sharply.

"Says they're bad, the lot of them. Easy as cheese to get through. Went into town this mornin', he did, and bought a bunch of good ones." He nodded knowingly. "Need a blowtorch to get through these ones. Knows his work, Hollister does."

"Hollister?" Linn's voice rose slightly. "Damn it, he can't just—" She stopped, breathing heavily. "Just what is it that Hollister does for a living that makes him so knowledgeable about locks?" *And so handy at running other people's lives,* she almost added.

Toomey beamed. "Writes them Steele books."

"Steel?" Linn blinked. "He's in construction?"

Toomey gave her a pitying look. "Steele: Man of Action," he explained scornfully. His estimation of her, not high to begin with, had obviously dropped another point or two. "Must have about eight out now, and all bestsellers. *Steele Connection* is the best, I figure. 'Course, there's *Hot Steele*, and *Steele Vengeance*, and—"

"I get the picture," Linn said quickly. "Men's action-adventure, aren't they? Espionage, mercenaries and mayhem?"

Toomey gave her a sharp look. "Bestsellers, all of 'em," he repeated, as though nothing more needed saying.

"So our Mr. Hollister is a novelist, is he," Linn mused aloud. Strange, that didn't fit the image she had of him at all. He'd struck her as the kind of man more comfortable behind the controls of a fighter jet or a race car than a typewriter. Hollister, man of action. Yes, he definitely *was* that, all right.

"Wouldn't plan on going over there and botherin' him about it. Keeps pretty much to himself, he does." He eyed her with mild hostility. "Can't remember him *ever* letting a woman inside. House is kinda his private domain. Off limits to them of the female persuasion, as it were. Not," he added hastily, "that he don't like women. Fact is, he likes 'em a lot. Just not at *his* place."

"I *get* the picture," Linn repeated frostily. "How much longer are you going to be with that window?"

"As long as it takes," he replied tartly. "Window's as good as fixed already, and it won't take long to replace the locks." He speared her with a speculative look. "Whatever it is you want to keep out, I wouldn't worry about it now. Not with Hollister watching over you."

Linn just nodded, biting back her irritation. She was, quite frankly, getting a little tired of hearing about Trey Hollister and everything he could do.

Old Toomey might not know a great deal about women, Linn had to admit that evening, but he certainly knew what he was doing when it came to house repairs. She'd spent most of the afternoon out on the beach with Nathan, and when they'd come in, Toomey and his gigantic toolbox were both gone.

He'd done a perfect job of replacing the broken pane in the kitchen window. As well, it and all the other windows in the house had been outfitted with heavy-duty catches that looked strong enough to keep out bears. The three exterior doors not only sported new locks, but safety chains you could haul logs with. And to top it off, he'd even installed wide-angle peepholes in both the front door and the one leading from the kitchen to the carport.

"I don't believe that guy," she whispered as she tested the new lock on the sliding door to the deck.

"Who, Aunt Linn?" Nathan peered around her, munching a peanut butter cookie. "Mr. Toomey?"

"Our new neighbor." She put her arm around Nathan's shoulders absently as she gazed at the beach. There was a man down there, dark-haired and deeply tanned, walking just along the edge of the water. There was a big German shepherd bouncing along beside him and as she watched, he picked up a piece of driftwood and flung it down the beach. The dog exploded after it and the man continued walking, limping slightly, alone and thoughtful.

Suddenly restless, Linn drew the grass cloth drapes. She'd lighted the fire earlier and it crackled and muttered comfortably on the hearth; now she added another piece of pine to it, then wandered along the well-filled bookcases built into one wall. The man who owned the beach house was a psychology professor at the University of Victoria, and although he'd left the place filled with reading material, most of it was too technical to be of much interest to the layperson.

There were a number of novels, as well, book club bestsellers for the most part, but Linn had already worked her way through the few that interested her. She'd noticed the shelf of hardcover political thrillers and mysteries before, but hadn't paid too much attention. They caught her eye tonight, though, and she wasn't surprised when she spotted a familiar name. Smiling, she reached down and pulled the book from the shelf.

The cover was dramatic, black profiles on silver: a man's face, a smoking gun, a beautiful woman, a file dossier stamped Top Secret. The title, *Steele Connection,* ran across the top in black, no-nonsense square letters, and under it, in smaller print, the author's name, T. C. Hollister.

Well, well. She opened it curiously, not surprised to discover Trey's name scrawled across the inside below a dedication to someone named Paul. She flipped the book over and found herself face-to-face with Hollister himself.

It was a good picture, head and shoulders, shot head-on. He seemed to be staring right into her eyes, as though it wasn't just Hollister's likeness in her hands but Hollister himself. And the effect was slightly unnerving. The photographer had somehow managed to perfectly capture that essence of power and danger and raw sex appeal that was as much a part of the man as those odd gray eyes. It occurred to Linn that in trying to get a picture designed to appeal to as wide a range of readers as possible, he had probably come closer to portraying the real man than anyone had intended. Trey Hollister radiated competence and the kind of self-confidence that is often mistaken for arrogance, and there was enough sensual promise in his half smile to make even her heart give a little thump.

The bio blurb inside didn't tell her much she didn't already know. Famed writer T. C. Hollister, author of seven bestselling Steele: Man of Action novels, was born in Lubbock, Texas, and although an American, had made his home for the last six years in the isolated Canadian West Coast fishing village and tourist resort of Tofino.

An ex-marine who had brought home an impressive collection of medals from two tours of duty in Vietnam, he'd disappeared into the mystique and shadows of something called military intelligence for nearly ten years. His first novel, *Steele Gambit,* had hit the stands seven years ago, and after whetting the reading public's thirst, he had been writing ever since.

She looked at the back cover again. His eyes seemed to lock with hers, looking right through the lies and the fabrications to every secret she'd ever had, and she subdued a little shiver. You're good, she told him silently. You're damned good. But there's nothing T. C. Hollister, or even Steele, both men of action, can do to help me. I'm on my own.

She carried the book to one of the love seats bracketing the hearth and sat down, tucking her feet under her and drawing the knit afghan, the one her mother had made last Christmas, around her shoulders. Nathan was stretched on his stomach in front of the fire, playing with a complicated array of toy trucks, and she watched him for a moment, then opened the book at the first page.

Linn didn't know what woke her up. One minute she'd been sound asleep and the next she was wide-awake, every sense alert, ears straining to hear something in the stillness of the night. Frowning, she sat up and looked around the dark room. The wind had picked up and she could hear the cedars whispering outside the window, all but drowning the pervasive pounding of the surf. She tossed back the covers and slipped out of bed, reaching for her robe, and made her way to Nathan's room.

He was sleeping soundly, brows tugged together as though he was dreaming about something that worried him. Not surprising, Linn thought, tucking the blanket more securely around his shoulders. He was probably going to have nightmares for the rest of his life, thanks to his father's obsession with putting Santos away.

She made her way down the dark corridor and into the kitchen, checking the living-room door and windows on the way just from habit. Moonlight flooded the kitchen, and she didn't bother turning on a light as she ran herself a glass of water and stood by the sink for a minute or two, drinking it slowly. The cedar just outside the window cast a grotesque shadow on the far wall as it moved in the wind and she watched it only half consciously, idly thinking about Hollister's book.

It was good. Incredibly good, actually. The writing was much like its creator, blunt, hard-hitting and vitally alive, yet with a gentleness and poetic beauty in places that had left her breathless. His characters, too, were fantastically drawn, every nuance of human behavior revealed with a magician's skill. It was his hero, Steele, who troubled her. Steele, the man with one name who never seemed to linger too long in one place, the lone-wolf righter of wrongs who could handle any weapon, drive any vehicle, love any woman better than she'd ever been loved....

The shadow on the wall shifted suddenly, seeming to coalesce into a finite shape, and Linn froze, glass poised against her lips as she stared at the unmistakable silhouette of a man.

The boughs of the cedar shifted in the moonlight, running the patterns together like ink, and when they stilled, the shape was gone. Linn dropped the glass into the sink and spun from the window, her heart hammering so hard that she could scarcely catch her breath.

Don't panic!

She closed her eyes, fighting the terror clawing at her throat. As long as she didn't panic, she had a chance. How many times had she heard her father say that? *Don't panic. . . .*

Soundlessly she slipped across to the carport door and leaned toward it, listening intently. All she could hear was her own heart pounding. But then, very faintly, she heard something else. Footsteps, maybe. Soft, cautious footsteps, betrayed only by the rustle of the dried leaves and pine needles that had blown inside.

Something moved again outside the door, so softly she couldn't be certain it was even real. She eased herself nearer and put her eye to the viewer. All she could see was part of the carport and the tail end of her rental car, both distorted by the lens.

Then, suddenly, someone stepped in front of the viewer. Linn recoiled so violently that she hit her hip on the edge of the counter, and she gave a gasp of pain, clasping one hand over her mouth to stifle the sound. Her heart was pounding against her ribs so hard that she felt light-headed, and she had to struggle to catch her breath, staring numbly at the doorknob as it started to turn.

That was what finally galvanized her into action. She wrenched the nearest drawer open and snatched up the big butcher knife, then headed for Nathan's bedroom. Astonishingly, he was still asleep. For a moment she contemplated waking him, then decided against it. Toomey had installed double catches on his window, which, because of the way the house was built on the sloping hillside, was itself a good twelve feet above ground level. For the moment he was safer here.

She pulled the drapes tightly across the window, then quickly went across the corridor to her own bedroom and the nearest telephone. She'd jotted Trey's number on the pad beside her bed and she dialed frantically, swearing with frustration as she misdialed and had to start over.

Her hand was shaking as she held the receiver to her ear and she prayed silently for him to pick it up as the phone at his end started to ring. "Come *on*," she whispered urgently. "Please be there. Please, *please . . . !*"

She could just see a corner of the house through the trees, rising solid and reassuring against the moonlit sky. So near, yet so impossibly distant. "Please answer... please...."

She heard a noise, a twig snapped by a careless footfall, perhaps, or a branch hitting the side of the house. Then, with no warning, someone stepped in front of her.

It was a man, and he rose tall and solid on the other side of the glass, looming against the shadows and sky like something out of a nightmare. He reached toward her and Linn flung herself backward with a soft cry, sending the phone and the knife, her only weapon, flying out of reach.

Chapter 5

"Linn!"

The urgent voice, even through glass, was familiar. The tall figure leaned forward and gestured impatiently for her to open the window, and in that moment she was able to see his face as the moonlight fell across it.

"Damn you!" She pressed the back of her hand to her mouth to stifle a sob and managed to get across the room and fumble with the unfamiliar catches to release them.

But she was shaking so badly by then that she couldn't lift the window. Trey did it from the outside and eased himself in through the narrow casement like a dark, lithe shadow. "Damn it," he breathed, reaching for her, "I didn't mean to scare you. I thought you'd seen me out there...."

It was the most natural thing in the world to find herself in his strong embrace, his arms wrapped tightly around her. He was bare to the waist and his skin was smooth and hot and scented with sea air and clean sweat; his masculine warmth wrapped around her like a cocoon. He was breathing quickly and she could feel the fast, rhythmic beat of the pulse in his throat against her cheek, the taut, hard lines of muscle in the arms holding her so closely.

Those strong arms tightened and he buried his face in her hair. For a moment all the fear and the horror vanished and there were just the two of them, man and woman in a long, aching embrace that encompassed all that words never could. It was apology, forgiveness, comfort, understanding and a hundred other things; just two people reaching through the darkness for the touch of another.

Linn drew in a deep breath, feeling her heartbeat finally start to slow, and Trey stirred slightly. The pressure of his arms eased, and in that instant something subtly changed. It wasn't just a pair of arms around her, holding out the night, but Trey Hollister's arms.

And it was Trey's hands on her back, so real that she could feel the pressure of each individual finger through the filmy fabric of her robe and nightgown. She could feel the slick film of sweat on his chest, the rough pressure of the waistband of his jeans against her stomach, could even feel the hard, cold band of his wristwatch.

And it was a good feeling, Linn realized with surprise. It was solid and real and incredibly masculine; it had been too long since she'd been all wrapped up in a man's embrace. Much too long.

But this wasn't the time. Nor, perhaps, the man.

She drew back almost regretfully. She heard Trey draw in a deep, careful breath, running his hands lightly down her arms as though reluctant to let her go. "Are you all right?"

Linn managed a rough laugh. "You need a new opening line, Hollister. You ask me that every time you see me."

"Usually with reason." He glanced around the room swiftly, his expression preoccupied and frowning. "You don't have company tonight, do you?"

"Company?" Her voice held a tremor of laughter until she realized he was serious. "Of course not. It's after midnight."

"I meant all-night company." He was still looking around the room assessingly, then his gaze swung around and locked on hers. "You're a big girl. It's allowed."

For some reason it annoyed her. "Is there a local ordinance about overnight guests or something? And have you been appointed to peek in bedroom windows to make sure none of the local women are entertaining someone they shouldn't be?"

Ignoring her, he walked to the bedroom door and looked into the corridor. His back was swathed in moonlight, strong and well-muscled, a sweep of smooth, tanned skin that was marred by only one thing.

Linn stared at the grip of the small revolver tucked into the back waistband of his jeans. "Trey, what are you doing over here? And why are you carrying a gun?"

He glanced around, then reached behind him to check the gun. "Sorry. You weren't supposed to see that. I didn't want to scare you."

"Damn it, Trey, you've already done that! What's going on?"

His eyes met hers again and held them for a fraction of a second, then he padded across the hallway into Nathan's room. He checked the window swiftly, pausing to look down at the sleeping child for a moment, then he was on the prowl again. He moved through the darkness like something wild and stealthy, gliding from shadow to shadow, his moccasined feet soundless on the hardwood floor. Linn followed him silently, watching as he checked every window and door, tugging the new locks, testing the latches on the windows.

Jack had been like that. A perfectionist himself, he'd never entirely been able to trust anyone else's workmanship, and he'd driven her crazy by insisting on double-checking things she knew perfectly well were all right—only to discover more often than not that they weren't all right at all.

Finally he stopped, standing by the sliding glass door in the living room and staring intently at the beach. Linn went over to stand beside him, rubbing her arms lightly, chilled. "All right. You've checked every window and door in the place. Now would you like to tell me what's going on?"

He eased a noisy breath between his teeth and flexed his shoulders, looking very large and dangerous in the dim light. "Murphy woke me up a few minutes ago, barking and carrying on. I got up to have a look around. There's a car parked up on the road, halfway between your place and mine. Lights off, doors locked. But the engine's still warm, so it hasn't been there for more than twenty minutes, half an hour at the most. It's a rental—no ID inside."

"Inside?" Linn looked up at him. "You said the door was locked." His eyes met hers, curiously flat in the moonlight, and she realized very suddenly that she didn't want to hear an answer to that. "And you thought . . . ?"

"I thought I should drop by to see if you were all right," Trey said quietly. Her eyes were very wide and dark and her hair spilled around her face and shoulders, gleaming like black satin in the moonlight. She was wearing something filmy that wafted around her like mist, and he remembered how it had melted around his hands, what her skin had felt like through it.

For an instant he was tempted to reach out and draw her back into his arms, wanting to touch her again, but he fought it down.

"It may just be someone going down to the beach."

It took him a moment to realize she'd said something. He shook himself free of his wandering thoughts and forced himself to look out into the night, away from that upturned face so temptingly near. "Could be," he said doubtfully.

"Or kids. Looking for a place to... well, you know."

He had to laugh, looking down at her in amusement. "What does a nice girl like you know about things like that? I can't imagine you sneaking down to a cold beach to... you know."

Her mouth curved in a smile. "You're right. But it wasn't prudishness. I just never got asked." She gave him a sidelong look. "When your girlfriend is the police chief's daughter, hormones are no match for blatant fear."

Trey looked down at her curiously. "So. You're a police brat." That explained a few things.

She was frowning very slightly, as though regretting having said anything, and Trey decided not to push it. He looked back toward the beach, very conscious of her standing beside him. The moonlight was behind her and it was hard not to notice the slender, naked form silhouetted against the window. He could see the long sweep of her legs, the curve of a hip, the indented curvature of her back and shoulder. And the clean, perfect outline of one breast, full and lush under the loose folds of her night clothing, so perfectly detailed that he could see the thrust of the small nipple against her nightgown.

His mouth went dry and he forced himself to look away. "I... uh... think I'd better go." She looked at him in surprise, probably hearing the hint of desperation in his voice, and he managed a careless smile. "It's late. If anyone was around, Murphy would have flushed him out by now."

She nodded and gave him a faint, wry smile in return. "I hope you're not going to feel obligated to tear over here for a bed check every time Murphy spots a squirrel or woodchuck."

"I was in the neighborhood," he said easily, smiling down at her. Then he drew in a deep breath and headed back toward her bedroom. "I may as well go out the way I came in—saves messing around with the door locks."

"Thank you, by the way," she said quietly, following him down the corridor. "For the locks and everything."

"Self-preservation," he said carelessly. "I'll be able to sleep nights, now."

"Like tonight?" she asked dryly.

He had to laugh. "Tonight was a...test run. Now I know you're locked in tight, I won't be worrying about you." Which was a damned lie. Who was he trying to convince, her or himself?

Her bedroom was dark and silent, the curtains wafting gently in the breeze coming in the open window. The bed was rumpled, and he could see the shallow indentation in the pillow where she'd been lying, swore he could catch the faint perfume of her hair. In fact the entire room seemed filled with her scent, sweet and evocative, and he looked around curiously, taking in the cut glass bottles on the dresser, the laundry basket by the door filled with small, lacy things. There was something about a woman's bedroom he always loved, and this one was no different, filled with intimate secrets and female mysteries that no man could ever fathom.

The phone, beeping madly, was still lying on the floor where she'd dropped it. He picked it up and put it on the wicker table beside the bed, noticing his own phone number written on the pad of paper. It pleased him more than it probably should have and he gave himself an impatient mental shake, reaching down and scooping up the butcher knife lying near his foot.

He tested the blade against his thumb, then flipped it around and held it out to her, handle first. "You . . . uh . . . always greet your gentlemen callers with one of these?"

"My gentlemen callers normally use the door."

His eyes caught hers. "I tried the door," he said softly. "It was locked."

He heard her swallow. "I thought you wanted it that way."

Her voice was just a whisper, caught with something halfway through. The silence grew, enveloping them, and Trey found it difficult to breathe. "I don't know what I want," he murmured truthfully, his eyes locked with hers. "But locked might...be best."

"Yes."

It was a whisper of sound, almost lost beneath the whisper of the curtains in the breeze and the whisper of silk as he reached out and brushed the robe from her shoulders. She started slightly, not from cold or fear but from something else, standing very still as he drew the filmy fabric from her and let it fall. He ran his palms lightly down her arms and tugged her closer, putting her hands on his own waist, then ran his hands up to her shoulders.

Her skin was like hot satin and he slipped his fingers under the thin straps of her nightgown and drew them over her shoulders, lowering his mouth to the nectar of her skin. She flinched at the first touch of his tongue and he heard her breath catch over a tiny groan, felt her fingers flex spasmodically on his hips. He started kissing her shoulder and the long curve of her throat, sucking gently at the sweet, perfumed flesh, and she shivered as he drew his tongue up the side of her throat to her ear. Her breasts brushed his bare chest and he could feel the tips of them puckering, felt a responding surge of pure desire race through him.

It was crazy, taking it even this far, but Trey could no more have stopped himself from touching her than he could have stopped the moon's pull on the great oceans. He'd been going out of his mind for days now, dreaming about the touch and taste of her, knew instinctively that she'd sensed it, too. It was as though each had recognized something within the other that first night on the beach when their eyes had caught and held in the moonlight.

And maybe, he thought dimly, that was what all the anger had been about that night. Maybe they'd been fighting it even then, both terrified, for their own reasons, of what they knew had to happen. Was happening now....

He moved his mouth across her cheek and found her lips with delicious ease. They parted instinctively, welcoming him, and he ran the tip of his tongue along her upper lip. She captured it, drew on it gently, her own tongue touching, seeking. Trey felt reason start to slip and spin away.

He wanted her in that moment more than he'd ever wanted a woman in his life. Wanted to ease her back across the bed, slide his legs between hers and plunge himself so deeply into her that he wouldn't be able to tell where he stopped and she started. It would be exactly what they both wanted, what they both needed: pure, raw sex, with no apologies, no explanations, just hard and deep and driving, the kind of spontaneous, high-octane passion that explodes between two people with no warning at all.

It would have been effortless. She was as ready as he was, woman enough to recognize the moment for what it was, woman enough to enjoy it. She wouldn't expect a damned thing from him when it was over, no more than he'd expect from her, and they'd both face tomorrow with the knowledge that it had been a one-time thing, never to be repeated, never to be mentioned. Never even to be remembered, except for the occasional secret smile.

And, damn it to hell, it wasn't what he wanted at all.

He'd never dreamed he had the willpower it took to ease himself away from her, but somehow, in the end he did. Teeth gritted so hard they ached, he drew in a deep breath and stepped back from her, tugging the straps of her nightgown back over her shoulders. She grabbed his arm as though suddenly afraid of her knees giving away, and Trey slipped his arms around her and cradled her gently against himself, feeling the raging need within him slowly ease.

After a long, long while, he was able to unclench his jaw. "Damn it." It was just a harsh whisper and he drew in another deep, uneven breath. "That would be too easy, wouldn't it?"

He heard her swallow. "Much," she whispered unsteadily.

He drew back far enough to look down at her. Her eyes were still slightly heavy and her mouth, that incredibly kissable mouth, looked swollen and lush. "It would have been good," he said very quietly. *Still could be....*

Even in the moonlight he could see the blush spread across her cheeks. She lowered her lashes, managing to look both shy and provocative at the same time. "I... suspect it might have been," she whispered.

There was still time. It would be different now, slower and more sensual, probably even better. He could see the pulse at the base of her throat racing and ached to lower his mouth to it, to taste her, to feel her heartbeat against his lips.

But it was too late. Done now, their lovemaking would be something altogether different. Not less satisfying physically, but fraught with questions and expectations and a whole complicated array of social rituals. It would still be sex, but of a different kind.

The kind he didn't want anymore. The kind he suspected she'd never experienced but would hate fully as much as he. The kind, he reminded himself wearily, that left you avoiding your own eyes in the bathroom mirror the next morning, knowing that if you looked too closely, you'd see something there you didn't particularly like.

He whispered a weary, profane oath, then picked up her robe and draped it carefully around her shoulders. "Somehow, Mrs. Stevenson, I think I'd better go home."

"Stevens," she said in a voice so soft he almost didn't hear her. "My name is Linn Stevens."

"And . . . Mr. Stevens?" he heard himself asking, his voice very casual.

She looked up at him, her eyes filled with a tangle of emotions he couldn't even begin to decipher. Then, very softly, she said, "there is no Mr. Stevens. Not . . . anymore."

Trey eased his breath between his teeth, not realizing until that instant how important the answer had been. He smiled at her, then lowered his face and kissed her gently—and briefly—on the mouth. "Good," he said with quiet conviction.

Then he straightened and tugged the robe more tightly around her shoulders. "I'm going home before I get myself into serious trouble, and I want you to lock that window behind me." He turned away and stuck his head out the open window, giving a piercing whistle.

Murphy appeared a moment later, tongue lolling, panting hard. Trey pulled back and snapped his fingers, and the big dog leaped effortlessly in through the window. He stood in the middle of the room and looked expectantly from one to the other of them.

"I'm leaving him here tonight," he said in a tone that brooked no argument. "And in fact, I'd sleep easier if you kept him over here every night."

Linn shook her head impatiently. "Trey, don't be ridiculous. I'm perfectly safe over here—my God, Toomey rigged the place up like Fort Knox. I half expected him to dig a moat around the place and stock it with alligators."

Trey gave a snort of laughter. "We thought of that, but good alligators are hard to find these days." Then he let the smile fade. "I'm serious, Linn. Murph's been dying to get back over here to play with Nathan, and I'll lay odds the kid feels the same way. I can bring his food and—"

"No." Linn said it firmly, with enough steel in the one word to tell Trey that she meant it. "You've done enough for me already." Too much, in fact, she advised him silently. It was just too dangerous to let him get any more involved. If Santos's men found out Trey was helping her, they wouldn't think twice about killing him.

"I'll keep Murphy tonight, but I'm sending him home in the morning and I don't want to see him—or you—again." He drew in a deep breath to protest and she held up her hand, stopping him in his tracks. "If I need help, I promise that you'll be the first person I'll call. If I see anyone suspicious hanging around, or if I wake up in the night and need—" A slow smile brushed his strong mouth and she felt herself blush. "If someone tries to break in and wakes me up," she corrected, "I'll be on that phone so fast the wires will smoke."

"Promise?"

"Cross my heart and hope to—die." Bad choice of words. She frowned, swallowing a sigh. "I know you're just trying to help," she said softly, "but the most help you can be is none at all."

His eyes held hers intently and for a moment she thought he was going to argue, then he just nodded. He turned back toward the window, but something caught his eye and he paused, then reached out and picked up the book lying on her night table.

"Slumming?" He glanced around at her with a faint smile.

"Don't fish for compliments. It's good, and you know it."

"Good enough. But not what most women look for in a book. Especially for bedtime reading."

"I'll admit it's a bit gory in places, but no worse than prime-time television. Why didn't you tell me you were the world-famous T. C. Hollister, creator of the equally famous Steele, Man of Action?"

"The topic never came up." He stared at the cover for a moment or two, then tossed the book down. "I'm glad you're enjoying it," he told her quietly.

"He's...lonely, isn't he?" Trey glanced around at her, and Linn nodded toward the book. "Steele. There's always a lot going on in his life and he doesn't lack for adoring females, but underneath it all he strikes me as being a very lonely man."

He shrugged. "Typical loner, I guess. Happier by himself than with people. Finds it hard to open up."

"Like I said," she told him with a faint smile, "lonely."

"Aren't we all, at some time or another?" he asked softly.

"Well, yes," she admitted doubtfully, "but—"

But she was talking to herself. Trey had slipped through the open window and vanished, appearing a moment later to look in at her. Murphy had leaped to his feet, but Trey held up a restraining hand. "Murphy, stay. Guard." The big shepherd whimpered once, then sat down again and gazed expectantly at Linn, tongue lolling. "Lock this window after I've closed it."

"I'd rather leave it open a bit. I hate sleeping with the—"

"Lock it." He bit each word out, and Linn swallowed the rest of her protest and nodded. He pulled the window down with a bang and waited impatiently for her to flip the latch closed and lock it, then he rattled it fiercely. It didn't budge, and he nodded in satisfaction. Then in the next instant he was gone.

Linn stared out the window for a long while after he'd left, trying to convince herself that the hollow little emptiness she felt was just the residue of fear. And embarrassment. My God, she'd come apart in his hands tonight like a poorly knitted sock. She'd been her usual collected, well-controlled self one minute and a sex-starved nymphet the next, ready to toss upbringing and personal standards right out the window for one explosive night of sheer, uninhibited lust.

And he'd been right—it would have been good. Better than good. There was something about Trey Hollister that made her think he would be the perfect lover, as strong and fierce and uninhibited as she needed, yet gentle too, caring, even tender. He was the kind of man who would make damned sure his women left their bed satisfied, skilled and knowledgeable and self-confident enough to spare no effort to make their time together mutually enjoyable.

It was tempting, no doubt about it.

Yet there was no way she could fulfill even one of those fantasies. She couldn't afford the distraction, for one thing. How could she ever face Kathy and Rod or even herself if something happened to Nathan while she was indulging herself with her next-door neighbor? And there was Trey to think about, too. God help him if Santos found out he was helping her. Being on the run was bad enough; endangering innocent bystanders was unthinkable.

Just stay away from me, Trey Hollister, she whispered, resting her forehead against the cool glass. I'm more trouble than you need, believe me. More trouble than any man needs....

Somebody was watching the house.

Linn turned away from the window, rubbing her bare arms. She was sure of it now. That dark brown Chevy had driven by three or four times, cruising slowly along the gravel road that was the only access to this part of the beach.

It could have been tourists, of course. There was a path leading down to the beach just beyond her house that attracted the occasional carload of picnickers. Except that the weather today was anything but conducive to beach walks. One of the classic West Coast fog banks had crept in during the night, and the entire coast was cloaked in a pale batting as thick as flannel.

For that matter, it could have been sightseers. The expensive beach houses along this road drew realtors and would-be buyers and the simply curious like flies. But there was something about that car that set her teeth on edge. And then there had been that man yesterday. Just standing on the beach, staring up at her. He'd started toward the steps leading up to the house, but at the last moment had changed his mind and had wandered away. But she'd seen him much later, sitting on a gray, weathered log sticking out of a pile of driftwood, apparently enjoying the view but glancing at the house now and again.

She'd seen him again a few times over the past couple of days, never coming close or attempting to speak with her, but watching. Just watching.

Either she was under surveillance, or she was imagining things again. It wouldn't be the first time she'd panicked over nothing. But then again, she'd rather panic when she didn't need to than become complacent at just the wrong time. In fact, yesterday she'd been contemplating packing up and leaving. She'd even gone so far as to haul their suitcases out of the closet, but in the end she'd changed her mind.

Nathan loved it here, for one thing. Of all the places they'd been in the past month, B.C.'s Long Beach area was the nearest thing to home, with its wide expanses of sand and sea. The town itself was a plus, too, small enough for suspicious strangers to stand out like the proverbial sore thumbs, yet busy enough in tourist season for Nathan and herself to blend right in.

She glanced at Nathan. He was playing beside her on the deck, but not very happily. They'd had an argument not long ago over his going over to Hollister's to play with Murphy, and he still hadn't entirely forgiven her for saying no.

She should have let him, she supposed. It couldn't do much harm. She was certain by now that she could trust Trey, and it seemed cruel to keep Nathan cooped up here with her when there was a large, energetic dog right next door and a beach full of tidal pools and piles of driftwood to be explored. But again, there was that danger of becoming complacent and careless. And besides, if she let Nathan play with Murphy, she was going to wind up seeing a good deal of Trey. And there was a whole lot of reasons that wasn't a good idea.

Not that she didn't see him now. In fact, she saw so much of him that she was beginning to wonder how he ever got any writing done. There were the long romps on the beach with Murphy, the two of them tearing around on the beach right in front of her house. He'd glance up at the house now and again, and sometimes if she was on the deck he'd even lift his arm in silent greeting, but to her relief he never showed the slightest interest in joining her.

At other times she'd see him on his own sun deck, sometimes just sitting reading, chair tipped back, long legs braced on the railing. In the early morning he'd be out there doing some complicated exercise routine, a slow, graceful series of moves that was half ballet, half martial arts. T'ai chi, perhaps, or something similar that he'd brought back from his tour in the Far East. It looked both beautiful and deadly, his lean body wheeling and turning, long muscular legs arcing up and around in acrobatic kicks that always reminded her of that night on the beach when he'd brought Rolfson down with one.

There were times when she could have sworn he was actually watching over her. It had annoyed her at first. Kathy had always been the one who turned to the first man she could find when things went wrong, not her. And there was something irritatingly patronizing about a man who automatically figured no woman could handle trouble on her own. But after a few days she started to find it almost comforting.

"Aunt Linn?"

Linn looked around to find Nathan standing beside her, arms crossed on the deck railing, chin planted on the back of his hand. He was staring longingly at the beach, his face wistful and sad.

"Can't we go for a walk, Aunt Linn?" he wheedled gently. "There's nobody down there. And it's been *forever*."

Linn had to smile. "Nathan, the reason no one is on the beach is because the fog's so thick you can taste it."

"I think it's neat. Kinda spooky and stuff. Like the Everglades, almost."

She smiled again and smoothed his hair with her hand, knowing exactly how he felt. They hadn't left the house since the afternoon Toomey had been over to fix the windows, nearly a week ago.

It was utterly still. The only sound was the constant patter of water dripping from the big fog-wreathed cedars, their lacy boughs heavy with the drizzle that had been coming down on and off all morning. Now and again she could hear the high, thin cry of a gull and, muffled by the mist, the far-off boom of breakers.

"Oh, hell, why not?" she suddenly asked aloud. Much more of this exile and both she and Nathan would need straitjackets.

That brown Chevy had undoubtedly just been sizing up property values, and Nathan was right, there wouldn't be a soul on the beach on a day like this. They didn't have to go far—just down to the water, where Nathan could putter around collecting tidal debris and she could stretch her legs and shake loose some of this nervous tension.

"You mean it, Aunt Linn?" Nathan's face lit up.

"Yeah, why not? Let's get into warmer clothes and grab some plastic bags for shells and stuff." Nathan's enthusiasm was infectious, and Linn felt her spirits lift for the first time in days. She walked across and pulled open the sliding door into the living room, Nathan bouncing along beside her.

"Hey, Aunt Linn, I got a *great* idea!" He looked up at her, eyes bright with excitement. "Let's go 'n' ask Mr. Hollister if Murphy can come with us!"

"Oh, Nathan, I don't think that's a good idea," Linn replied automatically. But as she slid the door closed behind them, she suddenly wondered if Nathan wasn't on to something. Murphy would probably love going with them, Nathan would be in heaven itself, and there was no doubt that *she* would feel a lot safer with the big shepherd playing escort. She hadn't seen Hollister around for a couple of days, but he was probably just busy with the book.

"On second thought, maybe it's not such a bad idea." She dropped an arm around Nathan's shoulders and gave him a quick hug. "It can't hurt to ask, can it?"

"Great!" Nearly vibrating with sudden energy, he shot down the hallway to his room.

Linn followed at a slower pace, changing into jeans and sneakers and a fleece-lined sweatshirt, then pulling on a heavy wool sweater-jacket. She tied her hair back into a loose ponytail, then grabbed up the paperback novel lying on her bedside table and shoved it into her pocket and went back outside, where Nathan was already waiting for her impatiently.

There was a path that led through the pines to Trey's place, but Linn took one look at the heavy, wet grass lining the trail and the puddles of rainwater lying on the mossy ground, and took Nathan along the beach instead.

Like her place, Trey's beach house had a long flight of steps leading up from the beach. As they trudged up, trailing sand, Murphy suddenly appeared at the top. He uttered a bay of alarm that rose to a series of formidable barks and then, suddenly realizing who it was, he bounded down toward them, wriggling with embarrassed pleasure.

He shoved his broad head under Linn's hand for a pat, then swarmed over Nathan with a yelp of delight. Laughing, Linn squeezed by them and climbed the last three steps to the deck.

Trey was standing in the sliding door leading into the house, almost as though he'd been expecting her. He was leaning comfortably against the frame, one arm braced against the open door, the other holding a coffee mug. Barefoot, his hair gently tousled as though he'd just run his hand through it—or had just gotten out of bed—he was dressed in old jeans and a sloppy grape-colored sweatshirt with University of Texas written across it. And he looked, she thought idly, like every woman's fantasy come true.

"So. It *is* really you." He gave her a half smile. "When I looked out and saw you at the bottom of my deck, I thought I must be dreaming."

"Yes, it's really me." She smiled and tucked her hands into the pockets of her jeans, suddenly self-conscious. "I...uh, hope I didn't interrupt your writing or anything. I guess I should have called first. . . ."

"I wish all my interruptions were half as attractive," he told her with that same lazy half smile, "and half as welcome."

It was ridiculous, but Linn swore she could feel herself blushing. Trey eased himself away from the door frame and motioned her inside. "How about a cup of coffee?"

Linn shook her head, recalling what old Toomey had said about Trey never inviting people into his home. "No, really, I can't stay." She gestured a bit awkwardly. "Actually, I just dropped over to ask you a favor."

"Ask away."

"Nathan and I are going for a walk and . . . well, it was Nathan's idea, really, but we wondered if Murphy might enjoy a romp."

Trey nodded slowly, eyes thoughtful as they held hers. "A little wet for a walk, isn't it?"

"A little. But Nathan's got cabin fever, and I thought a walk would do us both good. Besides," she added, looking out over the fog-shrouded beach. "I love a day like this. It's so peaceful and still."

And deserted. It was as though he'd said it aloud, and in the moment his eyes caught hers, Linn knew they were both thinking the same thing. *Rolfson.*

"Taking Murphy is a good idea," he said quietly, his eyes holding hers. Then suddenly he smiled. "But how about a two-for-one deal? Could I talk you into taking me for a walk, too?"

"You?" Linn blinked in surprise.

"Nathan's not the only one with cabin fever. I just got back from two days in New York and could do with a romp on the beach myself."

Linn looked at him suspiciously. "You're not suggesting this just because you think I need protecting or something, are you? Because if you are, you—"

"Hey." Trey held up his hand, gray eyes serious. "There are no ulterior motives at work here, trust me. I've just spent two days with a literary agent and my publisher, hammering out a new contract. And I've spent the entire morning sorting through sixty pages of fine print and legalese, trying to figure out who's got who by the throat. Believe me, I need a break. If you don't want me to come with you, just say so."

Linn actually had her mouth half-open to tell him just that when she suddenly realized she'd be lying. "No," she said quietly. "It's all right. I just didn't want you wasting time keeping an eye on me when you should be working, that's all."

"Keeping an eye on you is *anything* but a waste of time," he said very quietly.

Linn's heart gave a peculiar little leap. "Are you flirting with me, Mr. Hollister?" she asked lightly.

"Absolutely," he said with a raking grin. "Though I don't know why I bother—it doesn't get me anywhere but in trouble."

"Which is exactly where it's going to get you this time if you're not careful," she advised him with a careless laugh. "And if you're serious about coming with us, you'd better hurry up. The natives are getting restless." She nodded toward the bottom of the steps where Nathan and Murphy were playing, obviously impatient to be underway.

"Five minutes. Come in and wait."

She wrinkled her nose, pointing to her wet, sandy feet. "I'd better not."

Trey laughed. "The reason they call this a beach house is because it's built on a beach. And a sandy floor is the small price I pay for the view. There's fresh coffee in the kitchen if you'd like a cup."

He disappeared into the house, leaving the door open, and after a moment of indecision, Linn kicked off her wet shoes. She slapped as much sand from her cuffs as she could, then stepped through the door and pulled it closed behind her.

Chapter 6

The first thing she saw was the raven.

Perched on the back of a wooden chair on the far side of the room, it was huge and glossy black. It glared at her malevolently and stomped back and forth, then opened its huge beak and gave a raucous shriek.

A combination of living and dining room, the space was huge, a full two stories high at the front, with open beams and a loft across the back. The entire front of the house was glass, and opposite the windows was a massive, free-standing fieldstone fireplace that separated the living area from the large kitchen that Linn could see beyond. It was rustic and comfortable and overwhelmingly masculine, upholstered in leather and tweed, with lots of tables and lamps and bright Navaho rugs.

The walls were covered with oil paintings and watercolors, many of which were the work of local artists, by the look of them. There were other pieces of artwork as well: stone carvings, a big wall hanging of woven leather strips decorated with fur and feathers and a collection of native wood carvings that would have fitted comfortably in any museum in the world.

There was a sudden whisper of wind right above her head and she recoiled as the raven glided past on huge, silent wings. It banked sharply and landed lightly on the mantel above the fireplace, fixing her with a beady stare. She eyed the creature mistrustfully as it clacked its huge, razor-edged beak, then it stretched its neck and gave a couple of loud, shrill caws.

"I see you've met Poe," came an amused voice from behind Linn. "I should have warned you about him. He can be a little unnerving at first."

Linn uttered a peal of delighted laughter and turned to look at Trey. "My mother used to keep budgies, and I had a friend years ago who had parrots, but you are the only person I've ever met with a pet raven!"

"Poe's not a pet," he said with a smile. "He's a watch bird. If I'd thought you could handle the racket, I would have sent *him* over to stay with you the other night instead of Murphy." He reached out and stroked the big bird's glossy head. Poe preened himself like a cat, clacking his beak softly. "Actually, he's a damned fraud. Bribe him with an oatmeal cookie and he'll let you strip the house bare."

As though to prove Trey's point, Poe hopped over to sit on his shoulder, trilling like a pigeon. Linn very tentatively reached up and he ducked his head toward her outstretched fingers, then clacked in pleasure as she stroked the smooth, glossy feathers.

"I found him in a pile of driftwood last spring with a broken wing and a half dozen BB pellets in him—some damned idiot had been taking potshots at him just for target practice, I guess. He surprised both of us by surviving, and he's been hanging around making a nuisance of himself ever since."

"I hate to sound unadventurous," Linn said with a laugh, "but is he housebroken?"

"Absolutely. I leave a kitchen window open and he comes and goes—usually to eat Murphy's food, but I think he enjoys dropping in now and again just to see what he can steal." He glanced at her small gold stud earrings. "Watch those earrings, by the way. He loves anything shiny. He'll rob you blind and leave a pinecone or a dead beetle in return."

"Oh, terrific," Linn said with another peal of laughter. She was stroking the downy feathers on the underside of Poe's throat and beak and the big bird was crooning like a baby, eyes closed.

"That's nice," Trey said softly. When Linn looked at him questioningly, he smiled. "Hearing you laugh. It's the first real laugh I've heard since we met."

That flustered her, for no particular reason. She avoided Trey's eyes and concentrated on petting Poe. "I guess I've had a lot on my mind," she said carelessly. No need to tell him the rest, she decided: that there was something about Trey Hollister that made her feel safe and out of danger. That when she was with him, she could feel the leaden cloud of constant worry lift, feel *able* to laugh.

She gave Poe one last pat on his broad head, then looked at Trey. "Ready?"

Murphy and the boy were waiting for them at the bottom of the steps. As Trey and Linn started down, Poe spread his shimmering black wings and sailed off Trey's shoulder to dive-bomb Murphy. The shepherd made a futile leap, jaws snapping on empty air, then yipping in frustration, stood watching the raven sweep through the trees.

"What a great crow!" Nathan exclaimed in astonishment.

"Almost," Trey said with a smile. "Poe's a raven. Do you know anything about Indian legends, Nat?"

"I know some stuff," Nathan replied happily, hopping a little to keep up with Trey's long strides. "But not about ravens."

As they started across the sand, the fog curling around them like dragon's breath, Linn smiled. She wasn't the only one who found Trey Hollister easy company. Nathan missed his father terribly, and although Trey certainly wasn't any Rodrigo Valencia—at least in Nathan's eyes—he was adult and male and plenty of fun. And he had a dog, which in itself is pretty wonderful when you're five years old and your world has been turned upside down.

"The local Indians call the raven the Jokester," Trey was saying. "And that describes Poe down to the last pinfeather. He spends his days thinking up new ways to torment Murphy, stealing his food, sneaking up when Murph's asleep and nipping his tail or ear. And that dive-bombing routine is a favorite, although he usually glides in from behind and startles the daylights out of poor Murph. I swear you can hear Poe laughing as he flies away."

"I think he's neat!" Nathan gazed up at Trey worshipfully.

"So do I," Trey told him confidentially. "The raven's an important figure in West Coast Indian myth. He's sly and crafty and he loves nothing better than to cheat and steal and play tricks—

that's why they call him the Jokester. Or the Trickster. And he's supposed to have supernatural powers. Another name for him is the Transformer, because he can transform or change himself into other shapes, pretending to be something he isn't. According to the legends, the Raven created the world, then he put the sun and moon in the sky, filled the rivers and sea with fish, then changed the people into various animals."

Nathan grinned with delight, and galloped off ahead. "Hey, Murphy! Let's go see where he went!"

"Nathan, don't you go too far," Linn called after him. "I don't want you to get lost in this fog!"

"Murphy'll look after him," Trey said quietly. "This is supposed to be a relaxing walk, remember?"

She laughed quietly and shoved her hands into her pockets, taking a deep breath of foggy air. "You're right," she said with a grin. "Time off. It seems like forever since I've wandered down to this end of the beach."

You've been afraid of getting too far from home, he told her silently. *Afraid of turning around on a lonely stretch of beach and seeing whoever you're running from standing behind you. Afraid of getting trapped out here.*

She looked so relaxed and happy that Trey found himself smiling for no particular reason, glad that he'd decided on the spur of the minute to come with her.

He hadn't been entirely lying when he'd told her he needed a few hours off. He, his agent and his publisher had spent two days slogging through the intricacies of his new contract. There had been dozens of trick clauses to be ironed out, compromises to be made, a little bit of old-fashioned horse trading to be done. In the end it had probably been worth it. But at the moment he was wrung out.

He flexed his shoulders to loosen the muscles across them and took a deep breath of fog-damp air, feeling it curl down his throat, as thick as candy floss. The tide was full and there was a strong surf running, the water surging in, then back out again like the inhalations of some giant beast. Massive gray breakers roared toward them out of the fog to pile up on the lower beach and send cascades of foaming water hissing within inches of their feet.

They walked in companionable silence. Nathan and Murphy hurtled back and forth like two juggernauts, half-wild with the excitement of sudden freedom.

"It's hard to tell which of those two gets more enjoyment out of the other," Trey said with a lazy smile.

"Poor Nathan's got a lot of energy to run off. He's been bottled up all week."

He avoided asking the obvious question, knowing damned well she'd clam up tight if she thought he was probing. He gave her a teasing sidelong glance instead, then bent and scooped up a handful of water as another wave broke beside them. "And what about his mother?" he asked, grin widening. "Does she have some energy to run off?"

"What are you—? Don't you *dare* throw that on me!" But she was laughing as she said it, already backing away, her eyes sparkling. And in the next instant she'd wheeled with a fresh peal of laughter and was pelting down the beach.

Trey took out after her with a whoop, sore leg and weariness forgotten, not surprised to discover she could run like a deer. Startled, Nathan and Murphy both stopped dead to stare after her as she tore by them. Then Nathan uttered a yell and started after her, Murphy leaping and barking and practically turning himself inside out with excitement at the lunatic behavior going on around him.

She'd have gotten away if he hadn't resorted to trickery. He moved between her and the water, and when she dodged behind him and into the deep, soft sand, he had her. He caught her easily around the waist and swung her to a stop, both of them nearly falling as they staggered through the loose sand. She was laughing and out of breath, cheeks glowing with the cold and damp. The clip holding her hair back had come loose and without even thinking about what he was doing, he reached up and pulled it free.

The rest of her hair spilled into his hands, as glossy as a raven's wing, and he ran his fingers into the thick tangles. They'd come to a panting stop, still clutching each other, and Trey looked down to find her face only inches from his, her eyes laughing up at him. Her mouth was red and lush, lips parted slightly, and he felt something pull wire-tight within him.

There was that momentary tension that always precedes a kiss, the awareness of each other that was half awkwardness, half anticipation. He could feel her breath against his mouth, the flex of muscle in the slim thigh pressed against his as she steadied herself in the loose sand. He tipped up her face and lowered his mouth.

He kissed her lower lip, the corner of her mouth, small, lingering kisses that were undemanding but incredibly sensuous. He moved his cheek against hers, his skin smooth yet undeniably male, then kissed her again, still gently, lightly. A slow, syrupy heat went spilling through Linn, so achingly familiar yet half-forgotten, the first hot tendrils of desire.

How long, she wondered dizzily? How long had it been since she'd been kissed—properly and thoroughly kissed by a man whose very touch made her blood take fire? How long since she'd felt a man's arms around her, had been drawn between silken sheets and into a demanding yet gentle embrace, had felt strong, male flesh cleave and . . . ?

"Please. . . ." She felt breathless and dizzy and turned her face away, too confused to even think straight. "I—I'm not sure I'm ready for this. . . ."

She could feel the tension in Trey's arms, the fight he was having to hold himself back. Her heart was pounding erratically and she felt weak and drugged, knew that if he made even the slightest effort to persist that she'd be helpless to stop him. Wished, down deep, that he would...that he'd just take decision and choice away from her completely. It would be so easy to just let go, to let this strange, erotic magic run its course and to hell with the consequences.

"Damn," he breathed against her ear, his own heart rate more rapid than normal. "Something's happening here. Something neither of us counted on."

"I...know," she managed to whisper, praying he wouldn't step back and let her go without warning or she'd fall flat on her face. "I'm...oh, brother!" She drew in a deep breath, wishing her heart would stop that insane pounding. "I'm not sure this is a good idea."

He gave a throaty chuckle, his arms tightening around her. "Actually, it's a hell of a good idea." He nuzzled the side of her throat. "I could make it good for you, Linn. However you want it, sweetheart. I can give you whatever you need. . . ."

"Trey, it's not that simple." She turned her face toward his, let her lips touch his lingeringly, aching for the taste of him. "It...just isn't a good idea at all."

"Not here, and not now," he murmured huskily. "But sometime soon, Linn. Sometime soon."

"No," she whispered doubtfully.

He heard the lack of conviction in her voice and laughed very softly, his eyes locking with hers, filled with erotic promise. "Yes," he told her quietly. "Oh, yes, Linn. This is definitely something you can count on...." Then, eyes still gently teasing, he let his arms fall away and stepped back. Smiling, not saying anything, he held out the clip he'd taken from her hair.

Just as silently, not even daring to meet his eyes, Linn took it and pulled her hair back again, her hands shaking so badly that she had trouble securing the clip.

This was crazy! She'd never fallen apart at the mere touch of a man's hands before... not since Jack, anyway. In fact, during the past four years, she'd found even the thought of being kissed repugnant. She'd forced herself to date a few times, more to keep her mother and Kathy off her case than anything, but they'd nearly all been disasters. Yet she seemed to turn into a puddle of overheated hormones every time Trey Hollister even looked at her the right way.

Or the wrong way, she thought with a sudden giddy urge to laugh. Whichever way he was looking at her, Trey was doing things to her that no man had ever done but Jack. And to think she'd almost convinced herself that all those old, magical feelings had gone for good....

She drew in a deep breath and finally managed to fasten the clip, then bent to brush sand from her legs just to have something to do. What she was feeling wasn't real. She was just vulnerable, that was all. Alone and lonely and frightened half to death most of the time. And Trey was... very special. You didn't have to know him any better than she did to realize that. And to know he could handle just about anything that came his way, which added to her feeling of security when she was with him.

Jack had been like that, the type of man who always knew what was wrong with the car when it wouldn't start, who knew exactly the right thing to say and when to say it, who could walk away from a fight and never leave a doubt in anyone's mind that he could have won. And, just like Jack, Trey radiated that kind of rugged masculinity that made a woman *feel* like a woman.

And it had been a long, long time since that had happened.

Small wonder she was having trouble keeping things in perspective.

Sometime during the last few minutes Trey had braided his fingers with hers, and Linn marveled at how natural and comfortable it felt to walk hand in hand with him. She glanced at him just as he looked at her, and they traded a wordless, sharing smile.

There were two huge pieces of driftwood wedged in the sand well above the high-tide line, and they strolled over and found a sheltered spot between them, where the sand was soft and dry.

Linn glanced around to check on Nathan. He and the dog were digging industriously in the sand only a few yards away; she sat down and leaned against one of the massive logs with a sigh. Trey dropped beside her, wincing slightly as he straightened his left leg.

"It's bothering you, isn't it?" Linn asked quietly.

Trey smiled grimly, kneading his thigh with his fingers. "No more than usual. The walking's good for it, but this fog and rain don't help much."

"An old war wound?" she teased gently.

"Something like that." He smiled again, dryly this time. "Let's just say I zigged left when I should have zagged right. Story of my life, in a way—always in the right place at the wrong time."

Like being here with me now, she almost said. In another place, Trey Hollister, and at another time, I could fall for you in a very serious way.

She shook off the thought, smoothing tendrils of damp, wind-tangled hair from her face as she stared at the water. She felt exhilarated and at ease for the first time in weeks, and as she watched Nathan rummaging through a pile of pebbles and shells, she smiled. "It's beautiful out here. Thank you."

"For?"

"For coming with me today. For showing me this." *For making me feel normal and happy and alive again, even for a little while.*

"Even if I did it for purely selfish reasons?"

"Well, you deserve it, too, after two days in New York."

"That's not what I mean." He reached out and brushed a wisp of flyaway hair from her cheek. "I did it because I like to see you laugh. And," he added more seriously, still massaging his thigh, "because when I'm with you I forget the ache in this damned leg, and forget I have a deadline coming up, and forget . . . well, just a lot of things."

Linn's heart did another one of those peculiar little cartwheels as his fingers touched her cheek and she forced herself to smile carelessly. "Speaking of deadlines, tell me about your new contract."

Trey had to laugh. "Basically it just says that my publisher is going to pay me an improbable sum of money to sit in my loft and tell a bunch of even more improbable lies about a guy who doesn't even exist."

"I hope that means I'll have lots and lots of new Steele novels to look forward to."

"Five, anyway. Don't tell me you're getting hooked."

"You'd better believe it!" Linn smiled at him, her eyes sparkling and warm. "As a matter of fact," she added, pulling a paperback copy of *Steele Horse* out of her jacket pocket and holding it up with a flourish, "I picked this one up in town last week. The woman in the bookstore assured me it's your best yet."

Trey smiled, shaking his head. "You're knocking my publisher's demographics all to hell and gone, lady. I spent three hours listening to his marketing wizards explain that my average reader is male, college educated, between the ages of twenty-six and forty-seven and probably, but not necessarily, with military service. They *don't* do well with women of any age."

"So sue me," Linn told him with a laugh. "Maybe knowing his creator makes it easier to be sympathetic, but I like Steele. I think he's lonely, and I think he deliberately keeps people at a distance because he's afraid of being hurt, but I still like him. The man has possibilities."

"Possibilities?" Trey arched a doubtful eyebrow.

"Steele's big problem," Linn said matter-of-factly, "is that he needs a good woman."

Trey gave a snort of laughter. "Sweetheart, Steele has nothing *but* good women."

She didn't let his words faze her. "*One* good woman, Hollister. Not a baker's dozen of gorgeous but deadly blondes . . . he does have a problem with blondes, doesn't he? They're either spies or double agents or in cahoots with the bad guys, and they spend the first half of the book trying to get him into bed and the second half trying to shoot him or stab him or blow him to bits."

Again Trey had to laugh. "I didn't realize I'd gotten so predictable."

"Trust me. He needs a woman."

"There was Sabrina in *Steele Connection*."

"Who got shot in Chapter Nine. That's the other problem with Steele's women—they never last long. I mean, this guy is the kiss of death! The bad guys kidnap them for bait to get Steele, or they step in front of a bullet meant for him, or—like poor Ashley in *Steele Maneuvers*—they just conveniently die of unrelated causes."

"I had to get rid of her before the next book."

"Like Dresden in *Steele Gambit*? She loved him, Trey! And Steele just walked out."

"She walked out on him," he reminded her gently.

"Because he'd made it obvious they had no future. He loved her—it was as plain as day. But at the end, faced with admitting it, he took the easy way out and cut and ran. Dresden may have left *physically*, but Steele had already left emotionally."

Trey looked at her for a moment. Then he smiled again, faintly, and looked out across the fogbound bay. "Maybe you have to believe in fairy-tale endings to be able to write them."

"Love isn't a fairy tale," Linn said quietly. "Love is the strongest, most real thing there is. Sometimes it's the *only* thing there is. It can get you through just about anything."

She frowned slightly as she said it, her eyes focused on something far away, and Trey found himself suddenly thinking of the expression on her face that first night, when she'd come into the room and had seen him in that old plaid shirt.

"He must be pretty special," he said quietly.

"He?" She looked at him, puzzled. "Who?"

"Whoever owns that shirt I was wearing the other evening."

A hundred emotions crossed her face in that split second: surprise, pain, love, hurt. Then finally, just an aching sadness so deep that it made something within him twist. "He was," she whispered, looking down at her hands. "Very . . . special."

"Was?" He said it very casually, hating himself for needing to know.

She nodded, still not meeting his eyes. He didn't think she was going to say anything, and then she took a deep breath and looked up. "His name was Jack, and I loved him so much I was dizzy with it. But he died. Four years ago."

Trey winced. He had a few memories of his own he preferred to have left undisturbed. "I'm sorry."

"So am I," she said softly. She was staring at the water, seeing something in another place, another time. "We'd been married for only six months when he got sick. We thought he'd get better, at first—I guess you always do." She smiled faintly, looking at him now. "It was harder on Jack than on me, really. It took him two and a half years to die. It's not...pleasant, watching someone you love waste away in front of your eyes, knowing there's not a damned thing you can do. But it's worse on the other end of it, slipping away a little more every day from everyone you love, knowing what kind of hell you're putting them through."

She smiled again faintly, her dark eyes shadowed with old pain. "I learned one thing, though: there are no atheists in the chronic care ward of a hospital. Everyone there is too busy making deals with God. You promise everything you can think of. Offer to trade places if He'll just make some of the pain go away. But..." She shrugged, letting her gaze fall again. "In the end you just live through it. One day at a time."

"Two and a half years," Trey murmured. "My God, how did you do it?"

Linn looked up at him as though the question surprised her. "I loved him," she said simply. "I'd married him for better or worse, had promised to love and honor in sickness and in health." She managed a wry smile. "Mind you, no one ever counts on having to make good on promises like that. But I loved Jack too much to turn my back on him when he needed me the most." She frowned slightly then and looked down at her hands. "But I'll admit there were times I wondered how I'd ever get through another minute of it. Especially near the end when he was in such terrible pain and the doctors couldn't do anything. I'd listen to him screaming for something to stop the hurting, and wonder how I'd ever get through it sane."

Trey whispered an oath, fighting a shudder of horror. "I don't know how you managed it, either," he told her quietly.

"I probably wouldn't have if it hadn't been for my family. My parents and younger sister were there for me every minute of those two and a half years."

She was, he found himself thinking, an extraordinary woman. How many young wives, six months married, would have found that kind of inner steel? And still be able to speak of the man four years later with such love in her voice?

A man would be damned lucky to find himself on the receiving end of love like that. It was the kind of love he'd only read about, had thought never existed anywhere but between the pages of a novel. Yet here it was, sitting beside him.

"I shouldn't have brought it up," he said quietly. "It can't be easy to talk about."

Linn smiled. "You didn't bring it up, I did. And I don't mind talking about him. Not now." Her smile widened, sweet with love. "It took me a long while, though."

Trey nodded, rubbing his thigh absently as he watched Nathan and Murphy playing nearby. "So Nathan's never known his father," he said thoughtfully. He found himself thinking of his own son. He, too, had never known his father, had never . . .

He shook it off and looked at Linn again. "Although it had to help you through some bad times, too. Having Nathan, I mean. At least you still had him."

Linn looked at him blankly for a moment, as though not understanding what he was talking about, then she flushed slightly and looked away. A frown pulled her brows together and she drew in a breath as though to say something, paused, then eased it out again with a little shake of her head, still not looking at him, the frown deeper.

And, suddenly, Trey understood. He cursed his own clumsiness, wondering how he'd possibly missed seeing it: Linn's dying husband hadn't been Nathan's father! By that time he'd probably been too ill to father a child, based on the few details she'd told him. So there had been someone else. Someone who had perhaps offered some sympathy and kindness when she needed it the most.

Trey glanced at Linn thoughtfully. She wasn't the type of woman who would turn willingly to another man to help ease the pain of watching her husband die. So whatever had happened, he'd be willing to lay odds it had happened only the once. And she'd have felt both betrayed and betrayer afterward, would have spent every day from that moment on filled with guilt.

But one thing was certain. Whoever that man had been, he had something to do with why she was here now, running scared and jumping at shadows. Why she never let Nathan out of her sight. Why he was going to wake up one day and discover that she had vanished into the night without a word, without a trace, gone from his life as mysteriously and silently as she'd appeared.

Trey found himself gazing at her, letting his eyes follow the curve of her cheek. What the hell was he going to do with her? She was going to vanish out of his life in a few days or weeks, so it was pointless starting something that could only end in disappointment. And yet there was something within him that didn't want to lose her. Something within him that cried out in the silences of his nights for her touch. For the kind of love that could go through two and a half years of nightmare and come through unscathed.

"Uh-oh."

Trey shook himself free of his meandering thoughts to find Linn looking doubtfully at the sky. Then he felt it too, the first cold drop of rain on his cheek, and he swore under his breath. He eased himself stiffly to his feet, holding out his hand to help Linn up.

"We'd better head back," he said with real regret.

She slipped her hand into his and he lifted her to her feet, found himself tugging her that one step farther into the circle of his arms. She stood there very quietly, gazing at him with those calm, sapphire eyes that seemed to draw him, tumbling, into their depths, and the next thing he knew he was kissing her.

Chapter 7

Her lips were wind-cooled and tasted faintly of salt, but her mouth was warm and moist and deliciously sweet. She opened herself to the first probing touch of his tongue as though, like him, she'd been anticipating this kiss all day. There was none of the awkwardness that sometimes happens, no holding back, just a slow, drugging kind of kiss that is usually the kiss of lovers or soon-to-be lovers, an erotic entanglement of tongue and breath and want.

He reached up and this time deliberately unfastened the clip holding her hair back, dropping it as her hair spilled around his hands, and once again he ran his fingers into the satiny mass. Her arms were around his neck now and her tongue moved in sinuous, silken swirls against his, drawing him deeper, promising more. Wanting more. Her fingers were in his hair, holding him fiercely, and he could feel the pounding of her heart, could hear the tiny whimper she made low in her throat as he thrust his tongue against hers and his kiss grew more demanding, more urgent.

He drew his mouth from hers and ran his lips down her throat and she arched her body against his, letting her head fall back, and Trey could feel the already thin threads of his control near the snapping point.

"I want you," he growled roughly. "I want inside you, lady, so deep I'm part of you. I want to lose myself in you!"

"Trey!" Her voice was a soft, breath-caught plea, more assent than denial; she brought her head up and started kissing his neck and throat, her mouth like flame against his skin.

He pulled her knit jacket open and slipped his arms around her, pulling up her sweater impatiently, wrenching her blouse out of her jeans. Her skin was velvet against his roughened palms and she gave a soft gasp as he cupped her breast, let her head fall back again as she pressed herself into his hand, the nipple sensitive and hard. He rubbed his palm against her, feeling the friction of the lace of her bra arouse her even more.

"I want to make love to you," he groaned against her mouth. "I want to fill you up with it, Linn. I want to feel you moving against me, taking what you want, touching me.... Touch me, Linn." He caught one of her hands and drew it down, cupping her palm around himself.

She whispered something in that breathy little voice and moved her hand slowly, knowledgeably, and he groaned, responding to her touch. It was driving him wild but he couldn't stop himself, couldn't stop her.

"I want you all wrapped around me, naked and soft and warm. I want you moving on me, melting around me. I want you...." He went on, whispering now, the words erotic and explicit as he told her exactly what he wanted and how he wanted it, made her whisper the same words back to him.

He eased his leg between hers and pressed his upper thigh against the softness between hers, bracing his other leg for balance in the loose sand.

She flinched, breath catching yet again, then caught her lower lip between her teeth and buried her face against his neck.

"It's been a long time, hasn't it," he murmured gently, kissing her throat, her ear.

She nodded, not looking at him, and he heard her swallow. "Four years," she whispered. "Longer even." She managed a tiny sob of laughter. "I feel so clumsy and awkward and out of tune with myself. I've forgotten how to...you know."

"Like riding a bicycle," he whispered. "If you've done it once, you never forget."

She gave another gasp of laughter, daring to glance up at him. "I don't mean . . . well, *that*! I mean I've forgotten all the social bits—the rituals of dating, all that stuff."

Trey looked down at her, holding her gaze. "This isn't a date, Linn," he told her softly. "We're way beyond that."

Her eyes widened slightly and he smiled, then drew her against him once more and nuzzled her cheek, moved his face into the soft curve of her shoulder. "Don't be shy with me, Linn," he whispered. "I want it to be good for you again. I want to show you what it can be like."

"But it's so fast . . ." she whispered, breathless.

"Because it's right," he murmured reassuringly. "Just let go, Linn. Let me take you there. . . . Just let yourself go and feel it all happen. Let me make you happy . . ."

He felt her fighting it and rubbed his thigh gently, firmly, between hers. "It's all right," he whispered, reaching again for her breast. Hard-tipped and lush, it filled his hand, and he heard her groan softly as he caught the nipple between the V of his spread fingers and gently massaged it. "There's nothing to be shy about. You're an incredibly alive woman, with all the responses and needs and wants of a woman. Just listen to yourself, Linn. Listen to what you need. . . ."

"N-Nathan!" she gasped, putting her hand on his wrist as though to pull his hand free. But she pressed it against herself instead, the muscles in her inner thighs tightening urgently around his. "W-we mustn't. Nathan—"

"Is about fifty feet away," Trey murmured, watching the boy over the top of her head. "He and Murphy are digging clams. Just relax and let it happen, sweetheart. You're so close. . . ."

"N-no! Oh, please . . . !"

Was she fighting him or herself or the memories of a man called Jack? Trey wondered. And if he took her the full distance, if he made her face those long-denied passions fully and without inhibition or holding back on this wild, windswept beach, would she ever forgive him?

"Help me," she sobbed against his throat. "Oh, Trey, I want you so badly. It's been so long. . . ." She moved helplessly against him, arching, straining as she sought release.

Trey put one hand on the driftwood beside him and braced his leg in the loose sand for balance, moving rhythmically against her.

"Just let go, angel," he whispered against her ear. "Just go with it... let me take you there. Just let go...."

"I can't! It's been so long and I... oh!" She clutched his shoulders suddenly, her eyes widening with shock.

Trey rocked his thigh between hers, watching her eyes widen even more, seeing the shock turn to sweet surprise, the surprise to wonder. Then she arched back with a soft, shuddering groan, her fingers clutching his shoulders. He felt it run through her, a deep, cresting tremor that made her throw her head back, eyes closed, as she strained against him. The second tremor was even stronger; it tore another cry from her and she clamped her thighs tightly on his, her pelvis flexing in tiny, convulsive thrusts.

Then she collapsed against him, sobbing for breath, and buried her face in his throat. Trey held her tightly, feeling the last of the little shudders work their way through her, feeling her slowly, slowly relax. She drew back after a few minutes, her cheeks flushed, unable to meet his eyes.

Trey gently lifted her face, lowered his mouth to hers and kissed her, slowly and lazily, reveling in the special intimacy they'd just shared. It had been incredibly erotic, holding her in his hands and watching her respond to his caresses and whispered, coaxing words. His own body was so aroused that it hurt just to breathe and he groaned as Linn's small hand reached down to touch him, half-tempted to let her bring him to the same cataclysmic completion she'd just experienced.

But he found himself wanting to hold back, relishing the near pain of it, the anticipation. He caught her wrist and drew her hand gently from him, eyes locked with hers. "I want to stay like this," he said in a gritty whisper. "So ready for you I'm half out of my mind with it." He pressed her palm against himself again, watched her eyes grow heavy-lidded, felt her breath catch slightly. "We're going to go home and we're going to have supper and put Nathan to bed, and then we're going to go into the bedroom and lock the door. Then I'm going to make love to you."

Linn closed her eyes for an instant, trying to breathe. As impossible as it seemed, she could already feel herself starting to respond to the promise in his eyes, his voice, his body. Passion had only been whetted, not quelled, and she wondered if it was possible to lose one's mind with sheer desire. "Trey..."

"The first time's going to be deep and hard and fast, and I'm going to set you on fire, sweetheart, like you've never burned before." Trey's eyes glittered, his husky voice more erotic than anything she could have imagined. "But the second time, Linn . . . the second time, I'm settling in for the long, slow haul. The kind that takes hours and only gets better." He lowered his mouth and kissed her lightly, his eyes never leaving hers. "I'm going to take you places you've only dreamed of, lady. And then I'm going to bring you back and we're going to start all over again."

"My God, Trey!" Linn sagged toward him, so weak-kneed she'd have fallen if he hadn't been holding her. She felt dizzy and breathless and shaken right to the core of her being; knew, too, that there was no way she was going to be able to deny him everything he was promising. It was wild and dangerous and completely crazy, but it was what she wanted, what she needed. She would worry about Santos tomorrow. Tonight there was just Trey Hollister. . . .

Somehow they got to her house, although the walk back was just a blur to Linn. A light, steady drizzle started coming down about halfway there, but all she could remember was the pressure of Trey's hand around hers and the way he looked at her now and again, his eyes smoldering with erotic promise.

Nathan wore out about the time it started to rain, and Trey laughed quietly as he lifted him up and carried him. "I think he's out for the count."

"Poor little guy." Linn smoothed Nathan's hair from his face as she followed Trey up the steps from the beach. The boy was sound asleep, arms locked around Trey's neck, his face serene and happy. "I feel guilty for having kept him cooped up in here so long. It's just that every time I thought of going down to the beach with him, I thought of Rolfson, and . . ." She shrugged, unlocking the big sliding door into the house.

That was only partly true. She'd thought of Rolfson now and again over the past week, but mostly it was Santos who filled her days and nights with fear.

"Do you want him in here or in his bedroom?" Trey turned to look at her.

"Bedroom, I guess. I'll just let him sleep for now and make supper when he wakes up. It seems silly to wake him now."

Their eyes held for a fraction of a second, then Trey nodded. Linn followed him silently, wondering what on earth she was doing.

Some tiny part of her mind kept telling her she was asking for serious trouble, getting involved with this man. Now. That until Santos was behind bars and her family was safe, she had no business losing herself in any man's arms.

But the need was too real to be denied. It had been four years since Jack had died. Almost five since they'd made love for the last time. She'd just turned off all the switches, and until now, until Trey, had all but forgotten what it was like to love. To be loved. Physically, at least. The deeper kind she didn't want to even think about right now. Couldn't afford to think about. When the nightmare was over, she'd sit down and sort through her feelings and find out what was going on. If it truly was love, she'd deal with it then. And if it wasn't . . . well, no one was going to get hurt.

She pulled back the covers of Nathan's bed and Trey laid him down gently. He sat on the other side of the bed and tugged the boy's shoes off, setting them aside, while Linn removed Nathan's windbreaker and heavy knit sweater. He snuffled and muttered but didn't wake up, and she smiled as she took off his socks and jeans, spilling sand. "I think he's gone for at least three hours."

"Good." Trey's eyes caught hers in the dim light, and he eased himself to his feet. "Don't take too long. I'll be waiting for you."

Linn swallowed, a little shiver of anticipation tingling through her. She brushed the sand from Nathan's bed and drew up the covers over him, pausing to rub a smudge of dirt from his chin. Murphy had ambled in behind them and was standing beside the bed, looking up at her, his tail wagging slowly.

"Do you want up here?" He barked softly and leaped onto the bed with surprising lightness, then lay down beside Nathan and stretched his head along his paws with a huge sigh, eyes already closing.

Linn pulled Nathan's door almost shut, leaving a wide enough crack so she could hear him if he called out, then walked across to her own bedroom. The drapes had been drawn and the bedside lamp was on, but Trey wasn't there. She slipped her jacket off and hung it over the back of a chair to dry, then took a towel from the linen closet, sat down at the dressing table and started rubbing her hair dry.

It was the click of the door lock that made her look up. Trey stood at the door behind her and their eyes met in the mirror. He smiled. "I told you it was a little wet out there for beach walking."

"It was perfect," she said quietly, trying to ignore the way her heart was racing.

"Almost," he said very softly, his eyes locking with hers. "*This* is going to be perfect." He moved slowly toward her, large and dangerous and male in the lamplight. He reached out and took the towel from her hand, dropping it onto the floor, and drew her gently to her feet.

He was still standing behind her and Linn watched their reflection in the mirror as he slipped his arms around her. He smiled, kissing the side of her throat. "Nervous?"

"Terrified!"

"Four years is a long time."

"Four years is forever," she managed to whisper.

The eyes in the glass held hers, serious now. Searching.

Linn held his gaze steadily. Then slowly, very slowly, she reached down and grasped the lower edge of her sweater, drawing it up and over her head. She gave her head a shake and her hair spilled around her shoulders, but Trey nuzzled it aside and kissed her just under the ear.

He started unbuttoning her blouse, his eyes never leaving hers, and when he'd slipped the last button free, he pulled the blouse from her shoulders and started kissing her, drawing moist little swirls with his tongue that made her melt inside. He slipped the blouse down her arms and let it drop, then slowly undid the hook on her bra.

Linn stiffened very slightly and he murmured something to reassure her, kissing her shoulder as he slowly nudged off one strap, then the other. Swallowing, she let the bra fall, baring herself to the waist, and she saw Trey's eyes narrow slightly as he studied their reflection. His hands were large and sun-browned against her pale skin; she watched them move slowly to the waistband of her jeans and part the metal snap and then, even more slowly, draw the zipper down.

He moved his hands back up, slowly, slowly, and cupped her breasts, and Linn had to fight to catch her breath. Seeing his hands touching her was somehow even more erotic than the sensation of roughened palm on already sensitive flesh. The chocolate tips of her breasts were full and slightly swollen and she flinched slightly as Trey brushed his thumbs back and forth against them. As she watched, the nipples grew hard, aroused as much by the sight of his caress as by his touch.

Trey's eyes glittered behind the half-lowered lids, and as he ran his palms down her belly, Linn swallowed again. He folded back the flaps of her jeans and started to ease them over her hips, revealing the narrow, blue bikini briefs she was wearing under them, and she closed her eyes as he knelt behind her and drew the jeans down.

He ran his mouth down her bare back, settling a little nest of warm kisses at the base of her spine, then starting to work his way up again as he straightened. The touch of his tongue sent little shivers through Linn and she let her head fall forward to bare the nape of her neck to his mouth.

She sucked in her breath as he cupped one of her breasts again, teasing the nipple with his thumb, and she arched her back very slightly, mesmerized by the sight of his hand as he caressed her. He slid his other palm down her stomach and eased his fingers under the elastic waist of her briefs. Linn stiffened and looked away.

"You don't have to be shy with me," Trey murmured. "My God, you're so beautiful, Linn. Don't be shy...."

She looked once more into the mirror, meeting his eyes. Trey's gaze moved down her body and she arched her back again, smiling, and reached up and behind her to rest her hands on his shoulders. The motion lifted her breasts as she offered herself to his hungry gaze, loving what she saw in those burning, silver eyes.

He inched the briefs over her thighs and Linn leaned back against him with a soft moan, catching her lip between her teeth as he ran his hand across her stomach and then down, fingers slipping into the shadowed place where her thighs met. She moaned again, her voice catching on his name, and arched back against him as that questing, gentle touch moved inward, touching the secret places he sought, leaving silken fire in their wake.

"Trey...!" The sensation was indescribable, so exquisite that she cried out a second time, remembering too late the sleeping boy in the other room. Trey's hand moved with wondrous skill and she relaxed against him, shyness gone, wanting only more of the magic.

She was only half aware of turning in his arms, of lifting her mouth for his hungry, urgent kiss as she unbuttoned his shirt impatiently. He helped her finally, wrenching off the shirt and flinging it aside, then struggling out of his jeans and briefs, all pretense at restraint gone.

"Hurry," Linn whispered, reaching for him, touching him. "Oh, Trey...hurry. Please...don't make me wait any longer." She slipped her arms around his neck and returned his kiss eagerly, cupping him between her thighs and pressing herself along the silken length of him again and again.

Trey's breath left him with an explosive groan and he kissed her hungrily, his mouth hot and urgent on hers; he lifted her against him, rotating his pelvis. He took one stride forward and reached out to sweep everything off the dressing table, then eased her onto the smooth, cool wood.

Panting, Linn tried to pull him down to herself, but he just smiled and ran his hands up her thighs, lifting her knees so that she was gripping him by the hips. Then he grasped her hips and pulled her firmly toward him; at the same instant he thrust himself forward, and Linn gave a moaning cry as he sank fully and deeply into her.

It was, as he'd promised, deep and hard and fast. Standing between her thighs, forearms braced on the dressing table on either side of her head, Trey made love to her with the driving, fierce passion they were both ready for, each strong thrust of his hips bringing them together as deeply as their bodies would allow.

As though a floodgate of desire had suddenly opened, Linn responded with joyful abandon, moving greedily under him, taking with the same enthusiasm as she gave. Her dark hair spilled across the table like water and she moved her head from side to side, lower lip caught between her teeth as she strove to catch the elusive wave he could sense building inside her.

He gritted his teeth, praying he could hold out long enough to carry her all the way. He'd been so ready for her that he'd nearly lost it all at the first silken plunge into her welcoming warmth, and at each long, cleaving thrust he was that much nearer. He concentrated on timing his movements to hers, sensing even before she did when that uprushing wave was ready to break. The rhythmic flex of her hips suddenly became erratic and she uttered a tiny inward moan, drawing up her legs and tightening her thighs on his hips.

He moved inward and down, holding himself there, rocking his pelvis against hers, and she sobbed his name as the crest caught her and swept her away.

He straightened and gripped her hips firmly in his hands and moved against her in a series of sharp, deep little thrusts, and a moment later everything around him simply exploded.

"Is Trey Hollister livin' here now?" Nathan peered suspiciously into his glass of orange juice, then extracted a floating seed with his fingers. Lifting the glass to his lips, he looked at Linn over the rim. "He's sure been here a long time."

"No, honey," Linn replied casually, "he's just visiting."

There was a movement at the kitchen door just then and Linn glanced up as Trey strolled in, looking very man-about-the-house in nothing but a pair of jeans, a good tan and a lazy, self-satisfied smile. His hair glittered with water from his shower and he'd obviously managed to shave, probably using one of her disposable razors and a can of foam that the previous tenant had left behind, she thought to herself. He ruffled Nathan's dark hair with his hand as he walked by the table, then slipped one arm around Linn's waist as he looked over her shoulder to see what she was doing.

"Blueberry *waffles*?" He drew her loose hair back with his fingers and kissed the side of her throat lingeringly. "Mmm. Not only is she beautiful and fabulous in bed...but she can cook, too. I think I've just died and gone to heaven."

Trading a private, sharing smile with him, Linn slid two waffles onto a warmed plate and handed it to him. "Eat. Nathan, do you have room for another one?"

"Yep." Licking orange juice off his upper lip, Nathan held his plate out and Linn slid half a waffle onto it. "If you an' Aunt Linn...I mean, if you an' Mommy get married, does that mean I can play with Murphy anytime I want?"

"Nathan, for heaven's sake!" Linn looked down at him in astonishment. "Trey is just a friend." Linn absolutely refused to look in Trey's direction.

"If your mother and I got married," Trey said quietly, "that would make me your father. And yes, you could play with Murphy any time you wanted to."

Nathan looked up, frowning, his fork poised over the waffle. "But I've already got a father," he said, obviously confused. "My real daddy's coming back, isn't he?" he asked Linn, suddenly looking upset and frightened. "Y-you promised he was coming back!"

"Nathan, it's all right." Linn put her plate down quickly and knelt by the boy's chair, giving him a reassuring hug. Brushing a cowlick of tangled hair from his forehead, she gave him a kiss, then looked down at him very seriously. "Honey, your daddy *is* coming back. Everything's just very complicated right now, but it will all work out, I swear it." *And if I'm wrong?* she asked herself brutally. If Santos finds Rod and Kathy and—?

She refused to let the thought even form, closing her eyes as a sudden, sick feeling washed over her. *Oh, God, Kathy, where are you? Be safe! Please, just be safe!*

She was aware of a touch on her shoulder and glanced up to find Trey squatting on his heels beside her. "Is something going on here that I—"

"No." She shook her head vehemently, refusing to meet his eyes. "Please, Trey, don't ask me any questions."

"I think," he said very carefully, "that I have a right to know at least one thing." He reached out and put his hand under her chin, turning her face so she was forced to look at him. "Are you married, Linn?"

She pulled away from his grasp. "Nothing's what it seems to be, Trey. I . . . I can't tell you about it. Not . . . yet."

"Damn it, Linn," he said with quiet intensity, "after last night, if you can't—" He stopped short, glancing at Nathan. He stood up, breathing heavily. "We'll talk about this later," he said shortly. "And Nathan, I didn't mean I was trying to replace your real father. Nobody could do that. But can we at least be friends?"

Nathan looked at him for a thoughtful moment, obviously still not certain he believed what he was being told. "Okay," he finally allowed doubtfully. "But my daddy's goin' to be back soon and then I'm going home."

Linn stared at her plate, knowing Trey was looking at her, his eyes filled with questions she just couldn't answer. She started eating mechanically, not tasting a thing, and the silence around the table grew steadily deeper. Nathan, seemingly oblivious to the sudden tension around him, started humming, eating happily and occasionally slipping a piece of waffle to Murphy, who was sitting beside his chair. There was no sound but the click of cutlery, overly loud in the uncomfortable stillness, and the foreboding heaviness of Trey's impatience.

Justifiable impatience, Linn reminded herself. If anyone in the world deserved to know what was going on, it was Trey.

Last night had been . . . magical.

There was no other word for it. He had touched something within her that hadn't been touched in years, loosing a passion so earthy and abandoned and reckless it had surprised both of then. Those few tempestuous minutes on the dressing table had just been the start, when she'd wrapped her legs around him and had simply given herself over to the pure physical pleasure of her own body.

They'd fallen into bed not long after that and had made love again, slowly this time, Trey being true to his word that he was going to take her further and higher than she'd ever gone before. They'd made love in the soft glow of the lamp for a long, long time, letting it build sweetly and naturally until at the end, when she'd arched under him with an indrawn moan of sheer ecstasy, she'd felt the chains around her heart break and fall away and had lain in Trey's arms afterward, swallowing tears of happiness while he'd murmured her name over and over.

Finally they'd gotten up and Linn had made supper, and after Nathan had gone back to bed, Murphy in tow, she and Trey had sat by the fire with brandy and had talked for hours. Until their eyes had caught in the flicker of the firelight and he'd reached for her hand and they'd walked down to the bedroom, saying nothing, turning to each other in the darkness of her room.

He'd slipped her robe off her shoulders and had made love to her on the big goatskin rug on the bedroom floor, then later making love to her again, in bed this time, teaching her things about her body and his that she'd never dreamed possible. Teaching her things about love she'd never known before, even with Jack.

And all the time the lies had been between them.

She hadn't meant it to happen that way. But the magic that had exploded between them had happened too fast and too strong to be denied, and she'd just never had time to tell him.

Damn! Why had she ever thought it was going to be easy?

". . . finished. Can I go out and play with Murphy now?"

Linn looked up blankly, then gave her head a little shake. "Yes, Nathan, go ahead. Just stay within sight of the house."

He nodded and leaped to his feet, grabbing his sweater from the back of his chair. Murphy went bounding after him and then there was silence again. She started to cut another piece of waffle, then put down her knife and fork, knowing she couldn't swallow.

Trey stood suddenly. He took his plate to the counter and set it down, then poured himself a cup of coffee and came back to the table, swinging the chair around and straddling it. He crossed his arms on the back, toying with a spoon.

"I was thinking of taking a couple days off from writing," he said quietly. "A friend of mine's got a big cabin cruiser that I can borrow. We could go down the coast for a few days. Get away."

Linn took a deep breath. "I—I can't, Trey." In one way it would almost be ideal. But she couldn't afford to be away from the telephone for longer than a day. Her one and only contact, Detective Don Rasky from Miami vice, had to be able to reach her at all times, in case there was news about Kathy and Rod. And she called him daily to let him know that she and Nathan were all right. He was the only link she had with her sister and Nathan's father. The only touch with reality.

Trey didn't say anything, but she could see a muscle pulse along his jaw. "How about camping, then? A couple of days up in the mountains, away from everything. No newspapers, no phones, no—"

"I can't." She just whispered it, staring at her hands. "Trey, please don't make this difficult. I'm just asking you to trust me."

"Trust you?" The words were clipped. "Trust is a two-way street, Linn. Why the hell can't you trust me with whatever's scaring you half to death?"

"Trey, please!" Linn got to her feet abruptly and walked to the sink, staring out at the cedars. She could *not* tell him. For Nathan's sake. For hers. And maybe, most of all, for his. "It's too dangerous," she said softly. "You have no idea what's involved, Trey. None at all!"

"Then tell me, damn it!" He reared to his feet angrily and raked back his damp hair with his fingers. "You can make love with me but you can't tell me what's going on, is that it?" He caught her arm and pulled her around to face him. "What the hell can be so bad you can't tell me, Linn? This is *me*, remember? The man you trusted enough to let into your bed last night. The man you trusted enough to let into your—"

"Stop it!" Linn wheeled away from him. "Stop badgering me, Trey. I will not—I *cannot*—tell you, and that's all there is to it. All I will say is that it doesn't have anything to do with you and me. I'm not married, I swear."

"You won't go sailing with me, you won't go camping with me. You're too scared to walk on the beach. When you're in town, you don't talk to anyone, you rebuff any attempt at friendliness."

Linn stared at him, feeling herself go pale. "You've been asking the townspeople about me?"

"I asked a few questions." He gave her an impatient look. "You're the original mystery lady, Linn. Naturally I asked around. Although it didn't get me anywhere. No one knows a damned thing about you."

Linn felt light-headed, fear a cold lump in her stomach. "Don't ever do that again, Trey," she told him with quiet intensity. "You could get me killed by asking too many questions."

Trey's gray eyes narrowed. "Who's after you, Linn? Organized crime? The cops? Just who the hell *is* Nathan's father, anyway?"

Linn turned away from him again, unable to face those angry eyes. She felt torn apart, half of her wanting desperately to blurt out the whole story, to lose herself in the safety of his strong embrace, the other half knowing she didn't dare.

There was nothing Trey could do to help her. And she'd already put him in more danger than she had a right to. He had no idea of the things the Colombians were capable of. No idea at all.

"I'm still waiting for some kind of an answer here," Trey said suddenly, his voice vibrant with anger.

"What do you want me to tell you?" Linn gestured impatiently. "I've already told you all I can!"

"Maybe you can start by telling me just what the hell last night was."

Linn just looked at him. "Last night was . . . what it was. Why do you have to complicate this, Trey?"

"Honey, I'm not the one complicating things," he told her in a soft, precise voice. "I just don't like being used."

"Used?" She looked at him sharply.

"Used." Hands planted on narrow hips, he stared at her from across the room as though daring her to challenge him. "You're scared, you're lonely—and I sure as hell was available. I can see where a pair of warm arms in the night would be hard to pass up.

Maybe a few hours of pleasant sex to make you feel safe and cared for." He gave a snort. "Hell, women have *married* men for less security than that."

Linn felt herself pale again. She stared at him, hardly able to believe what she was hearing. "My God," she whispered, "do you really think I made love with you just because you were *handy*? That last night was . . . was just 'pleasant sex'?"

His eyes locked onto hers. "I don't know what last night was for you, Linn. But I do know I'm not interested in just being some woman's part-time lover. Just a pair of arms to hold her in the night when the nightmares come."

"Damn you, Trey Hollister, don't you *dare* come in here and start making morning-after demands on my life!" The feeling of panic was growing steadily. She couldn't deal with this now! "I didn't play seductress yesterday and entice you into my bed for an evening of frolic and fun—you were *plenty* ready to get me in there. And believe me, you weren't used. You were an active and *very* involved participant!"

His eyes narrowed dangerously. "Just two lonely people who meet on a beach and wind up in bed, is that it? A few kisses, some fantastic lovemaking—nothing more than helping each other through the night." He shook his head slowly, eyes burning into hers. "I don't even know your real name."

Linn recoiled as if from a slap. She turned away and stood at the sink, fists clenched, filled with a sick, empty despair. "I told you my real name," she said in a whisper, trying not to cry. "Why are you doing this to me, Trey? How can you say that after last night?"

There was a long, taut silence. "I've got a book to write," he suddenly said, his voice clipped. "I'll leave Murphy with you. I'm going to be working crazy hours for the next few weeks meeting this deadline and won't be able to give him the attention he needs, and Nathan could use the company. I'll bring a couple of sacks of food over for him. If you leave before—well, when you leave, just send him home."

Linn swallowed at a thick, salty lump in her throat. "You don't have to do that," she managed to whisper. "I can manage on my own."

"I'm damned well aware of that," he snapped. "But I am leaving Murphy—and you are going to keep him without any argument, got that?" His voice was crisp with authority, the voice of someone used to giving orders, used to having them obeyed.

It made Linn look around at him. His eyes met hers, expressionless. "It isn't charity, if that's what you're worried about. Or even maudlin sentimentality. I just don't like the kind of people you're attracting to my end of the beach. And I don't like trouble. Not in my backyard. So as long as you're living next to me, lady, you'll do as I say, understand?"

"Perfectly." Her voice was just as crisp, just as matter-of-fact. It was better this way. The farther away he stayed from her, the safer he was. And last night was—

There was no point in thinking about last night.

Last night, and everything it could have meant, was over.

Chapter 8

She was raven-haired and blue-eyed, and from the first time he saw her, Steele knew she was the kind of trouble that no man needed. It came like that sometimes, gift-wrapped in satin and sin and long, smoldering glances that kept you coming back for more. The kind of trouble that left good men dead....

Yeah.

Trey drew in a deep breath and impatiently tossed the manuscript pages aside. He was supposedly proofing his draft of the first four chapters of *Steele on Ice*, but his mind kept wandering all over the damned place and he wasn't getting anywhere.

A package of cigarettes lay on the table and he stared at it, then swore savagely under his breath and took one out. He lighted it and drew the smoke deeply into his lungs, then eased it out again, squinting through it as he looked across at Linn's house.

It was quiet over there. Had been all day. He hadn't seen hide nor hair of her or the kid since early the previous afternoon, when he'd watched them walk down to the beach together, Murphy gamboling happily beside them. He'd stared down at her, willing her to look up, but of course she hadn't. Almost as though she'd known he was up there, as though she'd deliberately kept her back to him, straight and stiff. Unbendable.

"Stubborn as hell," he muttered under his breath, taking another drag on the cigarette. Stubborn and independent: admirable traits in the right place and at the right time, but they could get you killed. He'd seen it happen.

And he didn't want to see it happen here. Not with this woman. Because, like it or not, he cared about what happened to Linn Stevens, or whatever the hell her name was. Cared a lot.

Not that the fact pleased him. In fact, it downright depressed him when he thought about it too much. Caring meant worrying, and worrying meant thinking about *her* when he should be applying himself to other things. It didn't matter much right now, but what if he got a call from the field that someone needed Trey Hollister's special kind of services?

He rubbed his aching thigh, brooding. He'd damned near lost his leg on that Central America job. And for the same reason—a woman. A nun, that time. Some sort of social worker down there, caring for the children a particularly brutal little civil war had left homeless. She'd been taken hostage by a group of renegade soldiers-turned-rebels, the same rebels who'd been doing their damnedest to kill the man he'd been down there to protect. And *he*—breaking every rule in his own book—went playing hero!

He kneaded the scarred flesh. He'd been lucky that time. But what would happen if he went on a job like that now, with Linn Stevens on his mind?

Hell, he didn't even want to think about it!

He took another swallow of cigarette smoke, eyes narrowing. It had always been a hard and fast Hollister rule to hire only unattached men for the dirty jobs—the jobs where one slip could mean death for yourself or your client. Men with wives and mortgages and babies just had too much other stuff on their minds. And here *he* was, the ultimate lone wolf himself, finding his attention drifting at all the wrong times. Remembering the sweet glissade of flesh on flesh, the taste of her mouth on his, that special little catch in her breathing when he'd . . .

No. Trey sat upright with a soft oath, stabbing the cigarette out angrily. By God, he wasn't going to fall into that trap. He'd always managed to avoid it up to now. Like Steele, he loved 'em and left 'em, and that was just the way he liked it.

He reached out and picked up the manuscript, refusing to give in to the urge to glance at the other beach house again.

> Her skin was hot velvet, and when she moved it was like smoke and flame against him, and he burned. He was steel and she was fire, he cleaving, she engulfing, both blazing white-hot. And like the blade of a finely crafted sword, he felt himself folded into himself and folded again, strengthening with each layering until he was—

Where *was* she, damn it?

He tossed the pages aside again with a soft oath and gazed at the other beach house. He'd seen lights last night, so she was still there. The last one to go off had been the one in her bedroom, and he'd stood in the darkness of his house and had stared across, able to see a shadow move over the window occasionally. Remembering the taste and feel of her, naked and silken in his arms, the husky way she'd whispered his name just before she'd . . .

That was it!

He pulled his feet off the railing with a bang and stood up, gathering up the manuscript and his notes. The day was a write-off anyway, so why not make the best of it? Go into town and do some shopping. Drop by the pub. Maybe catch a movie. Then stop in at the Loft restaurant and have one of their fresh crabs with the works, a couple of glasses of good wine, a bit of innocent-but-not-*that*-innocent flirting with the good-looking blond waitress who, given the slightest encouragement, could become some pretty serious trouble herself.

He gave a snort as he walked into the living room. Believe that, Hollister, he taunted himself, and you'll believe anything. Like any man, he might try to delude himself now and again that he'd take what he could get, where he could get it, and that fast, easy sex was the best sex.

But that was a damned lie. He'd never been into that scene. One-night stands and empty affairs didn't fill a man's life, they just emphasized what wasn't there. And that one wondrous night with Linn had only proved what he already knew. He wanted what he couldn't have, wanted what probably didn't even exist. And all the pretty blondes and the not-so-innocent flirting in the world weren't going to take that empty ache away....

"Nathan? Nathan, where are you?" Breathing hard, trying to fight the panic clawing at her throat, Linn forced herself to stop and take a deep, calming breath. "Nathan!"

She looked around frantically, trying to catch sight of him through the racks of tourist T-shirts and display cases filled with souvenirs. This couldn't be happening! He'd been right beside her a moment ago, exclaiming in wonder over a book he'd discovered, filled with pop-up figures of whales and dolphins.

"Nathan, this isn't funny!" Her voice wobbled and two women looking through the racks of postcards looked at her oddly.

She glanced toward the window at the front of the store, but the man wasn't in sight. She'd noticed him in the ice-cream shop first, and then again when she'd popped into the post office to buy stamps. The same man who had been watching the house.

Taking Nathan's hand, she'd crossed the street and swiftly walked the other way, finally losing the stranger in the crowd around a street musician. Then suddenly he'd been there again, pretending to be engrossed by the display in the travel office window when she'd looked around. She'd dragged poor Nathan in one door of an antique shop and out the other, but the man had stuck to her like a burr. At last, in desperation, she'd popped into the gift and souvenir shop to gather her wits and come up with a plan to get back to the car without being seen. And now Nathan was missing!

"Excuse me, miss, but is anything wrong?" The soft voice at her elbow made Linn whirl around.

One of the young women who owned the store was looking at her in concern. Linn nodded. "I've just lost my little boy. He was here a minute ago, then I turned around and he was gone."

The woman's face cleared and she smiled. "Dark curly hair and black eyes and a face like an angel? Wearing blue cords and a heavy knit sweater?"

"Yes!" Linn's heart leaped.

"Oh, he's in the other half of the store—I know it's confusing, no one realizes that the men's clothing store next door and this store are really together." She pointed toward the back where Linn could see a wide doorway linking the two sides of the building.

"We carry a very good line of product over there if you're—" She laughed quietly. "Don't worry about your son, he's all right. Your husband's with him. I saw them walking toward the door just a minute ago, hand in hand, and—"

But Linn wasn't listening. She sprinted down the narrow aisle between the display cases at a dead run, dodging a baby stroller and the two gray-haired ladies at the postcard rack. There was a handful of people in the clothing store and Linn glanced around in desperation, seeing neither the stranger who had been following her nor Nathan. There was a young salesclerk nearby, talking to a customer, and Linn ran toward them.

"A little boy came in here a minute ago?" she interrupted. "Five years old, dark hair and eyes. There was a man—"

"Pardon me, madam, but I was—"

"Damn it, did you see him?" Linn's voice cracked through the store, turning heads, and she had to fight to keep from grabbing the man's suit jacket and shaking him. "Was he here? Did—?"

"Over there." Eyeing her warily, the clerk inclined his head toward the shoe section, stumbling back as Linn brushed between him and his customer. "Well, of all the rude—!"

She saw Nathan first. He was trotting along unconcernedly, his hand in the firm grip of the man walking beside him. They had their backs to her and were nearly at the door when Linn shot down the nearest aisle to intercept them.

"Nathan!" Her cry resounded like a whiplash and Nathan turned to look at her, his eyes widening as she lunged toward him.

She grabbed the man's arm just as he was turning around, but before she realized what was happening, he'd seized her wrist and had wrenched her back from Nathan so hard that she cried out. Blazing eyes met hers, narrowed and dangerous. Gray eyes that in the next instant widened with surprise.

They simply stared at each other for a stunned moment or two, then Trey let his fingers slide free of her wrist. He gave his head a slow shake, easing a tight breath between his teeth. "Lady, that is a good way to get yourself killed."

"I—" Linn closed her eyes, trying to get her own breath back. "I thought—there was a man, and . . ." She knelt on the floor and hugged Nathan, squeezing him so hard that he gave a squeak of protest.

"He turned up beside me with no warning," Trey said gruffly. "I was just setting out to find you when you bushwhacked us."

"I'm sorry." Linn looked up at him, giddy with relief. "When I turned around, he was gone and the salesclerk said she'd seen him with some man and—" She managed a rough laugh, giving Nathan another fierce hug. "It never occurred to me that it might be you."

He gave a snort of bitter laughter. "Forgotten that quickly."

Her panic had receded enough by now for other emotions to work their way through, and Linn flushed slightly. "No," she said quietly. "There's been a man following me this morning. And when Nathan went missing, the first thing I thought of was—"

"Man?" Trey looked down at her sharply. "What man?"

"I don't *know* what man," she snapped. "Just a man!"

He nodded thoughtfully, looking through the front display window into the street. Then he glanced back at her. Something gentled slightly in those fierce gray eyes. "You're as white as a sheet," he said more quietly. "Come on, I'll take you home."

"No." She glared at him, still not ready to forgive him for the scare he'd given her. Damn it, he should have known better! She reached down and took Nathan's hand. "My car's just across the street."

Trey whispered something under his breath that Linn didn't quite catch but which, judging by the look of admiration on Nathan's young face, must have been fairly colorful. He pushed the door open and held it for her, then followed her out of the store and across the street with a grim, no-nonsense expression that made Linn keep further arguments to herself.

She'd left Murphy in the car and he burst into excited barking when he saw them, tail windmilling. Trey whistled, the dog leapt through the open window, and they wrestled and played for a minute or two. He watched as she got Nathan settled in the passenger seat and secured his seat belt. Then he lounged against the parking meter as she opened her door and tilted the seat forward to let Murphy into the back, then slid behind the wheel herself.

"I don't suppose," he said evenly, "that there's much point in telling you to drive carefully."

"I appreciate the thought," Linn said shortly, starting the car. "But I make a point of driving carefully all the time."

His expression grew even grimmer. "And I guess *that* means I shouldn't bother asking if you'd like to come over for dinner some night."

It surprised Linn, but she managed to keep her expression blank. "That depends on you. If you're asking me over because you'd enjoy our company, I'd like to. But if you're asking because you want to keep an eye on me or you think I'm not eating properly or you're going to start interrogating—"

"Forget I asked," he growled, shoving himself away from the meter. "And drive carefully anyway, damn it."

Linn felt her cheeks blaze with sudden shame at her behavior. "Trey—"

He glanced around, his face and eyes suspicious and angry. *Forgive me,* she wanted to cry out. *I know I'm handling this badly, but I'm scared and I'm alone and I don't know any other way to handle it!* Instead she just sighed, shaking her head. "Nothing," she whispered, letting her gaze slip from his. "And I will drive carefully. Thanks for... just thanks." *Thanks for caring.*

Linn didn't notice the car behind her until she'd turned off the main highway, and even then she didn't pay much attention to it. It was a nondescript vehicle, pale blue or maybe gray, and it wasn't until it had settled in right behind her that Linn really gave it a serious look. There were two men in it, both youngish, she thought, although it was hard to tell, since both were wearing sunglasses. Normal-looking enough. But there was something about them, about the way they were following so closely, that gave Linn a prickle of alarm.

She eased her foot onto the accelerator and her rental car picked up speed. The gap between the two vehicles widened momentarily, as though she'd caught them by surprise, but then they surged up behind her again, even closer. There was definitely something wrong! If they wanted to pass, they had plenty of room and opportunity to do so. And they weren't local kids out for a romp, or they'd have been hooting and hollering and generally making nuisances of themselves.

No. These two were sitting back there for a reason.

She swallowed, tightening her grip on the wheel, and glanced at Nathan. "Is your seat belt good and tight?"

He checked it, nodding. "Yep. How come?"

"We . . . uh . . . might be going for a fast ride, Nathan," she said very calmly. "So I want you to hang on really tight, okay?"

But just going fast wasn't going to help. She was a good driver, but could she outmaneuver and outrun them? And where should she go? Home? They'd expect that.

Damn, why hadn't she accepted Trey's offer of a ride? Or better yet, why had he chosen *this* particular day to go into town? If he'd been home she could have gone there. She'd be safe there. Trey would make sure she was safe. . . .

She forced the thought away impatiently, her mind spinning with possibilities. Going back to town was the best idea, but there was no place to turn—not with them two feet off her back bumper. If she could only—

"Nathan, hang on!" Linn almost screamed, barely having time to brace herself before the car behind smashed into their rear bumper. The impact threw her against her shoulder harness and it snapped tight, keeping her from hitting the wheel but knocking the breath out of her. Something struck the back of her seat, there was a yelp of surprise and pain from Murphy and the sound of claws scrabbling for purchase on the rubber floor mats. Nathan uttered a wail of fear.

"Hang on, here they come again!"

The second impact was even harder and the car slewed, half out of control. The rear end skated sideways, sending up a spray of dust and gravel from the shoulder, and Linn fought the wheel. She got back onto the pavement, tires screaming as she floored the accelerator, and glanced into the rearview mirror in time to see them coming again.

But she was ready for them this time. She pulled left and braked hard, and they went flying by on the right. In that instant she whipped the car back to the right lane to give herself room, then wrenched the wheel to the left again and slammed the brake pedal down.

Tires howling, the rear of her car slewed full around, but at the critical instant, Linn released the brakes and floored the accelerator. The car fishtailed, tires smoking, then they got traction again and the vehicle shot down the road toward the highway.

Linn dared a swift glance into her rearview mirror. Her pursuers had turned nearly as quickly, and her heart sank as she realized her maneuver had bought her only a minute or two.

Not even that. Another glance into the mirror showed them right behind her and she braced herself as they pulled closer. But instead of smashing into the rear of her car, they pulled out and around and came up beside her. Linn gasped, realizing too late what they intended to do. She stamped on the brakes, hoping they'd shoot by again, but the driver of the other car was anticipating her this time and braked too, slamming his car into the side of hers.

Murphy was baying with rage in the back, snarling and snapping helplessly at the other car, and poor Nathan was howling in fear. But Linn barely heard them, too busy fighting the wheel to keep her car on the road. The other car plowed into her again and her right front tire hit the shoulder. She tried to get it back onto the pavement, but the other car hit hers again; in the next instant, her car was skidding into the shallow ditch.

It plowed nose first into the steep bank on the other side and Linn was thrown forward savagely. She struggled to get her seat belt undone and Nathan out of the car before the men could reach them. Murphy had been thrown to the floor again but he was on his feet and in full, murderous voice a moment later, practically chewing his way through the side of the car, and the instant Linn flung her door open he was out.

She caught a glimpse of a black and tan missile hurtling up the shallow bank of the ditch to the road as she flung herself at Nathan. She snapped his belt free, opened his door and shoved him out in one frantic motion. He hit the ground, still howling, but Linn was beside him an instant later, snatching him to his feet.

She saw one of the men pull a revolver from his coat pocket and dropped like a stone, covering Nathan's body with hers. The windshield of the car dissolved at the same instant she heard the crack of a gunshot. Hugging Nathan, she started wriggling backward, keeping the car between her and her assailants, praying that Murphy could keep them busy long enough for her to get into the relative safety of the heavy woods.

There was a scream and the sudden sound of a dog worrying something, then another gunshot and a yelping howl of pain from Murphy that went through Linn like a knife blade. There was another scream, human this time, then the shriek of rubber as a brown sedan—the same brown sedan she'd seen lurking by the house—came to a screeching stop right behind her pursuer's car.

Linn didn't quite know what happened next. Nathan was now bellowing in pain and fright, someone was shouting, someone else was screaming and there were more gunshots. The two men who had been chasing her were struggling back to the road, one half dragging the other. He was kicking and swearing at Murphy, who was snarling and snapping at them, seeming fully intent on eating the two of them alive.

Then someone else was there. A bright red Jeep came to a smoking stop right behind the brown car. Her pursuers had managed to get to their vehicle by then, but Linn realized that someone was running toward her. There was a piece of sun-bleached wood lying beside her; she picked it up and swung it at the looming figure, screaming at him to get away, almost blinded by her own hair and the tears that just wouldn't stop.

Someone grabbed her hands and brought them down, then two strong arms were around her, holding her tightly. "It's all right," a familiar husky voice murmured. "It's all right now, sweetheart. They're gone. He's safe—Nathan's safe."

"Trey!" And then, finally, she could cry.

She was, Trey found himself thinking, the most incredible woman he'd ever met. He'd seen that race-car-driver turn she'd pulled back there, had seen the dents and scrapes in her car and knew what they meant. He'd seen the expression of pure, murderous rage on her face when he'd come running toward her. It was the look of someone pushed as far as they can be pushed, that last-stand expression that means they've got nothing more to lose.

She was shivering uncontrollably now and still sobbing, her arms wrapped tightly around Nathan, whose own tears had stopped, although he was still pale and plainly terrified.

Trey rubbed her back and shoulders and after what seemed like a long while, she lifted her face and gazed at him through brimming tears. "W-where d-did you c-come from?"

He smiled, brushing her tear-damp hair from her face. "You're going to be mad when I tell you."

"You f-followed me."

"You got it."

She tried to look indignant, failed badly, and started digging through her pockets. He found a tissue and handed it to her and she blew her nose and dabbed at her eyes, still hiccoughing with swallowed sobs. "They sh-shot Murphy."

"Just grazed his shoulder. He'll be limping around as badly as I am for a few days, but he'll be okay. By the look of that guy's leg, though, he might not be so lucky. Murph really did a number on it."

"Hey, Hollister?" Trey looked around to see Joe Cippino jogging down the slope of the ditch, frowning. "Got a trace on the car plates, but it's like we thought—they rented it under false names. Came into Vancouver three days ago."

Trey nodded. "Okay, that pretty much confirms what we already know. Has Correlis found anything yet?"

Cippino shook his head, his glance drifting toward Linn. "If she is who she says she is, there aren't any warrants or anything on her. Not so much as a fingerprint on file."

Trey nodded slowly, blowing out a weary breath. Linn looked up just then, her eyes still bleary with tears, but when they settled on Cippino they widened with horror and she reared back so suddenly that Trey nearly lost his grip on her.

"That's him!" She tried to scramble to her feet, but Trey held her firmly. "That's the man who's been watching my house! The one who was following me this morning! He—" She stopped at Trey's snort of laughter, looking from one to the other with dawning horror.

Trey sobered instantly. "Hold it, Linn, it's not what you think! Joe's a friend of mine. He does security work for me sometimes and I—well, I..." He winced. "He's been keeping an eye on you for me. When I knew I was going to be in New York for a couple of days, I called him in. Just in case something happened while I was gone and you needed help."

She blinked at him. "You... hired someone to watch me?"

Joe gave a snort and rubbed the back of his neck. "As best as I could. You are damn near impossible to keep under surveillance, I'll tell you! Like trying to catch a gopher—while you're watching one hole, she's goin' out another!"

She closed her eyes, looking suddenly too weary to even stand up. "I want to go home," she said quietly. "Is my car drivable?"

Trey helped her to her feet. "Nat, can you walk up to the Jeep or would you like a hand?"

"I can walk my own self," the boy announced a little unsteadily, reaching for Linn's hand.

His expression of grim determination was a mirror of the one on his mother's face, and Trey had to bite back a laugh. God almighty, what a pair! Any man who decided to take these two on had his work cut out for him!

They got back to Linn's house about twenty minutes later, and Trey motioned for Joe to go ahead while he helped Linn and Nathan out of the Jeep.

They were nearly at the door when Joe stepped out of the house, looking grim and serious. "They must have come here first," he said quietly. "Broke this door in, smashed the big glass door leading in from the deck. Most likely when they couldn't find her and the kid here, they set up that ambush on the highway."

Trey swore. Linn was looking at him blankly, as though she hadn't quite comprehended what had happened. But her confusion didn't last long. Taking a deep breath, she pushed Nathan gently behind her and walked into the house.

The carport door leading into the kitchen had been taken half off its hinges, the frame splintered where Toomey's new lock had held but the wood around it hadn't. Not saying anything, Trey gave a nod to Joe to look around outside, then followed Linn, letting her have a good look at it. Hoping, finally, to shock her into opening up.

She walked into the living room and simply stood there, looking at the smashed patio door. Piles of broken glass lay in drifts across the carpet, glittering in the sun. Nathan leaned against her leg and she reached down almost absently and stroked his head.

"I'll get Toomey to put a sheet of plywood over that until he can order new glass," Trey said quietly.

Linn turned around and walked past him without saying anything, her eyes wide and dark. As she and Nathan headed toward the bedrooms, Trey watched her for a moment, then took a quick, thorough look around the house himself. Murphy had followed them inside, limping heavily, and when Trey knelt beside him he whimpered.

"You did a good thing today, old fella." Trey rubbed the dog's neck and throat. "You're a naturally heroic son of a gun, aren't you?" Gently Trey examined Murphy's wound. The bullet had torn a deep furrow through the muscular flesh of the dog's left shoulder, angling across his ribs. His thick fur was soaked with blood and he was shivering, whining slightly as Trey looked him over for any other injuries.

"How is he?" Joe squatted on his heels beside the dog.

"He'll be okay, but he's lost a lot of blood."

Joe stood up. "I'll get him to the vet and have him sewn up while you're sorting this out."

"Here, put this around him." Linn's quiet voice made Trey look around. She was carrying the comforter off Nathan's bed and she handed it to Joe, then knelt beside Murphy, cupping his broad face between her hands. "I haven't even thanked you, Murph," she whispered, her voice catching slightly. "You saved our lives. If—if you hadn't been there . . ." Her voice broke and she didn't even bother trying to finish, just slipping her arms around the dog's furry neck and giving him a gentle hug.

Then she stood up, wiping her eyes with the back of her hand; Trey snapped his fingers and led the dog to Joe's car. He got Murphy settled as well as he could in the back, wrapping the comforter around him to fight the danger of shock, then stood there for a weary moment and watched as Joe drove away.

Linn heard Trey come into the bedroom a few minutes later but didn't bother turning around. She scooped up a handful of underthings and stuffed them into the suitcase that lay open on the bed.

"He'll find you again sooner or later, just like he found you here," he said with an edge to his voice. "How long can you keep it up, Linn?"

"Long enough," she replied shortly, folding a pair of jeans and shoving them into the suitcase, too. She caught herself after a moment and took a deep breath. Running both hands through her hair, she straightened and turned to look at Trey. "I'm sorry. For getting you involved in this, for getting Murphy hurt, for... everything." She faltered slightly, turning her attention back to her packing.

"Running away isn't going to solve anything." His voice still had a rough undertone and he started prowling the room, dragging deeply on the cigarette in his hand.

"Running's all I've got." Maybe she'd come back. Maybe, when it was all over, she and Trey would be able to explore what was between them more fully. But not now. She had Nathan's well-being to worry about before she could allow herself the luxury of falling in love.

If it even *was* love, she reminded herself brutally, and not just a bad case of fear, lonely nights and opportunity. Only time would decide that.

"So that's it? You come into my life and turn it upside down, then just leave again without so much as an explanation?" He stared at her and she could see the look on his face that she'd half dreaded, anger mixed with bewilderment and bruised male ego and a hundred other things. But it was useless even trying to explain what was going on.

She recognized his type. Like Jack, he was a born knight errant, as stubborn as he was heroic. If he found out just how serious things were he'd feel duty-bound to protect her—and she'd get him killed. And there was no way she was letting that happen. Trey Hollister, man of action, was going to have to sit this one out.

He strode across and took her firmly by the shoulders, gazing down at her intently. "Damn it, Linn, I can help you. I can—"

"No, you can't," she told him with fierce certainty, pulling away from his grasp and continuing to pack. "Trey, believe me, you don't have even the slightest idea of what you'd be letting yourself in for. The longer I stay here and the more involved we get, the more danger you're in."

"I can handle the danger," he growled. "Trust me."

"No!" It was so tempting to believe him. But temptation made people careless, and carelessness got people killed. "I'm mixed up in something you don't even want to think about. If I stay here, I'm going to get you hurt—or killed. For your safety, for mine and for Nathan's, I have got to leave here and just disappear. Because I—" Her voice cracked and she swallowed, folding a sweater and putting it into the suitcase. *Because I already care too much. Because I think I've fallen in love with you, and I just won't risk getting you hurt because of it....*

He was silent behind her. So silent that for an instant she thought he'd left. Then a strong, tanned hand came from behind her and caught her wrist as she started to pull the suitcase closed. "For how long, Linn?" he asked softly. "If you won't think of your own safety, think of Nathan's—if it's as bad as you're saying, it's not right to endanger the boy."

"Oh, honestly!" She wrenched her wrist from his grip. "Why are you so determined to make this as difficult as possible? We had one night of magic, Trey Hollister, and I'll never forget it—or you. But that does not mean I'm going to let you— Damn it, what do you think you're doing?" Her voice rose in shock as he upended the suitcase and dumped her clothing over the bed.

He flung the empty suitcase violently across the room. "You're staying, lady," he told her bluntly. "I'm not letting you panic and run just because this guy's got you so scared you can't think straight. The only way you're going to be free of him is to make a stand. And I'm going to be right beside you when you do."

"A stand?" The word broke on a harsh, disbelieving laugh. "Trey, have you lost your mind? Do you have any idea of what—"

He gestured impatiently, "Of course I do! Do you think I'm blind? For whatever reasons, you've kidnapped your own son and his father wants him back. It happens all the time. Courts are giving custody to fathers who shouldn't have it, and more and more women just aren't taking it anymore. Hell, there's a new underground railroad running from one end of the country to the other, women taking care of women, sheltering them, hiding them." He caught his anger, looking at her seriously. "But you don't have to do it alone, Linn."

"That's not it." She said it quietly, but there was something in her voice that stopped Trey cold. His eyes narrowed slightly and she sat down on the edge of the bed with a sigh of defeat, shoulders slumping with tiredness and despair. "I wish it were that simple, Trey. I wish…" She shook her head slowly, rubbing at a grass stain on the knee of her jeans, trying to figure out where to start. There was no other place to start than at the beginning.

Chapter 9

"Nathan is not my son," she said quietly. "He's my sister's boy. Kathy is three years younger than I am, and she's married to a . . . a crusader!" She smiled faintly, glancing up at Trey. "He reminds me of you, in fact."

She let the smile fade from her lips and stared at the stain on her knee again, rubbing it absently with her fingernail. "Rod is a cop. Miami vice. He's been working under cover for nearly a year now, infiltrating a cocaine smuggling operation run by a Colombian drug lord by the name of Guillermo Santos. The police finally got enough to indict Santos, and they're bringing him to trial sometime later this month. Rod is their key witness."

Trey gave a long, low whistle. "I'm beginning to not like the sound of this."

"Santos's organization isn't the biggest or most powerful to come out of Colombia, but it's growing fast. He's young, mean and greedy—and scared. He got careless and trusted people he shouldn't have, and now he's looking at spending the next fifty years in prison."

"And he'll do anything to stop your brother-in-law from testifying."

Linn nodded. "He's already tried to kill Rod twice, and six weeks ago Santos's men made an aborted attempt to kidnap my sister, planning to use her to force Rod to change his mind." She took a deep breath, looking up at Trey. "But Rod doesn't scare easily. He and Kathy went into hiding, but they decided not to take Nathan with them. For one thing, he'd make them more vulnerable—Santos knows he's looking for a man and his wife and their five-year-old son. For another, he'd slow them down. And most important, they were worried what it would do to Nathan."

"So they asked you to take him."

"I volunteered to take him," she corrected. "It was my idea right from the start to split the family up. Kathy and Nathan aren't the only ones in danger—I am, our father is, anyone trying to help us is. We tricked Dad into going to Ireland for a couple of months. He's retired and Mother died last year, so I convinced him to visit relatives over there just to get him out of the way. Then I took Nathan.

"My original plan was to stay with friends in Missouri, near Lake of the Ozarks. They have a boy about Nathan's age—I figured it would be easier on him with other kids to play with, and lots of fishing and boating to keep his mind off . . . things."

"What happened?"

Linn shook her head. "I don't know. I left Fort Lauderdale—that's where I live—and everything seemed fine. But after I'd been in Missouri for a few days, I realized I'd been followed. I also realized I was putting my friends in danger and I left."

"So you came up here."

"Not at first. I headed out to California. But it didn't take long for them to find me there, too. So I rented a car and headed north—actually, I wound up touring eight different states, going in so many circles I made myself dizzy. When I was sure I'd lost whoever was tailing me, I bolted up here. Crossed the border on some logging road in the mountains and made my way out here. I figured nobody would *ever* be able to track me down."

"Wrong again."

"Wrong again," Linn echoed in despair. "They want Nathan as blackmail, of course, to keep Rod from testifying."

"Killing you in the process."

"They'll try."

Trey snorted as he strode across to pick up her suitcase where it had landed against the far wall. He tossed it onto the bed and started shoving her clothes back into it. "Where's Nathan?"

"In his room, getting his things together." Linn watched him as he pulled the last drawer out of the dressing table and turned it upside down over the suitcase, mashing everything together and zipping the case closed. "What are you doing?"

"Packing." He tossed the larger case onto the bed and opened it, then started stripping the closet. "We'll take all we can carry now, and Joe and I can pick the rest up later."

"Take?"

"You're staying with me."

"Oh, for—" Linn caught herself, taking a calming breath. "Trey, didn't you hear a thing I just said? This isn't some irate ex-husband we're dealing with here, it's a Colombian drug lord fighting for his life. Do you have any idea what these people are capable of? *Narcotraficantes* determine the way of life down there. They even have their own army, the *sicarios*: paid assassins."

Trey closed the second suitcase, then picked up both and carried them into the corridor. "Have you got your stuff out of the bathroom yet?"

"Did you hear what I said?" Linn's voice vibrated with impatience. "Damn it, taking care of things is my specialty! I've been taking care of things in our family for most of my life. I took care of a dying husband for two and a half years, I took care of my mother for six months before *she* died, and I'll damned well take care of this, too!"

"Not alone, you won't," Trey growled as he walked by her and across the corridor into Nathan's room. "How are you doing, sport? Got everything packed?"

Nathan was pulling his toys out of the cardboard box by his bed and putting them into his suitcase. Tears were running down his cheeks and he had to stop every now and then to wipe his eyes clear.

"You and your aunt are going to be staying with me for a while. How does that sound?"

Nathan shook his head, his lower lip protruding, face set with sullen anger and fear. "Don't wanna," he said in an uneven voice, casting Linn a hostile look. "I wanna go *home*. I want my *daddy*!"

"Well, I can sure understand that," Trey said softly, squatting beside the suitcase. "But we have a little problem. Murphy was hurt this afternoon. Not badly," he added quickly, seeing the expression on Nathan's face, "but it's going to slow him up some. And I was hoping I could convince you to help me take care of him. I'm going to be busy for a few days, and he's going to be feeling pretty down."

"Trey. . ." Linn's voice was vibrant with warning.

Nathan wiped his face on the sleeve of his jacket, giving Trey a disdainful look. "There's nothing *I* can do."

"Actually there's a lot you can do. Keep him exercising his leg, for one thing. Make sure he's eating and that he's got plenty of fresh water. For the first couple of days he's not going to be feeling very chipper, and I think just having you there will make him feel better."

"Trey, damn it," Linn exclaimed, "don't you do this to me!"

"Really?" Nathan's face brightened slightly.

"Really." Trey smiled and stood up, ruffling Nathan's hair with his hand. "So let's get the rest of this stuff packed, okay?"

"Trey, I am *not*—" Linn snapped her mouth shut as Trey suddenly wheeled around and stepped toward her, his face hard with impatience.

"Yes," he said in a soft, but steel-edged voice, "you are." His eyes locked with hers, intent and hard and utterly implacable. "I don't know how in the hell you've managed to stay alive this long, but your luck's running out fast. Nothing is going to stop these guys until they kill you and kidnap Nathan—and I am not letting you risk your life and the life of that kid in there, just because you can't stand the idea of accepting help, understand?"

"They're killers, Trey! This isn't some novel you're writing. This is *real*."

Trey's face was grim as he glanced around to check the room. "Okay, let's go."

"Trey! You can't possibly protect Nathan and me against—"

"Yes, I can," he said bluntly, meeting her eyes dead on. "It's what I do, Linn. And I do it well."

"But—" But nothing. There was no arguing with him, Linn realized despairingly. Or more correctly, she *could* have argued with him, but if she attempted he'd probably toss her over his very capable shoulder and carry her across to his place.

To Trey's satisfaction, Linn followed him to his house docilely enough. She didn't even protest when he and Joe went back a couple of hours later to bring over the rest of her things. Later she'd come into the kitchen and had wordlessly started helping him with supper, making a green salad while he'd grilled the salmon steaks he'd picked up that afternoon.

Murphy had come through his ordeal at the vet's like the old warrior he was, stiff and bruised and groggy with painkillers, but unbowed. Even Nathan had settled in happily enough. Worn out, he'd barely made it through supper before falling asleep. Trey had carried him into the living room and tucked him under a blanket on the sofa where Linn could keep an eye on him. Then he'd lighted a blazing fire and had poured Linn a glass of brandy and himself a stiff shot of whiskey, and they'd been sitting here in silence ever since.

He took a swallow of the liquor and leaned well back in the easy chair, bracing one foot on the wide hassock and gazing over his upraised knee at the woman curled up in the big armchair across from him. She was subdued and thoughtful, her forehead fretted with lines of worry, eyes shadowed with unease, but he was surprised at how well she'd come through everything that had happened.

No, he decided on second thought. Not surprised. He'd seen flashes of that steely inner strength before. Relieved was a better word. He'd half anticipated an all-out brawl over her staying here, but—for the moment at least—she seemed content to let him run things. Which probably *was* surprising, he thought with a sudden flash of humor. Linn Stevens didn't strike him as being the kind of woman who let anyone run her life.

As though aware of his gaze, she raised her head slowly and looked at him. "Where's Joe?"

"Outside, giving the perimeter alarms a final check."

She smiled very faintly. "You make this place sound like a fortress."

Trey didn't smile. "Close enough."

She nodded, looking at him for a silent while. "I think," she said quietly, "that it's time you told me just who you are. And why you don't even turn a hair at the possibility that Santos could have an army at the back door by tomorrow morning."

"First things first." He lighted a cigarette—his fourth or fifth of the day, but what the hell—and drew on it deeply, eyeing her through the spiraling smoke. "You're not really Nathan's aunt, are you?" She looked puzzled, and he smiled tolerantly. "You're damned good at this kind of thing. A little too good to be just a caring sister-in-law. Where did you learn to handle a car like a pro, for instance? I saw that one-eighty you did on the highway this afternoon. Either you're a cop, or you grew up running moonshine in the Arkansas backwoods."

She looked badly startled for a moment, then her laughter rose through the shadows. "My dad would be grinning from ear to Irish ear if he heard that." Still laughing, she shook her head. "But you're wrong. I am Nathan's aunt, and I'm not a cop. Not that I wasn't *supposed* to be, understand."

Trey looked at her quizzically and Linn smiled. "Right from the day I was born, Dad had it figured that I was going to follow in his footsteps—just as he'd followed in *his* father's. So I was more or less groomed for the job right from the start. He's the one who taught me to drive like a Brooklyn cabbie." Her smile faltered. "Although I was wishing the other night on that beach with Rolfson that I'd paid more attention to my karate lessons."

"So you were the son he never had."

"No, not really. He's just a strong believer in knowing how to take care of yourself—especially if you're a woman. He taught Kath and me how to 'discourage unwanted admirers,' as he put it, before we were even in our teens." She grinned. "*Disable* was more like it. He showed us a whole lot of dirty little tricks that would have scandalized our mother, had she ever found out. She thought we spent all those hours in the basement learning Latin verbs, and really Daddy was teaching Kath and me how to knee an unwanted admirer in the groin."

Trey winced, laughing. "Did you say he's retired?"

"Thank heaven! If he was still on the force, I don't know what we'd have done. As it was, Kath and I knew we didn't *dare* let him in on what was happening. If he had the slightest clue that his baby daughter and his only grandchild were being chased by Colombian *narcotraficantes*, he'd be taking them on single-handed. So we tricked him into visiting his brother in Ireland to get him out of the way until this is over."

"For his safety, too," Trey speculated quietly. "Santos wouldn't be shy about kidnapping your father and using him as collateral, either."

"Exactly. Uncle Rory knows the situation and he and some of his old street-warrior friends are keeping a close eye on Dad without letting him know what's going on." She managed another smile. "Even Santos's bunch are no match for that band of ruffians—old Sinn Fein and IRA types, the lot of them."

"Seems to me," Trey said slowly, "that you might have been smart to have gone over with him—and taken Kathy and Nathan with you."

She gave him an odd look. "Kathy wouldn't have left Rod. And I certainly wouldn't have left Kath. We toyed with the idea of sending Nathan with Dad, but sooner or later Dad would have twigged to the fact that something was going on." She smiled again. "Patrick Duffy O'Connor grew up near the Shankill Road in Belfast and was teethed on car bombs and assassination squads. To hear him tell it, the Colombians are just amateur upstarts in the terrorism department."

Trey gave a snort of laughter. "Sounds to me as though he passed a bit of that Irish orneriness on to his eldest daughter."

It made her smile. "Yeah, well, you wouldn't be the first person to suggest it."

Trey nodded, looking at her thoughtfully. "Your sister is asking a hell of a lot, as I see it. Seems to me she could have gotten Nathan put under police protection, and it would have been easier on everyone."

She looked at him as though she did not fully understand the question. "Kathy's my sister," she said quietly. "I love her. Nathan might have been safe with the police. Then again he might not have been—and who knows the psychological damage he'd have undergone, being left with strangers? If you can't turn to your family for help, who on earth *can* you turn to?"

Trey frowned, staring at the glowing tip of the cigarette. "I wouldn't know," he said with faint bitterness. "My family was never big on…caring." He looked up after a minute or two to find Linn gazing at him curiously and he managed a ragged, careless smile. "My old man drank. A lot. He wasn't around much when I was a kid, which was just as well—he was surly and mean and not shy about taking a swing at anyone who annoyed him. My mother died when I was about eleven and some relative took me in. But they had a bunch of kids of their own, and I was just one more mouth to feed. I took off when I was fifteen. Joined the marines as soon as I was big enough to lie convincingly about my age. . . ."

He was still staring at the end of his cigarette, as though lost in the past, and Linn found herself studying him thoughtfully. *Typical loner. . . happier by himself than with people. Finds it hard to open up.* He'd been talking about Steele when he'd said it, Linn recalled. But how much was Steele, and how much his silent, introspective creator?

"And from the marines," she coaxed him gently, "to a couple of tours in Vietnam. Then a stint in military intelligence, whatever *that* means. Which, I presume, is where you started doing whatever it is you do."

He looked up in faint surprise, then broke into a quiet laugh. "You have me all figured out, don't you?"

"Not even by half," Linn replied very seriously. "Tell me about it, Trey. Tell me why Santos doesn't scare you. Why your house is rigged up so it could withstand a marine assault force."

He shrugged, still smiling faintly. "Nothing mysterious about it. After I got out of MI I needed a job. Looking over my work skills, I realized they hadn't taught me a hell of a lot, other than how to kill efficiently. And how to keep people from killing me. I figured I could either become a professional hit man, or adapt what I'd learned to some other use."

He took a final drag on the cigarette, then leaned forward and flicked it into the fire. "I took a good look at the state of the world and decided security was a lucrative field to get into. So I put together a list of people with skills like mine and went into business. Antiterrorism, mainly. If a big corporation has a field office in a high-risk country, I go in and set up a security system to keep their employees safe from kidnapping, bombing, that sort of thing. I also work with foreign governments now and again—I designed the security system for the Canadian embassy in France a couple of years ago. And our own embassy in Spain has a few of my touches."

Linn simply stared at him. "That's how you knew. Right from the start you knew I was in trouble."

"I knew you were running scared from something."

"And why you started watching over me."

He smiled. "Some habits are hard to break."

"And your leg? When you zigged instead of zagging, that was business, wasn't it?"

Trey nodded, the laughter leaving his face. "Central America. I was down there trying to keep a peace advisor alive long enough to get negotiations started. There had been a military coup and the place was in chaos, the military on one side and rebel government sympathizers on the other. By the time we got down there, the country was in a shambles. There was this woman—a nun from a local mission. One of the generals had her kidnapped, planning on using her as collateral in the peace negotiations." He frowned slightly, staring into the fire. "I wasn't supposed to get involved, of course. We weren't taking sides, just trying to hammer out a workable compromise both sides could live with."

His profile was hard-edged against the flames and Linn traced it with her eyes. "But you did."

He smiled faintly, slipping her an amused sidelong look. "Yeah, old Trey Hollister can never keep himself out of trouble!" Then the smile slid away and he stared into the flickering flames, his face cold. "I got this sudden urge to play hero. It was crazy—if I'd been caught it would have compromised our credibility and the entire mission would have been in jeopardy." He uttered a snort. "Jeopardy, hell! We'd have been lucky to get out of the country with our skins intact."

"And?" Linn urged gently. "Did you get her out?"

"I got her out."

"And did they ever find out who did it?"

He shook his head. "They had their suspicions—particularly when I turned up the next day with my leg half shot off. But I told them I'd done it myself while cleaning my gun, and they couldn't very well come out and call me a liar without jeopardizing their own position."

Linn gazed at him, shaking her head slowly. She smiled. "And you had to ask why I volunteered to take care of Nathan? Seems to me you've got a pretty deep streak of caring yourself."

Trey gave her a sharp look. "That was business. What you're doing is just plain nuts."

Like watching over me was business, she felt like adding. But she didn't. You're a damned fraud, Hollister, she told him silently. You may have convinced the rest of the world you're as hard as nails, but I don't believe a word of it.

"So you can believe me whan I tell you that you're safe here," he said suddenly, his voice quiet. "Nothing's going to happen to you here, Linn. I'll make damned sure of that."

It wasn't until he'd said the words that Trey realized how much he meant it; his voice must have given away more of his feelings than he'd intended, because Linn gave him an odd look.

It was strange how life worked, he found himself musing. You could be going along minding your own business, pretty much doing what you wanted to do and thinking you were happy, and then up would pop a woman with eyes like deep water and a smile that could melt a man's heart where he stood, and suddenly you realized that what you'd thought was happiness was just acceptance.

And maybe habit, too. Sometimes you just got so deeply into your comfortable little rut that you didn't even see it *was* a rut until something came along to jar you out of it.

Nathan stirred in his sleep suddenly, muttering something, and Trey shook off his meandering thoughts. Linn got up and walked across to the boy and Trey, setting the glass aside, did the same. He looked down at the sleeping child and smiled. "Poor kid's had a rough day."

He looked at Linn then, reaching out to brush a tendril of dark hair from her cheek. She was very pale and delicate shadows lay under her eyes like bruises. "So have you. You look beat."

She nodded, smiling wanly. "I am."

He smiled and bent down to scoop Nathan into his arms. "Come on. I think it's time I put both of you to bed."

It was one of those innocent statements so loaded with possibilities that it practically gave off sparks. And Trey knew, by the thoughtful glance she gave him, that Linn was as aware of the underlying tension that had been between them all day as he was. But he forced himself to ignore the growing temptation to simply take her into his arms and kiss her with all the pent-up passion of a man closer to the edge of his self-control than he'd like to admit, and walked toward the stairs leading to the upstairs bedrooms.

Linn followed him wordlessly up the stairs and to the small spare room where he'd taken Nathan's things. She turned down the covers and Trey slipped the sleeping child gently into the bed, watching her as she tugged the boy's sweater and jeans off, then tucked the covers under his chin.

"You do that like a natural," he said quietly. "You and Jack didn't have children?"

She shook her head. "We thought we'd have plenty of time." She looked up at him, smiling wryly. "You always figure bad things happen to other people, and that your life is going to unfold exactly to plan. Jack owned a small local newspaper, and our dream was to run it together—we did, too, for a couple of years. That's how I met him, as a matter of fact, when he hired me as his assistant editor." She gave a soft laugh. "Although on a paper that size, an assistant editor does everything from proofing advertising copy to making coffee."

Her face was warm with memories. "We figured we had forever to do all the things we wanted to do together—having children, building our own home, buying a sailboat and touring the seven seas."

"Then he got sick."

She nodded, her expression pensive. "We didn't think it was anything serious at first. Even when the first test results came in, we didn't really believe them—you never do. But soon it became obvious that Jack was seriously ill and wasn't going to be able to continue working. He wanted to sell the paper, but I flatly refused. Somehow, in my mind, the paper had become the symbol for Jack's survival—if we kept the paper going, he'd *have* to get better. But if we sold it, it was as though we were giving up." She looked up at him again. "Silly games. Sometimes games are all you have left."

"But they didn't work," Trey said softly.

"I tried to hold on to him and that damned paper for two and a half years, and in the end I lost both of them." She was silent for a moment, gazing down at Nathan. "I kept the paper until three months ago. Then I realized one day that it just didn't have the same magic without Jack, and that I was just trying to cling to something that didn't even exist. So I sold it and the house we'd bought, and was trying to figure out what I wanted to do with the rest of my life when this business with Santos came up. I've been on the run ever since."

She gave herself a sudden shake, as though casting off the memories, and smiled at Nathan, smoothing a handful of hair off his forehead. "I learned one thing, though—don't wait for the things you really want. I've always regretted not having Jack's child. It would have been something, at least. As it is, all I have left of him are the memories."

"Most people don't even have that," he said almost absently. He tried sometimes to remember what Diane had looked like, feeling a jab of guilt when he failed. In fact he couldn't even remember what it had felt like to be married. Maybe he'd never really known.

He found himself gazing at Linn, marveling over the kind of love it must have taken to get her through those two and a half years of caring for, loving, a dying man. It was the kind of love that came along once in a lifetime. If a man was very, very lucky.

"I'm sorry about all of this, by the way."

Trey blinked, finding Linn still sitting on the edge of the bed, looking up at him. "For?"

"For everything," she said with a rueful laugh. "I ruined your entire day, for a start. I hope you didn't have anything planned for tonight."

"I didn't."

"And," she added with a deep sigh, "I'm sorry for turning your home into a Gypsy camp, and for getting your dog hurt, and for...oh, hell, just for all of it." Wearily she combed her hair back with both hands. "You had a nice, peaceful life here until I turned up. You're supposed to be recuperating. And finishing your book. And instead you're running around rescuing me—not to mention getting my locks changed, hiring people to keep an eye on me when you can't, playing surrogate father and big brother combined to Nathan."

"Peace and quiet are overrated," he said carelessly. "Trey Hollister, man of action, that's me."

She smiled, as though knowing damned well that he was lying through his teeth, and got to her feet. "Well, Trey Hollister, man of action," she said softly, "I'll never be able to thank you for it."

"If I were an unscrupulous cad," he murmured, reaching for her, "I'd play on that guilt for all I was worth and get a kiss out of it. Maybe even two...."

She stepped into the circle of his arms as though she'd been waiting for his touch all day. "What's a little unscrupulousness between friends?" she whispered, lips already parting.

Her mouth was like peaches and cream, and kissing her was like coming home. It was a welcoming, unhurried kiss, relaxed and deep and rich with sensuous memories. A man-woman kiss, filled with everything they'd been and everything they still could be, as evocative as a glance across a room, as filled with undemanding promise as a smile.

She drew her mouth from his at last and slipped her arms around his waist with a small, contented sigh, relaxing against him as though it was the most natural place in the world for her to be.

Which it was, Trey realized idly. She fitted into his arms and into his life with sublime perfection. It had been strange, seeing her there in the shadows and angles and familiar patterns of his home today. Normally he would have found the intrusion jarring, even irritating, and yet there had been a curious rightness to it that he hadn't even questioned.

He tightened his arms around her and rested his cheek on her hair, breathing in the perfume of her. "I've been wanting to do this all day," he murmured.

"And I was hoping you would," she whispered back, nestled against his chest. "This has gotten much more complicated than it was supposed to, hasn't it."

"Complicated can be nice." He ran his hands down the long sweep of her back. "You feel real good here, lady. As though you belong."

"It's strange, but I know what you mean. There was a long time after Jack died when I couldn't stand having a man even touch me, let alone kiss me. I never dreamed I'd ever be normal and happy again. That I'd ever want a man to make love to me. Yet the other night, making love with you was the most natural, comfortable thing in the world. As though we'd known each other forever instead of a few days."

"Right place, right time," he murmured.

"Right man," she whispered, her arms tightening around him. Then, before Trey could even fully take in what she'd said, she eased herself out of his arms and looked up at him, smiling wearily. "And thank you for *this*, too," she said quietly, nodding toward the connecting door that led to the other spare room where he had taken her suitcases. "I'll admit that when you first brought me over here, I was uncharitably suspicious about your intentions. But I . . . well, I appreciate the fact you didn't just *presume*. . . ."

"You've been through a hell of a lot," Trey said quietly. "It might be pushy, but I'd like to think I'm not completely obnoxious." Then suddenly he had to grin. "But I'd be a damned liar if I told you I hadn't thought about it." Linn's mouth curved up at the corners with a responding smile and Trey reached out and stroked her hair back from her face, letting his palm cradle her cheek. "In fact, I think about it a lot. That day on the beach with you and Nathan. Then later, that night, making love to you for what seemed like hours...."

Her eyes had widened slightly, so deeply blue now that they seemed almost black in the dim light coming from the hall, and she turned her face and kissed his palm. "So do I," she admitted softly, her gaze locked with his. "All the time."

Trey drew in a deep, careful breath. "This...could get even more complicated," he warned her in a ragged voice.

"I know," she whispered.

He eased the breath out between his teeth. "My room's down at the end of the corridor, on the right. But I want you to be sure, Linn. I don't want you having any doubts about it in the morning, hating me for making it too easy."

"I know," she whispered again.

Trey nodded, holding her gaze, then he turned and walked to the door. "I'm going to have one last look around." He glanced around at her. "And Linn...I'll understand if you decide not to. You have to be sure, sweetheart. You have to be comfortable with it. I want to make love to you so badly I ache with it, but I want you in my bed because you *want* to be there, not because you think you owe me something or because you think I expect it. We're both too old for those kinds of games."

She smiled gently, her eyes glowing in the shadowed light. "But if I were to be there when you came back... you wouldn't kick me out or anything, would you?"

"What do you think?"

His voice was just a husky, evocative purr that made Linn melt right to her toes. His eyes locked with hers for a heartbeat of time, then he slipped through the open door and into the shadows beyond and was gone.

Linn suddenly realized she was holding her breath. She eased it out shakily and adjusted the blanket around Nathan's shoulders again, her heart giving a leap as the bedroom door swung inward on silent hinges. But it was just Murphy, limping heavily and moving with infinite care as he made his way slowly across the room. He made an attempt to jump onto the bed before Linn could stop him and fell back with a yelp of pain. Whimpering, he rested his chin on the edge of the bed and looked up at Linn, his tail giving a couple of half-hearted thumps on the floor.

"Murph, you don't have to do this," Linn told him softly, her eyes prickling suddenly as she realized he'd made his slow, painful way up the stairs just to be with Nathan. "He'll be fine, I promise."

Murphy barked softly, staring at her intently, and she had to laugh. "No, I am *not* going to help you up onto the bed! If you have to get down during the night, you'll rip those stitches out. But I'll settle on a compromise." She gathered up the spare blanket lying on a nearby chair and spread it on the floor beside the bed, making it into a rough nest. "How's that?"

Murphy eased himself onto the blanket, turning around a couple of times before settling down with a quiet whimper. He reached out and ran his tongue across Linn's hand and she smiled at him, scratching between his big, bat-wing ears. "You're as big a sucker for damsels in distress as your owner," she told him quietly. "And you're both too damned heroic for your own good!"

Chapter 10

Trey's bedroom was exactly as Linn had imagined it.

It was a large room, spacious and airy and uncluttered. There was a sitting area at the near end with a fieldstone fireplace, thick rugs and a love seat and matching easy chair of tan leather, worn as supple and soft as velvet. The big built-in bookcases flanking the fireplace were stuffed with hundreds of volumes, and the walls were covered with Indian carvings and paintings.

Like the man who owned it, the room was uncompromisingly masculine. Yet there was a richness there, a complexity of interests that gave away more about his personality than he probably would have been comfortable with.

Maybe that was why he never brought anyone here, she found herself thinking. Because of the fear of giving away too much, the possibility of someone catching a glimpse of the real man behind the armored facade.

Two wide pine steps led to the sunken bedroom, and Linn walked down them slowly. The fawn carpeting was rich and deep-piled, the furniture heavy and solid, the ceiling open-beamed and peaked. The big bed was angled to capture the incredible view of the beach and restless ocean provided by the wall-to-wall windows across the far end.

The en suite bathroom was as spacious and well-appointed as the bedroom, with a multitude of skylights and mirrors and plants. A sunken whirlpool tub stood at one end with twin marble sinks and a huge, freestanding shower enclosure of smoked glass that captured Linn's attention at once.

She rummaged through a couple of cupboards until she found Trey's cache of spare towels, then quickly stripped and, after fiddling with the faucets until they relinquished a deluge of steaming water, stepped under it with a sigh of utter pleasure.

She hadn't realized just how much the day had taken out of her until then. Exhaustion rolled through her in leaden waves and she simply stood under the pounding water and let the heat relax the taut muscles across her shoulders and neck, feeling the aftereffects of terror slowly wash away.

It wasn't until she turned the water off and stepped out of the shower, wrapped in thick towels and wreaths of steam, that she realized Trey had been there. The untidy pile of clothing she'd kicked to one side was gone and in its place was a plush terry robe that she wrapped around herself gratefully.

A small gesture, Linn mused. Yet exactly the kind of thoughtfulness she'd come to expect. Still toweling her hair dry, she smiled and stepped into the bedroom.

Trey was standing by the windows, leaning lazily against the wall and staring out across the moonlit water. He glanced around as she came out of the bathroom and his mouth lifted in a slow, warm smile as his eyes caught hers, held them. "That's nice."

Linn walked across to him and slipped effortlessly into the curve of his outstretched arm. He drew her close and she relaxed against him comfortably. "What's nice?"

"Having you here." He slid his other arm around her and cradled her against him. "Just standing here, listening to the shower and knowing you were in there. Knowing you'd be coming out soon and I could touch you again." He nuzzled her wet hair, lightly kissing the side of her throat. "Knowing I'd be kissing you again. Making love to you again."

Linn laughed quietly and kissed his cheek. "Breaking all your own rules, aren't you, cowboy?" she teased gently. "I thought you made love to your women on *their* turf instead of bringing them up here."

He drew back and looked down at her so quizzically that Linn had to laugh again. "Toomey was filling me in the other day. He made a point of advising me that you didn't like houseguests."

"Toomey talks too much," he said with a scowl. "I suppose he gave you the whole ten yards, did he? The women, the affairs, the private jet, the group gropes in Cannes, the—"

"I think he overlooked those last two," Linn said with mock seriousness. "Group gropes?" She raised an eyebrow.

Trey gave a snort. "Toomey's grasp of reality sometimes slips a cog or two. He's got this fantasy that a writer's life is all hard liquor and fast women, and he doesn't let a little thing like the truth get in the way of a good story." He smiled at her, his eyes as warm as melted silver. "If I indulged in half the mischief he likes to think I do, I'd have died of exhaustion long ago."

Linn reached up to brush a cowlick of dark hair off his forehead. "You don't owe me any explanations, Trey. I'm hardly naïve. Or so insecure I need you to tell me I'm the first and only."

His own mouth curved slightly in response. "Not the first, maybe. But very definitely the only." His smile faded and he gazed down at her, eyes caught with what could have been wistfulness. "It's been a long time for me, too, Linn," he said very softly. "Longer than a man likes to admit. I could give you a hundred high-sounding excuses, but the truth is it's been a long while since I met a woman who makes me feel like baying at the moon. Who makes me feel even close to how you make me feel."

His mouth was on hers, warm and questing, and as she opened herself to his deep, drugging kiss, Linn's firm resolve not to fall too heavily under Trey Hollister's formidable spell all but vanished. She'd made up her mind when she'd come in here tonight that what she wanted—what they both wanted—was a simple and loving affair, uncomplicated by promises or dreams of tomorrow. Tonight—tonight was all that mattered.

And yet as his arms tightened around her, she found herself thinking of what it would be like to spend the rest of her life with this man. Of what it would be like to fall in love and marry again and have all the things this time around that she and Jack had been cheated of. Children. Growing old together. Sharing all the things that can be shared by two people so much in love that it hurt just to imagine it.

"Ohh, honey—I've gotta go." Giving a laughing groan, Trey gave her one last fierce kiss, then eased himself away from her. He rubbed his chin, fingers rasping on a late-day growth of beard. "I've got to get rid of this, for a start, or you'll never forgive me." He grinned at her, his eyes teasing, yet wary, too. "You're not going to get cold feet or something while I'm in the shower, are you? I'd hate like hell to come back and find you'd gone."

Linn reached up to outline his lower lip with the tip of her finger. "I'll be here," she whispered. "Waiting. . . ."

He groaned again, obviously torn between going and staying. But in the end he did go, and Linn, still smiling to herself, walked to the big bed. She tossed the robe aside and slipped between the cool sheets, stretching languorously, loving the feel of the cool sheets against her naked skin. Trey's sheets. Touching her where Trey would be touching her. Caressing her breasts and thighs and belly and . . .

She shivered in anticipation, her body responding to even the memory of their lovemaking so vibrantly that it made her catch her breath. She could remember with distinct, wondrous clarity the instant he'd brought their two bodies together that first time, that moment of cleaving and acceptance, of taking and surrender.

It had astonished her how easily her body had accepted him, anticipating some last-minute doubt, if not actually discomfort, after all that time. But there had been none. It had been like the first time all over: the anticipation, the complete trust, the certainty of how right it was.

And the . . . love?

Now don't go start making things more complicated than they already are, she warned herself fiercely. She had a million things to worry about right now without tossing love into the equation: getting Nathan safely back to Kath and Rod after the trial, figuring out where she was going to live now that she'd sold the house, deciding what she was going to do with her life. She was at a crossroads, with possibilities and options running in all directions, and the last thing she needed was a major distraction while she was trying to make up her mind. And face it, she reminded herself with a smile, Trey Hollister could become a major distraction.

She was still thinking about that a few minutes later when she happened to turn her head and saw the photograph. It was sitting unobtrusively on the bedside table, just a small oval frame holding the snapshot of a child. A little boy, Linn decided, with wide blue eyes, a shock of black, curly hair and a slightly uncertain expression, as though he was trying to decide whether to laugh or burst into tears.

She rolled onto her side and picked it up curiously. It took her a moment or two to realize that the picture had been cut down from a larger one and that in the original, the boy had not been alone. All that remained of that mysterious other person now was a slender hand cupping the child's shoulder. A feminine hand, Linn couldn't help noticing, complete with wedding band.

A shadow fell across her just then. She glanced up and found Trey standing beside the bed, naked but for the towel draped loosely around his hips. He was looking down at the photograph, his expression a curious blend of anger and pain, and after a moment he reached out and took it from her.

"I didn't mean to snoop," Linn said quietly, "but I happened to see it there and—"

Trey shook his head. "It's all right. I don't know why I keep it there, to tell you the truth." He sat on the edge of the bed and rested his elbows on his knees, holding the picture in both hands and staring at it in thoughtful silence.

He kept his expression carefully blank, yet Linn could sense more than actually see weary despair. Sadness. Regret. She put her hand on his shower-damp shoulder and started kneading it gently. "He looks like you."

He looked at her blankly for a moment, then gave his head a shake as though dispelling the past and smiled very faintly. "He should," he said softly. "He's my son." Then his eyes turned bleak and he looked back at the photograph. "Or... was."

Linn felt a chill go through her. "Was?" she asked softly.

"He was born during my first tour in 'Nam. A few months after this picture was taken, my wife—ex-wife—decided that I wasn't the kind of man she wanted to spend her life with. Or the kind of man she wanted helping raise her son. So she took him when she left me, and I haven't seen him since."

"Oh, God," Linn whispered, feeling half sick. "Trey... I—I don't even know what to say! How could she just take him away from you? I mean, how could a mother do something like that?"

Trey's expression was haunted in the soft glow of the lamp as he gazed at the picture in his hands. "I can't blame her. Hell, maybe I'd have done the same thing. We got married three months before I shipped out to 'Nam, and when I got back a year later, she. . . well, I'd changed." A muscle in his cheek pulsed and Linn tightened her grip.

"We both had. I was in the marines when I married Diane, and she used to say it was the uniform that had won her over. That it was the uniform she'd really married, and had just taken me as part of the deal." He smiled fleetingly. "When I came back from that first tour, she was wearing love beads and granny dresses and talking about peace marches. She'd let her hair grow halfway down her back and went around with flowers painted on her cheeks, and she had a couple of doped-up, spaced-out hippies camping in the damned basement.

"I'd heard about all the antiwar demonstrations and everything while I was in country, but hell, it didn't make much sense. But I hadn't been home ten minutes when I got my first taste of it. A friend of Diane's came over—I swear he had hair longer than hers—and to say he and I didn't hit it off would be the understatement of the century." He gave a snort of rueful laughter. "He called me a baby-killer and I called him a long-haired freak, and things kind of deteriorated from there. I wound up punching him through the front window, with Diane screaming and crying and the two basement hippies waving incense sticks at me and chanting mantras."

He gave his head a wondering shake. "How I ever got out of there without killing the lot, I'll never know. But I did. I stayed with a buddy of mine that night, and by morning I'd cooled off enough to go back and talk with Diane. But she wasn't in a talking mood. She was packing and waiting for her friend when I got there. I tried to stop her, but it was...well, there was just no point, I saw that quickly enough. The last straw came when she told me she'd legally changed Craig's name to Rainbow SunChild, that she was moving to a commune and that if I ever tried to contact her *or* Craig, she'd have me arrested. She didn't want—as she put it—a baby-killer being anywhere near *her* child."

"Oh, Trey," Linn whispered, "I don't know whether to laugh or cry!"

He gave her a lopsided grin. "Neither did I at first. So I did the only thing I knew how to do—re-upped for a second tour, and went back to fighting Vietcong."

"But when you got home finally, didn't you—?"

"No." His voice was rough and he stared down at the picture cradled between his two sun-browned hands. "I wasn't in great shape when I got back," he said softly. "I spent about ten months in a VA hospital, getting rid of the shakes and the cold sweats and the nightmares, learning how to handle real life again. I'd been wounded just before my tour was up and had some trouble getting off the drugs they were giving me for the pain. Then after I got off that, I had some trouble with liquor...."

He was silent for a long moment, then gave his head a shake and looked at her. "By the time I got myself back together, I realized I'd all but forgotten how to be a husband, let alone a father. I tracked Diane down and discovered that I was divorced. I didn't even remember signing the papers. That was the kind of shape I'd been in." He managed a fleeting smile.

"And... your son?"

"Diane had met someone—her pediatrician, as a matter of fact." That fleeting smile brushed his mouth again. "His wife had died and left him with a couple of kids, and he and Diane found they had something in common and started seeing one another. One thing led to another and they fell in love. She'd held off marrying him until she'd talked to me about it—she didn't owe me a damned thing, but she... well, she'd grown up a lot by that time, too."

He was silent for a moment. Thoughtful. "I met Ken—oddly enough, we hit it off all right—and we talked about Craig. Ken wanted to adopt him, but only if I was happy with the decision. Diane had been given uncontested custody, considering the shape I'd been when we were divorced, but they were willing to give me partial custody or visiting rights or whatever I wanted." He stared again at the photograph, caressing the frame with his thumb. "But hell, I wasn't in any shape to take on fathering, even part-time. Ken could provide the two of them the stable kind of life I'd never had—the kind I figured she and the kid needed and deserved. I didn't want my son growing up in a torn-apart family like I had. So I let him go...."

The admission was torn from him, and the pain in his eyes and voice was raw. He drew in a deep, careful breath. "It was better that way—for all of us. Diane said that when he turned eighteen she'd tell him about me, about what happened, and that if he wanted to track me down it would be all right with her. I said I'd leave the decision up to her. And him. And I have."

"So he could turn up one day. Wanting to know all about his father." Linn smiled and ran her fingers through his hair. "When he does, he's going to find he's very lucky to have you in his life, Trey Hollister. You're an incredible man. . . ."

"I abandoned him," he said softly, his voice raw.

"No. You loved him." Linn kissed his shoulder and slipped her arms around him, holding him tightly. "No son would ever mistake what you did for him as anything but love, Trey." Reaching out, she took the photograph gently from his fingers. She laid it on the table and then leaned across and snapped the light off, leaving them in pale, moonlit darkness.

"Make love to me, Trey," she whispered, drawing him around and into her arms. "Let's leave the past back there where it belongs and take tonight for us."

The tide had come in.

Trey stood in the darkness, staring down at the moon-silvered water, seeing and yet not seeing the huge breakers crashing onto the beach. He drew deeply on his cigarette and blew the smoke out slowly, watching it spiral upward. So much for good intentions. He'd sworn he wasn't going to have another.

But then he'd also sworn he wasn't going to let himself get involved with his raven-haired, blue-eyed neighbor.

He smiled in spite of himself and looked toward the bed. She was sound asleep, hair pooled around her face and shoulders, the sweet curve of one dark-tipped breast limned by moonlight.

Involved, hell. He was halfway to being in love with her.

He took another drag on the cigarette, eyes narrowing against the smoke as he blew it out in a thin stream, and thought of what she'd told him about her husband.

Two and a half years! She'd loved a dying man for longer than he and Diane had even been married.

What would it be like, being loved like that?

Linn stirred in her sleep, murmuring something, and he watched the moonlight play across her breasts and flat stomach and felt his own stomach tighten a little in response. Could she ever love *him* like that?

Or maybe the question was, could he ever let her?

He ground his cigarette out in a nearby ashtray and padded back to the bed, covering her lightly with the sheet, then easing himself under it, trying not to wake her. She murmured again and turned toward him and he cradled her against him.

It had been different tonight. There had been passion and excitement and even moments of abandon, but their lovemaking had been sweeter than their first time together, gentler. She'd reached out to him and had enfolded him in such tenderness and caring that it had started unraveling a tightness within him he hadn't even been aware of. It had been a healing kind of love, a filling kind of love, and for a while, lost within the sweetness of her, he'd felt whole for the first time in his life.

And now?

What happens now, Hollister? he asked himself, staring past Linn's shoulder into the darkness. What the hell happens now?

"What happens now?" Linn shoveled a half dozen sizzling slices of bacon onto the plate in her hand, added two eggs and toast, and handed it to Joe. "I can't just hole up here forever."

"Why not?" Trey accepted the next plate and gave her a very warm, very private smile.

Linn's heart gave a foolish little leap that she pointedly ignored; she walked to the big kitchen table with her own breakfast. Nathan, sitting between Trey and Joe, with Murphy at his side, was munching happily on a piece of toast, and Linn frowned. Everyone seemed ridiculously congenial this morning.

"I don't know how you two can just sit here as though everything's normal!" She stabbed a slice of bacon with her fork. "Santos knows I'm here. God knows what he's going to try next."

"Relax," Trey told her calmly. "We know what we're doing. Trust me. And we've contacted the Canadian authorities. They'll be on the lookout for Santos's men at the border."

"I got across without anyone knowing it," she reminded him pointedly. She nibbled on the bacon, distracted and restless. "I've got to call Kath this morning. She'll be half out of her mind, knowing I didn't check in last night."

Both Trey and Joe looked at her sharply. "What do you mean, 'check in'?" Trey asked. "I thought you didn't know where your sister and her husband were."

Linn looked at him. "I don't. Rod's partner is acting as go-between, so we're always in touch with each other in case . . . well, in case something happens. Rod gave me a special phone number, and every day I call about midnight their time and leave a message, saying I'm all right."

Trey was looking at her intently. "And how do they get in touch with you if they have to?"

Linn glanced at Joe, then back to Trey. "I leave a phone number where I can be reached."

Trey swore under his breath, trading a look with Joe.

"No, you're wrong," Linn put in quickly, realizing what they were thinking. "Only Don Rasky has access to that information. And he wouldn't sell out. They're partners!"

Trey's eyes were hard in the morning light. "Anybody can be bought if enough money's involved."

"Partners don't sell each other out."

"Maybe not, but there's a leak somewhere. Didn't you say that Santos's men have followed your every move?"

Linn nodded grudgingly. "I knew the phone calls were risky," she admitted softly, "but I didn't know what else to do. You don't really think . . . ?"

"I don't know, but we're not taking any more chances. And you're not calling *anyone*, got it? I'll handle it from here on in."

"But—" Linn bit off the rest of her protest as Trey's eyes met hers, as intractable as gray stone. Arguing with him was pointless. He was as bad as her father when he had his mind made up about something. And the irritating part was that they were usually both right.

"Well, I'm going to turn in." Joe swallowed the rest of his coffee as he was getting to his feet, sparing Linn a smile. "That was delicious, Mrs. Stevens."

He gave Nathan a friendly pat on the shoulder as he walked by, moving wearily toward the spare bedroom at the back of the house.

Linn watched him for a moment, then looked at Trey. "He was up all night, wasn't he?"

"I spelled him off for a couple of hours," he replied calmly, his mouth tipping in a lazy smile. "You mean you didn't even notice I was gone? That's great for a man's ego."

"I would have slept through an earthquake. And trust me, Hollister—your ego has nothing to worry about."

"Glad to hear it." His eyes glinted with devilry. He finished his own coffee as he shoved back his chair and got to his feet. "Well, I've got a book to write, among other things. Do you want a hand with the dishes?"

Linn shook her head. "It'll keep me busy for a few minutes. There isn't anything else you want done, is there? I'm going to go nuts sitting around here with nothing to do."

"I can think of two or three things I'd like done," he murmured, slipping his arm around her waist and planting a lingering kiss on the side of her throat. "But they'll have to wait until tonight, after somebody's in bed." He glanced meaningfully in Nathan's direction. "Unless I can get Joe to take him for a walk later this afternoon."

Linn gave a throaty laugh. "Your mind just never quits working out all the angles, does it?"

"Nope." He patted her bottom lovingly. "Especially when you've got such *great* angles." His eyes held hers for a long moment, then he put his other arm around her and drew her gently against him, suddenly serious. "I sure do like having you around, lady. And I don't mean just at night, although I'm not complaining about that, either. But it feels good having you here with me, Linn. Damned good."

"It feels good being here," Linn told him softly.

The skin around Trey's eyes tightened slightly. "Don't tell me I might just be in the right place at the right time for a change," he said carelessly, his voice at odds with the sudden seriousness in his eyes. "That would be a first."

Linn felt her heart give an erratic leap. What did he want her to say? That—as impossible as it was—she'd defied all the odds and had fallen in love with him? Or did he simply want her laughing reassurance that she wasn't getting serious at all, and that his precious independence wasn't being threatened?

"I think," she finally said, very carefully, "that the only person who knows the answer to that is you."

His eyes held hers intently. "What would you like it to be, Linn?"

She stared up at him, her mouth suddenly dry. "Trey, what are we talking about here? What—just what are you asking me?"

He went very still, his eyes still locked with hers, and she could feel a sudden tension running through him, as though he were fighting some great inner battle. Then abruptly he uttered a snort of laughter and released her, turning away. "You serious about wanting something to do?"

Linn drew in a deep breath, her gaze following Trey as he strolled across the room to put his plate and cup into the sink. Fight it, damn you, she told him silently. One of these days, Trey Hollister, you're going to discover that admitting you care for someone doesn't hurt a bit! But all she said aloud was, "Yes. What did you have in mind?"

He poured himself another cup of coffee and turned to look at her, his expression carefully noncommittal. "You told me you have a good background in editing and proofreading."

"That's right." Her voice was a little more controlled than it needed to be, and Linn took another calming breath.

"How would you like to take a run through the first eight or nine chapters of this book I'm working on? Ordinarily I do it myself, but I'm really bucking the deadline on this one and I could use the help. And I wouldn't mind someone going over it with a critical eye and pointing out some of the rougher spots—the writing's pretty erratic. I've had a lot of interruptions, between this damned leg acting up and . . . other things."

"Other things being me," she said with a smile. "I'd love to go through it, but are you sure you want me to? I spent nearly six years editing and proofing a little backwoods newspaper, Trey, and before that I worked with technical books. Fiction, especially men's action-adventure, is a whole different thing."

"I might be on a tight deadline, but I'm not masochistic enough to let someone mess around with my work if I didn't have confidence in them. You've read most of my books, you seem to have a good understanding of Steele and what makes him tick. Maybe a little *too* good at times," he added with a fleeting smile. "And I trust you. It's that simple."

"With an endorsement like that, how could I refuse? When do we start?"

"How about right now?"

Chapter 11

The next two days dragged on interminably.

It seemed inconceivable, but Linn discovered it was possible to be happy, scared and mind-numbingly bored, all more or less at the same time.

The tension was the worst: knowing that Santos's men were out there somewhere, knowing that sooner or later they'd make their move. Every noise made her jump; every time Joe or Trey were gone for longer than fifteen minutes she was certain they'd been ambushed and killed. She found herself wandering aimlessly from window to window, not even realizing what she was doing until Trey would point out, none too patiently, that she was wearing ruts in his hardwood floors and would she for God's sake *sit down*!

Both men seemed unfazed by either the odds that Santos's men could appear at any moment, or by the fact that they were all prisoners to some degree. Trey spent most of his time at his computer, banging out page after page of *Steele on Ice*, and Joe spent the greater part of his waking hours playing endless games of solitaire with a dog-eared deck of cards that went everywhere he did.

To Trey's credit, he seemed to understand what she was going through and tried his best to keep her occupied. He kept coming up with an endless array of things she could do for him: filing, writing out checks for a stack of bills, taking care of updating his business accounts, sorting through seven months of unfiled receipts for his income tax records.

And making love, Linn reminded herself with a secret smile. That was one distraction he took very special pains with.

In fact, it was their nights together that made this whole nightmare tolerable. They'd slip upstairs after Nathan was in bed and Joe had discreetly withdrawn and lie in the dark for hours, making love and talking and laughing and making love again. They even managed to escape a couple of times during the day when Joe, with a knowing wink in Trey's direction, had taken Nathan down to the beach to run off some excess energy.

It seemed impossible, but every time Linn was convinced that it couldn't get any better, it did. Trey was an incredibly skilled, patient and attentive lover, releasing a passion within her she had literally never dreamed she'd ever experience again. It was a part of her nature she'd never even known about until she'd married Jack. And after his death—before, actually—she'd simply closed it off, finding it too painful to remember what they'd once shared physically while watching him waste away a bit at a time, until all that remained was the shell of the vital and passionate Jack Stevens she'd married.

It had stayed closed off. Until now. Until Trey had found the key and given her back the magic of being able to love again.

If only he could find that key for himself, she found herself thinking idly. If only he could just let himself believe in that magic, believe that it *could* be his.

She tossed aside the manuscript pages she'd been proofreading and stretched, yawning and glancing at her watch. Five minutes later than when she'd looked at it the last time. At this rate, the afternoon was never going to end.

She looked at the pages scattered across the sofa beside her: chapters fourteen and fifteen of what was turning out to be a superb book. Different from his others in a way, although that could simply be her perception of it, based on the way she felt about its creator. But it seemed somehow to be a gentler book, without the bitter edges his earlier ones had. Even Steele was different.

Trey was letting more of his hero come out, for one thing. Tidbits of information about Steele's past that explained so many things, the occasional bit of insightful dialogue that provided clues to a complex and interesting man. Steele seemed to be a little less arrogant, a bit more open to the possibility that he might not know all the answers. His methods were still as brutally matter-of-fact and unorthodox as ever, but this time around he was experiencing some guilt, some doubt. And, just maybe, even some love.

Linn smiled, fingering through the pages until she found the one she wanted.

> He watched her walk to the door, feeling something tight and hot spill through his chest. He didn't want to lose her.
>
> For a moment he toyed with telling her what she wanted to hear. What the hell would it matter if he meant it or not? It would keep her here. Telling her he loved her would keep her here.
>
> But for how long? Until she read the lie in his eyes one day and simply turned and walked away? What the hell did a man do then? Invent another lie, then another? When did the lying ever end, once it started?
>
> And if it wasn't a lie? If he really did love her? Would that make it any more certain that she'd stay?
>
> Hell, there were no guarantees. There were never guarantees.
>
> She paused at the car and looked back. He could see the tears on her cheeks, even through the rain. And the tightness, the heat in his chest, pulled even tighter.

Just tell her, you idiot, Linn advised him impatiently. She tossed the page down and got to her feet, shaking her head at Steele's inability to recognize the real thing, even when it was right in front of him.

She walked into the kitchen and poured herself a glass of orange juice, leaning against the counter as she drank it and staring out the big window above the sink. Poe was perched in a half-dead pine and broke into raucous cawing when he saw her. She leaned across and unlocked the window, pushing it open for him. He swooped down and landed on the wide sill, then gave another caw and hopped over to sit on the faucet, tipping his head and eyeing her impatiently until she reached over and turned the water on for him. The moment it started to trickle into the sink he went crazy with delight, screeching and bobbing up and down, trying to catch the stream in his huge beak.

"You're a cheap date, Poe," Linn told him as he finally settled down to drink his fill. His blue-black feathers glistened like coal in the sunlight and she ran her fingers down his back, marveling at the size and strength of him. He murmured with pleasure, then hopped into the sink and proceeded to have a bath, flinging water in all directions as he shook his wings out.

"Hey! That's enough of that!" Linn reached across and turned the water off, whipping her hand back as Poe took a spiteful peck at it. He uttered a loud, angry caw and took off with a strong downbeat of his wings, spraying her with water.

"Keep it up, bird," she called after him, "and you'll be trussed, stuffed and roasted by suppertime!" Swearing under her breath, she mopped herself dry, then picked up her glass of orange juice again.

"You and Poe having a disagreement?"

Trey's quiet voice startled her so badly that Linn's heart very nearly stopped on the spot. The glass went flying out of her hand and hit the edge of the sink, spraying both her and the counter with orange juice, but she just stood there for a moment, eyes closed, trying to collect her scattered wits.

"Relax, Linn," Trey drawled, starting to wipe up the spilled juice. "It's just me."

"Damn it," she whispered through clenched teeth, "will you *stop* sneaking up on me like that! Can't you clear your throat or cough or wear creaky shoes like normal people?"

"Maybe you should just lighten up a bit," he growled. "I told you no one's going to get in here."

Heartbeat still erratic, Linn snatched the cloth from his hand and started blotting orange juice off her sweatshirt. "I know, I know. It's just that this waiting is going to drive me crazy!" She flung the cloth into the sink and leaned back against the counter, taking a deep breath as she combed her hair back with both hands.

Then she sighed and looked at Trey. "I've spent half my damn life waiting and I hate it. Waiting for Dad to come home safe every night—they say that being married to a cop is rough, but it's no joke being a cop's kid, either. After Kath married Rod, it was the same thing—waiting for her to call to say he's been shot or killed or has just gone out on one of his undercover jobs and disappeared. Waiting for Jack to get better, then after the final diagnosis came in, waiting for him to die. Then going through the same thing—the same waiting—with Mother."

"Maybe you just worry too much," Trey told her calmly.

Linn glared at him angrily, then, in spite of herself, had to laugh. "That's what Dad says. He calls me the Official Family Worrier—says it takes the pressure off him because I do enough of it for everyone."

"You and your dad are pretty special to each other, aren't you?" Trey's voice was quiet.

Linn nodded, smiling. "Yeah. A father's bonding with his firstborn and all that. He adores Kath, of course, but they've got more of an ordinary father-daughter relationship. He used to buy her pretty dresses and tease her about boys and stuff like that, but they were never as close as he and I are."

She looked at Trey. "Dad's always treated me like a...a friend, I guess. I was still very much his daughter—I had to toe the line and do as I was told, and heaven *help* me if I stayed out too late. But we've always spent a lot of time together, talking about...oh, just things. Politics, religion, the state of the world. And more personal things, too. If I had a problem with a boy, for instance, it was always my dad I went to for advice. I always figured he knew just about everything there was to know."

Trey smiled faintly, staring out the window at the wind-teased pines, and Linn put her hand on her shoulder, rubbing it gently. "It must have been rough, growing up with no one," she said softly. "I can't even imagine what it would be like, not having someone there you can count on to love you, no matter what. Not having someone to share good news with, or someone who'll comfort you when things get bad."

She drew her hand down his arm, smoothing the dark hairs on the back of his wrist. "I don't think I'd have made it through those two and a half years with Jack if I hadn't had Mom and Dad and Kathy. There were some nights when all I could do was cry, and Dad used to hold me for hours and hours, not saying anything because he knew words wouldn't help. But just *being* there."

"You're an incredible woman, Linn Stevens," Trey murmured, slipping his arms around her and cradling her against him. He rested his chin on the top of her head and she felt more than heard him sigh. "I don't know how you did it, either," he said half to himself. "Where you ever got the strength. . . ."

"I loved him," she said simply. "When you love someone, it isn't hard at all—because there are no questions, no decisions, no doubts. It's just all there."

"I guess I wouldn't know about that," he said almost roughly. Then he shrugged carelessly, smiling. "But you don't miss what you've never had."

"But your wife loved you once," Linn said softly. There was something in his eyes, his face, that tore at her. "And you must have loved her—enough to marry her. To have a son with her."

His eyes hardened slightly. "I might have loved her once—or thought I did, anyway. Maybe I was just looking for someone to hold in the night, I don't know. But whatever it was, it didn't last." His eyes met hers, bleak and cool. "It doesn't come with guarantees."

"You're starting to sound like Steele," she teased, thinking to herself that it was probably the other way around. "Life doesn't come with guarantees," she added more seriously. "No one's standing there the day you're born, promising satisfaction or your money back. You take what you're given, and you do the best you can with it. And it's the same thing with love. It's a rare and a precious gift, having someone love you and loving them back. It doesn't come with guarantees, you're right. But if you really want it, you have to simply trust and jump right in. It's only when you stop holding back for fear of being hurt and just open yourself to everything it can be, that it *will* work."

"The ultimate act of faith?" he asked with a faint smile.

"That's right," Linn said softly. "No reservations, no keeping back little bits of yourself, no dipping your toe in the water—it's all or it's nothing."

"Seems to me like a hell of a risk. No smart person jumps into unknown water without checking out the bottom first."

"That's just the point—there is no bottom. Love is as deep as you need it to be. As deep as you want to make it."

He was staring down at her, his eyes troubled, his face pensive. Then he gave a snort and stepped away, reaching for the carton of orange juice. "You're getting too metaphysical for me, sweetheart. Maybe the kind of work I do for a living makes me a little more skeptical—or a little more realistic. But I like to know where the hell I'm going to land before I jump." He lifted the carton and took a deep swallow of juice.

Linn gazed at him, feeling a kind of weary despair drift through her. What was the point? He'd closed himself off too well, had locked the door and tossed away the key, and odds were he was never going to find the way out. She had thought—had hoped—that if he'd just open enough to let her slip through the barricades around his heart she could start the healing process. He needed to accept love before he could give it, but she was beginning to think that maybe he was too far gone even for that.

"What do you think so far?"

She shook off her brooding thoughts. "About what?"

He looked at her with mild impatience. "*Steele on Ice.*"

"I think it's great. Probably your best yet."

His eyes narrowed very slightly. "But?"

"But what?"

"You tell me. There was a distinct *but* in your voice."

Linn glanced at him, tempted to shrug it off. But then she decided to toss caution to the wind. "Okay, you're right. I do have a problem with the end of chapter fourteen, when Steele's lady—and that's something else. Why doesn't she have a name?"

He shrugged. "I liked the idea of this beautiful woman coming into Steele's life and then leaving, and him never knowing her name. So he can't even track her down if he wants to."

Linn looked at him with growing exasperation. "Honestly, you think of everything, don't you! Everything to keep Steele from having to make a choice, that is. Or a commitment. Kill them, leave them or lose them—is that *your* philosophy about women as well as Steele's?"

A look of irritation flickered across Trey's handsome face. "That's the way life works sometimes," he said gruffly. "You said you were having a problem with something in chapter fourteen?"

"A continuation of the same problem. Why does Steele let her go? My God, the man's hopelessly in love with her! Why doesn't he just come out and tell her?"

Trey's eyes held hers for a long, taut moment. "Maybe he just doesn't know how," he said in a soft, rough voice. "Not everybody does, Linn."

"All you have to do is say the words," she replied very quietly. "That's all it takes, Trey—just the words." And with that, she turned and walked back into the living room, knowing that if she didn't leave now, she was going to say something she'd undoubtedly regret. Like *I love you*, for instance. Just to prove how easy it was.

But it wasn't easy at all. Not loving someone who couldn't love you back, anyway.

All *you* have to say...? Trey stared out the window above the sink again, feeling restless and suddenly on edge. Now just what the hell had she meant by that? He took another swallow of the orange juice, not really tasting it. If either of them was having trouble spitting out what they wanted to say, it was her. He'd left it wide open that morning, had stood there *willing* her to say she wanted to stay here with him, that she figured they had a chance together.

But she hadn't. Those sapphire eyes had held his almost accusingly and she'd turned it right around on him, sidestepping the issue as though it didn't even exist.

Damn it, what did she want from him? Sure, he could tell her he loved her if that was what she wanted. But why mess up a good relationship with a lot of words that could someday come back to haunt them? Words didn't mean a damn thing. Feelings did. Those feelings he experienced every time he looked at her, every time he touched her, every time they made love. The feelings he'd had just that morning when they'd turned to each other in the faint light of dawn and he'd eased himself into her slippery warmth and they'd lain there wrapped around each other.

He'd moved gently, almost freeing himself and then pressing deeply, slowly inside her again, watching her face as that familiar, elusive tension built within her. And he'd sensed a corresponding tension within himself pull suddenly so tight that he'd thought he might explode. It hadn't been simple sexual tension—that was building, too—but something else, deeper and more profound. And it was still there. Even now, just thinking about her, he could still feel it. A deep, aching *want* unlike anything he'd ever experienced. A want so great that he felt torn and shaken apart by it.

He had that to give her. So why were the damned words so important?

He took another swallow of the orange juice, then folded the top of the carton and put it back into the fridge. Words were just—

things. He used them every day, was familiar, comfortable with them. He knew their powers and limitations.

And he knew only too well the kinds of trouble they could get a man into if he wasn't careful. Words like *love* and *forever*, for instance. Love was something that only happened to other people, and forever didn't exist. Just more lies.

Murphy came into the kitchen, hobbling along on three legs, his ears drooping, tail lifeless. He limped over to his dishes and started lapping up water, and Trey smiled.

"We make a hell of a pair, Murph. You'd think we'd be smart enough to keep ourselves out of trouble by now."

Murphy glanced up at him, managing a single waft of his tail, then turned and limped back into the living room.

They made love that night, as they had each night that she'd been there, but this time it was different. It was good—Linn couldn't imagine it being anything but good with Trey—but there was something subtly wrong. Trey seemed slightly preoccupied, for one thing, and although he was certainly there physically for her, she kept having the feeling that something was weighing on his mind.

For her part, Linn had to admit that she kept thinking about Steele and his beautiful lover. The lady with no name. The lady who had captured her man's heart but not the man himself. Like the chameleon that would shed its tail to avoid capture, Steele would rather shed his very heart than give in to love.

She lay in Trey's arms afterward, still brooding about it. If he noticed, he didn't mention it, appearing lost in his own faraway thoughts, and after a long while Linn drifted into sleep.

She didn't know what it was that wakened her. The moon was up, and the room was filled with a ghostly silver light that made everything look eerie and unfamiliar.

Trey was gone. It didn't alarm her at first, because he often got up during the night to check the house or spell Joe for a few minutes. But then she heard Murphy's deep-chested bay of rage and, almost lost in the barking, the distant but unmistakable sound of a gunshot.

She was out of bed and into her jeans and sweatshirt in an instant, and down the corridor and into Nathan's bedroom in the next. He was there, awake but groggy, and looked up at her grumpily as she burst through the door.

"Get up, Nathan," she ordered, already tossing the blankets back. "Come on, honey, hurry!"

He gave a sleepy mumble or two of protest, his voice inching toward a whine, and Linn reached down and lifted him bodily onto the floor, giving him a firm shake. "Nathan! Wake up!"

It was her voice more than her actions that got through to him finally. The sleep vanished from his eyes and was replaced by fear. "What's the matter? How come we're gettin' up?"

"Come on—quick!" She took him by the hand and started back toward Trey's big bedroom. "There's someone downstairs."

Murphy was barking almost hysterically now, and she could hear the sound of running footsteps, a shout, another gunshot, nearer this time.

"The bad men after my daddy?" Nathan broke into a trot, his voice wavering. "The men who bumped our car into the ditch?"

"I don't know," she replied tightly, casting a quick glance behind them. "Quick, in here!"

She ran across to Trey's huge walk-in closet and wrenched the double doors open. There was a big cedar blanket box sitting against the back wall, half hidden under jackets and hiking boots and sweaters. She pulled everything off it, then opened the box and started emptying it. "Nathan, I want you to get in this box and *keep quiet*! I'll toss some of this stuff back over it, and I don't want you to move until I come back up here and get you, understand?"

Nathan peered fearfully into the box, and in the single shaft of moonlight coming through the closet door she could see his chin wobble. "I'll snuffocate!"

"You're not going to suffocate," she told him gently, trying to calm him even as she neared panic herself. Murphy's ferocious baying was reaching a crescendo, and there was the sudden crash of breaking glass. "The lid's not that heavy—you can lift it easily from the inside. And I'll prop it open a bit." She urged him forward. "Nathan, get in! I don't have time to argue!"

He gave her one last frightened look, then obediently clambered into the big box and huddled down, and the last thing she saw as she lowered the lid was his pale, terrified face. She propped the lid open a scant half inch with a paperback copy of *Steele Gambit* she found lying on a nearby shelf. Then she tossed a couple of armloads of the discarded blankets and clothing back over the box, praying no one would think to root through the clutter to open it.

Praying no one got this far.

There were more running footsteps downstairs, another shot, then another, both right outside. What should she do? she wondered frantically. Stay there in the moonlight and darkness and wait? Phone the police? Or grab the revolver out of Trey's night table and go down and help?

She wet her lips, taking only a moment to decide before diving across the bed. He'd shown her the gun their first night together, as well as where he kept the extra clip and shells, and had told her it would be there if she ever needed it.

To her relief, it was. She checked it swiftly, then pulled back the bolt to put a shell in the chamber. It gave an evil snick and she shivered slightly, making certain the safety was on, then grabbed the extra clip and tucked it into her pocket.

She hated guns. But hate them or not, she knew how to use them. Her father had spent countless hours teaching her how to handle just about any handgun and rifle on the market, badgering her to improve her accuracy and competence until they'd often wound up in shouting matches. But tonight, as she walked swiftly down the corridor toward the stairs, she whispered a silent prayer to the stubborn Irish cop who'd made certain his daughter could take care of herself in a tight spot.

Because they didn't get much tighter.

She tiptoed halfway down the open stairs, then stopped, listening intently for any sound that would give her a clue as to what was happening. But there was nothing. Even Murphy had fallen silent, although she thought she heard the quick, predatory click of clawed paws on hardwood somewhere in the darkness.

Not even breathing, she eased herself down the rest of the steps, the revolver braced firmly. She swallowed as she reached the bottom, pausing to get her bearings, then she started moving silently toward the back of the house. Trey... where was Trey!

Linn didn't even know what happened next. There was a gunshot—outside, by the sound of it, but very close—then a slim shadow shot by her, so close she could have touched it if she'd had any warning. It vanished toward the corridor leading to the back bedrooms before she could even swing the gun around, and she stepped forward just as another shadow hurtled out of the darkness and as she scrambled after it, another shadowy form came charging toward her.

Her hand closed on the gun and she swung around just as the shadow paused, breathing heavily. Now Linn could see his face. "Trey!"

He whirled, crouching and bringing the gun in his own hands swinging toward her. "Linn?" His voice was a whisper of astonishment and shock. "What the *hell* are you—?"

"Nathan! *Nathan!*"

It was a woman's voice, coming from the back of the house, and Linn went rigid with shock.

Trey straightened with an oath. "Stay down," he hissed. "Murphy!"

The dog surged to his feet with a roar just as the woman called again, her voice rising in panic and desperation. Linn screamed "No!" just as Murphy took a leap toward the shadow that had suddenly appeared in front of them. She caught the big dog by the scruff of his neck and somehow managed to wrench him to the floor.

"Trey, don't fire! Stop, Trey, for the love of God! It's Kathy! It's my sister!"

Chapter 12

There was a split second of stunned silence, then Trey was bellowing at Murphy to get back and someone else—Joe, by the sound of it—was shouting something from the kitchen.

"Linn?" It was a small, shocked voice, and the shadow stepped forward tentatively. "Is it really you?"

Trey snarled something and moved forward, wrenching the small figure into the moonlight. It was Kathy, all right, scared to death, her eyes and mouth dark circles in her small, pale face.

"What are you doing here!" Linn's voice was rough with shock. "Where's Rod? What's happened?"

"H-he's outside," her sister stammered, "S-somebody started shooting and—"

"Is anybody else out there?" Trey snapped.

"N-no." Kathy's voice wavered and she stared up at Trey in wide-eyed fear, trying to pry his fingers from her wrist. "Linn? Wh-who is this man?"

"Trey!" Now it was Linn's turn to move, her heart pounding. "Rod and Joe are out there shooting at each other."

Trey dropped Kathy's wrist and headed for the door with an oath. He glared at Linn. "You keep her the *hell* inside, got it?"

Then he was gone at a sprint, the gun in his hand gleaming wickedly.

"I knew we should have just gone to the police!" Kathy exclaimed with a sob. "I knew we shouldn't have tried to do it by ourselves."

"Kathy, what in God's *name* are you doing, sneaking around like this!" Linn's own voice was unsteady. She groped for one of the small tables and switched on the lamp. "It's a miracle you didn't get shot! My God, I could have killed you myself!"

Two large tears trickled down Kathy's cheeks. "We didn't know what else to do! You'd disappeared, and th-then this man called and said he was holding you and Nathan and—" She swallowed a sob, shivering so badly that her teeth were chattering. "W-we knew it was probably a trap, but—"

There was a shout outside and another, then the kitchen door flew open with a crash. Someone snarled an oath and someone else started shouting; then three voices were lifted in a cacophony of threats and angry cries that was followed by the distinct thud of a fist meeting solid flesh. More crashes, this time of someone falling. Then finally, only the sound of heavy breathing and a few muttered curses.

Rod appeared first, stumbling heavily into the room as though he'd been given a ferocious shove from behind. He was cradling his bloody mouth and chin, and his dark, handsome face was livid with fury. Joe came in next, looking rumpled and out of breath, and Trey brought up the rear, flexing the bloodied knuckles of his right hand as he stalked into the lamplight, his eyes narrowed and glittering. There was a scrape along the side of his jaw, which was already discolored and slightly swollen, and he was probing his lower lip with his tongue.

"Are you all right?" Rod walked across to Kathy and put a protective arm around her shoulders. She nodded mutely and he looked at Linn, his face haggard and gaunt. "What about you? They haven't hurt you, have they? And is Nathan okay? Is he here with you?"

"Yes." Linn managed a rough laugh, giddy with relief at seeing the two of them alive and unhurt. "And he's fine. We're both fine!" She took two steps and embraced Kathy fiercely. "My God, I'm so glad to see you! And I'm sorry for shouting at you, Kath, but you scared me half to death! If I hadn't grabbed Murphy he would have—" She didn't even let herself finish the thought, giving Kathy another fierce hug instead. "I can't believe it's really you. Both of you!"

Relief had eased some of the harsh lines in Rod's dark face and he enfolded Linn in a smothering embrace. "Thank God you're all right. We've been going crazy with worry for the past week."

Linn hugged the two of them tightly, half laughing and half crying with happiness. "How on earth did you find me? What are you doing here? And why are you sneaking around in the dark like two burglars?"

"That," Trey growled from behind them, "is a damned good question. Valencia, what's going on here?"

"That should be obvious," Rod snapped, his eyes narrowing dangerously. He eased himself away from Linn and Kathy and put himself solidly between them and Trey. "It's me Santos wants, not my family. Let them go and we can talk a deal. But hurt one hair on the head of anyone in this family, and I swear I'll get you. Even dead, I'll get you. There'll be a Valencia on your trail before I'm cold, and they'll follow you to hell itself."

"You've got the wrong man, Valencia," Trey replied in the same chill tone. "I don't work for Santos."

"No?" Rod stared at Trey with hostility. "Then just who the hell *do* you work for? Why are you holding my son and sister-in-law here?"

"Rod," Linn said quietly, "Trey's been helping me. And Nathan and I aren't being held here against our will—we're both here very willingly, in fact."

Rod gave her a hard look, clearly skeptical, and Linn smiled and stepped around him, moving to stand beside Trey. "This is Trey Hollister—and if it hadn't been for Trey, Santos would probably have Nathan right now and I'd be dead. He's been protecting us, Rod. And that's Joe Cippino, a business associate of Trey's."

Rod gave a snort. "Hired thug, you mean. What business are you *in*, Hollister? As though I can't guess. You've got trouble written all over you. And I swear if you've laid a hand on Linn, I'll—"

"Why, you—!" Trey stepped forward on the balls of his feet, fists clenched.

For a fraction of a second Linn thought the two men were going to take each other on there and then. They stood eye to eye, faces hard with anger, and she readied herself to intervene.

"Mommy?" The small, tremulous voice made all four of them swing around. Nathan was standing on the stairs, still in his pajamas, scrubbing at his tear-stained face with his fist.

"Nathan!" Kathy catapulted across the room and scooped the boy up in her arms, and in that instant the tension in the room subsided.

Rod strode to his wife and son and wrapped his arms tightly around them. Linn eased out her breath between her teeth and suddenly realized that if she didn't sit down, her knees were going to give way. She walked to the stairs and sat down harder than she'd intended to, feeling numb.

Trey raked his hair with his fingers, then tucked his gun into the waistband of his jeans, shaking his head wearily as he walked toward her. "What the devil are you doing with that?"

Linn looked down stupidly and discovered she had pulled the revolver out again and was holding it. "I...mmm...thought you might need help."

Trey swore and reached down to take it from her. "It didn't occur to you that Joe and I might have things under control, did it? That you just *might* be safer staying upstairs with the boy?"

"Don't you shout at my sister!" Kathy gave Trey a furious look. "And why did you hit my husband?"

"I'm *not* shouting at your sister," Trey bellowed, "and I hit your husband, lady, because he was trying to kill me!"

"Hey, buddy, that's my wife you're talking to, not some—"

"*Stop it!*" Linn's voice brought instant, startled silence. Taking a deep breath, she stood up and held out both hands. "Just stop it, all of you! Rod, Kathy... Trey is not a hoodlum or gangster, and in fact he's saved my life a couple of times over the past few days. And he's the one you should be thanking for keeping Nathan safe, not me. And Trey, my sister and her husband have been through hell for the last month, and neither of them are acting rationally. So would you all please just calm down, because you're giving me a *headache*!"

Rod glared at Trey and a taut silence crackled between them. Then he mumbled something that could have been an apology, casting a hostile glance in Joe's direction. Trey mumbled something back, and the two of them eyed each other like strange tomcats, bristling with anger and belligerence and too much adrenaline. Finally Rod shoved out his hand and Trey, after a tense moment or two, grudgingly accepted it.

"I think you have my gun," Rod said with precision.

Trey stared at him for a moment longer and then, even more grudgingly, took Rod's service revolver from the waistband of his jeans and handed it to the other man. "RCMP know you're packing this, Valencia? They take gun control seriously up here."

"*Detective* Valencia," Rod snapped, taking the gun and spinning the barrel, checking it before slipping it into the shoulder holster under his leather jacket. "And I have a carry permit." He looked evenly at Trey. "And you still haven't told me who the hell you are. This place is rigged with more alarms and booby traps than Fort Knox. You're either into something that makes you very nervous, Hollister, or you're one unfriendly son of a—"

"Oh, for crying out loud," Linn interrupted, "It's what he *does*, Rod—security, antiterrorism, specialized alarm systems. Would you both just lighten up?"

"So y-you haven't been kidnapped or anything?" Kathy was still kneeling on the floor, cradling a sleepy Nathan against her shoulder. "We thought—"

"Of course I haven't been kidnapped," Linn said impatiently. She was still shaken, remembering how close she'd come to firing at that slender, elusive shadow that had bolted by her in the darkness. "Do I look kidnapped?"

Kathy glanced at Rod. "I told you we were panicking for nothing. I knew she was all right. Daddy's always said Linn would make a better cop than most men on the force."

Rod snorted, looking at Linn with a faint, wry smile. "It's not that I doubted you could take care of yourself in a tight spot, Linn—hell, you've got three generations of Irish cop in you. But when you just disappeared like that, with no word in three days, we...well, we just assumed the worst."

"And then we heard from some man—" Kathy spared Trey a suspicious glance "—saying you were with him now."

"And you thought it was Santos."

"Of course we thought it was Santos." Kathy shot Trey another hostile glance. "He said the only way we could contact you was through him."

"And you traced the phone number to here," Trey said mildly.

"Eventually." Rod looked at Trey. "You're damned good, Hollister, I'll say that for you. It took every resource I had, legal and otherwise, to track you down."

Trey just smiled.

"So you two came charging up here to rescue me," Linn said in disbelief. "Even though it could have been a trap."

"Rod said we couldn't risk wasting time with paperwork."

"Miami vice cops can't come up here to Canada and start operating as though they're on home turf," Rod explained calmly. "Coming up in an official capacity meant notifying the local authorities, and that would have meant bringing people in at a federal level. The whole thing would have turned into an international incident. And while the bureaucrats were arguing over who had jurisdiction to what, you and Nathan could have been murdered or... God knows what."

"So you decided to cut a few corners and free-lance." The corner of Trey's mouth tipped up with the barest hint of humor. "I like your style, Valencia. I think you're crazy, but I like your style. If you ever decide to leave Vice, let's talk. I may have a job for you."

"And speaking of crazy, Kath," Linn said in exasperation, "just what were you doing tearing around here in the dark? I can understand Rod breaking in to look around, but—"

"That's a damned good question," Rod put in. "What *were* you doing up here? I thought I told you to stay in the car and radio for help if I got into trouble."

"I heard shooting," Kathy whispered, hugging Nathan a little tighter. "I couldn't just wait there, not knowing what was happening. I had to find Nathan. I *had* to."

Rod's expression turned grim. "I'd expect a lunatic stunt like that from Linn," he muttered. "That's why I agreed to this entire plan in the first place, because I knew she could handle herself in a rough spot. But, damn it, I expected *you* to know better!"

"Three of the four people I love the most in this world were in this house," Kathy said with conviction, her eyes daring anyone to argue. "I was not going to just sit out there doing nothing when for all I knew, you, Linn and my baby were fighting for your lives in here. You're *family*. And—"

"—family takes care of family," Rod completed with a smile. His eyes were warm as he gazed down at her. "You know," he added softly, kneeling beside her, "there's maybe one woman in a thousand who'd be willing to stick with her man through what I've put you through these past couple of years. Who'd support him in every decision, even when it meant risking her life and the life of their child. I'll never know how the hell I got so lucky, Kath...but I love you all the more for it."

Kathy smiled up at him, and Trey felt something tighten in his gut. Her face held the same radiance that Linn's had that first night when she'd walked in and seen him wearing Jack's old shirt. That expression, he knew now, was simple love.

Simple? Trey snorted quietly. There was nothing simple about either of these women—or the love they had for their men. It was the kind of love a man could build a life on, knowing the foundation was strong, the girders unbreakable. The kind of love that could go through hell itself and come out stronger.

The kind of love, he found himself brooding, that a man only dreamed of finding....

He shook the thought off roughly, like a dog shaking off water, and turned to look at Joe. "Everything secure out there?"

"Shipshape." Joe nodded toward Rod and Kathy, his eyes faintly troubled. "What are we going to do with them?"

"Damned if I know," Trey breathed, shaking his head. Linn had moved to stand by her sister and as she and Kathy embraced, with Nathan between them, Rod slipped his arms around the three of them and hugged them tightly.

Family taking care of family. It was a tight little group, strong and self-sufficient, fortified against the world. He looked at Linn's dark head and found himself wondering where he fitted into the equation now. If, in fact, he fitted there at all.

He rubbed the back of his neck wearily, feeling at loose ends for some reason. There didn't seem to be a hell of a lot left for him to do, but in spite of that he felt oddly reluctant to just wrap it up and call it quits. It somehow didn't feel . . . finished. As though there were still things that needed resolving, bits here and there that needed nailing down.

"So how do things stand now, Valencia?" The three of them were still in a tight little knot that seemed to exclude him and the rest of the world, and Trey felt a jab of irritation. "What's your plan?"

Valencia lifted his head slowly, as though almost too exhausted to make the effort. "Plan?" His voice was hoarse.

"Plan," Trey repeated impatiently. "You *did* come up here with a plan, didn't you?"

Valencia's mouth twisted with a wry smile. "I never thought that far ahead, Hollister. Plans are for people with a future—I've just been living day to day, making it up as I go along." Trey swore quietly and Rod's face darkened. "Don't you worry about me. I'm doing fine."

"I'm not worried about you," Trey replied flatly. "I'm worried about the three people depending on you. You're so tired you're practically sleepwalking, and your wife's out on her feet. I didn't risk my neck keeping Linn and your kid alive just to have you fall asleep at the wheel and put your car over a cliff."

"I've been tired before. And I can still do whatever I have to do to keep my family safe, you can count on it."

"For how long?" Trey asked bluntly. "The shape you're in, you may as well just turn yourself over to Santos and save him the chase. You need help, Valencia. And you need it bad."

Rod gave an exhausted snort. "Yours, I suppose."

"That's right." Trey looked at him evenly. "I do this kind of thing for a living. And I'm damned good at it."

To Trey's relief—and admiration—Rod didn't refuse outright. He looked at Trey for a long while, as though weighing all the options, and Trey's grudging respect for the man took another leap. It wasn't everyone who could accept help when it was offered, even when it could mean the difference between life and death. Especially when his family was looking on.

But maybe in the end it was concern for his family that made him nod warily. "What did you have in mind?"

"You're safe here—safer than out there on your own, anyway. I've got spare beds and plenty of firepower, and I've already alerted the RCMP to what's going down. They've got extra men out, and a special watch set up on the border for any of Santos's people. If anything starts, they'll know about it."

Rod's eyes narrowed. "We're under Canadian jurisdiction up here. How do we know they'll cooperate?" Trey simply smiled, and

Rod eyed him with renewed speculation. "Someday I'd like to hear just what it is exactly that you do, Hollister."

"Does that mean you're staying?" Trey asked blandly.

Rod stared at him for a moment longer, then finally nodded, combing his hair back with his fingers. "As long as you know what you're letting yourself in for. Odds are that Santos already knows I'm up here—he seems to know what I'm doing even before I know it myself. If he does, he's going to be coming in here with everything he's got. And these boys play rough—even with the government crackdown on the Colombian drug cartel, they have enough manpower and arms to outfit an army."

"I have a few resources of my own," Trey told him calmly.

"I should call Don—Don Rasky, my partner. Let him know where we—"

"No," Trey said flatly. "No calls."

"Now wait just a—"

"If you stay here, Valencia, you do it my way, got that? No calls in, no trips out. As far as anyone out there knows, you've just fallen off the edge of the world."

Rod started to get that look on his face that Linn recognized only too well, and she stepped smoothly between the two men. "Rod, the man knows what he's doing. Trust him. Trust *me*."

Rod glared over her head at Trey, but he subsided after a moment or two, easing his breath between his teeth. "No calls."

"How long's it been since you had any sleep?" Trey asked calmly.

"A couple of days."

"Three," Kathy said quietly, her own face gray with exhaustion.

"Then why don't you catch a little shut-eye? We'll all be looking at things more calmly with a bit of rest under our belts."

Linn looked at Trey, her eyes warm with gratitude, and he felt his breathing catch in that odd little way it always did when she looked at him like that. It suddenly occurred to him that their sleeping arrangements might lead to more speculation than she'd be comfortable with and was just going to suggest that he'd take the living room sofa so Kathy and Rod could have his room when Linn said, "I'll put them in the room off Nathan's. That bed isn't being used."

Her eyes held his for a meaningful heartbeat, making his grand gesture a little superfluous, and he found himself smiling to himself at how easy she made it. He watched as she led Kathy and Nathan up the stairs, then looked at Rod. "Before you turn in, I want to know everything you know about Santos—right down to how he thinks. And then I want to beef up our perimeter alarms and—" He stopped dead, frowning. "Which reminds me—how did your wife get in here, anyway?"

Rod snorted. "Don't ask me, man! As far as I knew, she was waiting in the car, about half a mile up the road."

Kathy paused halfway up the stairs. "The kitchen window was unlatched. I just pulled it open and wriggled through."

"And nearly got yourself shot," Linn said disapprovingly.

"But I latched that window myself," Trey protested.

Linn winced. "I...mmm...that was my fault. I opened it to let Poe in, then forgot to lock it."

"I need a drink," Trey said wearily, rubbing his eyes. "Or a cigarette. Anyone got a cigarette?"

"Who *is* that man?" Kathy muttered as she followed Linn upstairs and down the corridor to Nathan's bedroom. "He just walks in and takes over, as though the whole universe runs on his say-so."

"Parts of it, anyway," Linn said with a smile. "Okay, Nathan—back to bed."

Nathan clambered onto the bed agreeably, yawning. "Mommy, are we going home soon?"

Kathy smiled at her son as she tucked the blanket around his shoulders. "Soon, honey," she said softly. "We're all going to stay here for a few days first, though. Daddy has some... some business to take care of, then we're going home."

"Is he gonna kill Santos?" he asked sleepily.

Kathy traded a grim glance with Linn. "I hope not," she told him quietly. "Killing is never an answer, Nathan. Even when it's someone like Santos."

"But Daddy's killed bad men before," he murmured, already half-asleep. "I heard him say so."

"Yes, he has," Kathy said after a moment, frowning as she reached out to stroke Nathan's cheek. "But it's not something he ever *wants* to do, Nathan. It just happens that way sometimes. If he has a choice, he'll arrest Santos and take him to jail."

"Trey'll help him," he whispered, eyes sliding closed. "Trey an' Murph will help Daddy. And Santos won't ever hurt anybody again. . . ."

Kathy stood up slowly, gazing down at her sleeping son. "My God, what's this doing to him? What's it doing to all of us?"

"Come on," Linn said gently, steering Kathy into the adjoining bedroom. "Don't worry about Nathan—he's handling things just fine. Aside from a couple of bad scares, it's been one long adventure to him. But right now it's *you* I'm worried about."

"I don't know how to thank you for keeping him safe," Kathy whispered, sudden tears welling in her eyes. "I knew you would, but I was so scared. And these last two days have been—" She shook her head, swallowing a sob.

Linn gave her a comforting hug. "It's all right now, Kathy. You're safe. Trey and Joe know what they're doing."

"I've never met anyone b-bossier," Kathy said through a sob. "Is he really as good as he says?"

"Better," Linn told her reassuringly. She pulled back the comforter and sheet on the big bed and plumped up the pillows, then started rummaging through her suitcase. "I'll give you one of my nighties, and I want you to get into bed and sleep the clock around. You look as though you haven't slept for a week."

"I haven't," Kathy said with a damp laugh, wiping her eyes with her sleeve. "We've both been catnapping in the car, mostly. I don't know how Rod's managed to stay on his feet."

"Well, you can sleep as long as you want now," Linn told her. "With Trey watching over you, we've got nothing to worry about."

"You sound as though you almost like him," Kathy muttered accusingly.

Linn smiled to herself. "I do," she said very quietly, not looking at her sister. *A lot,* she added silently. *In fact, more than a lot. . . .* She found the nightie she was looking for, shook the wrinkles out of it and handed it to Kathy. "The bathroom is across the hall. Do you want shampoo or anything?"

Kathy shook her head, frowning as she looked around the room. "These are all your things in here, Linn. Rod and I can't take your room—where are you going to sleep?"

"I . . . mmm . . . haven't been sleeping in here," Linn admitted quietly. To her amazement, she felt a blush pour across her cheeks.

Kathy looked at her for a puzzled moment, then her eyes widened. "Oh, my God!" Her eyes widened even more and she sucked in an astonished breath. "You're not—!"

Linn had to smile at Kathy's expression. "'Fraid so."

"Linn!" Kathy looked so sincerely shocked that Linn nearly laughed aloud. "Linn, you can't be serious! Are you telling me that you and...and that...that *man* are—?" She stammered to a stop as though unable to even bring herself to say it aloud.

"I'm a big girl," Linn reminded her dryly. "These things *do* happen."

"Well, I know," Kathy said, still sounding shocked, "but not to you! I mean, in the four years since Jack died I don't think you've even dated more than once or twice. And I certainly never thought you were . . . well, doing *that*."

"I wasn't," Linn said calmly. "Don't play the prude with me, Kath. I used to cover for you when you stayed over at Rod's before you were married, remember?"

"That was different," Kathy protested. "We were engaged!"

"You and Richard Cordston weren't engaged," Linn reminded her pointedly. "I used to tell Dad you were staying with Mildred Jones, remember? If he'd ever found out the truth, he'd have killed both of us. Not to mention what he'd have done to Richard."

"That wasn't the same thing and you know it," Kathy said tartly. "Richard and I had been dating for nearly two *years* before we slept together, and besides that, we'd known each other forever. You've barely even met this man. How long have you known him? A week? Two?"

"It seems like I've known him all my life," Linn said quietly. Then she sighed and sat on the edge of the bed. "Don't give me a hard time on this, Kath, please. I'm as surprised as you are, to tell the truth. I was afraid that—well, after Jack died, all those feelings died, too. I was beginning to think I'd never be . . . normal again. Then I met Trey, and one thing led to another, and suddenly all those feelings were back. . . ."

She shrugged, not looking at her sister. "Jack was the only man I ever loved, Kath. And that part of the love—the physical part—was wonderful. But it ended long before he died, and I guess I never thought it could ever be as wonderful again. But I've discovered that it can be. Trey's made me feel like a woman again. Alive and happy and . . . whole." Finally she looked up, meeting

Kathy's gaze evenly. "I'm sorry if this has upset you, but I'm not going to apologize for it. And I'm not going to sneak around behind your back, pretending nothing is going on. You're my sister and I love you, but this isn't any of your business."

Kathy was silent for a moment, her eyes searching Linn's. Then she smiled ruefully and sat down beside her. "You're right," she said very softly. "And I'm sorry. I didn't mean to sound like a disapproving mother—heaven knows, I've spent enough time trying to convince you to go out and start living again. It just caught me by surprise. I mean, with all that's been going on, the last thing I figured you'd have time for was . . . well, finding a man."

Linn had to laugh. "I'm still a little shocked at myself, to be honest. Or at least at how easy it was. I always thought I'd be racked by guilt, feeling unfaithful to Jack and everything, but when things got to...well, to that point, it was the most natural thing in the world. In fact, I swear I can feel Jack's approval. This sounds absolutely crazy, but I just know Jack would tell me it's okay if he could. I know he'd approve of Trey, too."

Kathy nodded thoughtfully. "He reminds me of Jack a little. Not his looks or the way he talks or anything, but there's a bit of Jack in the way he takes control of things." Then she gave a soft laugh. "Mind you, there's a lot of Jack in *Rod*."

"And a lot of Dad in all three of them," Linn added with a mischievous grin. "You don't suppose there's something Freudian going on here, do you? Daughters falling in love with their fathers and all that heavy-duty psychological stuff?"

Kathy laughed again. "I always thought it was just that we're cowards—just to avoid the fireworks if we brought someone home who didn't meet his standards." She glanced at Linn, looking as though she was wondering if she should ask the next question or not. "Are you in love with him, Linn?" she asked quietly. "I'm not asking as a sister, now. But as a woman."

Linn frowned slightly and rubbed at a grass stain on her denim-covered thigh. "I don't know," she finally said thoughtfully. "At times I *think* I am. But at other times I think that it's just the situation that's brought us together. He's strong and he's protective and I feel safe with him." She smiled faintly and looked at Kathy. "I guess women are always attracted to men who make them feel protected, aren't they? It probably dates back to prehistoric times when our lives, and our children's lives, depended on having a mate who could keep us safe. But it's more complicated today. And I don't know if what I feel for Trey is really love, or just hormones and genetics."

Kathy uttered a peal of laughter and hugged Linn tightly. "There's something to be said for hormones, sister dear. And I'm darned glad to see yours are working again!"

"What's this about hormones?" Rod stepped through the door leading from Nathan's room, thoughtfully rubbing one side of his jaw.

"Linn's hormones," Kathy said blithely, standing up and reaching for the nightie Linn had tossed onto the bed. "She and Hollister are sleeping together."

Linn yelped in protest, but Rod just nodded grimly. "Yeah, I know."

Linn felt her jaw drop, but Kathy just looked at him curiously. "How did you find out?"

"Gut instinct," Rod rumbled, still rubbing his jaw. "So I asked Hollister straight up. He didn't bother denying it."

"And he hit you?" Kathy looked at her husband with interest.

"No." Rod's dark eyes flashed. "I told him if he did anything to hurt Linn, I'd kill him—and *that's* when he hit me."

"Good grief," Linn muttered. "As glad as I am that you two are safe, I'm beginning to think life would be simpler as an only child!"

Kathy just grinned at her. "You'd better get some ice for Trey's hand—Rod's got a jaw like cement." She stood on tiptoe and planted a lingering kiss on her husband's cheek. "You and Hollister had better learn to play nice. I think she's serious about him."

"Kathy..." Linn started wearily.

"The man hits like a street fighter," Rod rumbled, glowering in Linn's direction. "Don't tell me you're thinking of marrying a man who packs a gun."

"I am not—"

"I married a man who packs a gun," Kathy reminded him sweetly. "And so did our mother. Are you saying Mom and I made bad choices in *our* men?"

"I am going back to bed," Linn said with precision. She strode out the door and down the corridor to the accompaniment of Kathy's soft laughter, feeling her cheeks burning. But in spite of herself, she felt her mouth twitch with a smile. At least the horror of the past three weeks hadn't dimmed Kathy's spirit—or dampened that irrepressible sense of mischief!

Chapter 13

Trey was in the kitchen when Linn walked in, swearing creatively as he fumbled one-handedly with the ice tray. His right fist—still a little tender from connecting with Rolfson's jaw—throbbed like a sore tooth, the knuckles already swelling, and he didn't argue when Linn took the tray from him. Wordlessly she gave it a twist and spilled ice cubes into the bowl sitting on the counter. Then she wrapped his bruised hand gently in a dish towel and eased it into the ice.

Trey gritted his teeth, breath hissing, and Linn looked at him. "Did you break anything?"

"No," he growled. "That damned brother-in-law of yours just has a jawbone like braised steel."

"He doesn't think much of you, either," she replied mildly. "That's the same hand you used to hit Rolfson, isn't it?" When he nodded, she gave him a look of mild exasperation. "If you're going to continue battling for my virtue, Hollister, you'd better think about learning to punch left-handed."

He grunted noncommittally. "He always that protective?"

"Since Jack died." Linn filled the ice tray and slid it into the freezer compartment. "Actually he started playing big brother about the time Jack was diagnosed as being terminal. Part of it's the cop in him, I guess—making sure the people in his precinct are safe. And part of it's just that he's a really nice guy.'' Linn's mouth curved into a smile. ''A little blunt, maybe. But nice.''

Trey grunted again, flexing his fingers experimentally. The ice seemed to be numbing some of the pain and would hold the swelling down, but he was going to pay for that rash punch for the next few days. Valencia *had* been blunt. Damned blunt. He'd looked Trey squarely in the eye and had demanded to know what his intentions were, and when Trey had suggested it was none of his business, Valencia had advised him in a cool, matter-of-fact voice that if Linn got hurt—physically *or* emotionally—Trey Hollister was a dead man.

In spite of the pain in his hand, Trey had to smile grimly. It was hard not to respect a man who cut through to the bottom line like that. He shouldn't have been surprised. It made sense that the fierce loyalty and love that Linn felt for her sister and Valencia ran both ways. Like elephants who pull into a tight, defensive circle when one of their own is hurt or threatened.

Did the herd take in strangers? he suddenly found himself wondering as he let his gaze rest on Linn. Or was he forever cursed to remain on the outside, looking in?

He shook off the idle thought, realizing that Linn was looking at him with an oddly thoughtful expression. ''I'm going to get a couple hours of shut-eye,'' he said gruffly, breaking eye contact. He picked up the bowl with his left hand, keeping his right submerged in the ice. ''Everything's locked up tight, and Joe has things under control down here.''

Linn nodded, not saying anything, and they walked into the living room together. ''Is this going to be a problem?'' he asked. ''The sleeping arrangements, I mean? Because if it is, I can take the sofa down here.''

Linn's smile was mischievous. ''Rod making you a little nervous?''

His eyes captured Linn's. ''It would take a hell of a lot more than an overly protective brother-in-law to scare me off you, lady. But if it's going to make things hard between you and your sister, I can take a cold shower and bunk down here.''

''Kathy's not a child anymore,'' she said simply. ''I might have been a little more discreet a few years ago, but there's no need for any of us to be coy at our ages. She knows the situation between you and me, and I think it would upset her more to discover you were sleeping on the sofa." Her smile turned mischievous again as they started up the stairs side by side. "Kathy is, when all's said and done, an incurable romantic. Don't be too surprised if she starts making noises like a prospective sister-in-law."

Trey's stomach gave an odd little wrench and he looked at her quizzically, something in his expression making Linn laugh quietly. "Oh, don't worry," she teased gently, giving him a sultry, sidelong look, "you're not going to wake up face-to-face with the family shotgun."

"That's...good." It occurred to Trey, even as he said the words, that they didn't sound as filled with conviction as they should have. But he was thinking of the expression on Kathy's face tonight as she'd looked up at her husband, that wordless look of unconditional love that held no demands, no expectations.

"They seem to have beat the odds," he said half to himself. As they walked into the bedroom, he realized Linn was looking at him questioningly. "Your sister and Valencia," he explained. "A lot of women wouldn't have put up with having their lives threatened and their families torn apart."

Linn just shrugged. "She loves the guy. And she knew what she was getting into, remember. She grew up watching Mom pace the floor nights, and has watched a lot of Dad's friends go through divorces over the years. Kath might come across as a bit of a scatterbrain, but she's a realist. She went through a lot of soul-searching before she agreed to marry Rod, wanting to be absolutely sure she could deal with the kind of life she'd be letting herself in for. And once she made up her mind to make it work, she learned to deal with the problems as they came up."

Trey looked at her thoughtfully. "Like you learned to handle Jack's illness."

Linn smiled faintly. "I didn't handle it as well as you seem to think I did. One of the reasons I married Jack—I mean other than the fact I was crazy in love with him—was that he wasn't a cop. I'd decided years ago I wasn't going to put myself through that kind of grief. So I married a nice, peaceable newspaperman, thinking the worst I'd have to deal with was a deadline crisis now and again."

She stood by the dressing table, running the brush through her long, thick hair almost absently, her eyes focused on something faraway. Then she gave her head a little shake and looked at Trey. "There was a while at the beginning when I figured fate had really double-crossed me. Then I realized I didn't have a choice—Jack was going to die, and I could either deal with that or run away from it."

"I can't see you running away from anything."

"I was tempted once or twice," she said very softly, staring into the mirror. "But he needed me. I couldn't leave him to deal with it alone." She was silent for a long while, frowning slightly, then took a deep breath and looked at Trey, as though shaking off the past. "Like I said a couple of days ago, love doesn't come with guarantees."

Again Trey just nodded. He sat on the edge of the bed, nursing his throbbing hand, trying to convince himself that the weariness he felt was nothing but the natural result of being up half the night.

"Thank you, by the way."

He looked up just as Linn tucked one foot under herself and sat down beside him. "For what?"

"For helping Rod and Kathy."

He shrugged, easing his hand out of the bowl of melting ice. "Like I told Valencia, this is what I do for a living."

"True." Gently she started unwrapping the cloth from his swollen hand. "But this isn't the same as being hired to help someone. And bringing us all into your home goes above and beyond the call of duty."

"I have to sleep nights," Trey drawled. "Valencia's in no shape to hold off Santos by himself. If I let him take you out of here, I'll just be helping him get you all murdered. I don't particularly want that on my conscience."

But was that the real reason? he found himself wondering grimly, or did it have something to do with the gaping emptiness he felt every time he thought of Linn leaving? She'd be gone for good once he let her go. She'd return to Florida and pick up the scattered threads of her life and he'd never see her again. He wasn't entirely sure he was ready for that yet. For cutting it off so quickly, so cleanly. . . .

"I feel guilty for dragging you into this mess," she said quietly, not looking at him as she examined his scraped knuckles. "It's not fair, getting you involved in my family's problems when the risks are so high. If anything happens to you or Joe because of me, I'll never forgive myself."

"Hey..." Trey tipped up her face so she was looking at him. "I didn't come into this with my eyes closed, lady. I had a hundred opportunities to back out—I stayed with it because I wanted to."

"But—"

She was frowing and Trey smiled, kissing her lightly on the mouth. "But nothing, sweetheart. Call it pride, call it ego—a man likes to think he's needed. And even though you don't need me now that Rod's here, how about letting me hang on to the illusion for a while longer?"

Her gaze moved across his face like the touch of a moth's wing and he could feel the warmth of her breath on his mouth. "I do need you," she whispered, her eyes soft and warm in the golden lamplight.

Trey felt something inside him pull impossibly tight and he lay back against the pillows, tugging her down and across him. Her dark hair spilled over his face like perfumed silk and he heard her sigh as he eased the sweatshirt over her head and caressed the smooth sweep of her bare back with his hands.

"No more than I need you," he whispered, finding her mouth and kissing her deeply, drugging both of them with that sudden, urgent need. Her hands were at the buttons of his shirt, then the zipper of his jeans, and then she was touching him, loving him, her hands and mouth and body enveloping him in magic.

He could hear someone groaning softly and realized it was his own voice as the silk of her tongue sent him swirling to the edge, and he reached up and found her again, naked now, the touch of her skin on his like the kiss of flame.

"I need you more than life itself," he murmured, the words catching as she eased herself down over him, silk on steel, wrapping him in herself. "My God, Linn, I don't know what you're doing to me...."

But there was only a breathing of laughter in the darkness as she started to move, loving him in ways he'd only dreamed of, touching him in ways and places he'd never known existed. She was witch fire and moonlight, surrounding him not just with satiny flesh but with the very essence of herself, sheathing him in an erotic fantasy of need and want and desire.

She took what she hungered for swiftly, deftly and he listened to her soft, tiny cries with pleasure and satisfaction. And then, with a breathless laugh, she started to give and give with a selfless joy, filling him with it, taking him further than he'd ever been before.

There was a moment or two when he instinctively fought it, struggling for control, fearing the consequences should he just let go and let himself be swept away. But then it suddenly didn't matter anymore.

He gave himself over to it with a reckless laugh, trusting in that moment more than he'd ever trusted before. He could hear her whispering his name and could have sworn the sound came from within his own skull, felt the beat of her heart, the rhythmic surge of her blood, the deep flex of muscle as she moved, all within himself. He called out to her and she answered, reached out for her and she was there, not separate, not simply female flesh and sweet laughter in the night but *there*, a part of him like the breath in his lungs, the blood in his veins, soul perfectly meshed with soul.

And then it broke, and breaking, broke again, and he was swept away on a riptide of physical sensation so crystalline it made him cry out. It was a primitive shout that was half conquest and half surrender and as he listened to his own voice, he found himself wondering dazedly if he could ever dare take all this woman had to offer, if he would ever survive the letting go it would demand. But if he didn't, would he ever be able to forgive himself?

"It's nice, isn't it, being one big happy family like this." Kathy helped herself to a slice of crisp bacon and neatly nipped the end off it, chewing thoughtfully. "We've been here four days now and so far Santos hasn't found us, you and I haven't argued even once, and Rod and Trey haven't killed each other yet. All in all, it's worked out better than I'd hoped."

Linn smiled as she started buttering the last slice of toast. Kathy was right: it *was* great having the family together again. Even Trey and Rod had settled down after the first couple of days, managing to be at least civil to one another if not actually friendly. "The problem," she said dryly, "is that they're both used to being in charge."

"That and raw pride. Rod sees himself as protector of the family, and feels his role is being threatened by Trey's relationship with you. And Trey figures that he, not Rod, should be protecting you."

"Nathan seems right at home, anyway." Linn nodded her head toward the far end of the kitchen where Nathan was sprawled on the floor beside Murphy. He was telling the big dog an involved story about a group of space-faring rabbits, and Murphy seemed to be listening intently to every word.

Kathy smiled as she watched her son, then she looked at Linn again. "I think Trey feels left out, if you want the truth."

"Left out?" Linn gave her a skeptical look. "He's pretty much running the show, in case you hadn't noticed."

"Yes, but you and I and Rod and Nathan are a fairly tight little group, and Trey's on the outside looking in."

"By choice," Linn said quietly. But she knew what Kathy meant. She'd sensed it herself at times, noticing how Trey would never join them after supper when she, Rod and Kathy would take their coffee into the living room. How he always managed to be elsewhere when they started playing one of the silly word games they'd invented just to keep boredom at bay. She'd seen him watching sometimes, off in the shadows, his expression carefully closed as he listened to their laughter and comfortable teasing. It was almost as though he was deliberately holding out on them, keeping temptation at bay.

"Are you going to stay up here with him when this is all over?" Kathy asked suddenly.

Linn gave her a startled look. "I don't know. I never really thought about it."

Kathy's gaze held hers. "You'd better *start* thinking about it, Linn. I see the way he looks at you. Especially when you don't know he's watching. Jack used to do the same thing—follow you around with his eyes, as though he just couldn't get enough of you."

Linn frowned slightly, wondering why Kathy's directness made her uncomfortable. Maybe because she didn't *want* to think about leaving. Maybe because, in spite of the ever-present threat of Santos and his people, she was finding it all too comfortable to simply let the days slide by one by one, enjoying Trey's undemanding companionship without having to face the unanswerable questions the relationship posed.

But they were going to have to be faced sooner or later, she reminded herself with an uncharacteristic sense of gloom. She couldn't stay in limbo forever, making no decisions about her life.

She'd sold the business, the house, her very future before this nightmare with Santos started, and that was going to have to be dealt with. And that was going to mean dealing with her feelings about Trey and his about her. How they fitted into each other's life and future. More questions than she had answers for at the moment. More questions than she might *ever* have answers to.

Linn shook her head sharply, annoyed to discover she'd been staring out the kitchen window, lost in thought. Kathy was still watching her, her expression speculative, and Linn picked up the plate of cooling toast and shoved it into her sister's hand. "Don't get on my case, Kathy," she said with quiet warning. "I'll live my own life, thank you. You've got one of your own to worry about."

Kathy's mouth tightened and Linn regretted her sharp tone immediately. She had her own mouth open to apologize when Kathy tossed her head and wheeled away. "Well, excuse me! I didn't realize it was a crime to care about your own sister!"

"Kath..." Linn started after her, then subsided with a sigh. Stress was taking its toll on all of them. It wasn't like her to take Kath's head off over a bit of well-meaning meddling, and it wasn't like Kath to get onto her high horse like that, either. They were both reacting more to tension than to each other, the same way Rod and Trey were getting on each other's nerves.

"What was that all about?"

Trey's quiet voice made Linn glance around. He was leaning against the counter, eating a slice of bacon he'd taken off the plate beside the stove, watching her curiously. Just seeing him filled her with a sudden warm happiness and she smiled as she walked across to him. "Nothing much. Cabin fever, I guess."

He nodded and drew her gently against him so that she was standing in the cradle of his long, outstretched legs, slipping into his embrace as naturally as breathing. She rested one hand on his shoulder as she combed a tangle of dark hair off his forehead with the other. "Hungry?"

"Uh-huh." His dark eyes held hers, filled with mischief. "For more of you, mostly," he murmured, tugging her against him. "I just got my appetite whetted this morning when our guests started stirring and you felt obligated to jump up and make breakfast."

Linn gave him a slow smile and slipped her arms around his neck, toying with a tangle of hair at his nape. "We were well past the whetting stage when I heard Kath and Rod getting up," she reminded him softly.

Trey chuckled and lowered his mouth to hers, kissing her gently. "It was kind of good this morning, wasn't it?" He nuzzled her hair, rubbing his freshly shaven cheek against hers. "So good it begged for seconds. In fact," he added softly, running his hands down to caress the sleek contours of her denim-clad bottom, "I was thinking that we could—"

"No, we couldn't," she told him with a laugh, giving his hair a gentle tug to lift his head as he started kissing her throat.

"Inhibited all of a sudden?" He looked at her in amusement. "Rod and your sister know we're sleeping together. And I presume they're both bright enough to have figured out by now that's not *all* we're doing every night in that big bed."

Linn had to laugh, surprised to find herself blushing lightly. "I know. It's just that she's my *sister*."

"I've got news for you, sweetheart," he said with a chuckle. "I think your baby sister knows all about these things. I doubt they found Nathan under a cabbage leaf."

"That's different," she said with another laugh. "They're married."

"Is that a hint?"

Trey's tone was still amused and teasing, but there was something else in it that made Linn draw back to look up at him. "Of course not," she said in honest surprise. "I thought you knew me better than that by now, Hollister. If I figured you should be making an honest woman of me, I'd come out and say it, not drop oblique little hints here and there, hoping you'd fall over one."

One corner of his mouth tipped up in a wry half smile. "Rebuke accepted and duly noted," he assured her. "It's just that your brother-in-law seems to think I'm taking you for a ride. He advised me yesterday that you're still pretty vulnerable after losing Jack, and that if he finds out that I've wooed you into my bed with false promises, he'll use his service revolver on me. And I have a feeling he wasn't planning on shooting me in the *head*."

Linn had to smile. "I think Rod's having trouble dealing with seeing me with another man, if you want the truth. He really liked Jack. And even though Jack's dead, it's sort of like catching me in adultery. I know that sounds silly, but families are like that." Her smile widened. "Mine, anyway."

"So a man has to marry you to be considered honest, does he?" He was smiling as he said it, but his eyes were watchful.

"Not as far as I'm concerned," Linn told him easily, wondering even as she said it why his words left her feeling strangely empty. She'd entered this relationship with no illusions, no motives, no plans. How could she feel a sense of loss for something she'd never had?

"Good," Trey murmured, giving her a lazy, comfortable hug. "I had a bad feeling that things were suddenly going to get complicated or something."

"Not with me," Linn said lightly, easing herself out of his embrace. It was silly—the last thing on earth she'd ever contemplated was marrying again—but his easy dismissal of it sent a tiny jab of hurt through her. She shook it off impatiently and picked up the plate of bacon. "This is stone-cold by now, but it'll have to do. I just have to put Nathan's porridge in a bowl, and I'll be right in."

Did he really give her an oddly thoughtful look as he turned away? she wondered, or was she just imagining things? Linn watched him as he strode into the dining room, then shook her head again and turned back to the stove.

Without even planning to, she found herself suddenly thinking about their lovemaking that morning. He hadn't been worried about complications then. And neither, for that matter, had she. In fact, they'd come together in the pale light of dawn with nothing more complicated between them than blunt physical need.

They'd already been making love when Nathan's young voice filtered through the heavy bedroom door, and had been for what seemed like a long, sweet while, Trey's body so deeply joined with hers that Linn hadn't been able to tell her heartbeat from his. He'd been moving slowly and rhythmically, each unhurried thrust of his body like silken fire, and Linn had been responding in erotic counterpoint, legs drawn up over his hips, the covers thrown back to give them more freedom.

The only sounds had been the whisper of flesh on flesh, Trey's deep breathing and the tiny, muffled groans that Linn hadn't quite been able to bite back. She'd heard Nathan running up and down the corridor, had heard Kathy's quiet attempts to shush him, but absolutely nothing had been more important at that moment that the man locked in her arms and the spiraling tension centered within her, building with every passing moment.

She'd deliberately held herself back, so familiar now both with Trey and herself that she had no doubt of attaining that sought-after release, and concentrating instead on drawing out the last few minutes for each of them. And Trey, knowing exactly what she was doing, had laughed quietly and cupped her bottom in his hands, shifting his weight and his movements to correspond to hers, watching her through heavy-lidded eyes that smoldered with his own hunger.

But it had finally got away from her and she'd arched under him with a moan, straining and writhing against him as the tautness was pulled that last desperate distance, sending her senses and control and willpower spinning away. Then it had broken in a hurricane uprush of sensation so powerful it had made her cry out and she'd only dimly heard Trey whispering to her, urging her on and on and on.

She'd still been half-dazed with the power of it when Trey's movements had suddenly become rapid and erratic. Then he'd thrust himself against her with a breathless exclamation, his head thrown back so she could see the cords in his throat standing out. As skilled a lover as Trey was, he didn't always manage to bring them to satisfaction as one, and they'd relaxed in each other's arms, laughing and savoring the specialness of it. And then, regretfully, Linn had finally eased herself out of his arms and bed to dress and come downstairs.

A scant hour ago, she reminded herself. And she still tingled from the wonder of it, every nerve ending more sensitive than normal, the muscles in her inner thighs still tender enough to bring an evocative smile to her mouth. Damn that man! All it took was one look, one touch, one smile, and she turned to melted butter. If this wasn't love, it was a pretty good imitation. And maybe that was all she needed for now.

She was just turning away from the stove with Nathan's porridge when she heard the car and glanced out the window above the sink just as Murphy came hurtling into the kitchen. He started into a deep-chested baying that was nearly deafening in the confines of the room, and before she'd even finished drawing in a breath to call Trey, he and Rod were there.

They seemed to fill the room with a deadly competence, moving like cats, quickly, silently, guns out, eyes cold, in tandem like a well-matched team, neither getting in the other's way, seeming to know without words what the other was going to do, where he was going to step. Trey silenced Murphy with one sharp word and positioned himself at the door as Rod crouched low and eased himself toward the sink. He dared a swift glance out the window, then dropped like a stone, gun hand braced.

"One car," he said softly. "Gray four-door. Driver and a passenger, both male."

Trey frowned, searching his memory for a description of the car. He shook his head. "You get a good enough look at them to recognize them?"

Rod shook his head, wetting his lips.

Trey moved quietly away from the door. "I'm going to go out onto the deck and slip around behind them—I think I can make it without being seen. But if—"

"Rod? Hey, Rod, you in there, old buddy? It's Don!"

Trey saw Linn stiffen in disbelief and looked down at her. "It's Don Rasky," she said in astonishment. "Rod's partner."

"Rasky?" Rod sounded as surprised as Linn. He glided to the window and ventured another quick glance outside. "Well, I'll be damned. It *is* him!"

"Hold it!" Trey's hand shot out and grabbed Rod's arm as he started for the door. "It could be a trap."

Rod's eyes glinted. "He's my partner, for—"

"I don't like it," Trey said with quiet urgency. "How the hell did he find you?"

"Because I told him," Rod said with precision, wrenching his arm out of Trey's grasp. "I called him a couple of days ago."

"Damn it, Valencia, I told you not to—"

"You're not my keeper, Hollister." Rod shoved his revolver into his shoulder holster. "You might be hot stuff with security systems, but Don Rasky and I have been partners for five years. And we've been fighting garbage like Santos for the same length of time. So don't tell me how to do my job!"

For a brief moment Trey was tempted to toss Valencia right through the damned door, just for the satisfaction it would give him. But he dragged in a deep breath and forced himself to relax, reminding himself that it *was* his fault the man was here in the first place. No two ways about it: he was getting too old for this kind of—

"Rod, you haven't stayed alive this long by being careless." Linn eased herself between them, her tone placating. "It can't hurt to be extracautious, can it? Let me go out and meet him, and—"

"No way!" Both men snapped it out at the same instant, trading hostile glares over the top of her head.

"I'll go," Trey growled, shoving Linn behind him. "Valencia, you—"

"Butt out," Rod snarled in return, roughly shouldering by Trey. "It's safe, I tell you! He's too damn good to let Santos put a tail on him."

"It's not a tail I'm worried about," Trey told him angrily, reaching across to unlock the door. He met Valencia's furious stare evenly. "It's your neck, *Detective*. But if something goes wrong, hit the deck and hit it hard—because I'm going to be right behind you, and I'm going to be firing at anything that moves. Got that?"

Rod's reply was an unintelligible mutter, but the pugnacious look he gave Trey needed no translation. And Trey, for his part, very nearly landed a knockout punch on the other man's chin there and then. He knew if he did there'd be hell to pay when Rod came to, but at least it would get him out of the way for long enough to confirm that everything was safe. And maybe save his damned life into the bargain. It wouldn't be the first time he'd had to use brute force to protect a man from his own stupidity.

As though knowing exactly what Trey was thinking, Rod eased his weight back, balancing himself on the balls of his feet, eyes narrowed as though waiting for Trey to make a move. They faced each other for a tense moment, then Trey whispered a savage oath under his breath and wrenched the door open.

"Just keep your eyes open, Valencia," he snapped. "I don't relish having to tell Nathan he has to face the rest of his life without a father because his old man was too damned thickheaded to listen to reason!"

Rod didn't answer. But he did, to Trey's approval, draw his revolver before stepping into the carport. "Don!" he called. "What's up?"

"We, uh . . . we've got news. About the trial. New information." Rasky wet his lips and glanced around nervously. "You up here alone, buddy?"

Something was wrong. Trey eased himself through the door, gun hand braced, safety off. Rasky was scared—so scared Trey swore he could smell it. And why didn't he step away from the car? If these two were such good friends, there was no need for that much caution. Rasky's eyes kept darting this way and that and he was sweating heavily, even in the cool morning air. He looked like something trapped and afraid, backed so far into a corner that he knew there was no way out.

"Valencia . . ." Trey kept his voice low, but he knew Rod heard him. Knew too he'd heard the warning in it, and the fact that he stopped abruptly told Trey that he'd also sensed something wasn't quite right. Trey glanced around swiftly, unable to see Joe but knowing the man was in position.

"What's going on?" Rod asked calmly. "Who's that in the car?"

"You . . . okay?" Rasky seemed to be having trouble swallowing.

"I'm fine," Rod replied. "Are you coming in or what?"

Trey honestly didn't know if he actually saw the car door open, or if some gut-level instinct told him what was going to happen before it actually did. But he was moving before he'd even consciously made the decision to do so. His mind separated two distinct images as he dived toward Valencia: one of the car door swinging open and the figure of a man stepping out, the weapon in his hands turning toward Valencia, the other of Rasky wheeling around with his arms outstretched, his mouth wide as he screamed something.

A warning, maybe. No one would ever know. Even as Rasky flung himself at the man with the weapon, it swung up, fired a short burst and Rod's partner spilled back across the hood of the car, as limp as a rag doll. Trey only saw it happen from the corner of his eye; he tackled Valencia low and hard and they both went sprawling across the floor of the carport.

The assault rifle was firing as they dropped and Trey heard bullets stitch the air above their heads. The doors on the far side of the car opened and two men piled out, both holding small automatic weapons. Trey started firing even as he rolled free of Valencia, scoring at least one hit; he could hear Joe opening up from one of the upstairs windows on what sounded like an AK-47.

One of the gunmen sagged against the car door and for an instant there was a lull as Joe pinned down the remaining two. Trey was on his feet in a heartbeat, grabbing a stunned Valencia by the arm and dragging him toward the door. Trey gave Valencia a ferocious push that sent them both sprawling, a spray of gunfire coming so close behind that the edge of the door frame exploded into slivers of wood even as Linn was slamming the door shut.

Chapter 14

To Trey's relief, the metal lining in the door—untested until now—held firm against the barrage of bullets, and he breathed a prayer of thanks to whatever whim had made him install it in the first place. The glass in the window above the sink was bulletproof too, and although it had crazed badly it seemed to be holding. Long enough for them to get their wits collected, anyway.

Abruptly the shooting stopped. Trey cat-footed to the window and looked out, just in time to see the car backing rapidly up the narrow, tree-lined driveway. It vanished around a curve and a moment later he heard the engine stop. They, too, were clearly taking time to regroup.

Valencia was slowly getting to his feet, his face gray, looking so ravaged by disbelief and the shock of betrayal that Trey almost felt sorry for him. "You . . . you saved my life, man," he croaked, looking at Trey numbly.

"If anyone has the pleasure of killing you, Valencia, it's going to be me," Trey told him gruffly. "You hit?"

"No." Rod shook his head slowly. "You're bleeding pretty bad, though."

Trey blinked, then looked a trifle stupidly at his left arm, realizing that blood was dripping off his fingertips into a growing puddle by his feet. He flexed his fingers, relieved to discover nothing was broken, and peered gingerly at the deep gouge on the inside of his upper arm. There was no pain yet. Adrenaline, fear and shock were numbing everything but a peculiar heaviness in his arm, though he knew from experience that it would wear off all too fast.

Linn was there a moment later, looking grim-faced and pale; she ripped away the torn, blood-soaked shirt sleeve and wrapped a pressure bandage around the wound with the swift competence of someone used to medical emergencies. Suddenly he found himself thinking of Jack, wondering if she'd looked at him with the same fear in her eyes, and became aware—as she obviously already was—just what a close call he'd had. The bullet had passed between his arm and his body. A few inches to the right, and it would have been game over for one Trey Hollister, man of action.

"A little close for comfort, but I'm all right," he said quietly, holding her gaze. "How about you?"

"Scared," she said succinctly. "Joe called someone by the name of Ryerson, and apparently help is on its way. Thirty minutes at the outside."

Knowing he didn't have the time to waste, he slipped his right arm around Linn and held her against him, breathing in the wind-and-sea scent of her thick hair, letting her body warmth flow through him like a calming wave. He could feel her trembling slightly and tightened his embrace.

"We're barricaded in here pretty solidly. All we have to do is hold them off till the cavalry gets here."

She drew back after a moment, smiling humorlessly. "You're a damned liar, but I appreciate the thought." Then her smile faded and she looked up at him, eyes very calm. "I know what these guys are capable of, Trey. They've got the latest in sophisticated military weaponry—most of it bought from American suppliers, and all of it the best money can buy. Grenade launchers, rocket launchers...and every other kind of high tech killing toy available. And they're not going to wait around out there for the police to show up. Joe said another car came in a few minutes ago, so they've got reinforcements." She swallowed. "They're going to hit us with everything they've got. And I—"

"Linn..." He stopped, not even knowing what he wanted to say. She was right. And they both knew it.

"I know this is incredibly corny," she said softly, "but if we don't get through this, Trey, I want you to know that you've made me unbelievably happy for these past couple of weeks."

"Linn, we're—"

"Shh." She put her finger across his lips. Her eyes searched his, such a clear blue they were almost azure, and he felt something pull tight in his gut, a desperate kind of ache that was half wonder, half despair. "I do love you, Trey Hollister," she whispered. "No matter what happens, at least I've had that."

The words hit him like a fist, knocking the wind—and whatever he'd been about to say—right out of him. He had to fight to catch his breath while his mind spun with a hundred possibilities, none of them making the slightest bit of sense. And it occurred to him that it was a little like getting shot again, every nerve ending as numb as stone.

Linn's mouth curved in a beguiling smile. "Don't look so scared, Hollister—I'm not putting you to the test. If we don't make it through this, it won't matter. And if we do, we can just put it down to the usual irrational things people say when they think they're going to die, and pretend it never happened, okay?"

He should be saying something, he knew. Something very wise and reassuring and preferably heroic. But the only words that kept spilling through his mind were the wrong ones, full of rash promises and hasty declarations he doubted he could ever live up to. The tangle of emotions within him seemed to wrap itself around his heart, a Gordian knot of wants and wishes and crazy, hopeless dreams, and for a split second he very nearly said the words he knew she wanted to hear, the words that kept filling his mouth with their sweetness.

"Damn it, Linn," he managed to growl, "this isn't—"

"They're starting to make their move." Joe's quiet voice brought Trey's head up, eyes narrowed, every sense alert. Joe was standing in the doorway, his arms full of weapons. "I counted six of them, but there may be more. Enough artillery to start a war. They've split up—two coming up from the beach, two from the north, two coming in through the trees at the front."

The icy knot in the pit of Linn's stomach tightened and she glanced around to find Kathy standing near the stove, her eyes wide and frightened, hands convulsively clenching and unclenching on Nathan's shoulders.

Trey nodded authoritatively. "Okay. I'll take the beach side. Joe, you take care of the ones coming from the north and—"

"I've got the front covered," Rod said grimly. He seemed to be over the worst of his shock now and although he was still pale, there was a glitter of healthy malevolence in his eyes that hadn't been there before. Joe tossed him a stubby, evil-looking weapon of some kind. Rod fielded it easily, then took the handful of magazines that Joe held out for him. "In case we don't make it out of this, Hollister, I want to thank you right now. For taking care of Linn and Nathan. For taking Kath and me in. Not many men would have done what you've done, knowing the odds."

"Forget it," Trey growled, slapping a full magazine into the weapon Joe handed him and checking it. "I didn't do it for you, I did it for me. And the kid." He flashed an unexpected smile at Nathan. "How are you holding up, sport?"

"Are those bad men going to kill us?" Nathan's voice was just a whisper.

"Not a chance," Trey said grimly. "Your dad's too good a cop to let that happen."

Rod cast Trey a startled look. Then he smiled faintly in appreciation. "I owe you, Hollister."

"Damn straight," Trey assured him with a reckless grin. "And I intend to collect, Valencia. So let's get it done. Linn..."

"Right here." She stepped forward and took the revolver he handed her, checking it expertly. "Where do you want me?"

Trey held out a plastic card. "Take this. It's a coded access card to a security room built in behind the sauna." Linn took the card, looking at him questioningly. "The linen cupboard swings out from the wall," he went on with quiet urgency. "The release catch is just inside the frame, about waist height. Swing the cupboard out of the way and you'll find a steel door—that card slips into a slot and unlocks it.

"Inside there's a couple of small rooms. It's built like a bomb shelter, sheathed in a special high-grade steel and stressed concrete, and can withstand even a direct rocket hit. Once the door is closed it's impregnable. The air is filtered and recycled, so it's completely self-sufficient. You can hole up in there for weeks if you need to—there are a couple of camp cots, a chemical toilet, food, water...everything you need."

"Trey..." she started warningly.

"I want you to take your sister and Nathan and lock yourselves in there," he said flatly. "No arguments, Linn. We don't have the time. Just do it. And take Murph with you," he added. "I don't want him hurt, either."

"I will not leave the three of you out here with—"

"Linn, do as the man says." Rod looked at her beseechingly. "If there's a chance to get Kath and Nathan through this . . ."

He didn't need to finish. Linn nodded once and wheeled away, smiling with false calm as she reached for Nathan's hand. Tears prickled behind her eyelids, hot and sharp, but she held them back through sheer force of will, refusing to look around. No goodbyes, she told herself fiercely. Goodbye means you don't expect to see them again. Goodbye means . . .

"Come on, Nathan," she said lightly. "We're going to find Trey's secret hideout."

He took her hand trustingly and Kathy stepped toward Rod, her eyes swimming. "Rod, please. I can't just—"

"Do it," Rod said roughly, scooping her into a fierce embrace, his own eyes squeezed shut. "Just do it, Kath. When this is over, I'm going to take you and Nathan for that tour of Ireland we've always been talking about. And Hawaii."

"I don't want to go to Ireland," Kathy whispered brokenly. "Or Hawaii. I just want to go home with you. So don't you do anything stupid and heroic, hear me?"

"We're running out of time," Joe urged tightly.

Kathy turned away from Rod and stumbled toward Linn, chin wobbling, trying not to let Nathan see her crying, and in that moment Linn's eyes met Trey's. They burned into hers, filled with all the things they'd never said to one another. Then he too turned away and walked from the room.

Linn, fighting to hold back her own tears, started for the back of the house where the sauna was. "Don't any of you do anything stupid and heroic," she told Joe sternly. "Murphy, heel!"

The linen cupboard built into the wall between the sauna and a luxuriously appointed bathroom ran from floor to ceiling, the shallow shelves filled with a rainbow of towels, scented candles and soaps, shampoos and other toiletries. Linn fumbled inside the door frame for the hidden lock, finding it easily.

It gave a muted click when she pressed it and the entire linen cupboard swung away from the wall on silent hinges, revealing the heavy, gray steel door that Trey had described. Her hand was shaking so badly that it took her two tries to slide the thin plastic code card into the slot, but it finally sank home and she could hear another quick click as it released some locking mechanism embedded deep inside the thick blast door. The door glided partly open, as silent as death, and Linn swung it the rest of the way back.

When the door opened, it activated a low-intensity, battery-operated lamp mounted high on one wall; the three of them peered mistrustfully into the dim interior. Cupboards lined one wall, presumably holding the supplies Trey had mentioned, and there were a couple of camp cots as well as two or three folded canvas chairs.

"Not exactly the Holiday Inn, but it's nicer than some of the places Rod and I have been staying," Kathy said with a forced smile. "Come on, Nathan."

"Take this." Linn held the revolver toward Kathy, who looked at it as she might regard a live viper. "Damn it, Kathy," she urged impatiently, "this isn't the time to be squeamish! You know how to handle one of these—Dad taught you, too, in spite of the fact you fought him tooth and nail over it. Now take it!"

Kathy took it distastefully. "Why? You're the Annie Oakley in this family."

"Because I'm not staying with you," Linn said calmly. "Murphy, get in here. And guard, do you understand me? Guard Nathan!"

The shepherd gave a sharp bark and Linn nodded, looking at her sister. "Okay, you'll be fine in here. The door unlocks easily from the inside—see the catch? But don't open it unless you're absolutely sure you know who's out here."

"But..."

"See this monitor screen?" Linn pointed to a small screen set in the wall beside the door. On it she could see the doorway where they were standing. "He's got a camera out there somewhere, focused right on this door so you can monitor who's outside at all times." She gave a soft, strained laugh. "Damn, he's good! He's thought of everything."

"Linn, you heard what he said! You've *got* to—" There was a sudden chatter of gunfire in the distance and Kathy flinched.

"You'll be as snug as a baby in bunting in here." Linn started to swing the door closed. "Now remember what I said—don't open it unless you're absolutely sure who's out here."

"Linn, you're going too far this time!" Kathy caught the edge of the door before it closed, her face grim with determination. There was more gunfire, accompanied by the sound of breaking glass. "I am not letting you risk your—"

"Kathy, I'm not risking anything I haven't risked for the past month. Now the only thing that got me through it—that has gotten Rod through it—is knowing that Nathan is safe. That's all that matters! You get in this shelter and stay there!"

The door clicked shut, cutting off Kathy's protest in midword, and Linn watched it for a mistrustful moment, half expecting Kathy to fling it open again. But she didn't. Linn stepped back and swung the linen closet into its niche. It fitted smoothly, with just a faint click, and all evidence of Trey's little bolt hole vanished as though it had never existed. Then, tucking the plastic access card into the pocket of her jeans, she turned and started making her way cautiously back to the kitchen.

There were more shots, coming from both inside and outside the house, and Linn ducked instinctively. She eased herself along the corridor, trying not to flinch every time a burst of gunfire shattered the stillness. It was coming almost continuously now and she could hear bullets raking the side of the house like hail, ricochets whining off the stonework of the foundation.

There was a resounding crash just outside the carport door, then a burst of gunfire; the bulletproof glass in the window above the sink, already badly crazed, seemed to crumble like old cheese. It sagged inward and spilled into the sink and Linn dropped like a stone as a spray of automatic weapon fire stitched across the far wall, filling the room with flying plaster, dust and noise.

It stopped after a moment and in the deathly silence that followed, Linn peeled herself off the floor and scrambled into the relative shelter of the island, pausing there to catch her breath and try to steady her shattered nerves.

Her knees were shaking so badly that she was afraid to even attempt standing up, so she just knelt there, wishing she hadn't been so damned impulsive. What in God's name had made her think she might be able to help? Sure, she knew how to handle a gun, but all her father's training and advice had in no way prepared her for facing a South American death squad! Even if she didn't get herself killed, she was liable to distract Trey or Rod at the wrong moment and get one of them killed.

She knelt there for another moment or two, trying to work up enough courage to make a dash for the living room. Trey would be there. And for some reason it seemed very important to be with him. Even now. Or maybe especially now.

She'd actually gotten her feet under her and was just about to bolt for the door when someone started firing through the window again and the row of brightly painted ceramic canisters right above her head exploded. She dropped back to her knees, arms around her head, as fragments of glazed earthenware poured around her. The filter coffee machine was the next to go and Linn sucked in her breath as she was showered with hot coffee and shards of glass.

She didn't even notice the man come through the window until she caught a movement out of the corner of her eye and glanced around the end of the island in time to see him jump lightly from the countertop to the floor. He crouched there for a heartbeat, glancing around swiftly to check his surroundings, and Linn flattened herself against the side of the island with an indrawn gasp.

He hadn't seen her! Linn's heart was pounding so hard that she was certain he must be able to hear it; she crouched there, absolutely frozen, not even daring to breath as every nerve ending screamed at her to head for cover.

But she ignored the impulse, knowing that if she ran the deadly looking weapon in his hand would swing around and he would bring her down with no more than a flex of his trigger finger. *Just please don't let him come around this end of the island,* she prayed silently. Why, oh, why hadn't she stayed with Kathy and Nathan, hidden and safe and . . . ?

The man moved, his feet crunching through the broken glass, and Linn stiffened. But he didn't move toward her. Instead, gliding as stealthily as a hunting cat, he started to make his way toward the door leading into the living room.

Paralyzed with relief and raw terror, Linn couldn't move. She was certain that if she so much as took a deep breath she'd shatter into a million pieces, so fragile was her control. Then she heard Trey's voice as he shouted something to Rod or Joe, and realized with sudden, brutal clarity that he had no idea their barricades had been breached.

Keeping the island between the intruder and herself, she peeked cautiously around the corner. He was in the dining room now, heading swiftly and silently for the living room. She could see someone beyond him, someone crouched by the ruins of what had once been the patio door, his broad back undefended.

Trey, Linn realized dimly. He had his weapon up and was firing through the shattered glass of the big door, spent shell casings raining onto the hardwood floor around him. The intruder paused at the door to the living room and stared at him, then, as though in slow motion, he raised his own weapon and aimed it right between Trey's shoulder blades.

Linn didn't even realize what she was doing until she was in motion. Without conscious thought she was on her feet and sprinting toward the crouched figure as though her very life depended on it, screaming *"Behind you!"* before she'd even cleared the kitchen door.

The intruder turned awkwardly and she was on him before he'd gotten the gun swung all the way around. If he hadn't been coming out of a crouch, it wouldn't have worked. But he was off balance and her flying tackle sent him staggering back against the wall with a grunt of pain, very nearly knocking the semiautomatic rifle out of his hands.

She caught a glimpse of Trey leaping to his feet, his face white with shock, heard him shout something... and then the intruder brought the butt of his weapon up and around so fast that it was just a deadly blur. In the next moment the very universe exploded and she was being sucked into a spinning vortex of bright-spangled darkness; she could hear her own cry hanging disembodied and distant in the air as she slid down and down and down....

"No...!" Trey's shout of anguish and rage echoed through the room, too late. He saw Linn's head snap back, watched her sag bonelessly to the floor and felt something within him tear loose, the pain more real than anything he'd ever experienced. He was still on one knee, knowing he was never going to get his own weapon up to snap off a shot before the intruder killed him. He watched the barrel of the semiautomatic arc smoothly toward him, thinking very calmly that it was all right, that there really wasn't a hell of a lot to live for without Linn, anyway....

"No! *No...!*"

It was a woman's scream this time, half terror and half fury, and for a split second Trey thought it was Linn's voice. But she was still sprawled limply at the intruder's feet. He blinked, realizing with some tiny, rational part of his mind that the shout had been real—real enough to make the gunman falter once more and glance around.

It was all the opening Trey needed. Bringing his gun the rest of the way around, he moved out of instinct and habit, but before his finger had even tightened on the trigger, a single shot cracked through the room.

It was followed almost instantly by another, the roar of Rod Valencia's service revolver this time, coming from so close behind him that Trey flinched, half-deafened. The intruder was slammed back against the wall so hard that the house shuddered, then he fell sprawling, the stubby weapon flying out of his hand and spinning across the polished hardwood floor.

There was a heartbeat of utter, stunned silence. Trey stared at the fallen gunman, then lifted his gaze to look at the woman standing in the kitchen doorway. It was Kathy, in perfect shooting stance, arms outstretched, left hand bracing her right, and she was holding the small revolver he'd given Linn. She was staring at the fallen man blankly, as though not really comprehending what had happened, and Trey heard someone behind him whisper a shocked oath.

Slowly Trey became aware of other sounds. Sirens, this time. And the thunder of a helicopter, the pulse beat of its rotors all but drowning the amplified, authoritative voice that was ordering everyone to lay their weapons down....

Trey closed his eyes for an instant, then lowered his own weapon and set it aside. It was over. Somehow, impossibly, they'd managed to hang on long enough.

Not wanting to startle Kathy, Trey gently eased himself to his feet. Rod stepped by him and walked cautiously toward his wife, holding out his hand. "Give me the gun, honey," he said quietly. "Come on, Kath—swing it down and put the safety on and hand it to me. You can do it, honey."

Kathy blinked, then looked at the gun in her hand as though seeing it for the first time. A look of revulsion crossed her face and she opened her fingers and let it drop, the sharp thud when it hit the floor making them all jump.

"I—I killed him," she whispered, starting to shake violently. "M-my God, I killed him...."

"No, you didn't," Rod said reassuringly. "It was my shot that hit him. You missed him by a country mile." He bent and retrieved the gun, then eased his arms around Kathy and drew her close. "I love you, honey, and I appreciate the gesture...but you're still one hell of a lousy shot."

Which was as fancy a bit of lying as he'd heard in a long while, Trey mused as he swiftly checked the gunman. The man was dead, all right, but it would take a forensic lab to tell which of the two bullets had actually killed him. Kathy might be a lousy shot—but when it counted, her aim had been as true and deadly as her husband's.

He touched Linn's cheek with the back of his hand, relieved at the warmth that rose from it, then placed his fingertips on the side of her throat. Her pulse was strong and regular and he let his breath out tightly, not even aware until then that he'd been holding it. There was a gash on her temple and her hair was sticky with blood, but it had obviously been a glancing blow, looking worse than it was.

"She isn't dead?"

It was Kathy's voice, tremulous with fear, and Trey shook his head. "No, but once she comes to and that headache sets in, she's going to wish she were." He brushed a strand of silken hair off Linn's cheek and gazed down at her, still aching with that deep, knifelike fear that had cut through him when he'd seen her fall. The realization, in that instant, that if he lost her, everything else just made no sense at all.

There were the sounds of running footsteps outside, someone bellowing orders through a loud hailer, someone else banging on the door and demanding to be let in by the authority of the Royal Canadian Mounted Police and half a dozen other enforcement agencies and official-sounding government departments.

Trey looked wearily at Rod. "How would you like to let those boys in before they bust my front door down?"

"With pleasure," Rod said just as wearily, walking across the room. "With pleasure."

The room was dark. Or almost so, illuminated only by the warm glow of naked flame. Someone had lighted the fire and Linn watched the flames weave intricate patterns on the ceiling. She could hear the murmur of voices nearby, blending with the murmur of the fire into a comfortable background noise that made her feel very safe and warm.

Her head had stopped aching. Or rather the potent little capsules that the doctor had ordered her to swallow had kicked in, and their narcotic haze simply made the ache bearable. She reached up very gingerly and touched her right temple, fingering the thick wad of gauze, and wondered if she dare try to sit up.

"Don't even think about it," a quiet baritone said from the shadows beside the fireplace. "You're supposed to be playing invalid."

"Trey?" Her voice sounded dry and raspy.

A lean shadow eased itself from the darkness just beyond the ring of firelight and Trey crouched beside the sofa, his dark eyes filled with concern. "How are you feeling?"

"Like I got run over by a herd of stampeding buffalo," she muttered.

"How many fingers am I holding up?"

Linn squinted at his hand. "What fingers?" The concern in his eyes turned to outright worry and she had to laugh, immediately regretting it. "Joke," she whispered hoarsely. "My God, it was just a joke!"

"Damn it, Linn," he protested tightly, "this is no—"

"Three fingers," she said consolingly. "But if you start asking me to count backward from fifty or repeat my name and address a dozen times, I'll strangle you."

He managed a fleeting grin. "Sorry. The doctor said your X ray came back clean—nothing cracked, concussed or bent out of shape. Except your sense of humor," he added as a dark afterthought. "And I still wish you'd stayed in the hospital overnight for observation like the doc wanted."

"No." Linn fought a sudden shiver. "I hate hospitals. I've spent too much of my life in hospitals, watching the people I love die."

He nodded, and she could see by his eyes that he understood. His face was pale and drawn, the lines bracketing his mouth deeper than she'd ever seen them, his hair matted with dried sweat. He looked worn-out and worn down, and she put out her hand and touched his cheek with her fingers. "Are you all right? No more bullet holes or anything?"

"Nope. Everyone's fine."

"And Kathy? They told me what happened . . . that she saved your life. And probably mine."

"She's okay. Pretty shaken up, but we all are."

Linn smiled. "She's something else, isn't she?"

Trey gave a snort of wry laughter. "You're both something else! What does it take to get either of you to do what you're told?"

"Whatever it is," someone growled from behind him, "I've never discovered it." Rod stepped into the firelight and grinned down at her. "How are you doing, Sis?"

Linn stared at him. "What happened to your eye?"

Rod grinned sheepishly, touching the puffy, bruised skin around his right eye. "Nothing much. Just stepped in front of an unfriendly fist, that's all."

"You and Trey weren't—!"

"Not Trey," Rod assured her. "Some government type in a shiny blue suit who kept getting in my way when we were trying to get you into the ambulance."

Trey's mouth canted to one side. "This brother-in-law of yours packs a pretty mean wallop. He just about caused an international incident, mind you, seeing as the guy he took a poke at was RCMP, and they're already a little ticked off at all the ruckus and paperwork we've caused."

"Are we all under arrest or anything I should know about?"

Rod snorted. "Trey seems to know everyone worth knowing in this part of the country. He spent the last couple of hours smoothing ruffled feathers." He gave Trey a speculative look. "One day, Hollister, I want to hear what you *really* do for a living. That guy was on the phone checking your credentials for about two minutes flat before he was standing at attention, calling you *sir* and doing everything but saluting every time you looked at him."

Trey just smiled lazily. "I write books, Valencia. I already told you."

"Sure," Rod said in a disbelieving drawl. "And my sister-in-law here is just another pretty face."

"Well, I won't argue with that." Trey gazed down at her, his eyes suddenly serious. "You saved my life, lady," he said very softly. "That guy had me cold. I'd have been dead before I hit the floor if you hadn't been there."

Linn shivered suddenly. "I don't even want to think about it. I've never been so scared in my life." Trey reached out and meshed his fingers with hers and she smiled, wondering what was going on behind those private, silver eyes. She still couldn't tell what he was thinking most of the time. Even now, even after what they'd been through, he had the barricades up, the action as automatic as breathing.

She stifled a sigh and turned her mind instead to other, more immediate things. "So what happens now? Can the police up here guarantee Rod some protection, or are we—?" She stopped dead, intercepting the look that Rod traded with Trey.

"I guess no one got around to telling her," he said with a faint, tired smile.

Linn looked at him sharply. "Telling me what?"

"It's over, Linn," Trey said quietly. "Santos is dead."

She heard the word, but her mind kept fumbling it like half-frozen fingers fumbling a ball. "Dead?" Even when she said it herself, it didn't sound entirely real. "You...don't mean that man who broke in here, the one I tried to stop, was—?"

Rod shook his head, managing a smile. He moved the big hassock across to the sofa and wearily sat down. "It would have made my day if it had been, but no such luck. That guy was just a hired gun." He blew his breath out and scrubbed his fingers through his hair, raking it back.

"One of Santos's competitors saw his chance to take over Santos's empire—just another two-bit hood with a billion or two to spend on weapons and hired assassins. He and his army took Santos down early yesterday morning. It happened in Santos's Caribbean stronghold, and not much news of it leaked out—which is why we hadn't heard anything."

"But if Santos was dead, why did these guys—?"

"They didn't know about it, either," Trey said. "Santos had dispatched this team three days ago, right after he'd found out that Rod was here. They were operating on their own, with no contact with Santos to minimize the chance of a leak."

"Dead," Linn whispered, feeling stunned. "I can't believe it."

"Believe it," Rod told her grimly. "From the pictures the RCMP showed me, it was a bloodbath. There aren't more than half a dozen of Santos's men still alive, and there are contracts out on all of them. The three that got picked up here are so scared, they're spilling everything they know, just for the promise of some protection."

"So... it's over." Linn drew in a careful breath, afraid of jarring her head. It didn't seem real, somehow. None of it seemed real.

"It's over," Trey repeated quietly, his fingers tightening on hers. His gaze seemed to burn into hers, seeking while giving away nothing, and she realized he was thinking the same thing she was. *Over. It's all over....*

Chapter 15

"What are you two doing?" Kathy's voice was brisk with impatience, and Linn looked over Trey's head to see her sister bearing down on them like a wrathful spirit. "My God, I don't believe this! The doctor told you she had to have plenty of rest, and the minute I turn my back you're in here pestering her!"

"Filling me in," Linn protested with a smile. "How's Nathan?"

"He and Murphy are tearing around the beach like nothing has happened," Kathy said with a wondering shake of her head. "The first thing he asked when Rod told him Santos was dead was if that meant he could go outside and play now."

Linn smiled drowsily, the fire's warmth and the medication she'd been given making her so sleepy that she could scarcely keep her eyes open. "The kid's just got his priorities straight, that's all." She gazed up at Kathy for a long moment. "When I gave you that gun, you were supposed to use it to protect yourself and Nathan, not take Santos's men on single-handedly."

"I just got tired of you grabbing all the heroics for yourself," Kathy said lightly. "I thought it was about time Patrick Duffy O'Connor's younger daughter showed she was made of the right stuff. After all, a cop's daughter who's married to another cop shouldn't be hiding when trouble hits."

Kathy's smile was careless, but Linn could see the horror still lurking in her eyes, knew it was going to be a long while before either of them could get through a full night without meeting Santos in their dreams.

"You don't have to go proving anything to me," Rod grumbled, reaching out and taking Kathy's hand.

"I was proving it to myself," Kathy said quietly.

Rod smiled at her, then looked around at Trey. "That's quite a little bunker you've got built in there."

"In my line of work it's handy to have a secure place where you can stash someone and know he's safe. Politicians marked for assassination, court witnesses with a price on their heads—" he paused to give Rod a wry smile "—potential kidnap and ransom victims...." He shrugged. "Whatever."

"Whatever." Rod smiled and shook his head slowly. "Just a natural extension of the bulletproff glass in the windows and steel cladding in the doors and walls, right?"

"Right."

"Which is fine, providing the person you're hiding stays hidden." Linn gave Kathy a pointed look.

Kathy smiled faintly. Then the smile faded and she looked at Linn seriously. "I'd have lost my mind in there, not knowing what was happening. I just knew that if it was as bad as I suspected, Rod and Trey would need all the help they could get. I always swore I'd never have a gun in my hand, but when the people you love are in trouble..."

She shrugged, reaching down to run her fingers through Rod's thick hair. "I can't remember being as mad in my life as I was when I stepped through that door and saw that man hit you with his gun. And I knew Trey didn't have a chance—" She stopped again, shuddering lightly. "Anyway, it's over. I don't want to talk about it. Linn, are you hungry? I've made some soup."

Linn shook her head, wondering drowsily if Kathy really believed Rod's well-intentioned lie about having missed her target, or if she suspected the truth. Maybe she'd ask one day. Years down the road when the horror had finally faded.

Then she looked at Rod, knowing she had to ask, wishing she didn't. "And Rasky?" she asked softly. "He really was helping Santos, wasn't he?"

Rod's face went hard and cold. "Yeah," he said roughly, the disgust on his face almost palpable. "He was the key man—he knew every move we were making."

"But he was your partner," Linn whispered. "Partners don't sell each other out."

"Partner, friend," Rod said bitterly. "What's friendship and honor compared with a million in cold, hard cash?"

Linn closed her eyes, opening them a moment later to look at Trey. "You knew all along, didn't you? Both you and Joe. That's why you wouldn't let me call in anymore."

Trey's face was as hard, as cold, as Rod's. "I'd hoped I was wrong. But it was the only thing that made sense. I could see you letting Santos get the drop on you once, but not a second or third time—you're just too damned good for that. But from what you'd told me, every time you made a move, Santos's men would be there before you'd even unpacked. That information had to be coming from inside—and Rasky was the obvious choice."

"We could use you on the Miami force, Hollister." Rod gave Trey a humorless smile. "It was right in front of me—and all the others—and we couldn't see it."

"In my business you learn not to trust anyone," Trey said quietly. "I've seen brother sell out brother for a pocketful of cash."

"They'd planned to grab Nathan and use him to bring Rod out of hiding." Kathy stroked Rod's hair. "But catching you didn't turn out to be as easy as they'd thought." She laughed quietly and looked at Linn. "You outwitted Santos's hired muscle at every turn. You've been driving them crazy for three weeks, staying just out of reach."

"I wonder why Rasky didn't just take care of you himself," Trey said with a glance at Rod.

Rod managed a bitter smile. "I have a feeling that's why he was up here—that he hadn't delivered me as promised, and Santos sent him up here to finish the job in person." He stopped, a muscle along his jaw rippling.

"But he couldn't do it," Trey reminded him sofly. "At the end he tried to stop them. He died trying to save you, Valencia. It's not much, God knows, but you have to give the man that."

"He's been hooked on cocaine for the last year," Kathy put in. "His wife suspected that something was going on, but she couldn't pin it down. Even a couple of officers who have been working with Rasky while Rod's been handling the Santos investigation had a feeling he was into something heavy."

"One of them called a couple of hours ago to say that they found a note in Rasky's locker that suggested he was considering suicide," Rod added. "I guess the stress was getting to him, between being so strung out he'd hock his own grandmother for a few grams of coke, then selling me out to Santos."

Kathy looked at Linn, her expression cold. "I know I should feel sorry for him, but I can't. I can understand someone getting in too deep. I can even understand him being afraid to ask for help. I can't understand him selling out his own partner."

Rod shook his head wearily, shoulders sagging as though weighed down. "I don't know, man. Maybe if I hadn't been so obsessed with this Santos case I'd have seen something was wrong. Been there to help when he needed it. That's what partners are for. . . ."

"It's over," Linn reminded them quietly. "We'll never know what demons were chasing Rasky, but I suspect he's more at peace now than he's been for months. And you can't start blaming yourself, Rod. Whatever turned Rasky bad came from the inside, not the outside. If he really wanted help, he knew all he had to do was ask and you'd be there for him."

Rod nodded, still staring at the carpet between his feet, and Kathy stroked his hair gently, looking pensive and sad.

"Why don't you catch some shut-eye?" Trey murmured, giving Linn's hand a gentle squeeze before unbraiding his fingers from hers and getting to his feet. "You've had one hell of a day."

Linn thought about arguing, wanting to hear more about what had happened to Santos, about what had gone on while she'd been unconscious. But her eyes kept sliding closed and finally it was just easier to leave them that way. She thought she felt the feather touch of Trey's lips against hers, but then they were gone and before she could catch herself, she felt herself slipping swiftly into the oblivion of sleep.

* * *

"We're really going home?" Nathan's small, dirty face was radiant with happiness as he gazed up at Kathy. "And Grandpa's coming home, too?"

"Yes, honey," Kathy assured him, "your grandpa's coming home. And your Aunt Linn's going to be staying with us for a while, too. So we're going to be a family again." Grinning broadly, Kathy looked up from her packing. "I honestly can't believe it's over, Linn. No more running and hiding. No more waking up in a cold sweat in the night, expecting to see Santos standing there with a gun."

She continued her packing, then looked at Linn. "Rod's quitting Vice."

"Quitting?" Linn stared at Rod in astonishment.

He nodded, his face grim. He still looked tired and haggard, and when his eyes met hers, they were the eyes of someone very old and very embittered. "It's a war zone out there," he said simply. "And it's no place for a thirty-five-year-old man with a wife and son. This last year working undercover on the Santos case made me look hard at my life. And one thing I realized is that a dead Rodrigo Valencia isn't a hell of an asset to anyone." He smiled at Kathy. "And my wife deserves more than I've been able to give her lately. A lot more."

"We want another child, for one thing," Kathy added. "We talked about it a lot during the last few weeks on the run from Santos. Neither of us is getting any younger, and I think Nathan's at a good age to really enjoy a brother or sister."

"A baby? And Rod quitting Vice. Good grief. . . ." Linn looked from one to the other.

"The word 'quit' is purely relative," Rod told her with a smile. "We're putting together a new drug crime task force that will be working hand in hand with the feds, and I was asked if I'd like to head it up. I wasn't sure at the time—I was still too caught up in this Santos thing—but I've decided to take it."

"I'm glad," Linn admitted quietly. "My heart's in my throat every time the phone rings—I always expect it to be Kath, telling me something's happened to you."

"For a cop's daughter, you sure worry a lot."

"That's *why* we worry a lot!" Linn and Kathy chimed in unison.

"I got us seats on a three o'clock flight out of Vancouver, and a charter flight out of Tofino harbor at noon. That sound all right to everyone?"

"Yeah!" Nathan bounced around the room as though he were on springs, radiating boundless energy and excitement. "Wait'll Gandpa sees all the shells I found!"

"And I think one of the first things we have to do when we get home," Rod said with great seriousness, "is get you a dog."

"A dog?" Nathan stopped dead, his eyes widening. "For real? Do you mean it? A *dog*?"

"I think you're old enough to take care of one, don't you?"

"Yeah!"

Linn smiled to herself, watching the three of them. Kath and Rod had obviously used their time in exile to sort out their priorities and were bursting with renewed energy and ideas, anxious to get on with their lives. But she hadn't given the future a lot of thought at all. Content, she reminded herself, to simply take each day as it came. To savor this wonderful and completely unexpected magic she'd discovered....

Her heart gave a sudden thump. She swallowed, knowing she couldn't put it off any longer. "I'll... be back," she said quietly, looking at Kathy. "I have a couple of things to do before we leave."

Kathy's eyes held hers. "There's no rush, Linn."

Rod looked up. "We have to be in Tofino in an hour."

"Shut up, Rod," Kathy said calmly. "Like I said, Linn—there's no rush."

Rod opened his mouth to protest, then shut it firmly at a glare from Kathy, and Linn took a deep breath and started for the stairs.

Trey had opened the outside door of the kitchen and was standing in it, leaning against the frame and staring out toward the beach. The sky, a deep, sultry blue, promising late-day heat, was curdled here and there with clouds and the morning air was cool and smelled of sea salt, tidal beaches and forest. It was an earthy, primitive scent, one Linn had never entirely gotten used to, and she breathed it in deeply as she strolled across to stand beside him.

The tip of his cigarette glowed like a small jewel against the sky as he drew on it, eyes narrowed against the smoke. "So. I guess this is it." He didn't look at her as he spoke. He braced his forearm on the door frame, the cigarette in his hand, and stared at the rising smoke.

"Yes, I guess it is. Kathy's packing Nathan's things now."

He nodded, still not looking at her. "You're going, aren't you?"

Linn frowned, hearing something in his voice she couldn't quite pinpoint. Anger, perhaps. Wistfulness. "I have to. Kath could use a hand getting things back in order, and with Dad coming home and everything . . ."

He nodded again, taking another deep drag on the cigarette. He blew the smoke out slowly, watching it drift upward. "I guess neither of us really gave much thought to this part, did we?"

"No," Linn lied, her voice just a whisper. She'd thought of it a lot, wondering how—when the time came—she was ever going to leave. Wondering how much of herself she was going to leave behind. Wondering if . . .

"Trey, I . . ." She paused. "I don't even know where to begin thanking you," she finally whispered.

"I already told you I had my own reasons." He glanced aside at her, smiling very faintly. "Mind you, I'll admit I was hoping it was going to last longer."

"Me, too," she whispered.

"Damn it, Linn—" He stopped, swearing softly, then tossed the cigarette down and ground it out with his toe. "I don't want it to end like this," he said quietly, turning to look at her. "When I told you at the very beginning that I didn't want to be just a pair of arms in your night—damn it, I meant it. I thought you understood that."

"You've been a lot more than just a pair of arms in my night, Trey. And you know it."

"But you're leaving."

It was more accusation than observation and Linn frowned, not knowing what he expected her to say. What he wanted her to say. "I have to, Trey. My whole family's been torn apart, and we need time to get things back to normal."

He was looking at the sky again and she watched him for a silent moment, wishing he'd turn and look at *her*. There was anger in the set of his shoulders, in the way he held his head as he stared out at nothing, narrow-eyed and silent.

"And I . . . have things I have to sort out, too. Where I'm going to live, what I'm going to do. I just had to leave everything up in the air when this Santos mess happened, and I have a thousand decisions to make and . . ." She shrugged, willing him to turn around to look at her. To say something.

"You're not making this any easier," she said after a moment or two, her voice quiet. "We both knew this was going to happen, Trey. Sooner or later."

"Yeah." His voice was rough.

Linn ran her hand up his arm. "You . . . mmm . . . could always ask me to come back." She smiled, daring to touch his cheek with her fingertip.

"What's the point?" He turned his head from her touch and pushed himself away from the door, brushing by her as he walked back into the kitchen. A battered pack of cigarettes lay on the counter and he picked it up and shook it, swearing when it relinquished nothing but a few shreds of tobacco. He crumpled it angrily and tossed it away, pacing restlessly.

Linn felt a jolt of responding anger and tried to ignore it, knowing it was nothing more than a gut-level reaction to Trey's behavior and refusing to give in to it. "A lady sometimes likes being asked." In spite of her best efforts some of the anger got through, giving the words an edge she hadn't intended.

Trey gave her a sharp look. "I'm not into games, Linn."

"I'm not asking you to play games!" She caught the anger and swallowed it. "I'm just asking you to talk to me, Trey. I think I deserve some sort of . . . of explanation."

"For what?" He started rummaging through one of the kitchen drawers, not looking at her.

"For why you're acting like this!" She stared at him in frustration. "Why are you doing this to me, Trey? Why are you making it sound as though it's my fault we're arguing? As though I've broken some sort of promise I don't even remember making?"

Finally he found what he was looking for. Opening the pack of cigarettes impatiently, he took one out and lighted it, drawing on it deeply.

"Damn it, Trey, will you talk to me!"

"What the *hell* do you want me to say?" He wheeled toward her angrily, expelling the smoke in a thin stream. "You've already made up your mind, so what's the point in discussing it?"

Linn stared at him in exasperation. "So this is how it's going to end? Thanks for the memories, it's been nice . . . if you're ever in the neighborhood again, give me a call?"

His chin lifted fractionally and he held her gaze with faint defiance. "You're the one calling the shots, babe."

Linn turned away and walked to the open door, blinking back a prickling of tears. "You really know how to make a woman feel cheap, Hollister," she whispered, rubbing her bare arms against a sudden, deep chill. "I don't deserve this and you know it. I didn't just pick you up on some beach and take you to bed. It *meant* something. And you're turning it into something tawdry and . . . empty."

"You're the one who's leaving, not me," he said in a low, rough voice. "You're the one who's calling it quits."

"I'm not calling it quits!" Linn turned around to look at him, gesturing angrily. "My family *needs* me!"

"Damn it, *I* need you!"

His words rang through the kitchen, clipped with his own anger, and Linn glared at him. "Trey—don't *do* this to me! Don't make me decide between you and my family. It's not fair!"

"I'm not asking you to *decide* anything," Trey said tightly. "It's just that I thought we had something here. Something good. Something that was working. And then I wake up one morning and you're packing to leave."

His words were filled with such bitterness that Linn simply stared at him. Then slowly she started to understand.

This wasn't about her at all. It was about an eleven-year-old boy whose mother had died, abandoning him to strangers. It was about a young marine coming home from the horrors of Vietnam to discover his wife was suddenly someone he didn't know. And a few days later, that same woman walking out of his life forever, taking the son he'd never gotten to know but had never forgotten, whose picture he still kept by his bed.

And how many others? she found herself wondering. He'd built those barriers around his heart tall and strong to protect himself from further loss, yet their very existence made that loss all but inevitable. How many other women had simply walked out of his life, unable to break through the barricades and weary of trying, bruised and wounded like moths battering against a window, trying to reach the candle's flame?

It chilled her to the bone, thinking of all that loss. All that leaving. . . .

"I just don't see why you're making it so damned difficult, that's all!" He stabbed the half-smoked cigarette into an ashtray. "We're good together, Linn. Hell, that's more than most men and women ever get. So why are you making it so hard?"

"Because I want it all, Trey," she replied wearily, wondering if he'd ever be able to understand.

"All? What the hell do you mean, all? All of what?"

"Of you." She looked at him calmly. "Trey, I'm not interested in a halfway love affair. I want something lasting. Something that's got the inner steel to withstand all the hard times."

"Damn it, do you want me to say I love you?" He sounded angry and confused, almost trapped. "If that's what you want, you've got it!"

"I don't need you to say it, Trey," she said softly, "I need you to *mean* it."

"Does anyone ever mean it?" he asked brutally. "You never know, Linn. It's like jumping into deep water blind, you told me that yourself. You take a deep breath and hope for the best."

Linn shook her head. "Not with love, Trey. You have to be ready to commit. Ready to *make* it work."

"Commit?" he barked. "Commit, hell, lady! *You're* the one who's running away."

"And you're not stopping me!"

"Didn't you hear what I just said? I said I love you! What in the hell else can I—?"

"Yes, I heard," Linn replied softly. "But they're just words, Trey. You say 'I love you' like it's some kind of magical incantation. But I don't think you really believe in it. And magic doesn't work unless you believe."

He was staring at her with such confusion and anger that her heart ached for him, yet there was no way she could make it easy for him. Or for herself. Because it would always be that halfway kind of love she swore she'd never settle for, requiring no more commitment from either of them but the assent of the moment.

"You said you loved me." His eyes held hers, almost daring her to deny it. "Didn't that mean a damned thing?"

"I do love you," she whispered. "Or at least as much as you'll let me. But that's the problem, Trey. You keep fighting me, holding me out."

"Fighting you?" He wheeled away with a bark of harsh laughter throwing his hands into the air. "God almighty, woman, what do you want from me?" It was a cry from the heart, a cry of anguish and anger and confusion, and Linn closed her eyes and turned away, her own heart aching.

"I want all of you," she whispered. "But you're fragmented and torn up inside, Trey. There's a vulnerable part—the part of yourself you never let me near. And a doubting, mistrustful part. It's as though there's another Trey Hollister inside you, detached and unaffected by everything that happens. I can sense him sometimes, even when we're making love, standing off to one side, watching and analyzing."

He stood there as though frozen, saying nothing, his face expressionless, and Linn felt a little part of her die as she realized he was doing it again: shutting her out, keeping her from getting too close to that vulnerable, private core.

Then he gave a snort and started pacing again. "If you think that's what love is like, you're dreaming," he said with a rough laugh. "No person can open up that much, Linn. You want something that isn't even possible!"

"It is possible, Trey," she whispered. "But this way it's just too... too one-sided. And I won't settle for that."

She'd thought she could. There had been a couple of times in his arms when she'd thought she might be able to do just that—to take the small bits of himself that he could bear to part with and make a life of it. To settle for *need* and *want* and *caring* instead of love.

But she knew now that it just wasn't enough. She'd had it all with Jack, and she wanted it all this time. Unless Trey could open up and accept her love, unless he could admit he loved her as much as she suspected he did, they simply had no future. It had to be real and it had to be forever.

"Will you be back?" His voice was ragged.

Linn looked at him evenly. "Do you want me to come back?"

There was a heartbeat's pause. "Do you *want* to come back?"

Linn simply stared at him, then she managed a sob of laughter. "My God, if you even have to ask, what's the point!" He was still staring at her, his eyes narrowed slightly now, and Linn sighed, suddenly so tired and dispirited she felt numb.

"Look," she said wearily, "if we keep this up, we're both going to say things we'll regret. We need time to work this out, and right now time is something we don't have. I'm going back to Florida to help put my family back together. And if you want me—*really* want me—you know where to find me."

She turned away and walked toward the door into the living room, willing him to call her back. Say it, damn you, she felt like screaming. Say it like you mean it, and I'll stay!

But he didn't.

And Linn somehow kept walking.

Chapter 16

Steele watched her walk to the door, feeling something tight and hot spill through his chest. He didn't want to lose her.

She paused at the car and looked back. He could see the tears on her cheeks, even through the rain. And the tightness, the heat in his chest, pulled even tighter. Then abruptly she turned, opened the door to the car and slipped behind the wheel.

"Wait!" He caught the door before she pulled it closed, and she looked up at him, startled. Steele braced one hand on top of the car and smiled down at her. "I don't even know your name. How will I find you?"

For one long moment he thought she wasn't going to tell him, that it had all been for nothing, after all. Then finally she gave him a small, wry smile. "I thought you'd never ask," she whispered. "And my name is . . .

What? Trey stared at the computer screen angrily. What *was* her name, this raven-haired beauty who had managed to send Steele into such a tailspin? Cleo, Damask, Rio... nothing seemed to fit. That was one of the reasons he'd left her nameless in the first place, because he couldn't come up with anything that felt right. There just didn't seem to be any name that captured the rarity and wonder of this very special woman.

Carolyn. Carol-Lynne. Linn....

Trey swore ferociously and shoved his chair away from the keyboard, reaching for the package of cigarettes. What the *hell* was the matter with him, anyway? Why was he having so much trouble getting this scene written? It wasn't even much of a scene—two pages maybe, three at the most. Yet he'd been grinding away at it for over two weeks now, ever since his household had gotten back to what passed for normal. He'd written the damned thing every way he could think of, and it *still* didn't work.

He toyed with the cigarette, then tossed it back onto the desk. It wasn't working this time, either. Another day wasted, and all he'd managed to do was get Steele out that damned door and into the rain, putting his heart and guts on the line.

There had been a time or two during the past few days when he'd been ready to throw the whole thing out. The problem was, he'd already made the mistake of letting his publisher see the first hundred or so pages. They were back there now talking about breakthrough books and fifty weeks on the *New York Times* bestseller list and publicity tours and God knew what else.

And here he was, sweating his way through three pages that just would not take shape.

He rubbed the back of his neck wearily, tempted to call it a day. Except that would leave him with nothing to do for the rest of the afternoon and evening. As long as he kept busy, he was fine. But when he had too much time on his hands, he started to think about Linn, about the hurt in her eyes when she'd turned away from him that last time. And that led to a whole lot of brooding and sleepless nights.

He wrenched his mind back from the course it was following and pulled his chair over to the desk, eyes narrowing.

> No. Steele gritted his teeth, strode down the stairs and out into the rain. No, damn it, he wasn't going to let her get away that easily. They had something, he and this raven-haired beauty, and he wasn't going to let her just slip through his fingers....

"I cannot believe you just did that."

Linn glanced at her sister. "Did what?"

Hands planted on hips, Kathy gazed at her in exasperation and Linn looked at the wall she was papering. And realized, after a moment or two, that she'd put the last strip on upside down.

"Oh, brother," she sighed. "Sorry. It's still wet—I can pull it off and turn it around."

"I'll pull it off and turn it around," Kathy said none too patiently. "Honestly, Linn, what is the *matter* with you? It's been a month since we got back, yet you're still wandering around in a fog."

Linn brushed her hair off her forehead with her wrist, eyeing the upside-down tulips with annoyance. "Look, you go on back to your painting—I'll fix this. You wanted this paper on all four walls, didn't you?"

"No," Kathy said succinctly, taking the ladder and moving it. "The tulips go on these two walls, the coordinating stripe on the other two." She looked around. "Linn, don't take this the wrong way or anything, but I wish you'd go on a long vacation or get a hobby or just go read a book—because you're driving me crazy!" She gave her stomach a gentle pat. "I've only got eight months before the kid is born—and with the kind of help I've been getting from you lately, I'll still be papering this room when the contractions start."

"Sorry," Linn muttered. "I guess I was just thinking about something else. . . ."

"No kidding," Kathy said dryly. "I'd never have guessed."

Linn looked at her sharply, then gave a rueful laugh. "You and Rod have been wonderful, letting me stay here while I figure out what I want to do. But I'm beginning to think it's time I got a place of my own." She sighed and tossed the wallpaper smoother into the bucket at her feet. "That editorial job they've offered me at *Florida Straits* magazine is a good one, and I've pretty much decided to take it. It'll mean moving down to the Keys, but I've always loved it there. I was thinking about heading there next week to look for a place to stay."

"Linn, I was *not* hinting that I want you to move out. I love having you here, you know that. It's just that you seem to be in some never-never land half the time." She smiled. "I'm worried about you, that's all."

Linn smiled thinly. "I'm just tired. And it's been odd, coming back to nothing—no house, no job, not even a family crisis that needs handling." She managed another wan smile. "Once I get back to work, things will settle down to normal."

"I don't think it's that at all," Kathy said with a shrewd look. "I think it's Trey Hollister. I think you're in love with him."

"Kathy..." But she sighed and turned away, not even having the energy to lie. She walked to the window and stared out at nothing. "It's the first time since Jack died that I found a man I could honestly care about. And I guess it's not written anywhere that just because I fell in love with him he has to love me back." She laughed ruefully and glanced around at Kathy. "If love ran that smoothly, all the country and western singers would be out of work."

"Are you really all right?" Kathy's voice was soft.

Linn swallowed, nodding. "I will be. It hurts like hell, that's all."

"Oh, Linn." Kathy came over and slipped her arm around Linn's shoulders. "I wish there was something I could do. I remember all those boyfriends and broken hearts I went through before I finally met Rod, and you were there for me every time. Now it's you who needs someone to hold your hand and pass you tissues and tell you what a bastard he is... but I don't think I'm doing a very good job of it."

Linn had to laugh. "You're doing fine. And I'll live. I went through this a time or two myself, remember, before Jack and I got married." Although not like this, she reminded herself. She'd been a girl back then, brooding over lost boys. But this was a woman's loss, a woman's hurt.

"Linn..." Kathy paused, biting her lip. Then she swore with uncharacteristic fervor and took a deep breath. "I wasn't going to bring this up, but... why are you still here?"

Linn blinked. "Here? Because you—"

"Not *here*," Kathy interrupted impatiently, her gesture taking in the entire house. "I mean here in Florida. Why aren't you up there with Trey where you belong? You've already admitted you're in love with the guy. So—"

"He's not in love with me," Linn said quietly. "And I'm not so desperate for a man that I'll go chasing after some poor guy who doesn't want me."

"Oh, for—" Kathy bit it off. Took a deep breath. "I was up there with the two of you, remember? I saw the way he looked at you. And you can't tell me he doesn't love you, Linn."

Linn smiled wearily. "Oh, I think in his own way he probably does—as much as he can let himself love anyone. But it's not enough, Kath." She got up and wandered toward the window again. "Maybe I am being unrealistic, I don't know. But I want the kind of love I had with Jack. The kind that Mom and Dad had. The kind that you and Rod have. Open and sharing and—"

"Do you really think that Rod and I got to where we were today without a lot of hard work?" Kathy moved to stand beside Linn. "Rod's got a lot of Latino machismo in him, Linn, don't let him fool you. It took two years for him to really relax and open up with me. But I knew I had to give him time to get used to being loved. It takes a while sometimes for a man to really trust something like that."

She looked at Linn. "You were lucky with Jack—he was open and loving right from the start. But a man like Trey needs patience, Linn. That's part of what loving him means. You stayed by Jack's side because you loved him—and because you never gave up hope. Yet you're giving up on Trey after only a few weeks. It just doesn't seem fair, if you ask me. If he's worth loving, it seems to me he's worth a bit of extra effort."

Linn looked at Kathy quizzically. "So you're saying I should go back."

"I think you should give the guy a chance."

"And if he can't do it? Even if I go back and he keeps me shut out?"

"I can't answer that, Linn. You'll have to decide for yourself how much you can live with. But it seems to me you've written him off without even giving him a chance to show you he can change."

Linn opened her mouth to protest, then closed it again thoughtfully. Maybe there was a kernel of truth in what Kathy was saying. Love was something she'd always been comfortable with, but it was an alien emotion to Trey, something never given freely, always suspect. A man—even one as strong and single-minded as Trey Hollister—would have trouble turning that around in a mere three weeks. *If he's worth loving, he's worth a bit of extra effort....*

She looked at Kathy. "Are my suitcases in the basement?"

A slow smile lifted Kathy's mouth. "I'll bring them up while you have a bath and wash the wallpaper paste out of your hair. And I'll call my travel agent and see what kind of connecting flights you can get to Vancouver tonight."

Linn slipped off the old plaid shirt of Jack's she was wearing as a smock and draped it over her shoulder, smiling as she headed for the bathroom. No doubt about it, pregnancy had brought Kathy's nesting instinct up to a full boil.

If he's worth loving, he's worth a bit of extra effort....

If he let her, she reminded herself. But who knew what had happened in the month since she'd left? All those barricades might have gone back up again, twice as high, twice as thick. And this time, abandoned once too often, he might not be inclined to let her anywhere near his heart again.

She ran the water deep and hot and sank into it with a sigh, deciding it was pointless trying to second-guess how he'd react to seeing her again. But Kathy was right about one thing—she owed it to him to at least give him a chance. And if it didn't work...well, there was always that job with *Florida Straits* to come home to. And broken hearts, after all, did eventually heal.

The hot water made her drowsy and she relaxed against the bath pillow and closed her eyes. Nathan was playing just outside the window and she could hear him and the kids from next door chattering happily, their laughter punctuated with excited yips from the pup Rod had brought home three days ago.

She must have dozed, because she didn't hear what had started the commotion. She'd been vaguely aware of hearing the doorbell ring, had heard the sound of running footsteps as Kathy had sprinted down to answer it, but then she'd let her mind drift again.

"But you can't go in there!" It was Kathy's voice, right outside the bathroom door, and it snapped Linn wide-awake. There was an indistinct reply, then Kathy's voice again, edged with laughter. "I'm serious—she'll kill me if I let you in there!" She was reaching for the towel when the bathroom door burst open. She uttered a gasp of shock and instinctively submerged to the shoulders as Kathy backed into the room, obviously trying to block the intruder's path.

"Daddy's going to be here any minute," she was saying, "and if he catches you in here with—"

"Lady," grunted a husky, familiar baritone, "you're in my way." Two tanned hands gripped Kathy's slender shoulders and moved her gently but firmly to one side. Trey stepped fully into the bathroom, his lean, handsome face set with what bordered on defiance as he gazed down at Linn. "I have to talk to you."

Linn stared up at him in utter astonishment. "What in heaven's name are you doing here?"

"Getting himself arrested if he doesn't get out of here," Kathy said, still laughing. "My God, Linn—Dad and Rod are due back any second! If Dad finds Trey in here, and you as naked as the day you were born—"

Trey turned and gently pushed Kathy from the room, then pulled the door closed and pushed the knob to lock it. He took a deep breath, as though bracing himself, and turned back to look at her. "I finished the book."

Linn blinked. *"Steele on Ice?"*

"*Steele and Flame.* I changed the title."

"Oh." Linn blinked again. "And you came all the way down here to tell me that?"

"No. I came all the way down here to tell you that you were right." Trey squatted on his heels beside her, seemingly unperturbed by the fact he'd caught her in midbath. He set a large manila envelope on the side of the tub and drew out a sheaf of paper. "Page 234."

"Katherine!" It was her father's voice, coming from the front door, and Linn winced. "Who owns that car in the driveway?" Linn could hear Kathy's voice, too faint for her to make out the words, then a querulous reply.

But she ignored it and reached around Trey for the towel, drying her hands before taking the page Trey was holding for her. "Kind of a long way to come for editing services, isn't it?" she teased gently. "What if I don't like it?"

"You'll like it," he said softly, his eyes locked with hers. "After all, you helped me write it."

"He's *where*?" It was her father's voice again, in the corridor now. "She's *what*?"

Steele watched her walk to the door, feeling something tight and hot spill through his chest. He didn't want to lose her.

She paused at the car and looked back. He could see the tears on her cheeks, even through the rain. And the tightness, the heat in his chest, pulled even tighter. Then abruptly she turned and opened the door of the car and slipped behind the wheel.

"Wait!" He caught the door before she pulled it closed. "It can't end this way," he said roughly. "I don't want to lose you, Rebecca. It's . . . hell, it's just too easy this way."

"I can't stay," she whispered. "You know I can't. . . ."

"I love you." The words came easier than he'd ever dreamed possible. They sounded natural and right on his tongue, as though weighted with honey. "Damn it, Becky, I love you. And you can't just leave. Not without giving it a chance."

Linn looked up and met Trey's eyes across the manuscript page. "So. He actually did it."

"Yeah." Trey slipped the sheet of paper from her hand and put the manuscript aside, catching her hand and braiding his fingers in hers. "It took me nearly three weeks to write that scene. I finished it two days ago. And caught the first flight down here I could get."

"Aislinn O'Connor Stevens, just what in the good Lord's name is going on in there?" Her father's bellow made the door rattle. "Talk to me, girl!"

"It's probably going to be a bestseller."

"Marry me."

Linn looked closely at him. "I . . . pardon?"

"I asked you to marry me," he repeated quietly.

"I . . . well, yes, that's what I thought I heard," Linn allowed.

"Linn! Linn, darlin', it's your father! Just hang on, girl, and I'll be getting that madman out of there. Katherine, will you stop your bleatin' and get out of the way!"

"Daddy, for heaven's sake," Kathy was saying, "don't you dare try kicking that door in! I tell you, it's perfectly all right!"

"All right?" her father roared. "My daughter's in there naked and drippin' wet with a strange man, and you're telling me it's all right?"

"I love you, Linn." Trey cupped her chin in his hand and turned her face so that she was looking straight at him. "I have never said that to a single person in my entire life. Not even to Diane. But damn it, I do love you. I never knew what it felt like to love someone—or what it felt like to have someone love me. It spooked the hell out of me, Linn. I felt wide open and more vulnerable than I've ever been in my life. When you were standing in my kitchen looking at me that last morning, it was as though you could see right through into my soul. There were things in there I'd never shown to anyone. Things I never even looked at too closely myself. And it scared me to death."

Linn simply stared at him, scarcely daring to breath.

"It wasn't until you walked out that I realized how deep you'd touched. I don't want to lose you, Linn Stevens. You've changed me in ways I still only half understand, and if I lose you, I'm losing part of myself. And I don't want to live like that anymore. I don't want to be just half-alive anymore."

"Linn!" Her father was pounding on the door now. "Linn, damn it, if you don't talk to me I'm going to—"

Linn's heart did a slow cartwheel and she slipped her arms around his neck, heedless of dripping water, heedless of the pounding at the door, heedless of everything but the unconditional love glowing in Trey Hollister's eyes. "We should discuss this, you know. There are hundreds of things we've never talked about. Kids, for instance."

"As many as you want, as soon as you want." He kissed her gently. "I've wasted my life running from myself. From feelings I didn't understand and didn't want to understand. But I don't want to waste any more time, Linn. I love you. I want to have children with you and grow old with you and hell, even fight with you now and again. I want to wake up in the morning and find you there beside me, and I want to look across the room and see you there. I want kids underfoot, and an Irish flatfoot and a Miami vice undercover cop as in-laws.... Say you'll marry me."

There was a ferocious banging on the door. "I've got a gun and at the count of three I'm kicking this door in. *One....*"

"Speaking of Irish flatfoots," she murmured, "that'll be one now. I think you're about to meet your future father-in-law."

"Two!"

"Can he shoot straight?"

"I'm afraid so." Laughing, she lifted her mouth from his. "Dad, I'm perfectly all right! And for heaven's sake, don't try kicking that door in or you'll sprain your bad knee again."

"Kathy says some madman's gone charging in and—"

"His name's Trey Hollister, Daddy." Linn smiled, eyes locked with Trey's. "And you can't shoot him because I'm going to marry him."

The silence outside the bathroom door was deafening and Trey smiled. "Was that a yes?"

"A definite and absolute yes, Mr. Hollister. And if you'll hand me that big towel over there, I'll get out of this bath and introduce you to your new family."

"Sainted Mary and Joseph," came a bemused voice from outside the door. "Kathy, would you mind tellin' your old man what's goin' on here? Does she know him, do you suppose?"

"Of course she knows him Daddy! She loves him."

"Does she?" whispered Trey as he wrapped the towel around Linn, brushing her lips with his.

"She does," Linn murmured back. "Yes, I think she does...."

Epilogue

It came in the morning mail, and Trey smiled as he read it. Picking up his cup of coffee, he carried it and the letter across to the sliding door leading to the big sun deck, standing there for a moment to look out at Linn.

She was sitting cross-legged in the sun, nursing the baby, and as it did every time he saw her, his heart took a leap. The sun surrounded her like a mantle of gold, making the loose torrent of dark hair spilling around her shoulders gleam, and she was smiling down at the child cradled in her arms. The small, dark head at her breast moved and he saw a tiny fist clench, heard the music of Linn's soft laughter, and he found himself having to swallow at a sudden thickness in his throat.

It caught him unawares like that sometimes. All it took was a sidelong glance from Linn, filled with unspoken love so deep that it never needed words. Or the unexpected sound of his new son's laughter. Or just waking in the night and seeing her lying there beside him, smiling in her sleep, and knowing that smile was for him.

You're a hell of a lucky man, Hollister, he told himself silently. To finally be in the right place at the right time....

Smiling, he pulled the door open and stepped into the sunshine. He held up the clipping. "It came."

Linn's eyes widened. "And?" she urged gently.

Trey's smile widened. "It's... good."

"Read it to me!" She bent to kiss the baby's head, smiling down at him. "Listen up, kid—the *New York Times* has reviewed your daddy's new book."

> "In *Steele and Flame*, author T.C. Hollister has given us one of the best reads of the entire year. And certainly one of the best books of his career. That Hollister has reached a new plateau of excellence is an understatement—this book isn't just a rousing good action story, it's a story of life, of change, of growth and, yes, even of love."

Trey skipped a few lines. "He runs through the plot, tells what's going on...."

"Get back to the good stuff."

> "There are segments in this book that makes this reviewer wish he could read it all over again for the first time. Hollister has reached down so deep inside himself—inside all of us—that it is not merely a story but a reflection of life itself. The reflection of a man finding himself through love. There is a sensitivity never seen in his writing before, passion and compassion, a sense of wonder and joy that have always been missing in previous Steele novels. It is, quite simply, the story of how love can transform a man's life. Steele will never be the same. And, based on the dedication Hollister has made to 'the woman who loves me, and made it all possible,' neither will his creator. Thank you, T. C. Hollister."

Trey smiled and leaned across to kiss her. "All he needed to add," he murmured, "was that they lived happily ever after...."

He drew back after a moment and gazed down at his son, smiling. The baby was still nursing, making soft sucking noises as he tugged gently at Linn's breast. "I got a letter from Craig today," he said quietly, stroking the baby's cheek.

He sensed more than heard Linn's breath catch slightly. "I wrote to Diane a few months ago," he admitted softly. "I didn't tell you because I didn't want you worrying about it. Worrying about me." The baby gripped Trey's finger fiercely and, as always, he was astonished at the strength in that tiny hand. "She wrote back telling me she was glad things were working out so well. And she said that she thought it was time she had a long talk with Craig. She said that he knew about me, that she'd told him years ago. But he'd never seemed very curious about what happened, and she'd never pressured him."

"And now?" Linn asked softly.

"He...uh...wants to come up. Next month, maybe." He looked at Linn, grinning. "He's getting married, can you believe it? He wants to bring his fiancée up and get to know us. Get to know... me." He gave his head a wondering shake, laughing. "I've barely got used to having one son, and suddenly I've got two."

Linn smiled, reaching out to run her fingers through his hair. "It's called a family," she teased gently. "And they're pretty nice to have around...."

"I know," Trey whispered, leaning down to kiss her again. Knowing, too, that the peace he felt was real. And forever.

* * * * *

A Note from Emilie Richards

Dear Reader,

All love demands a certain amount of trust, but Tate Cantrell is sorely tested when the man she will soon come to love introduces himself at gunpoint. It takes a heroine like Tate, formerly a street-smart teenage runaway, to master the challenge of a man like Simon. Their dilemma is a dream come true for this incurably romantic author. The solitude of Ozark autumn nights. The danger that lurks around every corner. The doubts and fears of two people caught up in something bigger than both of them. Still, like all of you, in real life I've happily settled for a man without an alias, a man I did not meet while I was staring down the barrel of a gun.

I chose the fictional town of Mountain Glade as the settting for *Fugitive* as a tribute to the wonderful months I spent years ago as a VISTA volunteer in Stone County, Arkansas. I lived in a remote mountain cabin on a road much like Kalix Road, attended hootenannies in front of the courthouse and met some of the finest people I have ever known. Those memories are still deeply treasured, and I am pleased and proud to have the opportunity to share a taste of them with you in this story.

Emilie Richards

FUGITIVE

Emilie Richards

Prologue

In the forgiving embrace of rose-tinted twilight, the gun towers rising above High Ridge Penitentiary resembled the turrets of a fairy-tale castle. The man with *Petersen 94729* stenciled above the pocket of his khaki work shirt knew better. High Ridge was neither a castle nor the setting of a fairy tale. It was hell, pure and simple, where the damned learned to placate the devil or died trying.

Inmate 94729 had been a quick learner. In his three months at High Ridge, he had learned everything he had to know. The problem was that he had learned too much, and sometimes knowing too much was more dangerous than not knowing anything.

He watched as guards vacated the two closest towers. Both the prison workday and supper were over, and apparently the inmate count had just been cleared for the night. No prisoners were on this side of the vast High Ridge complex to worry about now—at least officially.

At the sound of footsteps, the tall, blond prisoner straightened and cursed softly. "Damn you, Josiah Gallagher." He thrust one hand in his pocket and ran the other over the neatly trimmed beard he sported in a prison where clean-shaven men were the rule. The beard was just one example of his exalted status at High Ridge—a status that could backfire in the worst way, if he didn't take some action.

"Talkn' to yerse'f, Petersen?" The tobacco-chewing guard stopped and leaned on the doorjamb, watching curiously as Carl Petersen walked back to the computer and away from the window that looked out over a thicket of small pine trees and neatly trimmed yews. The landscaping was part of the fairy-tale illusion, too. The trees and hedges had been planted to hide the fourteen-foot Cyclone fence behind them—not to mention the thick coils of razor wire beyond that, or the second fence rising just beyond the wire.

The prisoner spoke. "Go away, Cooney. You bother me."

The guard chortled good-naturedly. Jim Cooney was one of the few good-natured men at High Ridge. His boss, the warden, Captain Roger Shaw, was not one of the others.

"I've got work to do," Petersen said.

"Now, *you* know I can't go away. Captain Shaw likes you well enough, but he likes you here, not hoppin' away to the briar patch."

Ignoring the guard, Carl Petersen silently damned Josiah Gallagher once more. Gallagher had left him here to rot. Gallagher, his trusted friend—which just went to prove that nobody—*nobody*—could be trusted. Not ever.

Cooney chortled again when Petersen didn't answer him. "Now me, I don't think you got rabbit blood. You won't run. Too civilized, that's what I think. Too educated. Never did see no educated rabbit."

Petersen spun his chair around. The chair, like everything else in the warden's office, was state-of-the-art. "I'm not going to get this finished if you don't stop chattering. Didn't I hear you were supposed to feed me tonight? Baked chicken and fresh asparagus?"

"Don't eat like no rabbit I ever seen, neither." Cooney's gaze roamed the room. Apparently satisfied nothing was amiss, he left to retrieve the tray that had been brought over from the kitchen half an hour before.

"And don't forget to warm it in the microwave," Petersen called after him. He was out of his seat and across the room again before the words were out of his mouth. The silver letter opener with the warden's initials flashed as he wrenched it from his pocket and twisted the last bolt from the air conditioner covering the bottom half of the one window that wasn't barred. Then, as satisfied as he could be under the circumstances, he strode across the room and melted into the crack between the door and the wall. He didn't have long to wait.

"Ham hocks and turnips, tops and bottoms," Cooney called out as he entered the room. "Don't need no microwave. Still as hot as a hooker's—"

"Just set it down, nice and easy," Petersen said from behind him. He stepped forward and pressed the letter opener against Cooney's throat.

Cooney didn't move. "You got no call to hurt me, son. And you ain't got no way a'tall of gettin' out of here 'cept in a pine box."

"The way I've got it figured, some of the poor bastards who end up in this hellhole don't even *get* a pine box." Petersen slid the letter opener lightly back and forth against the guard's throat to make sure Cooney knew he meant business. He had been sharpening both sides for days, every time he was called to the warden's office. Now he drew tiny beads of blood. "Now set the tray down."

"I'm doin' it, I'm doin' it." Cooney bent over and set the tray on the floor.

As he did, Petersen slid his hand down the guard's side and took his .44 out of his holster. Then he removed Cooney's two-way radio. "Turn around slowly. Hands over your head."

Cooney did as he was told, but his fingers passed lightly over his throat as he raised his hands, as if to be certain the cut was really bleeding.

"You'll live, if you're careful," Petersen assured him. "And you'll have something to tell your grandkids."

"You ain't gonna make it. Even if you get out of the yard, they'll round you up afore daylight."

"Too bad you won't be able to watch." Petersen motioned Cooney to the closet. "Unlock the door."

"I don't carry that key."

"Yes you do. You'll unlock it right now and give me the keys. Then you've got one minute to strip."

Cooney seemed to know what was coming. "I'm three inches shorter and forty pounds heavier than you are, son."

"Fifty-four seconds."

Cooney gave up the argument. His tie came off first, then the blue shirt with the official High Ridge armpatch. Finally his pants.

Petersen stripped simultaneously, holding the guard's gun squarely on him the entire time. He pulled Cooney's clothes on as Cooney watched, cinching the holster with its rounds of ammunition in the last hole. Cooney's pants hung in folds around his narrow waist, but there was nothing to be done about it. Petersen held out his hand when he'd finished. "You forgot your hat."

Cooney's expression grew pained. "This hat's all broke in. Jus' the way I like it."

Petersen held out his hand, and a nearly naked Cooney removed the wide-brimmed felt Stetson. He watched as Petersen jammed it on his head. Petersen motioned him farther into the closet.

"The captain'll have your hide for this," Cooney said sadly.

"Tell the captain something for me, Cooney. Tell him I talk just as well as I run. And tell him I took a little present with me, will you?" Petersen lifted two five-inch computer diskettes off the warden's desk and slipped them in the neatly trimmed pocket of the uniform he now wore.

"You'll be a dead man for sure, son. Hate to see it."

Petersen slammed the door, cutting off anything else that Cooney might have wanted to say. He considered, just for a moment, taking the necessary time to shave off his identifying beard with the electric razor the warden always kept in the bathroom just off his office, but he decided against it. The time to make his escape was too short already.

In seconds he was prying the air-conditioning unit from the window using a jail-cell bar. The bar was a souvenir from another inmate's "run to the briar patch." It was one of Captain Shaw's favorite knickknacks. The inmate who had so neatly sawed it from his cell door hadn't lived to see it put on display. He had lived just long enough to see the captain lift it high and swing it toward his skull.

The air conditioner fell with a crash to the carpeted floor. Petersen waited tensely for an alarm or the clatter of footsteps in the hallway. But there was only silence.

As he lowered his legs out the window, he cleared his mind of all fears, all doubts. He would make this escape as he had made others. He was young, strong and daring enough to make this work.

There wasn't now, nor had there ever been, a building or a fence or a man who could hold him if he didn't want to be held. And he didn't want to be held at High Ridge Penitentiary any longer.

He had a score to settle with a man named Josiah Gallagher.

Chapter 1

"When the moon rides low in the night sky, like the biggest pumpkin in October's frostbit pumpkin patch, folks here about call it an outlaw moon. I call it the same. You would, too, if you'd been lucky enough to hear the tales I've heard.

"Once the Ozarks were the home of many an outlaw band. The James Gang, the Daltons and the Doolins all had hideouts hereabouts or down the road a wander. Every family I know can tell you about one of them, or about Belle Starr, the outlaw queen.

"There are caves in these hills where fugitives could hide until the law got tired and the moon got full. Then, by nothing more than moonlight, they could find their way to freedom.

"There's an outlaw moon hanging on the horizon as I write this. I can almost hear the whickering of the James boys' horses as they ride along my riverbank to Missouri.

"I wonder how the men in prison at High Ridge feel on such a night? Does the moon stir their blood as it once stirred the blood of their brothers? Do they wish that they, too, were following the river? Or do they sit patiently in their cells counting the days until they make parole? Is the outlaw moon shining through their bars only a sign that they are one month closer to freedom?"

* * *

"Not for one man, Millard." Tate Cantrell closed the leather-bound journal and spoke her thoughts out loud—although there was no one to hear them. "Just the day before yesterday one man at High Ridge got tired of crossing off days on his cell wall and slid out a window, instead. Jesse James would have been proud to know him."

She hugged the journal to her chest for just a moment as a shudder passed through her. Either the crisp air of autumn, the pumpkin moon just clearing the horizon, or the folk legend recorded in her father's painfully neat handwriting had precipitated the chill—not that it mattered which.

Tate set the journal on the kitchen table beside her half-eaten supper and went to look for her wool jacket. She would make a fire when she came back in from her evening chores. In the meantime she would bundle up and force the chill away. There was no one else to warm the house for. She was alone in an Ozark mountain cabin with only her father's written musings and one cinnamon-colored hound dog for company.

And that was all the company she needed—maybe too much, if she counted Cinn.

After a search of the cabin she found the red-and-black checkered jacket hanging from a wooden peg on the back porch. She remembered she had hung it there after her last trip to the outhouse. She shivered again before she could button it. The jacket had belonged to her father. She had never seen Millard Carter, hadn't even known his name until recently. Now the jacket was just one more piece in the puzzle that was the man who had sired her.

For a moment she stared at the orange moon and considered what she'd learned about him since the day three months before when she'd been told that the man she had long since ceased to wonder about had died and willed her everything he'd owned.

She knew that he had been a huge lumberjack of a fellow. The jacket she was wearing hung just inches above her knees, and the first time she'd put it on, she'd had to roll the cuffs half a dozen times to get them to her wrists. In addition to size, she had an idea of what he had looked like. There had been three photographs of him in the cabin when she arrived. One was of a young man just about her present age of twenty-one, one of a middle-aged Millard accompanying a newspaper article headlined "Ozark Folktales Kept Alive," and one of him in his coffin.

The last had given her nightmares for a week—until she realized it hadn't been left there to horrify her. Mountain Glade and the surrounding area overflowed with people who claimed to be Tate's kin. They were a silent lot—though not disapproving, exactly. "Watchful" was a better word. But although it was clear that the members of the Carter clan weren't sure how they felt about her, their feelings about her father were clear. They had respected Millard Carter, and the photograph was a mark of that respect.

Tate had put that final photo away and concentrated on the others. From them she had discovered that her black hair had come from Millard, along with her pointed chin. She wasn't sure about her features. It was difficult to look at the two-dimensional photograph and compare noses, brows and lips. Eye color was a mystery, since the photographs were black-and-white.

One thing she was sure of, however, was how her father had felt about the land stretching down from this porch to the river, a quarter mile beyond. Millard Carter's slice of the Ozarks had been his whole life. He had lived and died on his five hundred acres, and he had left them indelibly stamped with his personality.

Cinn chose that moment to howl. In the month Tate had been living on her father's land, she had never seen any real display of energy from the lop-eared hound. Yes, he breathed. And sometimes he slunk from shade tree to shade tree, when the afternoon sun changed positions. Once she had even caught him lapping at a mud puddle—as if the bucket of fresh water she provided was permanently out of reach instead of fifty yards away. But now he was howling.

"Thatta boy, Cinn. Liven the place up a bit, why don't you?" she called.

The noise, coming from somewhere in the distant shadows, ceased abruptly.

"Blew your cover, didn't you?"

Her only reply was the noise of wings as the small flock of geese that made their home in the pond behind the barn rose as one into the night sky.

Tate debated between going back in the house to finish supper or taking care of her chores so she would have the rest of the evening free. The chores were few, the meal meager. She decided to finish the first before the second. Then she could eat what was left of supper in front of a warm fire.

The outlaw moon had risen a notch. Tate thought about her father's journal entry as she walked along the path toward the barn.

The journal, begun just months before his death, was one of the only really personal things of her father's that she had found. She was reading it slowly—gleaning Ozark folklore and history, as well as a picture of Millard Carter. It was odd that she had chosen the outlaw-moon portion to read with supper. Odd because tonight's moon so closely fit his description, and odd because there really was an outlaw on the loose. A federal prisoner named Carl Petersen, computer criminal and murderer, had escaped from High Ridge Penitentiary, twenty miles away, just two days ago.

Her portable radio, Tate's only link to the world, had been full of details. Petersen was known to be armed, dangerous and wounded. He was thought to be headed back home to Houston—which was just fine with her, since Houston was far south of the prison and Mountain Glade was due east. There had been two reported sightings south of High Ridge and, this evening, one unconfirmed story that Petersen had been seen hitchhiking out of Little Rock.

Tate felt a twinge of sympathy for Petersen, who seemed to have the whole state of Arkansas on his tail. From experience, she knew what being on the run was like. And a man like Petersen, a man reported to know everything about computers and nothing about life, probably wouldn't have a prayer of staying free. High Ridge wasn't rumored to be a place where "forgive and forget" was a popular motto. When Petersen was returned to prison, his life would be hell. He would probably never see daylight again.

Of course, he had brought his troubles on himself. According to the radio he was a former bank official who had neatly embezzled a cool 1.2 million using a complicated wire-fraud scheme, then killed the man who tried to turn him in. And even though the murder charge had been plea-bargained to second-degree, he was still guilty of taking a life. She hoped that he wouldn't take others before he was captured.

Tate stopped just short of the barn door and took two metal buckets off a set of pegs. One of the things she *definitely* knew about her father was that he was a man who had eschewed creature comforts. "Simple" was itself too simple a word for the way Millard had chosen to live. The cabin had no electricity, no running water or plumbing of any kind, and no telephone. The drive leading from the unpaved country road back nearly a quarter of a mile to the cabin was nothing more than a parallel set of ruts etched from hillside and forest.

She didn't mind the austerity or the isolation, but there were times like now, when she was dead tired and needed a bath, that hauling water uphill seemed an injustice. Still, chastising a dead man was a waste of time.

Tate carried the buckets a few yards down the hill to the rock-lined basin where a galvanized pipe spurted pure mountain springwater to the rocks below. She set first one bucket, then the other, below the pipe, emptying them as they filled into a small wooden rain barrel mounted on a makeshift wagon. When the barrel was nearly full, she would trundle it up the gentle slope to her back porch, where two more buckets waited to empty it. And when she finished with that, there was still wood to bring in for the fireplace and cookstove, as well as geese and one stupid hound dog to feed.

As she worked Tate wondered why Millard Carter, the father she had never known, had struggled so hard to stay off the twentieth-century path of progress. At that moment, with the outlaw moon bearing down on her and a day's worth of strained muscles crying out for reprieve, the nineteenth century seemed anything but romantic.

She was halfway up the path with the rain barrel before a more obvious question occurred to her.

Why exactly was *she* living in the middle of nowhere, following inch by inch in Millard Carter's footsteps?

Inmate 94729 regained consciousness slowly. One moment the sun had hung heavily on the horizon, refusing to sink into oblivion, the next the sky was black except for a huge amber moon leering behind a patch of pine and sassafras. The hours in between were a void filled with nothing but pain and thirst.

He opened his eyes wider and increased his field of vision slowly, turning his head from side to side as he tried to remember where he was. "Why" he was there was impossible to forget. He remembered too well sliding through the warden's window and the minutes afterward when he had blended into the shadows, watching for the slim possibility that someone might have returned to one of the towers. There had been a sweet moment of victory when he had known for certain that he wasn't being watched.

He remembered the fence he had climbed, too. Not one of the insurmountable Cyclone fences; he wouldn't have made it halfway up one of those without being seen. But the grassy area outside the warden's window had led to a lower fence, marking the entrance to a staff parking lot. There had been no need for scrupulous security here. Every window in the warden's wing was barred—except for the one that had held the air conditioner. And prisoners were only allowed in that wing under armed escort.

Good luck had run out abruptly at that point. His escape wouldn't have been detected except that at the same moment he scaled the fence top, a guard who was either late for his shift or coming back for something he'd forgotten had driven into the lot and seen him.

After that moment of discovery, his memory was mercifully blurred. He had run toward the woods. There had been gunshots, but none from his own gun, because it would have slowed him down too much to draw. There had been a siren and searchlights. There had been the realization, after endless minutes of plunging through the forest, that his leg had been hit by a bullet some undetermined distance back, and he was losing blood at an alarming rate.

That discovery had marked the beginning of brief moments of lucidity alternating with moments when he hadn't been sure of his own name. He had bandaged his leg with a piece of his shirttail, and despite excruciating pain he had stumbled on in the direction of the river separating High Ridge property from the nearest town. He had known that come daylight trackers would be after him, if they weren't already. His best chance of remaining free was to float downriver as far as he was able, until he could be sure his scent was lost to the hounds. Then and only then could he rest and recover his strength.

He had followed his own plan, and it had almost killed him. Finding the river had taken most of the night. Once there, the water had been numbingly cold and the current faster than he had expected. With the vines of wild muscadine that he had sawed with the warden's letter opener, he had tied himself to a log he found at the water's edge. Then he had pushed himself out to the middle of the wide stretch of water and begun the long trip to freedom.

Sometime later, hours, days, years perhaps, he had washed ashore like a beached survivor of a shipwreck. The log had broken into pieces; his shoes were gone, Jim Cooney's uniform sodden and tattered. Somehow, before he had bound himself to the log, he had found the presence of mind to strap the gun belt to a branch rising high out of the water, and it had endured unharmed.

Inch by inch he had dragged himself into the shelter of the brush-covered riverbank. Shivering and half dead, he had clawed a hole in the coarse silt, pulling what he displaced back over himself, along with branches and pine needles, until he fainted from the effort.

His own moans had awakened him sometime later, followed closely by the sound of men's voices. He had been rational enough to force himself to lie quietly and wait. He had expected recapture. Instead he had gradually realized that the men were farmers, working on the far side of the slight ridge along the riverbank. As the day progressed and the sun warmed him, he had listened to the sound of their farm machinery and their occasional shouts. He had grown so hot he had dared throw off his makeshift cover; then he had grown hotter still, until the cold water yards away was a torment.

He had dragged himself to the river to wash and drink after the men had gone home and the sun had gone down. The strength he had hoped to recover was as elusive as the miles he had hoped to gain. The wound in his leg throbbed incessantly, and the flesh around it was swollen and angry.

Through sheer determination he had found a better place to sleep that night. An abandoned hay barn just over the ridge had sheltered him until the first light of his second morning of freedom. Then he had made his way to the woods behind the barn, leaning heavily on a branch he used as a cane. His first taste of food since the escape had been a handful of black walnuts, husked between two flat rocks. His stomach hadn't been able to handle them.

He had wandered, after that. The woods were thick, the land surrounding him harsh and wild. He had stopped to rest often, once in a shallow cave, once under a pile of brush. He had drunk from a shallow stream whose water tasted of decaying leaves, and his stomach had rebelled again.

He knew he had covered no more than a mile before the sun began to sink in the sky once more. And he had known, somewhere in between the chills and fever that constantly racked him, that he was going to die if he didn't find food and warm shelter. The night promised to be colder than any he had yet experienced. And the infection in his leg was raging out of control.

He had begun to find his way out of the woods, then. Where before he had stayed in the densest part of the forest, now he moved toward a section that had been recently cleared. His plan had been to find a house and wait until night to forage for food, clothes, money. He had weighed his chances and known just how slim they were. But he wasn't a man to give up. Hope just wouldn't die. There were people who could help him—Aaron could help him, if he could just get to a telephone. He still had Jim Cooney's gun. If he had to hold someone prisoner to save his own life, he would do it.

He struggled on, now using two sticks as crutches. Gauging the sun's position, he guessed it was near five o'clock when he reached the forest's edge. There were hills beyond, some planted in neat rows of evergreens. The land zigzagged like a crazy quilt of forest and field. But beyond the last stand of trees was an old log cabin with a wide front porch. Far below it was a blue ribbon of glistening water, the river that had carried him this far.

He had backed into the forest and begun to follow its edge until he found a better position for reaching the house. Then, after watching as carefully as he could for the cabin's inhabitants, he had taken a gamble and crossed the first field. The effort had cost him everything, and he had sunk into oblivion in the cradle of a leaf-filled pit. He had awakened later to watch the sun hover on the horizon.

And now the sun had been replaced by the biggest moon he had ever seen. There were details about his odyssey that he would probably never remember, but now his task was to bring it to a conclusion. Somehow he had to get into the cabin, find a change of clothing, first aid for his leg and food his body would tolerate. He would not die here, in some godforsaken hillbilly county, immersed in pine needles and fallen leaves.

He sat up slowly, pushing himself with both hands. The moon revolved in fiery comet streaks; the skeleton forms of the trees danced a bizarre tarantella. He waited, breathing slowly to force his dizziness away. His makeshift crutches lay on the ground beside him, but finally, with their aid, he was standing and moving toward the cabin.

There was no sign of life inside, only a dull glow from the back of the structure, like a night light, perhaps. There was no smoke from the chimney despite the rapidly falling temperature. There was no car or truck parked outside, no pack of dogs clustered on the porch, no farm animals begging to be fed. If he was lucky, truly lucky, the cabin's residents were away for the evening. He could break in, find what he needed, even call Aaron in Memphis, perhaps. He could give Aaron the phone number, and Aaron could find out just exactly where this place was. Then he could find a safe spot to wait until Aaron could get to him.

If he was lucky.

He used the tree line for shelter, until he came to the best spot for making a break for the cabin. He started across the clearing, his skin soaked in sweat despite the chill night air. Once his leg twisted beneath him, and only stern self-control kept him from giving in to the agony and falling. Each inch between him and the porch seemed a mile, each step a relentless torture.

He had reached the porch steps when he heard a dog's howl. He stumbled, falling forward to the bottom step,and the world went suddenly dark. Nausea gripped him, and bells seemed to clang in whirling frenzies of sound. He held onto the wooden plank and hung his head. From somewhere far away he thought he heard a shout.

It was a minute before the mists began to clear. He listened intently, but everything was silent. The shout was a mystery, perhaps real, or perhaps only a voice from his fever-riddled brain. Whichever it had been, he had to move on.

The steps seemed as numerous as the stars breaking out in the night sky. He dragged himself up them, one by one. On the porch he rested, too exhausted to continue, too relentless to quit. After a moment he clawed his way up the porch post until he was standing once more. Lurching unsteadily, he reached the door.

There wasn't a lock he couldn't pick, but he didn't relish trying this one with hands that shook like poplars in an autumn windstorm. He turned the knob, and the door swung in with a creak. Silently he blessed the trusting souls of country people.

Inside, the cabin was larger than he had expected and more rustic. There had been no attempt to cover the massive logs and mortar with wallboard. Abe Lincoln would have felt right at home.

A quick scan uncovered a doorway to his far left and told him that the cabin had at least one more room. The majority of the space wasn't divided by walls but by the placement of simple furniture. Opposite the front door was a round oak table, beside it an old-fashioned wooden icebox, a counter and sink. A cast-iron wood stove separated the kitchen from the living area to his right. A massive fieldstone fireplace covered that wall, with a sofa and chairs placed in front of it. Opposite the fireplace, above more chairs and wall-to-wall bookcases, was an open loft with stairs leading to it.

The dim glow he'd noticed from outside came from a kerosene lantern burning on the table. By its light he recognized the obvious. The cabin had no electricity. More important, a kerosene lantern needed tending. No one left a lantern burning, without staying nearby. Particularly not in a firetrap like this.

And there was food on the table beside it.

He leaned against the door and drew his gun. There was no one in this room. He was still alert enough to know that. But there was at least one room to his left, and a loft. As quietly as he could, he hobbled in that direction. He determined to try the room. Surely if anyone was in the loft he or she would have made a sound when a half-dead stranger dragged himself through the front door.

The room beyond the doorway was medium-sized, obviously a bedroom. There was a large ornate iron bed made up with a patchwork quilt. No one was in it.

He stumbled to a closet and opened it to see men's clothing, overalls, mostly, and plaid flannel shirts. He grabbed one of each, then rummaged in the chest of drawers by the bed for socks and underwear. Two of the drawers yielded only women's things, but the third produced what he needed. Encouraged that he had made progress so quickly, he searched the near-darkness for a telephone but found none. Out of the bedroom, he made his way across the room to the table.

Half a sandwich stared back at him from hand-thrown brown crockery. Most of a glass of milk sat beside it. His stomach lurched as he imagined trying either, but he forced himself to lift the sandwich and take a bite. He chewed slowly, willing his body to accept nourishment. He had to be strong, and he had to eat if he was going to survive.

He tried the milk next, but he could only manage a sip. Nausea and dizziness overwhelmed him, no matter how hard he tried to fight. He slid into the chair and used what remaining strength he had to lift the glass chimney of the lantern and blow out the flame. His head slipped to the tabletop, and he lapsed into unconsciousness.

Later—he didn't know how much—he came to again at the sound of a mournful whistle and the shuffle of footsteps. His fingers closed on the butt of his gun. With what failing strength he had, he pushed himself upright and struggled toward the back door.

The lantern had gone out. Tate stopped whistling as she glanced toward the window that had framed the outlaw moon at supper. She was surprised. She didn't think the lamp had been low on kerosene, and despite the cabin's one hundred-plus years, it was surprisingly draft-free and cozy. Still, kerosene lanterns weren't exactly high-tech. At least the preposterous pumpkin moon was high enough to light her way until she could get the wick burning once more.

Maybe she would light the other lamps, too. Kerosene wasn't expensive, not when she figured what she was saving on utility bills. There was something about this night that called out for light. She would start a fire right away, as well. She might even toast marshmallows and make s'mores. She had missed Girl Scouts and slumber parties as a teenager, but later, thanks to Kris and Jess, her adopted parents, and Stagecoach Inn, the home for runaways that they had founded, she had regained a little of those lost years.

Kris and Jess were sold on s'mores, she remembered fondly. They squashed toasted marshmallows and graham crackers and chocolate bars into sandwiches on autumn nights, as if they were a special remedy guaranteed to heal the saddest or most rebellious adolescent in Stagecoach Inn's care. And sometimes, s'mores—or maybe the love that went with them—even seemed to help.

Tate climbed the back steps, her arms filled with firewood. Some of it was from an apple tree, and she looked forward to the scent of applewood filling the old cabin. Simple pleasures, s'mores and applewood, but oddly comforting on a night such as this one.

She balanced the logs against her chest, leaning backward as she reached for the doorknob. She whistled to herself again as the knob turned. The song was one she had heard last week at a Mountain Glade hootenanny. She couldn't remember the title, but the words had told the story of the murder of a faithless wife. So many of the songs of the region had survived the trip to America from the British Isles virtually unscathed. And so many of them were about murder and mayhem. She remembered that this one had been sung by a long-faced old woman with the husky voice of a New Orleans chanteuse.

The door swung open an inch before she had to grab a falling log. She settled the wood firmly in her arms again and pushed the door with her knee. The door was heavy and handmade, and it moved only a foot. The whistled folk song changed to a softly voiced curse. She pushed the door with her elbow, and it swung a little wider.

She stepped into the cabin and started toward the fireplace. The cabin seemed colder than when she had left it, and strangely desolate. She would set her wood on the hearth and light the lamp closest to it. Then she would start a fire. By the time she returned with the next load, the room would be . . .

"Stand right where you are."

For just a moment Tate was too surprised to feel fear; then it set every nerve in her body twanging. She didn't move, but she wasn't sure whether it was the harshly voiced order or shock that made her stand so still.

"That's right. Now turn around slowly. Very slowly. I've got a gun, and I don't mind using it."

She forced herself to do as the man's voice commanded. She moved slowly, still clutching the load of wood. Finally she faced the door she had just entered. It was still open, and a man's figure was silhouetted in front of it. He was tall, and his hair and beard glinted gold in the light of the outlaw moon. He was wearing a tattered blue uniform and a gun belt, but the gun itself was in his hand and pointed at her chest.

She had never seen his photograph, but Tate knew the identity of the man who was standing in front of her. Carl Petersen—who had not, after all, headed straight for Houston.

"You're a woman." He sounded surprised.

"Last time I looked." Her eyes were drawn to the gun. Her life seemed to depend on its whims.

"Who else is out there?"

In fascinated horror she watched the gun barrel waver. "Nobody."

"Don't play me for a fool. You don't live here alone."

She debated the wisdom of telling the truth. Perhaps the threat of someone else would force him to leave. "You're right," she lied. "I've got family coming home any minute. If you're smart, you'll run while you can."

He gave a derisive laugh. "I'm not running so well about now."

The gun barrel did a right side step, then a left. "Take what you need and get out of here," she said as calmly as she could while she still watched the gun. "I've got no reason to report you. Whatever you've done is no concern of mine."

"This is a democracy, lady. You *are* your brother's keeper. Or didn't that lesson make it to the Ozarks?"

"I've got food and money. You can have as much of both as you can carry. But if you stay, you're going to be caught." She improvised. "My father won't take kindly to you being here."

Carl Petersen stepped forward. The gun barrel continued its unsteady dance. "Let's deal with you first, then we'll worry about your father."

Regrets flashed through Tate's mind. She wished she had been better about telling Kris and Jess that she loved them. She wished she had searched for her father while he was still alive. She wished she had made more friends, done more good, made love to a man. She was twenty-one, and life had seemed endless.

Carl Petersen took one more step. The gun wavered.

Tate hurled the pile of logs just as he took step number three. Then, as the firewood slammed against his chest, she turned and fled.

Chapter 2

Only the same will to survive that had brought him this far kept Carl Petersen from lapsing into unconsciousness when the firewood knocked him to the floor. Had he not been so ill, he would have dodged easily. As it was, he managed to protect his weapon and the arm holding it as he fell. He rolled to his stomach, propped himself on both elbows and steadied the revolver. "One more step and you're dead."

Tate stopped just inches from the door. She didn't turn.

"You try anything like that again and you won't live to see your family come home." He blinked and sweat dripped into his eyes despite the chill in the room. "Now turn around."

Tate debated. The man behind her was obviously near collapse. At best, his aim would be poor. She knew enough about guns to realize that television shoot-outs made the difficult look too simple. The room was dark, and Petersen was shaking so hard he could hardly hold the gun, if she ran and made it another twenty yards, he would never have the strength to come after her or the control to aim carefully.

If she made it another twenty yards.

She turned slowly, having calculated the odds and found them wanting. "If you kill me, there'll be a new trial. They won't call *my* death second-degree. Kill me and you'll spend the rest of your life at High Ridge . . . whatever life they leave you before your appeals run out," she added.

The room was revolving slowly. Petersen concentrated on the small figure of the woman wearing the oversize jacket and ignored the rest of the merry-go-round. "Do what you're told, and I won't kill you."

"And your word is good," she said, cynicism oozing from every word.

"Get over here."

Tate moved slowly back across the room. "What do you want from me?"

"Silence." Petersen slid to his knees. The pain that lanced through his leg made the room revolve faster. He concentrated on the woman as he reached inside his back pocket. Slowly, with the hand not holding the gun, he slid his hand deeper and drew out a pair of handcuffs. He debated how best to use them.

Tate had learned long ago not to show fear, but now the bravado she had been forcing wavered. "You don't have to use those. I'll do what you say."

He laughed harshly. "Yeah. You've proved that." He motioned with his gun to the bedroom. "Move, but not too fast." He staggered to his feet, trying not to put weight on the injured leg.

"My family—"

"Isn't here!" He started toward her.

Tate searched his grim face, then turned and headed slowly for the bedroom as he followed a short distance behind. "It's obvious you're a sick man. Give yourself up. Let me go for a doctor. You aren't going to make it anywhere in the shape you're in." Tate tried to sound calm, but she was afraid she was pleading. "You haven't hurt anybody, and I'll tell the authorities you didn't hurt me. They'll take you back to High Ridge, but at least you'll still be alive."

The cabin grew darker as they moved across it. There were no windows under the loft, not until the bedroom. Tate considered all her possibilities as she neared it. Petersen hadn't bothered to answer her. She suspected that the short walk was taking all his concentration and strength.

He was a sick man, and she was a healthy woman. He was holding a gun, but just barely. If she let him handcuff her to the bed—and she was certain that was his goal—she could be a dead woman. Even if he didn't shoot her, he might not make it, and then *she* could starve to death.

Two yards from the door she leaped forward, squeezing through the narrow opening between the slightly open door and the jamb, then slamming the door behind her. She searched for a lock, but there was none. Instead she jammed an old rocker beneath the knob and raced the short distance to the window, trying with all her strength to lift it.

There were sharp blows against the other side of the door, and the chair shook. Desperately she struggled with the window, but it remained firmly in place. She expected gunshots through the door, but instead the chair began to slide across the pine floor. Wildly she looked around for something, anything, to defend herself with, but the room was bare except for the iron bedstead. And the half-open closet.

She was almost to the closet when the chair skidded across the room, rocking violently. She jerked the closet door and dove inside. There was a crowbar behind her father's clothes. He had probably kept it there to pry open the window when the frame was swollen with humidity. She remembered seeing it before, a useless object she had paid little attention to because she had never needed it. Now her life depended on it.

She found it at the same moment that the bedroom door slammed against the wall. Her fingers closed around the thick metal bar, and she stood and swung when Petersen stepped into the room.

She missed him by inches, but the strength it had taken to open the door, then to dodge her blow, seemed to be his undoing. He fell forward, grasping the quilt to break his fall. His gun clattered to the floor beneath the bed.

The momentum of her swing had carried Tate forward. She fell against the wall, then braced herself and turned, the crowbar still in her hand. She swung low, but he rolled away.

This time there was no chance to reposition and try again. He grabbed her ankle and jerked, and she fell beside him, the crowbar clattering uselessly to the floor. He was on top of her in a moment, pinning her hands.

Tate twisted beneath him, frighteningly aware of the odds against her. He was exhausted and sick, but he also outweighed her by at least seventy pounds. She was in good physical condition, but his body, despite the trials of his escape, was all tough, lean muscle. She struggled, but he used his extra weight like a street fighter who wasn't afraid to use any advantage he had.

She had once been a street fighter, too. Her hands were pinned, but one leg was free. She bent her knee and brought it sharply against the leg where he had so obviously been wounded.

He grunted and sagged against her. More importantly, her hands fell free. She kicked again, and instinctively he drew himself up to protect his leg. She dragged herself out from under him and searched for the crowbar. It was just yards away, and she scurried toward it, grabbing it as she scrambled to her feet. She was moving toward him when she saw the glint of moonlight on the gun in his right hand.

"That's one too many strikes against you," he said in a voice so rough it grated along her spine. He slid to his back and held the revolver high, aiming it at her head. The safety moved under his thumb.

Instinctively Tate squeezed her eyelids shut and waited for the explosion. The sound, when it came, was as loud as a cannon shot. She heard the bullet plow into one of the huge chestnut logs from which the cabin was built. She waited for the searing pain that should follow.

She heard Petersen's voice instead. "There are more bullets in this gun. And right now there's one three inches to the side of your head. It's not there by accident."

In the mind-numbing shock of finding she was still alive, Tate felt sensitized to everything around her. She could feel the cool cabin air caress the backs of her hands, could smell the pungent odor of cedar that lined her father's closet. She opened her eyes. In the eyes of Carl Petersen she could see something that looked amazingly like regret.

"Why didn't you kill me?" She whispered the words. To her ears they sounded as loud as a scream.

"Because I'm hoping you just needed a lesson."

She nodded. In the aftermath of certain death averted, her knees began to tremble.

"What's your name?"

She moistened her lips. "Tate."

"I give one lesson per customer, Tate."

She nodded again.

"Drop the crowbar."

She did, and it clattered musically to the floor.

He sat up with a grimace, then pushed himself upright, using the bed as a prop. "Get on the bed." As if he knew her thoughts, he shook his head. "I could have killed you more times than once."

Whether or not he was telling the truth, Tate knew she had no choice but to obey him. She moved across the room and lowered herself to sit on the quilt.

"Get in the middle." He motioned with the revolver.

She slid to the middle of the bed.

"Lie down and put your hands over your head."

She didn't move.

"Now."

He was an escaped convict, filthy and undeniably hanging on to consciousness by a thread, but his voice held command, like that of a man who was used to being instantly obeyed. And her choices were limited to none. She lay on her back and slowly stretched her hands over her head until they touched the iron railing. Carl Petersen came toward her and grasped one hand. In a moment one cuff was snapped snugly on her wrist, the other on the railing.

He dropped to the edge of the bed beside her, as if his legs wouldn't hold him any longer. "Where has your family gone, and when will they be back?"

"To town, and any minute."

"You're a convincing little liar, but I've known better."

Tate didn't answer. She was all too aware of being under his control now.

"I'll ask again, and this time tell the truth. I'm not in much of a mood . . . for games."

She heard his voice waver, and saw his chin drop toward his chest. "Give yourself up, Petersen," she said, trying not to sound afraid. "Isn't it better to be alive in prison than dead on the run?"

"Your family."

"I'm telling the truth. They'll be home any minute."

With an effort he turned to look at her. There was no emotion in his voice. "Then if I leave the key to the cuffs on the table on my way out, they'll set you free sometime in the next hour?"

She didn't answer.

"It's your choice."

For the first time since moving into her father's cabin, Tate wished there really was a family coming home tonight. But she knew—and she suspected Petersen did, too—that there was no family. If he left, she would lie here for more than an hour. She would lie here until some member of the Carter clan recollected that they hadn't seen Millard's girl in town for weeks. Will Carter from the next farm over would be appointed to investigate. And what he would find would not be pretty.

"I live here alone," she admitted. "No one's coming home."

"What about the men's clothes in that closet?"

"They belonged to my father. He died almost a year ago."

"Why are they still here?"

Tate wasn't about to share the story of her life with the embezzler-murderer sitting beside her. She hadn't gotten rid of anything of Millard's yet. She was still trying to figure out who he had been, and she needed all the clues she had.

"I haven't lived here long," she answered instead. "And Mountain Glade isn't exactly brimming over with charities looking for overalls and flannel shirts."

He shrugged with an effort. "If someone did come home, it would be a simple matter for me to shoot them before they got inside."

"No one is coming."

Petersen tried to read her expression. He already knew a lot about the young woman he had cuffed to the bed. She was a survivor, just like he was, with unusual courage and a trace of foolhardiness. She was slender, but she was also strong. By anyone's standards but his, she was a good liar.

She was pretty, too, he noted dispassionately. Smooth black hair fanned out on the quilt under her head. She wore it one length, not short, not long, and with none hanging down over her forehead to mar her delicately arched brows and widely spaced blue eyes. Her nose was straight and narrow, her lips enticingly lush, and her chin the pixyish focal point of a heart-shaped face.

"You're not from here," he said. "The accent's different."

"I'm not from anywhere."

He felt a curious twinge at the words. Apparently his physical weakness was weakening him in other ways. But he wasn't from anywhere, either, and despite himself he felt a reluctant bond between them.

He turned away sharply. The movement made the room whirl again. The woman was no longer a threat. And he believed her latest story, although he could be making a mistake. Now he had to decide what to do.

Decisions floated around him. All of them seemed to hinge on one fact. "Where's your telephone?"

Tate was surprised. She had been expecting almost anything from the man beside her, but that question seemed so normal. *Where's your telephone, miss? I've got to call my mother and tell her I'm all right. Where's your telephone? The warden will be worried about me.*

"There's no telephone," she said, hoping the news wasn't going to send him into a rage. "No telephone, no electricity and no plumbing."

He didn't believe her. "You live here without a phone?"

"Why would I lie? You could find out the truth easily enough."

He let the news settle into all the corners of his mind. No family. No phone. No neighbors—at least none he had been able to see from his vantage point in the woods. "How close is the next house?"

Again this was a fact so easy to check that there was no point in lying. "A half to three quarters of a mile as the crow flies. Almost a mile if you go by the road."

He was beginning to wonder if the room's twirling dance was just the normal state of things. It had gone on so long, and amazingly he was still conscious. "How often do you get...visitors?"

"It depends."

He knew she could just as easily lie as tell the truth about that. "Anyone who came looking for you might get more than they bargained for," he warned. "Unless...I could plan ahead."

"I've got no visitors on my social calendar, if that's what you're asking."

He wondered at his luck. He couldn't seek Aaron's help, but he could stay here for a day and gather strength again. His fight with the hellcat now handcuffed to the bed had taken everything he'd had left...and then some. Realistically, he could go no farther until he recovered.

He was in the exact middle of nowhere. Surely there was no better place to hide until he was able to move on. "You know who I am. How?"

"I've got a radio."

"Have they... searched this area?"

There was no point in lying. Tate was sure he would be listening to the news soon enough. "They think you're south of here, heading for Houston."

The room no longer seemed able to decide which direction to take. The woman's voice came to him through a thick fog. "Houston... that's where he'd have gone, all right," he mumbled to himself.

Tate wondered if she had heard him right. Then curiosity was replaced by satisfaction as she watched his head drop forward. In a moment he had passed out beside her.

The outlaw moon had cleared the treetops before Petersen came to. He was disoriented at first, believing himself to be back at High Ridge. But the woman being over him, assessing him, was nothing like the wild-eyed gorilla who had been his cell mate. Memory layered memory until he knew who she was. "Let me guess." He licked his parched lips. "You got my gun."

"You dropped it on the floor when you passed out."

He swallowed, then lifted his head. She was still securely cuffed to the bed. "You didn't find the keys."

"Not for lack of trying," she said coldly.

He managed a dry laugh. "I've been out for an hour?"

"More like two." Tate moved as far away from him as the cuffs would allow. "My arm is getting numb."

"Then sit up." He didn't wait to see if she took his advice. He began the arduous process of trying to manage sitting up himself. The room was still whirling. And he was hot enough to set the cabin on fire. "I... need water."

"Uncuff me and I'll get you some."

He didn't bother to answer. The cabin seemed impossibly huge, the kitchen miles away. Still, he had no choice. He slid to his feet, holding on to the post at the foot of the bed. His leg throbbed unmercifully. He had to clean and care for it.

Tate watched him stumble toward the door. She felt a peculiar flash of pity. "There's water in the icebox."

He made it halfway across the cabin before he collapsed again.

* * *

The outlaw moon had risen so high it was no longer visible from the bedroom window. Tate had watched its climb as if her life depended on it. There had been nothing else to do. The bed was wide enough, the cuffs short enough, that she could only dangle her toes against the floor to the side of the bed. She had thoroughly examined the bed frame. The headboard was bolted to it with four rusted bolts that wouldn't budge under the mere pressure of twisting fingers. After an hour of concentrated effort she had given up the hope of marching her body, headboard and all, out of the cabin and over to Cousin Will's.

The cuffs themselves gave no quarter. Carl Petersen had snapped them on like a pro. They were just tight enough to keep her trapped, just loose enough to keep her blood circulating. And if the cabin had been warm enough, her blood probably would have moved right along like it was supposed to. Unfortunately, though, the cabin wasn't warm. The temperature was dropping quickly. And even under the quilt, she was freezing.

"Petersen," she yelled. She was beginning to get hoarse. She had been shouting for him since the moment she had admitted that escape from the bed was hopeless. She had heard him fall; then there had been silence. Her worst fear was that he had died. If that were true, she envied him the ease of it. Her death, chained to the bed frame, wouldn't be as quick or as painless.

"Petersen!"

Tate thought she heard a moan. It was the first positive sign since he had fallen. "Petersen!"

She heard a series of thumps and what sounded like something being dragged across the floor. There was silence, then more thumps. Silence, the swish of something dragging. Silence.

Just as she was about to call out to him again, she heard a click. He had made it as far as the icebox. Relieved tears sprang to her eyes. He wasn't dead yet, and neither was she. Her life depended on his now. "Petersen, you've got to uncuff me! If you die, I'll die here. Let me go and I'll see what I can do to help you."

There was no answer.

She repeated her plea into the silence. Just as she had decided he had fainted again, she heard the slam of a cabinet door. He was rummaging for food. Sometime later she heard the dragging sound again, the the unmistakable sounds of retching. Finally she heard his voice. "Where do you keep... medical supplies."

She was irrationally glad to be communicating. "There's a first-aid kit in the loft."

His answer was a mumbled curse. She thought she knew why. "Look, unlock these cuffs and I'll get you what you need. We both know you'll never make it up there and back."

"I'm... not crazy."

"Maybe not, but you are half dead." Tate watched the doorway. His voice had sounded close. As she watched, he materialized out of the darkness. She was surprised to see he was standing. "Look, you're not going to make it much longer like this." The pity she'd felt earlier sounded in her voice. "You've put up a great fight, but it's over now. If you die and I die with you, you haven't won anything. Uncuff me. You can hold the gun on me, if you want, while I take care of your leg and fix you some soup."

"And when I go under again... you'll go for the sheriff."

It would be foolish to deny it. "It's your only chance. Maybe you'll stay conscious long enough to chain me up again."

"I just need... rest." He lurched toward the bed. When he reached it, he shoved something toward her. It was the package of graham crackers that she would have used for s'mores. She couldn't believe he had given any thought to whether she was hungry or not.

His hands shook so badly that he could hardly unbuckle his gun belt, but after repeated fumbling, he managed. It hit the floor by the door, followed by everything in his pockets, including the set of keys that she guessed would unlock the cuffs.

He didn't stop there. He unbuttoned his filthy shirt, agonizing over each button. In the moonlight his chest was a warm golden tan brushed by hair a darker gold. He slipped the shirt over his shoulders.

"What are you doing?"

"I think... s'obvious." He pulled at his pants as if to unbutton them, but they remained fastened. He tried again and succeeded. They slid only as low as the scrap of cloth tied around his wounded leg. Fumbling badly, he loosened the shirttail bandage, and the pants slid to the ground over his shoeless feet. He stepped out of them, one foot at a time, pulling the bandage back over his leg and tightening it once more with a groan. In the moment he stood that way, Tate got a clear picture of why he was such a formidable opponent—even with infection raging through his body. Then, clad only in cheap cotton briefs and the filthy bandage, he fell to the bed and struggled to get under the quilt.

"Petersen. Listen," Tate said frantically. "You're dying. Are you too much of a fool to realize it? People don't get over gunshot wounds without treatment. This isn't the flu! For God's sake, get the damn keys and let me go! I'll do what I can for you, I promise."

He sounded halfway to hell when he spoke. "Not...going back...kill me."

"This is the twentieth century! They don't kill prisoners for escaping! You might get a year or two added to your sentence, that's all. And you'll probably still be eligible for parole about the same time, anyway!"

"They'll kill..." The rest of the sentence died away.

Tate slid as far to the other side of the bed as she could. The man beside her was unconscious again.

The sun hadn't risen, but the sky was growing lighter. Carl Petersen slept on, but Tate had not slept at all. Her eyes hadn't flickered shut; her body hadn't relaxed for even a second. The keys that could free her were on the floor by the door, but Petersen was between her and them.

Tate knew she could eventually slide the bed in that direction with a combination of bouncing and pushing against the wall. Then, with the help of a sheet or pillowcase, she might be able to fish successfully for the keys. It could take hours, but every inch would bring her closer to freedom. The problem was that Petersen might come to as she bounced and pushed. Gauging her intent, he might find the strength to rise and throw the keys into the next room.

As the night had progressed she had realized her only chance was to wait until he died.

"God, no!" The horror of it overwhelmed her. She could not bear even a few minutes of being chained in bed next to a dead man. And once she was sure he was dead, she would have to crawl over him for the keys....

He was still alive now. Tate turned so she was facing the outlaw beside her. Jesse James in the flesh wasn't nearly as romantic as the legend. Would an Ozark tale grow up around this? In a hundred years would the locals tell their children bedtime stories about Carl Petersen and the woman he chained up to die of terror in bed beside him?

"Petersen!" Tate stretched her arm toward him, swallowing hard as she forced herself to touch his shoulder. "Petersen, wake up."

He mumbled something. His shoulder felt as if it was on fire. He had tossed restlessly, mumbling incoherently for the last hour. Did people survive fevers of this magnitude without brain damage? He was a human being, and he was suffering. But whatever pity she would normally have felt was eclipsed by her need to be free.

She shook him. "You've got to uncuff me!"

He tossed his head from side to side, then turned and gripped her hand. "Double-cross..."

"Wake up!" Tate tried to free her hand, but he wouldn't allow it.

"Bastard... you bastard. Said a month. No more..."

Tate was only half listening, her concentration fixed on waking him. "Petersen, please! Wake up. You've got to get up and uncuff me while you still can!"

"You'll pay... Gallagher.... No wall could hold..."

"Petersen!" When he didn't respond, she tried his first name, hoping he might believe she was a friend. "Carl. Carl, wake up. You've got to let me go before I have to lie here with a corpse!"

His eyelids opened. His eyes moved back and forth as if he were watching a movie. "Gallagher... you bastard... a month. No more!" He gripped Tate's hand harder, and she winced in pain. "Left me there to die!"

"Petersen. Carl. Carl!" She was nearly weeping in frustration. "Please wake up!"

"Simon." He turned toward her. "Simon. My name..."

"Please. Get the keys! Carl, can you hear me?" She wrenched her hand from his and shook him.

"Not Carl... Simon."

She was in no position to argue. Whatever reason his fevered brain had concocted for the identity switch didn't matter. "Simon, then. Please, I'm begging you. Try to wake up. You've got to wake up and get the damn keys! If you don't, I won't be able to help either you or me! You're going to die."

"Die." The mumbled word seemed to penetrate his delirium. His eyes opened wider. "Die. No justice in justice."

"Yes, die! Your fever will kill you, if nothing else does first. Look, Car—Simon, whatever you call yourself. I don't want to rot here beside you. Understand? I don't want to be a damn folk-tale."

"Folk..."

"The keys. Get the keys. You're going to die if you don't!"

He raised his head from the pillow. His eyes seemed to struggle to focus for the first time. "You don't quit...."

"No, I don't. Please. Get the keys. It's over. You're not going to survive this unless you get help. And you can't leave me chained beside a dead man!"

His head fell back to the pillow and his eyes closed. "I'm not...die..."

"Just because you never *have* doesn't mean you're not going to!" Tate wondered if he was weakening enough to believe a lie. "I won't go for help. I'll take care of you myself."

"Accomplished...liar."

"I mean it."

"D'like you on my...side."

"I'll be permanently at your side, if you don't get me the keys!"

He managed the ghost of a smile.

"Please. Simon, let me go."

His eyes opened. "How'd you know...Simon?"

"You told me to call you that."

"Damn!"

"Look, I just want you to let me go. I don't care who you are, or anything else. Just let me go. If you've got any shred of humanity, do it."

He lay very still.

"I'll beg, if you want," she said.

"Listen..."

Tate instinctively drew nearer. His voice had wavered and become less than a whisper. "I'm listening."

"I'll be killed...if I go back. Innocent. I have to prove...That's why..."

Tate leaned over him. "Simon?"

"Escaped. To prove..."

Tate suspected that ninety-nine murderers out of one hundred at High Ridge would stubbornly proclaim their innocence, even if their victims came back to identify them wearing angel wings and halos. "Why will you be killed?" she probed.

"Captain Shaw . . . I've got something. . . . Look in my shirt."

"I can't look in anything! I'm handcuffed here beside you!"

He lay very still. Tate waited, uncertain whether he was lapsing into delirium again—or just considering. Then, just as she was about to shake him once more, his eyes opened. With what seemed a superhuman effort, he pushed himself to a sitting position. He slid off the bed and crashed to the floor beside it. Tate heard a sharply indrawn breath.

Despite herself, she felt sympathy. "Are you all right?"

There was no answer. She slid as close as she could to the side, hoping to get a look at him. "Simon?"

As she squinted into the darkness, he began to inch his way to the door. She knew the movement was agonizing, but he continued. Inch . . . stop . . . inch . . . stop.

Finally his arm stretched as far as the door. She held her breath as he grabbed his clothes and pulled them toward him. The keys were on top of his pants. At last they were in his hand. Slowly he propped himself with his back against the wall and tossed the keys to the bed. His eyes closed.

Tate wasted no time finding the smallest key on the ring. Unlocking the cuffs took longer than she wanted, and she fumbled repeatedly, sure that any second he would change his mind.

"I didn't . . . kill you," Simon said from the floor.

The cuff fell from Tate's wrist. She was surprised at the tears of relief that formed. "Thanks, I guess."

"I could have."

"I know."

"If you go . . . for help, you'll be killing . . . me."

Tate's eyes flicked to the gun. It was within his reach, although she imagined that in his weakened state it would take him so long to get it, she might have a chance to get past him first.

"You were tried and convicted by a jury of your peers, weren't you?" she asked, slowly lowering her feet to the floor.

"I'm not what you think. . . . I let you go . . . saved your life. Save mine." His head slid to the side. His lips parted, and his breathing grew shallower.

Tate realized her chance to escape had arrived. She could get past him now and grab the gun on the way. She stood and started toward him. His head lifted, and his eyes opened. As she watched in horror, he reached for the gun. Then, with a hand that shook so badly he almost couldn't lift it, he held it out to her.

"Take it.... Shoot me.... Turn me in.... Either way, I'm a dead man." The gun fell from his hand before she could take it. Then the man who called himself Simon sagged to the floor.

Chapter 3

The unconscious man on the cabin floor was an escaped convict. He had threatened her life repeatedly through the long night, and once he had even fired his gun to terrify and subdue her. So why, Tate asked herself, couldn't she just drag him a foot closer to the bed frame and handcuff him there until she could alert the sheriff?

Because he was suffering. Because the floor was freezing cold, and he was exhausted and wounded. Because he had spared her life, when a desperate criminal should not have. Because, damn all sound reasoning, she wasn't convinced he was lying about his innocence.

Because the law and the people who enforced it had never unduly impressed her.

Tate held the revolver in both hands, aiming it at Simon's head. She could fire if she had to. She *would* fire. She had learned much of what she knew in ghetto classrooms, in overburdened child-care institutions, on the streets. She had learned the hard way how to protect herself, and those lessons had never been forgotten.

So she would fire the gun if she was forced to, but as she stared at the fallen heap of masculinity on the floor, she knew she didn't have to worry. Simon—or Carl Petersen, or whoever he was—

wasn't going to fight her anymore. He had come to the end of his strength, and he had realized it. He had offered her the gun, and by so doing he had offered her his future.

She didn't want his future. She didn't want any part of him. But he was conveniently unconscious, and she was stuck with him for a while, at least. Now she had to decide what to do.

One thing was certain. She couldn't leave him on the floor. She had to get him on her bed, if only to wait for the sheriff. The cold floor would kill him quicker than his wounded leg.

She considered how best to work this miracle. He outweighed her by seventy pounds, at least, and unless he came to and helped, he would be deadweight. He was also nearly naked. Getting a grip on him was going to be difficult, but she had to try.

Tate set the gun on a closet shelf so she wouldn't tempt Simon to grab it from her. She knelt beside him and shook his shoulder. "Simon, can you hear me?"

He groaned, then lapsed into silence.

"Simon?"

She got behind him, and using her own body as a lever, she grasped his broad shoulders and began to push him to a sitting position. His skin was hot to the touch and surprisingly slippery. With dawn breaking and the room growing lighter, she could see how dirty he was.

"Come on, Simon," she said, trying to encourage him. "If we can get you sitting up, maybe we can get you back in bed."

He groaned again, but he seemed to be trying to help. At least he wasn't fighting her. She pushed, straining hard until he was propped against the wall. It was still too dark to get a good look at him, but she could see how pale he was. His whole body looked drained of color, like the white-marble statue of a Greek god. Despite everything that had happened, she felt a pang of concern. People died from gunshot wounds. *He* could die.

Tate gauged the short distance from the wall where he was propped to the bed. She could not move him that far without his help. She shook him, her fingers biting into his flesh. "Simon. Can you hear me?"

He groaned in answer.

She raised one hand to his cheek, slapping it lightly. "Look, you've got to get in bed. You'll die here. I can't get you there without help."

His eyelids flicked open, but he seemed unable to focus.

"I'm going to put your arm around my shoulder. Lean on me as much as you need to. Once you're standing it will only be a few steps to the bed." Tate crouched beside him and slung his arm across her shoulders. For all its muscled length, it flopped there uselessly. For a moment she considered abandoning him. He was a fugitive, and only hours ago he had threatened her life. What was she doing with her arm around his naked back, her fingertips lightly brushing the mat of golden hair on his chest?

He shook his head as if he were trying to clear it. She felt his body contract uselessly against hers. He was struggling to help because he didn't want to die. He was a human being, just like she was. She hugged him tighter and lectured him. "You've got to help. You're going to die if you don't."

"Die . . . if you turn me . . . in."

She was relieved to find he was conscious enough to speak. She tightened her arm still further. "Right now we just have to worry about getting you in bed. I'm going to stand on the count of three. You've got to help. Do you understand?"

His head fell forward. She wasn't sure if it was a nod or if he was lapsing into unconsciousness again. She began to count. "One . . . two . . . three." With all her strength she hauled him upward, bracing her hip snugly against his. "Come on, Simon!"

They struggled together. He was so weak he was little help, but at least he wasn't deadweight. Tate strained and pushed. Then, when he was almost standing, she began to move across the floor, half dragging him as she took the required steps. "Come on, Simon! We're almost there. Don't faint now."

At the bedside, he fell forward. "Can't . . ." he muttered.

"You're there already. Just lie there. I'll help you lift your legs. Just don't slide off! Understand?"

He didn't answer, but she didn't waste time asking again. Before he could slide off, she grabbed his good leg and a mighty effort lifted it to the bed. She was gentler but equally resolute with the other. He lay across the quilt at an angle, but at least he was no longer on the floor.

Tate rested for a moment, viewing her handiwork. The man on the bed was still drained of all natural color. She had a well-grounded suspicion that the dirty rag wrapped around his leg covered more than a scratch.

Holding her breath, she eased the rag to his ankle until the wound on his leg was in full view. It was an obscenely gaping flaw on something so otherwise perfect. The place where a bullet had entered his calf wasn't large, but it was ripped unevenly, and the skin around it was red and swollen. The swelling was rising toward his knee, and the wound still trickled blood.

She swallowed hard. She was no stranger to injuries and illness. In college she had trained as a medic at the local free clinic. Under the supervision of whatever physician happened to be on duty, she had helped with any problems that were presented. Once she had even assisted with a minor gunshot wound. But nothing she had ever seen had been this serious. A case like this would have been transported immediately to the local hospital emergency room.

And the emergency room was where Simon belonged. Except that if he went, it would be under police escort. And when he was well, he would go back to High Ridge. To be murdered?

The possibility nagged at her. This was the twentieth century, but like her father's cabin, High Ridge was said to be a nineteenth-century sort of place. She'd heard talk about it on her infrequent trips to town. A number of Mountain Glade residents worked at the prison, since it was one of the few employment possibilities in the region. Those she'd spoken to didn't say much—saying anything to strangers wasn't the style here—but what they did say indicated that High Ridge was the last place a convict wanted to end up.

But a tough prison and a prison where inmates were murdered were two different things, weren't they?

Tate went to the dresser and took out a clean bandanna. Wincing at the pain she must be causing, she bandaged Simon's leg, then worked the quilt out from under his body. He didn't move. She noted that his breathing was rapid and shallow. With her hands at his shoulders he was easy enough to turn, and she positioned his legs so that she could draw the quilt over him, tucking him in like a small child.

The handcuffs swung from the iron headboard where he had anchored them. Tate considered them carefully, then lifted his wrist and snapped the cuff over it. He was her prisoner now, just as she had been his.

As she was leaving the room she stumbled over the clothes he had discarded. She stooped and picked them up. The guard he had stolen them from wouldn't want them back, that was for sure. The clothes smelled worse than the prisoner himself, and they were in tatters.

Tate searched the pant's pockets as she walked through the cabin. There was a letter opener, engraved with the initials RS, but nothing else. She dropped the pants by the back door. Just as she was about to toss the shirt on top, she remembered that Simon had said something about looking in his shirt pocket.

Frowning, she lifted the flap and reached inside to pull out a small, plastic computer diskette. The label was blank. Unless the diskette was, too, it was probably a copy of a program. What was Simon doing with a computer diskette? The man the papers called Carl Petersen had been imprisoned for a computer crime, but why was this diskette in the pocket of the uniform he'd stolen from the guard?

Unless it really did have something to do with his escape.

The diskette was wet. As she lifted it to the light, water seeped from it. Whatever information it had contained was probably lost. But its mere presence made the mystery of the man in her bed that much more complicated.

After setting the diskette in the kitchen, she busied herself gathering the logs from the floor where she had thrown them the night before. As the sun began to rise in the sky, she lit fires in the fireplace and stove to hasten heating the cabin.

When she returned to check on her prisoner, she discovered that he hadn't changed positions. Briefly she monitored his pulse. He was still as hot as he had been, and his pulse was rapid, but strong. She knew she had to be concerned about blood poisoning and shock. The first was certainly a possibility, although she thought the wound would look worse if blood poisoning was developing. The second would be heralded by a drop in blood pressure.

She left the room, returning a few minutes later with the first-aid kit she had told him about. The kit contained more than the usual bandages and disinfectant. She had purchased her own equipment to use at the clinic, and she had a stethoscope and sphygmomanometer for measuring blood pressure. She lifted his arm and wrapped the cuff around it. Then she put the stethoscope to her ears and inflated the cuff.

His pressure was on the low edge of normal, not yet in a danger zone. He had certainly lost blood from his wound, and he was exhausted, both possible reasons for the low pressure. She pulled the quilt lower and listened to his heart. The beat was even, if too rapid.

He was a sick man, but she guessed—accurately, she hoped—that the major portion of his illness was caused by exhaustion, blood loss and dehydration. The wound itself looked serious but not life-threatening. With luck it would respond to good care.

She put her instruments back in her kit and covered her prisoner once again, adding an extra blanket from the closet. She would have to boil water to tend to his infected leg. She didn't want to disturb him now, nor did she want to take the time to care for it properly. Not until she knew what she was going to do with him. Whatever decision she made, she had to make soon. She didn't think he was in immediate danger, but without treatment in the near future, Simon Carl Petersen could die chained to her bed.

Mountains weren't new to Tate. Stagecoach Inn was in the Virginia Blue Ridge. She had gone to live there when she was fourteen, and despite a childhood spent in the flatlands, the mountains had seemed like home. Maybe that was because Stagecoach Inn was the first place she'd lived as a teenager that had *been* a home. Whatever the reason, though, coming to the Ozarks hadn't seemed strange, although the mountains themselves were subtly different, rockier and rougher hewn.

Now, as her Ford Bronco churned up a red dust cloud behind her, she sped around once more in the series of Kalix Road curves that would take her into town.

Kalix Road was a study in contrasts. The houses closest to Tate's cabin were modest, but the yards were neatly kept, and pride was evident in fresh paint and flower gardens. Farther along the road, the houses turned into shacks, and the children playing in front of them were dirtier. It was almost as if Kalix Road was divided into the have-nots who had quit trying and the have-nots who hadn't given quitting a thought.

The land in this section of the Ozarks was too rocky for lucrative farming, and the countryside was too inhospitable and remote for industry. But some of the families along Kalix Road fought the odds. They farmed, and they worked at any job they could find, no matter how dirty. They educated their children and supported their churches, showing a stubborn pride and intelligence.

When Tate turned, and the clay road changed into blacktop highway, the houses changed again. These home owners, the town merchants and professionals, were not wealthy by city standards, but the closer to town Tate drove, the larger and more modern their houses became. If she had just been a tourist passing through, she might never have known about the poverty that existed in these beautiful mountains or the people's day-to-day struggle to maintain their pride.

And of course if Millard's cabin had been anywhere else, she never would have been introduced to Simon Carl Petersen.

Mountain Glade was so small it would have been easy to miss, except that by now she knew every inch, every shop, every café. It was a picturesque little mountain town with brick and frame buildings, wooden sidewalks and a character or two in constant residence. She had learned where to buy groceries, and where to park if she was attending the Friday evening hootenanny. She knew the bank's hours and policies, and where to get change for the laundromat.

She knew where the sheriff's office was.

Tate slowed to the required twenty-five miles an hour as she crossed the town boundaries. Mountain Glade was a sleepy town by anyone's standards, but it was no sleepier at eight in the morning than at high noon. The best parking places on Main Street were already taken, mostly by pickups. The largest number of vehicles were clustered in front of the Sassafras Café.

She parked in front of Allen's Pharmacy, but she didn't get out for a moment. Instead she reviewed the decision she had reached as the morning sun finally broke free of the horizon. She had decided *not* to decide her prisoner's fate—at least not by herself. There was too much she didn't know, but there was one person who might be able to enlighten her.

Her adopted father, Jess Cantrell.

Jess was an extraordinary resource. Not only did he direct Stagecoach Inn along with Krista, but he was also a journalist who'd written best-sellers. Jess always had his ear to the ground. And if there was something he didn't know, he knew someone who did. Jess was the perfect person to provide information about Simon, if she could just nudge him past the fact that she had a dangerous criminal handcuffed to the bed in her peaceful mountain retreat.

Tate grimaced as she silently practiced framing the bad news. Neither Jess nor Krista had been thrilled about her decision to spend several months alone in the Ozarks. They had been concerned about her isolation here. Nothing they'd said had been discouraging, but Tate had known them both too well not to understand their real feelings. Now they were going to be sure their concern had been justified.

She was no longer the fourteen-year-old waif they had rescued from the streets, but she supposed that, like parents everywhere, they were having trouble coming to grips with her maturity.

Still, even if this set them back a decade, she had to ask Jess to find out what he could about the man who had escaped from High Ridge. Consulting Jess was the adult thing to do. She just hoped he and Krista realized it.

There were two public phones in Mountain Glade. The one in front of the gas station had been out of order since she arrived. The second was inside Allen's Pharmacy. It was a wall phone, installed just inches from the counter where pharmacist and customers traded prescriptions, medication and gossip.

Wally Allen, the owner and sole dispenser of advice and medicine, was middle-aged, red-headed and the nosiest human being Tate had ever encountered. The telephone's proximity to his listening ear was no accident. Wally kept a willing finger on Mountain Glade's pulse. At a moment's notice he could tell you who was doing what with whom and where they were doing it. Tate sometimes wondered if Wally kept a diary, readying himself for an early retirement funded by Mountain Glade residents willing to trade cash for pages.

Today Wally seemed in rare form, performing happily for a dour-faced old woman. In a county with only two overburdened physicians, Wally functioned as the third. To his credit, Tate had never heard him give bad advice. He had filled a local doctor's prescription for her once when she'd had a sore throat, and his helpful hints had been useful.

He was expounding on the merits of fiber therapy when she approached his counter. Tate had overheard this particular lecture before. She guessed she might have as much as five full minutes on the phone before Wally would stop long enough to listen to her conversation.

She guessed wrong.

"Morning, Miss Tate."

Tate reminded herself that someday she might have to get a prescription filled again, and she smiled pleasantly. "Good morning, Mr. Wally."

He grinned, showing every tooth he had. "Still enjoying your stay?"

She wasn't about to tell him that her stay had suddenly become something less than enjoyable. "The fall colors are lovely, aren't they?"

"Nothing like them in the city." Wally watched Tate lift the receiver. "Need a phone book?"

She forced another smile before she turned away. "No thanks." There was silence behind her as she dropped her quarter in the phone. Pretending to fumble in her handbag for a phone number, she shifted so that she could see Wally and the old woman in front of the counter. Both of them were staring openly at her. There was no way she could call Jess now to ask him for information about an escaped convict..In ten minutes, everyone in town would know about the call. In twenty, the sheriff would be at her door.

Instead she consulted a blank memo pad, then dialed a string of ones. As she had expected, a recorded message told her to try again. She hung up as if no one had answered and retrieved her quarter. "I guess I'll have to try later," she muttered.

"Early bird catches the worm," the old lady said, as if she had just coined the phrase.

Hoping that Wally would be busy filling prescriptions soon, Tate nodded and left the pharmacy.

How long could Petersen go without treatment? He was obviously a strong man, but even strong men died. She decided to wait half an hour, then return to use the telephone again. If Wally was still eavesdropping, she would have to rule out getting additional information from Jess and make a decision on her own. In the meantime, she would force herself to join the crowd at the Sassafras Café and have some coffee. She hoped her stomach, which was clutching convulsively in anxiety, could handle it.

There was nothing extraordinary about the café. There were several others in town with similar menus and prices. The building itself was just one of a connecting string, with a plate-glass view of Main Street. Apparently, however, Mountain Glade residents knew their country cuisine and had given the Sassafras a five-star rating. And to give the residents their due, the few times Tate had eaten there, she'd had to admit the food, though simple, was tasty and plentiful.

With her mind whirling with thoughts of Simon, she opened the door. She scanned the room before entering, to be sure that there would be space for her. But it wasn't until she was inside that she realized a sizable portion of the vehicles parked in front belonged to her relatives.

The room didn't grow silent, but it did grow quieter. Since it was too late to leave, Tate walked to the large table holding six of the Carter clan to dutifully say her good mornings. She had never felt less like a family reunion.

Will, a gaunt string bean of a man, stood as she approached. As her closest neighbor, Will had seen more of Tate than the other Carters had. It had been Will who had shown her around her father's property and cabin when she first arrived in town. Unfortunately, it had also been Will who had suffered the greatest loss at her sudden appearance. Had she not been located and told of her inheritance, Will would eventually have owned her father's acreage.

Tate tried to sound glad to see them. "It looks like everyone's enjoying breakfast." She scanned the table. Will's wife, Dovey, more than pleasingly plump, sat beside him like an illustration for the nursery rhyme "Jack Spratt." Beside her was Dovey's mother, Zeddie, who resembled a bulldog more than an old woman.

Across the table and closer to Tate were three more Carters: Canna, Andy and Esther. They were older than Tate, but of her generation. Canna, an attractive blonde, worked as a teller at the bank. Andy and Esther were married and owned their own broiler house about two miles from Tate's cabin. They were all related to Tate, but she wasn't clear how.

"Pull up a chair and join us." Before Tate could refuse, Will was beckoning the one harried waitress toward the table. "Don't worry about me. I don't want to interrupt," Tate protested, but the waitress was at her elbow before she could continue.

"Coffee?" The waitress, who looked a bit like Zeddie, held out the pot as if she were waiting for Tate to cup her hands. Will had already dragged another chair up to the table. He took the paper place mat and silverware that had been in front of it and set them in front of Tate, along with a clean cup and saucer.

Aware that she'd been bullied into submission, Tate nodded. She was relieved when the coffee was directed into the cup.

"Want the special like everybody else?" the waitress asked. She left before Tate could respond.

"I guess I'm having the special," Tate said. She hoped she could choke it down.

Zeddie scrunched her face into even more wrinkles. "You need it."

Tate tried to think of something to say, but a sleepless night and a problem she hadn't yet solved kept her mute.

"So what do you think of Mountain Glade?" Canna asked.

Tate wished she could really tell them. *I think it's a little close to High Ridge for comfort.* "I like the mountains," she said instead.

"Are you makin' out all right at Millard's place?"

Notwithstanding the fact that a convict was sleeping in her bed at that very moment, Tate wasn't sure how to answer. If she pointed out that it was a little rough, she might be stepping on toes. For all she knew, the entire Carter clan lived as simply as her father had. "I've got everything I need," she said. *And one living, breathing thing I don't.*

"Winter's comin'," Will said.

Tate expected him to say more, until she realized everyone was waiting for her to answer. "Indisputably," she agreed.

"Gonna be a bad 'un."

Tate wondered if Will predicted the weather with the help of woolly worms and the breastbones of geese. Her father's journal had been specific about weather-forecasting superstitions. "How can you tell?"

"Oh, Will keeps charts," Dovey said breezily. "Got charts of all the weather for years back. Knows more than a weatherman."

Despite her preoccupation, Tate was impressed. Will looked embarrassed. "You can't know what a winter's like here, 'less you been through 'un."

Tate sipped her coffee. "What should I know?"

"Roads get so thick with snow, only a truck'll pass. And you've gotta have wood cut. Lots of it. Or I reckon you'll freeze. And you gotta have food stored by. Don't have it, you'll go hungry, that's for sure."

Tate realized she was being warned away. She hardly knew these people, and she felt no kinship to them. But somehow, the warning rankled. She had as much right to be here as they did. She wasn't going to let them scare her back to Virginia.

God knows, if she could be easily scared, she would be out on the highway right now hightailing it for Stagecoach Inn.

She finished half her coffee before she spoke. "Well, you don't have to worry about me. My car has four-wheel drive and all-weather tires, so I'll be able to get around. Millard cut enough wood before he died to keep me warm for three winters. But thanks for the tip about storing some food. I guess I'd better be sure to lay in a couple of bags of canned goods in case I can't get out to the store for a week or two."

No one smiled. Every eye at the table looked right through her. Tate thought about all the years of her childhood, when she had yearned for a big family, for grandparents and cousins, aunts and uncles. Krista often told the girls at Stagecoach Inn to be careful what they wished for, they might just get it. Tate wished someone had warned her earlier.

Breakfast came, to Tate's relief. The special turned out to be beaten biscuits with gravy, eggs and hickory-smoked bacon. She steeled herself and ate it quickly, not pausing once to savor the wonderful flavors. She was acutely aware that enough time had passed that she could reasonably try to use the telephone at the pharmacy again. The man handcuffed to her bed could wait no longer.

Conversation went on around her, but just as she was about to excuse herself, Will addressed her again.

"Noticed you put in trees."

Tate knew "noticed" was the wrong word. She and Will were next-door neighbors, but their houses were almost a mile apart. The only way Will could notice anything was to come on her property and spy. The thought sent a chill through her. If he was going to spy, he couldn't have picked a worse time.

"That's right." She didn't elaborate.

"Wondered why."

"I guess I was just finishing what my father started," she said, stressing the word "father," in case they needed a reminder of her right to do anything she wanted with the property. "I know from his journal that he wanted to plant the acres in front of the cabin with white-pine seedlings. The world can always use more Christmas trees."

"They take tending," Dovey said.

Tate wondered why they didn't just come out and ask her how long she was going to stay. "Yes, I know." She stood and lied, "I hate to rush right off, but I've got to get back. I need to use every bit of daylight if I'm going to get the rest of the seedlings in by the end of the week." She nodded pleasantly. "Thanks for inviting me to eat with you."

Will stood. "You know there's a man on the run from High Ridge, don't ya?"

Tate wondered if this was more scare tactics. She made herself nod, as if it were no concern of hers. As if the man in question wasn't handcuffed to her bed, dying.

Will nodded, too. "You need me, just give a holler."

She was surprised. For a moment Will had almost sounded as if he were concerned. But his face showed no expression. She wondered if her father had ever smiled. "Thank you," she said. She lifted her hand in goodbye to everyone else and went to the front counter to pay her bill.

There was more traffic, both foot and vehicle, when she emerged from the restaurant and headed quickly for Allen's. Silently she prayed that Wally would be busy filling prescriptions now that the town was waking up. Amazingly, he wasn't even behind the counter when she reached the telephone.

She deposited her quarter, then spoke in low tones to the operator, giving the Stagecoach Inn credit-card number to pay for the call. The phone rang repeatedly. Since Virginia was an hour behind Arkansas, Tate could just imagine Jess grumbling as he came awake enough to answer it.

But it wasn't Jess who answered. "Hello."

Tate recognized Krista's voice. "Hey, Kris," she said. "Did I get you up?"

Krista laughed huskily. "Hey, sweetheart. Everything all right?"

Tate hesitated, but she decided not to answer honestly. Krista was much more her best friend than her mother. Still, the fact that less than a decade separated them didn't stop Krista from worrying like a mother. Jess, on the other hand, was capable of a bit more objectivity. She would let him break the news about Carl Petersen to Krista. "Everything's fine. I was in town, so I just thought I'd call."

"It's wonderful to hear your voice."

They chatted for a few minutes, catching up on gossip, before Tate came to the real reason for the call. "Is Jess there?"

"You haven't gotten his letter?"

Tate frowned. There was no mail service on Kalix Road. And she hadn't been to the post office in a week. "I guess not. It's probably waiting in my box."

"He's out of the country, Tate. He wrote you before he left. It was pretty sudden. An old friend of his phoned from Lebanon—"

"Lebanon!"

"There's a group there that claims to have three American hostages. They're promising to let them go if they get the publicity they want. They chose Jess as their publicist."

Tate tried to fathom all the implications of what Krista was saying. "Why?"

"Because of the work he's done in the past and because of his reputation. He's been promised safe passage and return."

"And what are their promises worth?"

Krista's concern for her husband seeped into her voice. "I can only hope they're worth what they say they are."

Tate wished she were there to offer comfort... and receive it. "How long is he going to be gone?"

"Two weeks... three at most. He'll be home for Thanksgiving. Will you be here, too?"

Tate wanted to say that Thanksgiving was the last thing on her mind, but one thing was for certain: Krista had enough to worry about now. Tate couldn't add to her troubles.

She was on her own, and a man's life was in her hands.

"Don't worry about Jess," Krista said, when Tate didn't answer. "He knows how to take care of himself. You will think about coming home for Thanksgiving, won't you?"

"Sure. Look, you can send telegrams here. I'm sure you can. I mean, Mountain Glade isn't that isolated. You send a telegram if you need me. Okay? And I'll call you soon."

They exchanged warm goodbyes before Tate hung up.

She stood staring at the telephone until a voice sounded behind her. "Waitin' for it to ring, Miss Tate?"

She turned to see Wally behind the counter again. She sucked her bottom lip between her teeth as she considered him. Considered all the things she didn't know. Considered the state of her life. Considered that she might be making a terrible mistake.

"Wally," she said at last, "I've got a problem."

He looked delighted to hear it.

"I've got this cut on my leg." She pointed high on her thigh so he wouldn't ask to see it. "I got it when I was splitting firewood, and I think it's getting infected. Now, I don't have all day to spend in town waiting for Dr. Monson to see me, but when I had that bad throat after I first got here, he prescribed penicillin and put a refill on it. Do you think if I get that refilled now, it'll take care of the infection?"

"Had a tetanus shot lately?"

Tate prayed that High Ridge routinely inoculated its prisoners. "Yeah."

Wally rubbed his hands together in satisfaction and began a lecture. Tate left Allen's Pharmacy half an hour later with enough advice, first-aid supplies and medication to care for a battalion of war heroes.

Chapter 4

Tate had carefully banked both the fire in the fireplace and the one in the cookstove before leaving for town. By the time she returned, however, both the glowing coals and hours of sunlight had heated the cabin. She quickly dumped new logs on the fire before going to check on Simon.

He was in the same position he had been in before she left. His eyes were closed, his breathing too rapid. His skin was still hot to the touch, but he shivered when she laid her hand on his forehead, as if he were chilled.

Briefly Tate considered her plan. This was a very sick man, and her ability to heal him was laughable. But if what he said was true, sending him back to High Ridge would mean sure death. Her own life experiences had taught her that things were often not what they seemed. What if he was telling the truth? Sure, the odds were against it, but what if he was?

He had spared her life, and he had turned himself over to her keeping. What could she do except give him a chance? She would give herself twenty-four hours with him. If he took a turn for the worse during that time, she would go right for the sheriff. If he didn't, and she was able to reduce the fever and the infection in his leg, she could take her time deciding. He was handcuffed to her bed, and she had his gun. Even if he improved rapidly and regained his strength, he wouldn't be able to harm her.

With her decision made and a timetable in place to review it, she set to work. Before she even touched Simon's leg, she had to get water, aspirin and a double dose of antibiotics down him. She was sure he was dehydrated. With a fever the magnitude of his, she doubted he could even drink enough liquid to keep dehydration at bay. Intravenous fluids were a better answer, but impossible under the circumstances, so she was going to have to make do with dribbling medication-laced liquids in his mouth.

She decided to try plain water first. She knew he had experienced some nausea, and she wanted to be certain water stayed down before she added the precious antibiotics. First water, then water with liquid Tylenol added to it, then water with antibiotics. She calculated that the process would take an hour.

She bypassed the water on the back porch and went straight to the spring for fresh. Surprisingly, Cinn, who had never gotten remotely close to the house, was on the porch when she returned. He lumbered inside when she opened the door and parked his red-brown bulk by the bedroom doorway. Shaking her head, she added ice to the water from the bag of cubes she had bought on the way out of town, then resolutely strode past the self-appointed guard dog.

Simon still hadn't moved. With the cabin filled with light, she could examine him closely. His hair and beard were ragged and dirt-encrusted, his skin waxy. Simon Carl Petersen would win no beauty prizes right now, but she wasn't so sure about his potential once he was well again. His features were purely masculine, yet refined . . . elegant, she decided. Intelligent. Of course, he was no commonplace liquor-store bandit. He was an outlaw of a higher order. A computer criminal, which obviously took intelligence, or at least a good education.

Tate set the glass of water beside the bed and left, then came back a few minutes later with a washcloth and a basin of water. The water was warm, taken from the cast-iron kettle she always kept heating on the wood stove. She sat down on the edge of the bed, dipped the washcloth into the basin, wrung it out, then began to smooth it over his cheeks.

At first he made no noise or movement. Then, after she had dipped, rinsed and wrung several times, he arched his neck, as if trying to avoid torture.

"That's right," she said softly. "Show me you're still alive."

She continued smoothing the cloth over his face, over his beard and mustache and down under his chin. Clean, the beard was a dark gold, a shade or two darker than his hair, or so she guessed. His hair was too dirty to be sure. She worked on his face until it was as clean as a washcloth could get it, then set the basin beside the bed and picked up the ice water.

She had decided on an eyedropper instead of a spoon because it was more difficult to avoid. "Simon," she said gently, "this is just ice water. You've got a high fever, and I've got to give you liquids. All you have to do is swallow." She accompanied her words with action, drawing water into the dropper and sliding it into the corner of his mouth. Drop by drop she dribbled water between his teeth, speaking reassuringly as she did.

The first two droppers went in with no difficulty, but then he balked, locking his jaw tight and refusing to part his teeth. Rather than fight him, she went into the kitchen and emptied the basin of water into the sink. Then she refilled it with soapy water and carried it back to the bedroom, stopping momentarily to add another log to the fire.

He was still, but as soon as she joined him on the bed, his head tossed restlessly on the pillow.

"That water probably steamed away before you could even swallow it," she lectured. "If we don't get more inside you, you'll dry up and the wind will blow you back to High Ridge."

Surprisingly, his eyes opened. But they stared straight ahead, as if he were watching something she couldn't see.

"Simon?" She touched the washcloth to his cheek. "Do you know where you are?"

His eyelids drifted shut.

Sighing, she continued to wash his face with the cool cloth. At least he wasn't trying to avoid it anymore. After a few minutes she began feeding him water with the eyedropper again and managed to give him the equivalent of a cup.

She waited to see if the water was going to stay down. As she waited, she smoothed the cloth over his cheeks again. Thanks to her diligence, he seemed cooler. Since the cabin was now a comfortable temperature, she decided to take the blanket off completely and fold the quilt down to his waist. Then, allowing herself only a brief thought about the strange intimacy of this, she began to wash his chest, shoulders and arms.

He was a tall man, but not heavy. He had the body of a runner or a major-leaguer, slender but muscular. She wasn't sure how long he had been in the penitentiary, but whatever the length of his stay, he had remained in shape... or gotten into it. She could almost picture him down on the floor of his cell doing push-ups. Had he spent that time planning his escape? Had he become obsessed with fitness because he knew that he had to be ready to break out of High Ridge?

She guessed that his superb conditioning had kept him alive. From the shape he was in now, she could only guess at what he had been through. A weaker man would have stopped when the bullet plowed into his calf. This man had kept going.

It felt odd to think of him as a strong man, when he was lying unconscious and burning up with fever. It felt odd to be caring for him so intimately. She owed him nothing, certainly not tender, loving care. But he was a human being, and so was she. He was a fine specimen of the human male—at least physically. And even if she didn't owe him anything exactly, wasn't it her human duty to keep him alive?

Tate smoothed the cloth over her prisoner's arms. Even relaxed, they were ridged with muscle. His forearms were covered with golden hair and tanned—apparently he had made good use of the prison yard while sojourning at High Ridge. She pictured him pacing its perimeter, plotting just how he was going to make his escape. Had someone helped him? The radio had been fuzzy on details. Had he escaped from High Ridge alone when, according to the news, no other prisoner in the penitentiary's history had managed the same feat?

She rinsed the cloth and began to wash a hand. It was broad, his fingers long and shapely. They were capable hands, hands that had held a gun and fired it three inches past her head despite a debilitating fever.

Silently she made a guess that the escape had been attempted without help. This was not a man who wanted to rely on anyone. Last night, he had believed until the bitter end that he was just going to sleep off the effects of the infection raging through his body.

Only when he'd realized that he had really lost, that not a shred of hope was in sight, had he asked for her help.

She moved to the other side of the bed to wash his other arm. Maybe she was tired—missing a night's sleep did that to people. Or maybe she was just crazy—after all, this was an escaped prisoner she was treating so gently. But whatever the cause, she was becoming increasingly aware of the bond that was forming as she washed him.

She was twenty-one years old, and there had been men in her life. But she had always called a halt to relationships before they built to a natural conclusion. She wasn't sure why. She liked to believe it was because she had never fallen in love. The alternative—because she was unfeeling, cold, even frigid, perhaps—was less appealing.

And yet considering her background, considering where she had come from and what she had come through, it seemed understandable that she would have trouble giving herself to anyone. She was cautious. Life had insisted on it. Maybe she would always be too cautious to fall in love or make love to a man.

Of course, a truly cautious woman would have run screaming into the night when Simon Carl Petersen, escaped convict and murderer, asked for her help.

Gently she stroked the washcloth over Simon's chest. There were scratches covering him that she hadn't been aware of until she'd begun to clean him up. The one deep groove on his side near his waist looked as if a bullet had grazed him. Had it been directed only inches to the left, he never would have made it to the cabin.

He was badly bruised, too. Sympathy grew as she tried to imagine his ordeal in the woods before he'd found her cabin. The past few nights had dropped to near-freezing, and the tattered uniform he'd arrived in would have done nothing to keep him warm. She felt compassion and just a trace of some other indefinable emotion as she brushed the washcloth over his chest once more. It seemed almost a shame that a man as physically perfect as this one should spend the best years of his life locked away in an Arkansas prison.

She realized just exactly where her thoughts were taking her and dropped the washcloth back into the basin. He was much cleaner, and the water had briefly helped cool his skin. She left the room, then returned with one more basin of water to rinse off the soap.

She worked efficiently and quickly, trying not to notice anything else about him.

When she'd finished, she diluted the correct dose of Tylenol in half a glass of ice water. Luckily he'd had no trouble with nausea since she'd given him the plain water. She just hoped that would hold.

"Come on, Simon. Cooperate just a little longer. Let's see if we can get that fever down." With absolutely no intention of taking no for an answer, she set to work.

He was in the tropics somewhere. He should know where; he was never lost. Madagascar, maybe. Or Brazil. Somewhere hotter than the hinges of Hades.

And he was in a jungle. Running, except that he could barely move. Cutting his way through rain forest, green everywhere, everything green. The machete they'd given him was dull and growing duller. He slashed, and the machete bounced against green, then ricocheted toward him, covered with green, dripping green. Blood. Green blood. A forest bleeding green.

He was bleeding.

Where was Josiah? Josiah had brought him to this forest, hadn't he? Left him here to find something, but what? The heat was dissolving his brain. Green everywhere. And something... something he was supposed to find. He chopped uselessly. His machete slid against the trunks of trees like the bow of a Stradivarius, searching for the perfect symphony. But there was no music here, only green. And something he was supposed to find.

Thirst swelled his tongue and narrowed his throat. Rain forest all around him, yet there was no rain. Living, breathing heat. Rain forest withering in sun, and sun that seemed to radiate from the ground at his feet. And where was Josiah?

He swallowed convulsively, and something cool trickled past the thirst knot in his throat. He raised his eyes to the heavens. In prayer? He hadn't prayed in a century. But there were clouds forming. He opened his mouth and rain, sweet, sweet rain, poured in.

He was afraid he could not swallow fast enough.

* * *

The Tylenol was gone. Tate knew Simon would take more water if she offered it. Toward the end of the dose he had seemed eager to swallow. He had even turned his head, making her job easier.

She knew better than to rush things, though. She would wait half an hour, then try the antibiotics. They wouldn't taste so pleasant, even though she intended to mix them with half a can of cola. If he couldn't keep that down, she would have no choice but to go to Will's and make a call to the sheriff. Simon had to have antibiotics, even if they were administered in the prison hospital.

In the meantime, she had to take a good look at his leg. She didn't know if the bullet was still embedded in his calf or whether the wound would conceivably heal without stitches. Now seemed a good time to make an assessment. He was still, as if too exhausted to toss and turn. Later her might be a worse patient.

Steeling herself for what was to come, she pulled the quilt and blanket from under the mattress and folded them back so that Simon's legs were exposed. Her eyes traveled the long length of them. Like the rest of him, they didn't seem to belong to a man the radio newscaster had dismissed as a paper-pusher. They were an athlete's legs, long and lean, and his thighs were muscular.

Her eyes flicked higher. His briefs were cheap, prison-issue cotton riding low on narrow, thoroughly masculine hips. The fabric stretched tightly across his abdomen and below, leaving no curve or bulge to her imagination. The girls at Stagecoach Inn would have glowing praise for a man endowed like this one.

She forced her thoughts back to the job at hand. Her first task was to clean the uninjured part of his leg, then strip off the bandanna and clean the infected area. To prepare for the chore ahead, she left the room to fire up the cookstove and begin boiling water. She thoroughly washed her hands and took a clean basin of soapy water back with her to begin the process.

Half an hour later she had already discovered good news. There were two wounds on his leg. The first and nastier was the entrance wound; the second—a smaller, neater hole—the exit. The bullet had gone through at an angle, apparently missing the bone, since his leg didn't appear to be broken, but badly injuring muscle and tissue. She knew little about such things, but she guessed that without physical therapy, Simon might never regain full use of the leg.

First and foremost, however, was to get rid of the infection so that no more injury could result. The area around the wound was hot to the touch and swollen, but it had stopped bleeding. She wondered what havoc her efforts might wreak. Might she be responsible for causing the wound to bleed again if she cleaned it and packed hot cloths around it to drain the infection?

The risk was certain, but she saw no other choice. Something had to be done or blood poisoning would be the result. Steeling herself for the task ahead, she sat so that she could take Simon's leg in her lap and hold it still as she worked. She only hoped he would remain unconscious until she was finished.

There was a house in the jungle ahead. No, not a house. A shack built into the towering, menacing green. It was constructed of bamboo and held together by crudely crafted jute rope. A parrot, with plumage so brilliant it seemed to undulate in waves of color, flew back and forth in front of the door, barring entrance.

He would find safety inside. There was shelter here, food and drink. And rest. He had never been so tired. His eyes were heavy with sleep, and as he shaded them against the glare of the bird's feathers, they grew heavier still.

Shelter. He hacked a path, but his arms were as rubbery as the trees he tried to cut away. For each tree he felled, two took its place after he passed. He could feel the jungle pushing him, propelling him toward the shack even as the trees in front of him barred his way.

He could die here, with the jungle closing in around him. Die here to nourish the trees, become yet another layer on the spongy rain-forest floor. He forced himself to strike one more blow, then one more, but as he tried to move forward, something gripped his leg. A vine, perhaps. His head dropped forward. Slowly, slowly. His gaze drifted downward.

The vine moved sinuously, stretching and contracting as it twisted around his leg. Gleaming reptile eyes smiled up at him. Scales glistened along the vine's surface.

He struggled to lift his leg, struggled to dislodge the vine-turned-python. Only when he no longer found the strength to struggle did the python slither away.

* * *

Tate hung her head over the kitchen sink and took deep breaths. During her years at the free clinic she had considered becoming a physician. Then an old man, a homeless wanderer who was regularly treated there, came in one morning, sat down in the waiting room and died.

She had known the man for months, traded stories with him, made him sandwiches and coffee, then more sandwiches to take with him when he left. She had done some volunteer social work, introducing him to a sympathetic counselor at the local welfare department, going with him to meet the owner of a boarding home for recovering alcoholics. But nothing she had done had helped. He had died, anyway, in the one place where he could be sure someone would mourn him.

She had taken weeks to master her grief. And when it was a tolerable ache inside her, she had realized that becoming a physician was out of the question. She had never thought of herself as a particularly emotional person, but the loss of the old man had nearly devastated her. How could she possibly handle the endless losses a doctor experienced? She knew of no specialty or position where she could be guaranteed that none of her patients would die.

Now she knew she had another reason for finding a profession other than medicine. She didn't have the stomach for it. She had cleaned and treated Simon's wound, but the memory of the pain he had suffered would haunt her forever.

She took another deep breath, then slowly lifted her head. Her nausea was passing, and her head was no longer whirling. At least she hadn't allowed her squeamishness to overwhelm her. And though her experience and knowledge were less than ideal, she thought there was a good chance that with the help of antibiotics he could fight the infection now, although he still needed stitches.

A moan echoed through the cabin. She splashed some water on her face from a jug by the sink and went to check on her patient.

Only his head moved, tossing from side to side on the pillow. She wondered if she dared try to give him the antibiotics now. Surely if treating his leg had sickened her, it had done more serious damage to him. She perched on the side of the bed and put her hand on his forehead. If the Tylenol had begun to work, it hadn't yet touched his fever. She soothed her hand along his brow.

It was a funny thing, how the intensity of caring for him was affecting her emotions. She felt bonded to him. He was totally at her mercy, and it felt strange to be so responsible for another human being's life. Too, it was particularly strange that the human being so dependent on her was an escaped convict.

Her hand halted on its gentle path. Was this the sort of relationship that sometimes developed between a kidnapper and his victim? Was she beginning to convince herself that he was really good, when all the evidence pointed to the opposite? She had always been a rebel. Was she making the ultimate statement now? Wasn't living in an old log cabin in the middle of nowhere good enough for her? Or did she have to go a step further and prove to the world that she honored none of its conventions?

She stood, trying to shake off the sympathy she was developing for the murderer, embezzler, escape artist, gun-toting terrorizer of isolated women. He probably didn't deserve her help; he most certainly did not deserve her sympathy. She was going to have to be careful. She obviously had a soft spot in her heart for people who were alone and in need. She'd better be careful that the soft spot didn't ooze right into her good sense.

With that thought to guide her, she went back to the kitchen to prepare the antibiotics.

Somehow, he made it to the shack. The parrot flew toward him in an agonizing flash of color, all wings and exquisite rainbow torture. He ducked, and the parrot soared into the jungle, where it was lost in relentless green.

He stumbled to the door and peered inside. The shack was dark, a deep, velvet black that sucked at him until he entered. It was cool inside, enticingly, insidiously cool. Cool, then cold. Cold as the jungle had been hot. His heated flesh contracted against the thick, frostbitten air. He tried to wrap his arms around his chest for warmth, but he remained statue-still.

He would die here, in the cold, just as he would have died of the jungle heat. He had struggled so hard, only to come to the same ending.

His eyes began to close. Slowly, slowly.

At first there was silence; not even his own thoughts could penetrate its shell. Then he heard a voice. He forced his eyelids apart. A woman was staring at him. He saw her, but he could not see her face. In the frozen darkness, he could only see all that made her human.

She stretched her hand toward his. "Come," she said. "I'll give you comfort."

His fingers began to warm. He moved them as his hand warmed, too. With growing strength, he stretched his hand toward her. The movement took time that wasn't. He was moving toward her, and she waited.

When their fingers touched, in whatever millenium they walked together, she led him back to the jungle. The trees burst with rainbow foliage and bent in quiet greeting as they passed. And then, beside a forest glade, they lifted their heads and tasted the sweet, sweet rain together.

Simon had swallowed the antibiotics and cola without incident, although twice he had opened his eyes and mumbled incoherently. Tate felt drained of everything inside her, but her prisoner was looking better. Peaceful, at least. He seemed to have fallen into a quieter sleep, now that she was finished.

She felt the satisfaction of a job well done. Was this the way a mother felt after caring for her new infant? The answer was obvious, if humiliating. She felt no spark of maternal pride. Even depleted and unconscious, this was not a man to stir that kind of emotion. She felt something entirely different. The man lying in her bed had roused some darker feeling, although she couldn't or wouldn't name it. She had touched him in ways and in places she had never touched a man before. And she had made a commitment to him that was more serious than any other she had ever made.

She had no resources left to question either the feeling or the commitment now. It would take time for the antibiotics to make a difference, but she was encouraged by his response to her care. He was certainly no worse. If he could continue to tolerate the liquids and medication, he had a good chance for recovery. On the other hand, she was going to hit the skids if she didn't get some sleep.

There was a bed in the loft; in fact, that was where she usually preferred to sleep, but now that was out of the question. She couldn't be that far from her patient. The next twenty-four hours were going to be crucial. She had to be alert to any changes for the worse. She contemplated the alternatives and realized there was only one. She had to make a bed on the floor for herself. Never mind that it was fast approaching an Ozark winter and the floor was the worst place in the cabin to be.

She climbed up to the loft and stripped the bed, returning to the bedroom with two blankets and a pillow. Then she went out to her car to retrieve an old sleeping bag that she always kept in the back. A few minutes later she had made a tolerable pallet on the floor, with the aid of three sofa cushions. She left the room, pulling the door only half closed in case Simon called for her.

She considered going to bed without taking a bath, but decided against it. Once Simon was alert again, bathing might be a problem; certainly it would be an inconvenience. She balked at the idea of hauling bucket after bucket and splashing them into the round washtub that was propped beside the fireplace. But a sponge bath just wouldn't do. She needed a real bath. For just a moment she let herself fantasize about the luxury of going into a bathroom and turning on faucets, from which would pour clear, steaming water. Mumbling insults to the father she had never seen, she opened the back door and set to work.

The jungle heaven faded, to be replaced by thick, ancient logs. For a moment Simon believed he was in a fortress. Pictures formed slowly, the truth settling over him at so torturous a pace that he could only grasp its end—its beginning was already out of reach.

He was in a cabin. He couldn't remember why. He was in a bed, but he was too tired to have slept. And he was bound to the bed, although he couldn't see how.

He was both hot and cold, but something told him that his suffering was less than it had been. His leg throbbed until each heartbeat was a torment, but the pain was confined to one place. Some intuition told him that was good, but he was too tired to explore just why.

His eyelids kept drifting closed, but he forced them open. He focused on a wall, a chair, then a door. It was ajar. He narrowed his eyes, like an old man squinting at the newspaper. Light floated in from the window. And through the crack in the door he saw puddles of sunshine on the cabin floor.

He seemed to be alone. He yearned for the jungle and the woman's hand in his. He knew that he was a man who never reached for anyone, yet he had in the rain forest, and reaching had been good.

His eyelids drifted shut once more until he heard a noise. He was in no hurry to respond. He listened. The noise was a song, a whistle that seemed somehow familiar. He opened his eyes and saw the woman from his dream. She was as far from him as she had been then, as strangely undefined. He could see only her outline, could only experience, somehow, all that made her human.

As he watched, her figure began to take shape, shimmering against leaping flames until, even with her back to him, she was flesh and blood and sweetly curving femininity. He saw that she was naked, that her skin was the color of snow against the blazing fire. Like a dancer she stretched her arms over her head and piled her black hair on top of it, holding the inky mass with one hand as she poised at the edge of a round metal tub. Then with infinite grace, she lowered herself into the water.

He saw the silhouette of a breast, small and firm, the perfect curve of a hip, the slender length of a leg. She merged with the water until all he could see was the smooth white breadth of her back and the coal-black length of her hair spilling over the side of the tub.

He knew what it would be like to touch her, to stroke his fingers through the silk of her hair, to brush them over the satin of her body. He yearned to reach for her, but he could not move. He yearned to call to her, but his lips made no sound.

He stared until she grew dim, and even then he struggled to see more, fought not to lose her. At last his eyes closed unwillingly. At once he fell into a dreamless sleep.

Tate came back into the bedroom after her bath. She straightened the quilt and felt Simon's forehead. He seemed cooler, and he was no longer fidgeting. He seemed to be sleeping deeply.

She reached for his wrist and wrapped her fingers around it to check his pulse. The beat was strong, still too fast, but slower than it had been an hour before.

She stood gazing down at him. There was something between them now. She could deny it, could chastise herself for caring, but a bond had formed. Later she would have to face what to do about him. Now she could only be glad that he seemed to have improved.

Gently she laid his arm back across his chest. Her fingers brushed his hand as she began to move away, and in the briefest of moments, her hand was captured in his.

The pressure of his fingers was slight; his skin was fever-coarse and dry. But he held her hand, not in protest or plea, but as if in gratitude. As she stood there, holding her breath in surprise, his fingers tightened around hers . . . only for a second, for so brief a time that she might have imagined it. Then abruptly her hand was released. His lay on the quilt, fingers curled.

She was so moved that for a moment she could not turn away. Fugitive, murderer, the same man who had fired a gun to terrify her. Yet even unconscious, he had found a way to show her he was more than that. He was a human being, and he was grateful.

And she was a woman who was in danger of giving in to emotion and exhaustion.

Tate turned away and forced herself to stare at the scar in the cabin wall made by a bullet that could have lodged in her brain. She stared at it until she felt everything but exhaustion drain away. Then she found her way to the cushions she had lined up at the foot of the bed and crawled under the blankets.

Chapter 5

By the next afternoon Simon's fever had soared and plummeted as often as a skydiving stunt team. Through the hours of sweats and chills he had never regained consciousness. He slept more easily when his fever dropped and tossed restlessly when it spiked, but he never opened his eyes and asked where he was. Tate was certain of that, because she hardly left his side.

When his fever had climbed the first time, she had considered, yet again, going for the sheriff. She had even decided on an arbitrary number of degrees that would signal the need for a trip into town, and she had taken his temperature faithfully, hour after hour. The thermometer, anchored tightly under his arm, had never quite climbed to the point where her decision would be made. His fever had hovered near crisis point but never exceeded it.

Tate had slept in the periods when Simon's temperature dropped and, depleted by his body's struggles, he no longer tossed and turned. When she was awake she did the most cursory of survival chores, hauling wood for the fireplace, cooking and heating water, putting out food for Cinn, who watched her every movement from his post at the bedroom door. But she never left Simon alone for more than a few minutes. By deciding not to turn him in, she had made a commitment to watch over him.

Now, more than twenty-four hours after deciding to care for him, she was exhausted and discouraged. His fever was rising once more, after hovering just two degrees above normal all morning. She knew fevers often rose in the afternoon, and that if this one wasn't accompanied by other symptoms, it might not be as bad as it seemed. But she also knew that if she didn't see a definite improvement soon, she was going to have to seek help. Eyedroppers of liquids were inadequate to stop dehydration, and antibiotic capsules weren't nearly as effective as injections and intravenous medication.

She was losing the battle.

Tate sank to the edge of the bed, too tired to stand any longer. Beside her, Simon tossed his head. Despite her efforts to keep the pillow plumped, he had worn a deep valley in its center. She knew he must be suffering, although she doubted that his mind registered it. Hours ago she had unlocked the handcuff, then snapped it to the bedsprings to give them both more freedom as she washed him once more. He was certainly in no shape to escape or to threaten her. At the first sign of returning strength she intended to lock him to the bed frame again.

She laid her hand on his forehead, brushing the lock of freshly washed blond hair away. She didn't need a thermometer to determine the obvious. Even though she had given him the maximum dosage of Tylenol half an hour before, he was not responding. Faithful Nurse Cantrell was going to have to bathe his skin again and force more fluids down him.

Telling herself that she would find the strength somewhere, she rose and went to the back porch for the water she had hauled earlier that day. The ice she had bought in town was gone, but the spring water was still cool, since the porch was in shade. She filled the basin and a pitcher and went back into the cabin, where she poured powdered lemonade in a glass and mixed it with water from the pitcher. It was the closest thing to glucose that she had.

She began with the eyedropper and told herself she was lucky he wasn't so deeply unconscious he couldn't swallow. Of course, if he had been, her decision whether to notify the sheriff or not would have been easy. He would be back at High Ridge now, and she would be in bed asleep.

Of course, if what he had claimed was true, he might be back at High Ridge in a coffin.

The small jolt of adrenaline that followed that thought got her through the next fifteen minutes and Simon through an entire glass of lemonade. With that behind them, she squeezed a washcloth out over the basin and began to wipe his cheeks and forehead.

Her movements were rote. She had done this so often over the past twenty-four hours that she knew all the contours of his face by memory. He was almost as familiar as an old friend, although to her knowledge none of her old friends was a fugitive from justice.

A dry chuckle squeezed from a body she had believed too tired to ever laugh again. The truth was that if she went far enough back in her life, plenty of the people she had once considered friends could be fugitives from justice. For all she knew, some of them could have ended up in prison like Simon—which was probably why she was sitting here sponging him off.

She moved down to his neck and began to smooth the cloth over it, then down to his chest. If any of the runaways she had met before going to live at Stagecoach Inn were criminals now, they would not have been convicted for anything as white-collar as computer crime. And though her memory of those years was fuzzy, she doubted that anyone with whom she had raided Dumpsters or fleeced tourists had grown up to look like Simon Carl Petersen.

In fact, very few males indeed grew up to look like Simon.

She was cooling the arm closer to her when he moaned. It was another sign that his fever was climbing. Unless she could keep it from climbing higher, he would probably begin to thrash about and mutter. That had happened on two other occasions, but both times she had been able to give him Tylenol almost immediately. Now she had hours to wait before that was an option.

She wondered if he would say anything she could understand. None of the words she had been able to decipher before had made any sense. He called for someone named Josiah, but not as if he expected rescue. And she thought once he had said the name "Erin."

She wondered if Erin was a girlfriend. She didn't think he was married. The radio had never mentioned a wife, and since they had no hard news to report, they dredged up details of his past life at every newscast, just to keep the story before the public.

She had heard his story told time and time again, but never once had a Josiah or an Erin been mentioned. Odder still was the lack of detail about his escape. Apparently no one at High Ridge was willing to talk about that.

Tate knew all about the 1.2 million dollars Petersen had stolen, though. He had been an officer with the highest security clearance at a Houston bank. With his good reputation, access to computer codes and electronic fund-transfer lines, and the help of a banking system so complicated that it made wire fraud nearly impossible to detect, he had coolly embezzled his small fortune over a period of three months.

And he wouldn't have been caught and convicted, wouldn't be lying in her bed, if an unlucky surprise audit hadn't uncovered his scheme.

The auditor, a man named Joe Masters, had been even unluckier. Thanks to his own careful investigation, he was now lying in his grave. According to testimony at the trial, Masters had decided that *he* didn't make nearly enough money for all the work he did and offered to relieve Carl Petersen of his newfound wealth in exchange for his silence. Petersen hadn't thought the swap a fair one, and instead he had bought Masters's silence with one perfectly placed bullet.

And Tate knew just how perfectly the man lying in her bed could place a bullet.

Petersen had almost gotten away with his crime. It had taken months before the police had zeroed in on him for either embezzlement or murder; then the trial itself had taken more months. The jury hadn't taken quite that long to make a decision, but there had been doubts that Petersen had killed Masters. No weapon was ever found; no evidence that Petersen had ever owned a gun or shot one had been presented.

In the end he had been convicted because of the testimony of the accountant who took over for Joe Masters and discovered the embezzlement, too. Petersen's motive was ironclad; his alibi was not. The aunt he had supposedly visited on the night of the murder admitted, when pressured in court, that she had not seen her wayward nephew for more than a year.

So, although there were some significant gaps in what Tate knew about her own personal fugitive, there was much she did know. One other important detail was muddy, however. Never, in any of the news reports, had the name "Simon" been mentioned. Fellow bank employees, neighbors, the grocer at the store he had patronized, had all been given a chance to spout their two cents worth about him. He had been Carl to all of them. Never Simon.

He was a man of mystery, a man of contradictions. He was a man lying in her bed and possibly dying, and she was a woman who should know better than to help him.

Tate sponged his chest, observing the way the golden hair swirled into plastered curls. If Erin was his girlfriend, was she worried about him now? How had she felt when he had been sentenced to High Ridge? How had he felt knowing that he wouldn't kiss her, touch her or make love to her again until he was old and worn out from his years in prison? Had his desperate escape been motivated by a love so strong he would risk his life for it?

Tate realized how sentimental her thoughts had become, spurred, she was sure, by the intimacy of stroking his body so tenderly. She wrung out her washcloth and hardened her heart. It was more likely that greed had motivated the man in her bed. None of the money he had embezzled had ever been recovered. It was probably squirreled away in a foreign country gathering interest. Was Erin there, too, watching it grow and waiting for her fugitive lover?

Simon moaned again, and his lips moved as if he were trying to speak. Tate leaned closer.

"Josiah . . . bastard."

"Who is Josiah, Simon?" she asked softly.

"Gallagher . . . bastard . . . get you."

"Mighty unchristian of you," she said, moving the cloth back to his cheeks.

A hand captured her wrist. His grip was surprisingly strong. "Why? Friends . . . You saved . . ."

Tate felt a spurt of fear. She wished she hadn't gotten so close. "I'm nobody you know," she said soothingly. "I'm not Josiah."

"Bastard."

"Bastardess." Tate jerked her arm free. "I'm a woman," she said. "A woman taking care of you while you get better. You've got to rest. You've been shot."

He turned his head away. "Kill me. They'll kill . . ."

"Nobody's going to kill you. Nobody even knows where you are. You're safe."

His head turned, and his eyes opened. He stared at her, but she knew he didn't see her. "Why?"

She couldn't answer a question she didn't understand. "You've got to rest. You're very sick, and if you don't get better soon, I'm going to have to get the sheriff to take you to the hospital."

He stared at her; she wondered whom he saw. He stared until his eyes glazed over and his lids drooped shut.

She pulled the sheet over his chest and racked her brain for something she could do to calm him. His eyes were closed, but he was so fitful she was afraid he might reopen the wound on his leg if he began to struggle. His fever was worse, but the wound looked better to her. If she could just keep him still as his fever peaked, he might weather this.

She wished she could sing, but her rough alto was guaranteed to send him back on the run. Talking to him didn't seem to help. No matter what she said, he seemed to suspect she was this Josiah person. She settled on whistling. She couldn't sing, but she remembered melodies, and her whistle was clear and accurate. She started on tunes she had heard at the last hootenanny. They were mournful and melodic, tailor-made for a whistler.

He grew calm almost immediately.

Someone had weighted Simon's eyelids. Hadn't physicians once put copper pennies on the eyelids of the dead? The reason for the bizarre practice escaped him, but the possibility he was dead did not. He could not open his eyes. Surely that indicated something out of the ordinary. And although death was an ordinary occurrence, it had never happened to him. At least, not while he was paying attention.

His head spun as he tried to order his thoughts. They were like waves washing over a beach. He couldn't catch them; he couldn't depend on them to do what he wanted. They surged through his head, and there was no rhyme or reason to any of them.

He forced himself to concentrate on his eyelids. He realized that they weren't open because he was just too tired to push them apart. But why was he so exhausted? He had never been this tired before, not even when he had been lost in the jungle, fighting his way to...

But that had been a dream. Hadn't it? And this wasn't. At least, he didn't think so. He tried to concentrate on what he knew. He was lying down, and something covered him loosely, like a sheet or blanket.

Or a shroud.

Surely he wasn't dead. Death was final. Kaput. You didn't think and you didn't feel. He was doing both. And in a minute he was going to open his eyes. Just as soon as he summoned the energy and the focus.

In the meantime, he listened intently. Someone was breathing. It could be him, and if it was, that was an excellent sign.

There were no other noises that he could hear. No cars rushing by, no crickets chirping, no jungle squawks and squeals. But then, the jungle had been a dream. Hadn't it? And what else had he dreamed?

A woman. And a haunting, twine-around-the-gut whistle.

He summoned all his strength and pried his eyelids apart.

At first he thought he had been unsuccessful. There was still nothing but darkness surrounding him. How could anything but death be this black? Then, slowly, images formed. A window with glimmers of light filtering through gossamer curtains. The footboard of an iron bedstead. A closet door, slightly ajar.

Not dead. By why was he in bed? And why did he feel as if every bone in his body was made of rubber?

Something moved beside him. He knew he should respond. Some instinct told him to be wary, but the best he could do was begin to turn his head to the side. Once past a certain point, gravity finished the job.

His neck was stiff, but his view was better, although better was a matter of opinion. Something *had* moved—or rather, someone. There was a woman beside him, a lovely young woman, sleeping deeply with her head on his pillow. It was probably her breathing he had heard.

She wasn't a stranger. That much he knew. Who she was danced somewhere at the edge of his consciousness. Why she was in his bed was a total mystery.

He considered his choices. But until he could remember who she was and why she was here, there was nothing he could do.

He was beginning to remember faces and scenes, although he couldn't sift through them yet to order them. He remembered prison and running. He remembered a searing pain in his leg, pain that was seated in the same location as the distant throb somewhere below the sheet covering him. He remembered woods and a river. He remembered a cabin.

He forced himself to concentrate. Flashes of memory tantalized him. Firewood flying through the air. The woman running. A gun in his hands and a bullet splintering ancient logs.

Lord, had he really shot at her? And if so, what was she doing breathing so softly beside him? Was she wounded? Dying? Had all this happened just minutes before?

She didn't look as if she were dying. She looked as if she was asleep. Deeply asleep. So deeply that he could push himself off the bed and steal away without her knowing. Of course, a man who had to summon all his resources to open his eyelids didn't have much of a chance of stealing anywhere.

Why was she sleeping beside him? Surely she knew who he was. He was wearing a prison guard's uniform.... He wiggled the fingers of one hand against his leg and contacted bare skin. He *had* been wearing a uniform. How long had he been here? And why hadn't she called the police?

As he watched her sleep, he listened intently for movement elsewhere in the cabin. The deep silence was broken only by the woman's breathing.

She was remarkably lovely. With light stealing across the room and touching her face, he could see the milk-and-roses complexion, the straight black silk of her hair, the delicate features. He couldn't guess her age, but she was younger than he had ever been.

So what did he do now? And where was Jim Cooney's gun? The light breaking through the window was sunshine, not the obscene gold of the moon that had guided him here. Broad daylight was no time to run anywhere, and it was doubtful he could crawl, anyway. Somehow he had to force her to let him stay and recover. Then, if he had even ordinary luck, he could find his way to Memphis and Aaron. He was sure that Aaron could be trusted. Of course, once he had trusted Josiah, too.

His plan hinged on knowing why she hadn't turned him in. He couldn't think of one conceivable reason. He had threatened her, shot at her and...handcuffed her to the bed! That was why she was sleeping beside him. She must still be cuffed there. And what if he had died? Could she have found a way to escape?

He tried to struggle to one elbow to see if he was right, but something held him to the mattress. At first he thought it was his own lack of strength; then he realized the truth.

He stared at the woman, and as if his struggles had wakened her, her eyes opened sleepily and she stared back.

"I've been told I'm good in bed...but no one's ever chained me up...to keep me there," he said. The words were halting. To his own ears his voice sounded as if it was coming from a tunnel.

Tate sat up immediately and moved away from him. She finger-combed her hair away from her face as she stared groggily. "You're talking."

"Have been for years."

"You haven't been, not for days," she corrected. She couldn't begin to deal with the fact that she had fallen asleep beside him. Close beside him! The last thing she remembered, she had been whistling "John Riley" for the fifth time, perched on the edge of the bed. With horror she realized she had probably fallen asleep in the middle of a chorus and just keeled over. And when had she snuggled up to him like her favorite teddy bear?

"Days?" he croaked.

She struggled for objectivity. "How do you feel?"

He didn't answer. Tate thought he looked like a man who was searching for his past.

She filled him in. "Do you remember coming here?"

He gave a curt nod.

"After you so sweetly introduced yourself, shot at me and chained me to the bed, you finally relented and gave me the gun and the key to the cuffs."

He grunted.

She could tell he was wondering about his sanity. She knew the signs. She was wondering about her own. "I've been taking care of you ever since. Your leg was badly infected, and you've had a high fever."

"How long?"

"Two days." Tate wondered if she dared feel his forehead. She decided against it.

Simon stared at her. Two days and she hadn't called the sheriff. By all rights he should be waking up at High Ridge right now. Waking up so that Captain Shaw could kill him with his own bare hands. "Why am I still here?"

Tate stood, brushing nonexistent lint off her jeans so she wouldn't have to look at him. She wasn't sure why he was still there herself. And to give him a truly good answer, she would have to tell him the story of her life. "Let's just say I'm probably a nut case and let it go at that."

"Nobody knows?"

"Nobody but me." She lifted her head. "I should have turned you in. We both know I should have."

"Why didn't you?"

She could almost see him trying to make sense of her answers. "Do you remember anything you said before you passed out?"

He shook his head, making a deeper well in the pillow.

She smiled a little. "Good. Then let's see if your story is the same this morning. Sort of an informal lie-detector test."

He shut his eyes and wondered just how many secrets he had spilled, when he was out of his head with fever and pain. The thought wasn't pleasant. He felt something touch his forehead, and his eyes flew open.

Tate backed away. "You actually feel cool. I think the antibiotics must have kicked in. Since you're awake, let's get some liquids down you. Feel up to swallowing?"

"Yeah. Just unlock the cuff and I'll sit up and drink a gallon."

"If you feel up to it, I'll help you sit up. And you can drink one-handed."

He didn't answer, although Tate wasn't surprised. He was beginning to look like a man who was about to fall asleep again. She watched his lashes droop over eyes that were an icy gray. His color was better now that his fever was down.

"Go ahead and get some sleep," she said. "I'll wake you up when I've something ready for you. Any chance you could handle some food?"

The last thing on earth he wanted to do was eat. But food was energy, and God knew he would need energy if he was going to get out of here. He managed a nod.

He knew when she was gone, even though she made no sound. He thought of the woman in his dream.

In the kitchen Tate leaned against the sink and closed her eyes. He was real. *This* was real. Lying in the bed only yards away was a fugitive, and she had been lying with him! She could no longer pretend to be Nurse Nancy tending to the wounded. There was a name for someone who hid a fugitive, and that name was "accomplice."

Simon Carl Petersen didn't look half so heart-wrenching, now that he was awake. He looked dangerous, even though he could barely keep his eyes open. He looked amazingly like the man who had blasted a bullet past her right ear.

Weren't there stories about women who fell in love with prisoners? Stories about death-row brides hopelessly infatuated by serial killers? She was a far cry from being in love with the man chained to her bed, but was she somehow connected to all those crazy women who liked their men best when they were dressed in orange jumpsuits stamping out license plates?

She opened her eyes and looked around the cabin. She had lived alone for weeks, making meaning from hauling water and chopping wood. Had she really lost her mind in the process? Had even a fugitive looked like promising company?

Tate pushed away from the sink. She would feed him and make sure he got enough to drink. Then she would question him. His answers would determine what she did next. It would be more than interesting to see what he told her. His future would depend on it.

And hers might, too.

It took her only minutes to assemble a light breakfast of poached eggs and toast. To finish off the meal she made hot tea to serve along with a glass of canned orange juice. She knew that even if he could take just a few bites, the food would do him good.

Back in the bedroom she watched him sleeping. He was no longer restless. Even if he began to run another fever she suspected it would only climb a few degrees. She knew that when she checked his leg she could find it much improved. He was a strong man; from this point on he would probably recover quickly.

"Wake up," she called softly. She waited, but he slept on.

"Wake up," she repeated. "Simon, wake up!"

His eyes opened, and he stared at her. "What?"

"I said wake up."

"What did you call me?"

She didn't answer. It appeared that the test had begun.

He continued to stare at her. She would have given anything to read his thoughts. "I must have thought you were worth trusting," he said at last, "to tell you that."

"Why do the papers call you Carl?" Tate set the tray on the edge of the bed, but she didn't move any closer.

His hesitation was so brief that it would have been nonexistent to a less wary eye. "Simon is my middle name. Only the people I'm closest to call me that."

"People like Josiah and Erin?"

"People like that."

His eyes were such a frostbitten flint that they were impossible to read. Tate had thought that after years of practice she could read anybody. How unfortunate to find at such a crucial moment that she had been wrong.

"Here poor Josiah calls you Simon and all you can call him is 'bastard.' " She folded her arms.

"You're entitled to the story." He took a deep breath, and the aroma of the breakfast almost overwhelmed him. Nausea played around the edges of hunger, then disappeared. "Could I eat something first?" he asked.

She almost refused, but she had cared for him too long to deny him something that would make him stronger.

"First, there are some rules," she said, "and some things you should know. Number one, both your gun and the key to the handcuff aren't in this room and certainly not anywhere on me. If you grab me, you'll be wasting your time. I couldn't free you even if I wanted to, which I don't. Second, if you grab me for any other reason, eventually you'll have to let me go. When you do, you'll still be cuffed to the bed and I'll be at the sheriff's office giving directions to this cabin."

"I see."

"Do you?"

"I promise on my word of honor..." He took a breath and rested for a moment, "...that I won't grab you."

Other than the absurdity of his having any honor, something else about his words struck her. He had just the slightest accent. There was something about he way he clipped his words that was distinctly European. She wondered if she was imagining it.

"Besides, if I grabbed you right now," he concluded, "I wouldn't have the... strength to hold on."

"That won't wash with me. I've observed firsthand what a fighter you are. You'd hold on, if you thought it would do you any good. I'm telling you it won't."

"I'm hearing you."

She believed him. "Good. Are you strong enough to hold a glass?"

He started to say "of course," but he realized it might not be true. He wanted to be strong enough to yank the handcuffs into half a dozen pieces, but he wasn't even sure he could tear a newspaper.

Tate watched his brief struggle. She was surprised he had allowed it to show. "On second thought, I'll hold it," she decided for him. "You need to save whatever strength you've got."

The chain between the cuffs was long enough that she calculated he could be propped up in a semi-sitting position. She took the second pillow from the other side of the bed and stood over him. "Can you lift yourself up enough for me to slip this under you?"

He did, with maximum effort and minimum gain. She considered helping him get into a better position, then decided against it. She still wasn't sure he wouldn't try something, and she didn't want to take any chances.

When he had propped himself as much as he was able, she sat on the edge of the bed and put the tray on her lap. "Let's start with the juice." She lifted the glass, turning so she was facing him. "This should be quicker than an eyedropper."

"Eyedropper?"

"That's how I got liquids in you. Slow but foolproof."

He looked disgusted, as if a real man should never need something so ridiculous. She almost laughed. "Quarts and quarts of liquid. Lemonade, water, cola. You burned it right off with that fever. I'd guess you're still a couple of quarts low."

"Like somebody's old jalopy."

A sense of humor, even a cynical one, was something she hadn't expected. She lifted the glass to his lips, keeping a wary eye on him as she did. Any sudden moves and she would be on the other side of the cabin in a flash. His first few sips were clumsy, almost as if his lips and tongue had forgotten how to coordinate, but he improved quickly.

When the juice was half gone, Tate set the glass on the tray and picked up the plate. "You can talk between bites. You shouldn't eat too fast, anyway."

Simon was grateful he had been given a chance to plan his story. His head still wasn't completely clear. He had the peculiar feeling he was floating somewhere just out of reach of good sense and caution. He knew one thing, though. He wasn't going to tell this woman any more of the truth than he had to. His life depended on lies. And increasingly, as his thoughts began to gel, he knew that her life might, too. There were times when telling the truth was nothing less than immoral. And stupid.

"What have I told you... so far?" he asked between nibbles of toast.

"Nice try, Simon."

The room was filled with sunlight now. He could see the woman as clearly as he had in his dreams, only now she had form and features and the softest mouth he had ever seen—even when it was twisted in a cynical smile. He wondered what gods or lack of them had brought him to this cabin.

"What's your name?" he asked.

"You asked me that before."

He shifted through his memories, then shook his head.

"Try this one. Do you remember almost blasting my head off?"

"'Almost' is the operative word, isn't it?"

She noticed the precise way he said "operative." "Were you trying to miss?"

"Would any rational man answer no?"

She considered that. "Tate."

He worked hard and finally found the proper thread of their conversation. "Odd."

She wasn't sure why she bothered to explain. "My grandmother named me Kate. As a child I could only manage Tate. It stuck."

"It suits you."

She was angry at herself for getting even *that* personal. "But at least *everyone* calls me Tate. The newspapers don't call me Elizabeth or Mary Jane."

"I'm Carl Simon Petersen. I suppose, in my way, I was letting you know I trusted you."

"I *don't* trust you."

"A wise move." He let her feed him bites of egg before he continued. "But even if you didn't trust me...you took me in and took care of me. Why?"

"This *is* story time, only it's your story we're listening to. Not mine."

He decided the rumors he had heard about Arkansas hill folk had highly underrated their intelligence. "How much do you know . . . about my reason for being sent to High Ridge?"

She decided that was a question it wouldn't hurt to answer. As she fed him more egg she told him what she had heard on the radio, since that was undisputed fact.

"I'm innocent," he said, when she had finished. "I didn't kill Joe Masters . . . and I didn't embezzle the money." He rested and cursed himself for not even having the strength to put two sentences together. "I was set up . . . and I can prove it if I can just get to Memphis."

Tate's fork stopped halfway to his mouth. "Memphis? You're supposed to be heading back to Houston."

"Does this look like the way to Houston?"

"It doesn't look like the way to anywhere."

He grimaced and closed his eyes. For a moment desolation washed over him. Never once in all his years had he believed he couldn't defeat whatever was blocking him. Now, for the first time, he realized how totally at this woman's mercy he was. His story had better be good, superlative in fact, or the next place he would be heading was High Ridge. And that would be his last stop.

"A man named Josiah Gallagher killed Masters," he said, admiring the irony of his own life. "Gallagher and I worked in the same department." He rested, then continued. "He worked for me, but as it turned out, he worked me over good. He . . . he embezzled the money, but he manipulated the records so it would look like I did it. Then he tipped off Masters so . . . he could do a surprise audit."

"And you didn't know any of this?"

"Not then, no."

"Funny. You don't seem like a man who would be easily taken by surprise."

He wished she weren't so perceptive. "I've learned a lot since then." He opened his eyes and accepted more food.

"So just suppose what you're telling me is true. Why didn't any of this come out at the trial?"

"My attorney swore I'd go free. There wasn't any concrete evidence to prove . . . either the embezzlement or the murder. And he said there was nothing to link Gallagher. It would just . . . be his word against mine."

"Why did Gallagher murder Masters, if Masters believed you were the embezzler?"

"Because Masters didn't...believe it. Not after I showed him how Gallagher could have done it himself. He went to Gallagher...and Gallagher killed him. But he set it up to look like I did."

Tate fed him the last of the egg. He looked as if the explanation had completely worn him out. "And I suppose Gallagher set up your aunt, too."

Simon swallowed. The food felt strange on a stomach that had been empty for so long. His head felt strange, too. Too strange to think fast enough. "I'm not sure what you mean," he said at last.

"I suppose you think I don't know anything about the trial." Tate lifted the tea. It had cooled to lukewarm.

He tried desperately to remember what *he* knew. Then it came to him. "I wasn't with my aunt, and I made a...mistake when I tried to get her to back up my story. But I couldn't...tell the truth in court."

"How inconvenient."

"I was with...a woman."

Tate nodded. "Erin. You've been calling for her." She tilted the cup so he could drink.

It took him a moment to understand. "Right. Erin...Gallagher's wife." He liked the twist. It was too bad Gallagher wasn't there to appreciate it, too.

"But why would that matter? If you had an alibi, you would have been set free. And if Erin was your alibi, she couldn't have been Gallagher's alibi, too."

He scowled. "You should have been my attorney. He... convinced me that I had nothing to...worry about and that when my trial ended, the district attorney would go after...Gallagher next." He paused in frustration. Neither his tongue nor his brain was working fast enough. And he had to convince Tate of his innocence or he could die.

He struggled to go on. "Only I didn't realize that some of Gallagher's new wealth was...lining my attorney's pocket. Erin disappeared...after I was convicted, but I know where she is. If I can just get to her...talk to her, I can convince her...to come back and tell her story. But I have to do it myself. She's afraid...of Gallagher, and...she has a right to be."

Tate weighed his story while she finished giving him the tea. He looked completely worn out, and she knew she couldn't continue to drill him for information much longer. The story made some sense, but that meant nothing. A clever psychopath could talk his way past St. Peter. What was a lie or two to a murderer? Could Simon really be expected to tell her he had killed Joe Masters and would do so again if given the chance?

She set the teacup on the tray and stood. "Even if all this is true, why was your life in danger at High Ridge? Gallagher got what he wanted, didn't he? You were safely behind bars."

"I could still talk. There . . . was a reporter looking into . . . the case. I found out last week that Gallagher paid an inmate...to kill me before the reporter . . . could interview me."

"Couldn't you go to the warden?"

"No."

She was surprised that one word could be so filled with contempt.

"Tate?"

She faced him.

"I didn't kill Joe Masters."

His story sounded too much like a television movie of the week to be believable. But for some crazy reason she couldn't accept the fact that he had murdered someone in cold blood. She didn't know why. Most of the time they had spent together, he had been unconscious. What did she know of him? What did she really know?

"Are you going to turn me in?"

She considered the question, just as she had been considering it for days. "I don't know."

"That's more . . . than I have a right to expect."

She nodded; then taking the tray, she started toward the door. "Get some more sleep. After you've had a nap, I'll have to change the bandage on your leg."

To his ears those didn't sound like the words of a woman expecting to make a visit to the sheriff. Simon thought how easy it would be to pick the lock on his handcuff. Surprisingly easy. But what would be the point? He was too weak to run, and Memphis and Aaron were light years away. He could think of no better, safer place to stay and regain his strength than this.

And if he was truthful with himself, he could think of no place he would rather be. Just why eluded him, though. It was just one more of those facts—or feelings—swirling in a mind too exhausted to grab and hold on to it.

Chapter 6

The next morning Simon was still sleeping when Tate appeared in his room, rattling a length of rusty chain like the Ghost of Christmas Past. She stood in the doorway observing her prisoner. The day before he had been awake several times after their breakfast conversation, but only long enough to exchange a few words and swallow more liquids. What little fever he'd had that afternoon had dropped by evening. The wound in his leg still looked as if it badly needed a physician's attention, but signs of infection were receding.

His color was better now. The gray, waxy hue that had worried her was gone, although he was still too pale. Under the patchwork quilt stretched over his lanky frame, his chest rose and fell in a natural sleep. He was recovering, as much because he was a strong man as because of the dedicated nursing care he had received.

Tate wondered what kind of nurse chained her patient to the bed? Simon's story had been going round and round in her head since he had told it to her. She was far from convinced he was telling the truth, but until she could decide, she was going to have to keep him a prisoner.

For the past few days he had been too weak to move. Now that he was feeling better, she knew he would be more restless, and being cuffed to the bed would be a prime frustration. She had finally thought of a way to resolve the dilemma. She had removed an old chain from the barn and a padlock from the smokehouse door. She would lock the chain to the bed frame, then lock his cuffs to the chain. That way he would have more freedom of movement. Whatever personal needs he had would be easier to take care of, too.

Now she just hoped she could rig the chain and cuffs before he woke up. There would be a second or two when he could get free. And although she had insisted she would not get near him with the handcuff keys, she had to have them to make the switch.

Dream on, she pleaded silently.

She walked softly toward the side of the bed by the window, the chain creaking ominously as she moved. Simon still seemed to be sleeping deeply. His breathing was even and slow, and not a muscle in his face twitched as she drew closer. She had given this decision a lot of thought, and she knew just where she wanted to lock the chain so he would have the most freedom. The corner of the bed was ideal. She could wrap the chain around the frame and through the metal headboard so that even if Simon was able to unscrew the bolts, the chain would still restrain him.

She reached the corner without waking him. Carefully, moving slower than she'd known she could, she began to wrap the chain. Iron scraped iron; the chain protested, creaking as it was forced to twist in ways it had forgotten. Simon slept on.

Satisfied, at last, that the chain was positioned correctly, she reached for the padlock, which she had set on the floor by the bed, and slipped it through two meshed links of chain.

Tate guessed that the padlock had hung on the smokehouse door for decades. Undoubtedly it was older than she was, and if there had once been a key, it had gone to key heaven. In her father's heyday the smokehouse had probably held treasures such as ham and bacon, and the padlock had been secured. Since the farm had become hers, the padlock had merely served to keep the door closed and had never been locked.

Now she struggled to snap it shut. It squealed like Cinderella's stepsister squeezing into the glass slipper, but each time Tate released her pressure, the lock popped apart. Finally, after she mustered every bit of strength she had, the lock held.

Simon slept on. Tate brushed back the fall of hair caressing her cheek. How could he sleep so soundly? She stared at him, but there was no flicker of awareness she was there. Sleep was the great healer; at the rate Simon was indulging in it, he would be well by noon.

Well, by noon or noon tomorrow or noon next week. Ready to hit the road again—if she let him. She pushed that thought out of her mind to concentrate on the trickiest part of her maneuver. Still watching Simon's face, she inched the handcuff key out of the back pocket of her jeans. Something tugged at her memory as she stared at him. She thought she remembered hearing his age on one of the radio newscasts. He was supposed to be thirty-seven.

He didn't look that old. With his face in repose he seemed younger, hardly more than thirty. Even after everything he had been through.

Of course, it was hard to tell what was behind the beard and mustache. Funny the way his face could be distorted by all that luxuriant golden hair. She had to admit the beard fascinated her. She knew its feel. It was surprisingly soft, even though it was not long. And it was as thick and sensuous as a golden ermine pelt, thick enough to fill in the contours of his cheeks. Perhaps even thick enough to make a thirty-seven-year-old man look younger.

Sleep made people look younger, too, because you couldn't see their eyes. Tate remembered clearly what Simon's eyes looked like. Frostbitten flint. Opaque. Impossible to read. Old eyes, generations older than thirty-seven, even if the face was younger.

His eyes remained closed, as she held the key in front of her and engaged in final debate. Should she risk unclasping the cuffs even for the moment it would take to snap them to the chain? She decided that it had to be now or never.

The key pinged against the cuffs as she inserted it. When the cuff opened the snap seemed as loud as a gunshot. Instantly, at almost the same second the cuff was free, Tate felt fingers form an iron band around her wrist.

The eyes she stared into weren't opaque this morning. They sparkled.

"So, you're going to let me go."

She echoed the words she'd thought earlier. "Dream on."

"The matter seems to be out of your hands." Simon yanked the cuffs toward him. Tate grabbed them and hung on.

They remained at an impasse for a moment; then Simon gave a fierce jerk, and the cuffs went flying from Tate's grasp. Simon's fingers bit into her wrist. He pulled her down to the bed beside him. She struggled, but his grip was a vise she couldn't escape.

"Let go of me!"

Simon's voice was calm. "I'm not going to hurt you."

"Damn right you're not!"

"Stop fighting me and listen."

She aimed an elbow at his ribs, but he rolled to one side, taking her with him. She sprawled awkwardly, half across the mattress and half across his chest.

He pressed his cuffed arm across her back and held tightly to her wrist. Tate didn't know where he had found the strength. She lifted her head and found her face was only inches from his.

He was looking at her strangely, almost as if he was seeing her for the first time.

"Let go of me!"

He didn't. "I've never known a woman with so much courage."

She glared at him.

"Or compassion."

"Stupidity!" Tate struggled once more, but he had her restrained, at least until his strength ran out.

"You saved my life. Do you think I'd hurt you now?"

"I think it's a distinct possibility!"

"Stop fighting me. Hear me out."

"You're going to get tired in a few minutes. How long do you think you can keep me here like this?"

He smiled, just the ghost of one, but a smile nonetheless. "As long as it takes to make you listen. Do us both a favor, okay? Shut up."

She pressed her lips together and let her eyes talk for her.

Simon admired the thickly lashed blue eyes spitting icy fire at him. She always brought with her the autumn fragrance of piney woods and clear mountain air, and he wondered if her finely textured skin would taste the same. Or would it taste of something more exotic, something even darker and more elemental?

Something passed through him. In another lifetime, before his months at High Ridge, he might have called it desire. Now he called it aftershock. Desire was a human emotion. Whatever had been human in him had disintegrated and died in Cellblock A.

What he felt now was a life trying to heal itself after being torn asunder. And the woman lying half across him, her delicate curves a growing, pleasurable torture, was a healer.

"I have to get out of here." Simon spoke softly. "I have to know if you're going to let me go. I'm not going to wait here like a sitting duck. I don't have much of a life left, but I plan to hang on to what's still there, if I can."

Tate wished she could lie with more aplomb, but Jess and Krista had loved the lies right out of her. She had learned to be brutally honest with herself, and somehow, in the process, she had forgotten how to be anything but honest with everyone else.

"I don't know what I'm going to do." She stared at Simon and knew lying to him wouldn't have done any good, anyway.

"Do you believe what I told you yesterday?"

"No."

"Then why haven't you gone for the sheriff?"

"Because there's one chance in a hundred it could be true."

"I didn't kill Joe Masters."

"So you say."

As she watched, fatigue seemed almost to crawl along his features. The arm clasping her to his chest trembled. "I have to get out of here." With a supreme effort he sat up and pushed her back to the bed, quickly pinning her with the weight of his body. He could feel her soft breasts flatten against his chest as she struggled. His head swam with the effort to restrain her.

"You couldn't make it to the next farm!" Tate felt panic well in her, but she stopped resisting. She knew if she didn't panic, she would be all right. She only had to wait for the right moment. One kick to the leg she had so tenderly cared for would buy her freedom.

Surprisingly, he nodded. "But I won't be your problem any more. I've got a fighting chance out there. Cuffed to this bed, the only chance I've got lies with you. I've asked you to be judge and jury. It's not your fault you can't be."

"You're concerned about my moral dilemma?"

"I'm concerned about staying alive."

Tate stared up at him. He loomed above her, very male, very dangerous, but surprisingly, she felt no fear. Before, his cold gray eyes had only been shadows of the man. Now she saw feeling there, although she couldn't name it.

"Let me up," she said at last. It was not a command.

Simon rolled away from her and shut his eyes.

She wasn't surprised he had freed her.

She sat up and turned to watch him. He was drained of what color he'd gained. "There's no easy way to Memphis from here. You'll die trying to get there."

Grim lips turned up in a mock smile. "Then your moral dilemma would be eased."

Tate knew the next move was hers. "Why my cabin, Petersen?" she asked wearily.

"Fate."

"It was that damn moon!"

"Will you give me a head start before you go for the sheriff?" He opened his eyes and turned them to hers. She saw defeat and determination there—a curious mixture. Tate knew he would go down fighting.

"I'm a fool," she said at last, "but not so big a one that I'd let you continue to stay here until you're stronger—not unless you're back in cuffs."

"And if I let you snap this cuff on the chain, you could waltz into town and get the sheriff."

"I guess you'll have to decide if you trust me."

"You're saying you won't turn me in?"

Tate had avoided making a commitment, hoping that something would come along to make her decision for her. Now she knew she wasn't going to be that lucky. Nothing in her life had ever been easy. This wasn't going to be an exception.

"If you want to stay here till you're stronger, you'll have to do it with the cuffs on. If you're leaving instead, go now. Either way, I'm not going to tell anyone about you."

He considered his choices, because he knew she would want him to make a decision quickly. His answer had to depend on whether he believed her, just as hers had depended on believing him. The similarity was ironic.

The pulse beating too loudly in his ears made his decision. He was still terribly weak. Just the brief tussle with her had worn him out. He wouldn't make it to Memphis this way. Not with the woods and highways teeming with men searching for him.

With the last of the strength that had carried him this far, he leaned behind her and reached for the chain. He felt along its length. Then, with the cuff still dangling from his wrist, he reached down and snapped it through a link.

Tate stood. He was her prisoner again. She hadn't expected to feel relieved that he was staying, but she did, even though she would have been better off if he was gone. "I'll make you breakfast. We've got to build up your strength so you can be somebody else's problem."

Surprisingly, he managed to smile. "I hope someday you'll know you made the right decision."

"I hope someday I'll forgive myself for being a fool."

Like a computer programmed for limited functions, Simon simply slept and ate for the next two days. As a result, Tate could almost watch him grow stronger. He sat up and fed himself completely now, and the hands that at first had trembled grew steady. As soon as his fever broke she had given up bathing him, but after breakfast each morning she brought him a pan of water, and with much muttering he managed the job himself.

On the third morning she came back too soon to retrieve the pan. He was sitting up with the sheet pushed low along his hips, taking a thorough sponge bath. His chest gleamed with a fine haze of water, and the golden hair arrowing toward his navel was plastered in swirls to his tanned skin.

He was no longer the desperately ill fugitive who had found his way to her cabin. The image of a lion caged and lying in wait for his keeper came to mind instead.

Other thoughts came to mind, too, thoughts like: why was she staring at him? Why hadn't she turned and left the moment she realized he wasn't finished? Why had she come back so soon in the first place?

All were thoughts to consider in the other room. She turned to go, but Simon stopped her.

"It's all right. I'm finished. There's not much I can do with a basin of dirty water."

She noted the broad *A* in "water" and the cleanly uttered *T*. She also noted his disgruntled tone. "Getting tired of being an invalid, Petersen?"

He wiped his chest with the towel she had provided. "Tired of being a cur on a chain."

She felt a pang of sympathy as she crossed the room. "Are you ready to let me change your bandage?"

He shrugged on one of her father's soft flannel shirts. She couldn't shake the feeling that he would look more at home in a custom-tailored tux. "It's about to drive me crazy."

She gathered the supplies she kept on a closet shelf. "Itching?"

He gave a curt nod. "It's healing."

"Maybe that's true, but it's a long way from being healed." She peeled the covers back, exposing his leg. "If you put any weight on it, it'll rip back open."

"I've been moving it as much as I can."

"Take it easy. You don't want to put yourself back where you started."

"I don't want to end up walking like a kangaroo, either."

"Kangaroos don't walk."

"My point exactly."

She glanced at him to see if the joke was a sign that his mood had improved, but there was no smile on his face. "As soon as you're able, you've got to see a doctor and start physical therapy."

"Sure. I'll just look somebody up in the phone book and walk right in."

He could be a murderer—probably was, in fact—but she still felt another surge of sympathy. He was a dangerous man to feel anything for, and all her best instincts told her so. But if he *was* innocent, his life had been turned upside down for nothing, and he still had a long road to travel before it was put to rights.

She snipped off the old bandage, but there was nothing she could do about the adhesive tape still clinging to his leg. She stripped it off, and although he didn't even grimace, she knew she had caused him pain.

The wound *was* healing. With a physician's care it might already have formed scar tissue. As it was, the most that had happened was that the infection had almost disappeared. He still needed time before he began to use the leg. She washed the area and smoothed an antibiotic ointment over it before covering it with a clean bandage.

She started to stand, but she felt a hand on her shoulder. Every separate finger seemed to make an impression, although he was applying no pressure. "What have you heard about the search?"

She lifted her head and stared a warning. "You're old news. There haven't been any bulletins."

He lifted his head. "What about the regular newscasts?"

"When you're even mentioned, they just say that the search is continuing. I don't sit around and listen. I know more about where you are then anyone, don't I?"

"I have to get out of here."

"I couldn't agree more." She stood. "But you're in no shape to go yet. Walk a hundred yards on that leg and you'll end up crawling."

"I don't plan to walk."

"There aren't any trains into this county, and the nearest airport is Memphis, where you're going, or Little Rock, where your picture will be on every wall."

He didn't answer.

"What are your plans?" When he still didn't speak, she hypothesized out loud. "Kill me and take my car?"

"It's a temptation. Except for one thing."

She stared at him.

"I don't kill people."

She remembered the light of an outlaw moon glinting off the barrel of his revolver. The night he had handed his gun to her, he could just as easily have killed her.

"So where does that leave you?" she asked.

"Do you really want to know?" He didn't quite smile as she made a face. "I won't touch your car."

"You won't touch anybody's anything. You're still my prisoner."

"You're going to have to let me go sometime."

She couldn't argue with that. She turned to leave.

"Tate?" There was a hesitation as he phrased his next words. "I haven't said thank you."

"Don't. I can't believe I'm doing this, anyway."

She felt his hand enclose hers. She was more than surprised; she was stunned. She had touched almost every part of his body, but this was different. Her hand fit in his as if it had been created to be there. He held it with the gentle firmness of a man sheltering a frightened bird.

Before she could pull away, she felt him lift her hand to his lips. They were warm and moist against her palm, and the impact of the kiss traveled like lightning to every nerve center. Then, as quickly as it had happened, it was over. He dropped her hand. "I won't say thanks," he promised. "I'll just say I've never met anyone quite like you before."

She was away from the bed like a shot. "I'm going into town. I've got to pick up some more supplies." She turned at the doorway. He was staring after her, his expression unreadable. "For what it's worth, I've never met anyone quite like you, either," she said.

"And you hope you never do again."

"I might not live through it the second time."

On a sunny day, Kalix Road could almost be considered picturesque. Today, with storm clouds menacing, it looked like what it was: a poor road in a poor county.

Of course, as Tate sped back home, she knew that her mood might be distorting what she got from the scenery. After everything she had just learned in town, heaven itself would have no appeal.

She had bought groceries and ice in Mountain Glade; then she had gone to the pharmacy. She had shopped there, waiting and watching for Wally to launch into a lecture to another customer, so that she could call Krista. She hadn't expected miracles, hadn't expected to find that Jess was safely home and able to find out about Carl Petersen for her, but it would have been nice. Instead she had discovered that Krista hadn't heard a word from Jess since she and Tate had last talked.

On the way out of Allen's she had stopped to buy the Sunday edition of the *Arkansas Gazette*, even though it was four days old. She was starved for some contact with the outside world besides her radio. At times, in the past few days, it had seemed that she and Simon were the only people in the universe, two eccentric pioneers in the wilderness, *Little House on the Prairie* run amok.

She had turned immediately to the section with state news, to find that the entire front page was about Carl Petersen's escape from prison. One article described High Ridge and alleged that conditions there were deplorable. Another hypothesized how the escape had been made and where Petersen might have gone. The third and most interesting was Carl Petersen's history. Carl *William* Petersen's history.

Even more upsetting than the discovery that Petersen's middle name wasn't Simon had been the photographs. The man in them was fifty pounds heavier than the man in her bed. True, the pictures had been taken at the trial. True, High Ridge was probably a foolproof weight-loss program. But even with fifty pounds of fat on the man she knew as Simon, that man wouldn't look like the man in the newspaper. That Carl Petersen had a rounder baby face. Tate couldn't picture him with Simon's elegantly sculpted bone structure, even if he lost a hundred pounds.

There was something soft, almost effeminate, about the photos in the paper. The man she knew as Simon was all rock-hard masculinity. Even when he had been dependent on her for survival, he had never lost his swift, almost feral responses. Two days ago he had struggled with her over the handcuffs, despite debilitating weakness. He had struggled for days alone in the forest, and Lord knew where else, before finding his way to her cabin. The man in the photographs looked as if he would give himself up without a fight. The man in her bed would never give up. Period.

Yet she couldn't dispute the obvious. Simon had shown up at her cabin wearing the tattered uniform of a High Ridge prison guard. He had held her at gunpoint, and somewhere on his journey he had sustained a gunshot wound in his leg. He had told her that he was Carl Petersen. He was blond and bearded like the man in the papers, and there was a resemblance.

And the man in the papers was missing from High Ridge.

Tate gripped the wheel harder as she hugged one of Kalix Road's narrow curves. A hairy black tarantula scurried along the roadside, just at the edge of her vision. It was a living pipe-cleaner monster from some child's Halloween fantasy, and she shuddered. The world was filled with things she would rather ignore. But those were the things that always seemed to parade before her. Simon was one of them. She hadn't asked for him, and now that she had made an uncomfortable truce with his existence, she hadn't asked to have the truce blown to smithereens.

But whether she liked it or not, Simon was very real and very much a problem. And if her eyes and her instincts were even slightly accurate, he was also very much a liar.

She pushed the accelerator to the floor on the last straight stretch before her house. She wanted to get the confrontation over with. She was going to give Simon one chance to explain himself. Then, if she wasn't satisfied, she was going to turn him in—or out.

She was almost to the road leading up to the cabin when she got the first premonition that something was wrong. She slowed until she was barely crawling, and used all her senses to try to discover what was out of place. At first she couldn't discern any changes. There was no one on the road, and although the sky was growing darker, no rain had yet fallen.

She came to a halt at the cabin road and rolled her window down, sniffing the air. But there was no strange scent on the rising wind. No smoke from a forest fire, no hint of pollution from the charcoal factory two counties to the west.

The cold air rushing into the car brought with it another clue, however. She listened intently and finally pegged what had alerted her to danger in the first place.

Dogs. A pack of them, somewhere in the distance, baying like the hound of the Baskervilles.

Will's dogs? She knew he had several, at least. Sometimes late at night, when it had still been warm enough to sleep with an open window, she had heard them barking. Noise carried in strange ways on mountain nights, and at times the dogs had almost sounded as if they were under her window. Cinn would join in for a bark or two when he was feeling especially energetic, and rather than annoying her, she had found the ruckus comforting.

This ruckus wasn't comforting, at all.

She shifted into first and started up the cabin road. The barking could mean anything. The mountains were full of strays. Sometimes they banded together and threatened livestock, until the local farmers hunted them down. Perhaps there was a pack wandering somewhere nearby.

But perhaps there was a pack nearby that wasn't wandering, at all. Perhaps they were doing what good bloodhounds were trained to do.

She shifted into second and sped up the road. Her Bronco bounced and shuddered like its namesake, but she didn't care. She wanted to reach Simon before the dogs did—if they did.

At the crest of the hill looking over her cabin, she slammed on her brakes. There was a white van parked in front. Beside it was a sheriff's car.

A man chained to my bed? You're kidding. I wonder how that could have happened.

She knew what it was like to be terrified; once, as a fourteen-year-old runaway, she had found herself in the clutches of a New Orleans pimp. Now she felt the same ballooning of fear as she looked down at the Arkansas law. What was she going to tell them, if they went inside and found Simon? Suddenly none of her reasons for not reporting him sounded good enough. Despite the fact that he was cuffed to the bed, who would believe she was anything but an accomplice to his escape? An accomplice with strange preferences, perhaps, but an accomplice, nonetheless.

She said a silent prayer of gratitude that the bedroom window was so high above the ground. The ground fell away on that side of the cabin, exposing a cobweb-ridden root cellar, and the window was almost two stories up. Maybe they hadn't tried—or been able—to peek inside. Maybe she could just talk to them and send them on their way.

It was obviously too late to back up and head for Virginia. The man who, even at this distance, she recognized as Sheriff Monroe Howard was pointing in her direction. She started down the slope toward her cabin. As she drew nearer, she realized that the other two men were High Ridge officials. She recognized their uniforms, although they weren't as tattered as the one Simon had arrived in.

She pulled in beside the van and turned off the ignition. She noted that the cabin door was closed. Cinn was lying in front of it, looking deceptively dead. She hoped his presence there had discouraged snooping.

Forcing herself to appear calm, she opened her door and swung slowly to her feet. "Sort of a gray day for a social call, isn't it, gentlemen?"

The sheriff approached. He was silver-haired but still built like a football player in training. Tate knew they were related, although how escaped her.

"Afternoon, Miss Cantrell."

"Afternoon." She paused, but he didn't say anything more. "Is there a problem?" she asked politely.

"You might say so."

One of the prison officials started toward her. Tate noted that the other one was working his way around the cabin.

"Afternoon, ma'am. I'm Jim Cooney, from over at High Ridge. We're searchin' the area for a man who escaped jus' about a week back. You heard anything 'bout it?"

Tate knew better than to play stupid. These men were slow-moving and slow-talking, but they were a long way from slow-witted.

"Petersen?" she asked. "I was just reading about him in the Sunday paper I picked up in town. Not exactly a tourist attraction, is he?"

Jim Cooney chortled.

She continued. "The paper said you were searching south of here." The paper had also said the search would probably be called off soon, but obviously that wasn't true.

"We was. Looks like we been wrong, though. Now we're thinkin' he might have come this way."

"Why? We're sort of off the beaten path, aren't we?"

"Some think he might've floated down the river. Found a scrap or two of cloth 'bout half a mile back yonder, when we was searchin' with the dogs. It looks like it come from a uniform." He laughed again. "He was wearin' a uniform. *My* uniform, to be exact."

So this was the man Simon had overtaken. She was surprised he could be so good-humored. "It seems strange he could escape, at all. How did he? The paper said he slid out a window, but aren't prison windows barred?"

Cooney began to look uncomfortable. "Most are. He found one that wasn't. What we need to know now, ma'am, is if we can search yer house and the other buildin's. We're coverin' the area with our dogs, but it takes time. If we find anything suspicious-like, we'll bring them right over to sniff it out."

Tate could think of nothing she wanted less. "Well, sure you're welcome to search, but I can save you the trouble of bothering with the cabin. I hardly ever leave it. There's not much chance anybody's in there."

"Well, sure, ma'am. But how long you been gone today? Since this morning? Someone could have gotten in while you weren't here."

She forced a light laugh. "With Cinn guarding the door? He's a killer."

"We'd feel better, ma'am."

And she was going to feel much, much worse.

Tate played her last card. "Well, I'm going to go on inside while you search the outbuildings. If I see anything strange, I'll give a yell." She slammed the car door, then turned to start toward the house.

Sheriff Howard was right beside her. "I'm not letting Millard's girl go inside that house alone. You may not think we're much of a family, but we watch out for our own."

She didn't have time to think about his words. She was searching for some way to discourage him. If she could just get to Simon and take off the handcuffs, she would have a fighting chance to help him hide. As it was, Simon was going to be a bit conspicuous.

Cinn was still sprawled across the doorway when they got to the front porch. Sheriff Howard looked as if he'd had dealings with Cinn before. With the toe of his boot he prodded the dog until his eyes opened a slit. "Go!"

Cinn's tail thumped against the porch, but he didn't move.

"He misses Millard," the sheriff said.

"How can you tell?"

"We all miss him." He opened the door, but waved Tate back when she started after him. "Let me check around."

"There's absolutely no need for all this," she insisted, as loudly as she dared. "I'm sure you're all exaggerating. A few bits of cloth don't prove anything, do they?"

"Might. They're being analyzed right now." Sheriff Howard moved inside, his gun drawn, now. Before Tate could stop Cinn, he pried himself off the porch and followed the sheriff inside.

The sheriff surveyed the room, his gun moving with his gaze. Then his head tipped back as he looked up at the loft. Most of it was visible from the doorway, but the corners farthest back were not. He signaled his intention to climb up and investigate, then crossed the room, Cinn right behind him. When she started to follow, hoping to get to the bedroom while he explored the loft, he motioned her back.

Her possibilities had narrowed to none. She could only wait now for Simon to be discovered.

The sheriff climbed down after just seconds upstairs. Then he started toward the bedroom, where Cinn was standing by the door. Tate disregarded him when he waved her back. She followed a distance behind.

He hesitated, then flung the door open, jumping back as he did, as if to avoid gunfire.

The cabin was silent. He leaned forward and peered into the bedroom, then moved inside, where the dog had already disappeared. Tate could do nothing but follow them.

From the doorway she saw an empty bed. It was neatly made, and the room was tidy. Nothing remained to show that a man had once been chained there. Cinn was lying on the floor beside it, nose on paws, looking forlorn.

The sheriff dropped down beside Cinn and peered under the bed, then crossed to the closet and opened the door. Stunned, Tate saw that even the basin and packet of medical supplies were gone.

As was Jim Cooney's .44.

"Well, you were right," he said. "Nobody's here. But it doesn't pay to take chances."

"I guess not."

"I don't like you being here without a phone, not while this High Ridger's on the loose. You're welcome to come stay with Jo Ann and me until he's been caught. I know Will and Dovey would have you, too."

Tate stared at him. She could hardly comprehend what he was saying. Finally she shook her head. "Thanks for the offer. But I've got a lot to do before winter hits."

"You're Millard's kid, all right. Just be careful." He tipped his hat and strode across the room, disappearing into the front room. The outside door slammed a few moments later.

She went through the motions of making and offering coffee when their search of the grounds was completed, and appeared to listen as all the men lapsed into guessing where Carl Petersen had disappeared to. She even waved goodbye as they drove away.

And through it all, she had only one real thought. Where in the world had Simon gone, and how had he managed it?

Chapter 7

Was it worse to have Simon in the cabin, a prisoner in the bedroom? Or was it worse to have him loose again, his presence lurking in every corner, behind every tree?

Tate wasn't sure. She only knew she didn't like surprises, especially when they involved armed fugitives. And Simon was obviously armed now.

The sun was sinking toward the ridge of trees on the western edge of her property, when she left the relative safety of her cabin to get a load of firewood. Cinn stared at her from the lengthening shadow of the smokehouse. She shook off the feeling that another pair of eyes was following her movements. Surely Simon—if that name had anything to do with the man who had inhabited her bed—was hobbling toward Memphis.

"What kind of a guard dog are you, anyway?" she called to the hound. Cinn's droopy eyes followed every movement, though he didn't move. As soon as he had sensed there was no longer a masculine presence in the cabin, he had deserted.

"Somebody could shoot me and you'd supervise the burial!" She realized she was taking out her frustrations on an extremely dumb animal, although it didn't appear to worry him.

At the woodpile she peeled off her father's plaid jacket and set to work splitting logs. It was backbreaking labor. The first time she had tried it, the ax had bounced off the log and headed straight for her foot. And if it hadn't missed, she might have died here alone. Just as she might have died the night Simon had come to visit, if he had been a different sort of man.

What was she doing in the middle of nowhere, with a murderer on the loose? What was she doing in the middle of nowhere, period? Had she inherited hermit blood from the man she'd never known? Insanity?

She poured her frustrations into her work, and had an armload of wood in minutes. She was practiced with an ax now. And she was an expert at making fires. She had learned how to plant pine seedlings and use her father's old hand plow to dig up the expansive garden plot for next spring's garden. She had learned the habits of geese and the names of the wild birds inhabiting the forest.

For what?

She carried the firewood toward the house. The sun still hadn't touched the ridge. The day seemed endless; the night would seem longer. Every sound, every shadow and movement outdoors, would be Simon haunting her.

And where was he now? His leg wasn't well enough to bear his weight. There were no freight trains to hop, no eighteen-wheeler outlaws to hitch a ride with. He would have to leave the county on foot. One foot. Hopping like a kangaroo.

She remembered his joke. She remembered lots of things about him, like the feeling she'd had from the beginning that he was more than he was supposed to be. Wasn't that why she had risked her own safety to care for him? Because she had believed, despite all the evidence, that he was an innocent man?

At the back door she balanced the load of firewood against her chest and slipped one arm from beneath it to turn the doorknob. Not too many days ago she had gotten a landmark surprise when she walked through the same door. She would be reliving that moment, and all the ones following it, for days to come. For better or worse, Simon had escaped from prison into her life. And along the way he had forced her to face the fact that she, too, was a fugitive from the life that others lived without question.

"I wondered where you'd gone."

Tate stood with the open door to her back. Two logs slipped from the pile in her arms and rolled across the floor to Simon's feet.

She momentarily closed her eyes in shock, but the picture of Simon standing before her, gun belt slung casually around his hips, danced along her eyelids.

"Sorry to startle you," he said.

"Hey, I'm getting used to it." Tate opened her eyes. The picture hadn't changed.

"Company gone?"

"I tried to get them to stay for tea, but you know how law-enforcement types are."

The flicker of a smile softened his face. "Better than almost anybody."

"You don't mind if I set these logs down, do you?" She walked across the room and deposited the logs at the side of the hearth. She reached for a poker and used it to stir up a few coals still glowing from the morning's fire. When she straightened, the poker was still in her hand.

She hadn't heard Simon come up behind her, but when she turned he was right there. He held out the two logs she had dropped.

She couldn't easily reach for them with the poker in her hand. She knew he saw her dilemma.

He tossed the logs to the hearth. "Tate, if I wanted to harm you, I've already had a hundred chances. Forget what you think you know about me, and concentrate on what you really know."

"I *really* know your middle name isn't Simon. And I know the photograph of the man who was on trial in Little Rock doesn't look as much like you as it should."

"Put down the poker and let me explain."

"You explained once. Remember?"

"I lied."

"Terrific. I feel better already."

"I've got to get off my feet." Simon turned, leaving himself vulnerable to attack if she dared.

Tate clenched the poker in her hands, but she could not make herself swing it. She watched as he limped to the sofa facing the fireplace. Before he sat, he unbuckled the gun belt and laid it on a nearby chair. Once he was settled, the gun was out of his reach.

She stood with her side toward the fireplace and threw crumpled newspaper and pine kindling on the coals. Then, when the pine was burning, she added the smallest log. Her thoughts raced in circles, as she watched the log catch. By the time she added another, she felt as if she were captive on the Indianapolis Speedway.

When there was nothing left to do, she chose the chair opposite the one where Simon had placed his gun belt. The poker leaned against the hearth, beyond reach.

"I give up," she said, when it was clear he was waiting for her to ask questions. "Where were you, and how did you get free?"

"I was under the bed."

"Don't give me that. Cinn and the sheriff looked under the bed. I was there."

"You don't know what's under there, do you?"

"Outer space? A new dimension in time?" she asked sarcastically.

"A museum."

Tate watched pain flash across Simon's face as he shifted. In the shock of finding him in her cabin again, she had almost forgotten his leg. She was up and across the space separating them before she thought about what she was doing. "Let me look at that." She knelt beside him and began to roll up the cuff of the overalls he had apparently taken from the closet.

"Aren't you afraid?"

She didn't spare the time for a retort. The bandage she had so carefully changed that morning was streaked with blood. "I told you not to put any weight on this! Now you're in for it."

"I would really have been in for it, if Jim Cooney had found me chained to your bed."

Tate sat back and put her hands around her knees. "How did you get away?"

"I heard the dogs barking about twenty minutes after you left." Simon leaned his head back against the sofa and shut his eyes in exhaustion. He was disgusted that the simple things he'd done that day had tired him so much. "I'd already picked the locks on the cuff and padlock with the inside of the ballpoint pen I found in your father's shirt."

She wasn't sure if she was more surprised that he had picked the lock, or that her father had used something as modern as a ballpoint. "Did you pick up that little tidbit at High Ridge?"

"There aren't any locks I can't pick."

"What did you mean about a museum under the bed?"

"There's a trapdoor. I wouldn't have found it, but after I'd dressed and gathered up the evidence that I'd been here, I heard the dog barking."

"Cinn doesn't bark."

"He did this time. I looked out the window and saw the prison van coming up your road. I knew I didn't have time to get away, so I started looking for a place to lose the chain and cuffs."

"And yourself."

"I was going to shinny up your chimney."

"Sort of Santa in reverse."

He smiled. It was the first real smile Tate had ever seen from him, and for a moment she forgot everything else in the wake of its captivating brilliance. But just for a moment.

"You are truly one of a kind." Simon opened his eyes and let his gaze rest on her. It wasn't a tiring task. Even in jeans, she was a lovely woman. This morning he had thought he would never see her again. He had *planned* to never see her again. Now, despite his frustration with the way the day had evolved, he almost felt like a reprieve had been issued.

"Why didn't you tell the sheriff about me?" he asked, when she didn't respond.

"What makes you think I didn't?"

He studied her some more as he explained. "You lost the chance a couple of days ago. Taking care of me would have been too hard to explain. But why didn't you turn me in, when you could have?"

"Your story's more interesting than my motives."

"I doubt it." He raised a hand to stave off her denials. "I was going to thread the chains and cuff up through the springs so no one could see them. Before I could, I noticed that all the boards for about three feet across met in the same place. When I looked closer, I realized it was a door going down to a cellar. It's very well hidden."

Tate frowned. "There's a root cellar, but it's not much deeper than a long closet. It doesn't extend that far over, and the one time I was in it I didn't see any trapdoor."

"It probably shares a wall with the museum."

"What museum?" she asked in exasperation.

"You're going to have to see it. I don't think I can explain."

She knew they had come to a dead-end. But as interesting as the subject was, there was one of greater interest. And much greater importance.

"Why did you lie to me before? And who are you?"

He was still studying her—almost, she thought, as if he were deciding what to tell her. "Don't lie to me again," she warned him. "I'm not in the mood."

Slowly he shook his head. "It'll be safer for you, if I make up another lie."

"But not safer for you."

"You may wish you didn't know." He paused. "And you may not believe it, anyway."

"You're probably right."

He was quiet for a full minute. Just as Tate was about to give him an ultimatum, he spoke. "I'm not Carl Petersen, although I look a little like he might if he was deprived of food for a month or two. My real name *is* Simon."

"So how come no one noticed?"

"No one at High Ridge had any reason to follow the Petersen trial, and there was limited coverage, anyway. The bank didn't want to broadcast the fact someone punched a few buttons and made off with over a million dollars of their account holders' money. After the trial Petersen was held in Texas for a couple of months. Then, as far as the world knows, he was shifted to High Ridge as a federal prisoner."

"Back up."

His eyes sparked in the firelight, although the rest of him looked as if he were in pain. "Petersen's under lock and key somewhere else right now. When this is over he'll be transferred to Leavenworth, where he'll be serving a shorter sentence because he cooperated with us."

"Us?"

"The Justice Department."

She stared at him. "Right," she said finally. "You're one of the good guys."

He grimaced. "A matter of opinion. Prison officials are supposed to be good guys, too, only sometimes they're not. Sometimes they murder inmates and embezzle funds, just like the cons they're supposed to be watching."

Tate let his story filter into all the corners of her mind. "So you're an F.B.I. agent, and you were put in High Ridge under an assumed name to nail some official there?"

He smiled at her cynical tone. "No."

"No to what?"

"I'm not an agent. I work for myself, and sometimes the Justice Department pays my fee."

"They don't have enough employees of their own?"

"Not like me."

She let that pass for the moment. "Why were you in High Ridge?"

"That's what I don't know."

Tate pushed herself to her feet and went to the fireplace. She was careful not to turn her back to him, as she chose another log for the fire. "You're not making any sense."

"There's not much sense to be made. A man named Josiah Gallagher, a Justice Department official, asked me to impersonate Petersen. Gallagher's an old friend." He laughed bitterly. "*Was*, I guess I should say. I owed him a favor, and he decided to collect. I agreed to go to High Ridge as Petersen. Justice wanted somebody on the inside to investigate allegations of poor conditions there. Gallagher also wanted me to get close to a couple of cons from Oklahoma City who were on their way to making parole. He needed some information about their plans after release. The theory was the Carl Petersen would be the kind of guy these two would talk to."

"Why?"

"Because Petersen is a computer criminal, and these guys needed advice to take their penny-ante smuggling operation into the twenty-first century."

"Seems like a long shot."

"Gallagher never misses."

Tate stood with her back to the fire. "Just supposing this isn't another one of your lies, what happened at High Ridge to make you escape? Why didn't you just give this Gallagher person a phone call?"

"I was supposed to be there a month, at most. It stretched to two, then three, without a word from Gallagher or anybody at

Justice. Nobody at High Ridge knew I was a plant. I got plenty of information for them, but nobody came to collect it. About the second week I was there, Captain Shaw took a shine to me."

As improbable as his story was, she was beginning to believe him. No mere actor could have uttered the last sentence with such restrained venom.

"Captain Shaw's the warden?"

"The same. He's also a murderer and a thief."

"You say."

"I have proof—or I did."

"You lost it, of course."

"There's something about floating downriver at midnight, half dead and dying another inch a minute that does that."

"What are we talking about here?"

His gaze was steady, locked with hers. Tate thought that if he was lying, he was far beyond accomplished—he was a master. "The good captain moved me into the prison office just as soon as he decently could. He said I ought to put my computer skills to good use. I wasn't there for more than a day before he moved me into *his* office, only not so anyone would know. Officially he signed me to use the law library every night between six and eight. Then a guard would march me down to Shaw's office, feed me supper and watch while I juggled the prison records."

"Juggled the records?"

"Accounts received, accounts payable, accounts going straight into Shaw's personal account." He nodded, when it was clear by her expression that she understood. "It's easy enough to do if you understand computers. And I do."

"You said he was a murderer."

"I'd been doing his dirty work for him for about a month, when he told me to start editing inmate files. Editing was his word for changing facts he didn't want in the permanent records, facts like number of escape attempts, cause of death, etc. I had to break codes, find passwords to get into the state system and sometimes the federal computers. It took an expert to do it. Nobody in his pay was good enough to do it for him. And an inmate was the perfect person for the job, because when he finished, he could just disappear." He snapped his fingers.

Tate felt chilled, despite her proximity to the fire. "'Disappear' as in murder?"

"I wouldn't have been the first. Two guys jailed for computer crime were supposedly killed by inmates, after working for the captain. Shaw thought their prison records had been appropriately adjusted so that no one would connect them with him, but I found a secret file. The second man had figured out what was coming, and he left data Shaw didn't know enough to erase. There's other information, too, that could nail Shaw."

"That's what was on the diskette I found in your pocket?"

He was silent. His eyes said it all.

"I found it," she acknowledged. "Did you think you'd lost it in the river?"

"I had two diskettes. Apparently I did lose one. And now you have the other."

"Would it be any use after soaking in the river?"

"Probably not. But Captain Shaw doesn't know that."

"Which is why such a massive search was mounted."

He nodded. "Petersen committed a white-collar crime. He shot the bank auditor when his own back was against the wall, but he's not a dangerous criminal. If men like Petersen escape, they usually get caught a few weeks afterward, anyway, even if no one is looking for them. They're stopped for traffic violations, or they try to cash a bum check. Nobody has anything to fear from a man like Petersen."

"Nobody but Shaw."

Simon stood, and Tate repressed the urge to tell him to stay off his feet. She had no control over him now. And she felt that piece of the truth dead center inside her. He started toward her, limping noticeably, and she toyed with the idea of reaching for the poker.

"I was next." Simon stopped just yards from her. "I had just about outlived my usefulness. Shaw would have arranged a convenient accident for me, and I would have been a memory."

"You still haven't said why you didn't just get in touch with somebody from the Justice Department."

"Phone calls at High Ridge are monitored and numbers are traced. After I started working for the captain, I wasn't allowed phone calls, anyway."

"Then why not by computer? Surely you could have contacted a Justice Department computer and sent Gallagher a message."

"Think about it. I was supposed to be there less than a month. I was there three, with no word from Gallagher."

"Maybe there was a mistake—"

"No mistake."

She tried to put the facts together, but it was too confusing.

"I'll make it easy," Simon said, limping closer to the fire to warm his hands. "Gallagher left me there to rot or be murdered. I don't know which, and I don't know why, but I do know I couldn't go to Gallagher then and I can't go to him now. He wanted me dead. I've no doubt some of the men out there searching these hills are on his payroll."

It was a preposterous story, yet unlike his last one, all the pieces fit. There was only one he hadn't addressed. "What about Erin?"

Simon leaned against the wall and lifted his foot to the hearth, so his weight wasn't on it. "Erin is Aaron, not Erin."

Tate exhaled in exasperation. "You're not making any sense."

"Aaron. With an *A*. Aaron Reynolds, of the male persuasion. He was an agent. Josiah, Aaron and I worked on a case that exposed a Mafia family forming in the Northwest. I was almost killed. Josiah saved my life, and Aaron's, too. That's what I meant about owing him a favor. Aaron retired after that. He's living in Memphis now. Runs a security-systems business and fishes every weekend, but if I know Aaron he's still got his finger on the pulse of Washington. If anyone can find out why Gallagher tried to put me away for good, it'll be Aaron."

If there were more questions that needed to be asked, Tate couldn't think of them. She stood watching him in silence.

Simon knew how his story sounded. And he knew he had used up his credibility by lying before. There were only a few people in his life whose opinion of him mattered. Surprisingly, he found he had added another, and she had gone directly to the top of the list. But there was no way to force her to believe him. She was a woman beyond force, anyway, which was part of her considerable appeal.

"This is where you pick up the poker and swing it over my head," Simon said at last. "It's now or never, Tate. Believe me or don't believe me, but now's the moment of decision. Now you know that chaining me up won't do you any good." He smiled a little. "Never did, in fact."

"Why did you stay here this evening? You could have gone out the front door when I went out the back a little while ago. You could have gone and never had to tell me any of this."

His answer was more painful than anything he had endured since his escape. "Because I can't get out of here on my own. Damn it, that's all I want, but it's impossible. I thought I could. I heard you drive away this morning, and I thought you wouldn't have to be involved anymore. I was going to shave off this beard, find my way to the next county and hitch a ride to Memphis. You never would have had to know the truth."

"Why didn't you tell me the truth in the first place? What good did it do to lie?"

"The truth could get you killed!" He ran his hand through his hair in frustration. "I've got God knows who after me, and eventually they may trace me this far. You'll be questioned by some of the best if they do. And who's to care if a young woman in some remote cabin in the Ozarks disappears after she's been found to know some things she shouldn't?"

Tate forced herself to ignore the shudder passing through her at the thought. "Jess Cantrell would care. And when Jess cares, the world tends to find out about it."

"Cantrell, the journalist? The one who writes the book-length exposés?"

"My father."

"I thought your father was dead!"

"It's a long story. Good old Uncle Grady would care, too. That's Grady Clayton, state attorney in southern Florida, about to run for the House, or so I hear. And then there's the Mountain Glade sheriff. He's some relative or other. He doesn't have Grady or Jess's clout, but he wouldn't be too lightweight to flash around if I needed him."

"How much family do you have?"

"More than I ever thought," she said with a tiny smile.

He assessed her, but he didn't ask what she meant. She was as private a person as he was, and until she trusted him she wasn't going to reveal anything. "These hills are full of men who want to kill me. You're vulnerable."

"You need my help."

"Yeah." He spat out the word as if it tasted bad.

"You don't ask for it very nicely."

"I haven't had any practice."

In the fading light of day tickling the cabin's interior, she saw his face grow paler, but he didn't move, didn't attempt to sit. She knew enough about him to understand that he would never show weakness until it completely overcame him. "What do you want me to do?" she asked.

"As I see it, you've got a couple of choices. You can use the poker and put me out of my misery, or you can hide me a little longer, until my leg is stronger and they aren't searching the immediate area."

"At least you've got the sense to see that you'd get caught if you left now."

"Oh, I've got plenty of sense. I just don't have plenty of options."

Her instincts told her to help him. She was no human lie detector, but everything she had learned about people told her that this time he was telling the real story.

But what if he wasn't? What if this was another tale, embroidered to make him look like a good guy when he wasn't?

As she contemplated his words and her choices, a third option occurred to her. "What if you didn't have to go to Memphis, at all? What if I went into town and called Aaron for you?"

"Then you'd know I was telling the truth."

She nodded. "And you'd have Aaron to help you."

"Good idea. Only you can't do it."

She lifted an eyebrow in question.

"If I could have gotten to Aaron right after my escape, that might have worked. But his phone will be tapped now. Gallagher will know Aaron is the first person I'd try to contact."

"But would that matter? If I'm calling from a public phone?"

"They'd trace me to this area. It would be a small matter to get a record of who used the phone and run them down."

"You sound like you know."

He gave a humorless laugh. "I know."

"There goes my chance to find out if this is a lie."

"Maybe not." He winced as he shifted his weight and damned himself when he realized he had shown his pain. "There's another call you can make. Go into town and call the number I'm going to give you. Don't say anything. Listen closely. With any luck what you hear might convince you."

She shrugged when he didn't explain further. "You're saying you'll be here when I get back?"

"I'm saying that."

She hesitated. "And you're saying I can take the gun with me, just to be sure I don't get shot coming back through the door?"

"There's an agency or two in the Washington area that could use your talents."

"I'd never survive the background check."

Simon reached across the space separating them and laid his hand on her shoulder. His fingers were a light caress. There was nothing in the movement to restrain her. "I don't want you hurt. If you decide not to help me anymore, I'll understand." He didn't drop his hand. He flipped it, then caressed the length of her neck with his knuckles.

Her breath caught, and for a moment she was completely vulnerable. If Simon was who he said he was, then he was highly skilled at getting what he wanted.

She wasn't Jess Cantrell's adopted daughter for nothing. Like Jess, she knew how to listen. Amidst the ambiguity of Simon's story had been an admission that he lived his life somewhere other than in full sunlight. He had told her he wasn't an F.B.I. agent, as if to reassure her. But she knew better than to feel comforted. This man would never submit himself to the restrictions an agency would impose. He wouldn't follow anyone's rules and regulations, not when it didn't suit him.

He had said it best. He worked for himself. And he made his own rules. What did the rules say about seduction?

He withdrew his hand. "Go. Make the call." He bent and tore off the corner of a sheet of newspaper beside the hearth, scribbling a phone number on it with a pen he took from his pocket. She wondered if it was the one he had used to pick the lock on the handcuffs. He straightened and held the number out to her. "If you want me gone when you come back, I'll be packed."

She took the paper, stopped for the gun and left.

Outside, the distant baying of hounds rose to meet the descent of evening.

Chapter 8

Allen's Pharmacy stayed open most nights until seven, although there wasn't much call for evening hours in a county where almost nobody punched a time clock. Tate figured that Wally stayed open because he was afraid he would miss some good gossip if he didn't.

Now she was glad he liked to keep his ear to the ground. One glance into the phone booth at the gas station told her that repairs still hadn't been made there. She was going to have to use the phone at Allen's.

Two little boys with candy sticks were coming out as Tate went in. One little boy wiped his hands against her jeans as they passed, and the other giggled. The Living Strings selection playing over the loudspeaker sounded as if it were winding through the tape deck at half the normal speed. Tate envisioned elderly couples waltzing to a tempo that gave "slow dancing" a new meaning.

In the back of the store, Wally was holding court with two of his cronies. One, a pot-bellied man with a long neck, reminded her of the central fixture of an old-time general store.

"Evening, Miss Tate."

She had hoped to escape Wally's eye, but she had known it was unlikely.

"Feeling better?" he called. "Leg better?"

"Lots better. You fixed me right up."

"You know, I been thinking. How could you chop your leg that high up, and all?"

She wondered how many conversations she had been the center of since Wally had filled the prescription for her. *Far as I can see, nobody could cut their thigh with an ax. A foot, maybe, or even a shin. Course there was a time that old Sam Turnbull down on Goose Creek Road...*

"I was swinging it," she demonstrated, making up her explanation as she went along. "And I picked it up like this. Then I brought it down too fast and lost control." She grimaced, as if she had just reopened a wound. "I guess I'm just not as good with an ax as I thought I was."

"You could kill yourself," the pot-bellied man said with enthusiasm. "Kill yourself and the buzzards would pick your bones before anybody would find you out there at Millard's place."

"What a story that would make."

The man nodded solemnly. "Too bad Millard wouldn't be around to tell it. Nobody could tell a story like Millard."

Tate couldn't respond to that, since Millard's stories were as much a mystery to her as the man himself. She forced a smile—it was a major effort, since all she really wanted to do was make the phone call—then she began to examine the aisle of shampoos and hair conditioners. It took a few minutes, but eventually the men lost interest in chatting with her. When Wally had launched into a hunting story and the other men were jumping in to add their own insights, she sidled toward the telephone.

The number Simon had asked her to call had an unfamiliar area code. She dialed the operator and gave the Stagecoach Inn credit-card number, then the phone number Simon had given her.

The number rang four times. As it did she debated what she would say. Simon had said she was to listen only, but she knew she would feel like a junior-high-school prankster if she hung up without speaking. She had settled on telling the party who answered that she had gotten a wrong number when the fifth ring was interrupted. There was a brief moment of silence; then a voice began to speak.

"Simon Vandergriff here. I'm not in at the moment, but if you leave a message, I'll get back to you at the first opportunity."

There was another pause, then a beep.

It had all happened so quickly that it took Tate a second or two to put together what she'd heard. She listened to the ensuing silence even though she certainly had no message to leave. The man belonging to the recorded voice was living in her cabin. The merest trace of an accent was unmistakable.

Simon Vandergriff. She tried to think of a reason, any reason, why Carl Petersen would have an answering machine somewhere to tell callers that he was Simon Vandergriff. If there had been any lingering question in her mind whether Simon and Carl Petersen were the same man, it disappeared.

But who was he? Was he the man he claimed to be, a man set up by one of his trusted friends to die in High Ridge prison?

She knew from experience that sometimes the most incredible stories were true. Simon's story was incredible, but he had delivered it without hesitation and with sincerity. Of course, he could be a liar. But if he was, he was superlative.

Again, she had come to a turning point. There was no restraining the man now, no false sense of security to be had from keeping him in handcuffs. If she went home to him, it would be a sign of good faith. She would be telling him that she believed him. Even more, that she trusted him. She would *have* to trust him to go back.

She realized she was still holding the telephone receiver against her ear. There was nothing else to be learned here. Simon had offered her proof—of a kind. Now she only had to decide whether to believe it.

There was a faint rustle on the line just as she was about to hang up. At first she thought she had imagined it. Then she heard voices, the same type of remote conversation that sometimes occurred on the long-distance line when wires were crossed somewhere.

"Did you get the trace?"

"Not yet. But the connection hasn't been broken."

She let a second pass, then another, before she realized what was happening. As if she could no longer hold its weight, she flung the receiver into its cradle.

Simon's telephone was tapped.

By why? Wouldn't anyone who was *that* interested know he was on the run? Surely his escape from High Ridge was no secret.

An answer occurred to her almost immediately. The phone was tapped because someone was hoping his incoming calls might provide a clue to his escape. Perhaps even because someone hoped that Simon himself would call in for his messages!

"Never got your party, did you, Miss Tate?" Wally called from behind the counter.

Tate turned around to face the men. "'Fraid not." She thought it was too bad she couldn't tell them about Simon. If she could, nobody in Mountain Glade would ever doubt that Millard's daughter had a few good folktales of her own.

The cabin appeared uninhabited when Tate parked her Bronco in front of it. Before leaving Allen's she had made several additional calls and discovered three more pieces of information. One was that the area code Simon had told her to dial belonged to Washington, D.C. The second was that directory assistance did have a listing for an Aaron Reynolds in Memphis. The third was that Jess was still out of the country, but Krista had heard from him and he was safe, although it would be at least three weeks before he returned to the U.S.

Tate wondered what Jess could have uncovered that she didn't already know. Not much, she supposed, although she knew she would have been in for a great deal of advice.

But she didn't need advice. She was a woman. Wary, worried, rebellious, still, but a woman capable of making a decision.

And she *had* made a decision.

Inside the cabin she scanned the main room. There was no sign of Simon, although she suspected he wanted to be sure she was alone before he showed himself.

"Simon," she called. "I'm back. By myself."

The door to the bedroom opened, and a man appeared.

For a moment she wasn't sure who he was. Then she knew. "You've shaved off your beard."

Simon watched her from the doorway. Moonlight struck her hair with a silver gleam and caressed the defiant cast of her head. She hadn't taken the time to change for her trip into town, but she had tied the tails of her black flannel shirt into a knot at her waist, pulling the fabric tight across her breasts. The shirt only accentuated how slender she was, and how perfectly proportioned. Without shirttails hanging over her jeans he could see their snug fit, the taper of her hips, the flawless curve of her bottom and length of her legs.

Something inside him tried to break free, some long-restrained, threatening part of himself. He leashed it with difficulty.

She had been gone more than an hour. He could remember no time when he had waited that long for someone else to decide his fate. Fifteen minutes into his wait, he realized that he trusted Tate as he had trusted few people. Half an hour into it, he had realized that he cared what she decided. She was not a stranger, whose opinion would have been worth less than yesterday's newspaper. In some ways he knew her better than he had ever known anyone.

He had found that realization disconcerting. Now he was more disconcerted, still.

He walked toward her, a towel dangling from his shoulders. His progress was halting. He stopped while they were still yards apart. "Carl Petersen wears a beard. I don't."

She wished it wasn't true. She had washed the beard and felt its soft, seductive attractions. More disturbing, though, was the change its absence made. He seemed both more austere and more ruthless, now. More the fugitive, less the man she had tried to heal. "So Simon Vandergriff is clean-shaven."

"Then you got my machine."

"I got more than that. I got tapped—or rather, your phone did." She told him everything that had happened.

He cursed softly, and his face settled into rigid planes.

Tate stared at him. The beard had disguised more than his identity. It had disguised his very essence. Now there was no mistaking what the man facing her was: a knight errant who could face down a prison full of criminals—on both sides of the bars—and still come out of it alive.

She had thought him handsome. Now she knew that handsome had no relevance. Dangerous? Yes, if you weren't on his side. Attractive? The term was too anemic. Compelling was closer, and so was desirable, although, like the man himself, that was too dangerous to consider closely.

"Did you hang up as soon as you heard voices?" Simon asked.

"It surprised me so much that I..." Tate saw his eyes narrow. "I didn't," she admitted. "I held the phone for a few seconds afterward. Then, when I finally realized what was happening, I hung up."

He didn't criticize. For someone without training, she had done well just to realize what was happening. "They sound like bunglers, anyway. Maybe they didn't get the trace. Not everyone in the agency is Gallagher's caliber."

"How's your leg?"

"How's your state of mind?"

He hadn't smiled since he'd come into the room. Tate realized he was waiting for her to tell him if she believed his story. "If I was sane, I wouldn't even give you a head start on an escape."

"Do you believe what I've told you?" he asked, getting straight to the point and moving closer.

"I do." The two words freed her in a way she hadn't expected. They were a commitment, just as the same two words signified a lifetime commitment in a wedding ceremony. Now that she'd said them, her decision was made. She wasn't going to indulge in any more doubts or confusion.

Simon knew the words for what they were. "Thank you."

Tate guessed he was a man to whom gratitude didn't come easily. Gratitude or illness or... bonding.

As she stood close enough to him to feel the heat of his body, she realized that the last had more to do with her decision about the truth of his story than anything she had heard over the telephone.

She cared about this man. She had watched over him when he was delirious with fever, used all her limited skill to guide him toward recovery, protected him when anyone else would have turned him in. From the beginning there had been a bond between them, pulling her toward decisions she shouldn't have made.

The bond was stronger now, and unlike the chain that had kept him bound, she doubted that he would be able to discard it easily. She had tried and failed. Even the lies he had told hadn't destroyed the link she felt with him.

"You're welcome, Simon Vandergriff."

"You may wish you'd never heard that name."

"I'm finished wishing. I think I'm stuck with you."

He smiled then, and without the beard she saw that his smile was more dazzling and dangerous, still. "Well, at least you won't be stuck with a grimy-around-the-edges ex-con. Primitive bath facilities you have here, but I made do while you were gone."

She tried to imagine him hauling water off the back porch and heating it. "You're really not well enough to push yourself that hard."

"There were parts you never seemed to get to when you bathed me."

The blush that tinged her cheeks was unfamiliar. She couldn't remember it happening before. "You were lucky I even bothered with the G-rated parts."

"I *know* how lucky I was. And am." He stretched his hand toward her, almost hesitantly. "You didn't know me. You had no reason to trust me, and lots of reasons not to. Even now, my story could be a lie." He told himself to move away, but he touched her cheek instead. His fingers weren't quite steady. "Maybe you should tell me why."

"Some people took a chance on me once, when they didn't have to. I was a pretty hard case, but they didn't care. They were there through all the bad parts, and they never gave up on me. Maybe I learned something."

"There're a lot of creeps out there who aren't worth taking a chance on."

"I've met up with my share."

"And learned to tell the difference?"

She shook her head. "Learned to try."

He started to drop his hand, but it lifted again to brush a lock of hair behind her ear. His voice was low; the words seemed to be wrung from some place deep inside him. "You fascinate me."

She had been admired and desired by men. But no one had ever told her that she fascinated him before. To herself she seemed the most straightforward of women. There was nothing mysterious or exotic about her. Yet she saw he wasn't lying, and she suspected Simon didn't fascinate easily.

She tried to make light of it. "If fascinate means I've been forced to think about you constantly, I suppose you fascinate me, too."

She wasn't transparent like many women he'd known, but right now there was no doubt in Simon's mind that she was uncomfortable. He had never been intrigued by innocence. He had lived too long on the edge to take the time to gently woo a woman. Now, for the first time in his life, he wished he had the time. She was a woman who wasn't quite sure of her effect on men, and he was a man who would be obscenely pleased to show her. His lips curved slowly into a smile that was all heat and feelings repressed.

"You find me funny?" she asked.

"I find you anything but. Shall I tell you what I find you?"

She was afraid to know. "I don't think so."

He stepped back to give her room—another inch or two. He was only too aware that it ought to be miles. Safe subjects seemed suddenly few and far between. He settled on food. "I can put together something for dinner."

"You're going to destroy all the good we've done for your leg if you don't get off it."

"You can stop mothering me. We're beyond that now."

Her cheeks heated for the second time. "Is that what I was doing?"

"It's easier to act like a mother than the alternative."

Again she didn't want to know what he meant.

"Friend," he explained, without prompting. "Shall we be friends, Tate?"

"How long are you planning to stay around and act friendly?"

"That depends on you . . . and the men searching for me."

"You can stay as long as you need to. I don't want you leaving until it's safe." She didn't add the idea that had been forming since she had begun to believe his story. She wasn't sure Simon was willing to accept more from her than a place to stay.

"You have a foolproof place to hide me in the cellar."

She had completely forgotten his story about the "museum." Now seemed like the time to explore it. "I'd like to go down there."

"The doors are hinged from below. They fold back like shutters so they'll open under the bed. When I went down it was very dark, even when there was light coming from the room above. When I closed the door, it was black as night. Now that it's dark in the bedroom, you'll have to take a lantern."

"I'll go down after we eat."

"Go now, while I get everything together."

"You don't want to come?"

He wanted some time away from her to purge himself of feelings he could never act on. "I think you should see it by yourself."

Tate realized this was a final test of faith in Simon. Once she was in the cellar, he could weight the door and she could be there until her bones were found by the cabin's next resident.

"I won't be long."

He smiled a little. "Is that a question?"

"If you want me out of the way, shutting me down there would be an easy way to accomplish it."

"But I don't want you out of the way...." He stopped. What had he been about to say? That he would never want her out of the way? And what did that mean, exactly?

Tate didn't ask him to say more. Their relationship was already complex to the point of absurdity. "If you wanted to get rid of me, you've had plenty of opportunities. I guess I'll take my chances."

Simon limped to the fireplace and took down one of the lanterns from the mantel. He took a match from the canister on the hearth and followed Tate into the bedroom.

At the bedside she frowned. "Shouldn't we just push the bed to the wall so the entrance is easier to get to? We could push it back after I come up."

"If this was a normal situation, yes. But if anyone comes in here looking for me again, I'd rather they didn't find scuff marks on the floor."

She started to protest, until she remembered that his career demanded attention to details such as that. The men searching for him would have the same keen eye. "You can hand me the lantern after I've dropped like a sack of potatoes to the floor and wiggled under the bed on my belly."

"I'll stand here and enjoy the sight."

Which was exactly what he did. He had proof of how far his recovery had come when he felt each sensuous twist and turn of her bottom in the place where she had never bathed him.

"Ready for the lantern?" he asked after she had disappeared.

"I don't see anything under here."

He struggled to the floor. "You're right on top of it. Slide back. See where all the planks line up? Midway along that line you'll find a depression along the side of one of the planks. It looks almost like a defect in the wood." He waited until she was out of the way; then he pointed. "There."

"I feel like an idiot." Despite that, though, she slid her hand along the plank he had singled out, until she found the depression.

"Push it toward me," Simon instructed.

She did, although it wasn't easy. Just as Simon had said, the section gave under pressure, folding like an accordion until a space was revealed. The other side did the same. Now a hole loomed in front of her. An unappealing, black-as-midnight, musty, suspicious hole.

"You never said what you found down here," she said slowly.

"No, I never did."

"I don't know much about my father."

"No?"

"He wasn't an ax murderer, was he?"

"I don't want to spoil your surprise."

"I'd be comfortable with a little spoiling."

Simon slid the lantern toward her, then handed her the match. "There's nothing to be afraid of."

"How long will this kerosene last, do you think?"

"Certainly long enough to get you down to light the lanterns that are already there. Turn around and lower one foot until you find the ladder. It's sturdy, maybe eight feet long. Feel your way down, a step or two, before you light the lantern."

"I'm planning to work up an appetite."

"I'll be ready."

Tate inched into position. Then, with hands grasping the edges of the folding doors, she started down the ladder.

Making a meal out of the meager supplies in Tate's kitchen was a challenge, but Simon liked challenges. He had cooked meals with the entire city of Paris as his pantry. He had cooked others, when the vegetation and creatures of the Brazilian rain forest had been his only ingredients.

Either challenge paled next to the possibilities present in this remote Arkansas cabin. In one cabinet there were a can of tuna fish, six cans of chicken broth, a jar of cheese spread, half a loaf of stale bread, and salt but no pepper. Two eggs nestled in what remained of a bag of ice in the icebox, along with a stick of butter and a bottle of lukewarm white wine. In canisters on a counter behind the stove he found flour, powdered milk, coffee, tea and rice. Beneath the sink there was a year's supply of graham crackers, marshmallows and chocolate bars.

He assembled cheese-and-tuna sandwiches and dipped them in a mixture of egg and powdered milk before he sautéed them in butter. He whipped the other egg and threaded it into boiling chicken broth for egg-drop soup, setting it on the side of the stove to stay warm after it was finished.

Tate still hadn't reappeared by the time the meal was ready. Simon hobbled to the back porch to get the wine that he had immersed in what was left of the water Tate had hauled earlier that day. The bottle was cold against his cheek. It was an Ohio vintage, cheap and probably too sweet for his taste, but after three months with nothing to drink but mud-black—and thick—coffee and watered-down tea, he wasn't about to criticize.

He opened the bottle and set it to the side of the fireplace before he went looking for Tate. There was no answer when he called her name in the bedroom. Thoughts of the dangers she might have encountered in the cellar—rats, hibernating copperheads—pushed aside the memory of going down the ladder with one good leg. He was under the bed and hopping from rung to rung in seconds.

He found her standing in the middle of the room, her head bent over a leather-bound volume. When she lifted her face to his, her cheeks were wet with tears.

Simon didn't know what to say. He cursed himself for sending her down here alone. All the objectivity he had struggled for disappeared.

"My father wanted me," she said. Her voice was steady, but the tears were there, shading each word. "All the years when I thought nobody did, my father wanted me."

Simon was at a loss how to answer her. "He left you this place, didn't he?"

"I didn't know why. Not till now." She smiled a little, and Simon felt something inside him twist at the sight. Knowing he shouldn't, he put his arms around her and pulled her close. Her body, soft and warm against him, seemed only an extension of his.

"Tell me about it." He felt her shudder, as if all the tears she still hadn't cried were battling inside her.

She tried to move away. "I can't."

He heard "not yet." "Then tell me about the book you're holding."

Tate knew she should push him away. Instead, she stopped struggling and circled his waist with her arms. Being held felt right. If it also felt confusing, even dangerous, that somehow didn't matter. "One of my father's journals. I didn't know it was here. There's a whole shelf of them in the corner, dating thirty years back. I never would have found them if you hadn't—"

"Hidden here?" He laughed a little. "Strange blessings."

"Your leg!" She tilted her face to his. "Coming down those steps must have—"

He hadn't intended to hold her. And now he didn't intend to kiss her. So much, he thought, for good intentions.

Her lips were soft under his, soft and pliable and young. She felt the same way against him. He had to bend his head to meet her; he had to bring her closer to arch her body against his. In the confused seconds that followed his senses seemed to expand, filled with the woodsmoke and fresh-air fragrance of her hair, the warmth and velvet texture of her skin, the tiny moan she uttered when his lips took hers.

He let her go the moment he felt her stiffen. No matter what happened between them, no matter what he felt, he never wanted her to be frightened of him again.

"That's not why I came down," he said.

Her eyes showed just how vulnerable she felt, though her words were determinedly casual. "For a man who's been in prison for three months, you haven't forgotten how to kiss."

"It's like riding a bicycle."

"I just begin to think I know who you are and something changes."

"I've never changed. The only thing that's changed is that I'm not lying anymore."

"What kind of truth is a kiss?"

"We could analyze it and find out."

"Let's not." Tate turned away from him. By wavering lantern light, the room seemed as much of a mystery as what had just happened.

The room was an airtight historical vault. For most of his life Millard had apparently zealously collected Ozark memorabilia, along with important records documenting the area's folklore. Then he had sealed off this section of the old root cellar and fashioned it into a crypt for a dying culture. The room was proof it hadn't been Millard's style to trust his records to the Smithsonian or a university collection.

Tate slid her father's journal back in place and forced herself to ignore the desire to turn and kiss Simon again.

He rested his hands on her shoulders. "What do you think of this room?"

Tate felt his warmth and support behind her. She wanted to lean against him, but held herself rigid. "I don't understand it."

"Shall I tell you what I think?"

"Why not?"

"I think the cabin's older than your father could have been. It's built from chestnut logs, and the chestnut forests died out in the early part of the century from blight. This room was designed as a place to store bootleg whiskey. White lightning. That's why it's so well-hidden."

"Well, that explains the jugs." Tate stepped away from Simon's gentle hold and started toward the far corner. She moved as much to put some distance between them as to explore. A dozen pottery jugs stood together in a neat row along the wall.

Simon followed and watched her lift a jug for his inspection. Carefully he pried the hand-carved cork from the jug's neck and sniffed. He was instantly racked with coughs. "This stuff defines rotgut," he managed.

She was glad to be talking about something so far removed from them. "You mean it's full?"

"Full and probably nearly as old as the cabin." He held it out for Tate to smell.

She waved it away after a quick whiff. "You think this was my father's secret stash?"

"I think your father was either a historian or one of those people who can't throw anything away."

She defended the man she hadn't known. "A historian."

"Then 'museum' was the right word."

"I'll have more of the answer after I've read his journals." Tate walked along the shelves lining the walls. Everything was almost compulsively neat, except for a thin layer of dust. The room was so well constructed and sealed that the air was surprisingly dry, though cool.

There were three shelves of books other than Millard's journals, which she had instantly recognized because of the one she had found in the loft. The titles indicated that most of the books were works of Ozark folklore. Some of them looked very old; some looked as if they had been bound by hand. She opened one and ran her finger down the page, aware, without looking, that Simon was beside her. "Did you know it's bad luck to change a horse's name?"

"How about a man's?"

She turned the page. "Don't know, but it is bad luck to wear another person's clothes—so you're in trouble, anyway." She replaced the book and chose another. She turned to a page at random and read for a moment. "It says here that Jesse James went undercover somewhere in the Ozarks and died a natural death."

"Definitely the best kind."

She hadn't met Simon's gaze since he's kissed her. Now she did. The flickering lantern light made it hard to tell what he was thinking, but she knew, even without visual proof. He was thinking about her and how odd it was that they had come together so easily. She knew, because she was thinking the same.

She turned back to the shelf and replaced the second book before she moved on to a shelf of carefully labeled tools. There were cast-iron kitchen gadgets that Simon examined with interest. "This peels apples. This pits cherries." He balanced one in each hand. Tate noticed that his injured leg was propped so that it didn't have to bear his weight.

"We ought to look for remedies for your leg. Everything else is here." She moved down the row a little farther, to a collection of handmade musical instruments, including a dulcimer that looked as if it might have been crafted from native woods.

Simon lifted a zinc-lidded Mason jar from a row of glassware and antique bottles. "This still has something in it. What do you suppose your father was preserving?"

"Botulism?" Tate could hardly absorb the impact of the cellar museum, not to mention the entries in her father's journal.

And then there was Simon's kiss.

Simon saw her bewilderment. She had the look of someone who had just discovered that nothing was the way it had always seemed.

He wondered if he did, too.

He stretched out his hand to her. She knew better than to take it. She was too vulnerable, too easy to hurt. From the beginning she had found his hands oddly compelling. Like the man.

Exactly like the man.

Unbidden, her hand lifted slowly until he had captured it in his. His eyes were shadowed. "We'll go back up, and I'll feed you dinner and ply you with wine. You'll tell me about your father, and I'll tell you that you have nothing to worry about from me."

"And will you be lying this time?" she asked softly.

He shook his head, answering his own silent questions, too. "I guess that remains to be seen."

Chapter 9

Tate spread a quilt over the rag rug in front of the fireplace. "I'm not trying to mother you," she told Simon, "but if you don't get off that leg you'll probably end up back in bed, and I'm tired of taking care of you."

She heard the deep rumble of his laugh somewhere behind her. It had taken him some time to climb the ladder, and she knew how his leg must be throbbing. "Go ahead and laugh," she said, "but see how funny it is, if your leg doesn't heal. Try hopping to Memphis and see how far you get."

"Do I detect a note of personal concern?" Simon lowered himself gingerly to the quilt. Once down, he knew he wasn't going to get up again for a while.

"For me or you? I'm sharing my cabin with a wanted man."

"That might not be bad, depending on *who* wants me."

"At this point, who doesn't? The state, the feds, the prison," she listed, ignoring the double entendre. "Tell me what I'm supposed to get for supper."

"There're soup and sandwiches on the stove."

"The man works miracles."

"The man would have to be a miracle worker to feed anyone with what he found in your kitchen."

"Next time break into a cabin with a larger pantry."

"And miss the fun I've had here?"

She risked a glance at him. He was watching her intently. Even when he was engaging in light banter, he never lost his intensity. She had the feeling that if someone broke down her front door at that moment, he would be ready for them before the door crashed to the floor.

"You stay put. I'll bring the food over."

"Start with the wine." He hiked a thumb over his shoulder in the direction of the fireplace.

"You just get one glass. It has to be rationed."

"*That* has to be rationed?"

"Do you know what I had to go through to get *that*?"

"Whatever it was, it wasn't worth it."

"This is a dry county. I had to drive to the next. They have one liquor store and it's on the worst dirt road you've ever seen, miles from anywhere."

"And you did that for Ohio wine? One bottle of Ohio wine?"

"Their selection left something to be desired. Wine's not their big seller." Tate got the bottle and the two glasses he had set beside it. "Oh, good—you left it to breathe. All the alcohol probably evaporated."

"Let's try it and see."

"Let me guess, you haven't had a drink in three months."

"They don't serve wine with meals at High Ridge."

He was trying to keep his voice light, but Tate heard the anger under his words. "It must be an awful place," she said, and both of them knew she wasn't talking about the beverages that were served there.

"No one deserves to live that way."

"You didn't know anything about the conditions before you were sent?" she asked as she poured the wine.

"Not enough." He held out his glass in toast. "To Tate, who saved my life."

Their eyes met, and she couldn't look away. They sipped their wine, still gazing at each other.

"Grape juice," Simon said at last. "But it's the best damn grape juice I've ever had."

"And you thought I wasn't a connoisseur."

"I think you're not a lot of things."

"Such as?"

"Half as cynical as you like to pretend, half as tough."

"So I cried a few tears down there. It's been quite a week."

He smiled, and there was no edge to it. "Get the soup and sandwiches, then tell me why you were crying."

"It might bore you."

"I don't think so."

Tate found that Simon had already mastered the wood stove, while she still routinely burned anything she tried to bake. "How did you manage to figure the stove out?" she asked, as she carried the bowls of steaming soup across the room.

Simon took his bowl and watched her go back for the sandwiches. He waited until she was seated to answer. "We had a wood stove in our country house when I was growing up. As a boy, I helped our cook stoke it. And when my mother and father weren't looking, she taught me to use it."

"Country house?" She whistled softly. "Somehow I don't think we're talking about a cabin like this one."

"Let's talk about you."

Tate understood secretive. For years she'd thought she had invented it. "Not if we're not going to talk about you, too."

"I've told you my life story."

"You forgot a part or two."

Simon stretched out, so that his injured leg was as comfortable as it could be. "You first."

She was halfway through her soup before she started. "I'm not sure where I was born. My mother worked in a carnival when she got pregnant. She had me on the road somewhere, and didn't stop to file any papers. I guess it was lucky for me that a couple of stops later she ended up in her hometown long enough to hand me over to *her* mother to name and raise. I didn't see her again until I was ten and my grandmother died. A neighbor found my mother's address in Grandma's papers and got hold of her. She came after the funeral and took me to live with her."

Simon kept his voice neutral. He knew that the slightest show of sympathy would halt her flow of words. "Was she still in the carnival?"

"She was a cocktail waitress, by then. I think she took two drinks for every one she served. By the time she got home she could barely make it into bed. I wouldn't see her in the mornings. I'd get myself off to school alone, but in the afternoons she'd be waiting for me." She finished her soup. These were memories she'd tried to put behind her. Now she was discovering that the feelings were still there.

"She hated me." She waited for Simon to jump in and tell her that was impossible, as so many others had tried before. She was grateful when he didn't. "I know now that she was a sick woman. But back then I never understood what was wrong with her, other than the alcohol and whatever pills she could get hold of. I thought it was me, that something was wrong with me."

"And now you know that's not true?"

She smiled at him, but she didn't answer right away. She set down her soup bowl and started on her sandwich, talking between bites.

"I've known that for some time. Kids don't make parents crazy. It works the other way, and that's what was happening to me before I decided to run away. When I was thirteen, I took off. I got caught and sent back, but I took off again. I was caught twice more and assigned new places to live, first a foster home, then a lockup for juvenile offenders. They weren't bad places, but by then I couldn't trust anyone, so I ran."

He was losing his struggle to sound objective. "You were young to be on your own."

She smiled sadly. "It was safer and better than living at home, but not safe and not good. I might not have made it, but I met a woman named Krista Jensen. I thought she was a runaway, too, at least at first. She was pretending to be one, so she could find her sister. She had teamed up with Jess Cantrell, who was out on the streets getting stories for a book he was working on."

Simon was beginning to understand. "They adopted you?"

"They couldn't find Anna, Kris's sister. At first I thought Kris wanted me as a substitute, but I discovered later that she and Jess really cared about *me*. They got married and started a shelter for runaways in Virginia, called Stagecoach Inn. I ran away from them, too, but I always came back. And one day I came back to stay. After that they started proceedings to have my mother's rights terminated. It was a nasty battle. My mother didn't want me, but she didn't want anyone else to love me, either. After a lot of expense, Jess and Kris won and adopted me. I never saw my mother again. She died about six months ago in a shelter for women."

"How does your father fit into all this?"

"I never knew who he was. Neither did my grandmother. My mother refused to tell anybody. When I'd ask, she'd say that he was a bastard and I was just like him."

Simon wondered how she had survived such abuse to become the bright, articulate, risk taker she was.

"I only lived with my mother for three years," Tate said, reading his expression. "My grandmother was a good woman. She was old and sick, but she never made me think the full-time burden of a grandchild was too much. If I hadn't had that, I'd be a different person." She held up her empty plate. "The cook taught you well."

"Someday you'll have to see what I can do when I have something to work with."

She got to her feet and reached for his dishes, waving him back down to the quilt when he tried to get up. "Next course. Don't go away."

He watched her journey to the kitchen. Her shoulders were thrown back, her chin tilted high. Her mother's hatred hadn't defeated her, but he knew that the pain of it would be with her always. That she had moved beyond it to come so far, was a tribute to her strength and intelligence.

She took her time returning. Talking about her childhood was never easy. And talking to Simon about something so personal put them on a new footing, although everything had changed when he'd kissed her, anyway.

When she finally crossed the room, she was carrying the ingredients for dessert. "Did your cook teach you how to make s'mores?"

"Apparently not."

"Then you've been deprived." She moved close to the fire and lowered herself to the rug, crossing her legs campfire-style. "A s'more is like a sandwich. You break a graham cracker in half—" She demonstrated. "Then you cover one half with a chocolate square." She stripped the wrapper off a chocolate bar and broke the bar into pieces, putting a square on her cracker. Then she did one for him. "Next you have to toast a marshmallow. You have to do this part yourself. There are two skewers here, one for each of us."

Simon moved closer, taking the metal skewer that she offered him. He followed her example and slid a marshmallow over its tip.

"Have you ever toasted a marshmallow?" she asked.

He shook his head, and she frowned. "You have so much to learn. What else haven't you done?"

His eyes traveled the length of her body, and his lips turned up in a slow smile.

"Never mind," she said, turning toward the fire. She wasn't sure whether the color rising in her cheeks was a blush or the impact of heat from the flames. "This is an exact science, so pay attention."

Simon could have told her that nothing was going to distract him from watching her, but he didn't.

"If your marshmallow catches on fire, the inside will still be cold and your chocolate won't melt," she instructed.

"Sounds serious."

She nodded, not looking at him. "And the chocolate won't melt, if you don't toast the marshmallow long enough."

"I don't know if I'm up to this."

She stopped trying to ignore him and shot him a high-voltage smile. "Just hold the marshmallow a few inches from the coals and keep turning it. When it starts to droop, you'll know it's ready."

"Droop?"

"You'll know. Trust me."

He had. With his life. But he didn't remind her. He moved closer, until their shoulders were almost touching. Together they thrust their skewers into the fireplace.

"How long does this take?" he asked.

"You have to have patience."

"I'm noticeably short on patience."

He shifted, and they were touching. "So tell me how you found out about Millard and this cabin."

She felt his hip and shoulder against hers, and wondered if he was trying to tell her he was there if she needed him. The effect, however, was only vaguely comforting and considerably disturbing..

"My mother told the whole story to a shelter worker, a Mrs. Phillips, before she died. I'd like to think she was sorry for the way she'd treated me, but I think she was probably just scared."

"Judgment Day?"

She rotated her marshmallow, and he did the same. "Something like that."

"What story did she tell?"

"Brenda, that was my mother's name, met Millard at the Arkansas State Fair in Little Rock. She was running a game on the midway, and Millard was telling folktales in one of the tents. Apparently they fell in love and conceived me. Millard wanted to marry her. He brought her here, but Brenda was appalled at the way Millard lived. I guess I'll find out more as I read his journals, but according to the story my mother told Mrs. Phillips, she wanted Millard to move to Little Rock, and he wouldn't."

"Not a big-city boy."

"I'm guessing he knew he'd be miserable in Little Rock. According to what I read today, he did promise to put electricity and plumbing in here and build another wing."

Simon pulled his marshmallow toward him to examine it. "But that wasn't enough for Brenda?"

"Nothing would have been enough." Tate reached for Simon's skewer, and her hand brushed his. She let it go immediately. "That's not ready. It has to cook some more."

Simon turned to watch her. She was young; he still didn't know how young. She was reciting the events of her life, as though they were an interesting story—perhaps she had more of Millard's talents than she had even guessed—but he knew the pain that must be associated with all she told him. He was not a nurturer, not a comfort giver. He had moved too fast, seen too much, too often, to have comfort to give. But now he wanted that to be different.

They finished toasting their marshmallows to a golden brown. "They're done," Tate announced at last. She pulled her skewer from the fire and lowered the marshmallow to the cracker and chocolate, sliding it off with the other half of the cracker. Simon followed suit. "Now you have to eat it while it's still hot."

Simon watched as she took her first bite. Chocolate and marshmallow oozed around the edges of the cracker. Her small white teeth closed over it, and her tongue licked its edges to catch the soft insides.

His reaction was visceral.

"Hurry and eat yours," she prodded.

He didn't tell her that watching her eat was more of a sensual delight than the s'more could ever be. He took a bite, but his eyes never left her.

"What do you think?"

For a moment he wasn't sure what she was asking. What did he think about her life story? He wasn't a vengeful man, but he wanted to resurrect Brenda and wreak vengeance on her for what she had done to her daughter. What did he think about Tate herself? He thought she had shown more courage in her short life than almost anyone he'd ever known. What did he think of the sweep of her tongue as she licked melted chocolate off her bottom lip?

"The s'more. What do you think of it?" she clarified.

"It tastes like more."

She nodded. "Exactly."

They finished without speaking, although somehow neither of them could stop watching the other. Simon finished first. When Tate had finished hers, he rested his hands on her shoulders and gently tugged her toward him. "Come here."

She was wary. "Why?"

"Because you need this." Before she could pull away he turned her and framed the top of her spine with his thumbs. Gently he began to knead. "You're as tense as a High Ridge lifer before his first appeal."

"If I'm tense, it's because you're doing that."

"Liar."

"The pot calling the kettle black." Despite her best judgment, Tate flopped into place in front of him.

Simon slid his fingers under her collar to get a better grip. Her skin was as soft as he had imagined. "This is like giving an anvil a massage."

"You can't insult an anvil."

"What did Brenda do, after she realized she couldn't get Millard to Little Rock?"

"She took off." Tate let her head drop forward so Simon could knead the muscles in the back of her neck. His fingers stroked along her skin as if he knew just where her tension lay. "She left one morning when Millard was busy somewhere else. She didn't leave him a note, or even an address where he could find her. She just disappeared, and she never contacted him again."

"So he had no way to find you?"

"Millard never knew if Brenda had given birth to his child or had an abortion. Apparently he tried to find her, but she hid herself well."

"And she never told anyone who the father of her baby was?"

"No one. Including the baby. I guess she believed the greatest punishment for Millard would be keeping me from him. He valued family. Every time she was cruel to me, it was almost as good as being cruel to him."

She managed to say the words dispassionately, but she was suddenly feeling anything but. She had been fine until Simon had touched her. Now she felt under siege. She didn't care about her mother. It was old news. She had long ago overcome the problems her mother had left her. Long ago...

Simon felt her shoulders tremble. He wrapped his arms around her and pulled her to rest against him. "Go ahead and cry," he said softly, his lips against her ear.

"There's no reason to cry! Just because I never knew my father...I'm sure he didn't sit around and wonder about me. He was busy—happy, as far as I can tell. He didn't even know if I was alive. He didn't know—"

He held her tighter. "Go ahead."

"This isn't a therapy group, damn it!"

"No, it's something private between two people who care about each other." He kissed her hair. Then, again, "Go ahead."

She felt as if she were strangling. The tears she had shed in the cellar were nothing compared to the torrent threatening now. She tried to shake off Simon's arms, but he held her easily.

"I'd cry for you if I could," he said.

The tears came then. Not a child's tears. Not the hurt tears of the young teen who'd been rejected over and over by a hate-filled mother. The tears were the tears of a woman who had only begun to count the things she had lost.

Simon turned her so that she was crying against his chest. Each of her tears seemed to wash something from him until the defenses that were as much a part of him as his arms and legs were gone. The man beneath was someone he didn't know.

"I don't want to cry!" Tate cried harder.

"I don't want you to. But you have to. And we'll get through it." Simon rested his cheek against her hair and felt her body shake against his. She seemed unbearably precious to him at that moment. She was everything that he'd almost forgotten existed. Courage and vulnerability. Strength and passion. Fire and tears. In his months at High Ridge he had forgotten. Perhaps before those months. Perhaps a long time before.

"I dreamed of my father," she said finally, choking back what was left of her sobs. "I dreamed he would come and take me away. It was a child's dream, but I gave it up once I began living on the streets. If I had only known . . ."

"How did you find out he left you this cabin?"

"Accidentally." She paused until she was able to speak more easily. "Someone from Mountain Glade ran across Brenda before she died. My father was dead, by then, but this man told her Millard had left his place in trust to me—if I existed."

She took a deep breath. Simon's hand was stroking her hair, and she began to relax against him. "My mother told him that she had given birth to Millard's daughter, but she wouldn't help anybody find me. I guess she thought she would make everything as complicated as possible. Will, my father's cousin, was set to inherit this place if I didn't appear sometime in the next ten years. If she'd denied my existence, he would have inherited it right away. As it was, he couldn't inherit, and neither could I, because I didn't know."

"It was too bad your mother couldn't turn her talents to better use."

"Well, at the end she repented. I suppose some might say that counted for something."

"Some might." From his tone it was clear that he wasn't one of them.

"She told Mrs. Phillips that I'd been adopted by Jess Cantrell. Jess is easy to find. The woman wrote him, in care of his publisher, and told him the whole story."

"And here you are." Simon understood so much more than he had before. Tate's story explained her willingness to live a Spartan life-style, but it also explained why she hadn't turned him in to the sheriff at the first opportunity. She had suffered. She knew what it meant not to be given the benefit of the doubt, and in her own way she knew what it was like to be behind bars. Some of her life had been lived outside the law. She had seen firsthand that trust was something to give those who deserved it, not those in positions of authority.

Tate moved far enough back to use the hem of Simon's shirt to wipe her eyes, then she pushed herself away. Reluctantly, he let her go.

"I'll bet you can't wait to get out of here, after that," she said, not meeting his eyes. "You escaped from prison right into a puddle of tears."

"I think I'd take this over High Ridge." He slid his hand under her chin and lifted it. "How old are you?"

"Twenty-one."

"Going on a hundred."

"Thereabouts."

"I'm ten years older than you are."

"Going on two hundred."

He smiled. "Thereabouts."

"The last time I cried like that was the day I asked my mother if I could come home. I was fourteen, and I'd been out on the streets for most of a year."

"Now you've evened it out. You've cried for your father, too."

"Living here had made a difference to me." Her gaze met his. "Of course, then you came along."

She was trying to look cynical, but she only managed wounded.

"I came along." He told himself not to reach for her again. Kissing her would be like taking candy from a baby. She needed to be kissed, needed to know how desirable she was, but he wasn't the one to do it. He had nothing to give her. His life was barely worth the few cents' value of the minerals in his body.

He kissed her, anyway. The kiss was neither impulse nor compulsion. He kissed her because nothing was ever certain, and because sometimes more damage came from denial than acceptance. She didn't protest. She moved into the kiss with the passion of a novitiate pleading for grace.

His hands settled at her waist, and his fingers stroked the flesh under her shirt. She pressed closer to him, draping her arms over his shoulders, and her lips parted. Desire, so intense it had no name, knifed through him. He clutched her tighter, and his hands slid higher.

Tate felt the warmth of their bodies fuse, until they no longer seemed separate but became two souls entwined by passion and compassion. Simon was no longer a stranger, no longer someone to be feared. He was part of her, in some way she didn't understand. His struggle was hers; her sadness, his. She explored the taste of him, the heat of him, without fear, and she exulted in the feel of his fingers moving against her skin.

Simon knew the exact moment when choice would no longer be theirs. There was a small part of him that watched, whose voice counseled him to pull back, to protect himself and the woman in his arms. That voice had saved his life more than once, but it only whispered now.

A whisper was enough. He pulled his mouth from hers and pushed her head to his shoulder. "We're asking for more than we can handle."

She felt as if he was asking her to return to a place she could never go again. "I wasn't asking for anything."

He cupped her face in his hands. "We were *both* asking. I want you. I feel like lightning just struck. But I've still got half the state of Arkansas on my tail. I'll go down fighting, but I'll probably go down, anyway. I don't want to be worrying about you when I do."

She stared at him, trying to find a way behind the shield he had erected. "You can't hide from me," she said finally. "You heard my life story. I live in the same shadows you do. Even if you weren't a wanted man, you wouldn't want this."

"This?"

"You walk alone. So do I. You act like you're not afraid of anything, but walking with me would scare you to death."

"I don't walk. I run, even when no one is after me."

She knew how many of his defenses he had breached to admit that. "You're afraid because I might keep up with you."

"I'm afraid for both of us."

She took a deep breath and released it slowly. "You know why I run, but you haven't told me why you do."

He smoothed back her hair and wished this could be easier. "My story's not as straightforward as yours."

"Nothing about you is straightforward."

He admired her. With the firelight flickering over her features and her lips still moist from his kiss, he thought her the most intriguing woman he had ever seen. But more than her physical beauty intrigued him. He was taken with her courage, her determination to make sense of a senseless situation, her commitment to him, despite all the reasons why she should push him away.

He could fall in love with her. He, who had believed that love was something a fugitive never found.

He tried to explain. "I always knew who *my* parents were. They're dead now, but not a day went by in childhood that I wasn't reminded of exactly who I was. I was born on the Hudson, on an estate established before the Revolution. Like all my ancestors, I was educated in England and the Netherlands. My blood's bluer than your jeans, and I'm on the charts of two royal families."

"That explains your accent."

He smiled briefly, and said a silent thanks that she was not easy to impress. "I speak five languages, four of them fluently. I had to be able to do the royal honors, just in case dozens of people were wiped out simultaneously and I was suddenly sitting on a throne somewhere."

"King Simon?" She considered. "Hard to imagine."

"Do you like this story better than my others?"

"Let's hear the rest of it."

"There's not much to it. I was expected to be someone I couldn't be, someone quietly, absurdly aristocratic. Instead I nourished myself on stories of my grandfather. He was a hero during the Second World War, responsible for rescuing hundreds of Jews and smuggling them from the Netherlands safely to Sweden, right under Nazi noses. He died for it, but that didn't worry me. I wanted to be my grandfather. So when I was approached at Oxford to do some espionage for a European government, I accepted."

"And your parents?"

"Didn't know. I'm not sure they ever suspected. They only knew I wasn't the son they'd wanted."

"Did you become a hero?"

He brooded over the question for a moment. "I've done some things I'm proud of, and I've never taken an assignment I didn't believe in. But I suppose somewhere along the way I discovered that you can't work at being a hero. Heroes don't get paid."

There were so many thing he hadn't said, but Tate understood them, anyway. She could picture the little boy of diluted royal blood, who could never please his ambitious parents. She could picture the young man who had chosen his own destiny, but could never please himself. And still he ran, a fugitive from the ordinary, with no place to go.

"Will you keep trying to be a hero until you die of it?" she asked, leaning closer to him, as if to hear his answer.

"I'm about to die of it, now! I could have died already if I'd detoured one cabin or two."

"Don't feed me that line about how your life was saved by coming here. You're much too ruthless to die and much too determined to live. Maybe you don't feel like a hero, but you don't hate what you do, either. You're scared I might get in your way."

His fingers threaded through her hair, but not gently. He wanted to hold her there, to make her face the truth. "I would hurt you. You're much more vulnerable than you think. Just let go of this now. We feel something for each other, but it ends here. I'm leaving tomorrow for Memphis."

"You heard the dogs today. You'll be caught if you try."

"I can't stay here forever!"

"Then let me take you to Memphis myself." She covered his lips with a finger, when he began to protest. Her eyes sparkled angrily. "No, hear me out. Give me a chance, Simon! I've thought this over carefully. Tomorrow night, after dark, we'll leave in my Bronco. I'll load the back with stuff from the barn, and we'll pack you in between so nobody can see you. It won't be comfortable, but it'll be safe. When we get to Memphis, I'll make contact with Aaron. I'll do it any way you say, but any way I do it will be safer than if you go alone."

He covered her hands and pulled them to his lap. "I won't involve you any more."

"Any more is right! You've already involved me up to my earlobes. Do you think I'm just going to let you hop out the back door, while I suffer here never knowing if you made it to Memphis alive? You picked my cabin to break into. It was my head you almost shot off, and my bed you handcuffed me to. Now you've got to let me help you one more time."

"Did you hear what you just said?"

"Simon!"

He wondered if he had already fallen in love with her. He wanted nothing more than to take her back in his arms and overwhelm her with the feelings erupting inside him.

It would be safer for them both if she drove him to Memphis, instead.

"I'll have Cooney's gun with me. If I'm found in your car you can say you were forced to drive me," he said.

She nodded. "There's a condition attached. After this has ended, when you're safe again, you'll come back here so I'll know."

"And if I don't?"

"Then I suppose I'll worry for the rest of my life." She hesitated for just a moment. "Or else I'll have to find Josiah Gallagher and see what he can tell me."

"Don't ever go to Gallagher! Do you understand?"

"I'd go to the devil himself, if I had to!"

He groaned and pulled her toward him for one more kiss. It tasted like desperation and regret. Then, before they could mire themselves more deeply, he pushed her away and got to his feet.

Tate watched the bedroom door close behind him.

Chapter 10

The next morning the hounds were closer. Tate knew the precise moment they began to bay, if not their precise location.

The night had seemed eternal, each minute gaining seconds until she was sure the sun would never rise again. And now it had, to light the forests and fields of the sleepy Ozark countryside, so that the men hunting Simon could close in on their prey.

She sat up in bed, pushing the quilt around her waist as she peered out the window behind her. From this perch in the loft she could see far into the surrounding hills. But not far enough. It was still too dark, and perhaps—if they were lucky—the dogs were still too distant.

"So you heard them, too."

Startled, she gasped, turning to find Simon materializing out of the shadows at the top of the steps. She reached for the blanket and tucked it under her arms.

"Sorry, if I startled you." He limped across the loft and dropped to the bed beside her. "Have you seen anything?"

He sat casually, as if he weren't the same man who had haunted her thoughts and dreams through the long night. He was wearing a pair of her father's jeans and a shirt, buttoned just partway, as if covering himself had been an afterthought. His hair was rumpled and his face shadowed with the night's growth of beard.

He shouldn't have looked so desirable. The clothes were too large, and he seemed paler than he had the day before. Yet everything about him called out to something long dormant inside her. And newly awakened, the feeling refused to be silenced.

She turned back to the window. Whatever she felt was less important than reality, and reality dictated reason and objectivity. Simon's life was in danger. Everything had to be that simple, and that complex. She spoke, without looking at him again. "I haven't seen anything. But they sound like they're coming closer."

"Do you always sleep bundled up like an Eskimo, or is that because I'm in the house?"

She was wearing nothing more than a knit undershirt with lacy straps and a pair of bikini pants. His voice had dripped with irony. "You give yourself too much credit," she said, still not facing him.

The sight of her, tousled and rosy from the cool morning air, was quickly heating Simon's blood. He wanted to reach for her, but even as his hands lifted he heard the baying of the hounds. His hands fell to his lap, and he knotted them into fists. "I think if I was going to be in the house much longer, we'd find another way for you to sleep."

She turned from the window. "Promises, promises."

Simon watched her hair glide across her cheek as she tossed her head. Her sensuality was as natural as some women's was rehearsed. He doubted she knew what she was doing to him. Reluctantly, he turned to the window. "They are getting closer. If they continue in this direction, they'll be here before noon."

"How can you tell?"

"Wind velocity, sound waves bouncing off the mountainsides, the number of dogs multiplied by the number of trees between here and the river."

"You're making that up."

"Right."

It was surprisingly easy to discuss Simon's situation, much easier than talking about themselves and their relationship had been the night before. Especially when he wasn't gazing at her. "What if the dogs catch your scent once they're on this property? Even if you're in the cellar, someone might know enough about the cabin to look there. I'm surprised the sheriff didn't find it yesterday."

"You may be able to keep them from catching my scent."

"How?"

"What do you clean house with?"

The question seemed irrelevant, but Tate knew enough about Simon to answer. "Something cheap that was here when I came."

"Know what's in it?"

"Ammonia, mostly. It burns my eyes when I use it."

"Perfect."

"What are you talking about?"

"About ammonia. Those bloodhounds are mostly for show, right now. They haven't picked up my scent because the trail's too old, and it's rained since I've been in the woods."

"But you have been outside. You've been on the back porch."

"I've been farther. I've taken the trail to the outhouse."

"I knew I'd find a sterling excuse to get indoor plumbing."

"Both porches and the outhouse entrance could use a good swabbing down this morning." He turned back to her. "Ammonia will ruin a dog's nose faster than anything. Mix up a bucket ten times stronger than you usually clean with, pour some on the porches and the ground around the outhouse. One sniff and the dogs won't be much good for a while."

She smiled a little. "How do you learn these things?"

"What do you think the men at High Ridge talk about at night?"

"Women?"

"And escape."

"You must be their hero."

"Let's see if we can keep it that way." Simon stood, forcing himself to ignore the pain shooting through his leg. He wasn't going to tell Tate that he had awakened earlier to find the bandage covering his wound wet with blood. Until he was safely in Memphis, his leg was the least of his worries.

She stood, too, draping the blanket sari-style around her. Simon thought any other woman would have looked silly, but she somehow managed it with grace.

From her shoulders to her toes Tate was covered against the cold, but the blanket didn't provide the barrier she wished for. She had slept little that night, knowing Simon was only a cabin's length away. Early this morning, she had begun to believe she had imagined the pleasure of his kisses.

Now she knew imagination had nothing to do with it. She had only rarely indulged in romantic fantasies; now she knew she had outgrown them completely. Simon was no fantasy. He was a man she never could have conjured up from a dream, because he was altogether too human and desirable.

She wanted to comb her fingers through his morning-rumpled hair, button his flannel shirt against the cold, stroke his beard-roughened cheeks. She wanted to kiss him, to savor the warmth of his lips and body against hers.

But there would be no savoring. As a child she had sometimes glimpsed the lives that others led: the special bond between mothers and daughters, the joy of piggyback rides on daddies' broad backs, the jokes and laughter of families around dinner tables. Now she felt as if she was once again being given a glimpse of what others had, the satisfaction of reaching for a man and finding his arms reaching out in return, the fulfillment of sharing lives, the ecstasy of sharing bodies.

Once again those simple human pleasure were out of her reach.

"I have a head start," Simon said. "I could be out of here in five minutes. You don't have to do another thing for me."

She realized he had no idea what she was really thinking. How could he believe she wanted him gone, wanted the complication of him out of her life, when the opposite was true? "Don't you know I'd do almost anything to keep you safe?"

"You looked so sad."

She risked just a little of what she was feeling. "Sometimes I think I'm on a carousel. I see everything I want, only it's standing just out of my reach on the ground, watching, while I go round and round...." She smiled to take the sadness from her words. "Someday I think I'm going to throw myself off, no matter how fast it's going. It might be worth the risk."

He groaned and pulled her against him, although every bit of caution he possessed told him not to. "You're too young to know what you want. You don't need a man like me in your life."

"I haven't been that young in a long time." Tate lifted her face to his. "I'm not asking you for anything, not to stop the carousel or even to catch me."

"You want me to remember you."

"You will."

As his lips took hers, hungrily, possessively, he knew she was right.

The dogs searched around the edges of Tate's property for most of the morning. She could gauge their location by their occasional blood-curdling howls. Once she heard a car on the road to her cabin, but either it turned or stopped midway, because no one appeared.

With Simon relegated to the cellar after a quick breakfast, she began her "chores." She had thoroughly mopped both back and front porches and deluged the path to the outhouse with cleaning solution, when she caught sight of two men on the hill above her house. They had three dogs between them. She dumped her bucket down the front steps and began to mop, watching them zigzag closer.

When they were close enough to see her, she waved.

One of the men waved back, then, leading two of the dogs, he came down the hill.

Even from a distance Tate could see that one of the dogs was a real bloodhound. The other was a mutt that resembled Cinn. As if he were aware of the kinship, Cinn—who had deserted the house the moment Simon disappeared into the cellar—dragged himself out from under her Bronco to investigate.

"I just hope their IQs are on a par with yours," Tate muttered as Cinn ambled past. The dog didn't spare her a glance.

"Mornin', miss." The young man leading the dogs waved again as he moved closer. His moon-shaped face wasn't familiar to her, but his uniform was. She wondered how High Ridge was keeping the rest of its inmates from escaping, when all the prison personnel were out searching for Simon.

"Morning. The sheriff said you might be stopping by today or tomorrow. I guess you haven't found your man yet." Tate leaned on her mop and watched Cinn introduce himself to the other dogs.

"Not yet. Found some more evidence he's been nearby, though."

"Oh? I didn't think anything exciting ever happened around here."

"You haven't seen anything?"

"Not a thing."

The young man's gaze was openly admiring. "You don't live here alone, do you?"

"I like it that way," she said pointedly.

"Mind if I check around the house?"

"Be my guest." Tate watched men and dogs approach. Both dogs had their noses to the ground. The man on the other end of their leashes was too busy gaping at her to pay them much attention. He looked up, though, when the bloodhound began to howl.

"What the . . . ?" He watched the dogs dance around the edges of the puddle at the bottom of the steps; then he knelt and scooped up a handful of mud. "Jeez, what's this?"

Tate attempted to look perplexed. "What's the problem?"

"This smells like pure ammonia!"

"I've been mopping, getting ready for the winter. I had birds nesting in the eaves of both porches, and you know what a mess they can make."

The man stood and jerked both dogs backward. "Well, if we were going to find anything around here, we sure can't now."

She continued to look perplexed. "Just because I've been cleaning? I didn't wash the whole outdoors."

"Ammonia'll wipe out a dog's sense of smell!"

"No..." She changed her expression to stunned. "I never knew that. Listen, don't take them down behind the house, then. I was scrubbing up around the outhouse, too."

The young man was obviously disgusted. "It's too late to worry. These two couldn't find a skunk in a toolshed, now. It'll be tomorrow before they're good for much."

Stunned progressed to contrite. "What a shame. I'm sorry. Really."

"We'll keep the other dog away from the house."

She shrugged. "Hope you have some luck. I don't like the idea of a convict hanging around here."

"Oh, if he's around, we'll find him. We've even set up roadblocks on some of the major routes out of here."

She made a mental note not to take any major roads tonight. "We're all glad you're working so hard." As she watched, he pulled the dogs around and started back toward the hill.

He called over his shoulder, "You hear anything or see anything, you give the sheriff a call. Don't take any chances."

She thought of all the chances she had already taken. The young man would be amazed.

She found more outdoor chores to do until the men were out of sight. Then she went inside and tapped on the bedroom floor. In a few moments Simon was beside her.

"They were here. They've gone." She told him about the ammonia.

He didn't spare a smile. "They'll be back."

"Why? They didn't find anything. I think you're safe now, safer than you'd be out on the roads, anyway. He said they're setting up roadblocks on the major routes out of here. If you stay for a few more days, they'll move on and it'll be safer to leave."

"Those guys were just the beginning. Gallagher's going to be along right behind them. And Gallagher's immune to tricks."

A shudder passed through Tate. "I'm going to put more wood on the fire. You'd better stay out of sight until it's dark and I can draw the curtains."

"I need Cooney's gun and holster."

"What for?"

"I'm going to make a shoulder holster to wear under my jacket."

She stared at him, but she knew nothing she could say would change his mind. "I'm sure you know where they are."

"I just didn't want you to be surprised when you found them gone."

"Nothing surprises me anymore." She watched him limp to the closet and dig under a pile of her father's clothing. "Simon, is your leg worse?"

"Don't worry about my leg."

"How are you going to fight off the bad guys...?" She paused. "Or is it the good guys?"

He straightened, the gun and holster in hand. "I don't want you worrying about me. Understand?"

"Fine. Great. I'll just pretend you were never here."

"That would be best for both of us." He stared at her and allowed not a flicker of feeling to show. "I never *was* here. You never saw me, never took care of me. You never kissed me. I'm nothing to you, because I never existed."

"Then why am I driving to Memphis tonight?"

"It's not too late to change your mind."

She was frustrated and hurt. Perhaps he could forget everything that had passed between them, but she couldn't. Not that easily. "Of course I'm not going to change my mind. But while you're still here, can't we at least be honest about our feelings?"

"It won't do either of us any good. You won't see me again after tonight."

"You said you'd come back when this was over!"

"No, you said you wanted me to." Simon looked up from the gun, which he had unloaded. "This was a dream. I'm not real. You can't call a dream back, Tate. It turns into a nightmare."

She wanted to curse him; she wanted to beg. Worse than either, she wanted to tell him she knew he was right. What reason was there to believe that something could come of their time together? It had been built on isolation and danger. What chance would they have in the real world, where day followed day and what to have for supper assumed paramount importance? No woman could hold a man such as Simon. No woman should want to.

"How will I know if you're all right?" she asked at last, trying not to sound as if she was pleading. "I deserve to know that much."

"I'll be sure you know."

Her face was as carefully blank as his. "Thanks." She had one foot over the threshold before she added, "You'll need some sandwiches to take with you, and some money. I'll get them together. I think we should leave as soon as the sun goes down, in case we have to take back roads the whole way to Memphis."

"I'll be ready."

"I'm going to make a run into town in a little while and see if I can discover which roads are blocked and which aren't. I've got some things to buy for the garden that'll make good cover for you tonight. I'll buy you some sturdy boots, if you give me your size."

Simon stared after her when she had gone. He believed everything he had told her. So why did he feel the same way he had the day he realized that Josiah Gallagher was never going to spring him from High Ridge?

By six the sky was dark. Tate fixed sandwiches to eat on the road, as well as some for Simon to take with him. She had seen little of him until sunset, but when she came in from hauling water to the back porch, he was dressed and ready to go. The gun was nowhere in sight, but she imagined it was close at hand in case he needed it.

He was wearing a clean flannel shirt topped with a blue, much-mended sweater and a khaki windbreaker. He was a tall man, but he still had been forced to roll up the cuffs on a pair of her father's jeans. Luckily, that never seemed to go out of style.

"I found these in a drawer." Tate handed Simon a pair of wire-rimmed spectacles. "They're not strong. They shouldn't bother your eyes." She watched as he slipped them on. He really didn't resemble the trial photographs of Carl Petersen, any more—if he ever had. But then, Josiah Gallagher wasn't looking for Carl Petersen.

"Where's your car?" he asked.

"I parked it out front. I thought I should go out first, then if it looks safe, I'll start to whistle. You can come out and get right in the back. I'll pack sacks around you."

"Sacks?"

"I told you I was going to the feed store. I bought some things to work into the garden to get it ready for next spring. And I got corn for the geese, birdseed for the winter."

"You sound like you're staying."

"I'm a long way from knowing what I'll be doing." She hadn't really looked at him as they'd talked. Now she did. "But I'll be here a while. Drop me a postcard."

"So you and everyone in town will know I'm all right?"

"Then make it a letter. They did teach you to write at Oxford, didn't they?"

Despite himself, he smiled. "I could probably piece together a sentence or two."

"We'd better get going." She started toward the door, but he caught her arm before she'd gone more than a few feet.

Her eyes fell to the fingers gripping her. They were long and tapered, almost deceptively slender. They were also as powerful as the handcuffs he had once forced her to wear. She stared at them and, finally, at him.

Their eyes said everything their voices couldn't. He pulled her close, like a man who had just lost a battle with himself. His hands framed her face, and his thumbs traced her eyelids, her nose, her cheekbones, before dipping lower. He caressed her bottom lip. She felt tears rising, and it was all she could do not to plead with him to stay.

He lowered his head and took her mouth with his. She circled his neck with her arms and rose to press herself against him. His lips demanded everything, as if he were absorbing the very essence of her to take with him.

How could something that felt so gloriously simple be so hideously complicated? The kiss should be a prelude, not a postlude. She struggled to get closer to him, to let her body, her lips, her hands, tell him what he had come to mean to her. For just a moment she believed he knew and that somehow, someday, he would find a way to come back to her. Then, abruptly, he pushed her away. His eyes glittered, but somehow, his feelings were still masked. Slowly he shook his head.

Tate stared at him, all too aware that her heart was exposed for him to see. "Go with God," she said at last. Then she started toward the front door.

The moon glowed behind angel-hair clouds. The night was a perfect one for secrets. Tate slammed down the backseat and juggled sacks in the rear of the Bronco. If Simon had to leave, it was best to get it over with quickly. When the wagon was ready and she was as sure as she could be that no one was watching, she swallowed hard and began to whistle.

She didn't even know that Simon had left the house, until he was climbing in the back of her car. The moment he was stretched out, she pushed a blanket toward him. He covered himself, and she began to pile sacks around him. When she was finished, the back of the wagon looked as if it belonged to a farmer, and nothing more. Unless it was closely scrutinized, no one would suspect that she carried a fugitive under the sacks of bonemeal and dried blood, sand and peat moss.

"Can you breathe?" she asked softly.

"Enough to keep me alive."

That was hardly reassuring, but Tate knew it would have to do. "Then we're off."

"Stay on the back roads."

She fought down her fear for him. "No kidding." She slammed the back door and started around the car. In a minute she was pulling up the drive toward the main road.

There were a variety of routes into Mountain Glade, although only one, Kalix Road, was well traveled. The others were variations of cow paths. Tate chose a meandering dirt road that followed the twists and turns of the river. She had taken it before, when she was in the mood for a scenic drive. Once—in a rainstorm—she had needed every bit of power and four-wheel-drive agility her wagon possessed, to make it over the mud-slick ruts. There was no storm tonight, however, not unless she counted the one raging inside her. There was only a hazy night sky and the light of a three-quarter moon.

There had been no one on the road earlier that day. The route was little used and little known. She had found it, by accident, because it cut across a corner of her land. Only later, where it joined another more-traveled road, would they be in any danger of detection.

Tate winced every time she hit a bump. The road was bad enough from the front seat, but she could imagine Simon's discomfort with fifty-pound sacks bouncing on top of him. She navigated carefully, particularly where the road began to edge up the mountainside. The road twisted and curled, a red clay gash in the midst of a pine-and-poplar forest. She shifted into second gear as she climbed higher.

Around one corner she could see the sparse lights of Mountain Glade. The view was to be her excuse, if she was stopped and questioned about why she was out on this road at night. Of course, an excuse wouldn't do her any good if the car was searched. Simon had told her to say he had threatened to kill her if she didn't cooperate with his escape. She wondered if anyone would believe that a man encased in fifty-pound sacks was dangerous.

The road wrapped around the mountainside once more, and she followed it slowly, the lights of Mountain Glade disappearing behind her. The lights appearing just beyond the next bend were a sobering surprise. So was the barking piercing the clear night air.

She began to whistle ferociously, and she took her foot off the accelerator so that the car, which had already been nearly crawling, almost came to a halt. From the rear of the car she heard a muffled, "Roadblock?"

"Yes."

"Don't hit your brakes. They'll know something is wrong."

She couldn't turn to see what Simon was doing. She was whistling and praying silently, until each shrill note seemed to be aimed straight for heaven. She was close enough now that she could see lanterns in the hands of the men standing on each side of a wooden barricade. They were waving them up and down to warn her to stop.

From behind her she heard a click. Nothing more. She knew the sound. Simon had gone out the rear door. On one side of her was a cliff, almost a sheer drop-off. On the other was the bleak wall of a mountain. She knew which side he must have chosen.

She prayed that he hadn't been seen, hadn't been injured, hadn't been killed. She prayed the wind wouldn't turn and blow his scent in the direction of the dogs. She prayed she would find a story good enough to explain why the dogs went wild when they smelled the inside of her car. If she didn't, the dogs could be turned loose—she would be turned in to the sheriff.

She reached the barricade much quicker than she wished, but she wasted time by rolling down the window at a leisurely pace. "Tell me you haven't stopped me for speeding." She gave the good-looking young officer at her door a tooth-jarring smile. He was not in High Ridge uniform. She guessed he was a state trooper.

He ignored the smile and the joke. "License."

She reached for her purse and pulled out her wallet, handing it over to him. "Is there a problem, officer?"

He didn't answer. "This says Virginia. You're a long way from Virginia, lady."

"I'm here temporarily, living just off the river. That way." She pointed over the mountainside.

He handed back the wallet, after making notes. "Registration?"

She got it from the glove compartment and gave it to him.

"What are you doin' out here tonight?" he asked, as he handed it back.

"I'm on my way into town. I like this road because the view is so pretty just around that bend back there. I come up here sometimes at night, just to see the lights."

"Do you know there's an inmate from High Ridge on the loose?"

"I know he's on the loose somewhere. He's probably in Timbuktu by now, don't you think?"

"What do you have back there?"

Tate wanted badly to swallow, but the trooper was watching everything she did. "Birdseed, fertilizer for my garden."

"I thought you said you were here temporarily."

"I haven't decided for sure. My father died. I'm here settling his estate."

"You won't mind if we check what you have?"

"Of course not. But would you mind telling me why?"

"You a lawyer or something?"

She was beginning to get angry, and anger might distort her good sense. She was about to need all the sense she had. "No, just a citizen," she said, with forced calm. "One who believes in the Bill of Rights and the Constitution."

"I told you, there's an inmate loose. We think he might be tryin' to escape by car, maybe with help. Now, are you gonna let us check, or are you gonna make us get a warrant, all official-like?"

"I said you could check. I just asked why."

The trooper said something to his partner on the other side of the car. Then Tate's heart dropped as the man gave a shrill whistle. From just beyond the barricade she saw another trooper leading a pack of dogs.

"The back locked?" the first trooper asked.

"I'm not sure." Tate turned around and saw that the lock wasn't engaged. "No. You can get in without the key."

"How about steppin' outside while we do?"

"There's not much room over there."

"Then slide on over and get out the other door."

Tate knew protesting was no use. Awkwardly she hitched her legs over the gearshift and moved to the next seat. Then she got out and stood beside the door.

The dogs might be the same basic species as Cinn, but they snarled and snapped as they passed her. If Cinn had possessed even a drop of their temper, he would have eaten Simon before he had broken into her cabin.

"Stay out of their way," the second trooper said unnecessarily.

"Good advice." Tate watched the trooper who had interviewed her start toward the back of the car. He opened the door and peered inside, while the trooper with the dogs held them several yards away. But at the first whiff of the car's interior, the dogs began to emit ear-splitting howls.

Tate widened her eyes innocently. "What a racket."

The trooper moved closer to her. "Any reason they should be barking?"

She shrugged. "They're your dogs. I don't know anything about them."

"They bark when they smell what they're trained to smell."

"They're dogs. Dogs bark at everything."

"Mind if we rearrange your load?" the trooper in the back asked.

"Just don't make it too hard for me to get everything out."

He was already piling sacks toward the front of the Bronco. The dogs were going wild. Tate prayed that Simon had left nothing behind to incriminate her. As it was, she was certain she had a long night of questioning ahead.

"Damn!"

Tate closed her eyes briefly, and wondered what Krista would say when she got to make her one phone call.

"Well, that's why they're barkin'." The trooper waved the man with the dogs back. Then he slammed the door and started around the car. "You got a sack of dried blood back there's been ripped open. Smells like a damned slaughterhouse to those dogs. Probably thought they were in for a feast."

For a minute Tate had nothing to say. She knew the sack hadn't been ripped when she covered Simon with it. In the few seconds he'd had to escape, he had thought of everything.

Where was he now?

"You go on ahead," the trooper continued. "Just stay off the roads for the next couple of days unless you want to be searched again. We're gonna get this no-good and get him soon, if we have to stop every car in the county."

Tate bit back every incriminating reply that came to mind. "Hope it warms up a bit for you," she said instead. Then, with a careless wave, she walked around to the other side of the car, forcing herself not to look over the mountainside, and slid carefully into her seat, rolling up her window once she was settled.

She started the engine and waited for the barricade to be pushed aside. When the road was clear she began to creep forward, but at the last minute the trooper who had checked her license waved her to a stop again. She felt ill. She had almost pulled off the deception.

He strolled around to her side and motioned for her to roll down her window once more. Her hand trembled, but she forced herself to take as long as possible.

"You stay in Arkansas," he said, when they were eye-to-eye once more, "and you'd better get an Arkansas license. You hear? Next time, somebody's gonna write you a ticket. And it might just be me."

Chapter 11

There were no more roadblocks on the road into Mountain Glade. Tate's intention had never been to visit town, but now she didn't want to arouse suspicion by turning around and going right back home. Simon was somewhere on a mountainside, struggling to make his way to Memphis. She had to protect him in the only way she could, even if that meant spending an agonizing hour in Mountain Glade.

She parked in front of the café and momentarily rested her forehead on the steering wheel. Where was Simon right now? Had he survived the dive from her wagon? She was helpless to do anything more than stay in town and look busy for a little while. There was no one she could safely alert, no way she could search for him.

No one she could safely alert.

She straightened and turned to stare at the sign in front of Allen's Pharmacy. There *was* someone she could alert. She had Aaron Reynolds's phone number. She could call him and tell him that Simon was on his way. His phone might be tapped, but if she only stayed on the line a moment, if she asked him to go to another phone where she could call him right back, they could safely have a conversation, couldn't they?

She knew her head wasn't as clear as it could be. She was worried sick about Simon and suffering the aftereffects of the encounter at the roadblock. But she couldn't just sit back and do nothing. Simon was alone somewhere in these mountains, fighting to stay alive. She had to do what she could, *anything* she could.

And besides, what difference did it make now if someone traced the call to Mountain Glade? Obviously the authorities believed Simon was in this area, anyway. What was one more piece of evidence?

Convinced that calling Aaron was the right thing to do, she got out of the car and headed into the pharmacy. Allen's was surprisingly busy, with half a dozen customers blocking the aisle leading to the telephone. Tate hoped they would entertain each other and Wally, and leave her to have her conversation with Aaron in privacy.

She knew so little about how a telephone was tapped or a call traced that she wasn't even sure how to take precautions. She did suspect, though, that using the Stagecoach Inn credit card might make Josiah Gallagher's job easier. So she bought a candy bar with a ten-dollar bill and begged the high-school student at the pharmacy counter for some of her change in coins. Then, after a few words of greeting to a harried Wally, she went to the telephone.

She couldn't seem to stop shaking, and lecturing her body to halt its flood of adrenaline didn't make any difference. She settled for dialing Aaron's number with an icy, trembling hand.

The number rang once. She remembered the last call she had made for Simon. Then she hadn't been sure that she wasn't being taken in by an expert liar. *The number rang twice.* She remembered how surprised she had been to hear Simon's recorded voice. *The number rang a third time.* She remembered how surprised she had been when she had realized that call was being traced.

And what if that trace had been completed? What if one of the people crowding Allen's Pharmacy, even now, was a buddy of Josiah Gallagher's? What if he or she was watching her at this moment—had been watching a moment ago, as she dialed?

As the number continued to ring she turned to investigate the people closest to her. None of them was familiar, but all looked as if they belonged there. One old man was bent, as if with arthritis, and his hands were leather-tough and stained. A young woman had a toddler in a stroller beside her. Another man had the baby-soft cheeks of a recent high-school graduate.

The number rang again. She had lost count by now. What would she do if Aaron wasn't home? Allen's would be closing soon. Should she drive to the next town and call again? What if Simon found his way back to her cabin and she wasn't there?

Hysteria was as foreign to her as waking in a lover's arms, but she recognized the feeling as it welled inside her. She took a deep breath and tried to force the hysteria away. The number rang again.

And then a voice spoke.

"Hello."

Tate was not so overwrought that she couldn't tell the difference between a man and a woman. "Hello," she answered, as softly as she dared. "I'd like to speak to Aaron Reynolds, please. This is an emergency."

There was a short silence. "Who is this?" the woman asked.

"I can't say. Please, may I just speak to Mr. Reynolds? It's very important."

Tate thought she heard a sigh, and then, "I don't know who you are, but obviously you haven't heard."

Tate waited, counting the seconds that ticked by, seconds that would make tracing her call easier.

The woman spoke again. "I'm Sylvie Reynolds, Aaron's wife. Aaron was killed several months ago," the woman said at last. There was no sorrow in her voice, just acceptance. "In a break-in at the store."

"No!"

"I'm sorry, but it's true. It's lucky that you got me at all. I'm in the middle of a move, and the telephone is going to be disconnected tomorrow."

Tate tried to hang on to her good sense. "You're moving?" She imagined Simon making his way to Memphis, only to be greeted by an empty house and the ghost of the one man he could have trusted.

"The van comes tomorrow." Sylvie paused. "Who is this?" she asked gently. "Are you a friend of Aaron's? Someone he worked with?"

"No." Tate wished she could say more, but she knew it wasn't safe. "I'm sorry to hear about your husband. I'm sorry I troubled you." She hung up before the other woman could answer.

Aaron was dead. Dead, and Simon was blindly seeking his help.

She wanted to cry. Instead, for the benefit of anyone watching, she casually flipped open the coin return on the telephone, as if hoping to find change, then strolled out of the store, stopping twice to price items on the shelves.

Outside, she debated heading straight to her cabin or wasting time at the Sassafras. She settled for ordering coffee and pie at the café counter, forcing herself to linger over a second cup to lessen her chances of looking suspicious.

"Cold out there, ain't it?"

Tate had been so deep in thought that she hadn't even realized the stool next to hers was now occupied. She turned to find the baby-faced man from the pharmacy. Coffee turned to acid in her throat. The man's words were down-home Southern, but to her suspicious ear, his accent was distinctly East Coast.

She swallowed more than the coffee. She swallowed fear. "It's usually cold in the fall."

"You're not from around here, are you?"

She raised one brow. "Are you?"

"I been here a while."

"I've been here a while, too."

"Do you like it?"

"What's not to like?"

"My name's Ben Kinney."

She'd just bet it was. Tate fished around in her purse for a couple of dollars and anchored them under her plate. "It's been nice talking to you, Ken."

"Ben. Ben Kinney."

"Right."

"You never told me yours."

"Right." She stood. "See you around." She was gone before he had a chance to answer.

There was no time in Tate's memory when she had felt so helpless. Even as a runaway, she had felt some sense of control over her own life. And in the worst moment of that life, Jess and Krista had been there to turn to when she could no longer handle her problems alone. Now there was no one to help her, and nothing she could do. She was compelled to wait for events to unfold by themselves. And she knew that she might never know what that unfolding would bring.

Simon was as good as dead to her.

She had taken a different way home from her involuntary trip to town, only to find her cabin empty and the ashes in her fireplace cold. She had busied herself making a new fire, hauling wood and water, coaxing a reluctant Cinn indoors to keep her company, but nothing had taken her mind off Simon.

She had lived almost twenty-two years. The days they had spent together were few in number, only a speck on the time line of her life, but she wasn't going to be able to fool herself into believing that the number of days mattered. She and Simon had lived an adventure together, but that was only a small part of what she felt for him.

She had never expected to fall in love. Love was for warmly nurturing women such as Krista and her sister, Anna. Love was for those who threw themselves into life, not for those who stood along its borders, watching and waiting.

And longing. Hadn't she learned that longing for something was the same as chasing it away?

Now, close to midnight, she sat in front of the fireplace, Cinn an arm's length to her left, and wondered how she could have failed to stop herself from falling in love with a man such as Simon. Perhaps she had even done it on purpose. She had never lived her life the normal way. Why shouldn't it follow that she would fall in love with a man she could never have and shouldn't even want?

Except that she did want him. And in the first hours of the life she would live without him, that knowledge was a jolting pain in the region of her heart.

She was about to bank the fire and crawl in bed for another sleepless night, when she heard a noise outside. If she hadn't been so ready to hear it, so attuned to every sweep of the wind and brushing branch, she never would have noticed. As it was, the shout, quickly chopped off, sounded like an explosion.

She was out on the porch in seconds.

The cobweb clouds that had hidden the stars earlier had solidified as night deepened. The moon, which should have illuminated the woods beyond her house, had been snuffed out. Her eyes adjusted slowly, but even when her pupils were at their widest, she still could see nothing out of the ordinary. Dried leaves blew in widening circles as the wind increased. A nighthawk rose from the limb of a nearby oak and soared overhead, disappearing in a graceful swoop to feast on some unseen forest creature.

She listened intently. From the pond behind the cabin she heard the honking of geese. The wind and trees moaned an atonal duet, but there was no countermelody of a human voice. She wanted to shout Simon's name, but she knew she could not. There were others who could be waiting in the woods.

She thought of her father's shotgun. Millard had shown a definite talent for hiding relics under beds. During her first week in the cabin she had found the ancient shotgun in the top of an old army trunk under the bed in the loft. She had left it there, since she hadn't known any safer place to keep it. Now she was glad she hadn't followed her first inclination and gotten rid of it. If Millard had kept ancient shotgun pellets to go with the gun, she had never found them. But now just the sight of the weapon might be good for something.

A few moments later she stood in the same spot on the porch, Millard's shotgun by her side. Nothing appeared to have changed, yet she sensed a change, anyway. The geese were quiet, and this time Cinn had followed her. He stood beside her, listening.

Just as she was beginning to believe her instincts were playing tricks on her, she heard another shout. She raised the shotgun to her shoulder and braced her leg against the porch railing. "Who's out there?" she shouted.

A figure condensed from the shadows. At first she wasn't even sure it was human. Then, as she watched, she realized it was a man. "Simon," she said softly. She dropped the butt of the gun to the porch and stepped forward.

It was then that she realized the man was not Simon. The man coming toward her, his arms stretched over his head, was Will. The man behind *him* was Simon, and Simon was armed.

Cinn barked in happy recognition. Tate stopped where she was and watched. She didn't know what to say, but she wasn't given a chance to speak, anyway.

"Drop the gun, miss," Simon shouted to her. "Drop it or I'll blow this man's head off."

She was surprised enough to do as he asked. *Miss?*

"Now put your hands over your head."

She did that, too. Beside her, Cinn's tail thumped rhythmically against the porch.

She watched, in silence, as Will came toward her. Simon was limping badly, but he managed to keep pace. The two men were climbing the porch steps before she spoke.

"Will, what's going on?"

Simon answered. "Your friend here was in the wrong place at the wrong time."

"This has gotta be the man who escaped from High Ridge," Will told her. "I saw him crossin' a field when I was out checkin' on my horses."

"And I saw *him* before he saw me." Simon motioned Tate against the porch wall. Then Will. "Now I've seen you both first."

Tate stared at him. Simon's face was covered with scratches, but his expression was as stiff as if it were cast in bronze. He hadn't once looked her in the eye.

"Be careful," Will said softly. "He's desperate."

"Is anybody else home?" Simon asked Tate. He ignored the dog rubbing back and forth against his good leg.

She just stared at him. Then, suddenly, she understood. She would have understood sooner, if she hadn't been so stunned. Simon had not changed into a desperate criminal; he was just putting on a good act. Once again. Only this time, it was for her protection.

"Dog sure likes him," Will observed.

Tate ignored him and spoke to Simon. "Nobody's home but me," she said.

Simon tried to nudge the dog away, but Cinn wouldn't budge. "Is that your car out front, then?"

She knew just what he was leading up to, and she knew she had to stop him. Simon was going to pretend to steal her car and drive to Memphis. Only Memphis was no longer the haven he had hoped for. Aaron was dead, and she was going to have to find a way to tell him.

"You won't get more than a mile down the road in it," she said.

"I'll take my chances."

"There's no place safe for you to go," she said pointedly. "There's no place you could drive it, where you'd be safe."

"I'll take my chances."

"Your record's stuck," she said angrily. "And you're not listening!"

"I don't have time to listen to you, sweetheart. I'm getting out of here right now." Simon motioned Will toward the door. "You go on in. The young lady and I will be right behind you."

For a moment Tate thought that Simon was going to hold her back for a brief conversation, but as soon as Will's back was turned, he motioned for her to follow him. She tried to catch his eye, but he was concentrating on Will.

"You're hurt," she said as she turned. "You won't make it anywhere. Next big city's Memphis, and they'll be looking for you there. You won't get any farther with that leg."

"Move it, sweetheart."

She felt such a surge of frustration that she lost all perspective. Whirling, she almost spat her words at him. "Simon, for God's sake, listen to me! You can't go to Memphis. Aaron's dead. I called there to tell him you were coming, and I talked to his wife. He was killed months ago when somebody broke into his store!"

The pain that twisted his features sent her into his embrace. She pushed his gun aside and wrapped her arms around his waist. "I'm sorry I had to tell you like that," she said, near tears. "But you weren't listening to me. I couldn't let you leave, knowing what I do about Aaron."

He put his arms around her and leaned heavily against her. Somehow she knew that he never cried, and that right now he was as close to breaking down as he would ever be.

"What the hell's goin' on?" Will demanded from behind her.

"Tate, you little fool," Simon said in a shaky voice. "You should have kept quiet!"

"And let you put yourself in danger?"

His arms tightened around her. "It would have been better than this."

"I'm not taking any chances with your life!" She turned to face her cousin. Simon kept his hands around her waist. "Listen, Will, this man is not who you think he is. He's not Carl Petersen, and he's innocent of any crime. He's proved it to me. Now you've just got to take my word for it."

"I don't take nobody's word for nuthin'."

Tate admired his courage. After all, he was the one being held at gunpoint. Despite herself, she also admired his stubbornness. It reminded her of her own.

"That's good thinking," Simon said. "There's not much I can tell you except that I was working for the Justice Department, undercover at High Ridge. I escaped, because something went wrong."

"What do you mean, somethin' went wrong?"

"They left me there too long and I'd learned too much. It was either escape or be killed."

"Killed, at High Ridge?"

Simon gave a curt nod.

"It's true, Will," Tate said. "He was half dead when he found his way here. He's been here since the escape until tonight." She told him of the attempt to get Simon to Memphis. She felt Simon's weight sag against her and knew that whatever reserves of energy he'd had were all used up. "Right now I've got to get him to bed and try to treat his leg."

"No. I've got to get out of here," Simon answered. "Can you keep your cousin here long enough to give me a head start?"

"You can't go anywhere!"

"I don't have a choice. Somebody's going to miss Will. And there'll be a search for him that will lead right here."

Will humphed. "Nobody's gonna miss me, 'cause I'm goin' right back home to get Dovey. She'll fix yer leg. She's a nurse, does most of the fixin' in this part of the county. Good as Dr. Monson. You think I'm too much of a hick to know the difference between a story and the truth? I've got kin workin' at High Ridge. I *know* what goes on there. If the Feds didn't send someone in to investigate, then *that*'d be the crime."

He dismissed Simon with a wave of his hand and turned his attention to Tate. "Now you, girl, I've had some doubts about you, make no mistake about it. You look like yer pa, but I haven't seen no sign of Millard in you. I reckon yer his kid, though. Only a Carter would do anythin' as stupid as this!"

Tate just stared at him, but that didn't deter Will.

"What were you thinkin', keepin' this man here with no help from us?" he demanded. "We're yer family, even if you don't seem to want to claim any of us. Millard was a hermit, but Millard asked for help when he needed it, and gave it back, too. He was family.

You better be more like yer pa if yer plannin' to stay, 'cause if you don't start actin' like a Carter, I'm gonna have to turn you over my knee!"

"Nobody turns me over their knee."

"Which might be half o' what's wrong with you!"

The events of the night had been too much for Tate. She blinked and realized her eyes were wet. "It wasn't that I didn't want to claim you, Will," she said tightly. "It's just that I didn't know how. And I didn't know you wanted me."

"Yer Millard's kid, aren't ya?"

Could it really be that simple? Was that all it took? All the years when she hadn't really felt a part of anything or anyone, she'd had a home and a family waiting for her, just because of one act of passion between her parents?

"I guess you didn't know," Will said gently, when she didn't answer. "But now you do."

She nodded, unable to speak.

"As for you," Will said, turning his attention back to Simon. "Go ahead and shoot me, if you think it'll help, but I'm leavin' now. And I'll be back with my wife, if you don't kill me first. Get off that leg while yer waitin'. Tate, girl, get him ready for Dovey. She'll fix him up, but I doubt it'll be much fun. You might want to give him some of Millard's home brew first."

"*Millard's* home brew?"

"I never did know where he kept it, but I know he always had a supply."

"My father made whiskey?"

"Oh, Millard practiced all kinds of old-time skills." He winked. "A real folklorist, our Millard."

Tate watched Will stroll toward the door. Only a brave man would turn his back on a gun-wielding Simon. Tate reached for Simon's gun and took it from his hand. The door slammed behind Will.

"You're safe with him," she said, turning to face Simon. "He's not going to turn you in."

"I guess I can trust him or I can trust him." A pale Simon lifted her face to his. "I didn't plan on seeing you again."

She rubbed her cheek against his hand. It was icy cold, and she could feel a slight tremor. "I didn't know if you'd survived your dive out of the wagon. I was so worried! And if the wind had been blowing in the other direction, the dogs would have picked up your scent."

"I've been up and down every hillside and hollow between here and the roadblock."

She covered his hands with her own. "I'm so sorry about Aaron."

"Gallagher had him killed."

"No!"

"He ran a security business. No ordinary two-bit burglar could have gotten the drop on Aaron. It had to have been Gallagher's men."

Tate watched him grow paler. The night had taken a terrible toll on his strength. She didn't even want to think what it had done to his leg. She slid his hands to her lips and kissed them. "Let's get you to bed. Lean on me, Simon."

She guided his arm over her shoulder until his hand dangled over her breast. He didn't protest; he was too exhausted to pretend he didn't need her. They moved slowly toward the bedroom. Tate guessed the trip would take them practically as long as it would take Will to reach his house.

"My leg's worse," Simon said unnecessarily.

He was leaning heavily on her, but she welcomed his weight. "I can tell."

"I've got to get away from here. It's only a matter of time until they close in on this cabin."

"Where will you go?"

"North. I'll find a place to stay, until I've got my strength back. Then I'm going after Gallagher."

"But if he's as dangerous as you say he is—"

"I'm just as dangerous!"

Tate had no reason to doubt him.

In the bedroom, Simon lowered himself to the bed. He squeezed her hand, and she knew the simple gesture took most of his remaining strength.

She sat beside him. "Unsnap your jeans, and I'll help you slide them off."

"I can do it myself."

"Don't get modest on me. You were practically naked the first days I took care of you," she reminded him.

"Out!"

Tate knew he needed a moment of privacy. He had to have some time to assimilate everything that had happened. "Then I'll get you something to drink. I don't want you to get dehydrated again." She wrapped her arms around him and gave him a fierce hug before she left the room and closed the door behind her. Ten minutes later she knocked and entered, carrying a glass of tea.

Simon had done as she'd ordered, managing the jeans alone. She lit the bedside lantern. His legs were bare, except for the blood-soaked bandage on his calf. She felt a shudder of foreboding as she gently stripped that off, too. As she'd been afraid, whatever healing had taken place was a thing of the past.

"It's got to be stitched," she said, pressing a clean towel against it. "If it's not, it's just not going to heal. There's nothing else I can do for you. You've got to see a doctor."

"I'm all the doctor we use in these parts, unless he's dyin'." Dovey bustled into the room, followed by Will. "Lord!" She stopped and stared at Simon. Tate wasn't sure it was his leg that interested her so much.

Tate conferred briefly with Dovey, telling her everything she had done. Will lifted the tea Tate had put by the bedside and sniffed, wrinkling his nose in distaste. He left for his car and reappeared a few minutes later with a bottle of Jack Daniels. "Didn't take me seriously, did you, girl?" he chided Tate as Dovey finished her exam. He held out the bottle to Simon. "Drink."

Simon assessed Dovey, who was rummaging through a well-equipped black bag. His gaze settled on Tate, whose face was paler than his own. With a nod to Will, he held out his hand.

Chapter 12

Tate added more logs to the fireplace and watched sparks scatter in iridescent spirals. There seemed little she could do for Simon tonight, other than keep the cabin warm and stay nearby if he needed her. Dovey had tsk-tsked and mumbled over his leg for the better part of an hour, but when she'd finished, the wound was cleaned and stitched, and Simon shot full of antibiotics.

Backbone, and more than a few slugs of whiskey, had gotten him through the operation. Now he was sleeping off the effects.

Or so she'd thought.

"Aaron!"

Tate hurried toward the bedroom. Simon hadn't shouted, but his voice had been loud enough to be heard if anyone was outside his window. She was apprehensive enough, by now, to believe that anything was possible.

She found him tossing restlessly. Memories of the fever and delirium he had suffered in his first days at the cabin came flooding back, and she was horrified. She lit the kerosene lamp by the bedside with trembling hands, then dropped to the bed beside him and touched his shoulder. "Simon," she called softly, "Simon, wake up!"

His hand gripped hers, and before she could brace herself, he had jerked her to the bed beside him. He rose above her and his eyelids snapped open, but his eyes stared right through her.

Tate rested her hand on his shoulder. "It's just me. You're safe. You must have been having a bad dream."

Little by little he seemed to focus. Tate's heart beat faster. At last he fell back against the pillow to stare at the ceiling. His free arm lifted as if to shade his eyes, but not from the moonlight filtering through the window. From the truth. He gripped Tate's hand harder, although she doubted he was aware of it. "Aaron's dead, isn't he?"

"I'm so sorry." Tate rolled to her side so she could watch him. "But you can't think of Aaron now. You've got to think of yourself."

He was silent for a while, but when he spoke it was clear who had filled his thoughts. "Aaron taught me to fish when we were up in Oregon working on the case I told you about. I hadn't fished since I was a little boy, but Aaron bought me enough equipment to catch a whale."

"Simon—"

"He was going to sell his business when he turned sixty and buy a house on a lake somewhere, so he could fish every day. Sylvie was going to weave, and they were both going to entertain their grandkids. He didn't see much of his own kids when they were growing up. He was hoping to make it up to them by being a perfect grandfather."

"It's hard to lose a friend, especially after what Gallagher's done."

"Gallagher." The three syllables were heavy with bitterness. "Aaron made Gallagher fish, too. Gallagher was like a son to him."

"Gallagher's a young man?"

"Not much older than I am."

"Simon, you're not going to..." She paused. She wanted to find a prettier word than avenge—or its soul mate, revenge. "You're not going to go after Gallagher, are you? Your only priority right now has to be your own safety."

"I'll never be safe, until Gallagher's been taken care of."

"What do you mean 'taken care of'?"

He shook off her hand. "It's late. You'd better go to bed."

"Look at me!" Tate held his face in her hands. "This has to stop somewhere, doesn't it? Aaron's dead, and you came a lot too close to death for comfort, yourself. Dovey says your leg's going to be fine now, but if the bullet had passed just inches to the left, the bone would have been shattered. You might have died out in the woods somewhere, trying to drag yourself to safety. At the least, you would have been caught."

He covered her hands and dragged them down to his chest. His eyes were the color of smoke. "This doesn't concern you."

"No?" Slowly she lowered her mouth to his until she was only a whisper away and showed him why it did.

"Go to bed, Tate."

"You concern me." She brushed her lips across his, then back again. "I was terrified all evening, wondering what was happening to you. I don't want to be terrified, and I don't want to be concerned. But I am."

"If you keep that up," he said harshly, "you'll be in this so deep you can never turn back."

"I'm already there." This time her lips lingered.

His hands dropped hers, and he reached for her shoulders to push her away. His fingers dug into her flesh, but he couldn't find the strength.

"I don't want to be terrified or concerned or in love with you," she said softly. "But I am."

"No, you're not!"

"No?" She brushed his hair back from his forehead. In the flickering lamplight, his face was a kaleidoscope of expression. Each changing nuance made it harder to read his feelings. "I don't want to love you. I don't want to love anybody, because I don't think I'll be very good at it. But I don't think I have any choice."

"You can get up from here and walk away. When I leave tomorrow, you can tell yourself it doesn't matter." He slid his hands under her hair. "And it doesn't, because I don't have anything to give you. I'm a walking dead man."

"You've stayed alive this long!"

Her hair slipped through his fingers. It was fine and silky, the color of night against her pale, worried face. He thought of all she had done for him, and all she still wanted to do. And he thought of all he could never do for her.

When he spoke, his voice denied his feelings. "I'm only alive because of luck, and because I've had nobody else to think about."

"You need to think about someone else," she said fiercely. "You need to remember that avenging Aaron's death is going to get you killed, and that someone will be left here to mourn you! If you go after Gallagher and he kills you, it will kill me!"

He gripped her head and forced her to look into his eyes. "You're acting like a little fool! I'm nothing to you. Nothing. And when I leave tomorrow, I'll still be nothing."

"Tell me again this is nothing!" Simon's fingers were tangled in her hair, holding her back, but Tate found his mouth, anyway. His lips were warm, but they didn't yield under hers.

He turned his head. "Stop it!" This time he found the strength to push her away. "You're not in love with me! You're still a kid, damn it. You've got a kid's fantasies, that's all. I'm some lousy fairy-tale knight to you. I brought excitement into a dull existence. But that's all I've brought, Tate. Maybe you want me—maybe you've never really wanted a man before. But wanting's a hell of a leap from loving."

"You're not a knight. I don't want you because you've spent your life running from human warmth and being a hero." She sat up. Her hair swung across one cheek, but she didn't shake it back. "And I'm not a kid. But maybe I am a fool."

Behind the veil of hair, he saw her pain. "You're also lovely and desirable, but that passion belongs to a man who can give you what I can't."

"Then maybe I'm more of a kid than I thought. I didn't know passion was a request to share the rest of your life. I didn't know that asking you to work at staying alive was the same as asking for a commitment."

"You're asking me to think of you!"

"I'd ask you for the moon and stars, if I thought it would keep you alive."

"Go to bed." Simon almost choked on the words. His voice was not as aloof as he had intended.

Tate stood and turned to face him. She knew more about rejection than most people learned in a lifetime. She also knew more about the horrors of running from it. She examined Simon as dispassionately as she could and wondered whether the pain would multiply if he continued to reject her—or if that was impossible.

Her hands rose to the top button of her shirt. "You've told me *my* feelings. You haven't told me yours." She pushed the button through the buttonhole and slid her hands lower to the next. "Have I just imagined that you want me?"

He gave a harsh laugh. "I'm a man."

The third button was unfastened, then the fourth. "Am I supposed to believe that all men want me?"

Simon sat up and grabbed her hand. "Cut this out!"

"This, Simon?" She didn't smile. "Am I asking you for something, again? Something you can't give me?"

"Damn it, Tate, you may be a kid, but I'm not!"

"A grown man driven wild by the sight of a child?" Her free hand unfastened the next button.

Simon jerked her back down beside him. "You're asking for sex, is that it? Nothing else?"

"I'm asking for whatever you can give me, and not one thing more." She stared into his eyes.

"That's not asking for much."

"Maybe it doesn't seem like it. But I've never asked a man for anything before."

Her message was unmistakable. Simon's breath caught, and for a moment he couldn't find words. Then he did. "Find someone who'll appreciate what you're offering. You're wasting it on me."

"I guess that's my right." Tate slipped her hand out of his and pulled the last button free. She shrugged, and the shirt glided down her back and arms. In the lamplight, her bra was only a shade whiter than her skin.

Simon stifled a groan. He hadn't remembered seeing more of her body than wrists and hands. But there had been one tormented dream where he had seen her naked, bathing in the firelight. Since that moment, he had wanted her—and now he knew it had not been a dream.

He was a strong man, a man for whom weakness was a deadly sin. But he wasn't strong enough to resist her. He wouldn't, couldn't, name his feelings, but he knew they had little to do with the absence of women from his life, or even the acute danger he was in.

He knew he should reach behind her and pull the shirt back over her shoulders. Instead, he watched silently as it fell to the floor.

Tate reached behind her for the clasp of her bra. Her fingers trembled, but the clasp fell free. She shrugged once more.

Her breasts were small and rose-tipped. They tilted up, as if in supplication. "Warm me," she said softly.

He tried once more. "You don't know what you're doing."

"No? Then you can show me." She moved closer. "Show me." She reached for his hand and hoped he didn't feel her trembling as she guided it to her breast.

He had never felt anything as soft. It seemed like forever since he had touched a woman. It *was* forever since he had touched a woman such as Tate. He didn't want to draw her close, but he did. He didn't want to circle her with his arms as she unbuttoned his shirt. But he did.

She lingered over every button. Simon's hands moved slowly over her back. He pressed his face into her hair, and she felt him shudder. She didn't know whether it was passion or regret.

Under her fingertips, his chest was hard with muscle. She had bathed him; he was not a mystery, but the things she felt as she touched him now were mysterious to her. Her hands glided from his waist to his neck, savoring each separate texture, savoring the heat of his skin. She lifted the shirt from his shoulders and pushed it down over his arms. Then she pressed herself against him.

He held her there, although he knew he should force her away. He felt her nipples harden, and he knew he was lost. "I don't want to hurt you," he said, swaying against her in unconscious caress.

"Then don't." Tate arched her back to be closer, still. "Don't. Just love me. Just for now. Just for tonight."

He wanted to warn her again. He wanted to make her understand that even this exposed them both to a danger she couldn't conceive of. But his lips wouldn't form a warning. Instead they moved over her hair, stroked the petal-soft skin of her forehead, grazed her cheeks and drew a shimmering welcome from hers.

He stroked her breasts as he kissed her. She lifted herself against his hands in invitation. Her lips moved, then parted against his. His tongue touched hers, and she sighed with pleasure and relaxed against him.

He knew she had been afraid he would continue to resist her. She had no idea of how powerfully he was drawn to her. She believed her feelings were her own; she didn't know that he shared them. Yet she had risked humiliation to come to him, to offer herself.

Beneath his wandering hands her frame was delicate, almost fragile. But he knew better. She was held together by steel. Perhaps she wouldn't break apart when he left her. She had more courage, real courage, than anyone he had even known.

"I just want to protect you," he murmured against her lips. "But I've wanted you since I first saw you."

She kneaded the muscles of his back and shut her eyes as he kissed her again. Sensation ran hot and liquid through her. Simon ran his thumbs along her spine until his hands cupped her bottom. He guided her against him, and even through the heavy denim of her jeans, she could feel his arousal. She flung one leg over him as he leaned back against the iron headboard.

His eyes were half closed, his lips pressed together as he fought for restraint. He was always a patient lover, able to keep enough distance to give pleasure as well as to take it. Now he wondered if there would be any distance between them tonight. He felt himself moving toward fulfillment, and they weren't even fully undressed yet.

She was so slight he could hardly feel the burden of her weight. But he could feel every heated inch of her skin, as she pressed against him; feel every silken hair that brushed his face. Perhaps she had never had a lover, but she was no tremulous virgin. She was sharing herself, her warmth, her emotion, with a generosity of body and spirit he had never known.

He turned her so they were on their sides, but she kept one leg thrown over his, afraid he would move away. She was drifting, drowning in the river flowing through her. When his hand caught in the waistband of her jeans, she leaned away to give him room to unsnap them.

"This is happening fast enough." Simon's hand dipped lower and unfastened her jeans, but he left them on. Instead, his lips began a slow journey. He found the drumroll pulse in her neck, and savored its wild rhythm. He found the hollow at her throat with his tongue, and heard her moan.

Her skin was so pale he could trace the fine network of veins beneath it. She tasted like warm cream and wildflower honey. He was wrapped in the scents of autumn, of sweet forest air tinged with pine and the fragrance of burning applewood.

She moaned again, when he drew the tip of her breast into his mouth. He buried his face against her, and for a moment the pleasure was too intense to bear. She moved against his hand, against his mouth, silently begging him for more.

He found her other breast with his lips. As sensation jolted through her, Tate wondered if she could die of such ecstasy. She hadn't known what she was asking of him. She had only yearned for something that couldn't be explained.

He lifted his head to look at her. Her lashes were dark shadows against her flushed cheeks. Her hair was a thundercloud against the white pillowcase. He was flooded with emotion that gave wings to his passion. She was no ordinary woman, and he was not just a man trying to hold on to a life that was rapidly slipping away. She was *his* woman, by her own words and by the emotions suffusing him. And she would always be his woman, whether he lived to see tomorrow or not.

She moaned his name and lifted her hips to meet his. There was so little he could give her, and nothing he could say. But he knew he could give her this night.

He pushed her jeans down, caressing her stomach, her hips, as he eased them off. She attempted to help him, but he captured her hands in one of his and kissed her. "Let me," he said.

"Your leg?"

"Was hurting like hell, and now I don't even feel it." He stretched half across her, pushing down the jeans just inches at a time and caressing the long, sleek length of her legs as he did. He brushed his hand over the dark triangle of her hair that was now his to touch. And then his hand settled there to caress her.

The sound she made was almost a whimper. Every touch of his hands trailed heat into new parts of her body. She pulled her hands from his grasp and wove them through his hair as his lips followed the path of his hands. Her body no longer seemed earthbound, and thought didn't exist. She floated, tossed from wave to wave of sensation. Simon had undressed her, before she realized it. Her hands were at the waist of his briefs before she knew she was undressing him.

Nothing had prepared her for the overwhelming perfection of their bodies together. She felt the beat of his heart, the heat of his skin, the rasp of his hair, all as if they were part of her. His chest was firm against the soft pressure of her breasts, his arms rigid with muscle. Her hands slipped lower. And stopped.

Simon's laugh was a harsh rumble. "Where's your courage, now?" He covered her hands and moved them lower still to cover the place she hadn't yet touched. Tate opened her eyes and stared into his, as she began to explore him. She watched his expression change by slow degrees. She felt suddenly, powerfully female. She was not the recipient of Simon's lovemaking, but a willing, eager partner. And perhaps what she didn't know, she would soon learn.

As he captured her hands again and moved them above her head, she arched her back, seeking, craving, the feel of his body against hers. Then she lifted her hips to meet his first ecstatic thrust.

The fire had almost died by the time Tate got out of bed to bank it. Simon was sleeping, and she had pulled on his shirt as a robe. She shivered in the cold air, and debated whether to throw more logs on the fire or to crawl back into bed and the warmth of his arms.

She compromised, using kindling and several small logs to revive the fire while she washed with water from the kettle hanging in front of the fireplace. But by the time she was ready to add hardwood that would burn all night, she found she had little desire to do so. Instead she pulled an afghan from the sofa and sat on the rug, staring into the flames.

She was Simon's woman now, although she knew he would never claim her. She had given herself to him, given everything she knew how to give. But what would Simon remember of tonight? Certainly not her prowess as a lover. She had been so bombarded by sensation that she had been at a loss to focus it, to use it to give him pleasure.

He hadn't complained, but she had seen the regret in his eyes afterward. She might be a kid, and she might be a fool. But she wasn't enough of one to believe that what they had shared had been enough for him. He had made love to her because she had begged for it. The most she had given him was sexual release after months of imprisonment.

There was no doubt in her mind that he expected more from a liaison. She had never asked him about his personal life, but there had to have been women in the past. And there would be more in his future—if he had a future.

She was left with a body that still throbbed from his lovemaking and a heart that was filled with despair.

Hands settled on her shoulders. "Is this a private party? Or can I join you?"

She had been so deep in thought that she hadn't heard him get up. "I . . . I was just warming the cabin a little before I banked the fire for the night."

"I missed you beside me." Simon lowered himself to the rug. He had felt Tate grow tense under his hands, and he was careful not to touch her now.

Tate glanced at him. He was wearing jeans and a blanket, Indian-style, around his shoulders. She turned back to stare at the flames, the picture of his broad, blanket-clad shoulders flickering brightly with them. "You need your sleep. You shouldn't be up."

He tried to fathom what she could be thinking. She sounded like the woman who had been his nurse, not the woman who had just been his lover. "You shouldn't be up, either. You could rekindle the fire in the morning."

She was silent for a long time, and he was silent beside her. When she spoke at last, there was little emotion in her voice. "Simon, I'm sorry."

He quelled the urge to shake an explanation out of her. "Are you?"

"I pushed you to make love to me. And I kept pushing."

He doubted that she was really apologizing for being too bold.

"I . . . you were right. It was a bad idea," she finished.

One minute she was staring into the flames, the next she was lying half across him, staring into his eyes. Simon's fingers dug into her upper arms. "All right," he said coldly, "let's hear you say that again."

"It was a bad idea! I know you regret it. I know I wasn't much good. I don't know what to do, what to feel. I was the kid you accused me of being!"

He stared at her. "Kid?"

"Kid. I'm not experienced. You know that now. I . . . I thought it didn't matter, but it did."

He struggled to make sense of what she was saying. "Are we talking about what you felt or what I did?"

"What you felt. I—"

He touched her lips with his fingertips. "How do you know what I felt? Let's forget that for a moment, anyway. Let's talk about what you felt."

She couldn't look at him, and she couldn't speak.

"It wasn't much fun, was it?" Simon cradled her face and brought it back to his. "I hurt you. I tried to be gentle, but I wasn't. I lost control before I could give you much pleasure."

"It wasn't your fault. It was mine. I thought I'd know what to do. I was sure—"

"You did everything just right." He caressed her hair and felt himself growing hard again. The conversation was an aphrodisiac; touching her was a reminder of how she'd felt, naked and soft against him.

"Look, I don't need to be reassured. I mean, I'm not some vulnerable—"

"Yes, you are. And yes, you need reassurance. So let me tell you what I felt."

"You were sorry you made love to me! I saw it in your eyes afterward. It can't be much fun to make love to a virgin. And not what you're used to."

Gently he pushed her to the rug and pinned her there with the weight of his body. Her insecurities were legion. He hoped he didn't neglect any of them. "I did feel regret. You're right. But not because we'd made love. Because I can't make love to you every day for the rest of your life. We didn't even hit the highlights tonight, and I didn't give you the pleasure you were entitled to, and I regretted that, too."

He kissed away her reply, until there wasn't even a rumble. "And yes, making love to a virgin has some drawbacks, but do you know how sweet it was to be your lover, anyway? To be the man to share that with you?"

He kissed her again. He knew she wanted to believe him, but she couldn't yet. "You gave me more pleasure tonight than I knew I could have," he said softly. "I'll never forget this. Never. And I'll never forget you." He began to unbutton her shirt, even though she tried to still his hand.

"You don't have to—"

"Don't I?" He raised one aristocratic brow. "You're not a virgin, now. And I'm not going to lose control again. We've got the rest of the night together. Let's see if we can rid you of your doubts, one . . . by . . . one."

The fire died, and the cabin grew cold. But it was only later, much, much later, that they found their way back to bed. Replete and satisfied with her ability to please Simon, Tate fell asleep immediately, wrapped tightly in Simon's arms. He lay against her, stroking her hair, and wondered if a hero could learn to be an ordinary man and a fugitive could learn to stop running.

Chapter 13

In the hour just before dawn, Simon eased his body from Tate's. She hadn't awakened during the night; he had hardly slept. Now she still lay sleeping, her body curved like a graceful willow branch, her hair a midnight cloud against the pillow they had shared.

Monitoring the deep, even rhythm of her breathing, he got up slowly, careful not to shake the bed. She slept with one arm outstretched. Who or what was she reaching for? Even in sleep, did she somehow sense he was leaving her?

He remembered the last words she'd spoken before falling asleep. "Let me help you escape," she'd murmured. "Let me try again. Promise you'll let Will and me find a way to get you to safety."

He had whispered that she wasn't to worry; she had been too exhausted to realize that he hadn't made a promise. She would know when she awoke, though; he just hoped she would also know why he had left without her help.

He had already put her in too much danger. Once, he had believed Josiah Gallagher was an honorable man. Now he knew that if Gallagher suspected Tate's involvement in his escape, he would stop at nothing to silence her. The only way Simon could keep her safe was to disappear. From her house, from Arkansas, from her life.

He didn't want to. He wasn't a man who lied to himself. He didn't want to disappear. Even now, with his life nearly a thing of the past, he wanted to slip back into bed beside her, to caress and kiss her into wakefulness, to merge with her so totally that nothing else—not danger, not fear—was real.

Instead, he stepped away from the bed, taking one long last look at her. Then he turned and carried his clothes into the living area to dress. His leg throbbed unmercifully, but for the first time he had faith it would heal. It bore his weight, and that was all he could ask for. Luckily he had found a way to leave that didn't require much walking.

Last night, as he'd painfully hobbled through fields and forest, making his way back to the cabin, he had encountered a boat shed at the river's edge. Gauging what he knew of Tate's property lines, he had suspected the shed was hers. The task of picking the lock and investigating had been a simple one.

Inside, he'd found a rowboat upended on sawhorses and a sturdy pair of oars. In the moonlight, the boat looked as if it had seen some use, but he hadn't been able to gauge its seaworthiness. Now he was going to take a gamble. Millard Carter had been a man to keep and care for everything that crossed his path. Even if Millard had never used the boat, he would have kept it in good repair.

He had probably used the boat often, though. The walls of the shed had been lined with fishing gear, including a collection of rods and lures, a fishing vest and a battered rain hat sporting a feathered fly on the brim. All testified to Millard's enthusiasm for the sport.

Simon planned to make good use of all that gear today as he drifted down the river to freedom. He was going to pose as an Ozark angler, an ordinary man taking one final fishing trip before winter set in.

He knew if he waited until dark to launch the boat his chance of escaping detection was better, but he didn't want to spend even one more day putting Tate at risk. He also knew enough about the river to realize that somewhere up ahead there was white water and waterfalls. People came from all over the country to raft the river rapids. Shooting them in a rowboat after dark was a wet, cold way to commit suicide.

He had no illusions that his pretense of fishing would be foolproof. His chances of escaping were fifty-fifty, perhaps even less, but he had no other choices. He was not staying in Mountain Glade even a day longer.

He dressed quickly, easing the jeans he'd worn yesterday over his bandaged leg. When he finished, he strapped the ersatz shoulder holster in place and checked his gun.

The sandwiches Tate had slapped together yesterday were still in the pocket of his parka. They were worse for wear, but they would have to do. He wanted to have the boat in the water before the sun rose.

The front door closed behind him, and he pressed his back to the log wall of the cabin, letting his eyes adjust. The silence of night was broken only once by the call of a wakening bird. Beyond him the forest was still, as if all its nocturnal prowlers were already in hiding and its day creatures not yet about. He listened hard, all senses alert, but only silence greeted him.

When he was satisfied, he crossed the porch and took the steps as quickly as he could, edging along the front of the cabin until he reached the corner. He knew he would be at his most vulnerable as he crossed the clearing to the grove of Christmas trees. He considered doing it on hands and knees, but decided against it. His leg wouldn't cope well with the strain.

He crossed the clearing as quickly as he could, leaning heavily on a large pine when he'd reached the safety of the trees. The silence still held as he gauged the best path to the boat house. He had two choices. One was shorter; one, under cover of the forest, was safer.

He chose the second. When he had rested, he wove his way through the Christmas-tree grove. There was another clearing to cross, and then, if he was judging correctly, he could stay in the woods until just before he reached the shed.

The journey took most of thirty minutes. As he traveled, the darkness seemed too quiet. Dawn was fast approaching, yet all he heard were intermittent bursts of birdsong. The forest seemed to be holding its breath, as if waiting for something.

As he drew closer to the river, he could taste its presence on the misty air, hear its subtle cadences. Days before, it had carried him to this place, to a woman he would wish for every day of his life, to a time of learning to share himself.

He was all too aware there was no guarantee it would carry him anywhere else.

Minutes later, he stood at the edge of the forest and stared at the boat shed. It was fifty yards away, bordered by brush and a grove of tulip poplars. A path had been cleared from another direction, obviously Millard's chosen route. Simon's only choice now was to make his own path. He stood quietly for a minute first, watching the river, watching the trees beyond him for any movement. Satisfied at last, he started through the brush.

At the shed he pulled the unlocked door toward him. The door opened with a rusty creak until he could prop it with a rock. Inside, the boat was just as he'd left it. He ran his hands over the keel, searching again, both with his eyes and fingers, for reasons to scrap his plan.

He managed to swing the boat off the first sawhorse without incident, although the increased pressure on his leg was agonizing. Before he swung it off the second, he gathered the supplies he would need: vest, hat, rods and tackle box. The vest fit neatly under his parka, the hat brim sank low enough on his forehead to help disguise his face.

When he was ready, he pulled the boat to the doorway and turned it on its side. Then, backing out, he slid it through.

A man's voice sounded behind him. "That'll do, Vandergriff. Just keep your hands on the boat, and don't move."

Simon didn't recognize the voice, but he recognized his own situation. It was a breath away from hopeless. He stood absolutely still, waiting for a gunshot. "At least let me see who you are," he said, buying time.

"Don't you know?" The man's voice sounded almost jovial. "I'm surprised."

"Let me turn around, and maybe we'll both be surprised."

"Put your hands over your head. Clasp them. That's right. Then turn slowly. No funny stuff, okay?"

It was more of a request than an order. Simon turned as slowly as he could. The voice hadn't been familiar, but the man it belonged to was. The last time Simon had seen him, the smiling young man had been in the company of Josiah Gallagher. He was chubby-cheeked and shiny-faced—and altogether deadly. "Barker," he acknowledged. "Where's your boss?"

Barker shook his head. "The name's Kinney today. Ben Kinney. Didn't the little brunette mention me?"

Simon never got a chance to answer. A figure materialized from the grove of trees behind Barker. The butt of a shotgun arabesqued through the air and descended across his skull. Barker crumpled and hit the ground before the shotgun had made a full arc.

"Thought you could sneak out on me?" Tate knelt over Barker, lifting his wrist to take his pulse, but her words were addressed to Simon.

"You could have gotten yourself killed!" Simon was beside her, lifting her up again before the words were out of his mouth.

"Your friend's going to have a heck of a headache."

"What do you mean, following me?" He shook her once for emphasis.

"You didn't even know, did you? That's how good you are at what you do. I could give you some lessons."

He didn't know whether to kiss her or shake her again. He pushed her away instead. "We've got to get out of here." Stooping, he grasped Barker under the arms and painfully began to drag him toward the boat shed. "Can you finish sliding the boat out? It's not heavy."

Tate beat him to the doorway and managed to move the boat. Then she watched dispassionately as Simon dragged Barker inside and left him there.

"Who is that guy?" she asked, as he slammed and locked the door.

Simon picked up the shotgun and tossed it into a patch of mountain laurel before he spoke. "Gallagher's right-hand man." He retrieved Barker's gun, which had fallen to the ground after Tate's attack, checked it, then handed it to her. "Do you know how to use this?"

She nodded. "Then Gallagher—"

"Isn't far behind." Simon drew his own gun and pulled her behind him. He started toward the woods, turning once to be sure she was with him.

"You were going to float down the river, weren't you?" she asked accusingly.

"Quiet!"

"You would have been a sitting duck!"

In the relative safety of the woods, he turned and jerked her against him. "Have you got any better ideas? I'm trying to get out of here. I'm trying to save your life."

"And what about your life? What good is mine, if you go and get yourself killed?"

"It's a life, which is more than I can give you if I stay around here."

"I told you, Will and I can get you to safety."

"You don't know who you're fooling with!" Simon dropped his arms. He was furious at her for risking her life for him, and he was furious with himself for ever involving her.

"I know your life's at stake. That's all I need to know." She stretched out a hand pleadingly, touching his cheek. "Let me help!"

"It's probably too damn late to help either of us." He shook off her hand and turned, limping through the forest as fast as he was able. His head turned from side to side, scanning the trees that bordered their trail. His gun was at his hip, ready to fire.

Tate stayed close behind him, Barker's gun dangling by her side. There was nothing she could do now, except shoot if she were forced to. She had probably just saved Simon's life, but if his words were true, she had also just delayed the inevitable. He was sure Gallagher was somewhere nearby, waiting to finish what his youthful sidekick had started.

She didn't dare speak, although she had a thousand questions, first and foremost why he hadn't said goodbye. Not that she really needed to ask. She already knew what Simon would say. The passion they had shared was over. She had willingly agreed to one night; he had never promised her more. Now all his energy was focused on escape, as it should be. Their time together had ended; no goodbye had been necessary.

Simon was moving as swiftly as he could, but it was still taking them too long to get back to the cabin. At one point she touched his shoulder and forced him to stop. "There's a better way," she whispered, pointing to a hollow to their left.

"You're sure?" he mouthed.

"When I was a runaway, my life depended on shortcuts and quick getaways." She took the lead, walking silently with a skill she'd acquired years before. Behind her, leaves and twigs crunched under Simon's halting steps.

The sun was rising, as they reached the last stand of trees before the clearing that led to the Christmas-tree grove. They waited, watching together.

"It looks okay," Tate said doubtfully.

"Okay is hardly good enough." Simon scanned the tree line and the clearing repeatedly, but his task was hopeless. There were more places to hide than there were people searching for him. "It looks like we're going to have to make a run for it. We'll do it in stages. Let's just get to the thickest part of the grove, then we'll do the last leg. I'm going first. You follow, if nobody starts shooting, but count to ten."

She held him back. "Let me go first. Nobody wants me. I'll just stroll out, like I've been for a walk in the woods. Then you can follow, if it looks all right."

He shook off her hand. "Nobody who's traced me here would be stupid enough to think you were out for fresh air." Before she could argue, Simon, bending low, started through the clearing. It was light enough now that he made a clear target, but no one seemed to care.

Tate counted to ten and started after him. He waited for her in the thickest patch of white pines. There was one more clearing to cross. From their vantage point it seemed a mile wide. "We'll do this the same way," Simon told her. "Wait until I'm almost to the porch."

She grabbed his arm. "Be careful."

"I've never needed anybody to tell me that," he said coldly.

"Somebody should have told you that before you let yourself get put behind bars in the first place!"

He wanted to be angry at her. Anger was the quickest way to sever the bond between them. But it wasn't anger that threatened to explode inside him. He was so worried about her that he couldn't concentrate. And he had never needed to concentrate more than he did now.

Anger wasn't going to work. Arrogance wasn't, either. Nothing was going to work. He could tell himself all the lies in the world, and when he was done, she would still fill his mind and heart. He covered her hand with his own and raised it to his lips. "Damn you," he said against her palm. "Just don't go getting yourself killed. Watch closely, and don't move if you suspect anything is wrong. Anything! Understand?"

"I've never needed anybody to tell me that!"

"Somebody should have told you that before you let a fugitive into your life, love." He dropped her hand. In a moment he was running low, zigzagging through the clearing.

She knew the meaning of "her heart in her throat" as she watched him cover the distance as quickly as he could. She couldn't breathe, and the pulse in her neck had the doomsday meter of a time bomb.

He was on the first porch step, when she began to follow. She imitated his crooked route, aware that it would make her a more difficult target if someone was going to fire.

The decision was a good one. She heard the unmistakable whine of a bullet as the ground her foot had just deserted exploded in a spray of rocky soil.

She didn't have time for fear, nor did she have time to trade fire. Instinctively, she knew that her best chance was to keep running. She put on a burst of speed. She heard another shot and realized Simon was firing from the porch. She ran faster, the ground beside her exploding once more.

She took the steps two at a time. Simon was behind one of the massive pillars supporting the porch roof. "Get inside!" he shouted.

There was no time to argue. She reached the door and flung it open, ducking behind it to wait for Simon.

"Don't even think about firing at me."

She heard the voice coming from the direction of the window behind her. Turning slowly, she saw a man, gun in hand, at the window's far edge.

"Simon, run!" she shouted, but it was too late. Simon was already inside, barring the door before the words were out of her mouth.

"I've got my gun on the woman, Simon," the man said. "Drop yours. You do the same," he said, motioning to Tate.

"Do it," Simon said from behind her.

She considered aiming at the man and firing.

"Do it, Tate!" Simon ordered.

She heard Simon's gun thud as it hit the floor. Reluctantly she dropped hers, too.

"Kick them this way."

Simon moved forward and kicked both guns toward the man. "Nice work, Gallagher. But you've got me now. There's no reason to hurt her." He continued to move, as he spoke, until he could rest his hands on Tate's shoulders. She felt the firm pressure and knew he was going to push her out of the way if Gallagher fired.

Gallagher, long awaited and finally here. Tate examined him with an objectivity that said everything about shock. He was Simon's height, but stockier. His hair was a mop of tamed chestnut curls, his cheekbones broad and strong, his mouth wide and unsmiling. He looked more like a tough Irish cop than a man who could betray his two best friends.

"Just what do you think I'm here for?" Gallagher asked. He looked more irritated than murderous.

"To finish what you started at High Ridge."

A shot rang out from the woods along the far side of the cabin. For a moment Tate didn't understand. Gallagher had the gun. But Gallagher wasn't shooting.

"Go ahead and call off your boys," Simon said. "We'll wait."

Gallagher's eyes flicked to the window. "I hate to break good glass," he said with distaste. "Old glass, too. That's the worst." In a minute, the pane was fragments on the porch floor and Gallagher was firing through the resulting hole.

There was another shot from the woods, then silence.

Gallagher spoke. "Not my boys, Simon. If I'm right, they're friends of yours. Hired killers. They've been after you for months."

"You've been after him!" Tate said.

"Shush, Tate." Simon moved her to one side, then behind him. Gallagher didn't seem to care. His gaze darted back and forth between them and the woods.

"What are you talking about?" Simon asked.

"The Knapp family. There's been a contract out on you for months now. One of the Knapps managed to arrange it from prison. There's one out on Aaron, too."

"Aaron's dead."

"Wrong. Aaron's in Hawaii, probably on a deep-sea fishing boat catching mahimahi at the taxpayers' expense. We'll never get him back to the mainland."

Gallagher turned his full attention to Simon. "Aaron's a lot smarter than you are. I could go to him, once I knew about the

Knapps, and I could tell him we were going to protect him. You? You were a different story. You've never let anybody help you. I knew you'd refuse. The Petersen thing came up just about the same time. We decided you'd be safer in High Ridge than anywhere else we could think of, so we hired you to go in undercover. Only nothing went like we wanted it to. These guys kept slipping through our fingers. I couldn't tell you. I knew you'd make us release you, and you'd have been dead the minute you stepped out on the streets."

"You expect me to believe this?" Simon asked.

"I expect you to use your head!" Another shot scudded along the ground, splintering a porch step. "You got a better explanation? Some reason I don't know about, why I'd want you and Aaron dead? I saved your neck once, remember? Why would I want to kill you, now?"

"You left me at High Ridge to rot! I'd have been dead in another month."

"I didn't know about Shaw, when we put you in! I knew he was harsh, but not corrupt. But I know now. We put Cooney on our payroll after you'd been there less than a week. He was watching over you all the time. With his help we would have gotten you out of there before anything happened."

"Why didn't he tell me, then?"

"He was under orders not to reveal anything. And you took him by surprise the night you ran." Two more shots were fired, and Gallagher fired one in return before he turned back to them.

Tate couldn't keep silent another moment. "Who are the Knapps?"

Simon didn't look at her. "The last case Gallagher hired me to help him with. A bunch of thugs in the Northwest."

"It looks like Aaron's fishing lessons took," Gallagher said, gesturing toward the hat Simon still wore. "But you look ridiculous." He stared at Simon for a moment, then, as if his assessment was positive, bent over and lifted both guns from the floor. He tossed one to Simon. "How well does she shoot?"

Simon caught the gun. "Ask her."

"Well enough to worry *you*," Tate said, holding out her hand.

"Can I trust her?" Gallagher asked Simon.

"Ask her."

"Simon, if he's telling the truth," Tate said, "Shaw's looking for you, and all the cops and troopers in Arkansas are looking for you, and the rest of Gallagher's men are probably still looking for you, and these Knapp characters are—"

"That's what it means to be wanted." Simon jerked his head toward Tate. Gallagher sighed and tossed the other gun in her direction.

She caught it and released the safety.

"Every bullet's going to count," Gallagher said, turning his back to both of them. "We tried to get to you before they did, and if you hadn't made it so damn hard, we might have. My men are combing the hills north of here. I've only got Barker with me, and I don't know where he disappeared to."

"He's taking a little nap," Simon said.

"Thanks a lot."

Simon grabbed Tate's hand, and then, bending low they ducked beneath the windows on the other side of the door. "Listen," he said, not sparing her a glance. "I want you to get in the cellar. The gun's to defend yourself, if somebody finds you who shouldn't."

"Dream on." Expertly she snapped it open and checked her ammunition. "I'm not leaving."

"Where did you learn to use a gun?" he demanded.

"Jess made sure both Kris and I learned, when he was afraid her crazy stepfather, the senator, was stalking us." She shot him a smile as she stationed herself at the side of the window. "My life's never been dull. And I'm still here. Breathing, too."

Simon knew they had no time to argue. "Just stay away from the window."

"I will. When I'm not shooting." She punctuated the last by shattering the glass on her side.

He finished the job, and the cabin sported another gaping hole. "You take any chances, and I'll throw you in the cellar!"

"We both know how easy that would be!"

"I do believe King Simon's met his match," Gallagher said from across the room. "If we get out of here in one piece, I want to hear this story."

"If we get out of here in one piece, you're not going to *stay* that way for long," Simon threatened.

"Hey, I only aimed to please." Gallagher gave one derisive laugh. "And right now I'm going to be pleased to aim."

Chapter 14

By the full light of morning it became obvious that three men, armed with semiautomatic weapons, were in the woods. If they were caught, neither they nor the imprisoned members of the Knapp crime family would ever see the light of day again as free men. But somehow, as bullets plowed into the cabin's thick log walls, that seemed a small compensation.

As he reloaded for the third and final time, Gallagher spoke. "How many bullets do you have left?"

"Enough to put two in every man out there," Simon said.

"Tate?"

"Three."

"Then we're going to stop firing. Let's draw them out."

"They won't fall for that, if they've watched even one old Western," Tate said, moving back against the wall.

"Put yourself in their shoes. They've got to make a run for us, sometime. They'll be most tempted, if we're not shooting at them. They're sure to be dressed for business. No bullet's going to get through the armor they're probably wearing." Simon lounged indolently against his portion of cabin wall, like a teenage thug on his favorite street corner.

"Then why have we been shooting at them?"

"We've been pretending. When they come for us, we'll be serious," Gallagher said.

"And you'll be in the cellar," Simon added, nodding to Tate.

She ignored him. "Where do I shoot? If they're wearing vests, do I aim for their heads?"

"She's good at heads," Simon told Gallagher. "She used the wrong side of a shotgun on Barker's."

Gallagher flashed Tate a smile. "Ever think about a career in law enforcement?"

"The two of *you* ought to think of a career in something else," she retorted. "You've botched this from the beginning."

"Tactful, too." Gallagher came to attention beside his window and pointed. "They're moving closer."

Simon peered out his corner, and Tate, hers. She saw several unnaturally swaying tree branches where Gallagher was pointing. "Will they rush us?"

"Most likely."

If they did, she wondered what the chances of survival were for anyone in the cabin. The three hit men were dressed and armed for deadly assault. She, Simon and Gallagher had only a handful of bullets between them.

She was still contemplating what seemed like the inevitable, when she realized Simon was at her side. No one seemed to be shooting at anyone anymore. She doubted that was a good sign.

"Will you stop being a tough guy for a minute?" Simon asked softly.

Tate's eyes flashed to Gallagher. He was pointedly looking away. She concentrated on Simon again. "I'm not going downstairs."

"Don't you get it? If you're up here, I'll be worrying about you. You'll be putting us both in danger."

She wanted to tell him to take a flying leap, but his concern was so obvious that the words died on her lips. "Maybe you're better at your job than I thought. You know exactly what to say, don't you?"

He brushed her hair back from her cheek and cleared his throat. "Maybe I haven't said enough. I'll say it now, even if it doesn't change a damn thing. I love you."

She was so caught off guard she could only stare. "Do things look that bad?" she asked at last.

"They don't look good."

"Most people say a prayer before they die."

"I just did."

She tried to smile. "I should have known it would take something like this to make you admit you loved me."

He tried to smile, too. "This or the apocalypse."

"I'll be a lot more frightened downstairs than I would be up here with you."

"If you're down there, I'll be a lot less frightened and a lot better shot."

She moved into his arms, and he kissed her with all the passion that had been missing from his voice. Then he pushed her away. "Don't disturb anything. Don't leave any clues where you've gone."

"We could all go down and make them crazy."

"If we all disappear, they won't stop looking until they've found us."

"Simon—"

He didn't let her finish. "Go!"

She held out her gun. "Take this."

"You might need it."

"If they found me, I wouldn't have time to get off a shot."

He accepted the weapon. "Now go."

"I love you, too." She turned and started toward the bedroom.

Simon watched her until she was out of sight.

"I hope you're not feeling quite as desperate as you sounded," Gallagher said dryly.

"Don't worry about your stinking neck, Josiah. I plan to pick off every last one of those bastards."

"She's something else."

"You always did have a way with words."

"Did I hear you say you loved her?"

"Only if you were eavesdropping."

"I was."

"Then you heard what you heard."

"Is it true?"

Simon answered with one of his most austere looks.

"She'd make a lovely queen, if they ever make you king of somewhere," Gallagher said with a laugh. "You've been on an emotional roller coaster, haven't you?"

"One of the first intelligent things you've said since our touching reunion."

"I never would have betrayed you." Gallagher wasn't laughing now.

Simon's eyes narrowed. "What you did was almost as bad."

"What I did, you made necessary."

"You could have come to me."

"And what would you have done?" Simon didn't answer, but Gallagher continued as if he had. "If I hadn't cared what happened to you, I could have let them kill you. You're good, Simon, but not good enough to have handled the Knapps on your own. You're not infallible. Never have been, never will be."

"I know."

"Do you?"

"I know." Simon bit off the words.

"Then that woman's taught you something." Gallagher turned all his attention back to the woods, and both men fell silent.

The cellar blocked all light and sound. With the trapdoor closed, Tate felt like the last person in the world—which, she suspected, was just the way Millard had wanted it.

Why else was the cellar so completely sealed and insulated? It was as impervious as a bomb shelter, a time capsule filled with all the life-enriching traditions of one mountain man's unique heritage.

Now, for good measure, crazy old Millard's museum might accidentally save the life of the daughter he had never been sure he had. Except that as Tate lit the one lantern she planned to allow herself, she felt anything but gratitude.

Nothing here could save the life of the two men above her. Nothing here could stop three hit men intent on earning their living. What good were dulcimers and carefully kept journals against the violence of semiautomatic weapons? She could sing every chorus and verse in the yellow shape-note hymnal lying on top of the pump organ in the corner, but it wouldn't keep Simon from dying.

Simon had said he loved her. Maybe he did, or maybe he had just said it to get her down to the cellar, but no matter which it was, Tate knew she had to find a way to help him. The last time she had sat quietly by and waited for someone to take care of her, she had been in a playpen.

Resolutely she began to investigate the shelves, one by one. Maybe dulcimers and hymnals weren't going to do the trick, but there had to be something here that could help. And with the age-old partners, imagination and desperation, she was going to find it.

"I think they're about to make their move." Gallagher squatted beside the window for better aim and protection.

"They're going to be coming from different directions."

"Damn! We need something to make them take notice!"

"How about a blonde?"

"How about an Uzi?"

"How about this?" Tate joined Simon at his window. It was a measure of the two men's concentration that they hadn't heard her coming back up.

"I told you—"

"To be a good girl. I was. I've been downstairs saving your lives." Tate thrust an antique bottle that she had filled with her father's homemade whiskey toward him. The neck had been plugged with a pair of her bikini panties taken from the bedroom dresser. "You'd prefer a blonde?" she asked, as Simon stared at her invention.

"What the hell is this?"

"Apparently you haven't been to any of the world's hot spots."

"You think this thing is a Molotov cocktail?"

"It's a bomb. Primitive, maybe, but useful. I didn't have time to split any atoms down there."

"What is it?" Gallagher asked.

Tate answered before Simon could. "Pure grain alcohol, as flammable as gasoline. The wick's one-hundred-percent cotton."

"The wick's a pair of your panties!" Simon said.

She shrugged. "I can buy more."

"You have one for me?" Gallagher asked.

"I've got one for each of us. I only had time to make three."

"Can you get it over here?"

"If Simon will let go of me." Tate shook the arm Simon had wrapped his fingers around.

"Let her go," Gallagher ordered. "There's not much chance they'll work, but we haven't lost a thing if they don't."

"You don't have time to drag me down to the cellar." Tate covered Simon's hand with hers. "I'm here. I'm going to stay long enough to throw my bottle."

"Then you'll go back down?"

"I promise." She didn't add that she'd be returning with another round of cocktails. He wouldn't be amused.

The moment he dropped her arm, she bent low and took one of the bottles to Gallagher. Then she returned to Simon's window, standing on the side that had recently been hers.

"I doused all the pants with some of Millard's mountain dew," she said. "They'll burn fast."

Gallagher sniffed his bottle. He spoke when he'd finished coughing. "What a waste of good corn whiskey."

Simon ignored him. "The trick's going to be throwing them at the right moment. Too soon, and the wick'll go out in midair. Too late, and it could go off in your hand. I'll say when to light and throw. When they're close enough, aim for the ground at their feet."

Tate looked at him with horror.

"They'll be rushing us any second," he affirmed.

"Then I was just in time."

"That's one way to look at it."

"Don't be mad."

"Then don't be stupid."

"I'll be careful."

"I'll bet."

A movement in the woods cut the conversation short. There was a burst of gunfire, and one by one the three men appeared.

"Get down."

"I'm down." Tate squatted beside the window, as Gallagher and Simon were doing. She prayed the chestnut timbers would continue to stop the killers' bullets.

"How far do you think you can throw?" Simon asked.

Her tongue felt like cotton, but she tried to sound brave. "I was pitcher on the Stagecoach Inn softball team."

"Why don't I feel better?"

"Because you never saw me pitch." Tate slid a pack of matches toward him. She didn't dare look out the window. Simon was keeping to one side, but he still managed a view.

"Damn, these guys are dressed like a SWAT team," he muttered.

"What are they doing?"

"Running for the Christmas trees."

There was another round of fire. "How close are they?" she asked.

"Almost there."

"I planted some of those seedlings myself!"

"I'll yell at them, if they step on any."

"You can be a real jerk, sometimes." Tate tore off a match. She knew the men would have to be almost halfway to the porch before she could throw. But she was going to be ready.

Simon slid the gun she had been using back to her. "Here. Just in case."

She waited, and refused to think that everyone in the cabin could be dead in minutes. She had to believe her homemade bottle bombs would buy them time, maybe even put one or two of the men stalking them out of commission.

Gallagher was first to predict the final rush. He shouted over the next round of shots, "Okay, get ready."

Simon needed no more direction than that. He struck a match, holding it well away from the wick, and waited. Tate did the same. She watched his face and knew the moment the killers began their last dash.

"Light," he said gruffly.

The panties flared like a sparkler on the Fourth of July. In less than a second, they were engulfed in flame.

"Throw!"

Tate rose and with one graceful movement swept her hand parallel with her shoulder. Then, with every bit of her strength, she heaved the flaming bottle out of the window. Ducking to the side she listened to the joyful music of three explosions. Like a burst of jubilant percussion, it could have been the central theme of a symphony.

Simon reported results. "One man's down. He won't be getting up."

Tate marveled at his calm voice.

"Second man's running. Third man's..." He raised his gun and fired.

Gallagher began shooting, too. Tate could hear shots being returned. She peeked out the window, gun in hand. One man was almost to the porch, face down on the blackened ground. It took her longer to find the others. She finally located them in the Christmas-tree grove.

"How long will they stay there?" she asked.

"Until we're out of ammunition . . . and whiskey."

"This isn't the Alamo! Somebody's going to hear the shots and come."

"It's deer season. Nobody'll give shots a second thought."

"Will will."

"That's quite a stutter." Simon aimed a terse smile in her direction. "You bought us some time," he said, before she could explode like one of her bombs. "Somebody might come."

Tate knew she was being placated. "What about you?" she said, spinning to face Gallagher. "You're supposed to have walkie-talkies or something. Can't you send for backup?"

"My radio doesn't work worth—" He stopped himself. "It doesn't work in the mountains."

"Bunglers, both of you!"

"Go see what else you can find in the cellar," Simon said. "We'll bungle better up here without you." There was another round of gunfire.

"Don't bother," Gallagher said. "By the mole on my sainted grandmother's nose." He pointed out the window. "That was the sound of shotguns. Will you look who's come calling?"

"I'll be damned." Simon lowered his gun slowly. "Will-will came through."

Tate knew better than to ask what was happening. One look was worth a thousand of Simon's explanations. The risk seemed minor compared to not knowing.

At first she thought nothing had changed. Two of the men were still in the Christmas-tree grove; one man was on the ground. She glanced away from them, her gaze darting toward the horizon. As she watched shadows began to move slowly toward the cabin.

Shadows with guns.

"Will . . ." She leaned back against the wall.

"Will and about ten of his friends." Simon leaned back, too. "Do you want to break the news, or shall I?" he asked Gallagher.

"Let me." Gallagher moved out of all range of fire. "This is Josiah Gallagher of the Justice Department. Throw down your weapons," he shouted. "You're surrounded."

The cracks of ten rifles from the forest beyond strengthened his words.

"We know who you are and who sent you," Gallagher shouted, in case the message hadn't been clear. "You won't get out of here alive, unless you put your guns down and your hands up."

The silence was as loud as the previous rounds of fire.

"This is going to take a while," Simon said, after a tense minute. "They were walking arsenals."

"Were? They're dropping their guns?" Tate abandoned caution and peered out the window. "They're dropping their guns!"

"They don't know who's shooting at them. They probably think it's cops or some more of Gallagher's men."

"They'd be better off with cops. Cops have some sense. I'm not sure my family does, but they do have guts, don't they?" Tate said proudly.

"Hillbilly justice."

"It saved your life."

"I've been lucky, from the start, to know the Carters, haven't I?" He didn't wait for a response. "Ready, Josiah?"

"I don't think they're bluffing, but let's be ready to shoot, anyway." Gallagher moved to the door and met Simon there. "Stay low, Tate. At least until we've got their weapons."

Simon and Gallagher hit the front porch at the same moment, their guns aimed at the men at the edge of the Christmas-tree grove. Like surrealistic sugar-plum fairies, the Knapps' hired killers swayed against the trees, hands over their heads and their feet wide apart.

The rest was over in minutes. Both men were efficiently searched as Tate's family, both male and female, swarmed out of the woods. Tate recognized Will and Dovey, Andy and the preacher of their church. She left the cabin and found herself in the embrace of people she hadn't even met. She ended up in Will's arms for a final hug.

"You saved our lives," she told him.

"You're Millard's girl. He'd a' done the same thing for one of mine."

"Would he?"

"Darn right."

"Maybe you can tell me some more about Millard?"

"Just been waitin' for you to ask."

She gave him one more long hug before he went to help Dovey, who was monitoring the pulse of the fallen hit man. Tate looked for Simon and found him off to one side talking to Gallagher. Before she could reach him, the wail of a siren silenced the excited, self-selected posse.

The siren grew louder, bouncing off the surrounding hills until siren and echoes were indistinguishable. Tate made her way to Simon's side just as the sheriff arrived.

"No one's ever going to believe this," she said, grabbing Simon's arm. "What if he tries to take you back to High Ridge?"

"You don't have to worry about that." He covered her hand, but he didn't look at her.

Monroe Howard eased himself out of his car and squinted at the crowd surrounding the men lying on their backs, hands folded as if in prayer. He muttered something to the deputy, who had gotten out, too. Both men looked distinctly disappointed that all the fun was over.

"Somebody gonna tell me what's going on?" Monroe asked.

Will strolled to the front. "Took you long enough to get here, Howard. That radio of yours still workin'?"

"We been down south of here…" His voice trailed off as he saw Simon.

Gallagher moved away from the others and reached in his pocket, flashing his badge at the sheriff.

Monroe nodded curtly. "I know who you are. You can put that thing away. We're informal-like 'round here. Just tell me he's not who he looks like." He inclined his head toward Simon.

"He works for me."

Monroe rolled his eyes. They were still rolling minutes later, when Gallagher had finished a short explanation. "Why the you-know-what didn't someone tell me what was goin' on? You Feds ever think about workin' with us locals, for a change? This top-secret stuff makes about as much sense as a pig in a penthouse."

"We didn't want any of this to get back to Shaw. With Simon's testimony, we've got a strong case against him. We didn't want him getting rid of any more evidence than he probably already has."

Monroe still looked disgruntled. "I'm no friend of Shaw's. He won't hear about it from me."

"We need your help to get Vandergriff out of here. I could drive him out in the trunk of my car, but his leg's been injured, and I'd rather not."

"Well now, that's something I can do. Not hard a'tall. When do you want to leave?"

"I've got a man lying around here somewhere with a bad headache. And these three have to be dealt with." Gallagher gestured to the men on the ground. "One of them's got some burns, but the woman over there tells me he's not hurt bad." He nodded toward Dovey.

"We'll load 'em up in my car." Monroe signaled to his deputy, who along with several Carter family members began the process of reading the men their rights and moving them.

"I sent somebody down to the boat shed to get Barker as soon as the shooting stopped," Tate said. "He'll take the short way, so he should be back in a minute." She followed Simon forward to join Gallagher and the sheriff. His hand was still clasped over hers.

Monroe gave her a long assessing look. "Carter through and through," he pronounced at last, shaking his head.

"Thank you."

"Don't thank me. It's a mighty heavy cross to bear."

She smiled. "I guess I'll manage."

"I guess you'll have to."

"Looks like the other problem's solved." Gallagher nodded to the forest break. Barker and a young man were coming through the trees. Barker looked like a freshman quarterback who had just suffered his first defeat.

They waited for him to join them. "If you'd held off bashing in my head just a minute more," Barker told Simon, once he was standing in the circle, "I would have explained what was going on."

"I held off," Simon pointed out. "She didn't." His hand still covered Tate's.

She felt the warm pressure all through her. Simon hadn't looked at her, but neither had he been able to drop her hand. She wondered just what he was feeling. "I'm sorry I hit you," she told Barker. "At the time, it seemed the thing to do."

He rubbed the back of his head, but he shot her a rueful grin.

"Barker'll go with you into town," Gallagher told the sheriff. "We'd appreciate you keeping our friends here in jail until we can get all the paperwork done."

"My pleasure." Monroe extended his hand, and the two men shook.

"You never said just how you were going to help me get Vandergriff out of here," Gallagher said.

Monroe nodded. "That's right. I didn't." He still didn't. Instead, he strolled over to his car and reached through the open window for his radio. He made brief official chitchat, then turned so that everyone could hear him.

"Listen, connect me to the search command center. I think we've finally got Petersen cornered. Yeah, Petersen." He lounged against the car while the connection was made. "Search command center's nuthin' but Glenn Austin's garage in town," he told Gallagher. "We had to call it that, to keep you Feds happy."

Another voice came over the radio, and he waited until it had finished. "Yeah, Sheriff Howard here. We've got the break we needed. Right." He listened to the static-laden voice, then cut it short. "Stop flappin' your gums, woman. Petersen's been spotted twice in the last ten minutes, down in the old stone quarry south of here. Yeah, the one down by Two Chimneys. He's done some shooting, too. Looks like it's gonna take everybody to get him."

He waited until the disembodied voice on the other end was silent once more. "That's right. Get everybody down there. All our boys, the troopers, the prison folks. Tell 'em to clear the roadblocks. No sense in anybody missin' out on the fun." He signed off and switched off the radio.

"The roads'll be safe in ten minutes," he predicted. "I just hope nobody gets killed racin' down to Two Chimneys."

"How far is it?"

"Fifty miles south. You'd better go north."

Gallagher nodded. "My car's parked down the road. I'm going to go get it. Then I'll come back and get Vandergriff."

The sheriff nodded. "The timing should be just about right."

Tate realized her neighbors were drifting back the way they had come. She pulled her hand from Simon's to say a final thank-you and goodbye to each of them, promising over and over again that she would come visit just as soon as things returned to normal. Last of all, she kissed Will's cheek and hugged Dovey. "I can't remember everybody's name," she admitted. "All those people are really related to me?"

"Some more than others. Kissin' kin, some of them," Dovey said. "You and Simon, you gonna be kissin' kin, too?"

"I . . . I don't—"

"Don't go nosin' where you're not wanted," Will warned his wife.

"If I hadn't gone nosin' this morning, this girl'd still be gettin' shot at."

"Dovey was the first one to hear shootin'," Will explained. "She'd picked up the phone and called everybody for a mile around before she even woke me up."

"We take care of our own." Dovey nodded toward Simon. "But there's nothing to do about that one, is there?"

"He takes care of himself. Usually," Tate added.

"C'mon. Shootin' makes me hungry." Will took Dovey's arm and gave Tate an exaggerated wink.

She watched them head through the woods toward their home.

Behind her an engine coughed and sputtered, then roared to life. She turned to see Monroe, his deputy, Barker and a backseat full of subdued bad guys crowded into the sheriff's car. She didn't envy any of them the trip into town.

Only Simon was left standing nearby, and she knew that was only for a few minutes. She joined him as the car pulled away.

"Gallagher's gone to get his car." He didn't touch her.

"Then you'll be leaving." She hesitated. It seemed so odd to be talking like two people who hardly knew each other. But she didn't know what to say in the short time left to them. "Do you have everything you need?"

"The only thing I need is the diskette." He fished it out of his shirt pocket and held it up. "You can keep the cuffs, but Cooney would probably like his gun back."

Her gaze met his and held. "There's something I want to know," she said softly. "What you said to me this morning. Was it true?"

"Tate—"

"No stories, Simon. And no promises. I just want to know."

"This wasn't real. Nothing that happened here was real."

"What you said wasn't real?" She watched him struggle—with himself, with his answer, with the seconds left to them.

"You have your whole life ahead of you," he said finally.

"We always have our lives ahead of us. Until the second we die. I'm asking you if you love me. You owe me an answer."

"What good are answers? If I said yes, you'd be waiting for me to come back."

"I haven't asked you to come back."

"You're a beautiful woman, everything a man could want."

"Spare me the compliments." She folded her arms and turned toward the cabin. "You're right about nothing being real this last week, Simon. I didn't even know who you were, not for a long time. Maybe I still don't."

She felt hands on her shoulders. Strong hands with strong, slender fingers. "You know who I am. You told me yourself once. I'm a man who lives in shadows."

"No, you told me the real answer. You're a man who plays at being a hero. I'll tell you about real heroes, Simon. They don't go off seeking adventure. They're men and women who can be honest about what they feel, who make commitments and share themselves, who deal with life's problems whenever they come up against them. They're men like Will and men like Jess."

She turned to face him. "You know, I never thought about it before, but you and Millard have a lot in common. He thought he was some kind of hero, too. He lived in his log monument to the past, telling folktales and cataloging bits and pieces of Ozark culture. He made a halfhearted effort to love my mother and even to find her when she vanished. But if he hadn't been so busy trying to be a folk hero, he would have found her and he would have known for sure about me. Then he really might have made a difference in the world!"

"I'm not your father."

"Maybe not. But you're like him. You're living proof that my mother and I had something in common, after all."

He thrust his hands in his pockets; his eyes were smoky and filled with secrets.

"I wanted to know if you loved me," she said, when he didn't answer. "I guess that's asking too much. But if my life's ever threatened again, if I need somebody who'll hijack an airplane or start a revolution, I'll be sure to look you up."

A nondescript blue sedan rolled over the last hill of her drive and pulled to a stop on the road beside them. Tate watched Gallagher get out and approach. It was better than watching Simon.

"Ready?" Gallagher clapped his hand on Simon's back. "We've got to get you out of here fast."

"I'm ready." Simon didn't take his eyes from Tate.

She looked at Gallagher as she spoke. "Have a safe journey."

"I'll take good care of him."

"If he'll let you." Her eyes flicked back to Simon, and she saw he was still watching her.

"For whatever it's worth," he said, "I meant it."

She stared at him, then shook her head slowly. "You're the only one who knows what it's worth, Simon."

He buried one hand in her hair and pulled her close. His kiss was hard and quick; then he let her go.

She didn't say a word as he limped to the car. Instead, she turned and started up the slope to the cabin. Cinn, who had survived the hailstorm of bullets from a safe vantage point, gave one mournful howl as Simon was driven away.

Chapter 15

"When one brilliant star hangs in the midnight sky like God's own night-light, folks hereabouts call it a wise-man star. I can't think of a reason to call it anything else, can you? Even the wisest of us needs help finding his way sometimes.

"There's always been a wise-man star on Christmas Eve as long as I've been alive—and sometimes I think I've been alive forever. The star has always been there, reminding me that there's something out there to search for, something that needs finding.

"The wise men weren't just wise, they were brave. It took courage to go looking for that tiny baby in the manger. Not because they could have gotten lost. No, getting lost was the least of their troubles. It took courage because the baby might just get himself found, and once he was, well, lives were going to be changed forever. The son of God can do that to you.

"The son of man can do that to you, too—or the daughter of man. Go looking for the baby in the manger or the hospital, or in the pitiful, thin arms of a starving mother, and your life is changed forever, too. Some of us can't find our camels to make that search. We sit home, and we search for the star instead. And when it hangs high in a Christmas Eve sky, then it's just the same thing as being told we're not all we were meant to be.

"But ain't it wonderful the way the wise-man star just goes ahead and shines on, anyhow? Every Christmas Eve it shines. Maybe it's God's way of egging us on. Or maybe it's His way of telling us He loves us, anyway, even if we've put our camels out to pasture this year.

"I'd like to think so anyway, wouldn't you?"

Tate stopped reading and closed her father's journal, setting it on the table at her side. For a moment, only the crackling of the logs in the fireplace broke the stillness.

Krista, who was sitting beside her on the sofa, covered Tate's hand. "What a wonderful legacy he left you. Not many of us ever know what our parents really thought about anything."

"I've got Millard's journals and Jess's books. I guess I'm extra lucky." Tate smiled at both Krista and Jess, who was standing behind his wife. Dark-haired Jess, still tan from his successful weeks in the Mid-East, was a perfect backdrop for Krista's pale-skinned, golden-haired beauty.

"Everything about this place is amazing," Jess said. "The cabin, the land, Millard's cellar. But his journals are more than amazing. They're priceless. They should be shared."

"I know. I've had time to study them lately. He had so much to say about everything. I guess living alone gave him a lot of time to think. Apparently he was good at it. Will tells me he could ask Millard a question and he'd be so deep in thought it would take him a week to hear it and another week to think of an answer."

Jess laughed. "It sounds like twisting words around runs in the Carter family."

"I live in fear that one day I'll wake up and start spouting tales."

"Well, the one about Simon Vandergriff wasn't bad for a start," Krista said, squeezing Tate's hand.

Tate felt a familiar stab of pain. She made her voice purposely light. "And it even had the requisite happy ending, didn't it? Captain Shaw's going on trial, and according to what Jess has been able to find out, Simon's back in Washington playing James Bond."

Krista sent Jess a quick worried glance before she answered. "I guess now the question is... are you happy?" She gestured to the interior of the cabin. Evergreen boughs hung in graceful, ribbon-bedecked swags on the mantel and around the door and windows. A huge pine reached from floor to ceiling in one corner, decorated with popcorn and cranberries and turn-of-the-century ornaments that Tate had unearthed from a box in the cellar.

"This cabin is amazing," she continued. "And the way you've fixed it up for the holidays is wonderful, honey. But is this enough for you? You're so alone here."

"Not as alone as you'd think. Now that the Carters are sure I want to be family, somebody's visiting all the time. I have to shoo kids and dogs out the door on an hourly basis."

She went on, before Krista could say more. "I can't do a lot with the land in the winter, but when spring comes I'll be planting more Christmas trees and making a garden. In the meantime, I'm going to start typing up some of Millard's journal entries to see if anyone is interested in publishing them."

"That's a good idea," Jess said. "I was going to suggest it."

"Then it must be a good idea," Tate said, sending him a grateful smile. "And you'll give me advice?"

"And contacts."

"You could come back to Virginia for the winter, bring the journals with you and work on them there," Krista said, worrying out loud.

"Kris, I'm almost twenty-two. You've got to let go." Tate put her arm around Krista and rested her cheek for a moment against her blond curls. "I'm not that raggedy kid from the New Orleans streets anymore."

"You're not a kid anymore, period," Jess said. He rested one hand on each of their shoulders. "I'm proud of you for living here and making something of this place."

"But all those bullet holes in the logs out front!" Krista shuddered.

"Not a one in me." Tate was glad Krista hadn't seen the condition of the cabin before new glass had been installed and the porch steps rebuilt.

"Kris is feeling a bit overly maternal these days," Jess apologized.

Tate hugged Krista. One day earlier Jess's words would have been a mystery to her. But yesterday, just after their arrival, Jess and Krista had popped the cork on a bottle of champagne to tell her that her status as an only child was about to change.

"I still can't believe I'm going to have even more family," Tate said. "Carters, Cantrells, not to mention the Claytons. When will it end?"

"We're planning at least two children, maybe three, one right after the other," Krista warned. "We're going to inundate you with sisters and brothers, so you'll have a reason to come back and visit."

"And as long as I stay here, you can bring them for an old-fashioned Arkansas Christmas."

Jess glanced at his watch. "Speaking of which, isn't it just about time for the Claytons to get here?"

Tate stood. Krista's sister, Anna, and her husband and son were coming to spend the holiday, too. "Will's supposed to be back from the airport with them anytime, now. Dovey wants us to go over to their house to wait. She's invited some of the rest of the Carters over to meet all of you. She's fixing squirrel dumplings for dinner."

Krista swallowed audibly.

"And chicken for the squeamish," Tate promised.

"It's snowing." Jess went to the window and peered out. "It's a perfect Christmas Eve."

Tate wanted to believe that. Jess and Krista were here, and Anna and her family were coming. With one exception, all the people Tate loved most in the world were going to be with her for the holidays.

With one exception.

"Let's walk over." Jess turned away from the window. "Do you feel like it, Kris?"

"I'd love to." She stood. "Tate, can you guide us?"

Tate tried to shake off the grief that always filled her when she thought about Simon. "Let me tell you how to get there. I'll be along in a little while. I've got some chores to do here first." She waved aside Jess's offer of help. "No, you and Kris go ahead. I want to change my clothes, too. You can have a romantic walk through the woods without me."

She gave them directions and watched as they buttoned themselves into winter coats. Jess wrapped a long yellow scarf around Krista's neck, gently lifting her hair over it. His tenderness tightened the knot in Tate's stomach. Not because Krista and Jess loved each other, but because of what was missing in her own life.

She called goodbye and watched from the porch to be sure they took the right path through the woods, since it was fast getting dark and she didn't want them to get lost.

She wasn't surprised that snow was already powdering the landscape. The smoke from her chimney had been rising in curls since that morning, and according to one of Millard's books, that was a sure sign that snow was expected. According to the same book, she should be able to tell how much snow they were about to get by the size of the snowflakes. She just couldn't remember whether big flakes or little flakes meant a heavy snowfall. Nor did she much care.

When was everything going to stop reminding her of Simon? Less than two months ago, she hadn't even known him. Why couldn't she go back to that time? Then a snowfall would have been just a lovely new way of seeing her surroundings. Now it made her feel lonely for warm arms around her.

She hadn't forgotten how Simon's arms felt, or how his kisses tasted. She hadn't forgotten lying together in front of the fireplace, their bodies entwined.

There were other things about him she hadn't forgotten, couldn't forget even if she had tried. His long, elegantly tapering fingers. The smoky warmth of his eyes. The unconsciously regal way he held his head. The broad, muscular expanse of his back.

Krista would never know how tempted Tate had been to take her up on the offer to go back to Virginia. The cabin was filled with too many memories, but even so, she couldn't bring herself to part with them yet. She wouldn't live here for the rest of her life. Someday the cabin would be nothing more than a summer place, a retreat from the frantic pace of the rest of the world. But now it was a museum to her memories, as well as to Millard's Ozark heirlooms. She wasn't ready to let go of the little part of Simon she still had.

When Krista and Jess were out of sight, Tate turned and went back inside. Just a brief spell on the porch had been enough warning that, heavy snow or light, the night was going to be cold. She had learned to live without central heat, but her guests were going to have enough hardships with outdoor plumbing and a wood cookstove. The least she could do was throw another armful of logs on the fire now and raise the temperature before she went to Will's. Then, with a good bed of coals waiting for her, she could make a fire quickly when she returned.

She threw the last of the logs from the hearth on the fire and drew the screen in front of it. She would need more wood to get comfortably through the night, and she slipped on her jacket and work boots to go out to the woodpile. There was water to haul and geese to ply with corn. And unless Cinn had followed Jess to Will's house, she had one chauvinistic hound dog to feed and bed down in the straw in the barn.

Chores, backbreaking and ever-demanding, had gotten her through the weeks since Simon and Gallagher had driven away. Now she was glad for the hard work ahead of her tonight.

Simon slowly threaded his way through the trees. There had been another night in the not-too-distant past, when he had made his way through these same woods by the light of a giant amber moon. As if to remind him, his leg throbbed. Actually, it was the temperature that caused it. The thermometer was dropping, and although his leg was completely healed, it was still sensitive to both heat and cold. Weeks of physical therapy had helped alleviate his limp, but it would be many more weeks before he could forget he had ever been shot.

Other things wouldn't be so easy to forget.

He wondered if he was on a wild-goose chase. What right did he have to think that Tate might still be here, waiting for him? He hadn't written; he hadn't tried to make contact through Will or the sheriff. He hadn't needed to ensure her of his safety, because he knew it had been obvious that with Gallagher's protection he was no longer in danger.

Six weeks ago he had left her, steeling himself against backward glances. He had told himself it was best that way. He had little to offer any woman, and nothing to offer one as intense and passionate as Tate. She needed commitment, stability and enough love to wipe away all the loneliness and trauma of her childhood. He was more experienced at rescuing people than loving them.

Funny, wasn't it, the things a man could tell himself when he was frightened?

He supposed it was also fear that had made him park on the road, instead of driving straight up to her door. This way he could hike the crazy quilt of forest and field until he had his first view of the cabin. He had no clear idea what clues he was looking for, or what would make him cross that last clearing and knock on her door. Perhaps he had just needed these extra minutes in the icy mountain air to rehearse what he would say. Or even to decide if he would say it.

Whatever the reason, he knew he was nearing the spot where he would be able to glimpse both the cabin and the river far below. Yesterday Aaron had informed him that the river held some of the finest bass and trout in the Ozarks. He'd even threatened to come and show Simon how to catch them, if Simon stayed a while.

Simon had told him not to pack just yet.

Leaves and finely powdered snow crunched under the soles of his boots. The moon was just peeking through the trees, but it shone with a soft glow put to shame only by one incredible star hanging over the cabin roof. Simon stopped and took in the scene of Christmas-card splendor. The cabin's tin roof was white with snow that glistened like billions of tiny diamonds under the caressing celestial beams. Smoke curled from the chimney, an encouraging sign, but no lights shone from within.

It was Christmas Eve. Tate might be anywhere, at church, in town, with relatives. There was a strange car parked beside the cabin. Perhaps she was showing company the sights. Perhaps her visitor was another man.

His eyes narrowed, as he considered that possibility. What did he know of her, really? Their time together had been so short. They hadn't talked of other loves. She had come to him a virgin, but he wasn't foolish enough to think he was the first man to pursue her. Even Gallagher and Barker mentioned her now, every chance they got, like two love-smitten idiots. Simon was beginning to think both men were envious of where danger had led him, never mind that he had almost died.

The night was too cold for him to stand and make guesses about where she might be and with whom. He could go back the way he had come and write her a letter, or he could continue on to find some answers.

The choice was the first simple one he'd made in six weeks.

Tate lunged for Cinn one more time, only to have him slip out of her grasp. He obviously had plans for the night, and they didn't include sleeping in the barn. He gave her a big-eyed, soulful stare, then turned his nose to the rising moon and howled.

Tate dusted her hands on her jeans and gave up the battle. Cinn hadn't slept inside once since Simon had left, but with Jess, Grady and Ryan sleeping in the cabin tonight, she imagined she could coax him in to the rug in front of the fireplace. Man's dog that he was, he would be in canine ecstasy. As she watched, he trotted off to the front of the cabin, almost as if he had read her mind.

She had hauled water and done what she could for the geese and dog. Now she had only to fill the wagon with firewood. In the first agonizing days after Simon left, she had split enough logs to last the winter. Tonight, everyone would benefit.

When all the wood was loaded, she began to pull the wagon up the slope to her back porch. She welcomed the heavy load as a job almost finished. Before she brought in enough logs to last the night, she would heat a kettle of water, so she could wash after she stacked the wood. Then she would change and drive over to Will's. A walk through the snowy, silent forest on Christmas Eve seemed torturously sentimental.

At the porch she anchored the wagon and began to haul the logs up the steps. When she'd finished, she grabbed one load to carry inside with her and opened the back door to start toward the fireplace.

A man stood in the center of the room, illuminated only by a thin, golden wash of moonlight. She stopped, but the panic she felt was different from what she'd experienced the first time she had seen him.

"Simon!"

"Aren't you supposed to drop the logs...or throw them at me?"

The firewood grew heavier in her arms, but she clutched it like a precious burden. His hair was longer now than the regulation High Ridge cut. He was wearing a dark wool overcoat with a subtly striped scarf and pants he hadn't had to roll the cuffs on. He stood even taller, weight easily distributed on both legs, as if he were no longer in pain.

He seemed untouchably elegant, the distant heir to a foreign throne instead of the man she had fallen in love with.

"You do have a way of sneaking up on people," she said at last. She started to cross the room to deposit her logs on the hearth, but he intercepted her, taking part of the burden to lighten her load.

His arms brushed hers, and she stepped away. "I saw a car out front," he said. "Is somebody else here?"

"Jess and Kris, but they're over at Will's right now. I'm expecting more company, but I wasn't expecting you." She dropped her logs on the hearth with a thud. "Damn it, Simon, I wasn't expecting you! You never wrote. You never tried to get in touch with me, at all. And now you just waltz into my house like I should be glad to see you!"

"Are you?" He dropped his logs and turned her to face him.

"I don't know."

"I couldn't stop thinking about you."

"You had a strange way of showing it." She crossed her arms and lifted her chin. "For all I knew, you were off in Europe doing your royal duty, or stealing somebody's computer secrets, or getting shot at again."

"I've been in D.C. You know where I've been, because you had Jess Cantrell check up on me."

Her chin jutted another notch. "I risked my neck more than once for you. I thought I deserved to know if *yours* was still in one piece."

"You had him check because you care about me."

"Never assume anything. Didn't they teach you that in Undercover 101?"

"You'd be surprised what I've learned. For instance..." One hand glided down her sleeve to her elbow. Gently he pried one arm from the other and stripped off her glove. "Your hands are cold."

She tried to shake him loose. "It's snowing outside."

"Yes, but your gloves are fur-lined. And the snow wouldn't explain why your hand isn't quite steady." He clasped it with his own.

She could feel the warmth of his skin flowing right through her, but she tried to ignore it. "It's not steady because you scared me to death."

"I probably do scare you. You scare me. When I'm with you, I don't know who I am."

"You could have solved that problem by not coming back."

He lifted her hand to his lips and kissed her fingers, one by one. She squeezed her eyelids shut and squelched the absurd desire to cry.

"I don't want to be a fugitive, anymore," he said, holding her hand against his cheek.

She swallowed hard. "I had to learn to stop running. Can you? It's not easy, Simon."

"You're running right now. I asked if you were glad to see me, and you ran."

"Yes. I'm glad to see you."

He pulled her into his arms and clasped her against him. "I've wanted to come back. Every day I've been away. I couldn't write, because I didn't know what to say."

"I never asked you to say anything!" She lifted her face to his earnestly. "I never asked you *for* anything. If you're here because you think you owe me—"

"I'm here because I want to be!" He cut off the possibility of an answer with a kiss. Then, for a long moment, there was no possibility of words, at all. Her scarf yielded to his fingers and adorned the floor at their feet until her jacket covered it. She was as greedy to touch him as he was her, and his coat and scarf followed the path of hers.

"I planned to do this with a little more finesse," he said shakily, his fingers tunneling through her hair, his lips against her forehead, her cheeks.

"I don't want finesse. I want you." She arched against him, emphasizing her words.

"I promise you both. Someday." He finished undressing her with the haste of a child tearing the wrapping paper of a Christmas present.

She tried to undress him, but he was too impatient to let her finish alone. The rug in front of the fireplace welcomed them as old friends.

She had wondered if memory had expanded the mystical pleasures of his hands on her body, but now she knew that memory was only a poor substitute. There was no way to recall such exquisite perfection. One moment built inexorably upon another. How could this be remembered—the slow upward climb, the intensifying of unbearable sensation, the yearning for, reaching toward, cataclysm?

She twisted and moved beneath him, above him, like a dancer so immersed in her performance she transcended the steps. Everything about him was familiar, yet altogether new. She absorbed the heat of his body, the smooth slide of his skin, the pressure of his lips against her breast. She felt the muscles in his back ripple against her fingertips as he lost patience completely and turned her back to the rug.

She watched his face as he slowly united them. Memory might capture only a wisp of truth, but at that moment she knew she would never forget what Simon's eyes told her as he began to move against her.

"I didn't know if I would ever see you again," Tate said later, still wrapped in Simon's arms. "But I told myself if I did, I'd be wearing a dress. You've never seen me in anything but flannel and jeans."

"I might have passed you right by and felt guilty I'd noticed you when I already had a woman I loved back in Arkansas."

She shivered and pretended she was cold. "Is that what you would have told yourself?" she asked lightly.

He wasn't fooled by her tone. He turned her to her back again and lay half across her, gazing into her eyes. "Why don't I tell you, instead? I have a woman I love right here in Arkansas. I want to love her forever. Will she let me, do you think?"

"How could she stop you?"

"She couldn't stop me from loving her. But she could stop me from being with her."

"Why would she want to?" Tate lifted her hand and brushed his hair off his forehead.

He took a long time before he answered, and he chose his words carefully. "I'm still the man I was. I'll probably die trying to be a hero. I'm planning for that to happen when I'm an old, old man, but . . ." He shook his head, and his meaning was clear.

"You're not going to change everything about yourself for me?"

Her tone had been neutral. He wasn't certain what she'd meant. "I want you in my life. It's selfish. I know I'm asking too much. But I finally realized this is your decision to make. I won't run from you again, but I'll leave if you tell me to go."

Her eyes widened. "No nine-to-five? No house in the suburbs?"

He smiled slowly, beginning to understand. "Just a man who loves you. A man who promises he won't take foolish risks."

"No bank president? No Boy Scout leader?"

He considered. "I could lead a unit or two on tying knots."

"And picking locks." She brushed back the same strands of hair once more. "There's not a part of me that expects or even wants life with you to be ordinary, Simon. I wouldn't know what to do if it was. I never want to chain you again. Can't we work out the other details as they come?"

"I want you with me!" He wasn't smiling now. Tate saw how much he meant his words, and how hard it had been to ask her to share his life.

She hugged him hard. "Then I'll come and be with you."

"What about the cabin?"

"Will and Dovey will look out for it. I've asked Will to use whatever portion of the land he wants anyway, so he'll be over here frequently. And we can come back for vacations."

"What will you do in Washington?"

"I'll ask Gallagher for a job."

He stared at her. "Gallagher?"

"He'd hire me in a minute."

He was afraid she was right—and not for office work. She had proven that fieldwork was her forte.

"We'd never be at a loss for something to talk about," she added, when he didn't answer. "Do you think you're the only person in the world who likes adventure?"

"Let's work out the details as they come."

"And if we don't agree?"

"I know how to compromise. Do you?"

"Sure." She smiled. "If I get my way."

"I have a feeling you will, more often than not." He lowered his head the necessary inches to kiss her, and for a long time they were silent.

"Shall we go tell your family we're going to be married?" he asked at last, his lips reading the pulse at her throat.

She pushed him away. "Married? Who said anything about marriage, Simon?"

"What did you think I was talking about?"

"Moving to Washington to be with you."

"Your life hasn't been ordinary, has it?" He cradled her face in his hands. "I'm past needing to try this on for size, love. I want you forever. People marry, when that's what they want. Even would-be heroes and heroines."

"I said I wouldn't chain you."

"Marriage is a bond, not a chain. Don't you know the difference?"

She felt something stirring deep inside her. "Are you sure you do?"

"When I finally stopped running, I began to understand."

As he kissed her again, she pulled him tighter against her. There *would* be time to work out all the details. Most important, there was nothing for either of them to flee again. Without looking over their shoulders, they could journey wherever life called them. Together.

She wondered if that was what Millard had meant about following the wise-man star.

"Millard would have been happy we found each other," she murmured against his cheek.

"Your father was a wise man."

"In a way, he brought us together."

"A very wise man."

She smiled and knew he was right.

Epilogue

"Anna, you anchor her headpiece. I can't get close enough to do it!" Krista stepped back and slapped her hands on her silk-covered hips.

Anna, a smaller, more vibrant version of her older sister, stepped forward to take the wreath of white roses out of Krista's hands. "Does she sound a little irritable to you, Tate?" she asked.

"I feel like a new moon in this dress," Krista said, holding folds of yellow fabric away from her body in distaste.

"You look like a woman about to have a baby any minute," Tate said, holding her head still as Anna began to anchor the wreath with hairpins.

"Not for another six weeks. And why are you so calm?"

"I'm just getting married." Tate watched herself being transformed from ordinary to extraordinary. Her dress was fragile white-tissue silk, cocktail-length and elegantly simple. The sweetheart neckline was adorned with a sapphire locket that Krista had worn at her own wedding. Tate had been her only attendant that day; now Krista would return the favor.

"Just?" Krista lowered herself to the side of the bed. "Just? Have you looked outside, by any chance? There are two hundred people trampling your wildflowers. There is a duchess out there," she said, lowering her voice in emphasis. "And not a bit of indoor plumbing in sight."

"Simon insists his relatives are all terribly stoic. And most of my guests live within a four-mile radius and won't need it, anyway."

"Krista's been reading up on how to be the mother of a bride," Anna said, poking one last pin in place. "Doesn't she do it well? Nerves, and all?"

"Someone has to be nervous. Tate is positively radiant."

Tate stood and adjusted her skirt. In the freestanding mirror that Dovey had donated for the occasion, she did look radiant. In the last five months Simon had frequently seen her dressed up, but she doubted that he realized she could look like this.

She doubted he had any inkling what she was feeling right now, either. Apparently no one did. Simon was probably somewhere outside with Gallagher and Aaron. For all she knew they were behind the barn swilling what was left of Millard's white lightning. Dutch courage was the appropriate phrase.

Simon had never flagged in his determination to marry her. She had given him every out, and he had taken none of them. But what was he feeling now that the event was almost at hand? She wondered if he felt like running; after all, she was bringing something to his life that he had never wanted. Surely this was the moment when the truth would wrap its tentacles around his throat and choke him.

She had spent the past five months trying to let Simon know he could still be free and love her at the same time. She had delayed their wedding, insisting that she wanted to be married when the wildflowers bloomed in the Ozarks. Now she wondered if she should have insisted on falling leaves.

It wasn't that she didn't want to marry him. Their lives had become more entwined, their lovemaking more exquisite. She was enthralled with Washington and her job with the Justice Department working on missing-children cases. Even Cinn seemed contented in his new Georgetown home—just as long as he got to sleep on the floor next to Simon's side of the bed.

She was happier than she had believed it was possible to be. Still, there was one, tiny nagging voice that eternally questioned whether marriage might kill Simon's love for her.

She turned and saw that she and Krista were alone. "Anna went to signal the musicians," Krista said.

Tate and Simon had compromised on music. She would walk up the flower-strewn hillside overlooking the river to the strains of a string quartet that Simon had imported from Washington. Then, for the reception, they would be entertained by local musicians, including a Carter or two.

"So soon?" she said.

"Are you ready? Jess is just outside." Krista lifted the bouquet of roses and lilies of the valley from the bedside table.

Tate straightened her skirt. She wondered what she would do if Simon weren't there waiting for her when she reached the hilltop. "I'm ready," she said.

"You're beautiful, sweetheart. I love you." Krista leaned over and kissed Tate's cheek. "I'm going to cry all the way up the hill." She sniffed, as if to prove a point.

"Don't you dare. Not one of the kids from Stagecoach Inn will invite you to their wedding if you cry at mine!" Tate sniffed, too.

Krista gave her a watery smile. "Let's go."

They walked to the door, and Krista stepped out first. Will was waiting on the porch to escort her up the hill—and Dovey was standing by, in case Krista went into labor on the way. When they were halfway there, Jess opened the door and held out his arm to Tate. "Come on, daughter."

She almost said no. He took in her suddenly pale face and smiled gently. "He loves you," he said. "Don't worry."

She searched his eyes. "I am worried."

"I know. I've known. You don't need to be."

She looked at the man who had been the only father she had ever known. For a moment her vision blurred and she saw the photograph of the father she'd never know, taken when he was just about Jess's age. For one crazy, heart-stopping moment they seemed to be the same man. "Come on, daughter," Jess repeated.

"Millard?"

He cocked his head in question.

She smiled shakily and shook her head. She extended her hand to Jess and rose on tiptoe to kiss his cheek once she was in place.

The walk took forever. The sun had never shone brighter; the air had never smelled sweeter. The fields were a carpet of gold and pink. As she walked, she understood why Millard had never left his mountains.

The trail took a turn, and Tate looked up to see her guests lining the hillside. Some were wiping their eyes; some were smiling. The group of girls from Stagecoach Inn was gawking at her, as if she had suddenly become a stranger. Gallagher and Barker were, out of long habit, assessing the crowd. Anna and Grady were holding hands, their other hands on a grinning Ryan's shoulders. Krista was waiting at one side, trying not to cry—and failing.

Tate couldn't look at Simon, because she was afraid of what she might see.

She slowed her pace. The music built in intensity; the sun shone even more radiantly. At last she had no choice. She and Jess were close enough that she could no longer avoid Simon's eyes. She knew that if he felt trapped or regretful, she would see it now.

She lifted her gaze and found him next to his best man, sun-wrinkled, balding Aaron. Simon was staring at her. Slowly his smile welcomed her. Then, with no regard for tradition, he strode down the path. One hand reached out, as if he were too impatient to wait for the steps that would bring her to his side. In moments he had pulled her close and swept away all her doubts forever.

"Take care of her," Jess said, leaning over to kiss Tate's cheek. Then he shook Simon's hand and went to stand beside Krista.

Tate gazed up at Simon. As if he knew what she had feared, he shook his head. Then he leaned down and kissed her.

"I think you're supposed to wait until we're married to do that," she said, when everybody laughed.

He tucked her hand under his arm and led her toward the minister. "Then let's get married and do it again."

And they did.

* * * * *